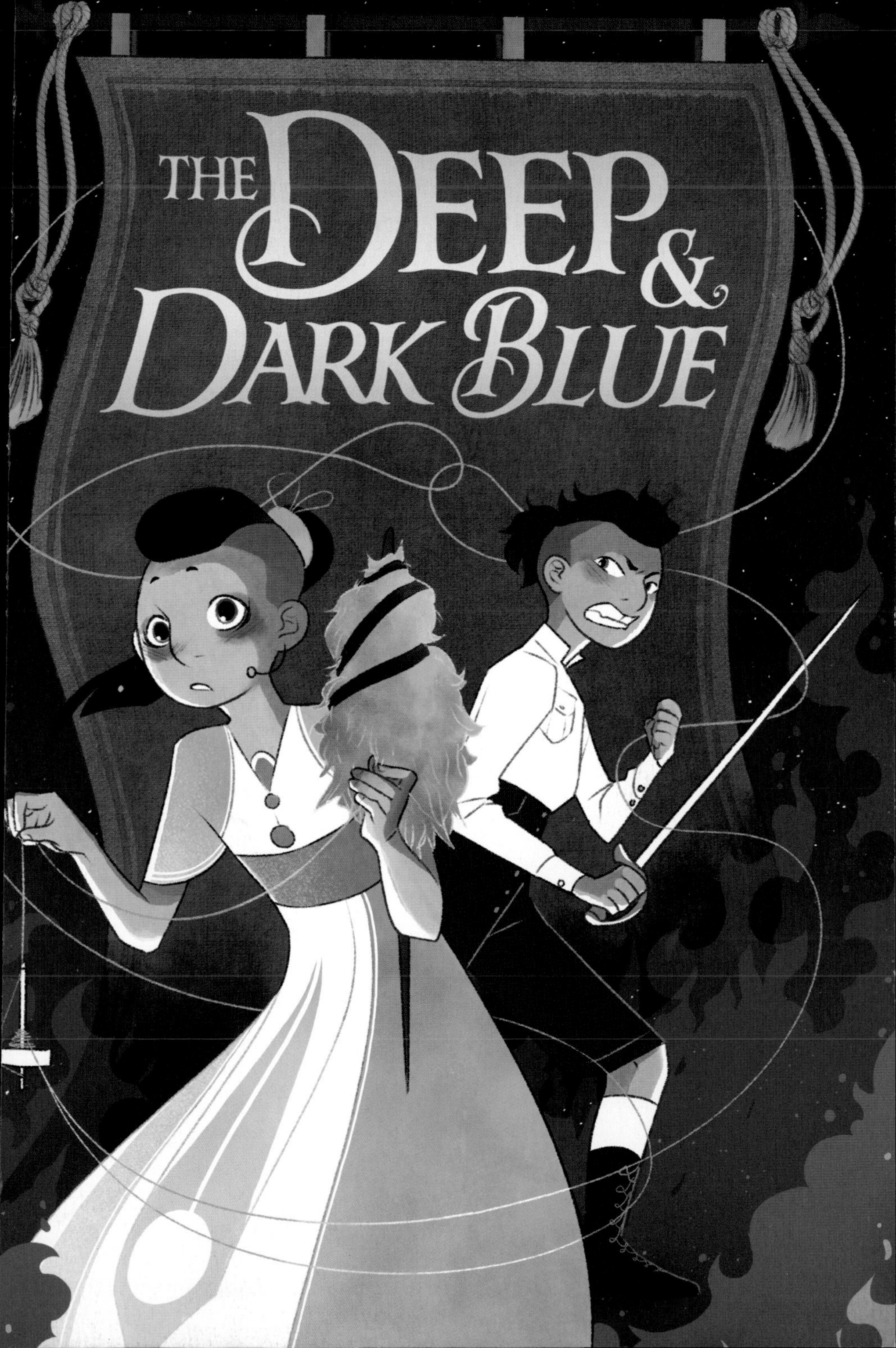
THE DEEP &
DARK BLUE

About This Book

The illustrations for this book were done in Clip Studio Paint and Adobe Photoshop. This book was edited by Rex Ogle and designed by Ching Chan. The production was supervised by Erika Schwartz, and the production editor was Annie McDonnell. The text was set in Claire Hand, and the display type is Yana B.

Little, Brown and Company
Hachette Book Group
1290 Avenue of the Americas, New York, NY 10104
Visit us at LBYR.com

First Edition: January 2020

Little, Brown and Company is a division of Hachette Book Group, Inc. The Little, Brown name and logo are trademarks of Hachette Book Group, Inc.

The publisher is not responsible for websites (or their content) that are not owned by the publisher.

Library of Congress Control Number: 2019941622

ISBNs: 978-0-316-48598-2 (hardcover), 978-0-316-48601-9 (paperback), 978-0-316-48602-6 (ebook), 978-0-316-48599-9 (ebook), 978-0-316-48597-5 (ebook)

PRINTED IN CHINA

1010

Hardcover: 10 9 8 7 6 5 4 3 2 1

Paperback: 10 9 8 7 6 5 4 3 2 1

THE DEEP & DARK BLUE

Niki Smith

LB
Little, Brown and Company
New York Boston

For my dad, who loved to dream.

Thank you to Mey Rude, Jo Kreil, and
Sarah W. Searle, for all your help and guidance.
And thank you, Kiri, for everything.

CHAPTER I

COUP

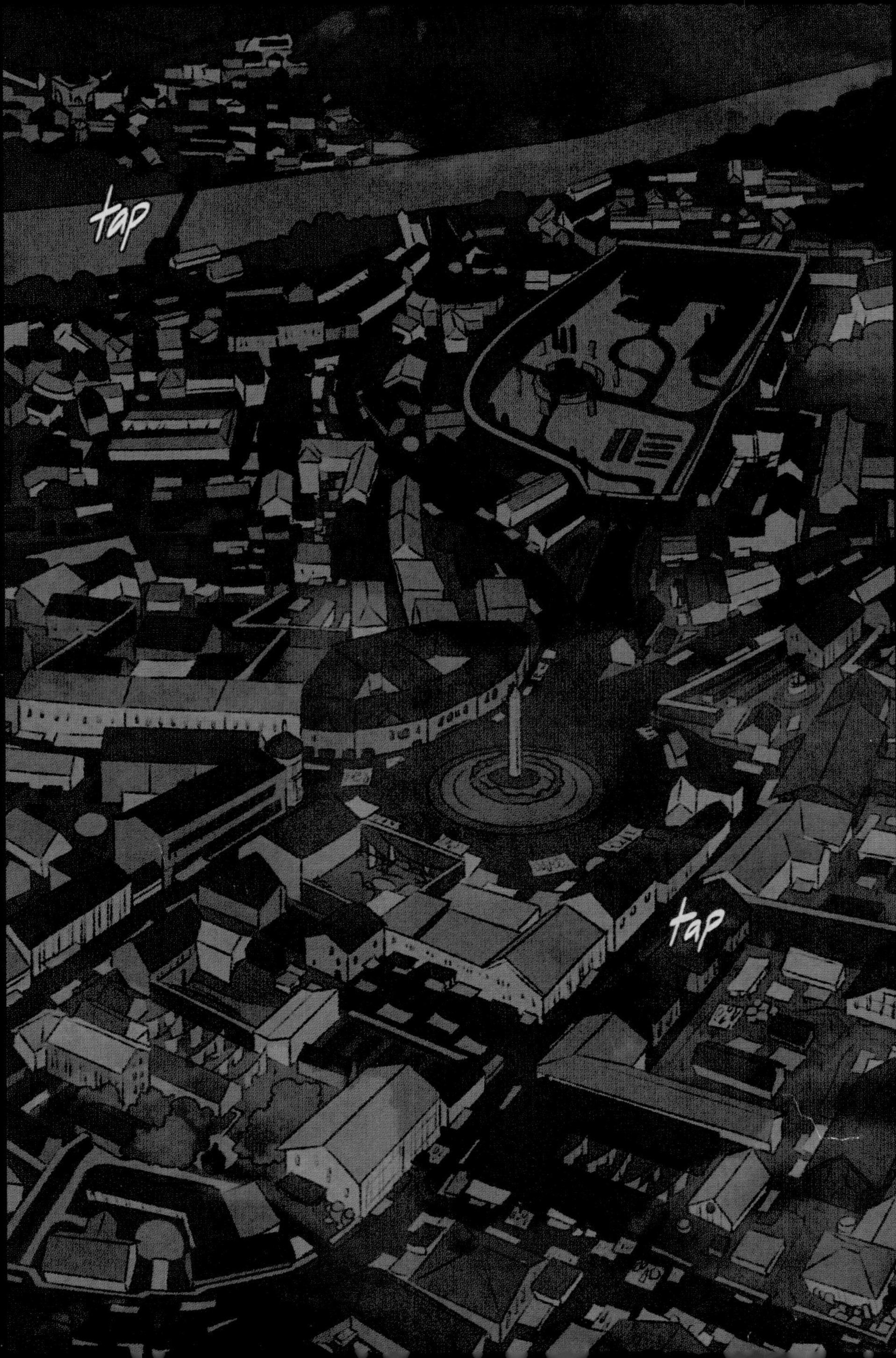
tap
tap

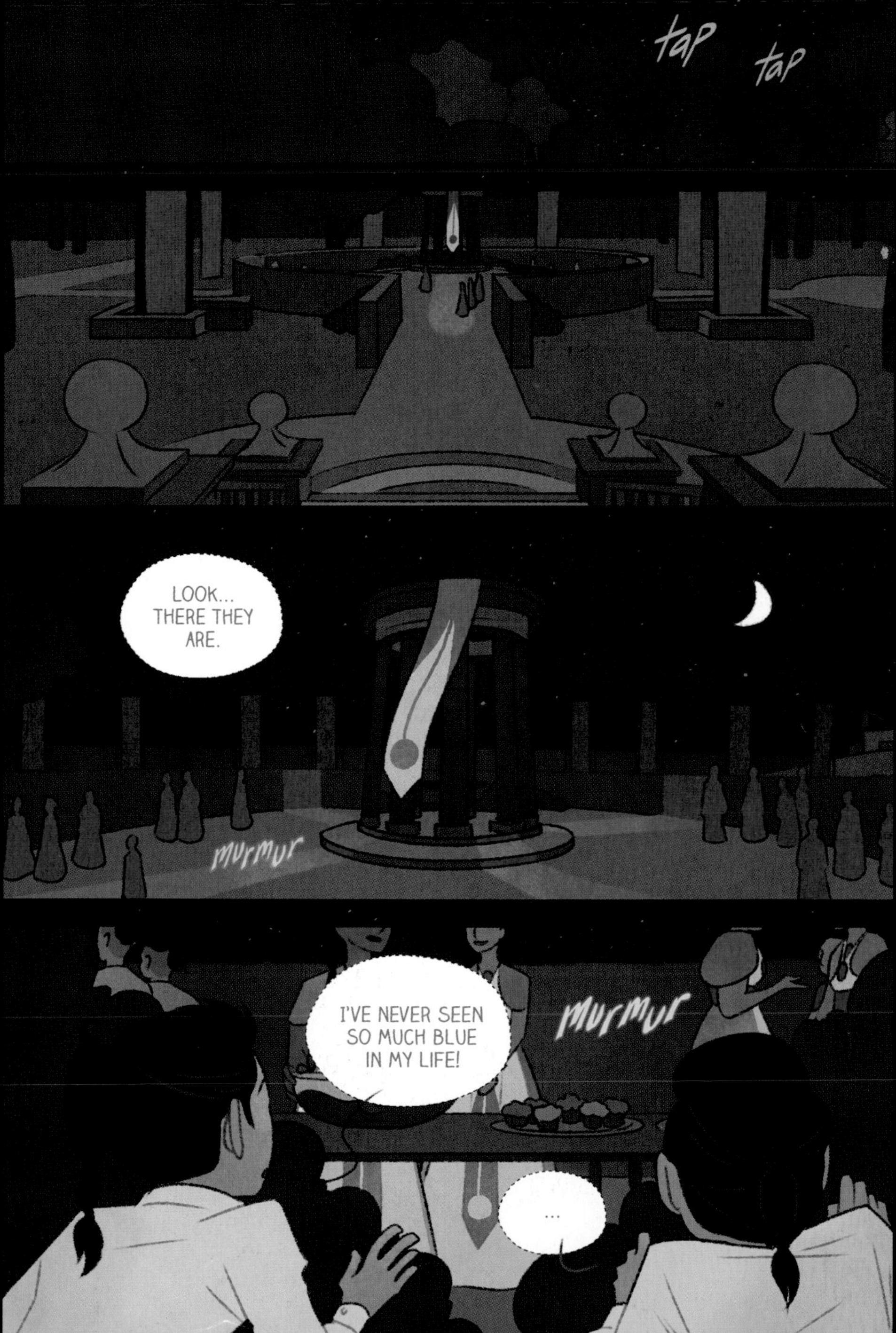
tap tap
LOOK... THERE THEY ARE.
murmur
I'VE NEVER SEEN SO MUCH BLUE IN MY LIFE!
murmur
...

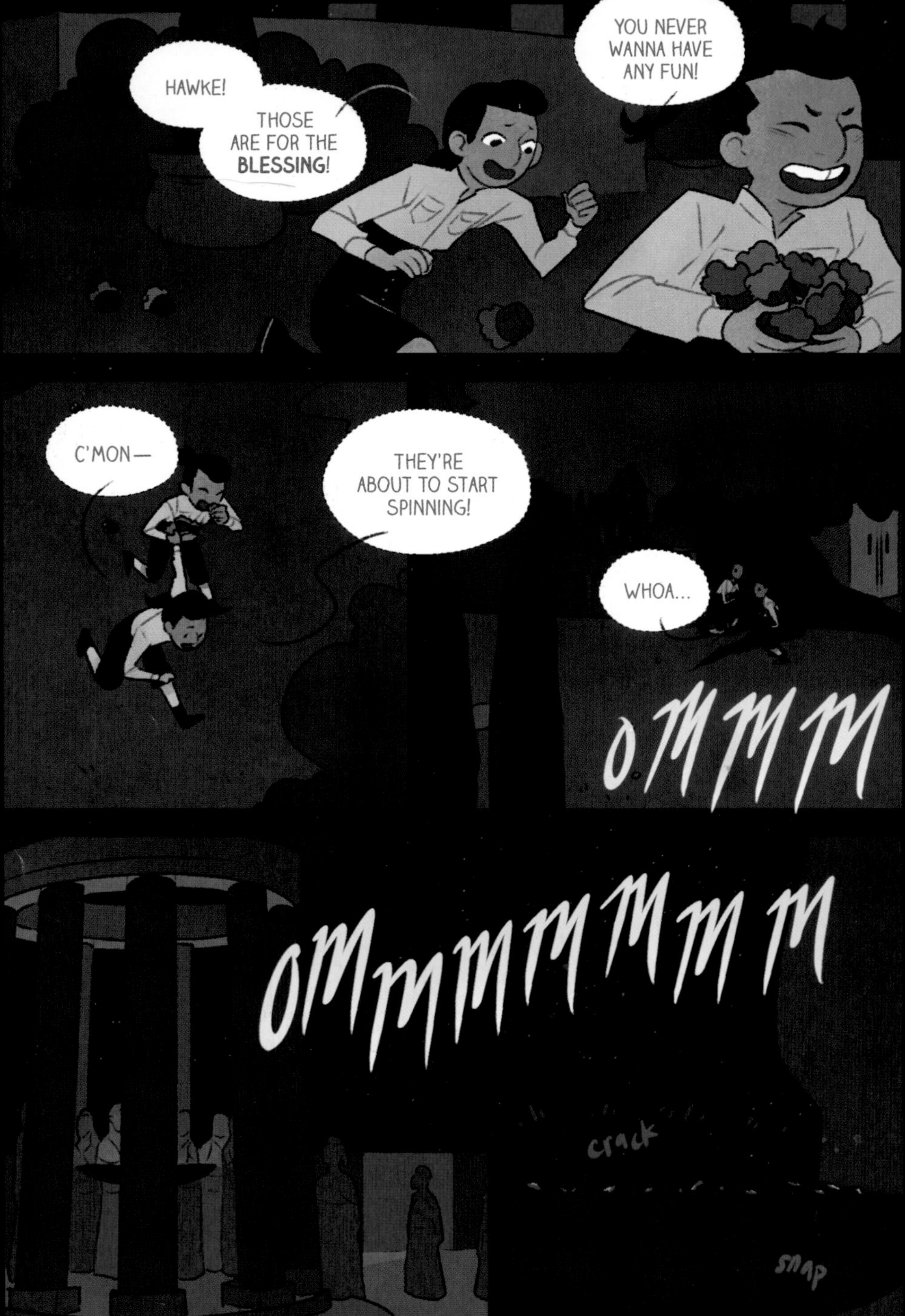
HAWKE!
THOSE ARE FOR THE **BLESSING**!
YOU NEVER WANNA HAVE ANY FUN!
C'MON—
THEY'RE ABOUT TO START SPINNING!
WHOA...
OMMMM
OMMMMMMMM
crack
snap

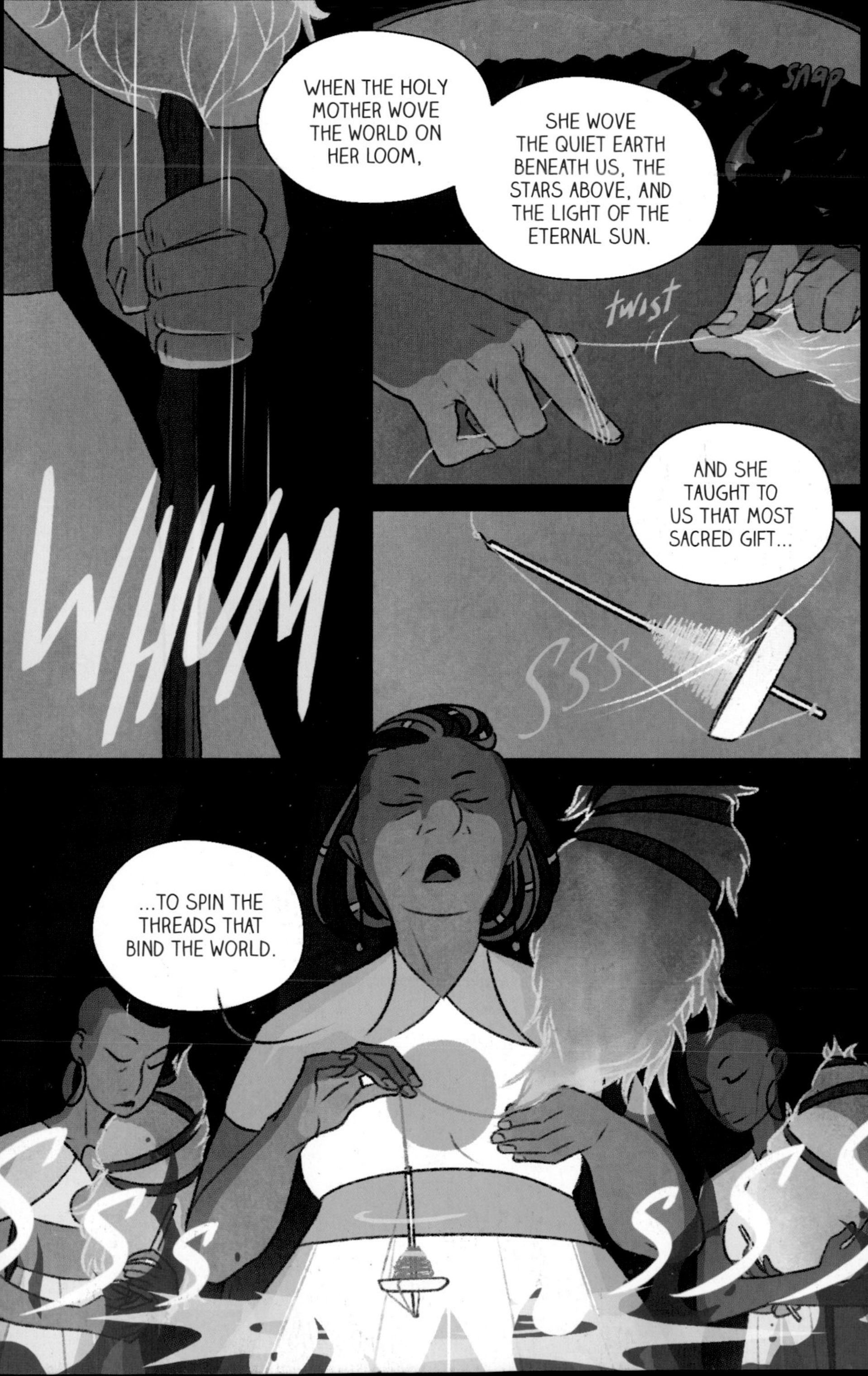
snap
WHEN THE HOLY MOTHER WOVE THE WORLD ON HER LOOM,
SHE WOVE THE QUIET EARTH BENEATH US, THE STARS ABOVE, AND THE LIGHT OF THE ETERNAL SUN.
twist
WHUM
AND SHE TAUGHT TO US THAT MOST SACRED GIFT...
SSS
...TO SPIN THE THREADS THAT BIND THE WORLD.
SSS
SSS

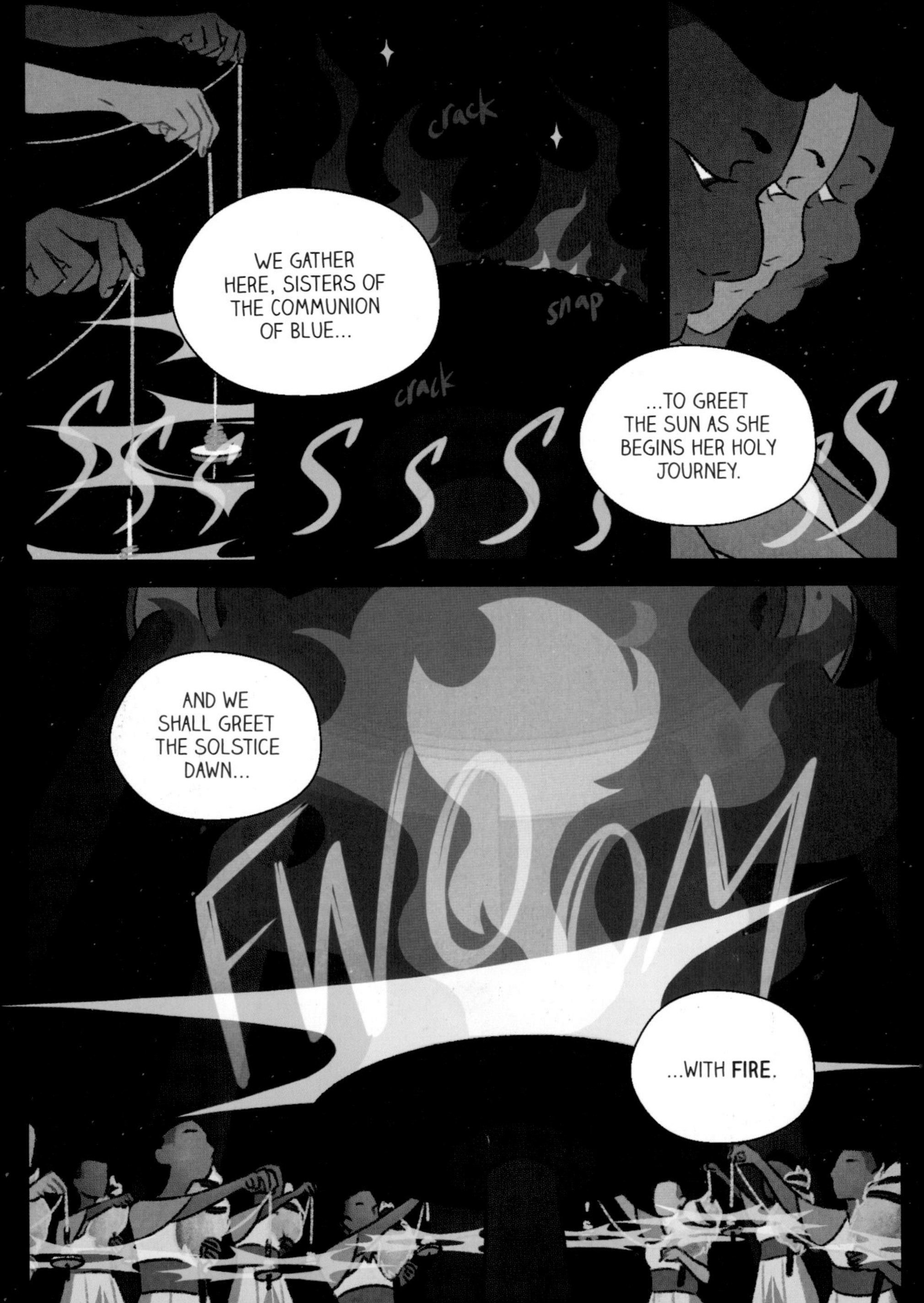
crack
snap
crack
WE GATHER HERE, SISTERS OF THE COMMUNION OF BLUE...
...TO GREET THE SUN AS SHE BEGINS HER HOLY JOURNEY.
AND WE SHALL GREET THE SOLSTICE DAWN...
FWOOM
...WITH **FIRE**.

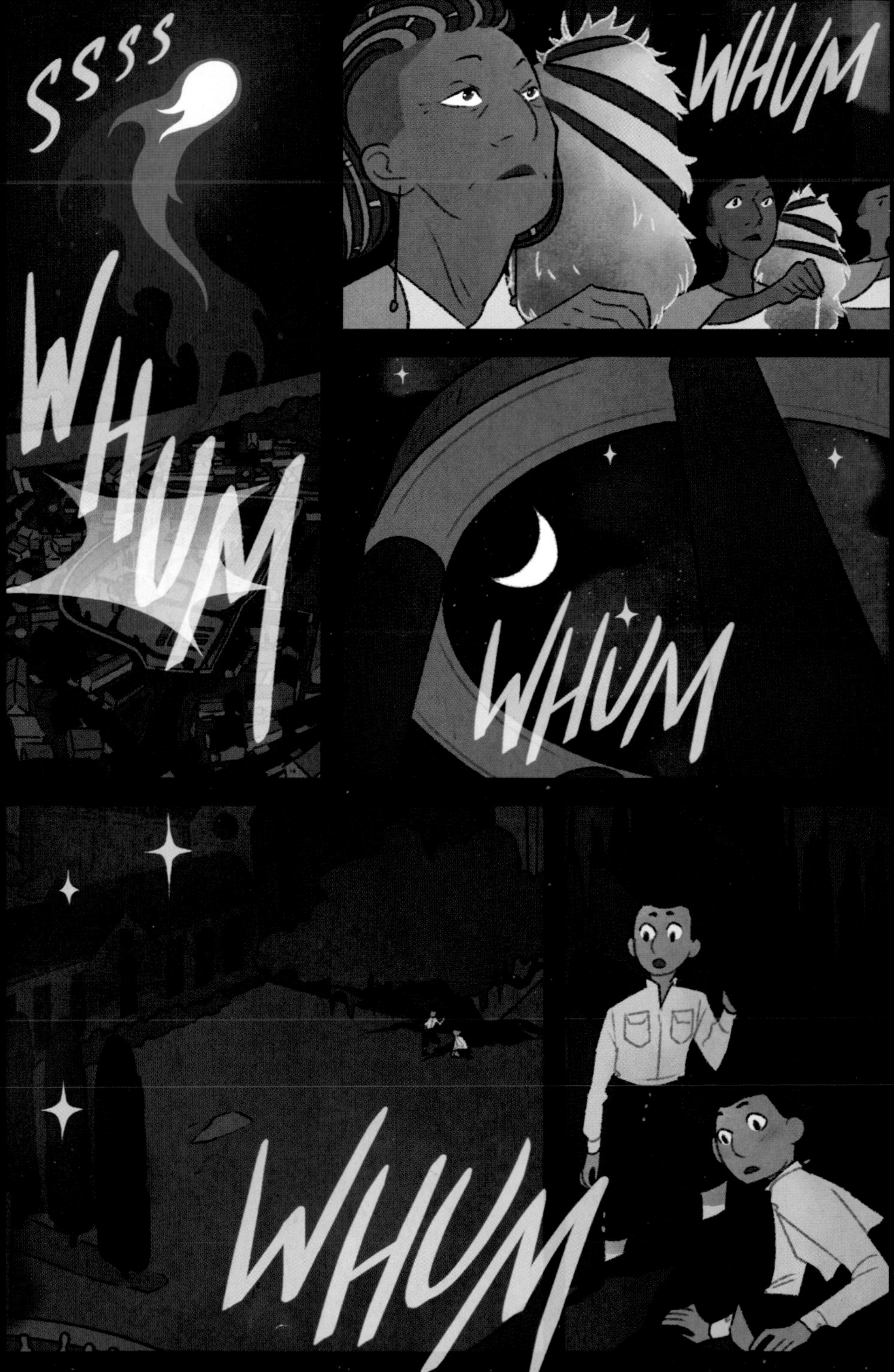
SSSS
WHUM
WHUM
WHUM
WHUM

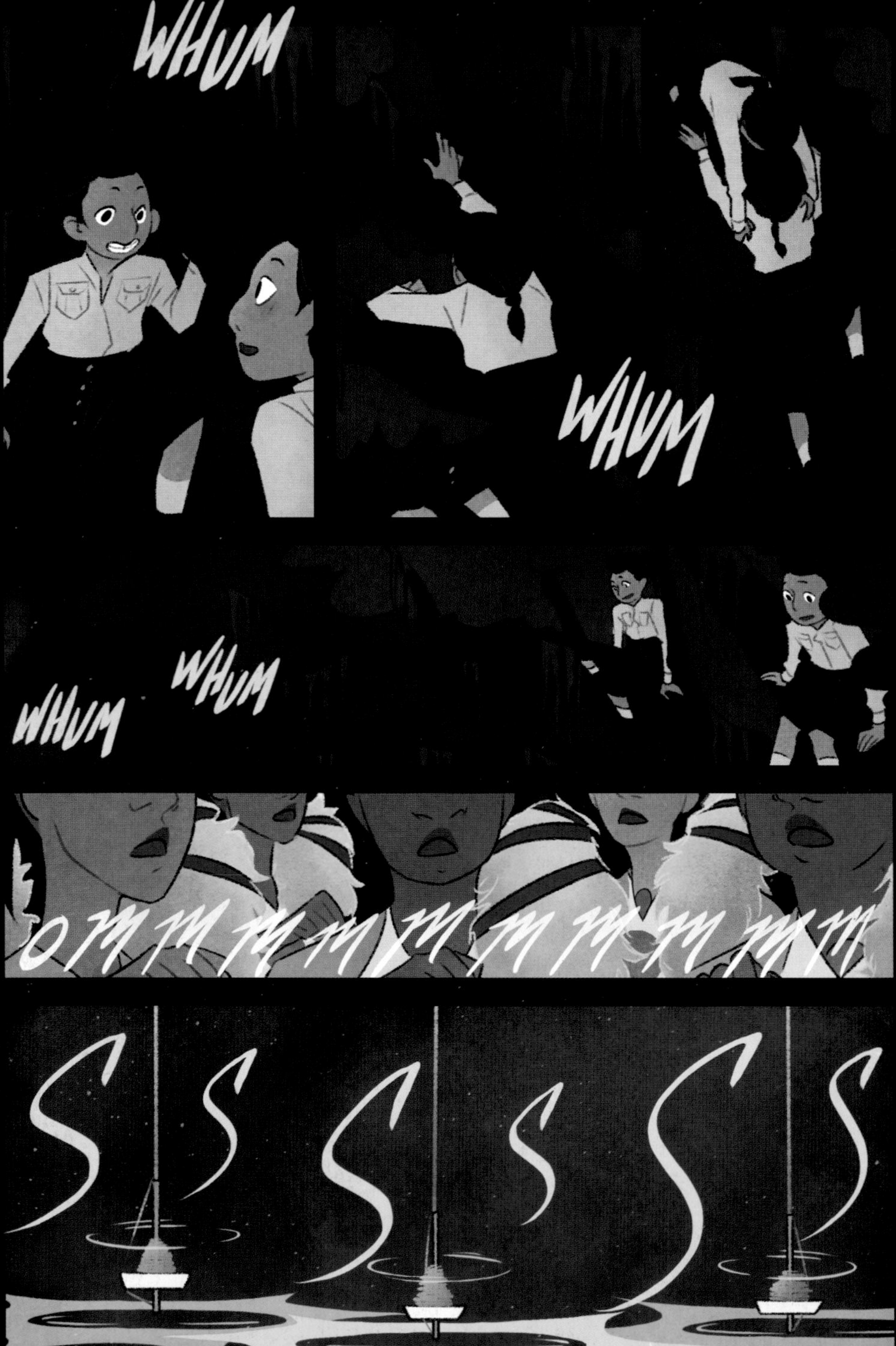
WHUM
WHUM
WHUM
WHUM
OMMMMMMMMMMM
SSSSSS

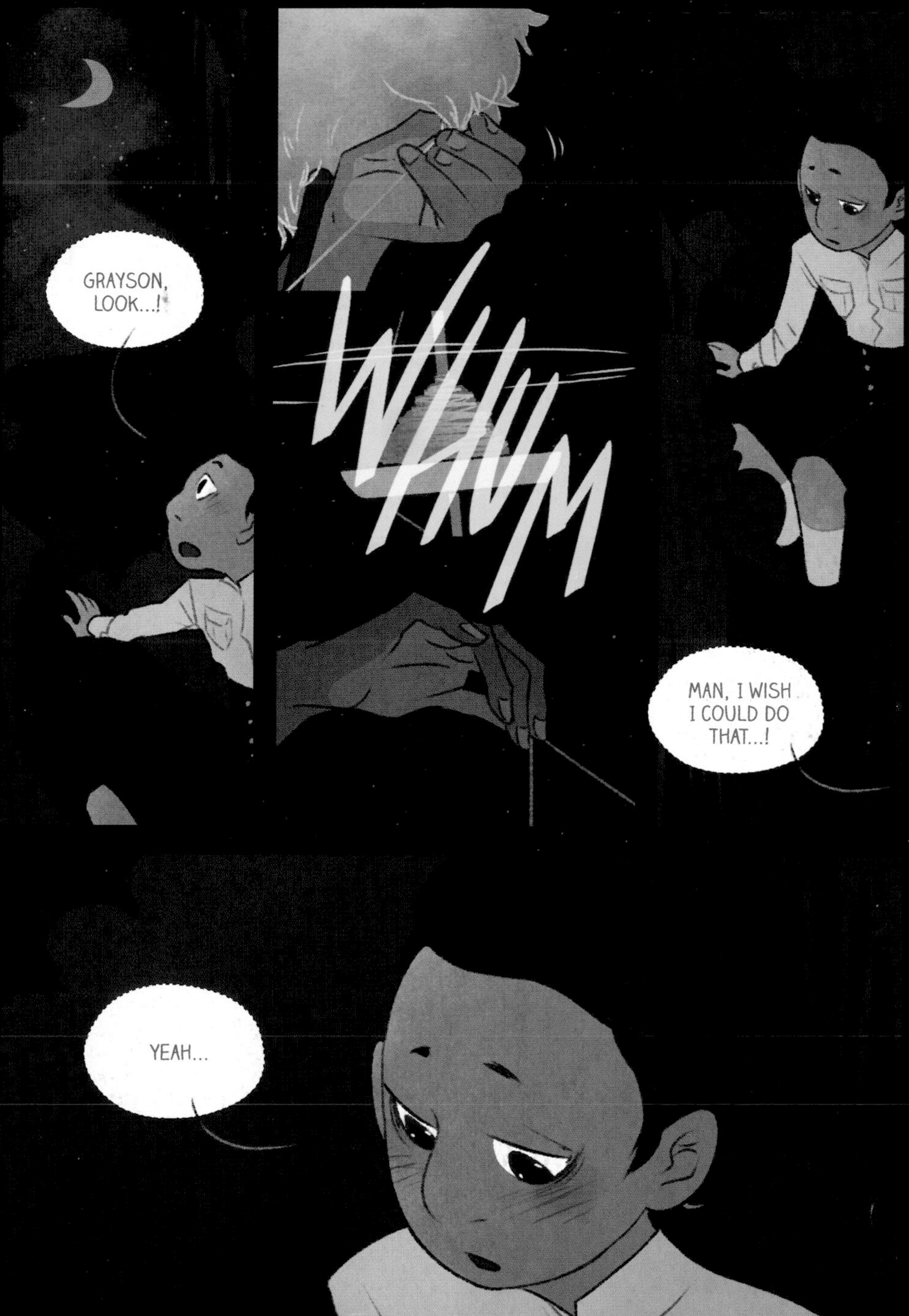
GRAYSON, LOOK...!
WHUM
MAN, I WISH I COULD DO THAT...!
YEAH...

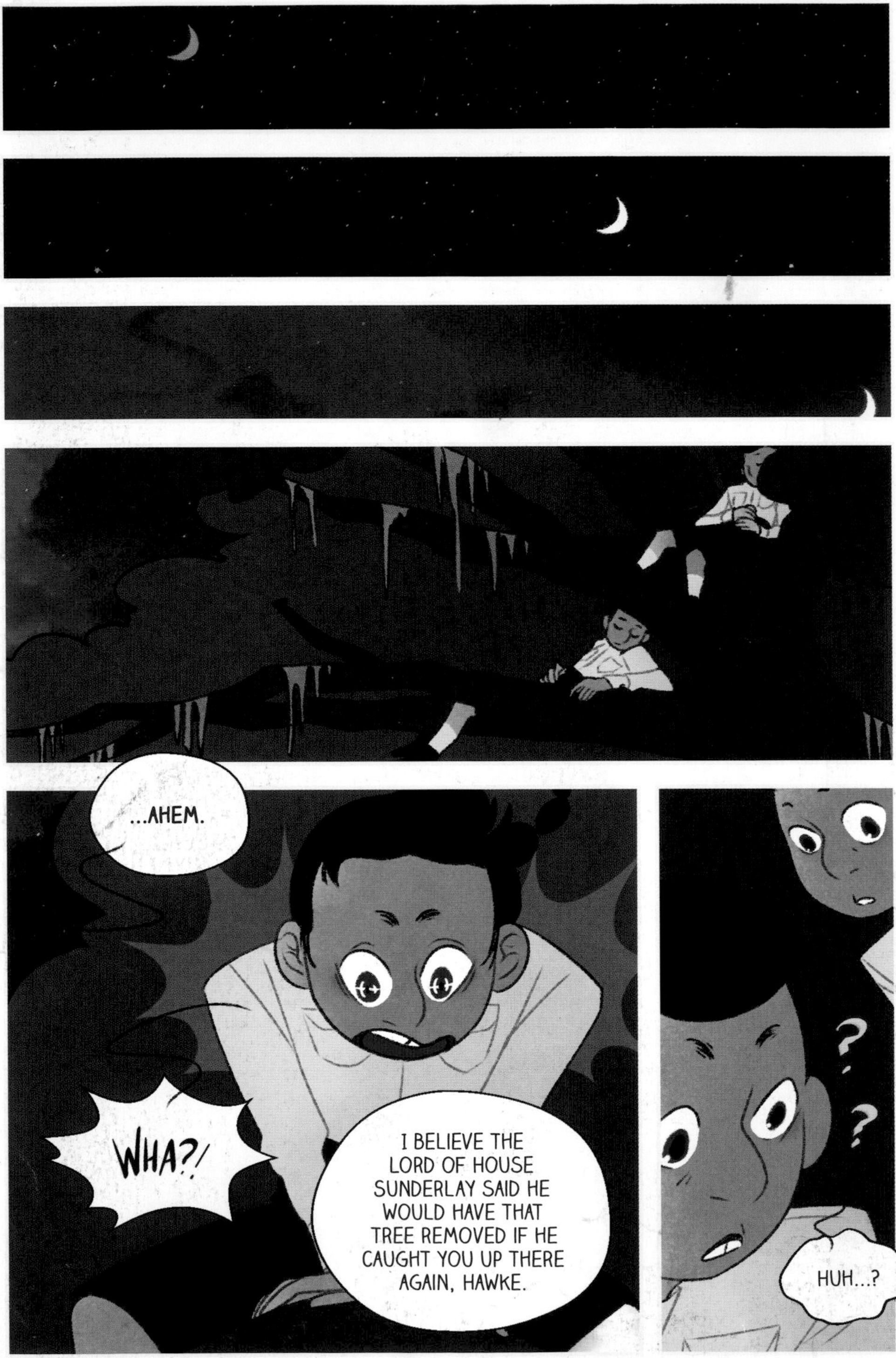
...AHEM.
WHA?!
I BELIEVE THE LORD OF HOUSE SUNDERLAY SAID HE WOULD HAVE THAT TREE REMOVED IF HE CAUGHT YOU UP THERE AGAIN, HAWKE.
HUH...?

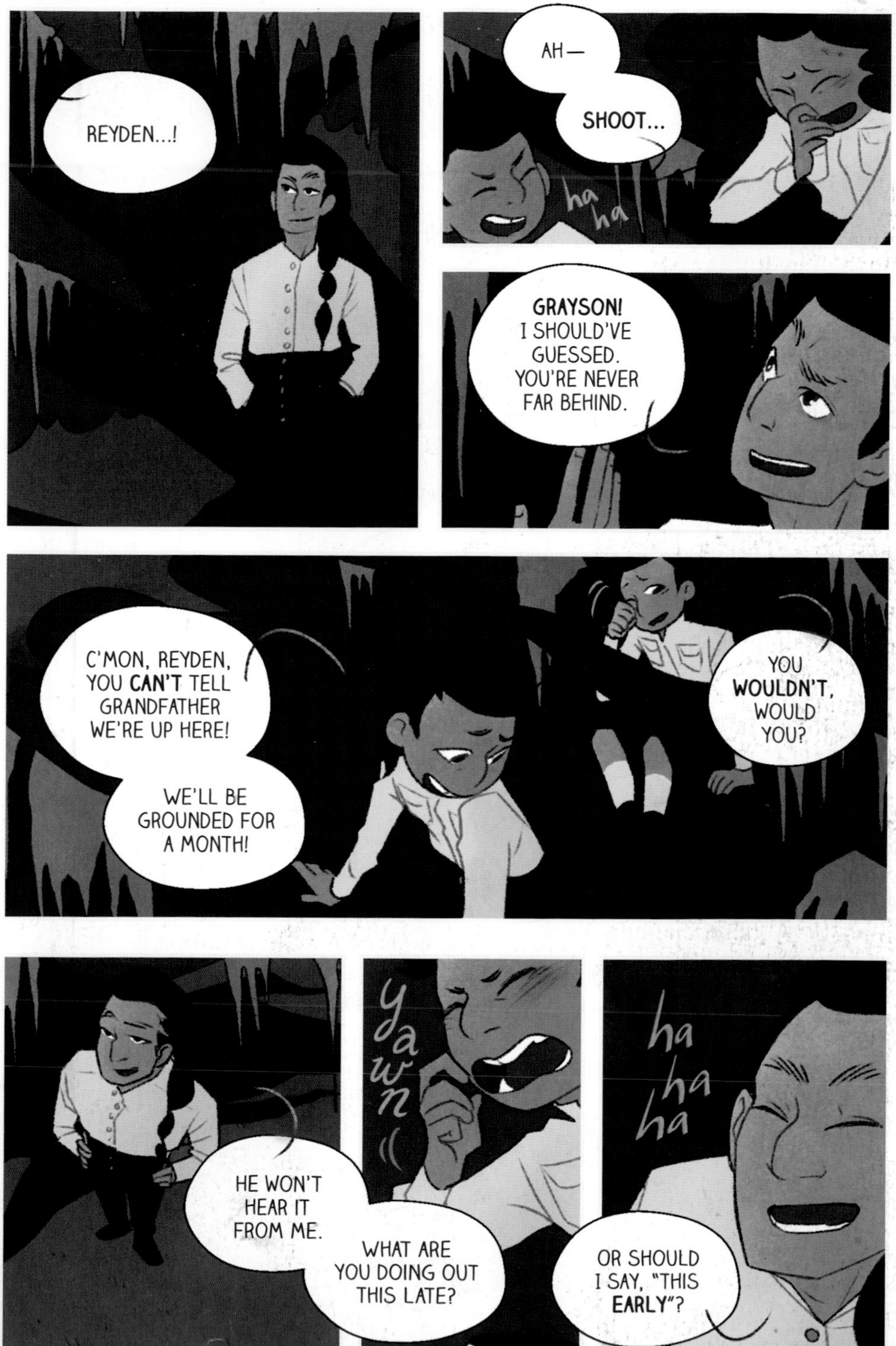
REYDEN...!
AH—
SHOOT...
ha ha
GRAYSON! I SHOULD'VE GUESSED. YOU'RE NEVER FAR BEHIND.
C'MON, REYDEN, YOU **CAN'T** TELL GRANDFATHER WE'RE UP HERE!
WE'LL BE GROUNDED FOR A MONTH!
YOU **WOULDN'T**, WOULD YOU?
HE WON'T HEAR IT FROM ME.
yawn
WHAT ARE YOU DOING OUT THIS LATE?
ha ha ha
OR SHOULD I SAY, "THIS **EARLY**"?

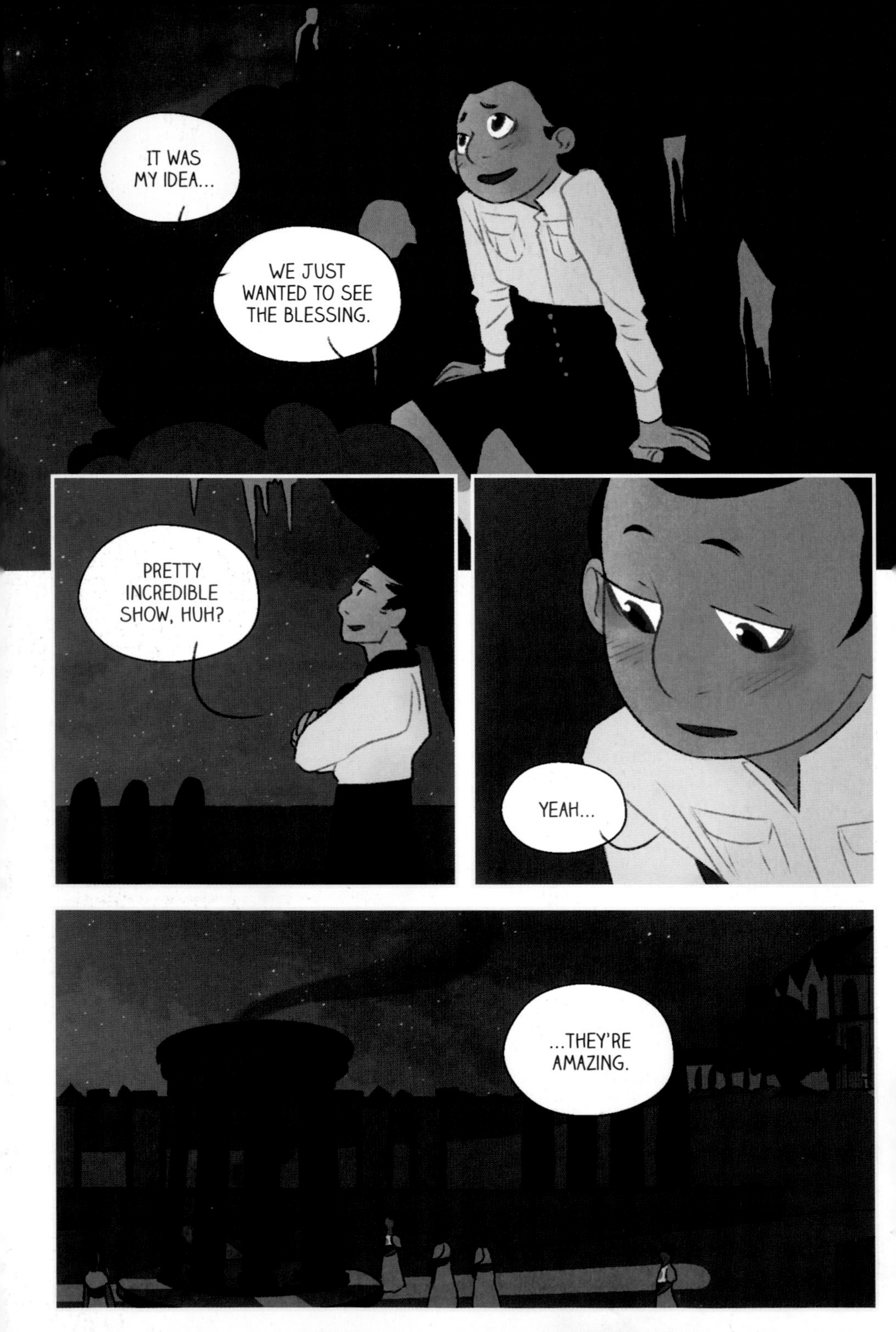
IT WAS MY IDEA...
WE JUST WANTED TO SEE THE BLESSING.
PRETTY INCREDIBLE SHOW, HUH?
YEAH...
...THEY'RE AMAZING.

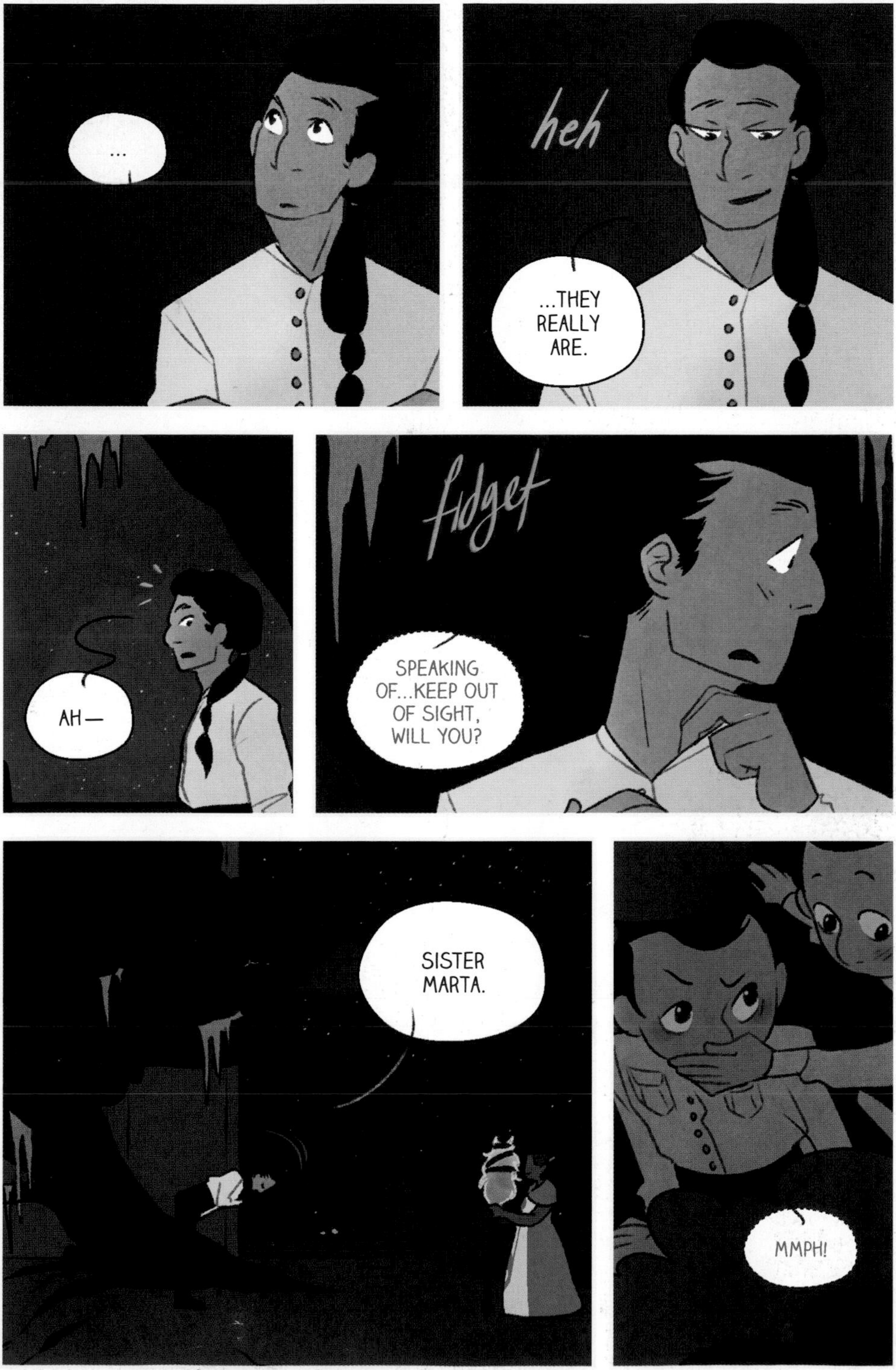
...
heh
...THEY REALLY ARE.
AH—
fidget
SPEAKING OF...KEEP OUT OF SIGHT, WILL YOU?
SISTER MARTA.
MMPH!

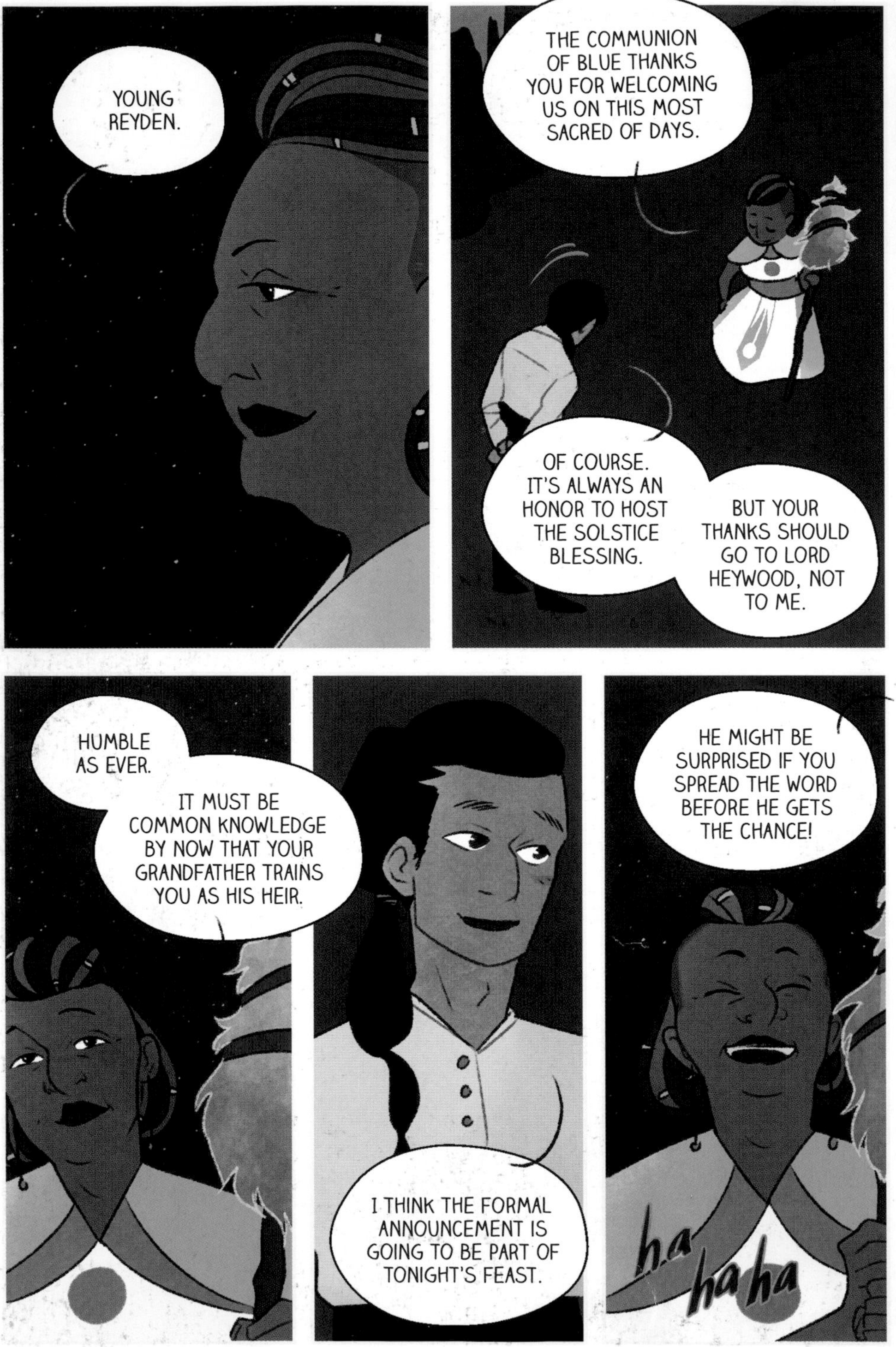
YOUNG REYDEN.
THE COMMUNION OF BLUE THANKS YOU FOR WELCOMING US ON THIS MOST SACRED OF DAYS.
OF COURSE. IT'S ALWAYS AN HONOR TO HOST THE SOLSTICE BLESSING.
BUT YOUR THANKS SHOULD GO TO LORD HEYWOOD, NOT TO ME.
HUMBLE AS EVER.
IT MUST BE COMMON KNOWLEDGE BY NOW THAT YOUR GRANDFATHER TRAINS YOU AS HIS HEIR.
I THINK THE FORMAL ANNOUNCEMENT IS GOING TO BE PART OF TONIGHT'S FEAST.
HE MIGHT BE SURPRISED IF YOU SPREAD THE WORD BEFORE HE GETS THE CHANCE!
ha
haha

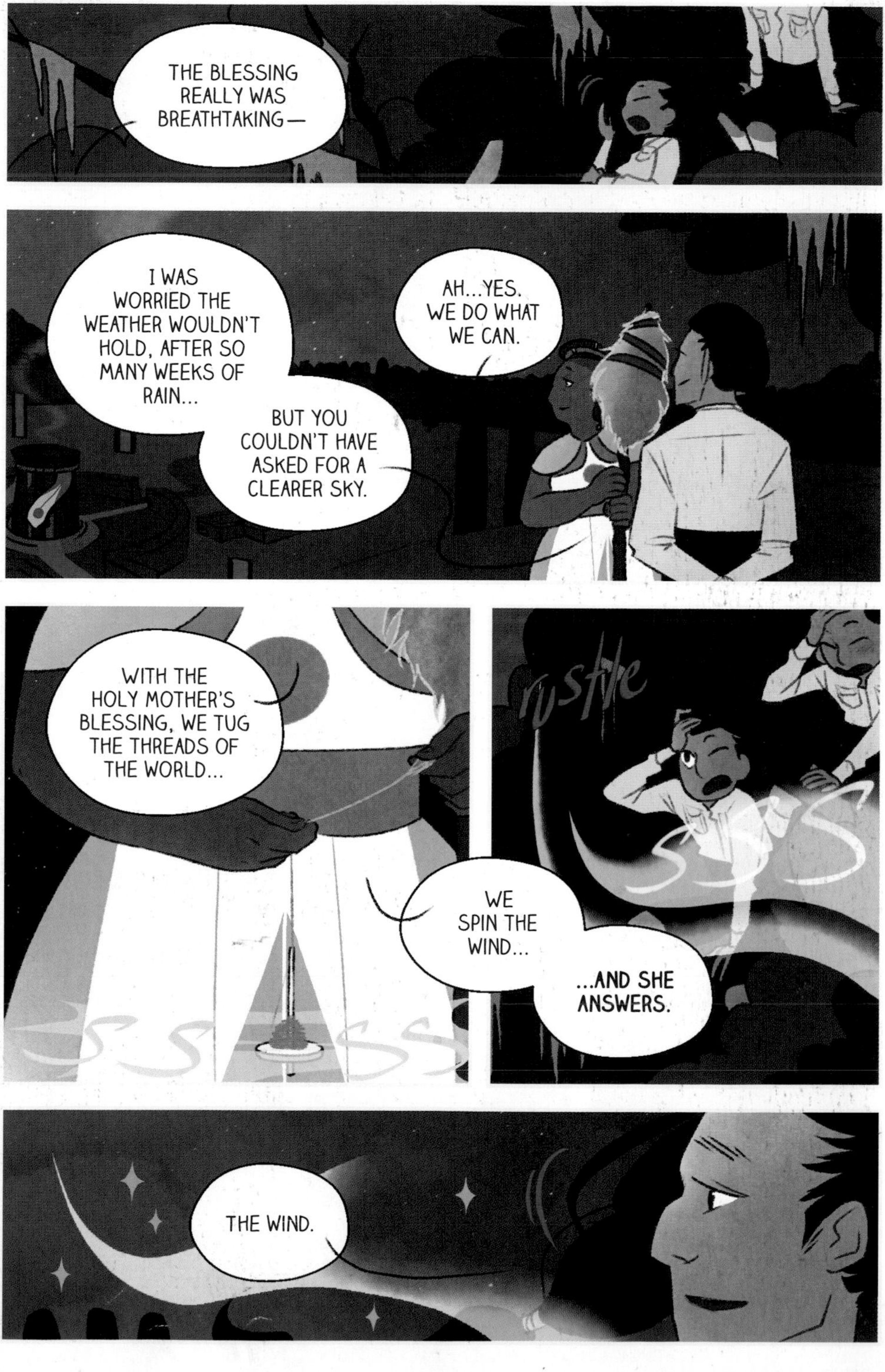
THE BLESSING REALLY WAS BREATHTAKING—
I WAS WORRIED THE WEATHER WOULDN'T HOLD, AFTER SO MANY WEEKS OF RAIN...
BUT YOU COULDN'T HAVE ASKED FOR A CLEARER SKY.
AH...YES. WE DO WHAT WE CAN.
WITH THE HOLY MOTHER'S BLESSING, WE TUG THE THREADS OF THE WORLD...
rustle
WE SPIN THE WIND...
...AND SHE ANSWERS.
THE WIND.

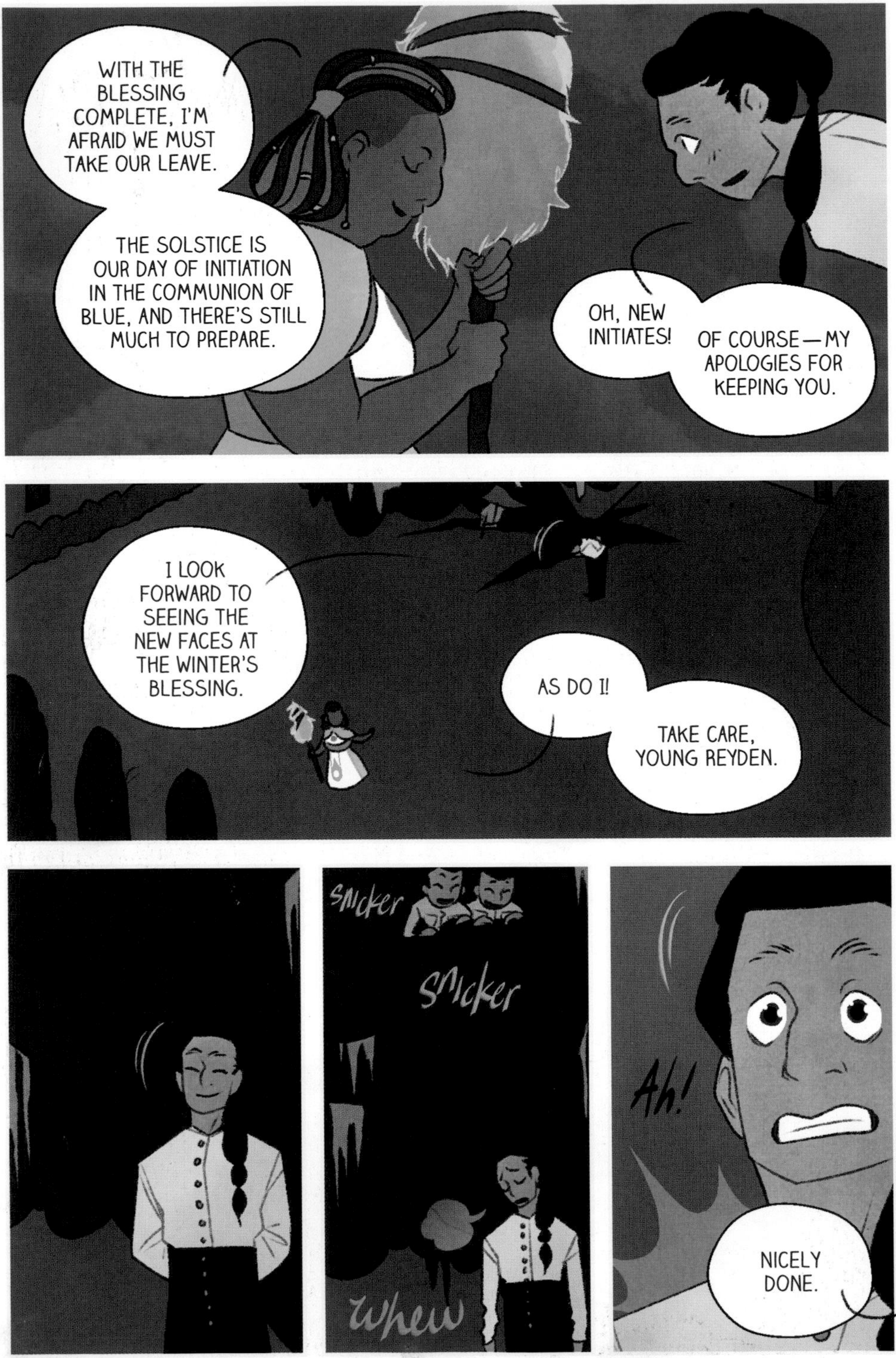
WITH THE BLESSING COMPLETE, I'M AFRAID WE MUST TAKE OUR LEAVE.
THE SOLSTICE IS OUR DAY OF INITIATION IN THE COMMUNION OF BLUE, AND THERE'S STILL MUCH TO PREPARE.
OH, NEW INITIATES!
OF COURSE—MY APOLOGIES FOR KEEPING YOU.
I LOOK FORWARD TO SEEING THE NEW FACES AT THE WINTER'S BLESSING.
AS DO I!
TAKE CARE, YOUNG REYDEN.
snicker
snicker
whew
Ah!
NICELY DONE.

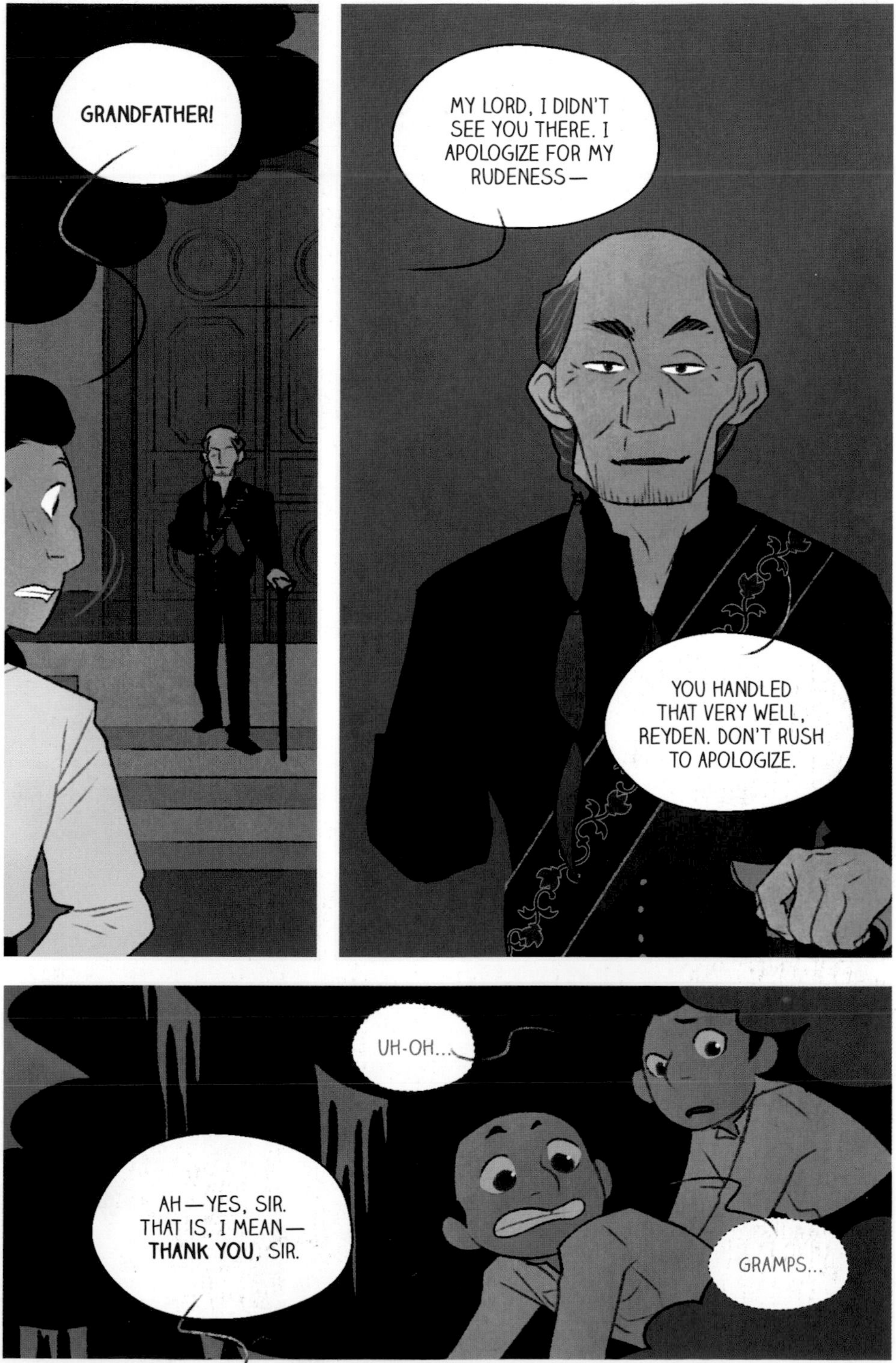
GRANDFATHER!
MY LORD, I DIDN'T SEE YOU THERE. I APOLOGIZE FOR MY RUDENESS—
YOU HANDLED THAT VERY WELL, REYDEN. DON'T RUSH TO APOLOGIZE.
UH-OH...
AH—YES, SIR. THAT IS, I MEAN—THANK YOU, SIR.
GRAMPS...

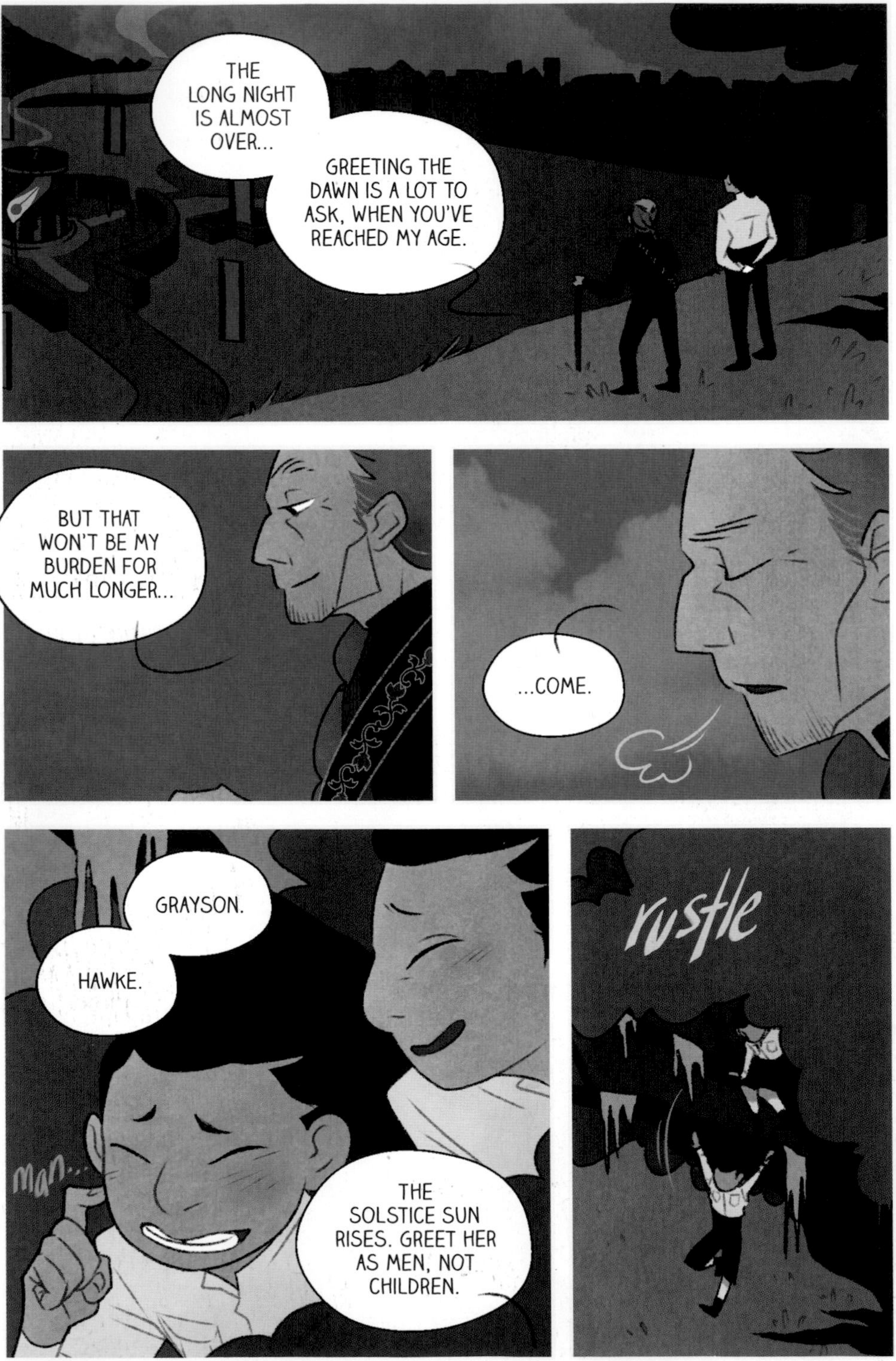
THE LONG NIGHT IS ALMOST OVER...
GREETING THE DAWN IS A LOT TO ASK, WHEN YOU'VE REACHED MY AGE.
BUT THAT WON'T BE MY BURDEN FOR MUCH LONGER...
...COME.
GRAYSON.
HAWKE.
man...
THE SOLSTICE SUN RISES. GREET HER AS MEN, NOT CHILDREN.
rustle

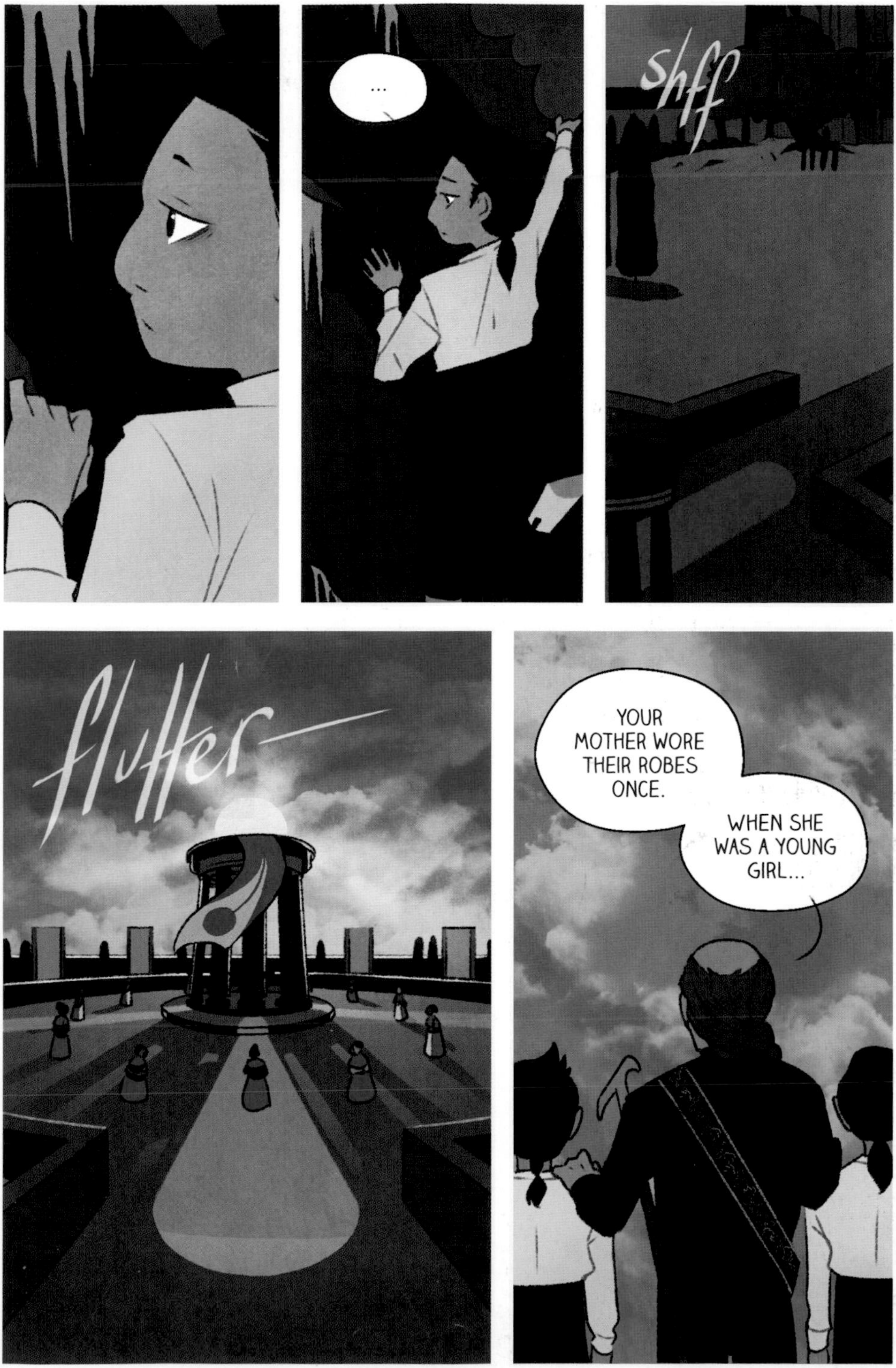
...
shff
flutter
YOUR MOTHER WORE THEIR ROBES ONCE.
WHEN SHE WAS A YOUNG GIRL...

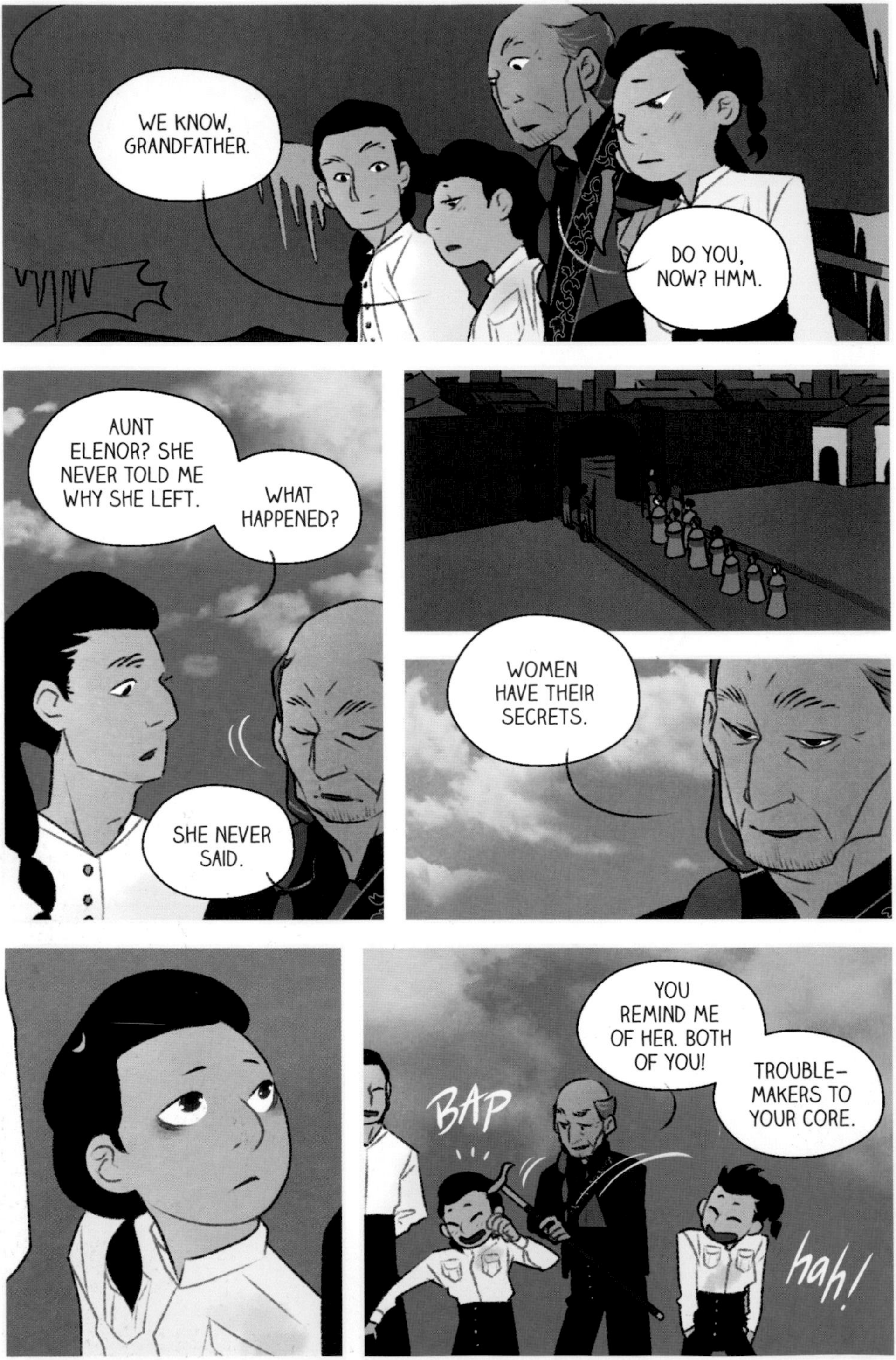
WE KNOW, GRANDFATHER.
DO YOU, NOW? HMM.
AUNT ELENOR? SHE NEVER TOLD ME WHY SHE LEFT.
WHAT HAPPENED?
SHE NEVER SAID.
WOMEN HAVE THEIR SECRETS.
YOU REMIND ME OF HER. BOTH OF YOU!
TROUBLE-MAKERS TO YOUR CORE.
BAP
hah!

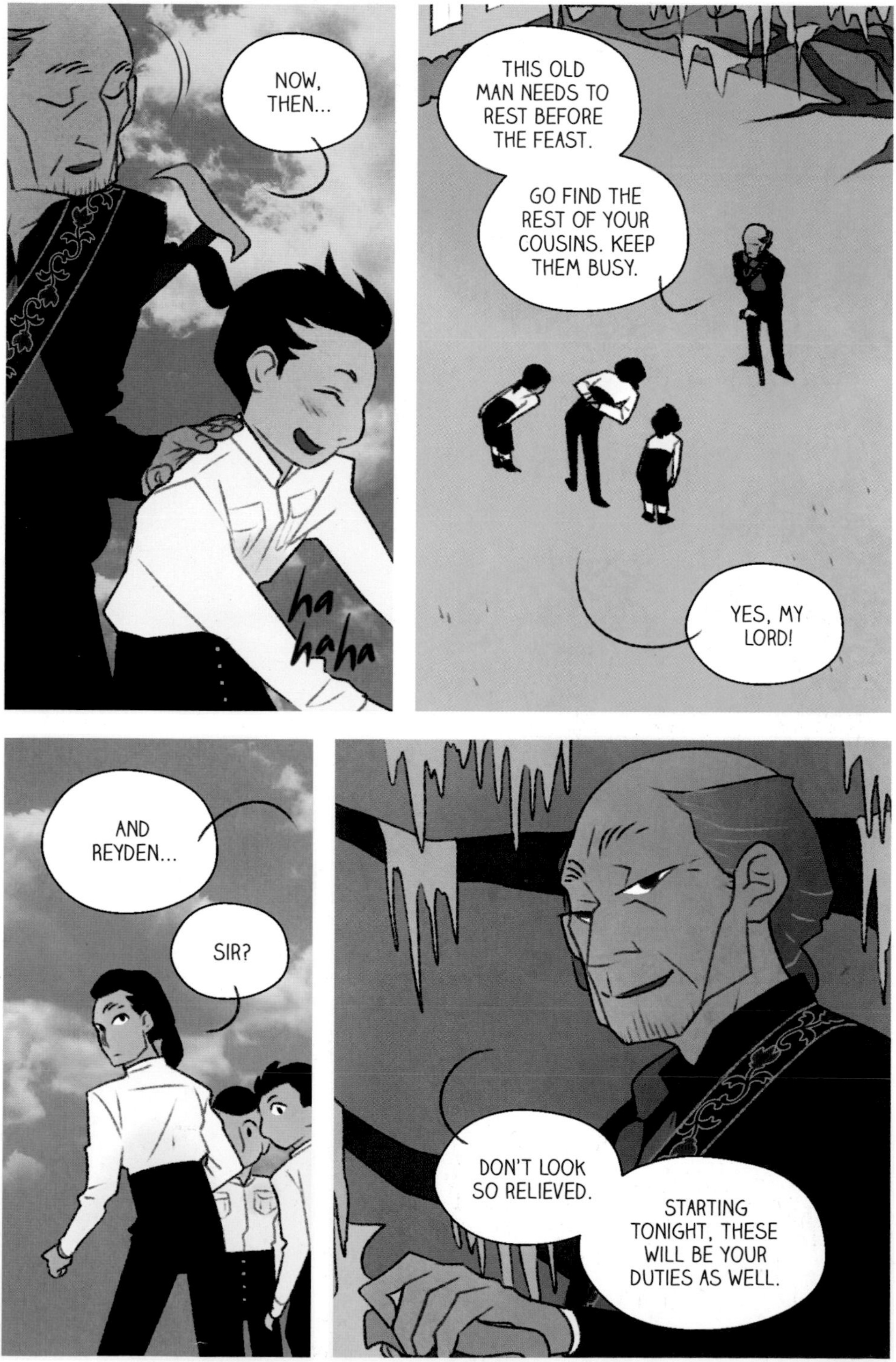
NOW, THEN...
ha haha
THIS OLD MAN NEEDS TO REST BEFORE THE FEAST.
GO FIND THE REST OF YOUR COUSINS. KEEP THEM BUSY.
YES, MY LORD!
AND REYDEN...
SIR?
DON'T LOOK SO RELIEVED.
STARTING TONIGHT, THESE WILL BE YOUR DUTIES AS WELL.

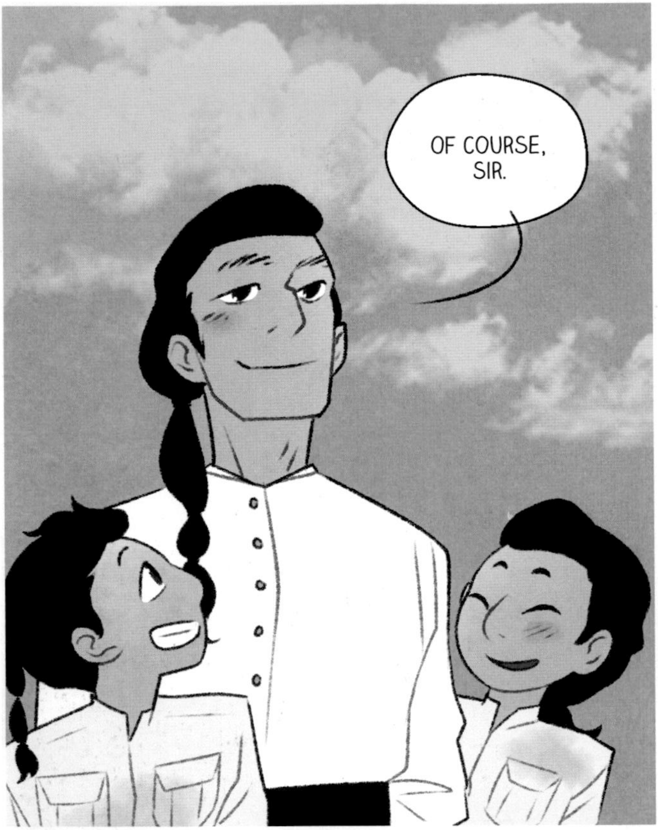
OF COURSE, SIR.

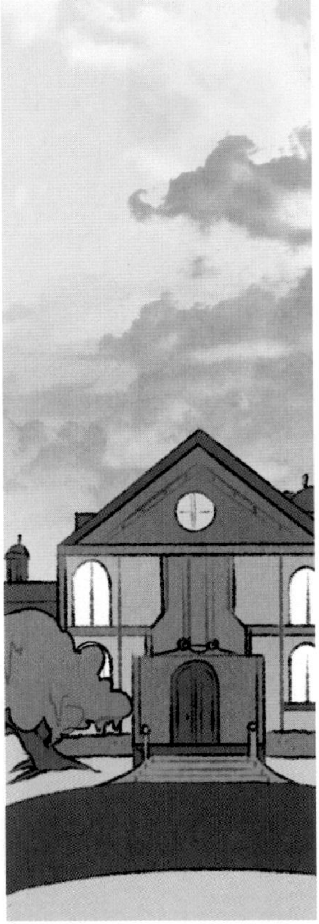

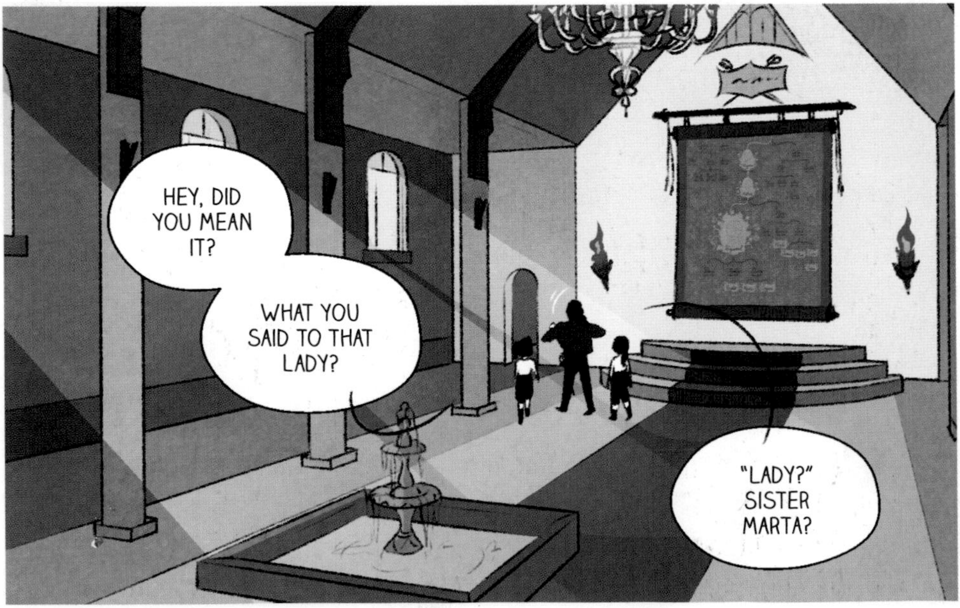
HEY, DID YOU MEAN IT?
WHAT YOU SAID TO THAT LADY?
"LADY?" SISTER MARTA?

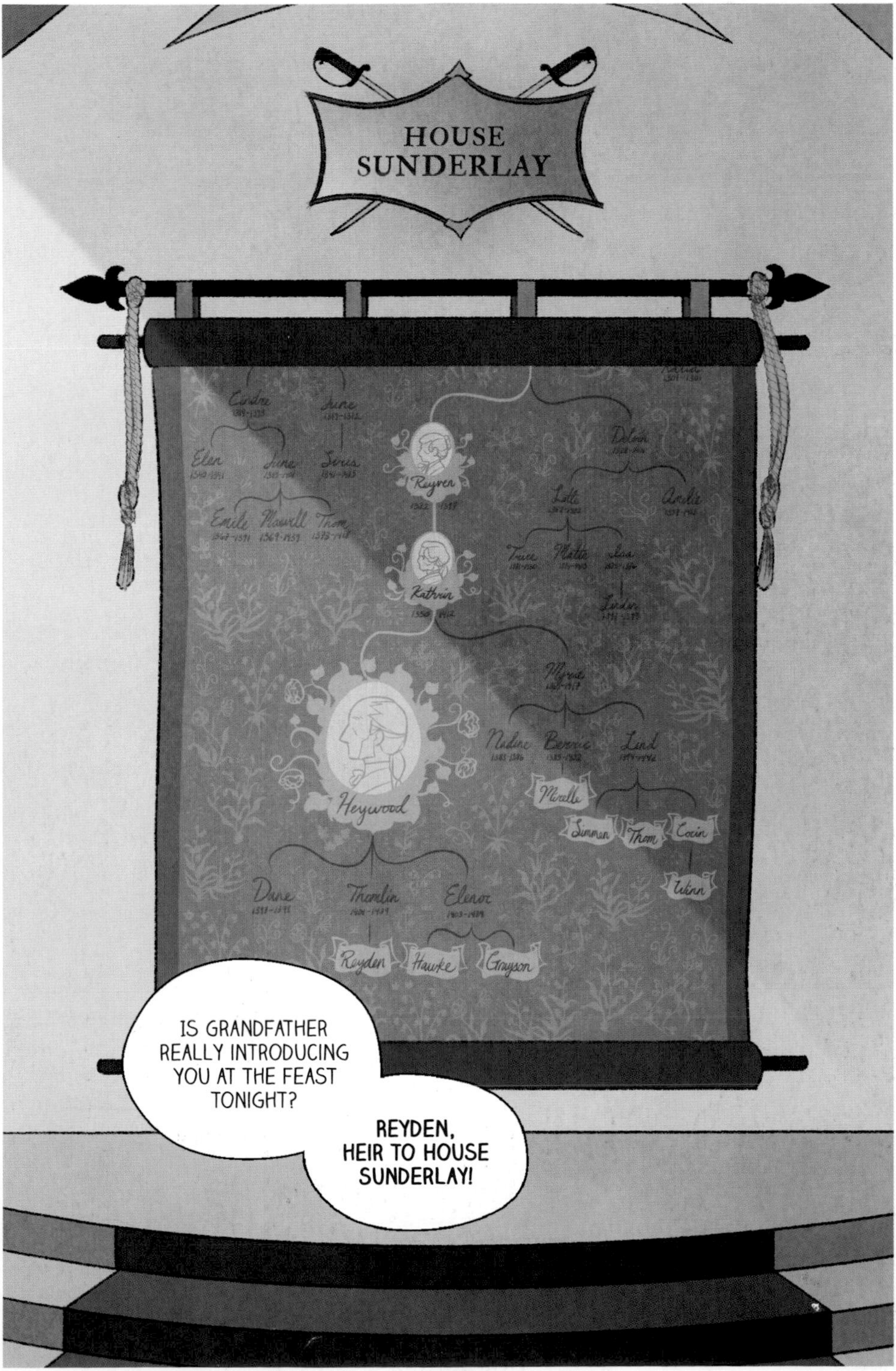
HOUSE SUNDERLAY
Reyren
Kathrin
Heywood
Reyden
Hawke
Grayson
IS GRANDFATHER REALLY INTRODUCING YOU AT THE FEAST TONIGHT?
REYDEN, HEIR TO HOUSE SUNDERLAY!

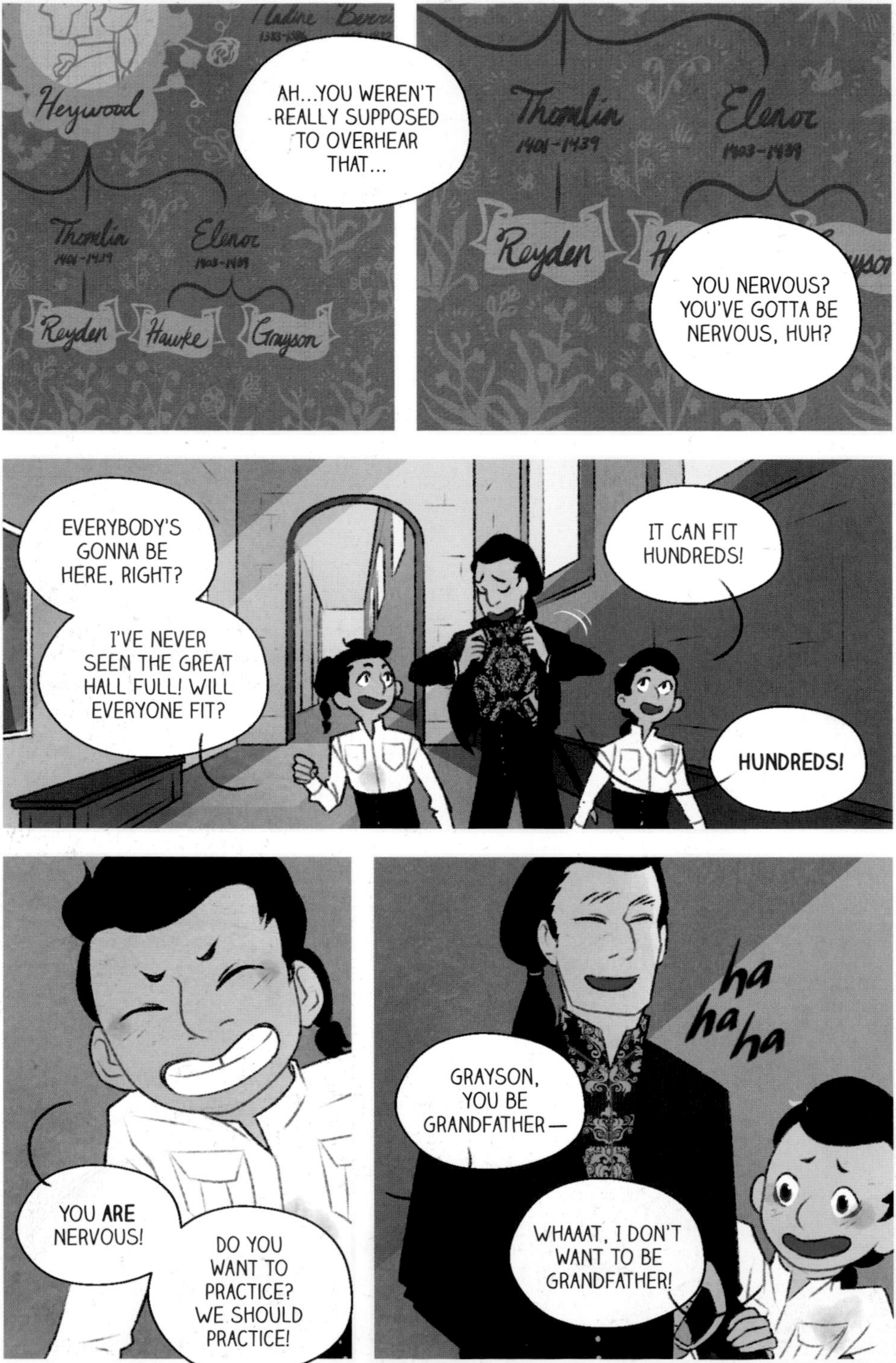
Heywood
Nadine
1383-1386
Thomlin
1401-1439
Elenor
1403-1439
Reyden
Hawke
Grayson
AH...YOU WEREN'T REALLY SUPPOSED TO OVERHEAR THAT...
Thomlin
1401-1439
Elenor
1403-1439
Reyden
YOU NERVOUS? YOU'VE GOTTA BE NERVOUS, HUH?
EVERYBODY'S GONNA BE HERE, RIGHT?
I'VE NEVER SEEN THE GREAT HALL FULL! WILL EVERYONE FIT?
IT CAN FIT HUNDREDS!
HUNDREDS!
YOU **ARE** NERVOUS!
DO YOU WANT TO PRACTICE? WE SHOULD PRACTICE!
ha ha ha
GRAYSON, YOU BE GRANDFATHER—
WHAAAT, I DON'T WANT TO BE GRANDFATHER!

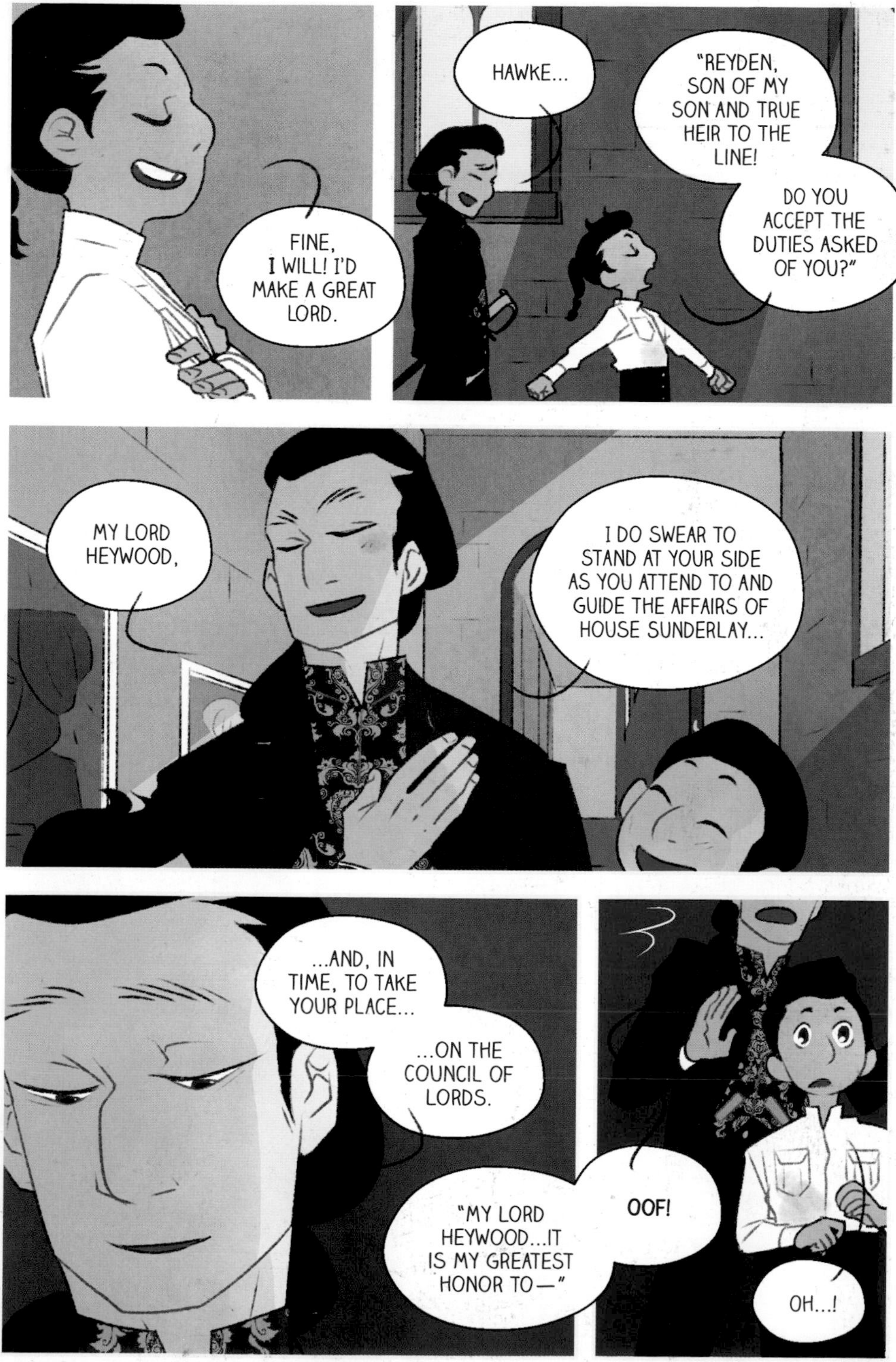
FINE, I WILL! I'D MAKE A GREAT LORD.
HAWKE...
"REYDEN, SON OF MY SON AND TRUE HEIR TO THE LINE!
DO YOU ACCEPT THE DUTIES ASKED OF YOU?"
MY LORD HEYWOOD,
I DO SWEAR TO STAND AT YOUR SIDE AS YOU ATTEND TO AND GUIDE THE AFFAIRS OF HOUSE SUNDERLAY...
...AND, IN TIME, TO TAKE YOUR PLACE...
...ON THE COUNCIL OF LORDS.
"MY LORD HEYWOOD...IT IS MY GREATEST HONOR TO—"
OOF!
OH...!

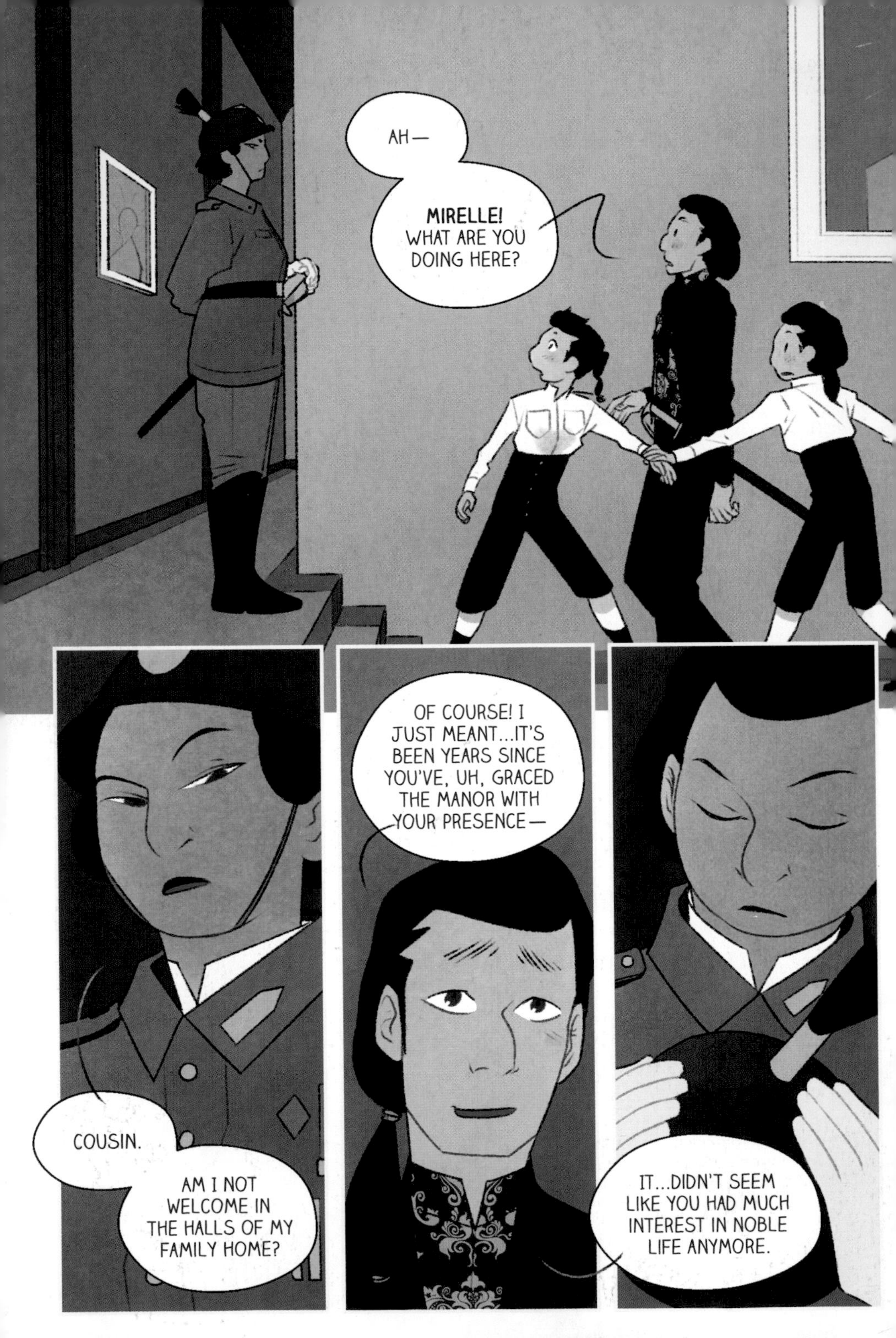
AH—
MIRELLE! WHAT ARE YOU DOING HERE?
COUSIN.
AM I NOT WELCOME IN THE HALLS OF MY FAMILY HOME?
OF COURSE! I JUST MEANT...IT'S BEEN YEARS SINCE YOU'VE, UH, GRACED THE MANOR WITH YOUR PRESENCE—
IT...DIDN'T SEEM LIKE YOU HAD MUCH INTEREST IN NOBLE LIFE ANYMORE.

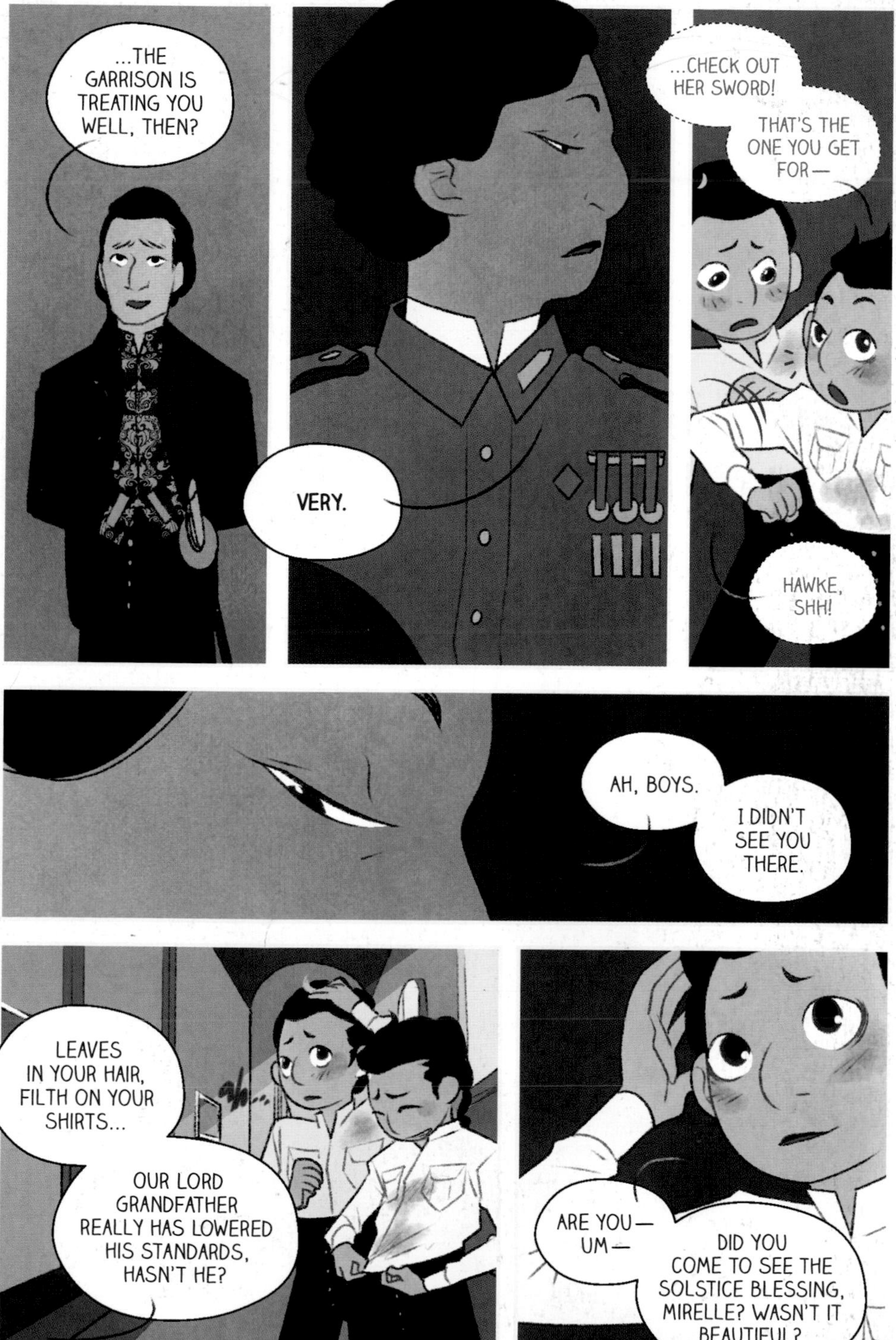
...THE GARRISON IS TREATING YOU WELL, THEN?
VERY.
...CHECK OUT HER SWORD!
THAT'S THE ONE YOU GET FOR—
HAWKE, SHH!
AH, BOYS.
I DIDN'T SEE YOU THERE.
LEAVES IN YOUR HAIR, FILTH ON YOUR SHIRTS...
OUR LORD GRANDFATHER REALLY HAS LOWERED HIS STANDARDS, HASN'T HE?
ARE YOU— UM—
DID YOU COME TO SEE THE SOLSTICE BLESSING, MIRELLE? WASN'T IT BEAUTIFUL?

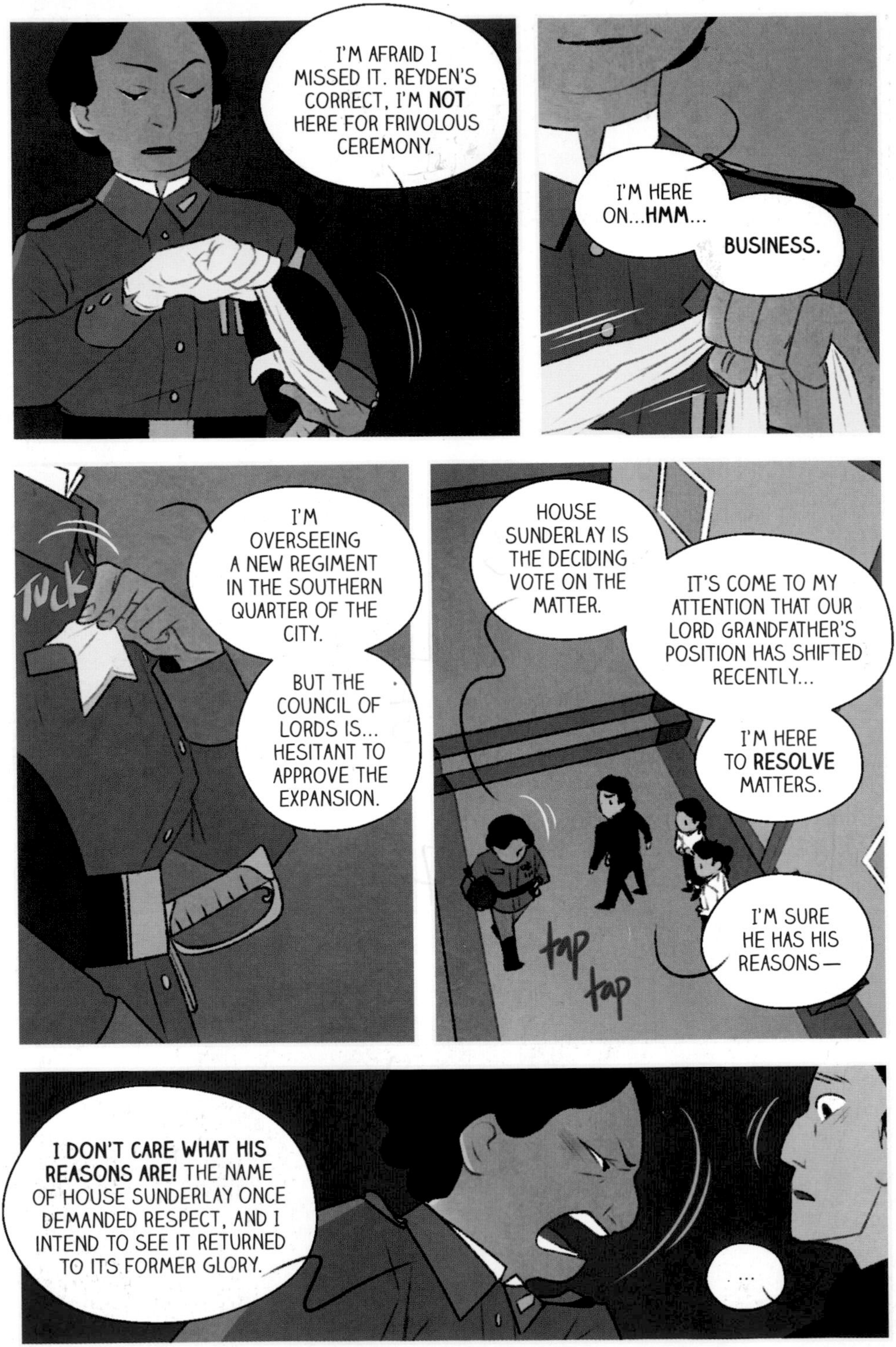
I'M AFRAID I MISSED IT. REYDEN'S CORRECT, I'M **NOT** HERE FOR FRIVOLOUS CEREMONY.
I'M HERE ON...**HMM**...
BUSINESS.
TUCK
I'M OVERSEEING A NEW REGIMENT IN THE SOUTHERN QUARTER OF THE CITY.
BUT THE COUNCIL OF LORDS IS... HESITANT TO APPROVE THE EXPANSION.
HOUSE SUNDERLAY IS THE DECIDING VOTE ON THE MATTER.
IT'S COME TO MY ATTENTION THAT OUR LORD GRANDFATHER'S POSITION HAS SHIFTED RECENTLY...
I'M HERE TO **RESOLVE** MATTERS.
tap
tap
I'M SURE HE HAS HIS REASONS—
I DON'T CARE WHAT HIS REASONS ARE! THE NAME OF HOUSE SUNDERLAY ONCE DEMANDED RESPECT, AND I INTEND TO SEE IT RETURNED TO ITS FORMER GLORY.
...

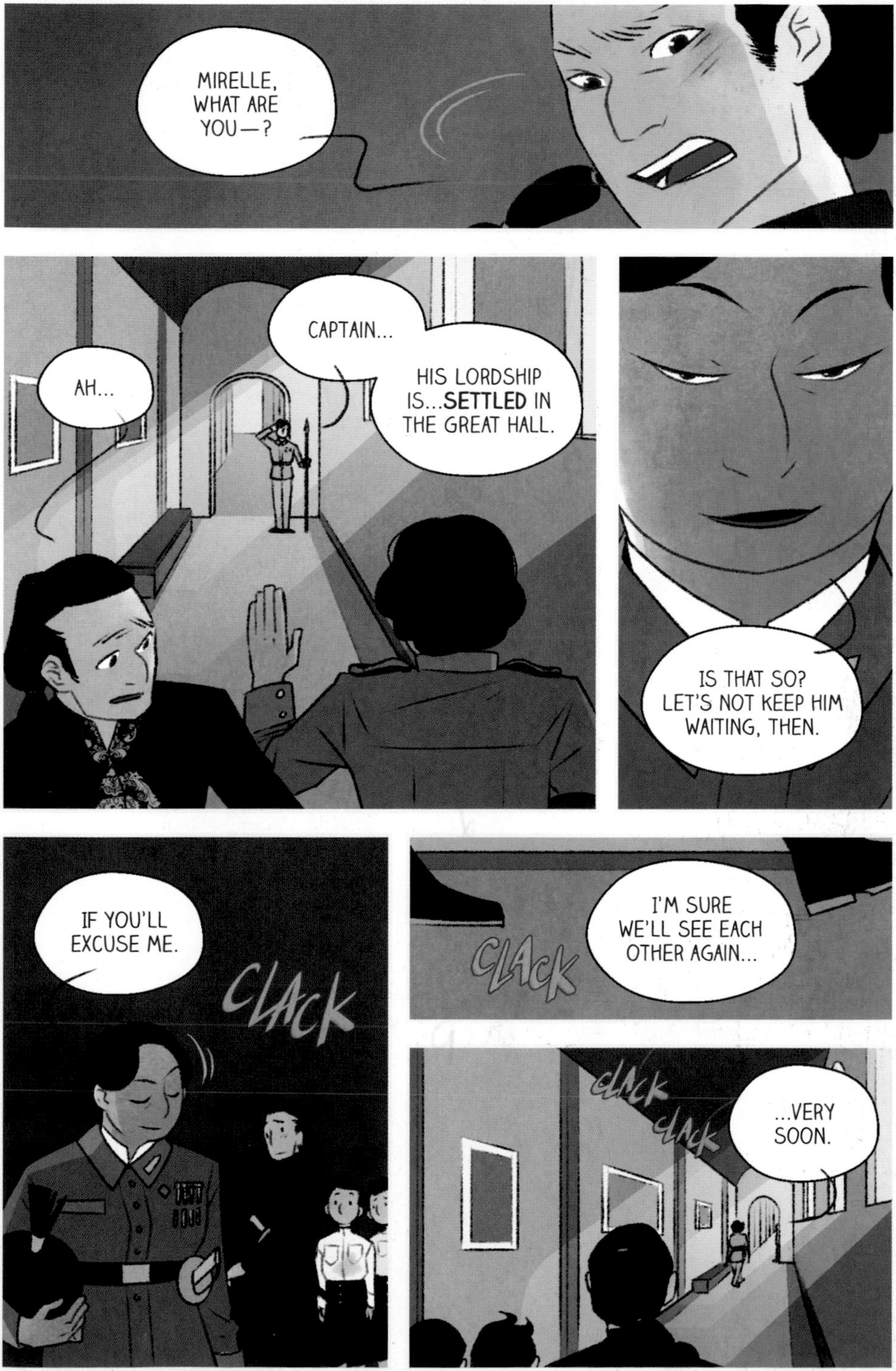
MIRELLE, WHAT ARE YOU—?
AH...
CAPTAIN...
HIS LORDSHIP IS...**SETTLED** IN THE GREAT HALL.
IS THAT SO? LET'S NOT KEEP HIM WAITING, THEN.
IF YOU'LL EXCUSE ME.
CLACK
CLACK
I'M SURE WE'LL SEE EACH OTHER AGAIN...
CLACK CLACK
...VERY SOON.

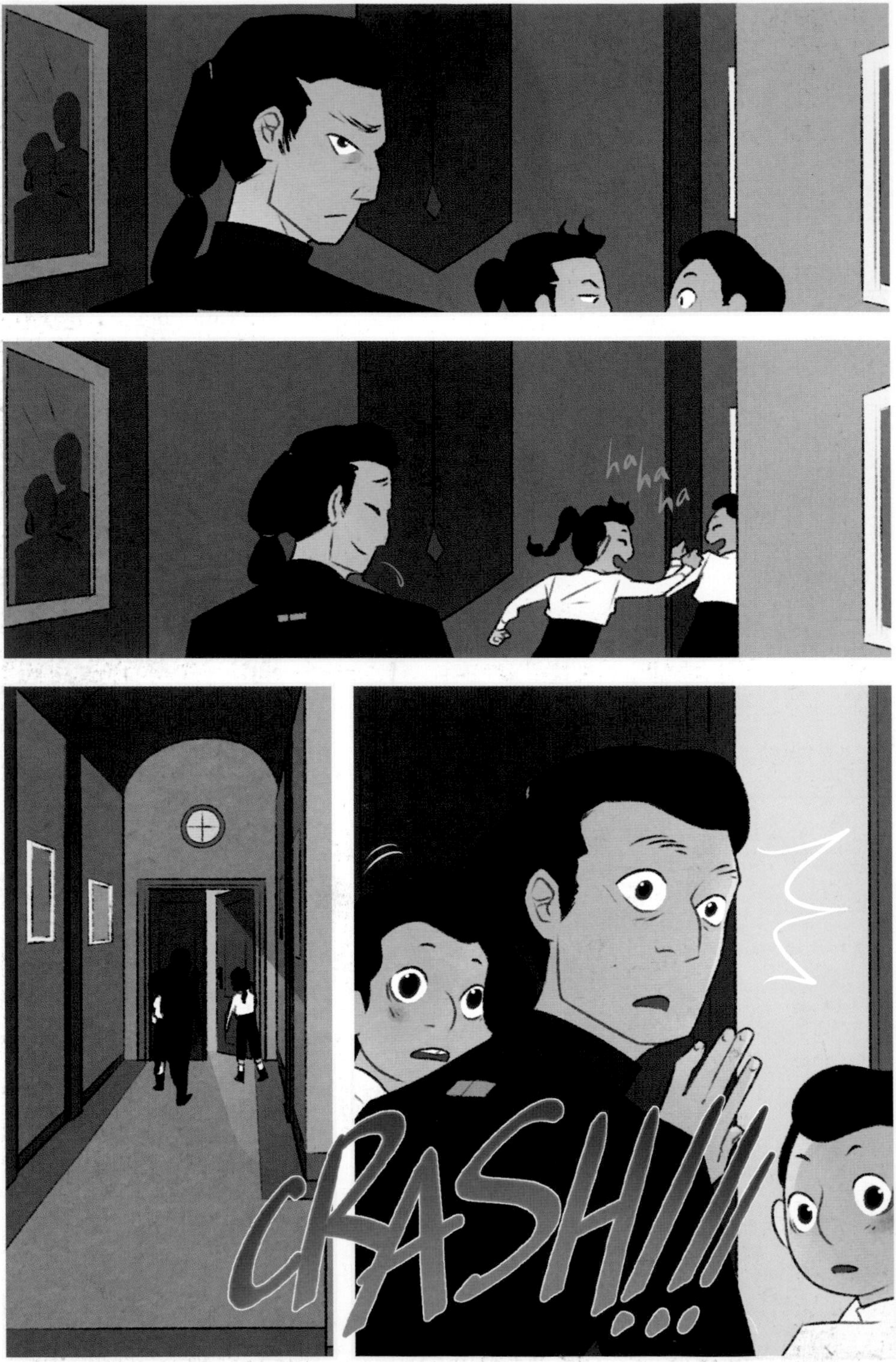
ha
ha
ha
CRASH!!!

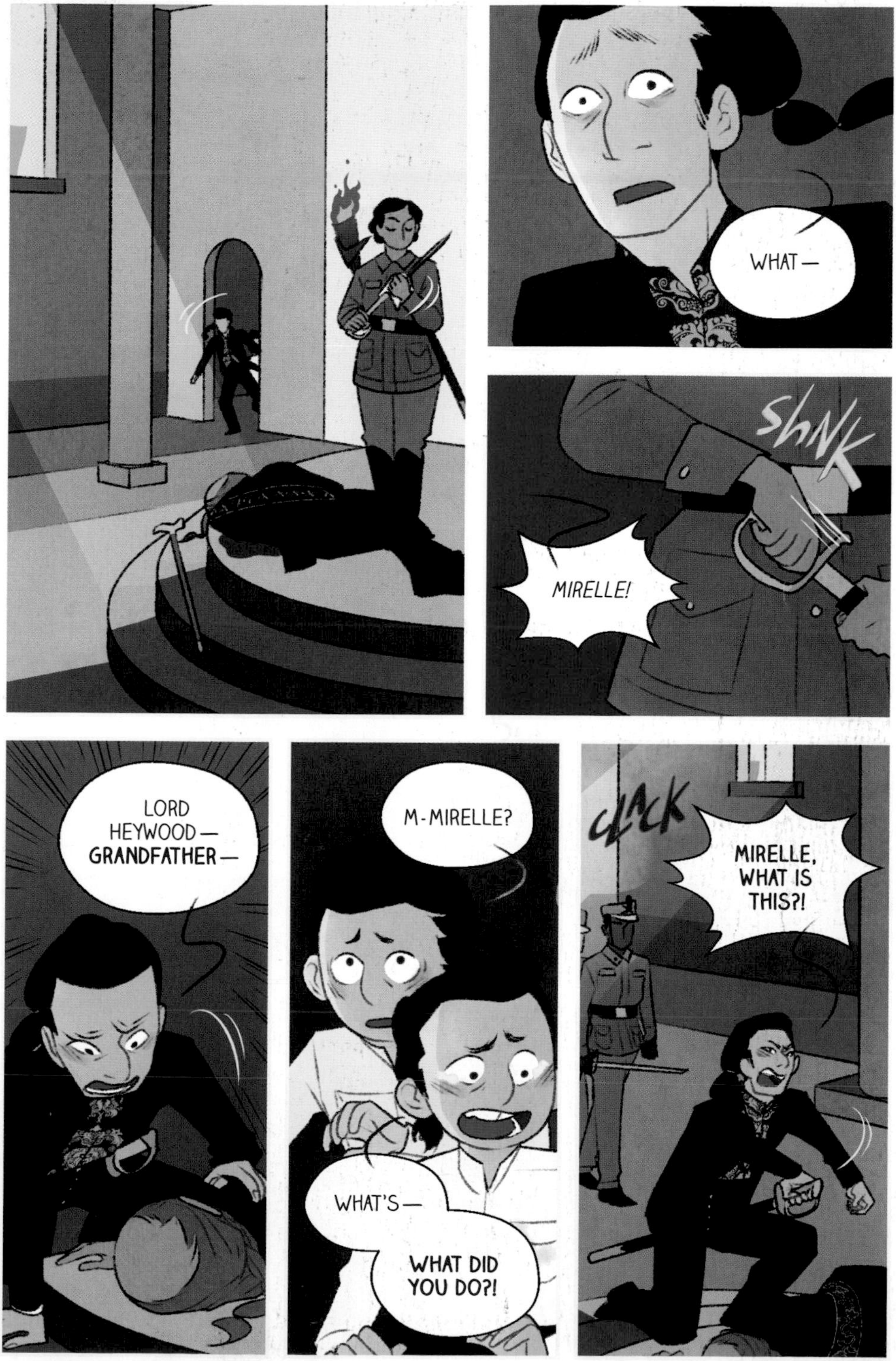
WHAT—
SHNK
MIRELLE!
LORD HEYWOOD— GRANDFATHER—
M-MIRELLE?
WHAT'S—
WHAT DID YOU DO?!
CLACK
MIRELLE, WHAT IS THIS?!

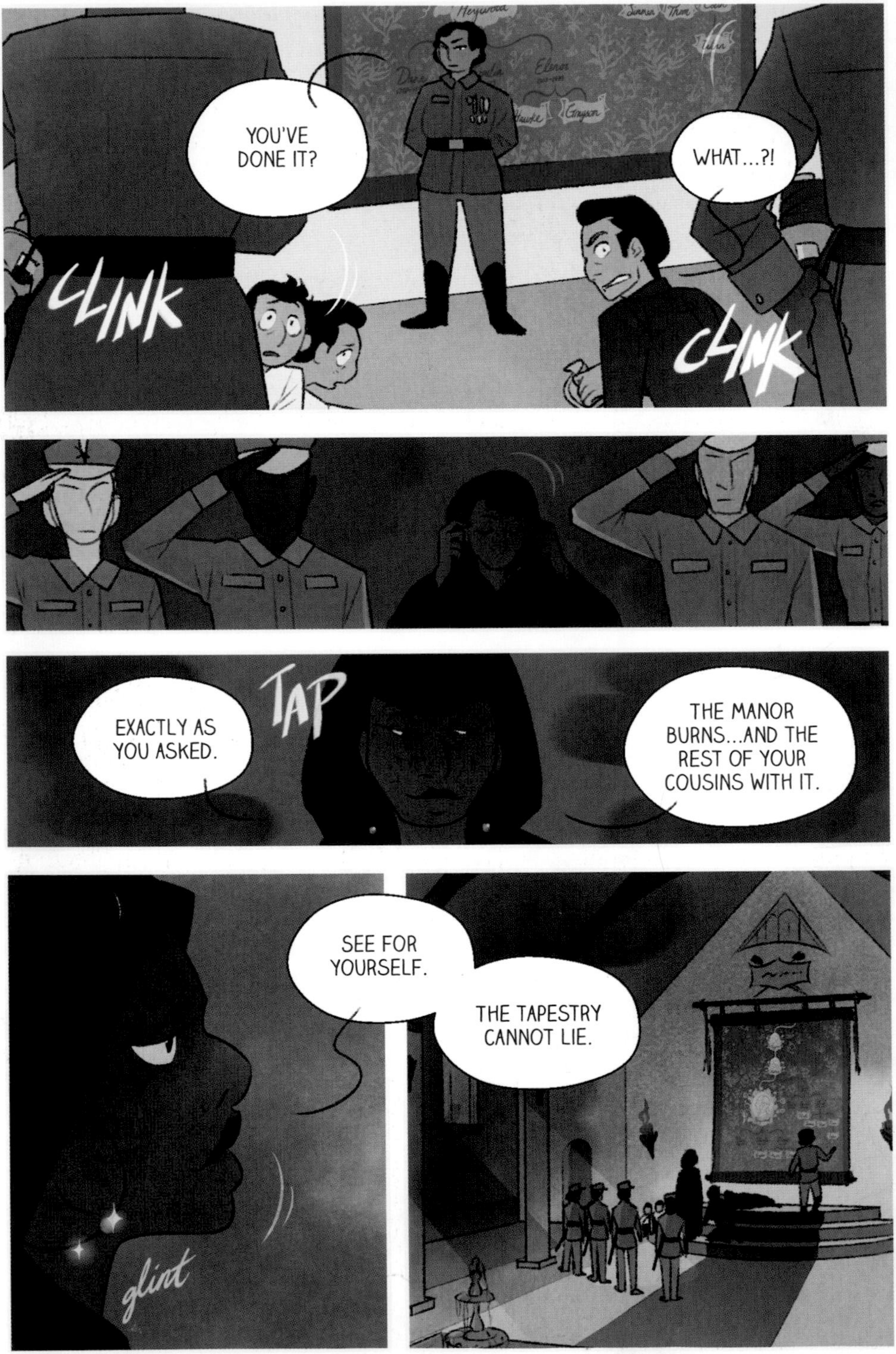
YOU'VE DONE IT?
WHAT...?!
CLINK
CLINK
TAP
EXACTLY AS YOU ASKED.
THE MANOR BURNS...AND THE REST OF YOUR COUSINS WITH IT.
glint
SEE FOR YOURSELF.
THE TAPESTRY CANNOT LIE.

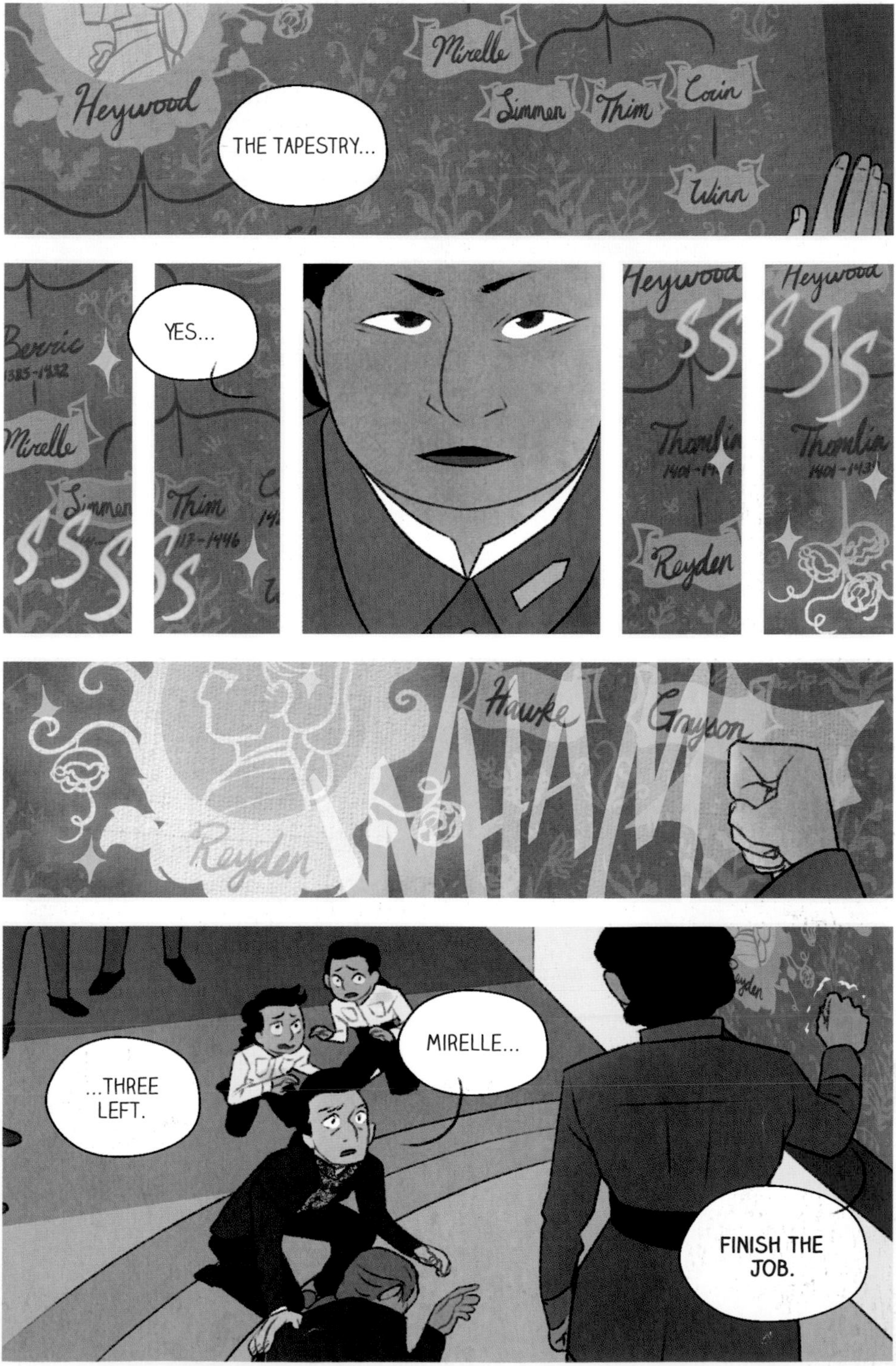
THE TAPESTRY...
YES...
SSSSS
WHAM
...THREE LEFT.
MIRELLE...
FINISH THE JOB.

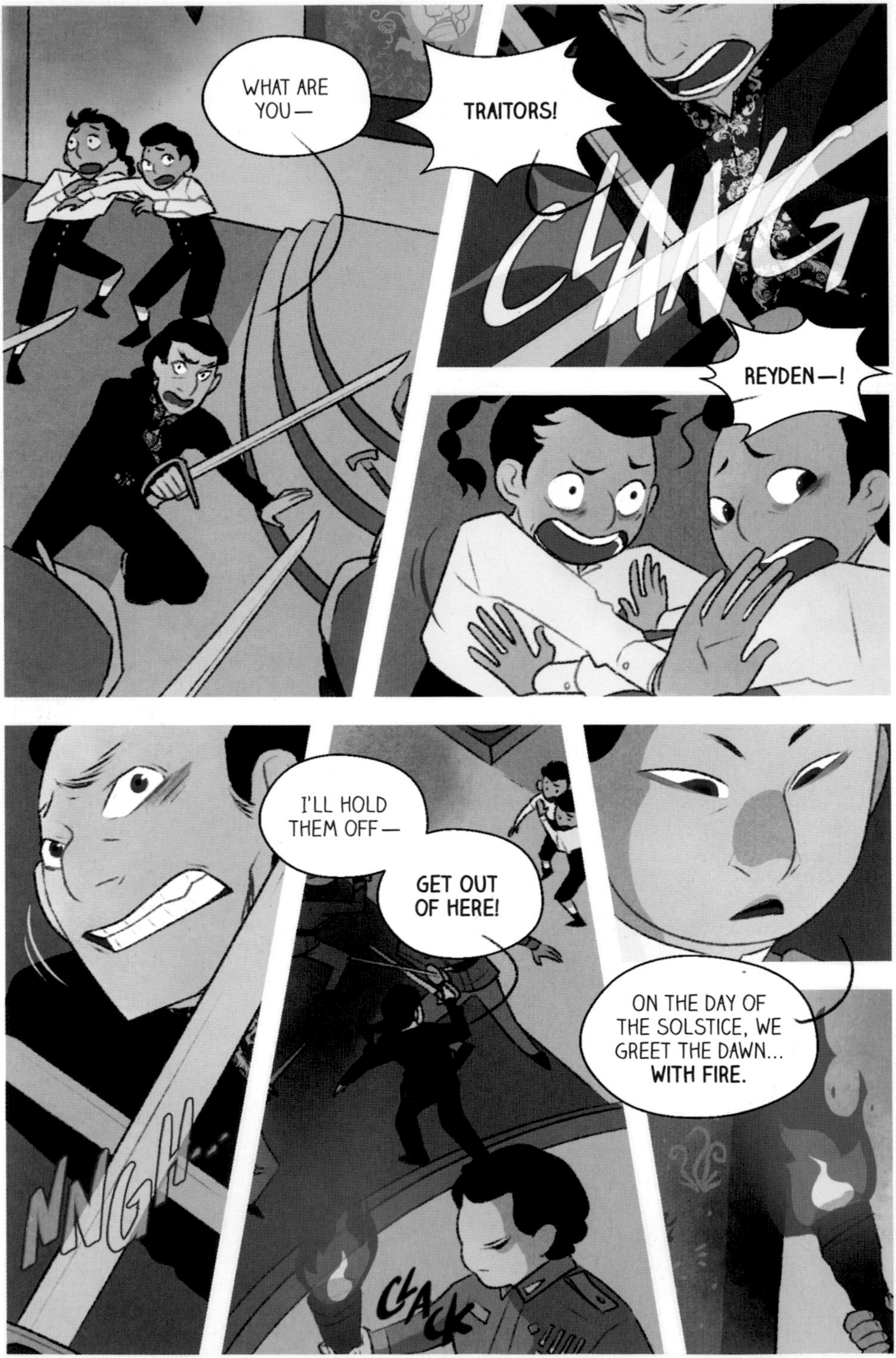
WHAT ARE YOU—
TRAITORS!
CLANG
REYDEN—!
I'LL HOLD THEM OFF—
GET OUT OF HERE!
ON THE DAY OF THE SOLSTICE, WE GREET THE DAWN... WITH FIRE.
NNGH...
CLACK

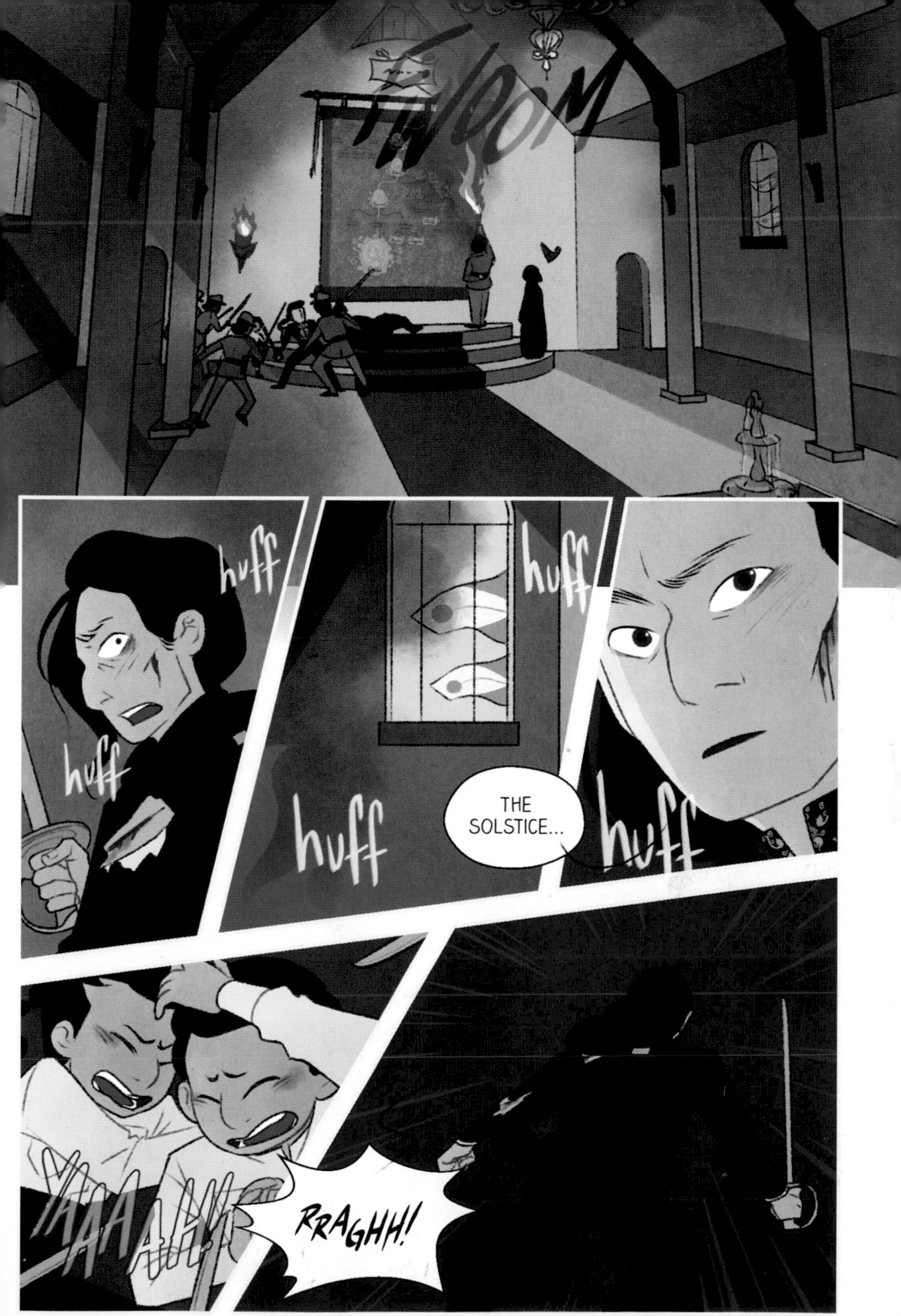
FWOOM
huff
huff
huff
huff
THE SOLSTICE...
huff
YAAAAH!
RRAGHH!

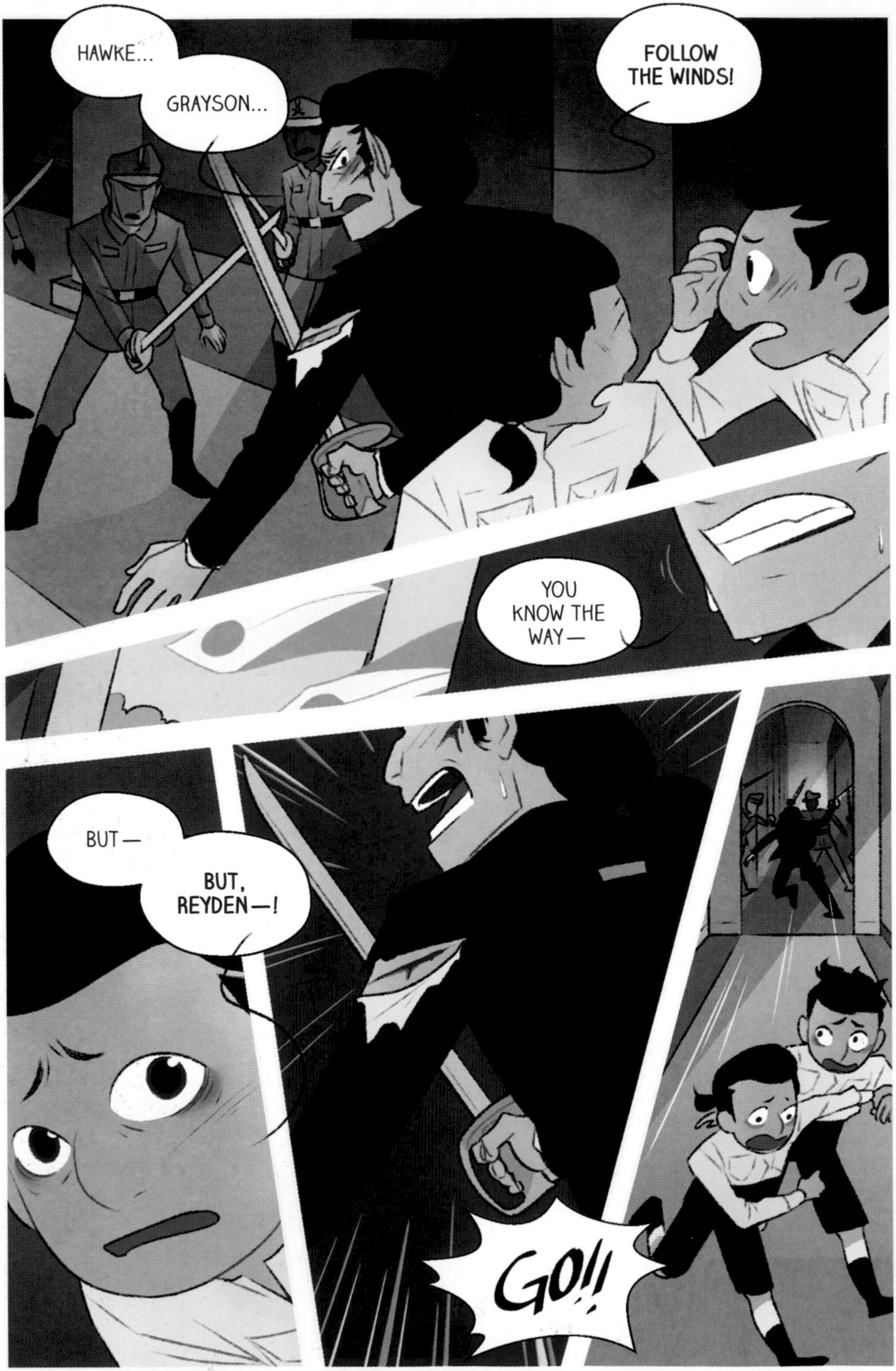
HAWKE...
GRAYSON...
FOLLOW THE WINDS!
YOU KNOW THE WAY—
BUT—
BUT, REYDEN—!
GO!!

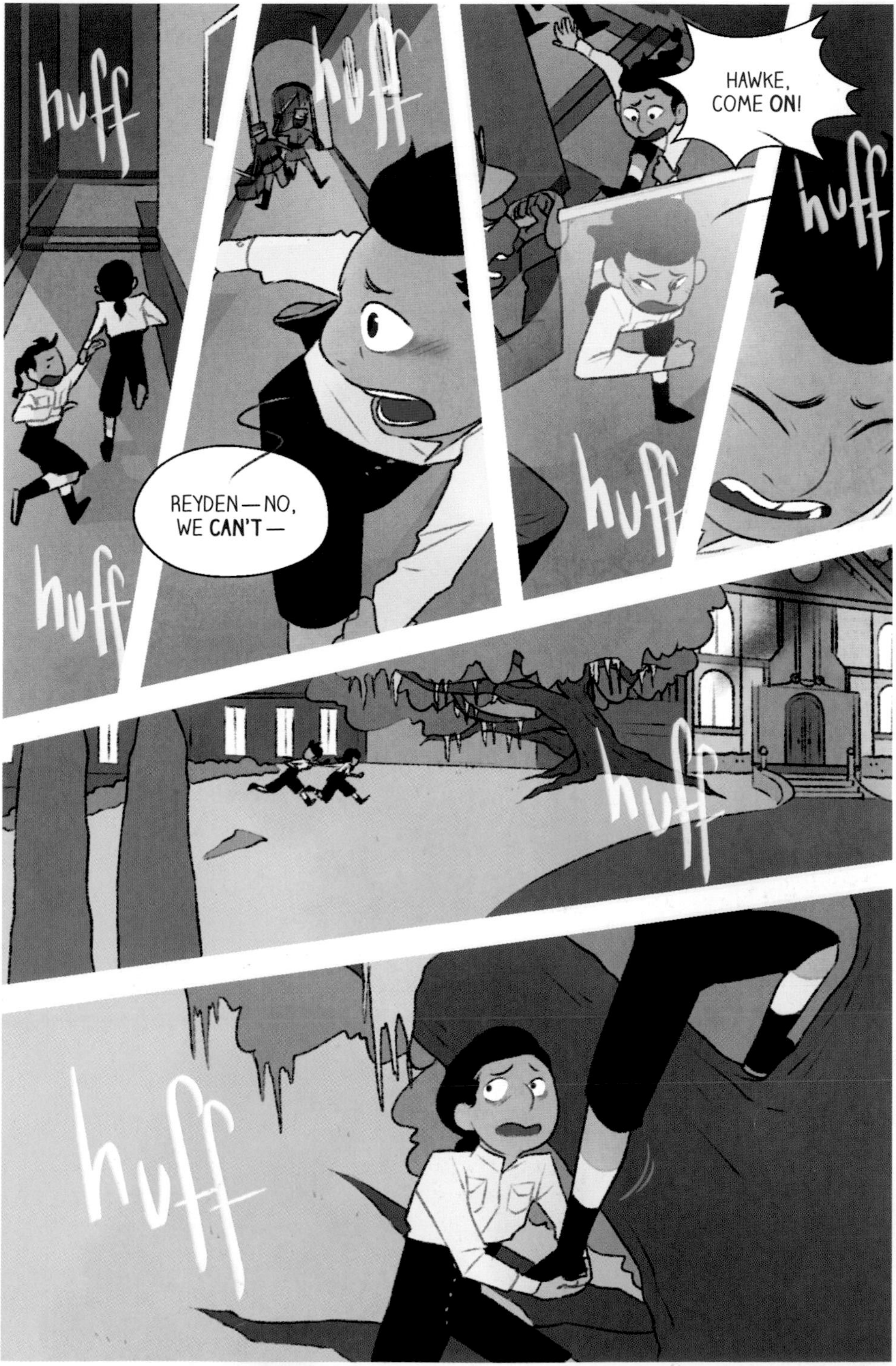
huff
huff
REYDEN—NO, WE CAN'T—
huff
HAWKE, COME ON!
huff
huff
huff
huff

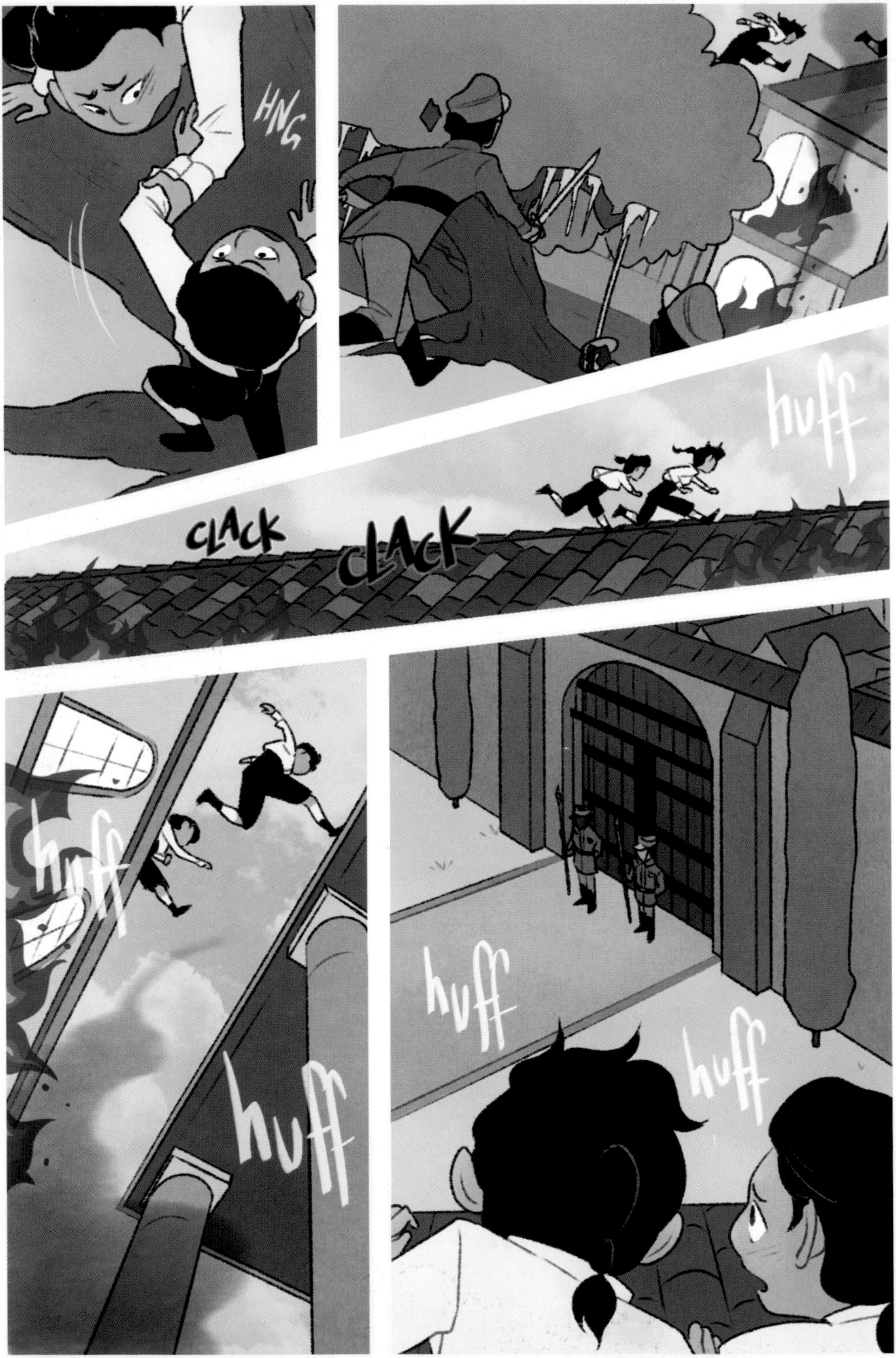
HNG
huff
CLACK
CLACK
huff
huff
huff
huff

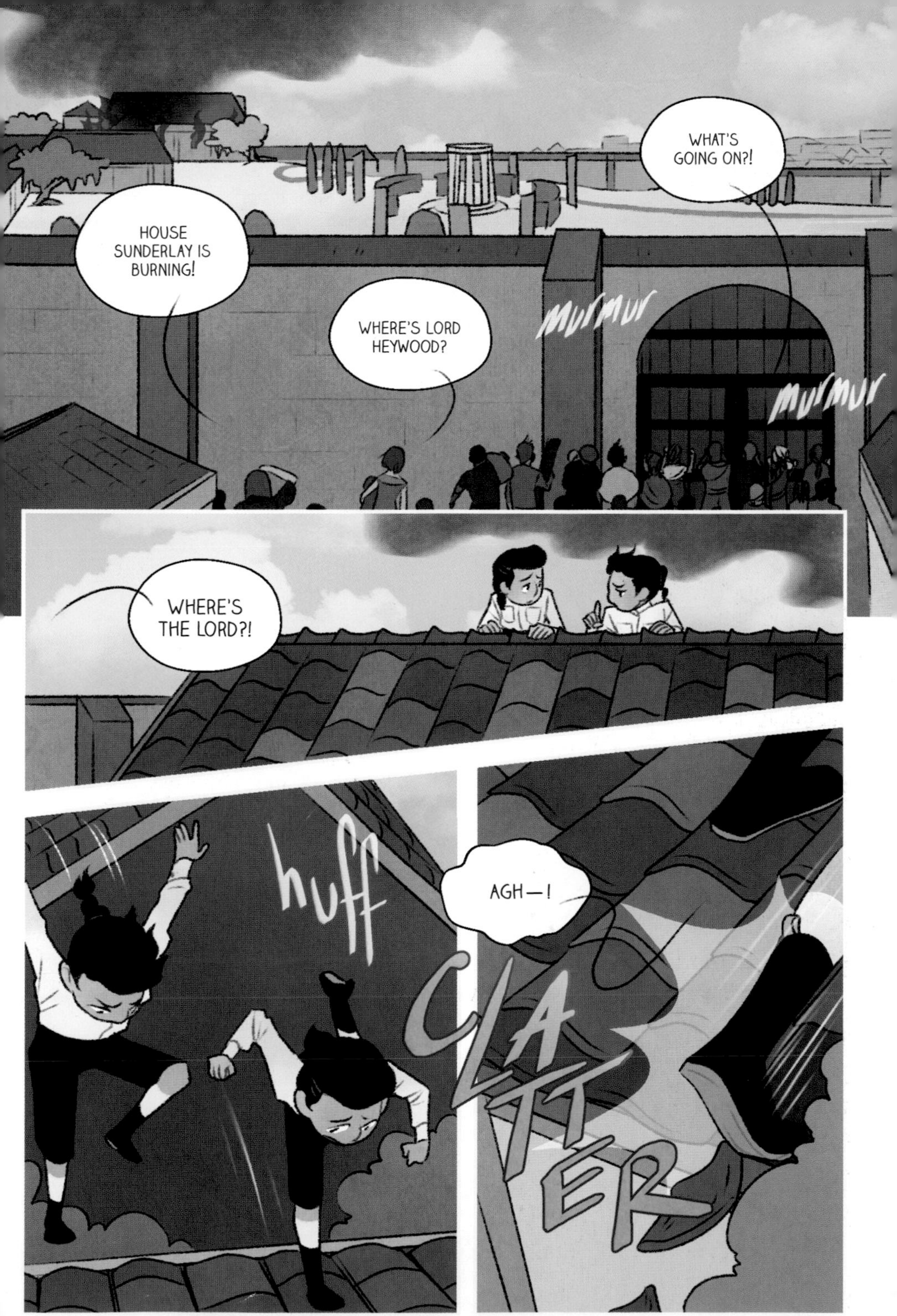
WHAT'S GOING ON?!
HOUSE SUNDERLAY IS BURNING!
WHERE'S LORD HEYWOOD?
Murmur
Murmur
WHERE'S THE LORD?!
huff
AGH—!
CLATTER

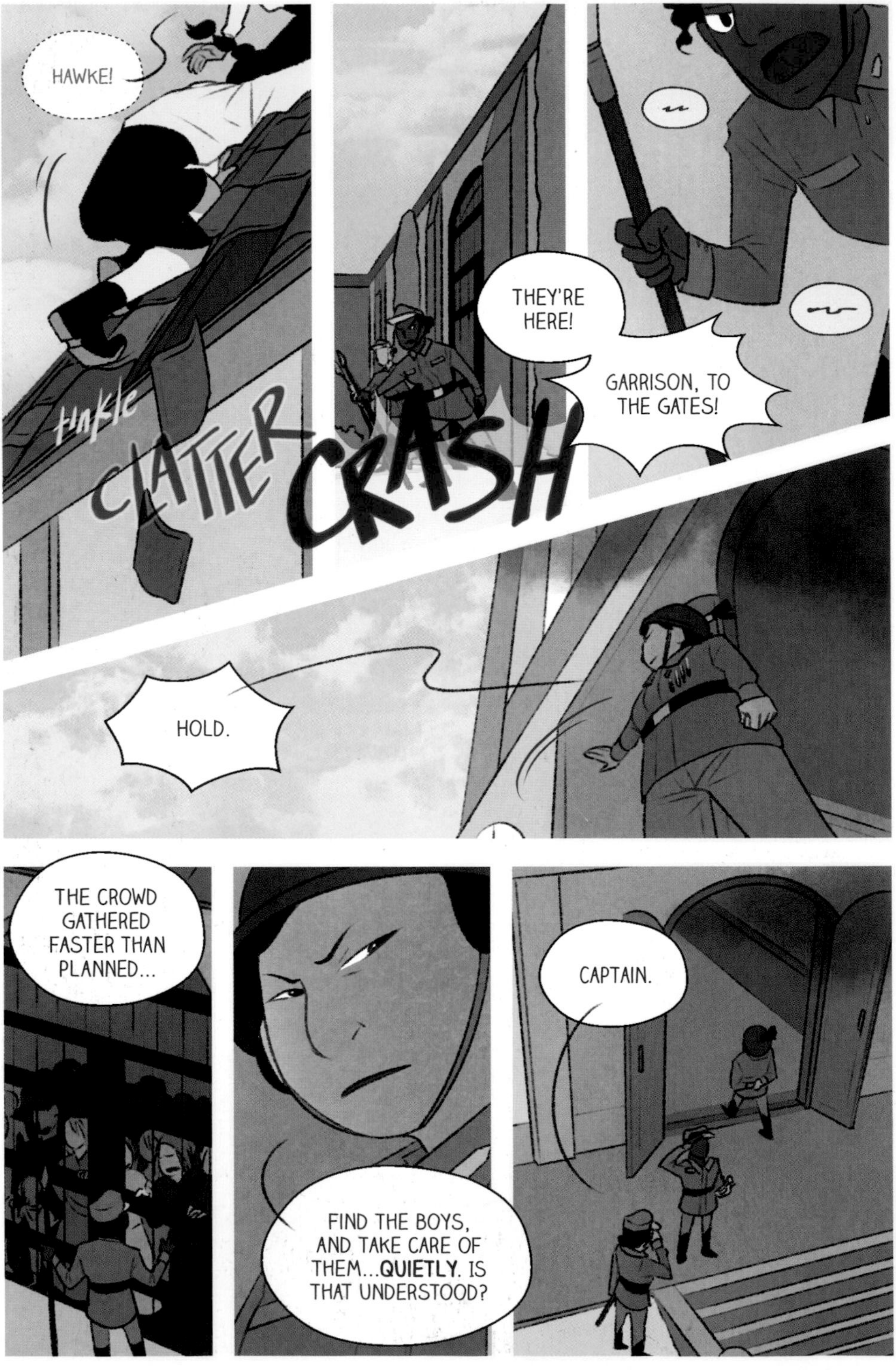
HAWKE!
tinkle
CLATTER
CRASH
THEY'RE HERE!
GARRISON, TO THE GATES!
HOLD.
THE CROWD GATHERED FASTER THAN PLANNED...
FIND THE BOYS, AND TAKE CARE OF THEM...**QUIETLY**. IS THAT UNDERSTOOD?
CAPTAIN.

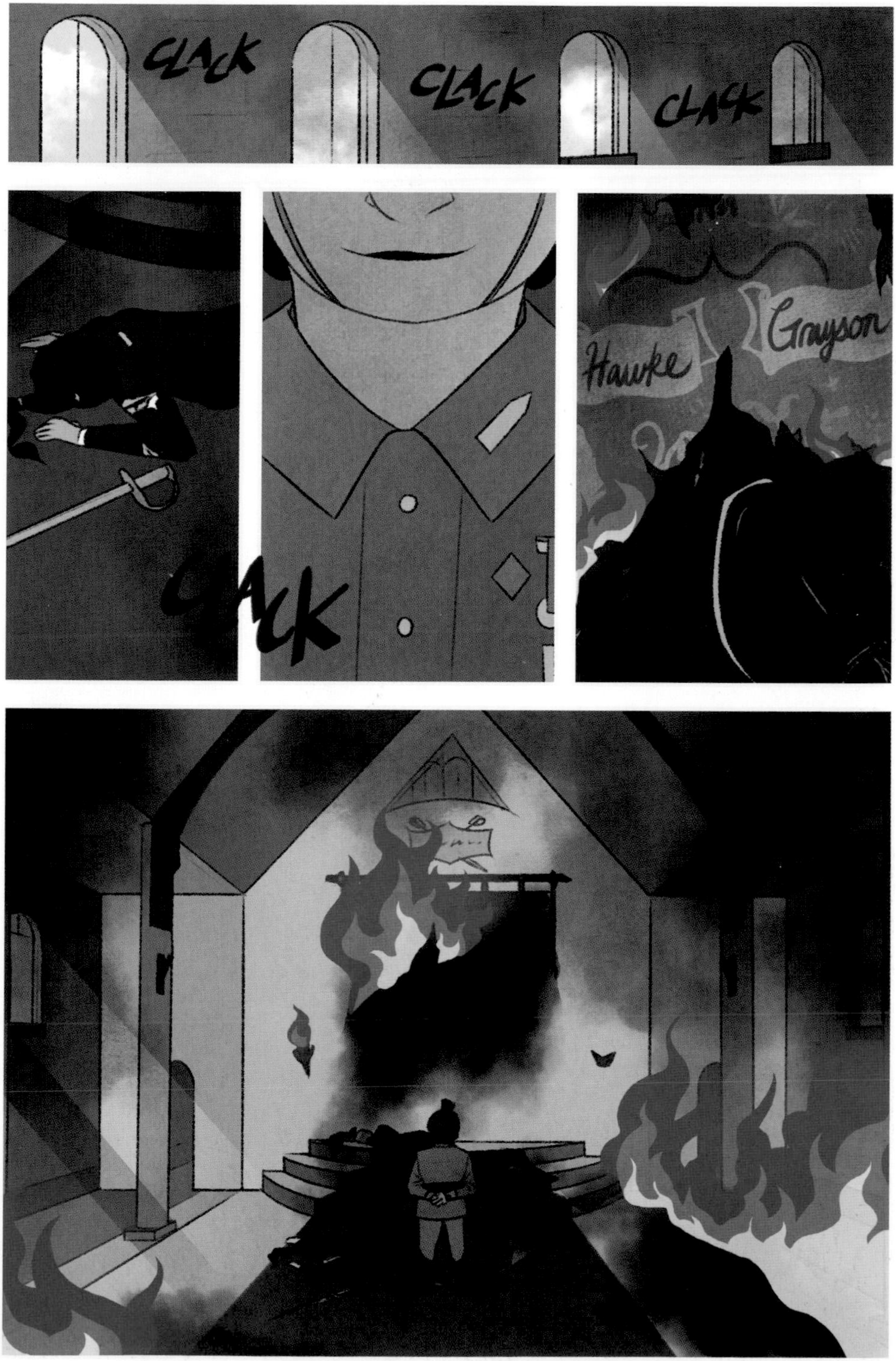
CLACK
CLACK
CLACK
CLACK
Hawke
Grayson

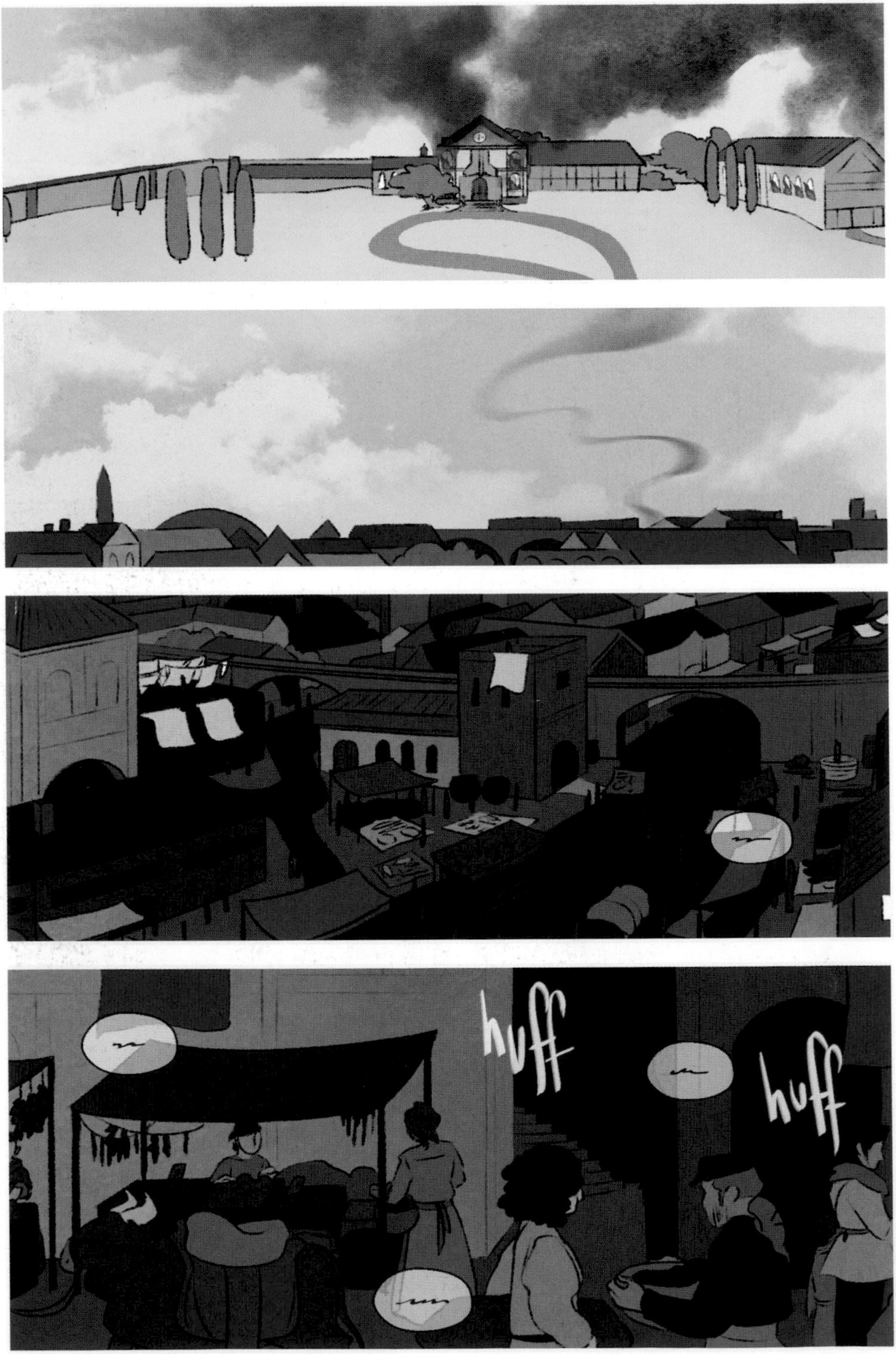
huff
huff

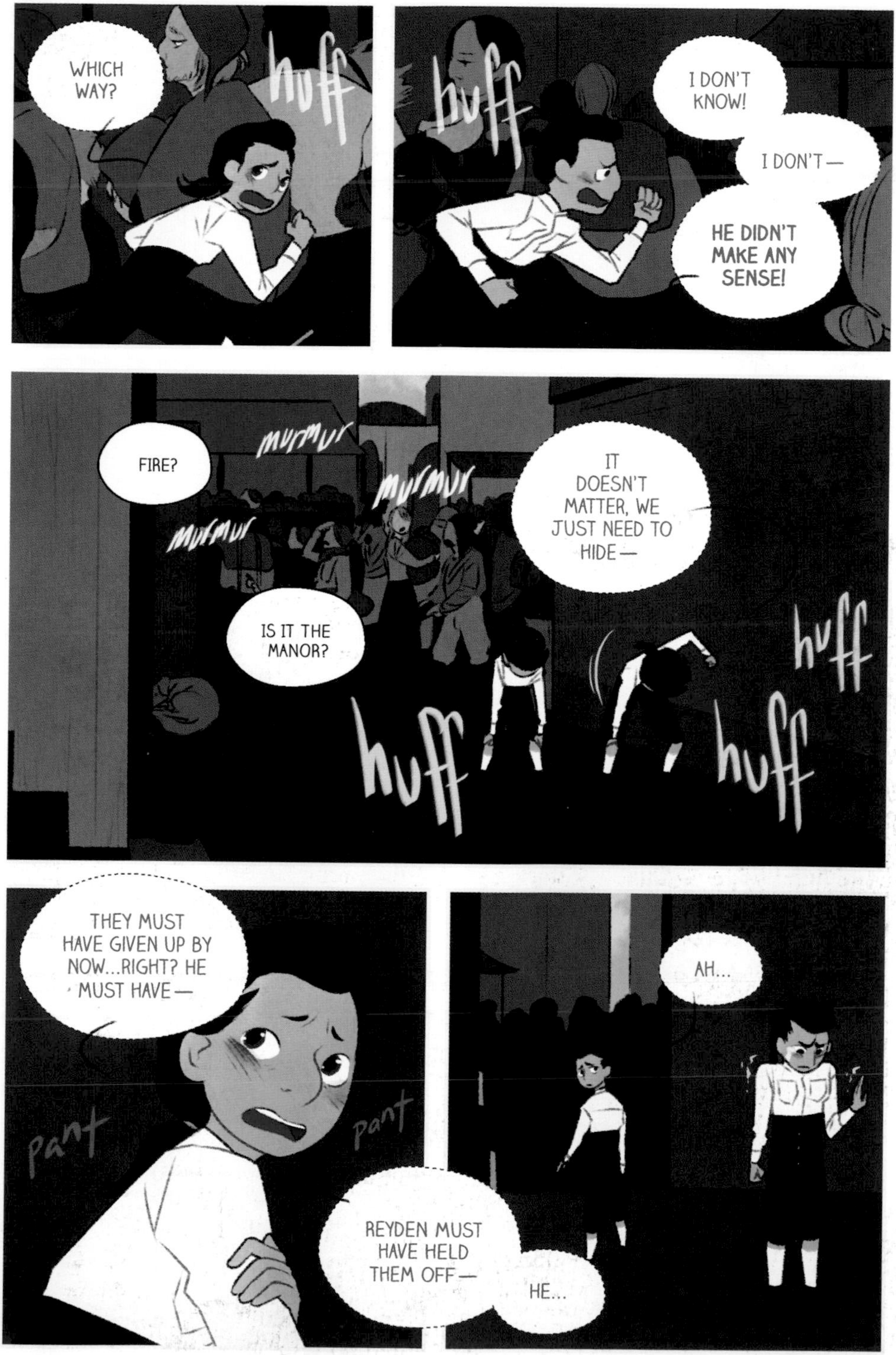
WHICH WAY?
huff
huff
I DON'T KNOW!
I DON'T—
HE DIDN'T MAKE ANY SENSE!
FIRE?
murmur
murmur
murmur
IT DOESN'T MATTER, WE JUST NEED TO HIDE—
IS IT THE MANOR?
huff
huff
huff
THEY MUST HAVE GIVEN UP BY NOW...RIGHT? HE MUST HAVE—
pant
pant
REYDEN MUST HAVE HELD THEM OFF—
AH...
HE...

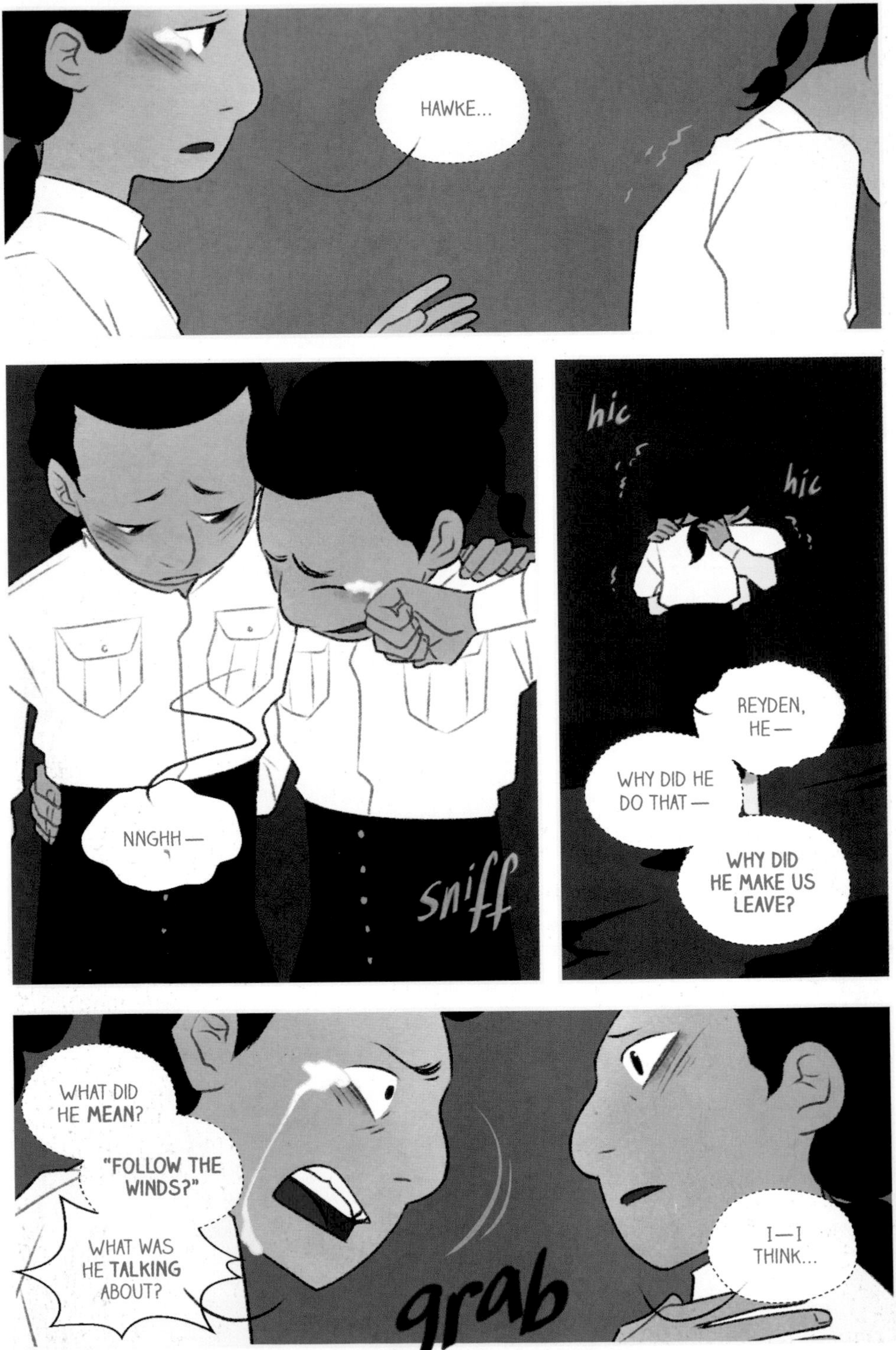
HAWKE...
NNGHH—
sniff
hic
hic
REYDEN, HE—
WHY DID HE DO THAT—
WHY DID HE MAKE US LEAVE?
WHAT DID HE MEAN?
"FOLLOW THE WINDS?"
WHAT WAS HE TALKING ABOUT?
I—I THINK...
grab

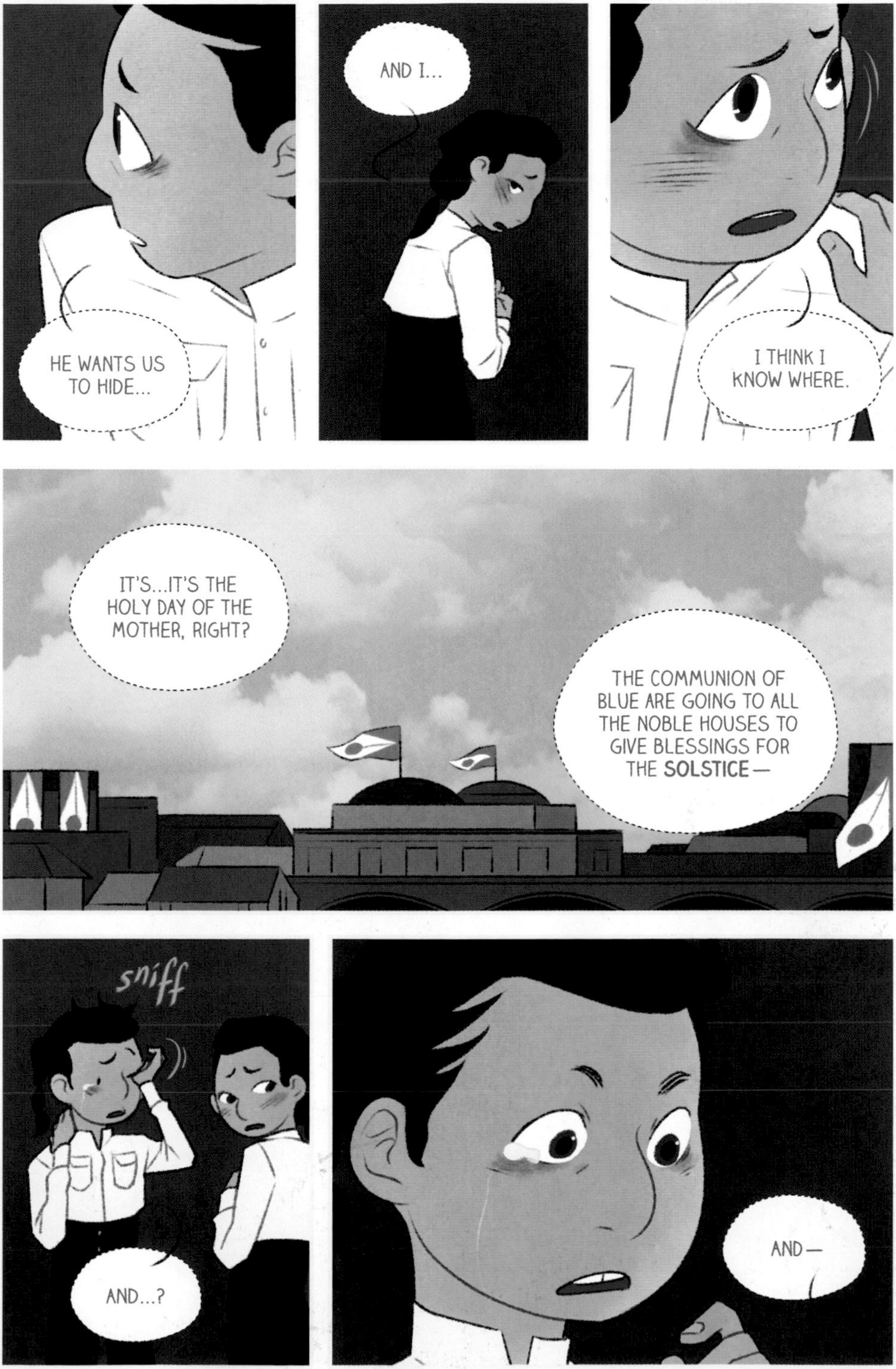
HE WANTS US TO HIDE...
AND I...
I THINK I KNOW WHERE.
IT'S...IT'S THE HOLY DAY OF THE MOTHER, RIGHT?
THE COMMUNION OF BLUE ARE GOING TO ALL THE NOBLE HOUSES TO GIVE BLESSINGS FOR THE **SOLSTICE**—
sniff
AND...?
AND—

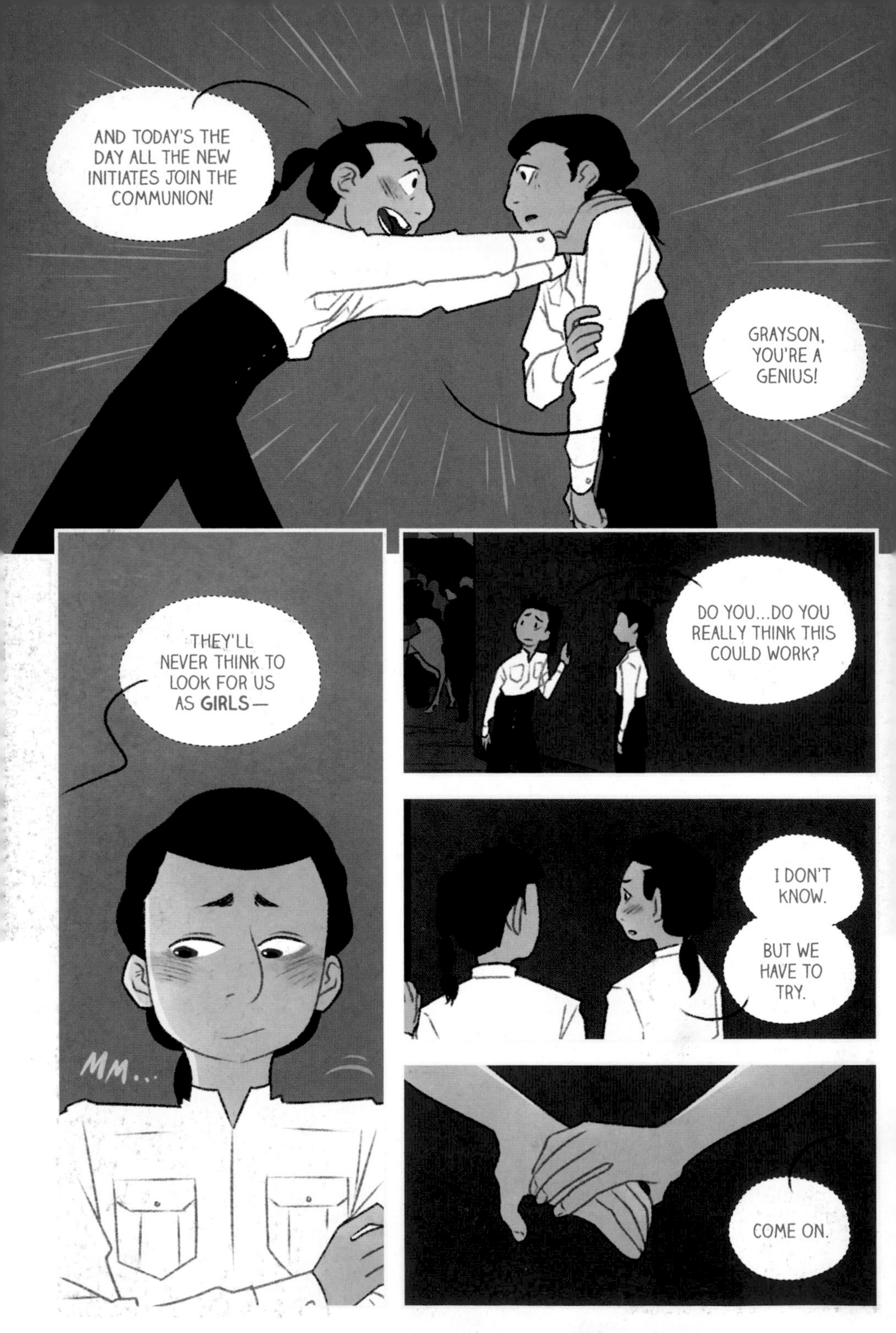
AND TODAY'S THE DAY ALL THE NEW INITIATES JOIN THE COMMUNION!
GRAYSON, YOU'RE A GENIUS!
THEY'LL NEVER THINK TO LOOK FOR US AS **GIRLS**—
MM...
DO YOU...DO YOU REALLY THINK THIS COULD WORK?
I DON'T KNOW.
BUT WE HAVE TO TRY.
COME ON.

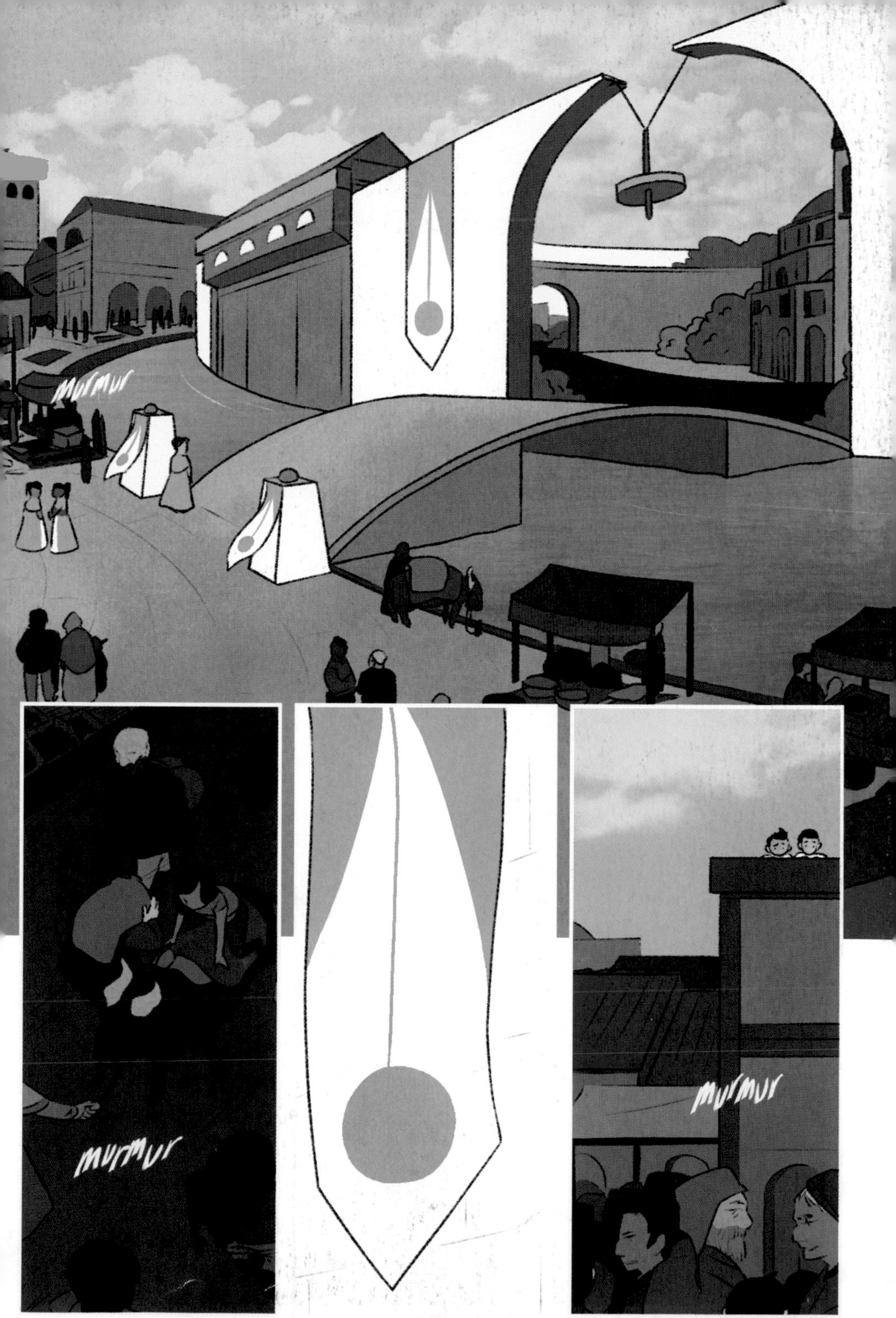
Murmur
murmur
Murmur

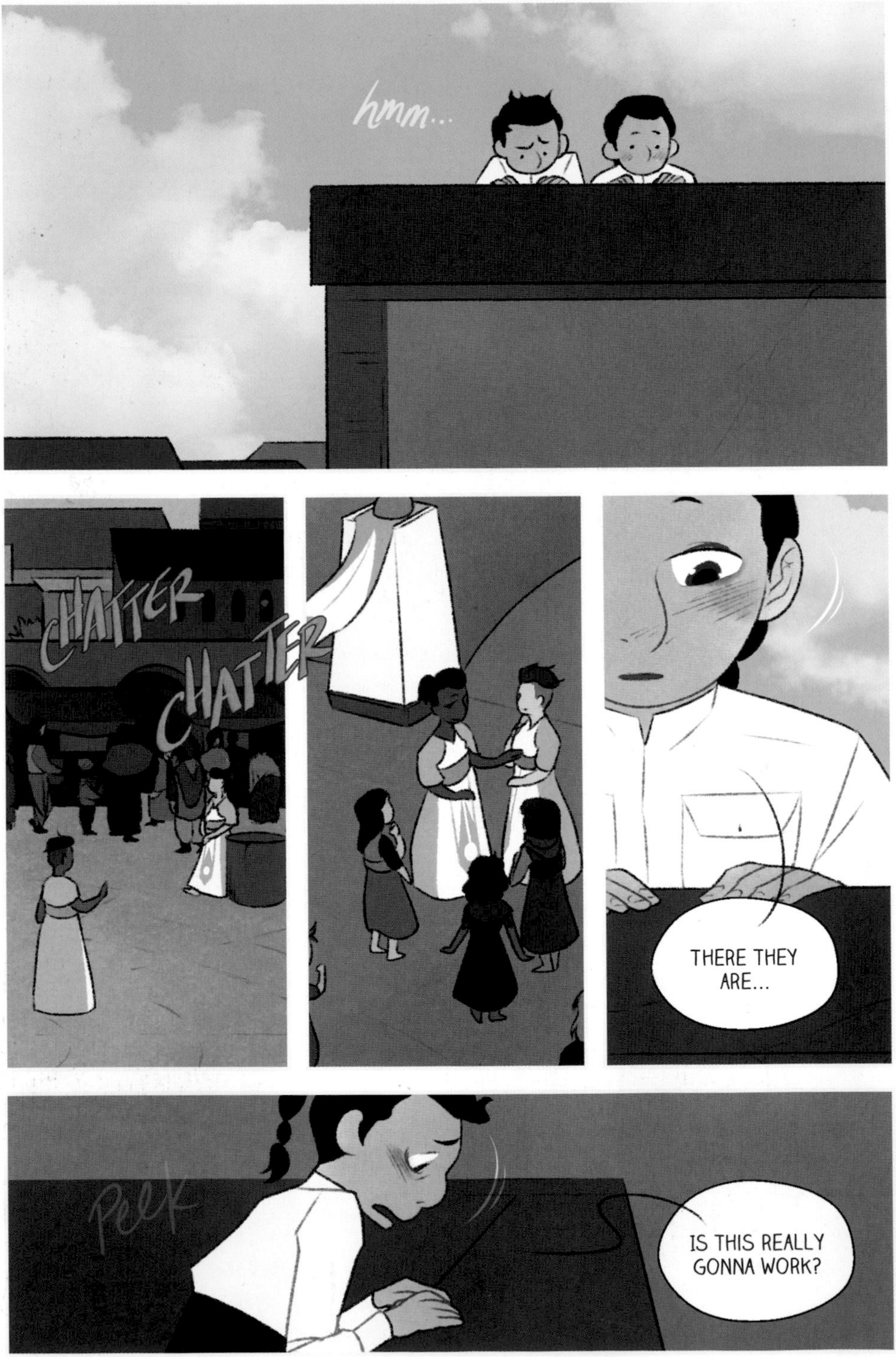
hmm...
CHATTER
CHATTER
THERE THEY ARE...
PEEK
IS THIS REALLY GONNA WORK?

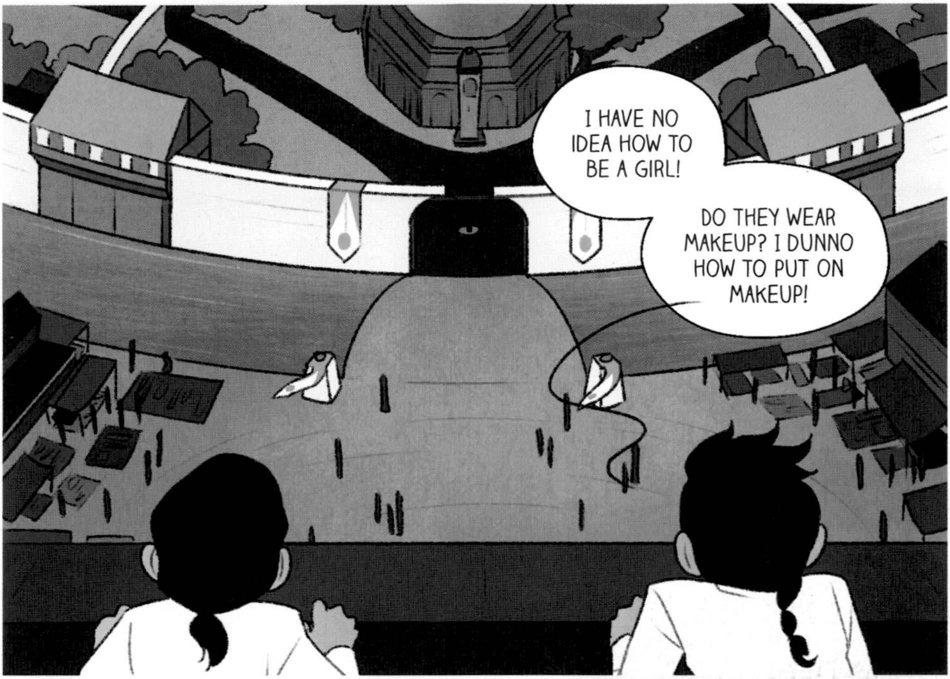
I HAVE NO IDEA HOW TO BE A GIRL!
DO THEY WEAR MAKEUP? I DUNNO HOW TO PUT ON MAKEUP!

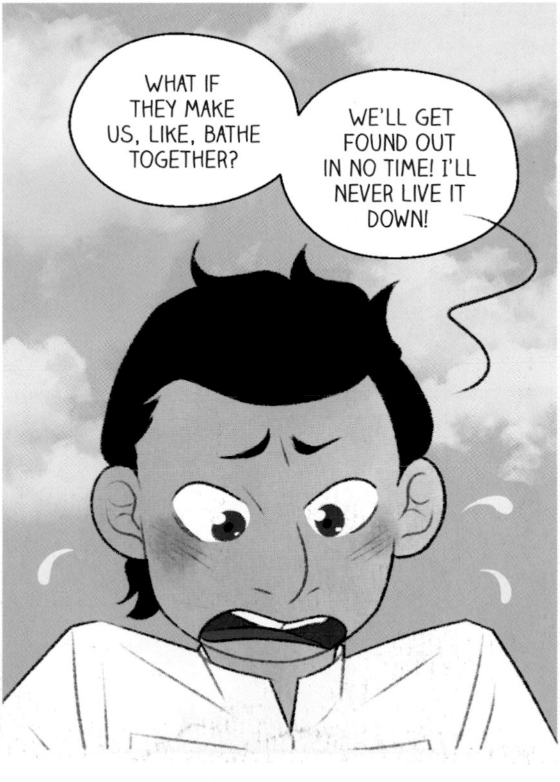
WHAT IF THEY MAKE US, LIKE, BATHE TOGETHER?
WE'LL GET FOUND OUT IN NO TIME! I'LL NEVER LIVE IT DOWN!

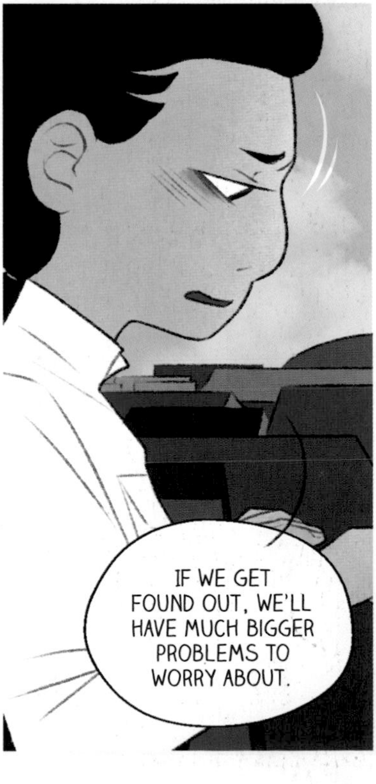
IF WE GET FOUND OUT, WE'LL HAVE MUCH BIGGER PROBLEMS TO WORRY ABOUT.

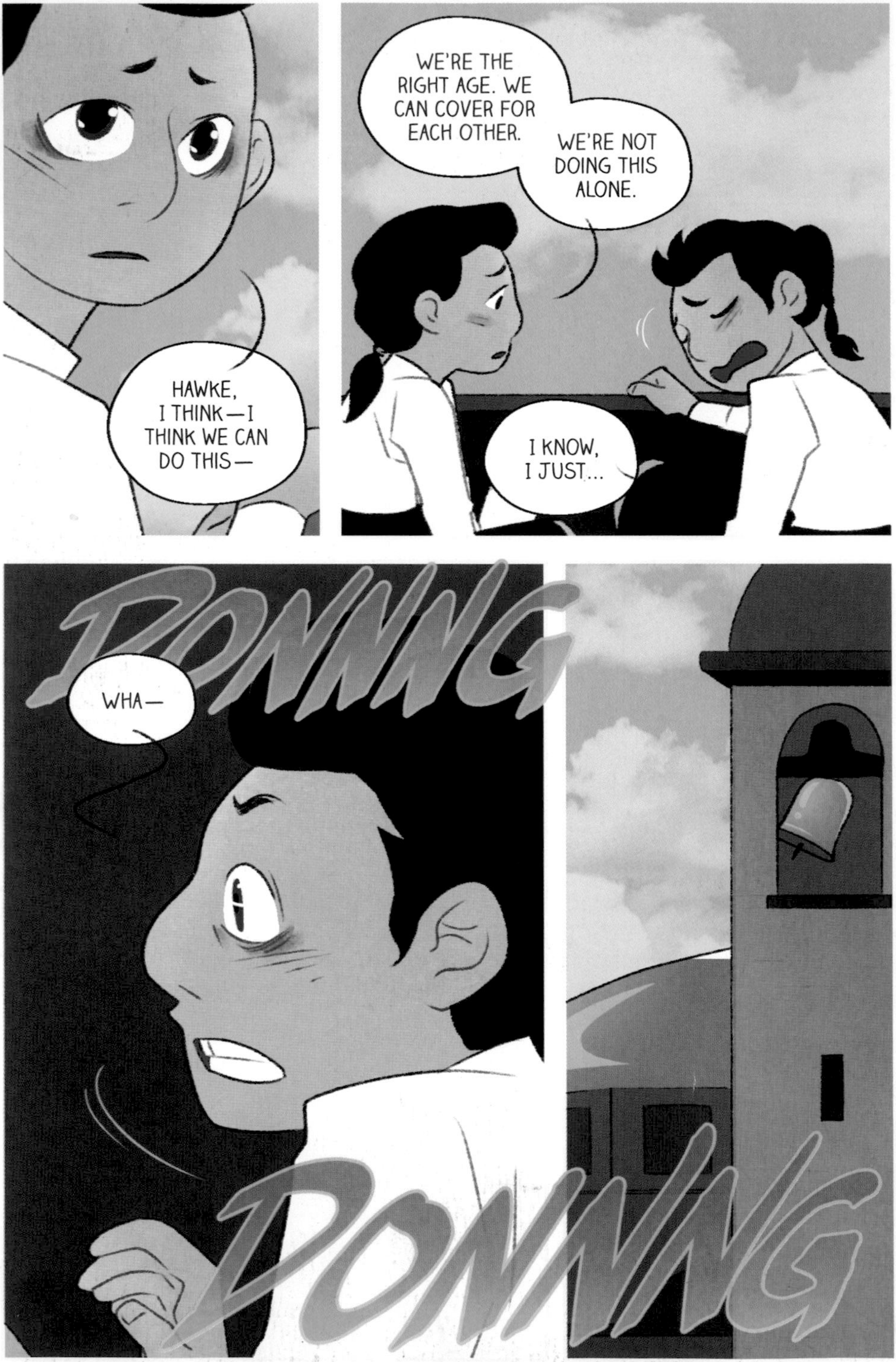
HAWKE, I THINK—I THINK WE CAN DO THIS—
WE'RE THE RIGHT AGE. WE CAN COVER FOR EACH OTHER.
WE'RE NOT DOING THIS ALONE.
I KNOW, I JUST...
DONNNG
WHA—
DONNNG

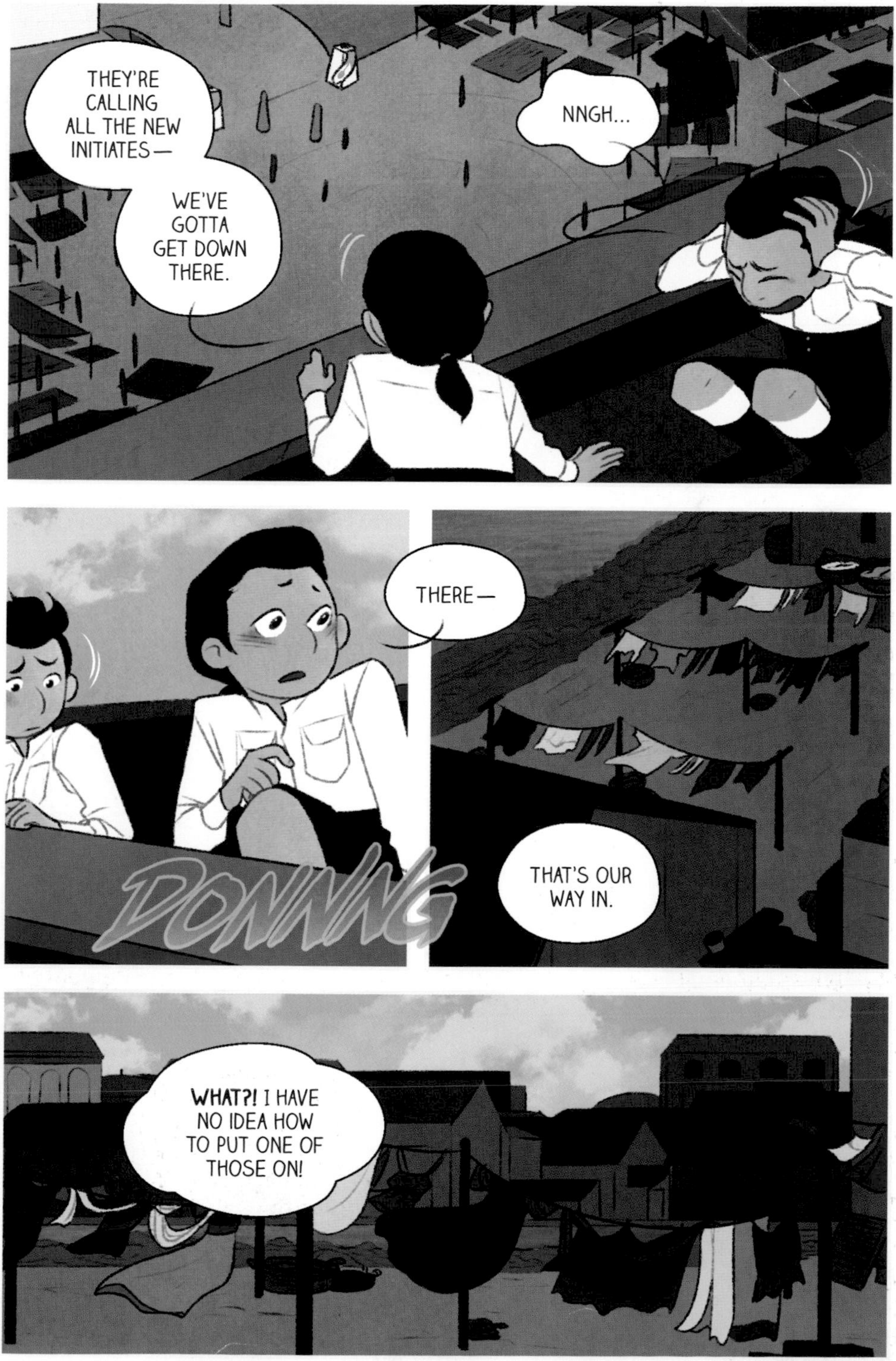
THEY'RE CALLING ALL THE NEW INITIATES—
WE'VE GOTTA GET DOWN THERE.
NNGH...
THERE—
DONNNG
THAT'S OUR WAY IN.
WHAT?! I HAVE NO IDEA HOW TO PUT ONE OF THOSE ON!

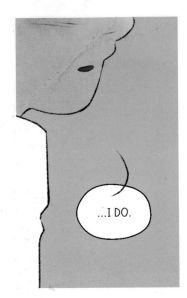

...I DO.

WHAT?! HOW?!

I HELPED MOM WHEN WE WERE LITTLE.

IT'S EASY ONCE YOU GET THE HANG OF IT.

JUST— JUST TRUST ME, OKAY?

I DO! I JUST—

OH NO...

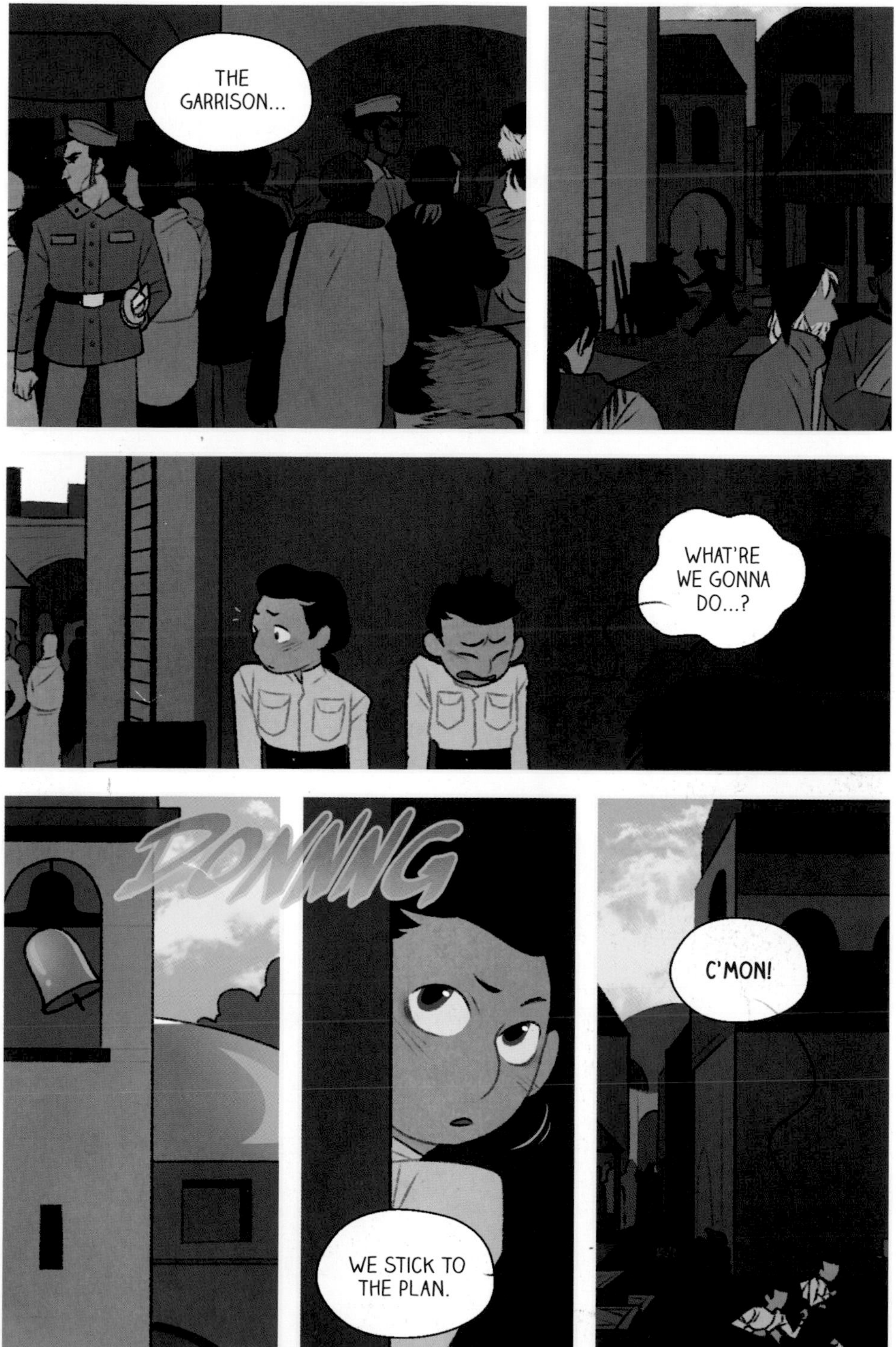
THE GARRISON...
WHAT'RE WE GONNA DO...?
DONNNG
WE STICK TO THE PLAN.
C'MON!

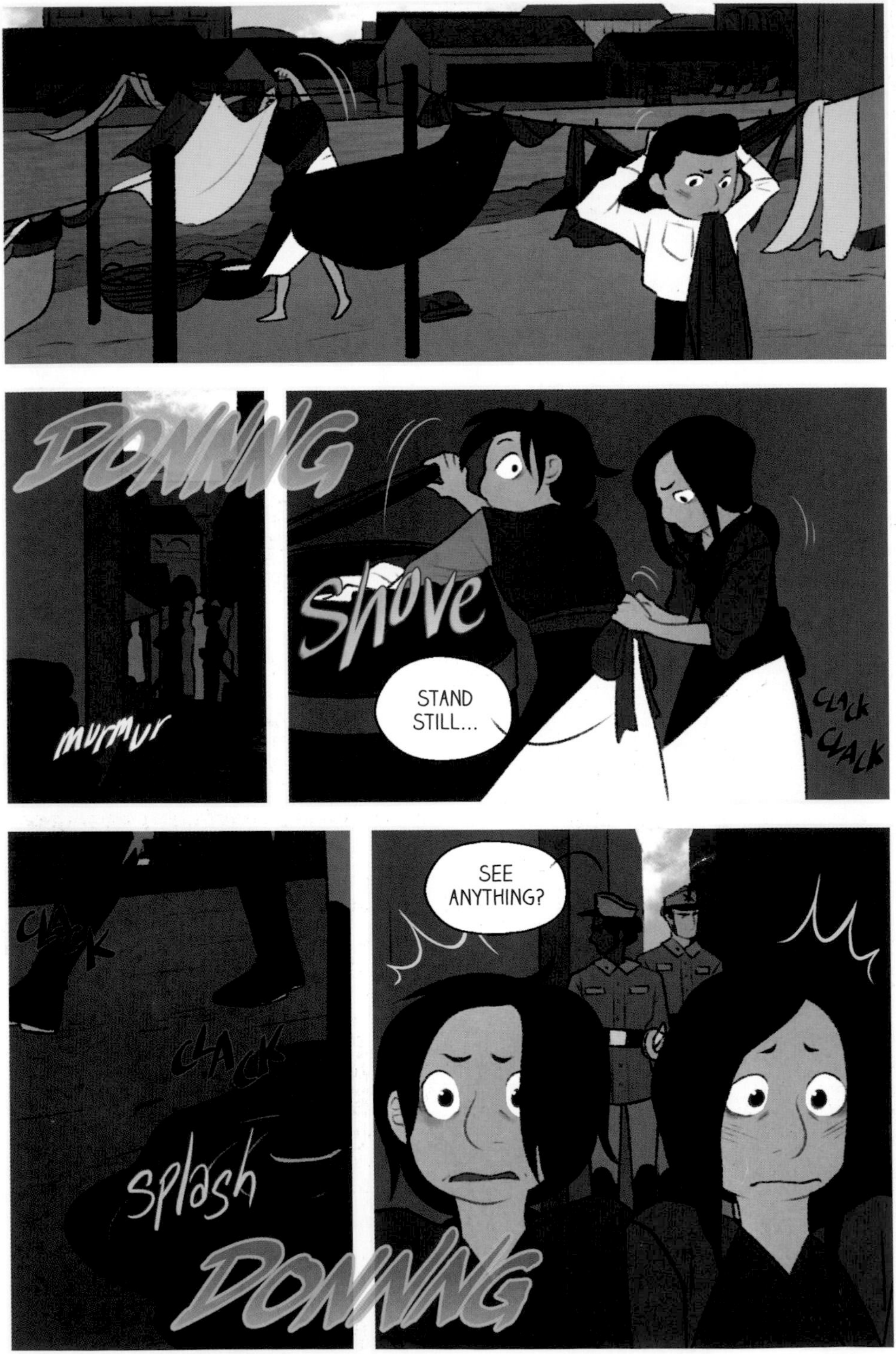
DONNNG
murmur
shove
STAND STILL...
CLACK
CLACK
CLACK
CLACK
splash
SEE ANYTHING?
DONNNG

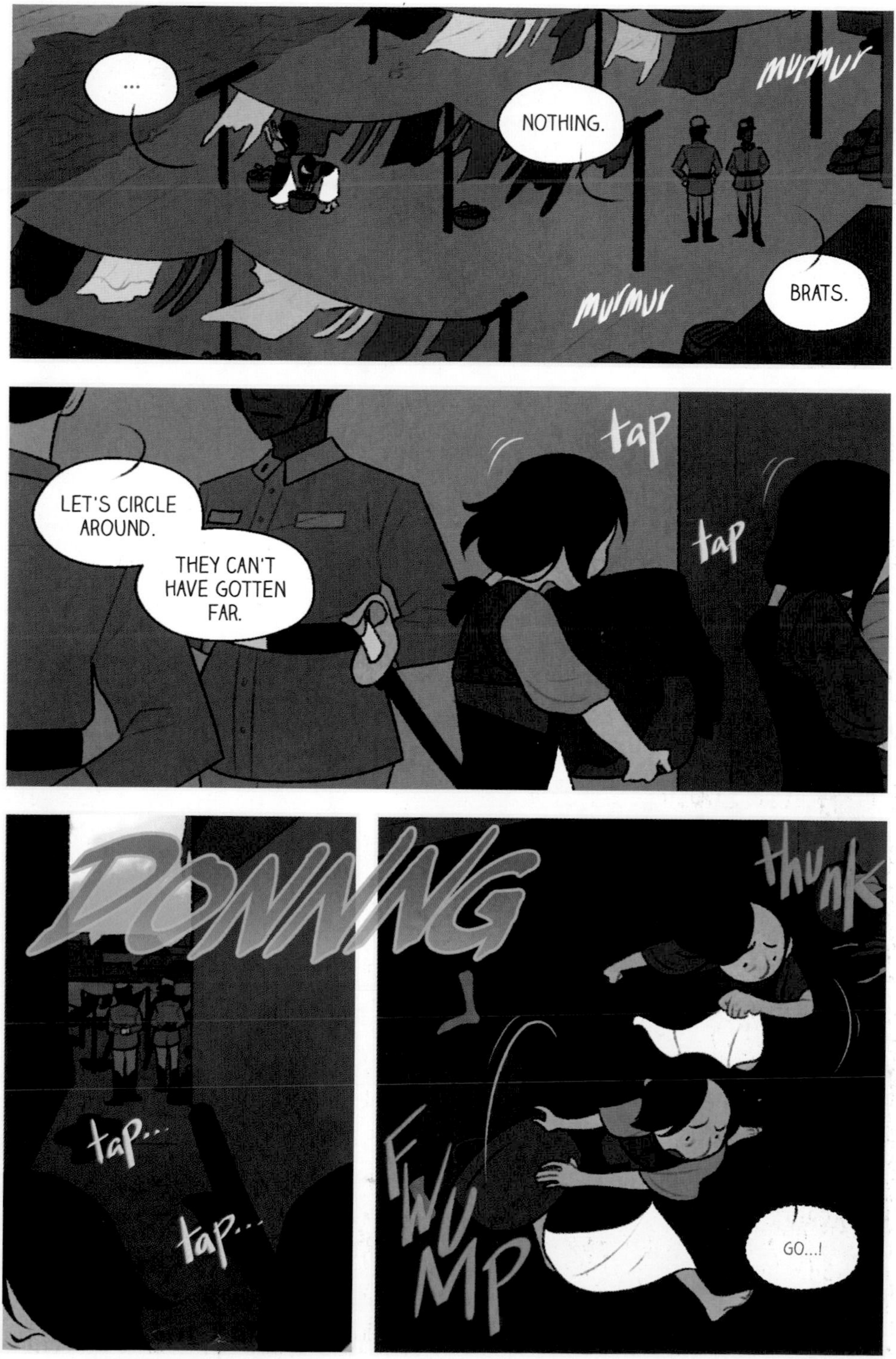
...
NOTHING.
murmur
murmur
BRATS.
LET'S CIRCLE AROUND.
THEY CAN'T HAVE GOTTEN FAR.
tap
tap
DONNG
tap...
tap...
thunk
FWUMP
GO...!

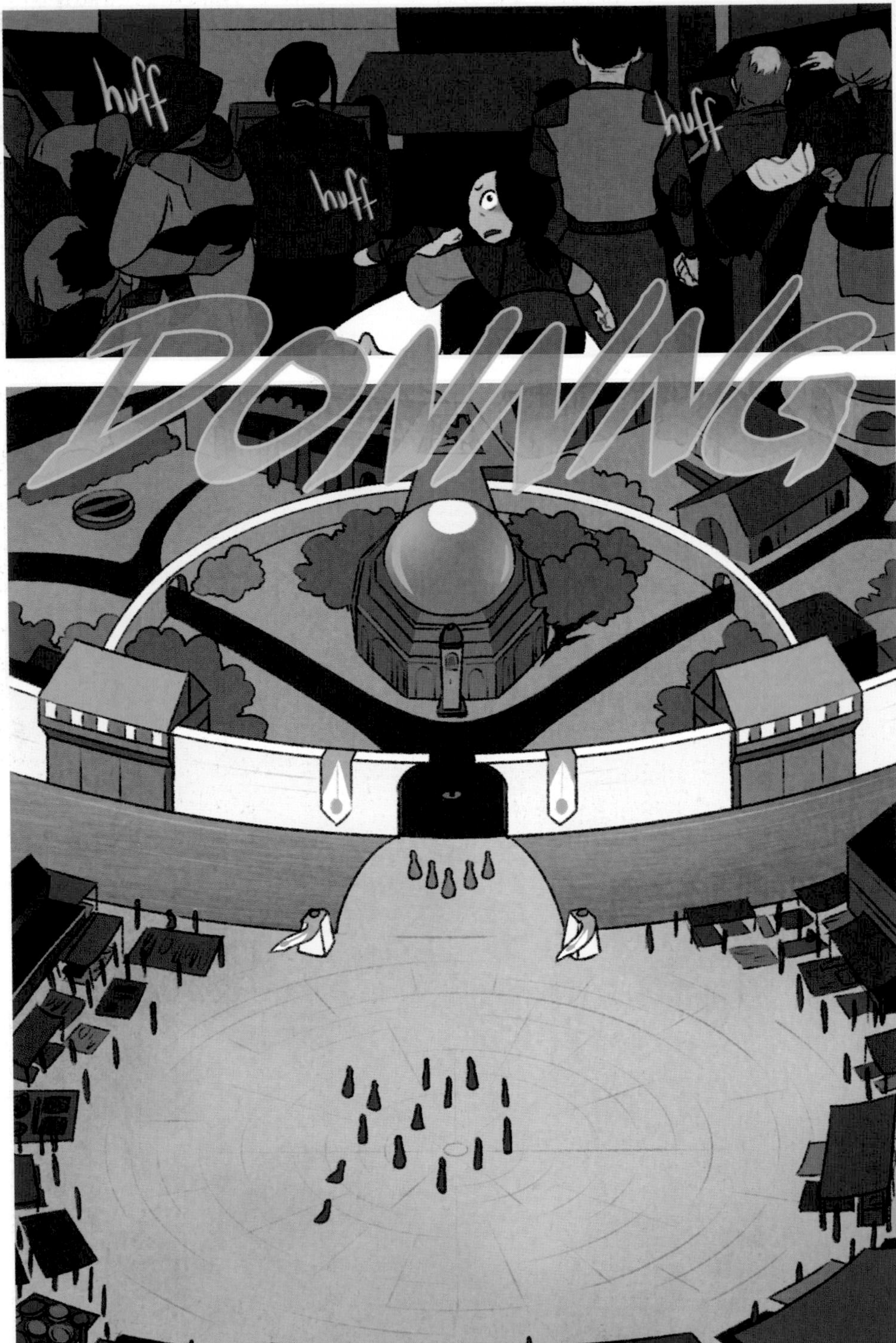
huff
huff
huff
DONNG

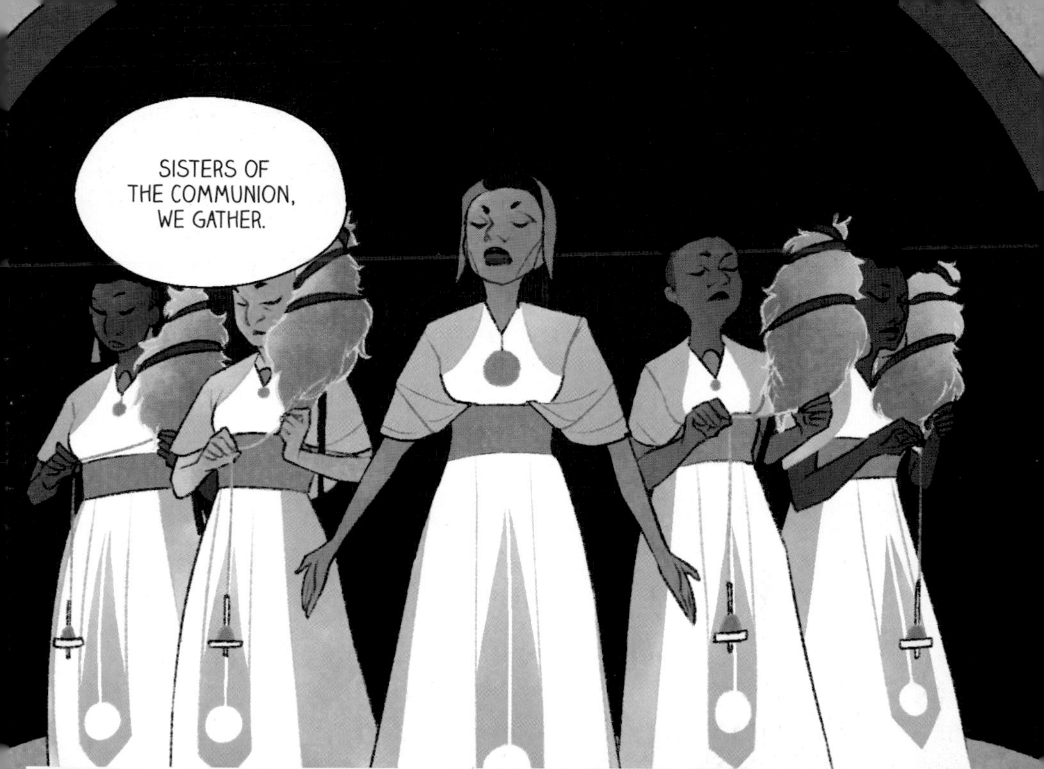
SISTERS OF THE COMMUNION, WE GATHER.

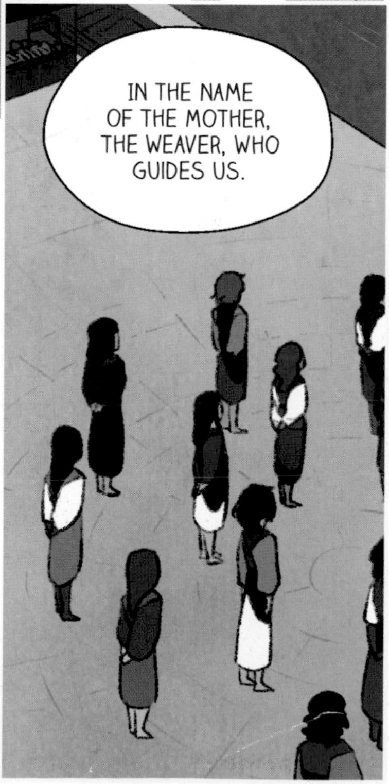
IN THE NAME OF THE MOTHER, THE WEAVER, WHO GUIDES US.

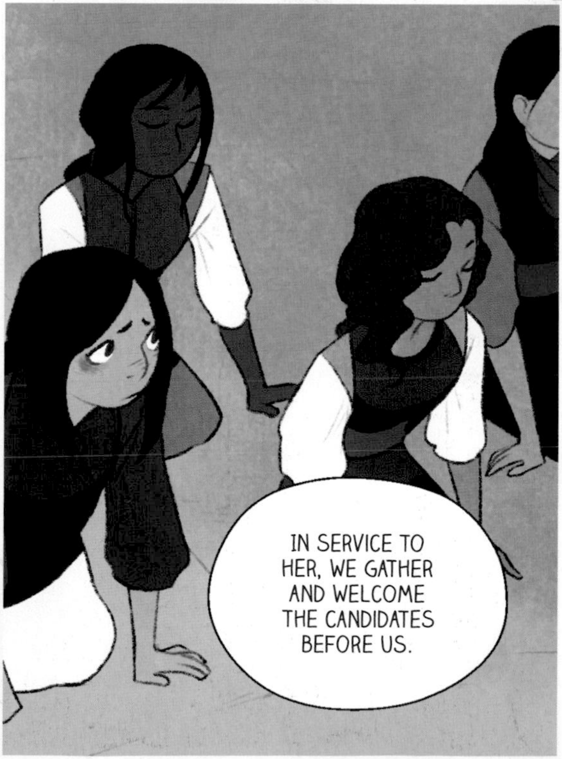
IN SERVICE TO HER, WE GATHER AND WELCOME THE CANDIDATES BEFORE US.

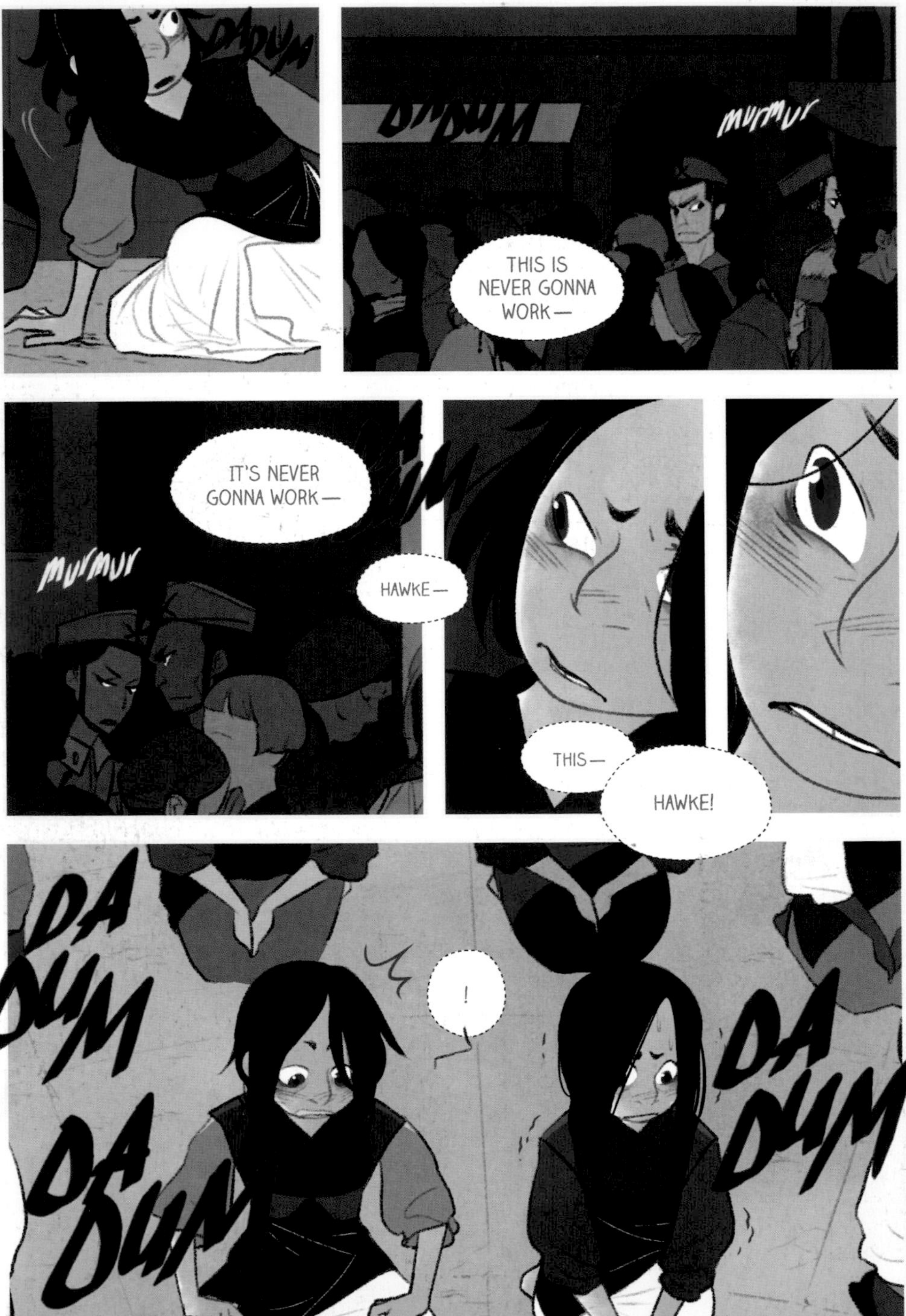
DADUM
DADUM
murmur
THIS IS NEVER GONNA WORK—
IT'S NEVER GONNA WORK—
DA DUM
murmur
HAWKE—
THIS—
HAWKE!
DA DUM
DA DUM
!
DA DUM

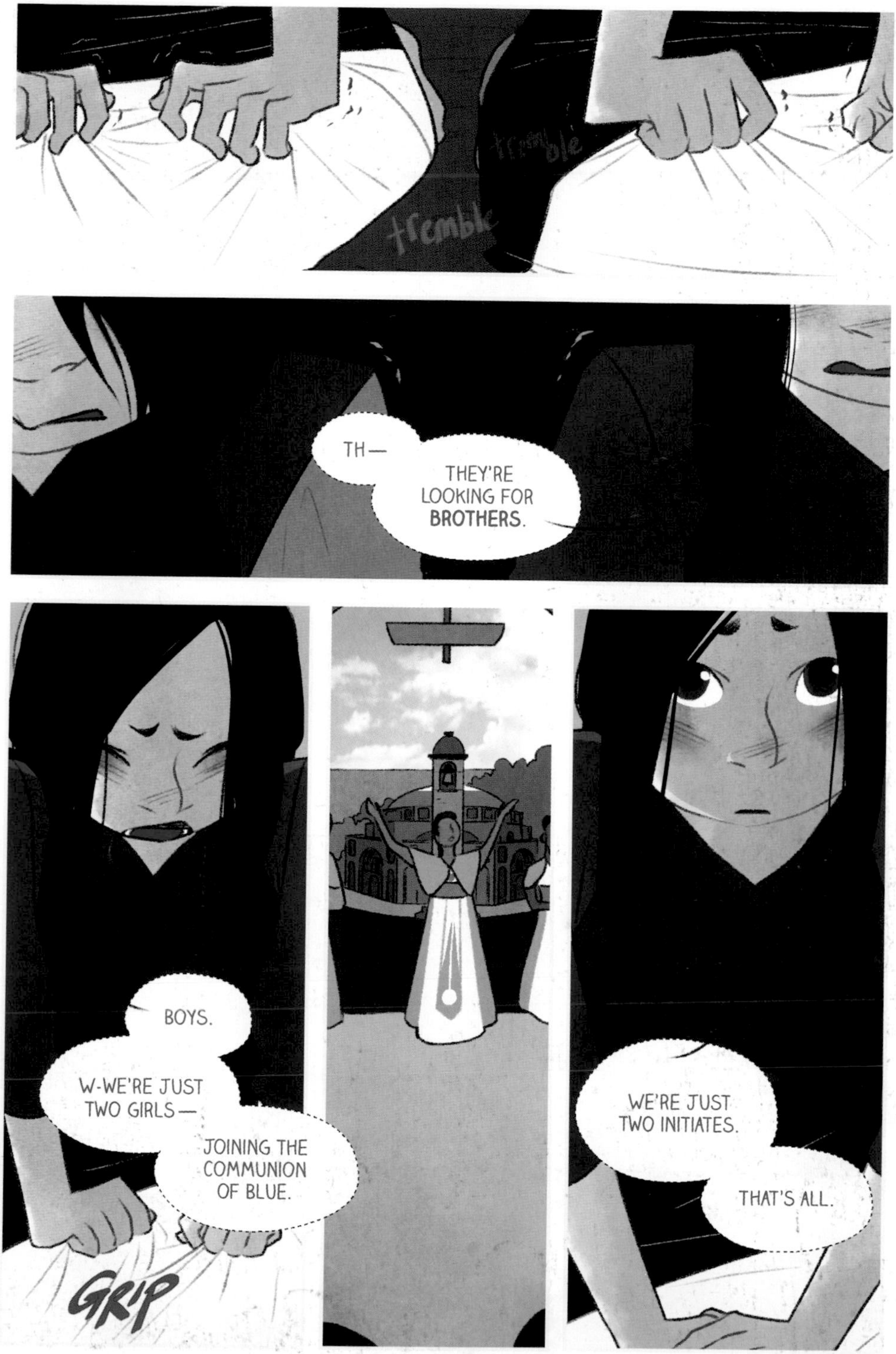
tremble
tremble
TH—
THEY'RE LOOKING FOR **BROTHERS**.
BOYS.
W-WE'RE JUST TWO GIRLS—
JOINING THE COMMUNION OF BLUE.
WE'RE JUST TWO INITIATES.
THAT'S ALL.
GRIP

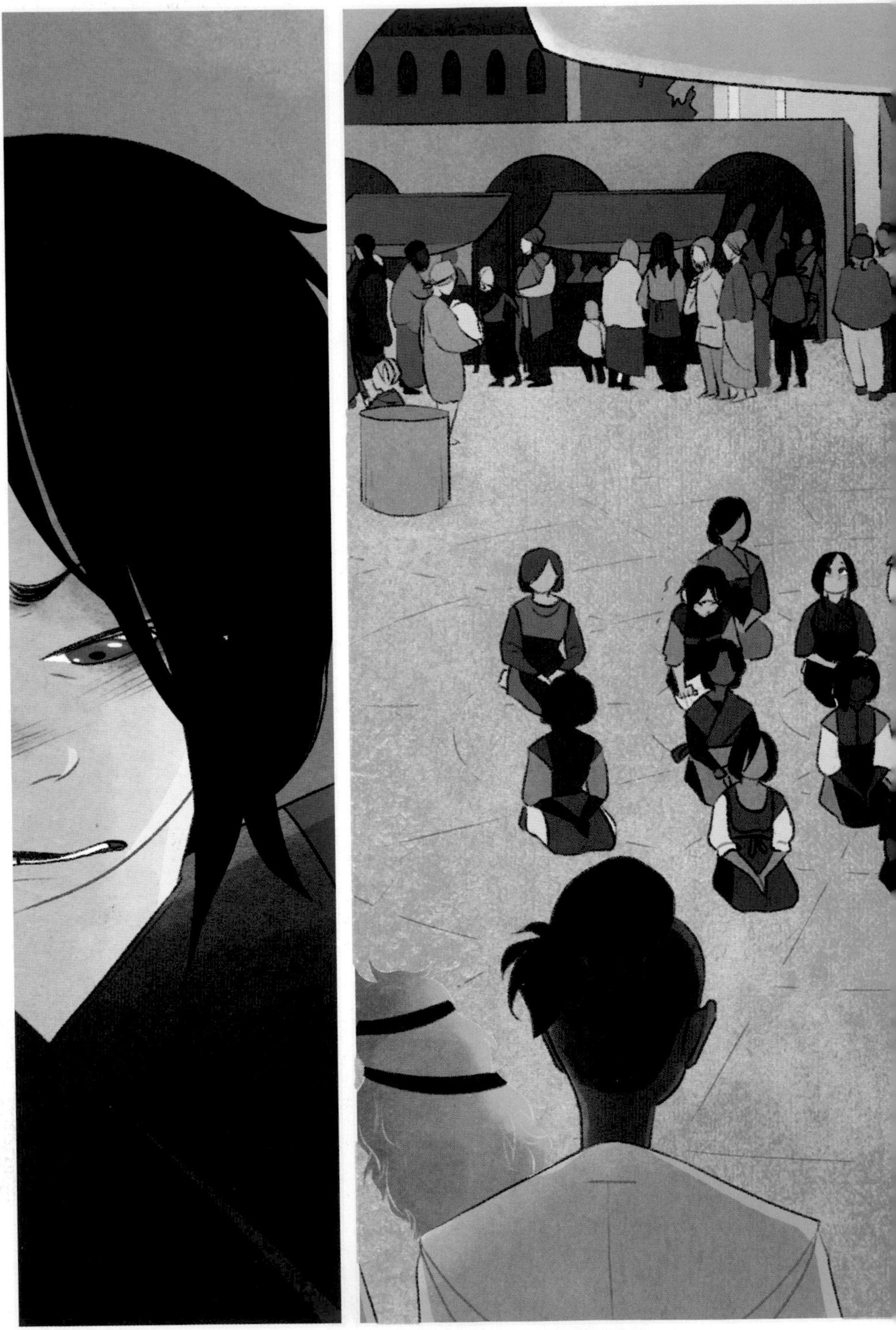

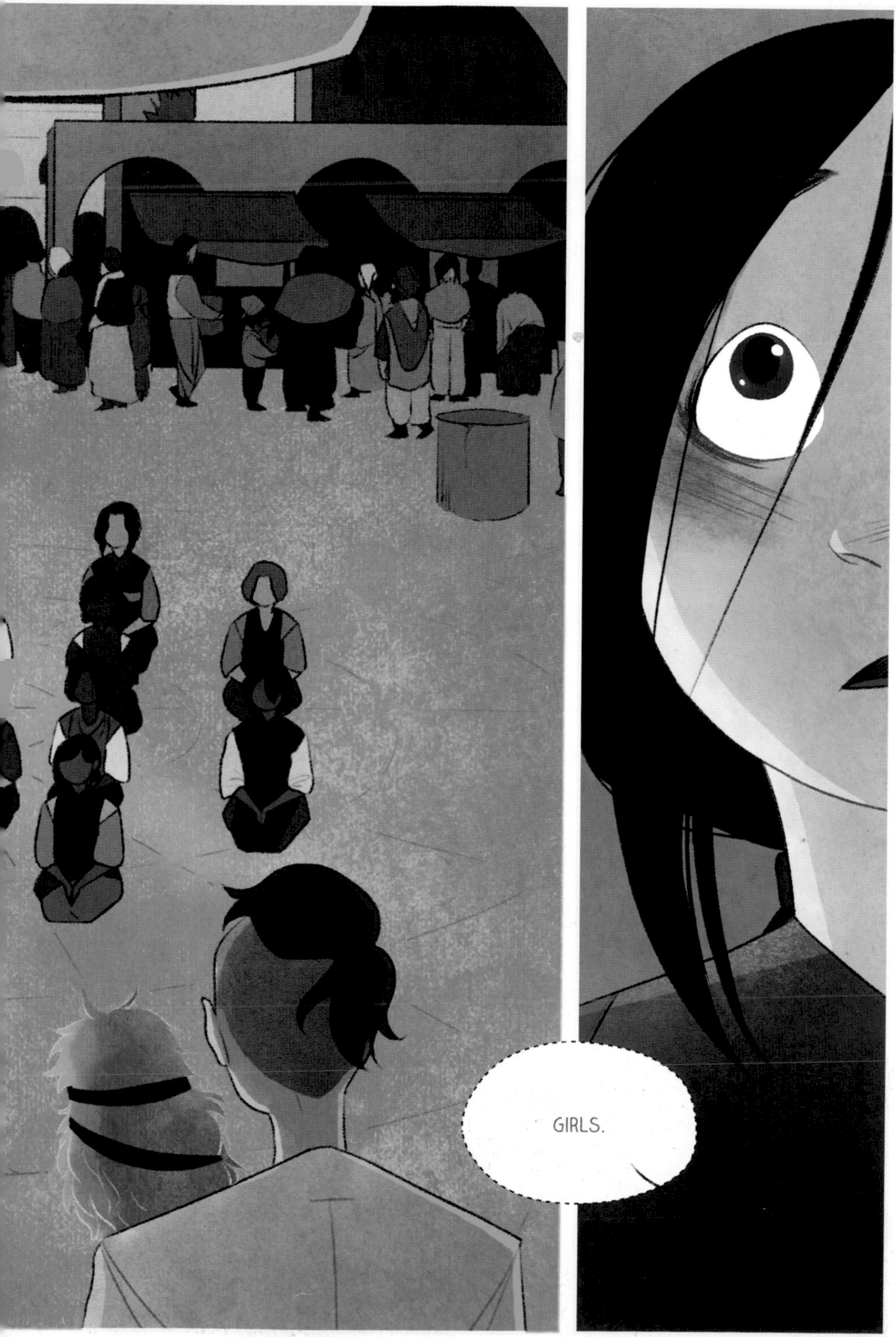
GIRLS.

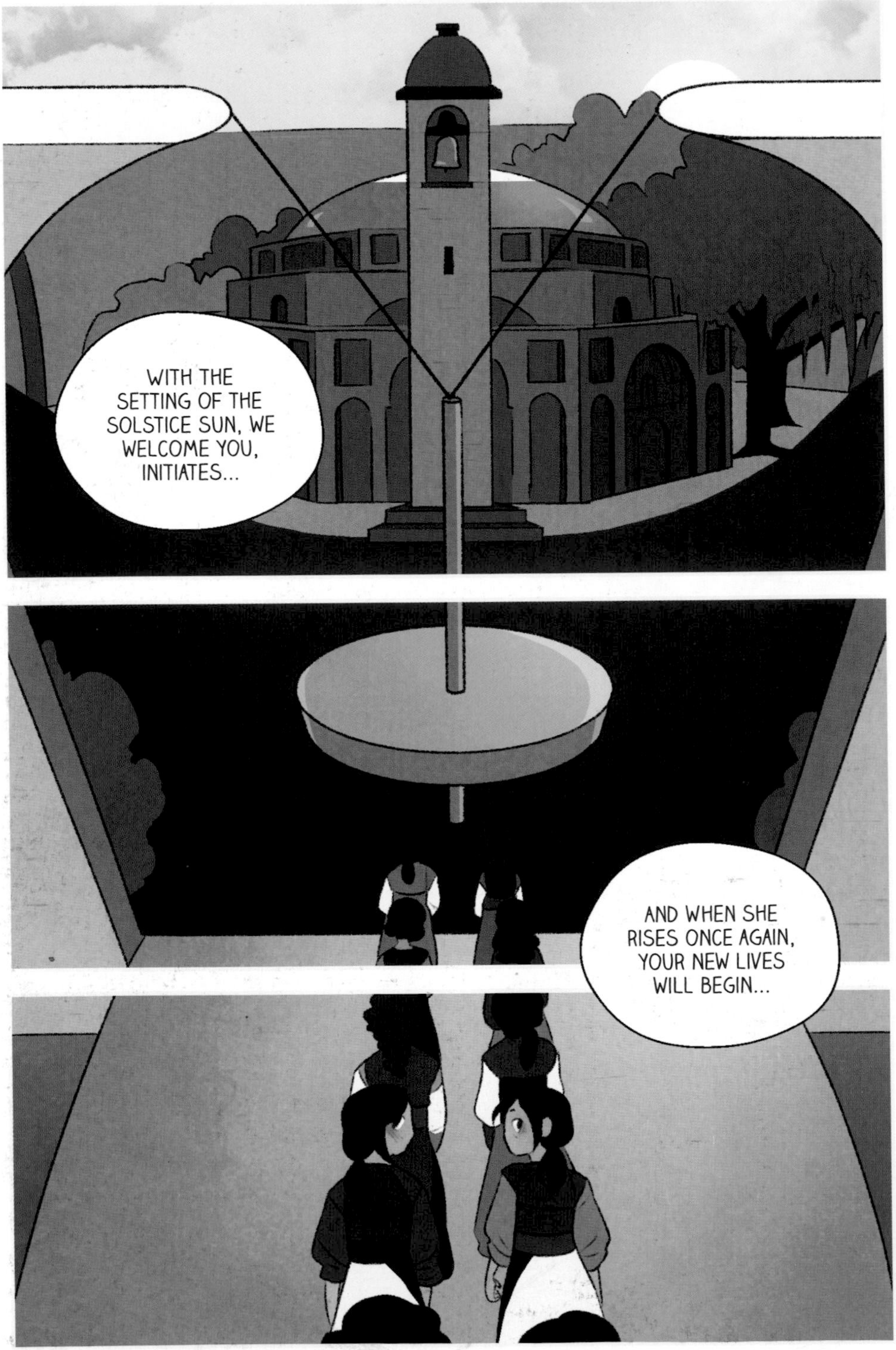
WITH THE SETTING OF THE SOLSTICE SUN, WE WELCOME YOU, INITIATES...
AND WHEN SHE RISES ONCE AGAIN, YOUR NEW LIVES WILL BEGIN...

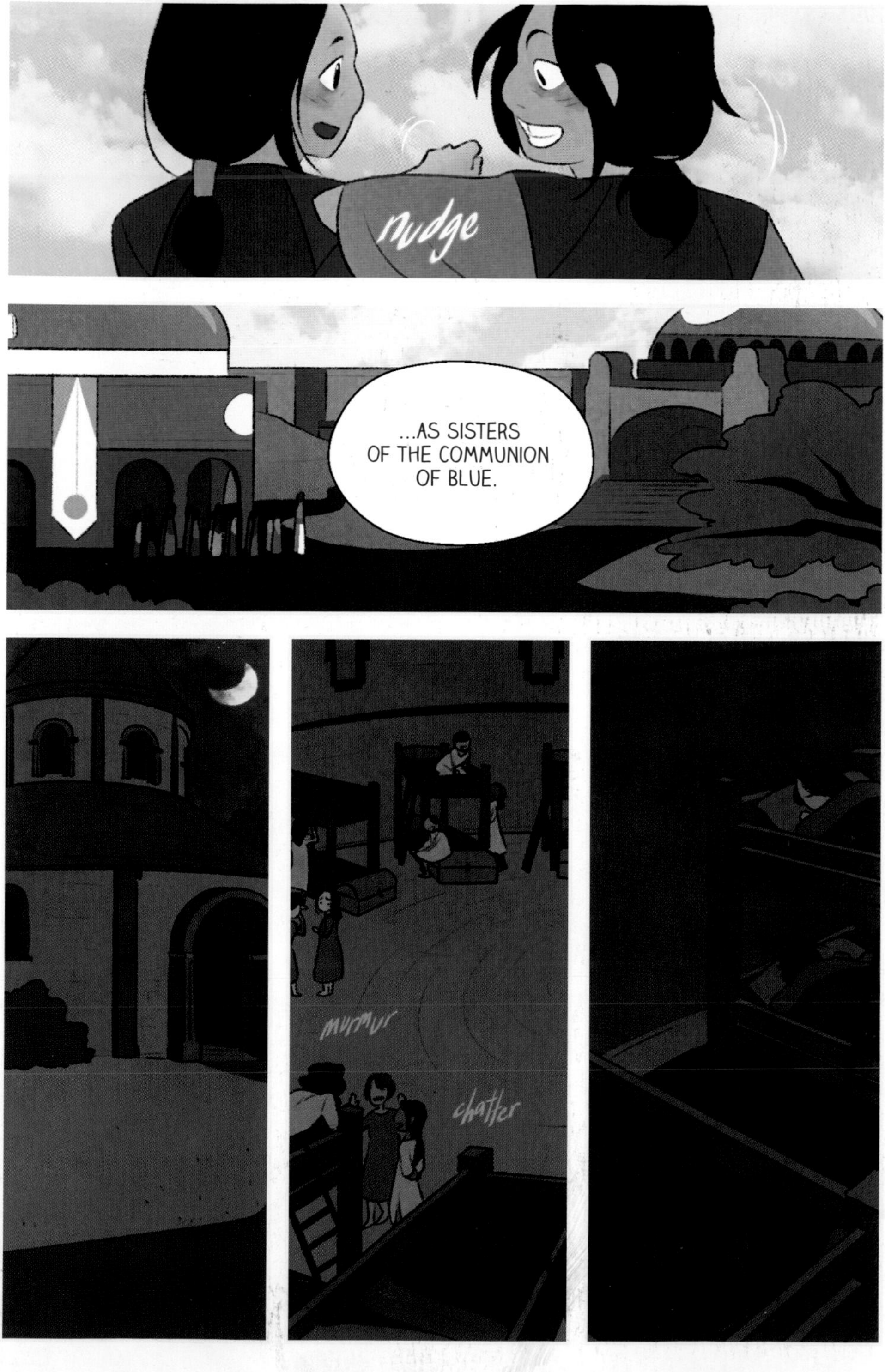
nudge
...AS SISTERS OF THE COMMUNION OF BLUE.
murmur
chatter

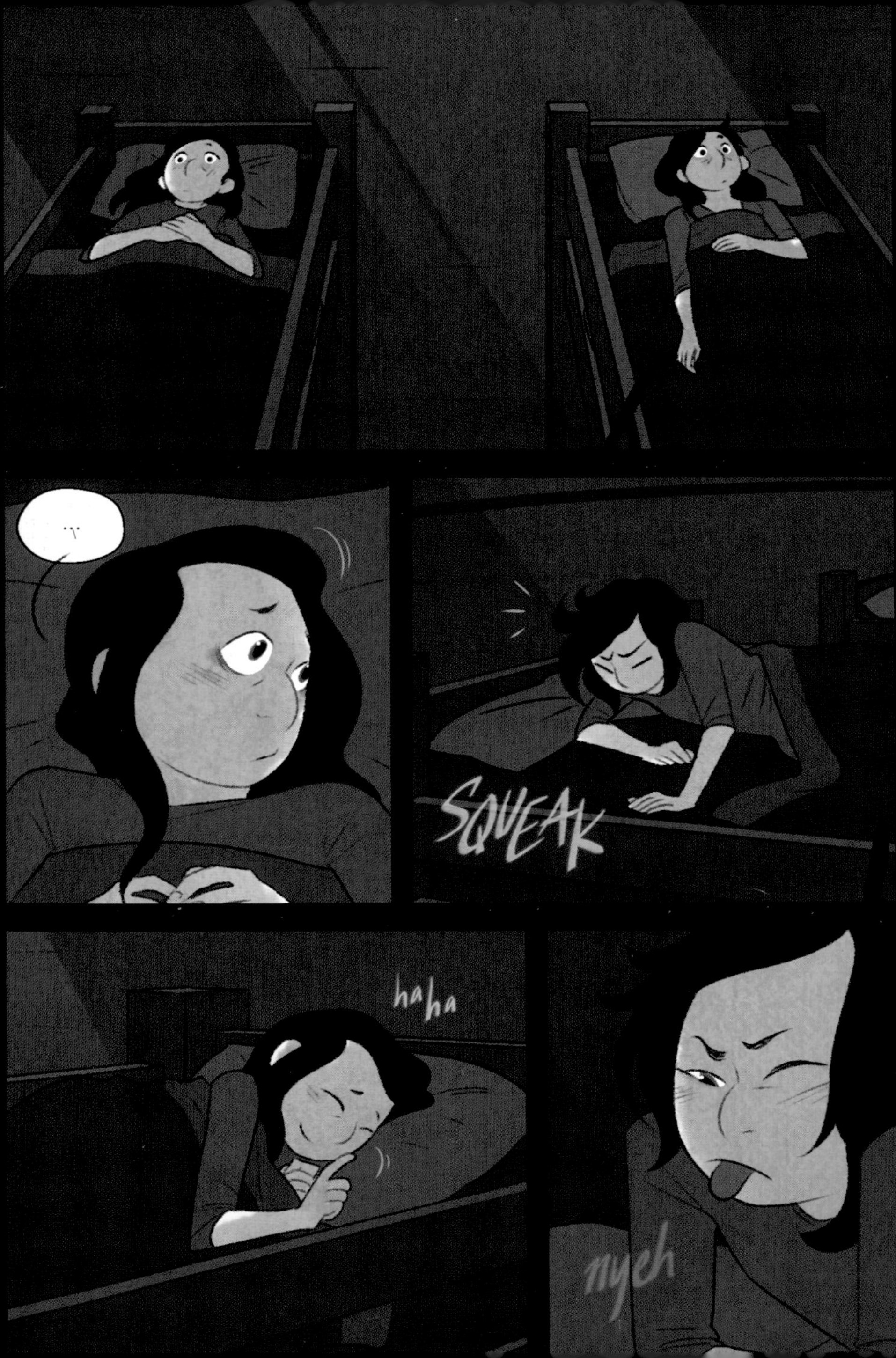
..
SQUEAK
haha
nyeh

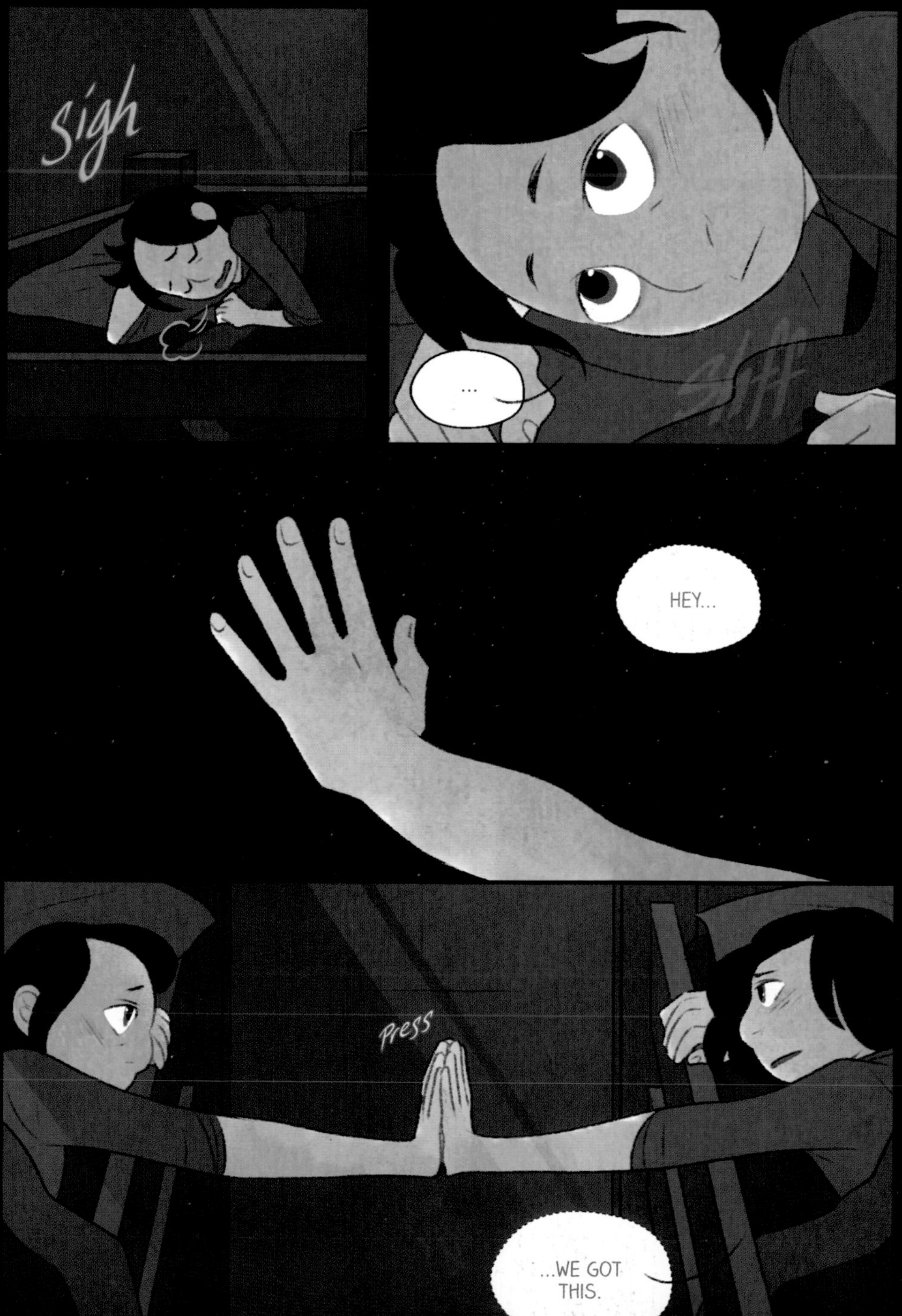

sigh
...
HEY...
Press
...WE GOT THIS.

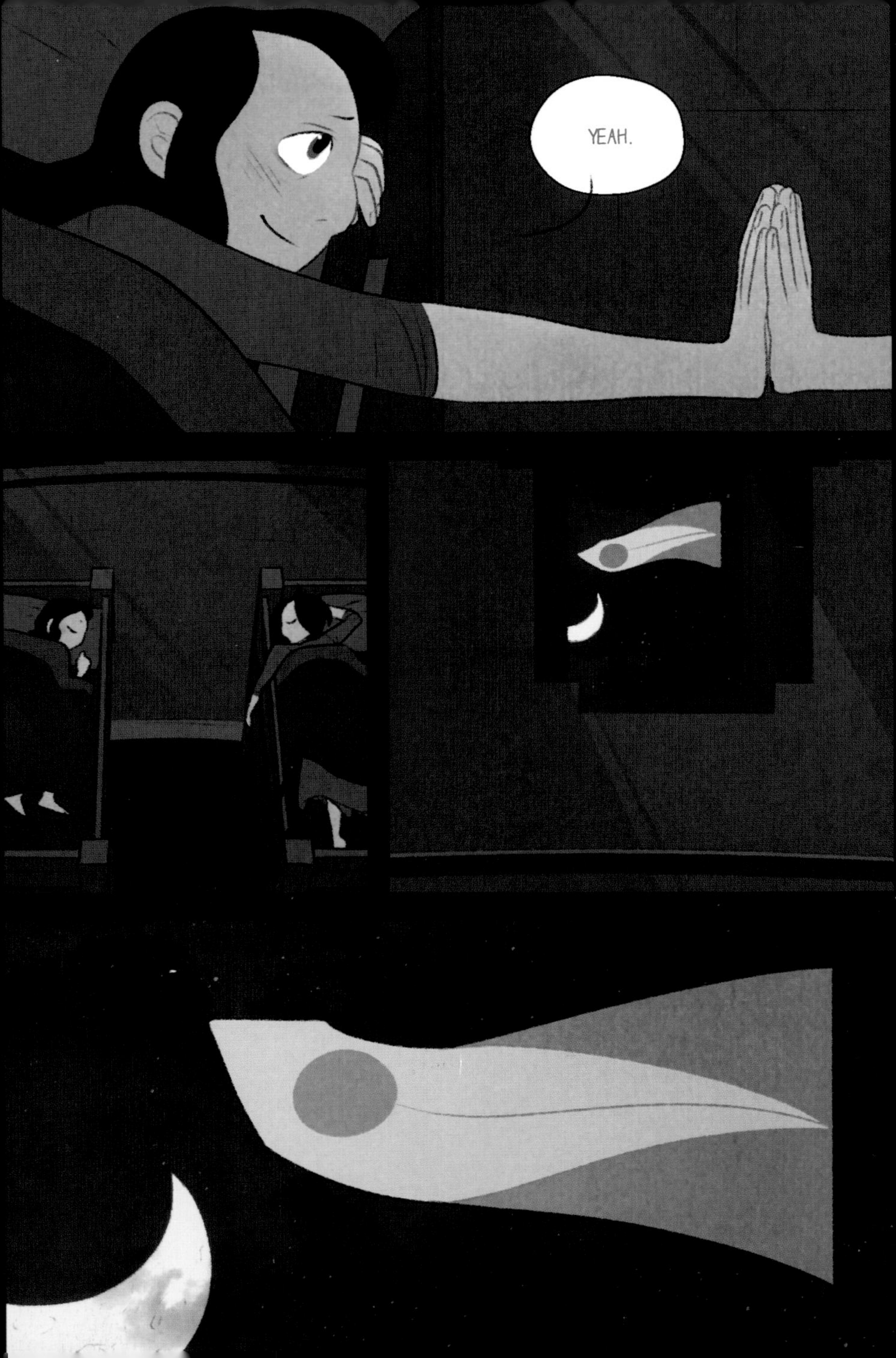
YEAH.

CHAPTER II
THE COMMUNION OF BLUE

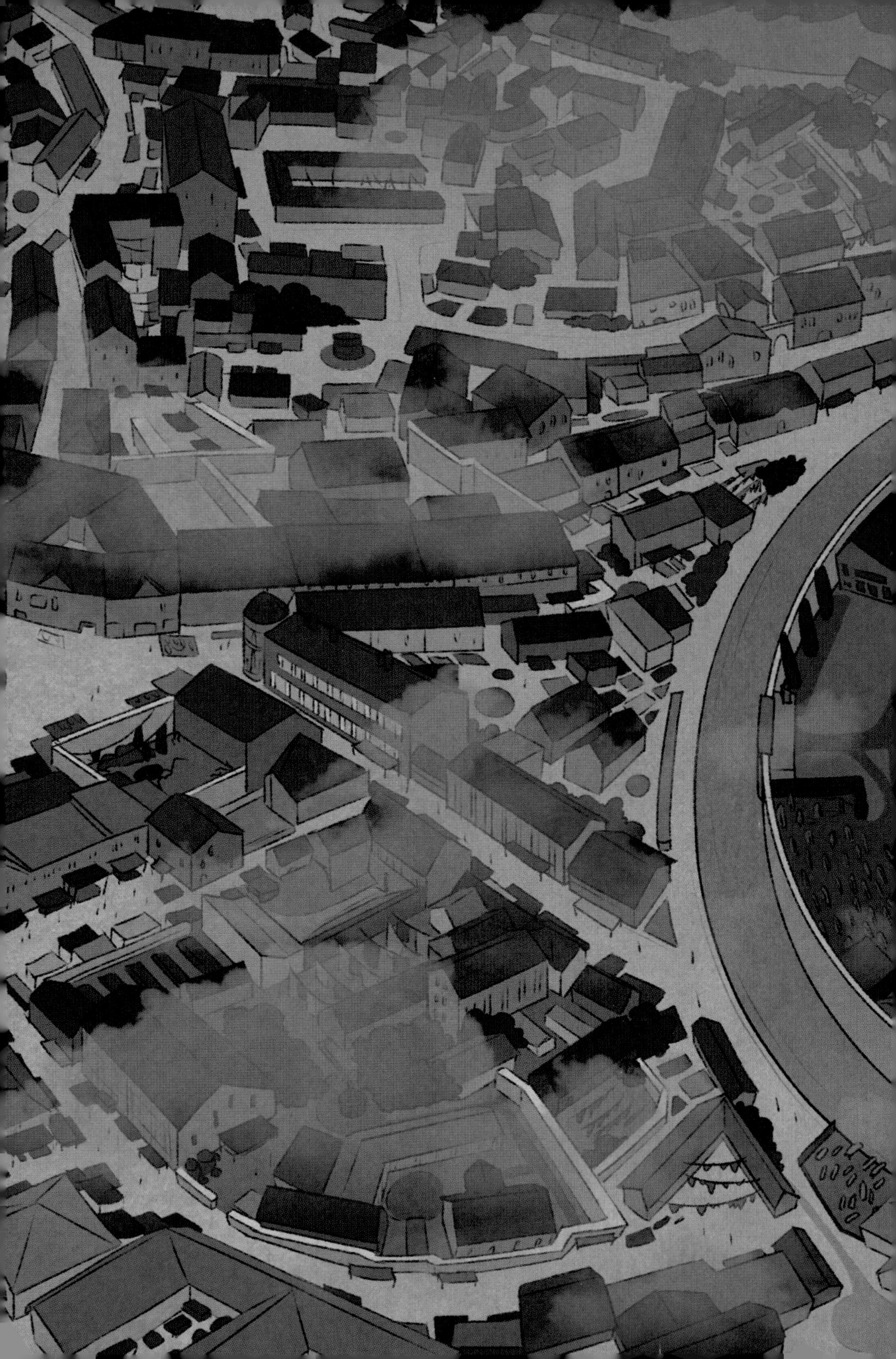

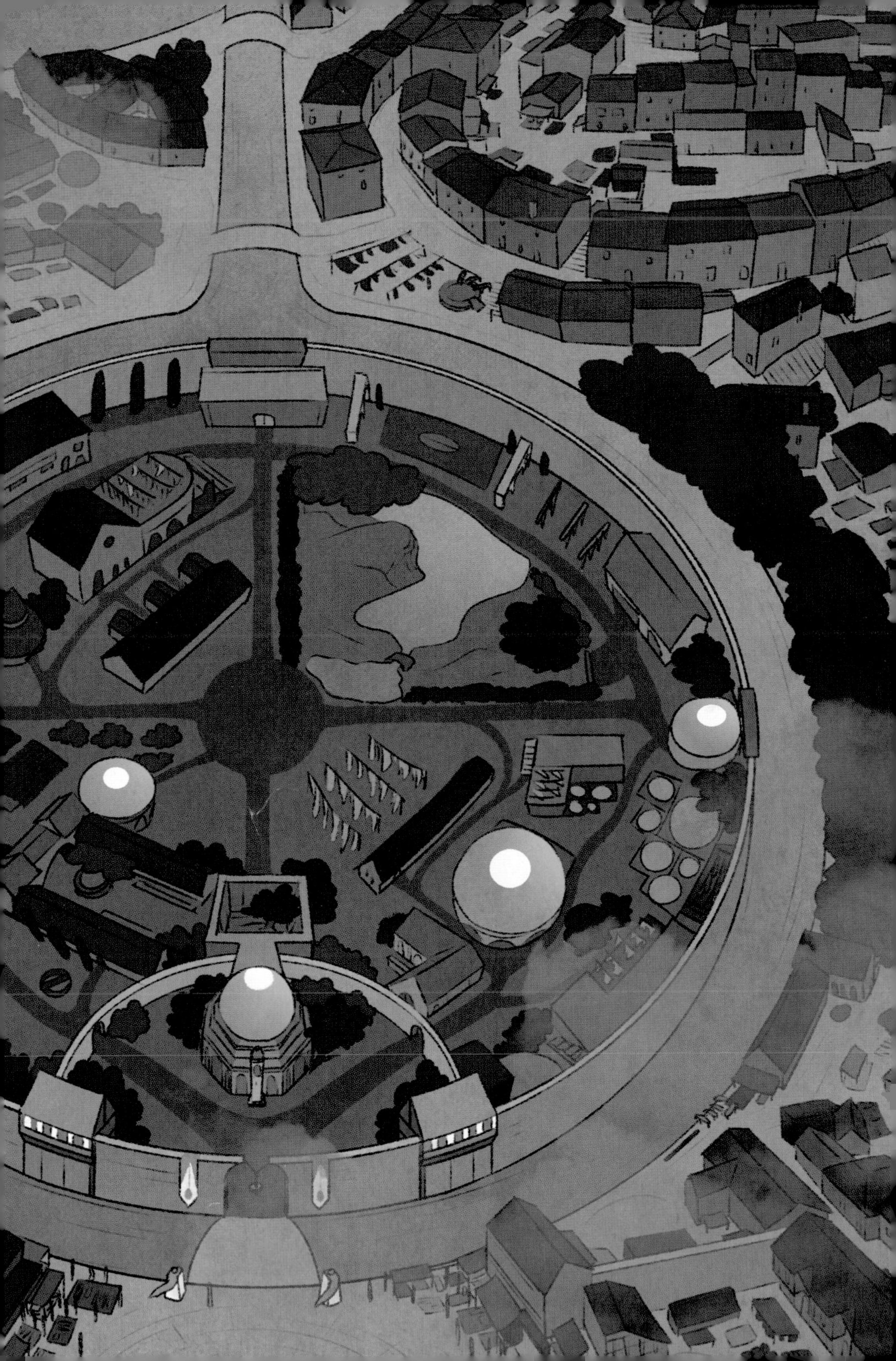

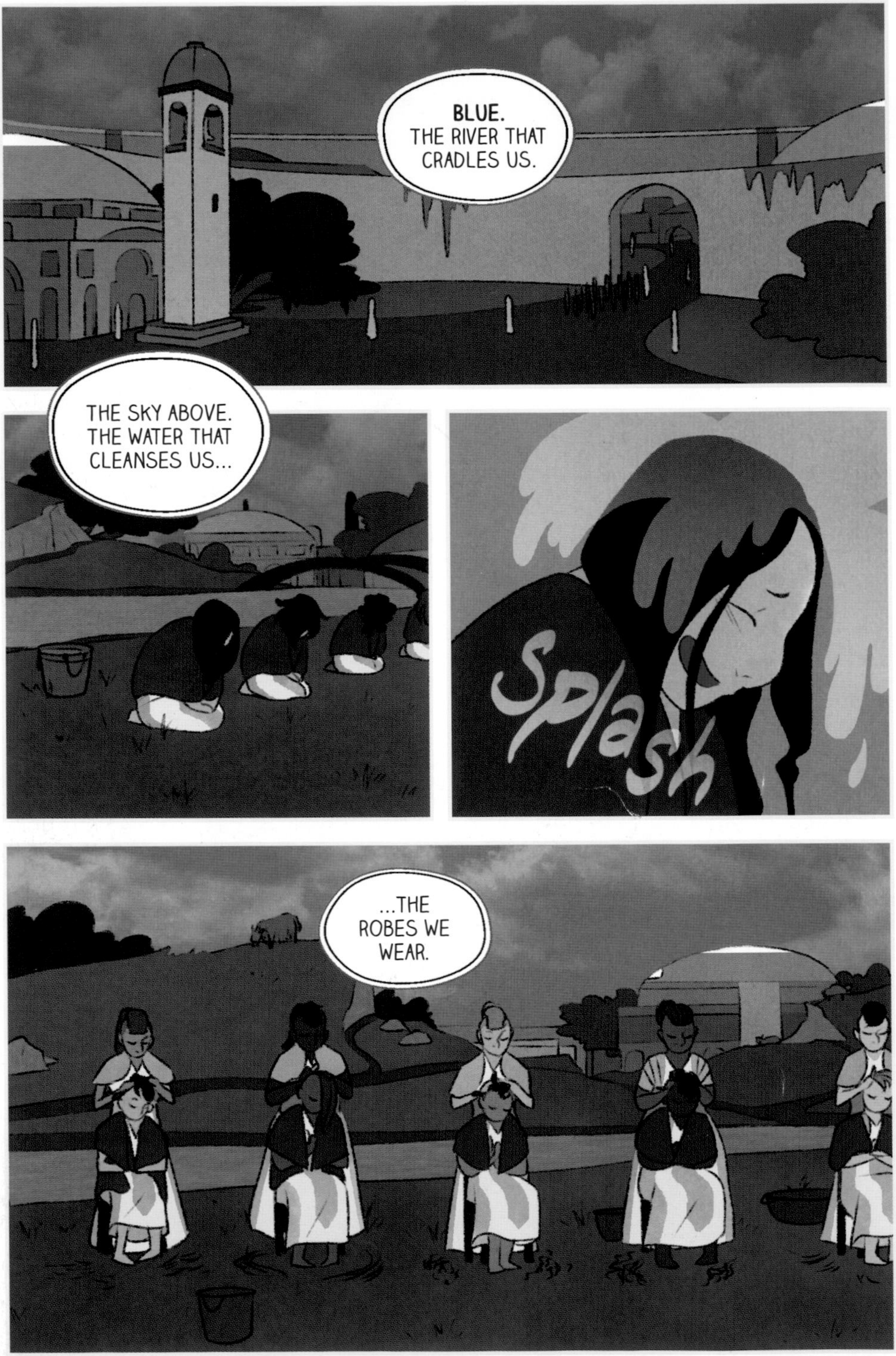
BLUE.
THE RIVER THAT CRADLES US.
THE SKY ABOVE. THE WATER THAT CLEANSES US...
splash
...THE ROBES WE WEAR.

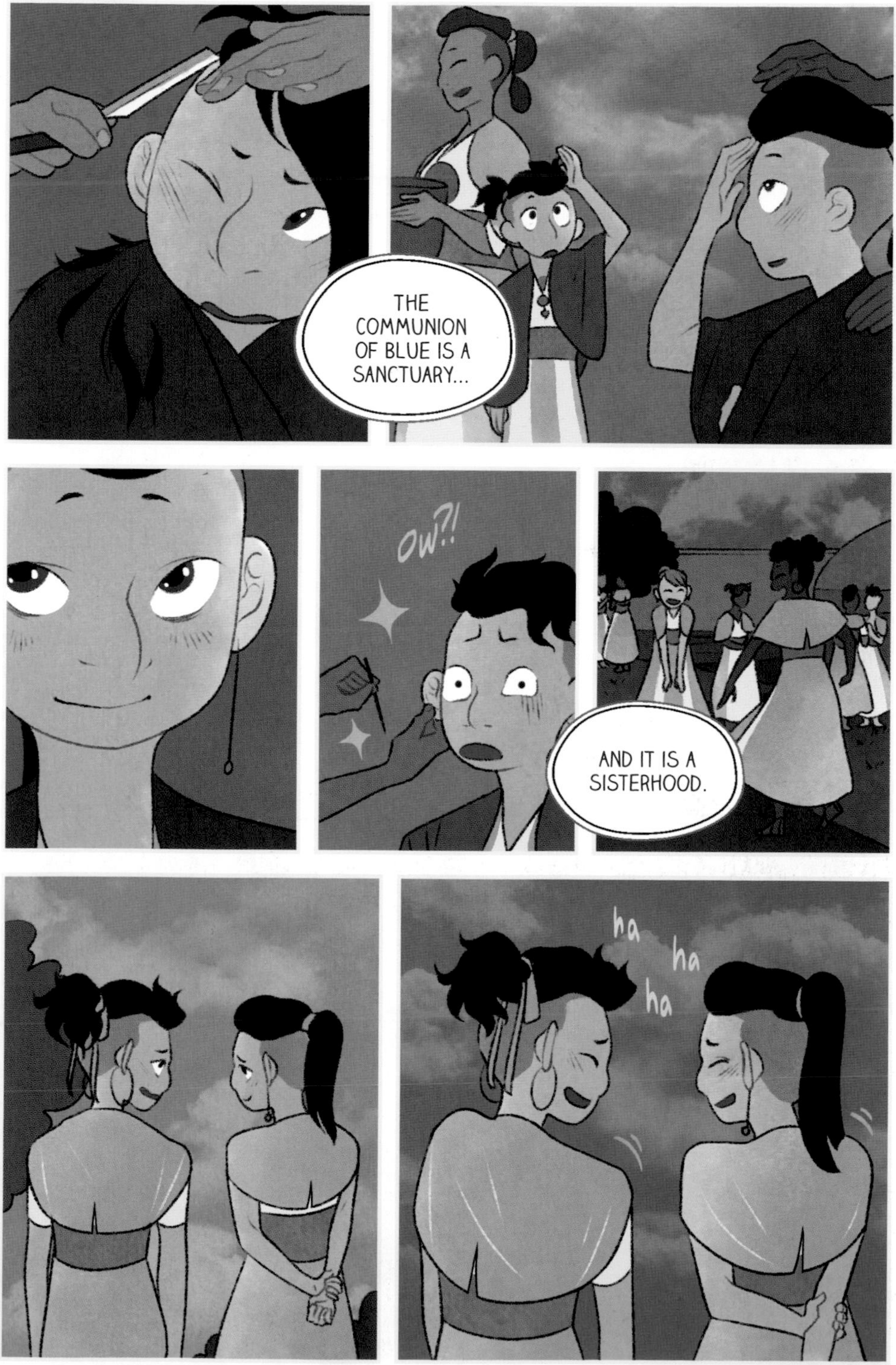
THE COMMUNION OF BLUE IS A SANCTUARY...
OW?!
AND IT IS A SISTERHOOD.
ha
ha
ha

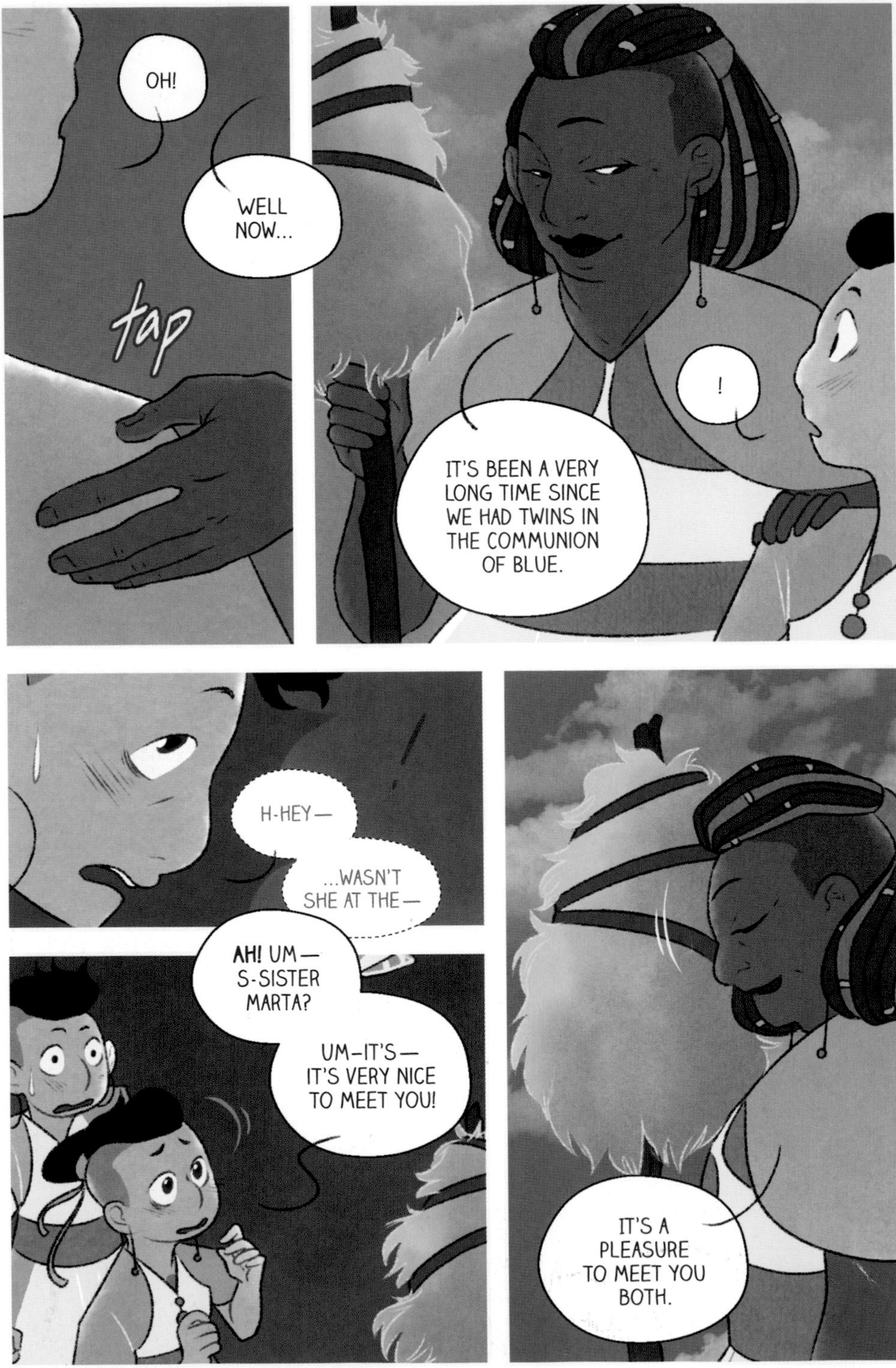
OH!
WELL NOW...
tap
!
IT'S BEEN A VERY LONG TIME SINCE WE HAD TWINS IN THE COMMUNION OF BLUE.
H-HEY—
...WASN'T SHE AT THE—
AH! UM— S-SISTER MARTA?
UM—IT'S— IT'S VERY NICE TO MEET YOU!
IT'S A PLEASURE TO MEET YOU BOTH.

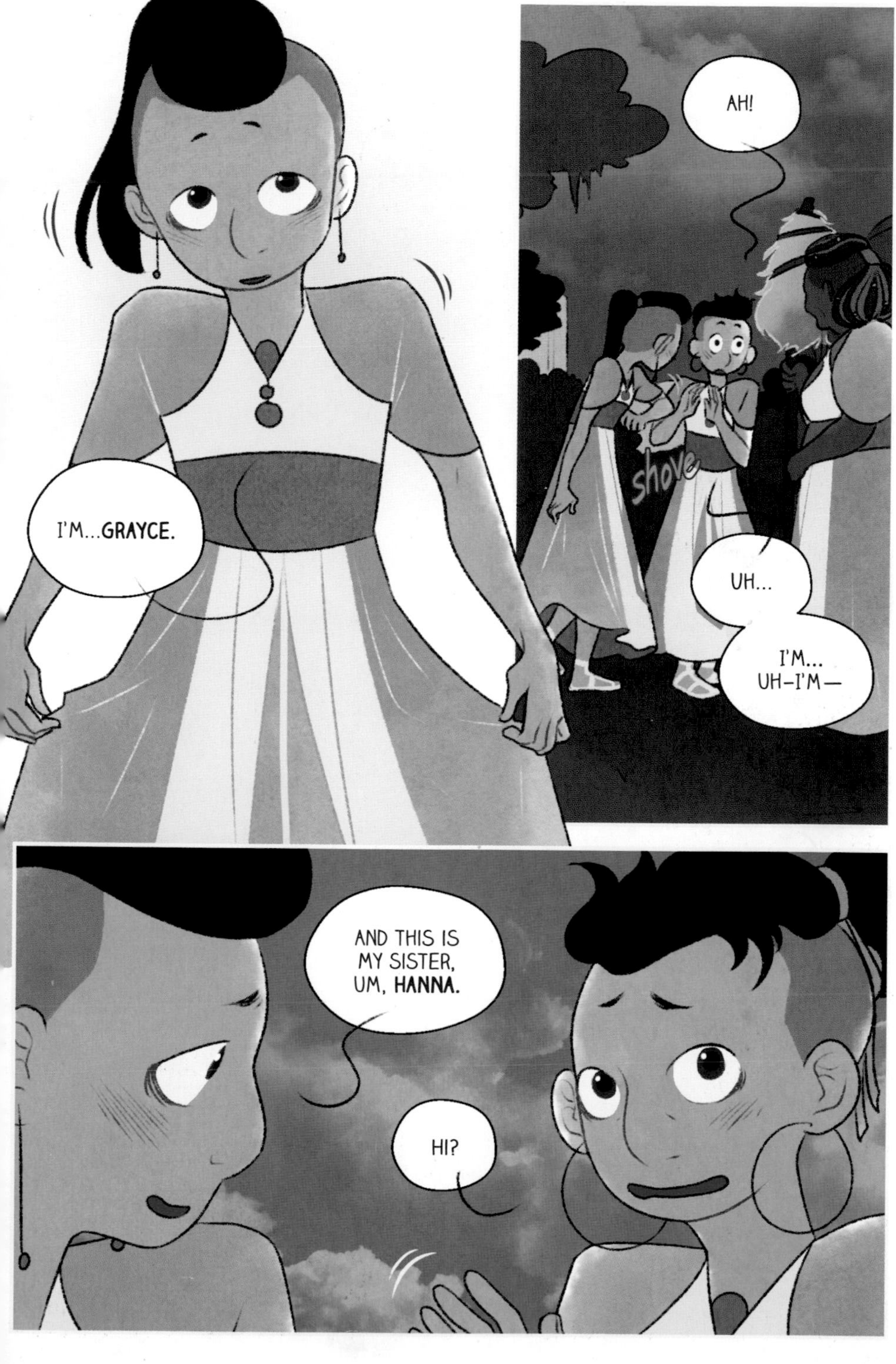
I'M...GRAYCE.
AH!
shove
UH...
I'M... UH-I'M—
AND THIS IS MY SISTER, UM, HANNA.
HI?

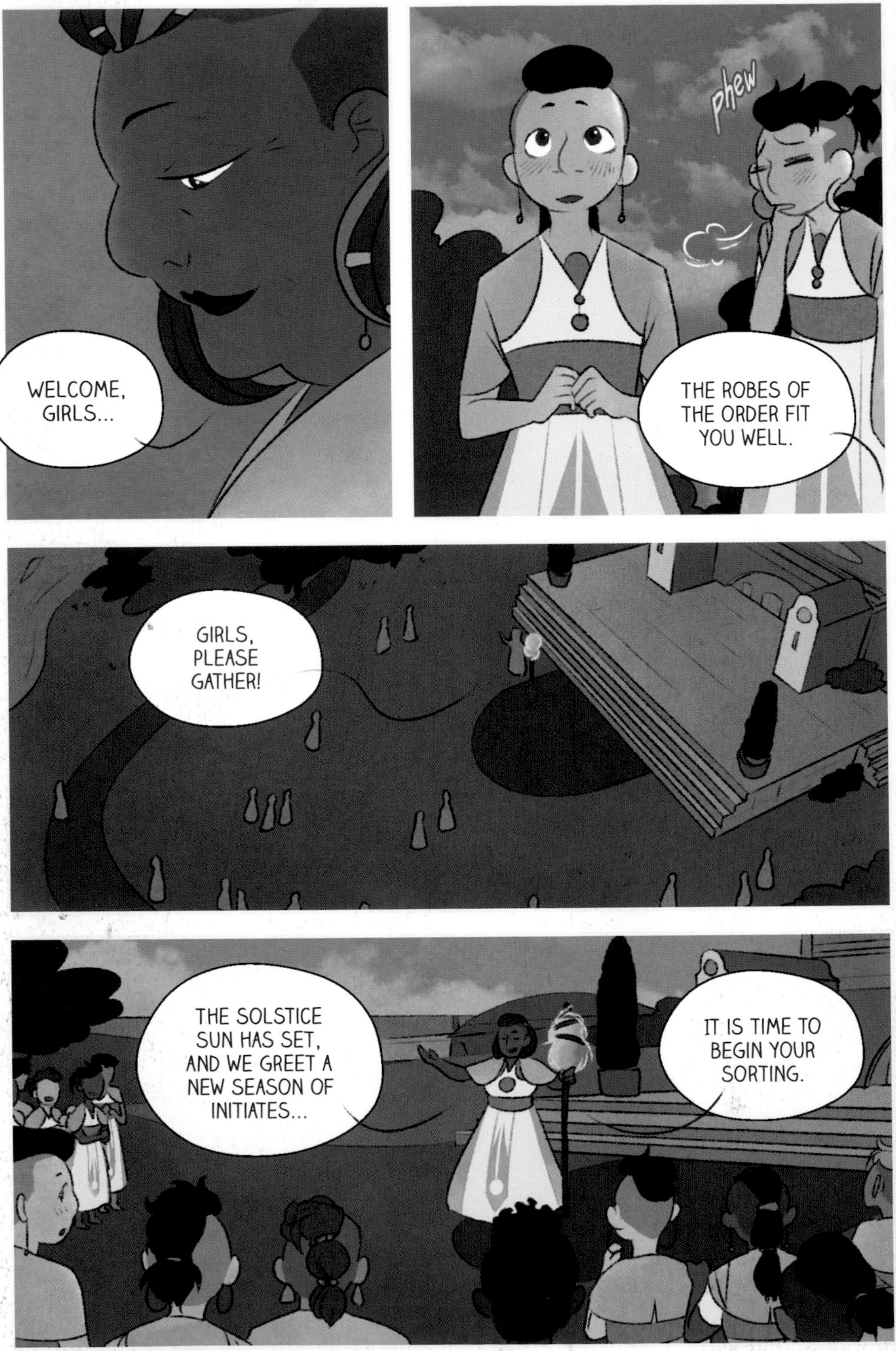
WELCOME, GIRLS...
phew
THE ROBES OF THE ORDER FIT YOU WELL.
GIRLS, PLEASE GATHER!
THE SOLSTICE SUN HAS SET, AND WE GREET A NEW SEASON OF INITIATES...
IT IS TIME TO BEGIN YOUR SORTING.

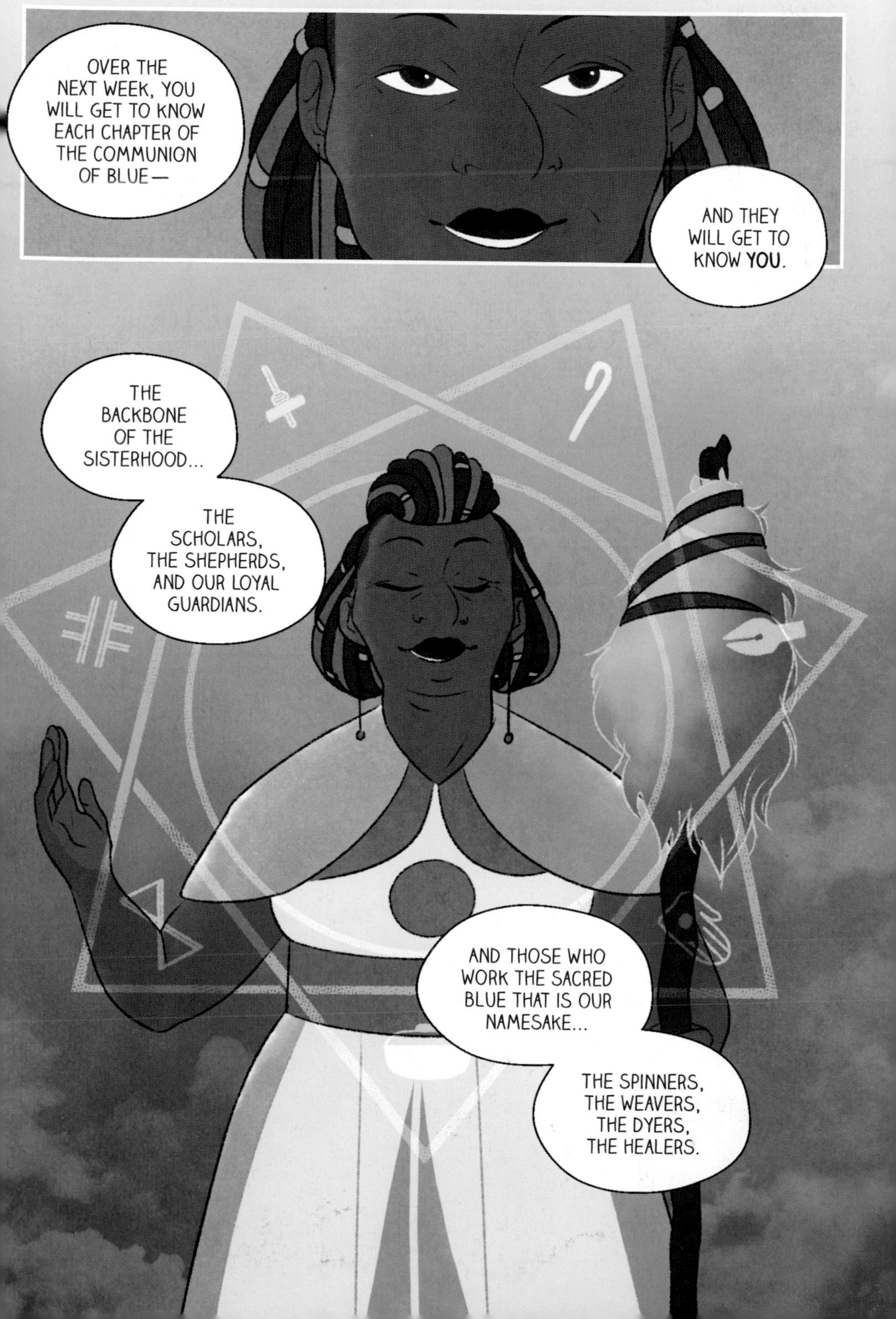
OVER THE NEXT WEEK, YOU WILL GET TO KNOW EACH CHAPTER OF THE COMMUNION OF BLUE—
AND THEY WILL GET TO KNOW **YOU**.
THE BACKBONE OF THE SISTERHOOD...
THE SCHOLARS, THE SHEPHERDS, AND OUR LOYAL GUARDIANS.
AND THOSE WHO WORK THE SACRED BLUE THAT IS OUR NAMESAKE...
THE SPINNERS, THE WEAVERS, THE DYERS, THE HEALERS.

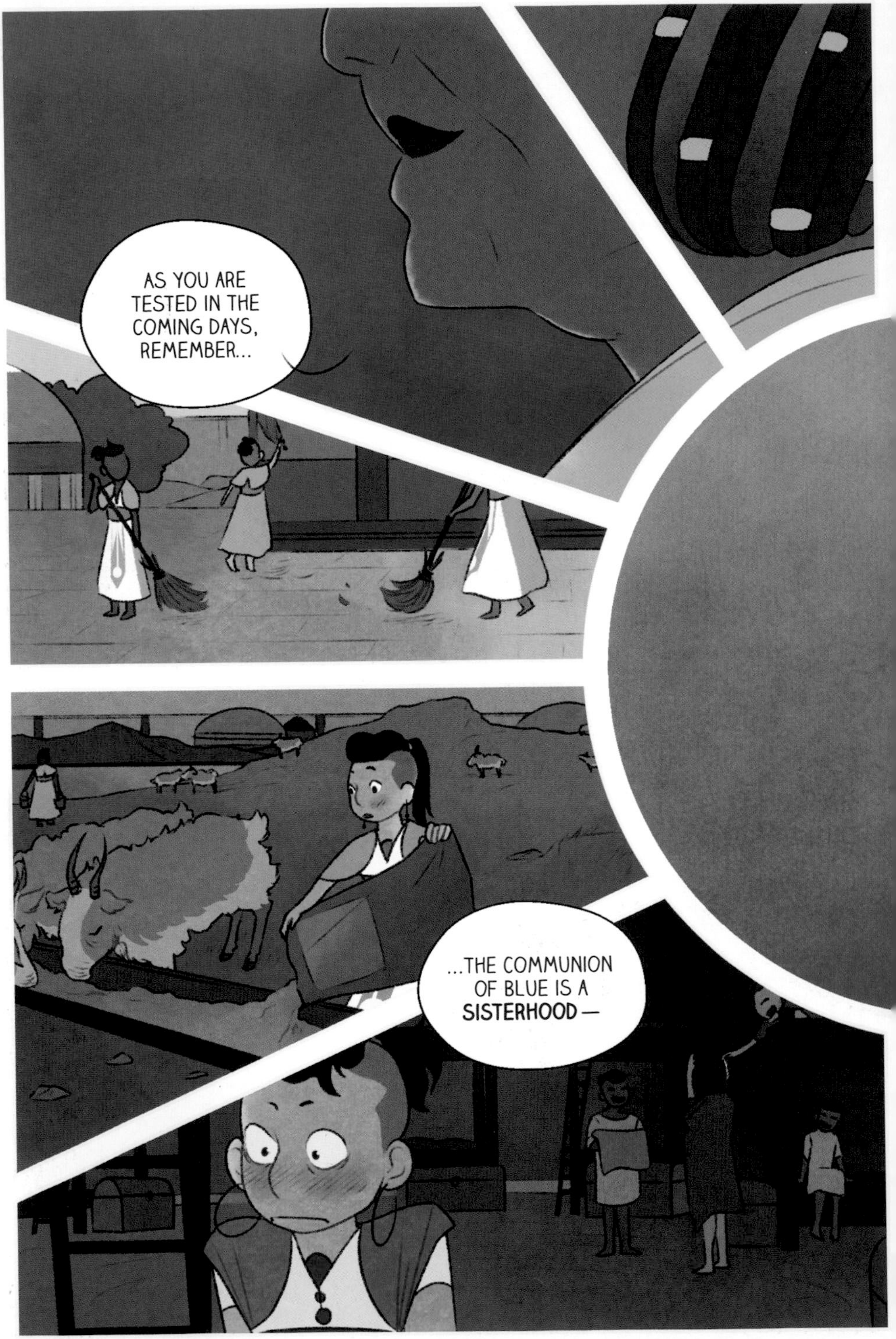

AS YOU ARE TESTED IN THE COMING DAYS, REMEMBER...
...THE COMMUNION OF BLUE IS A **SISTERHOOD**—

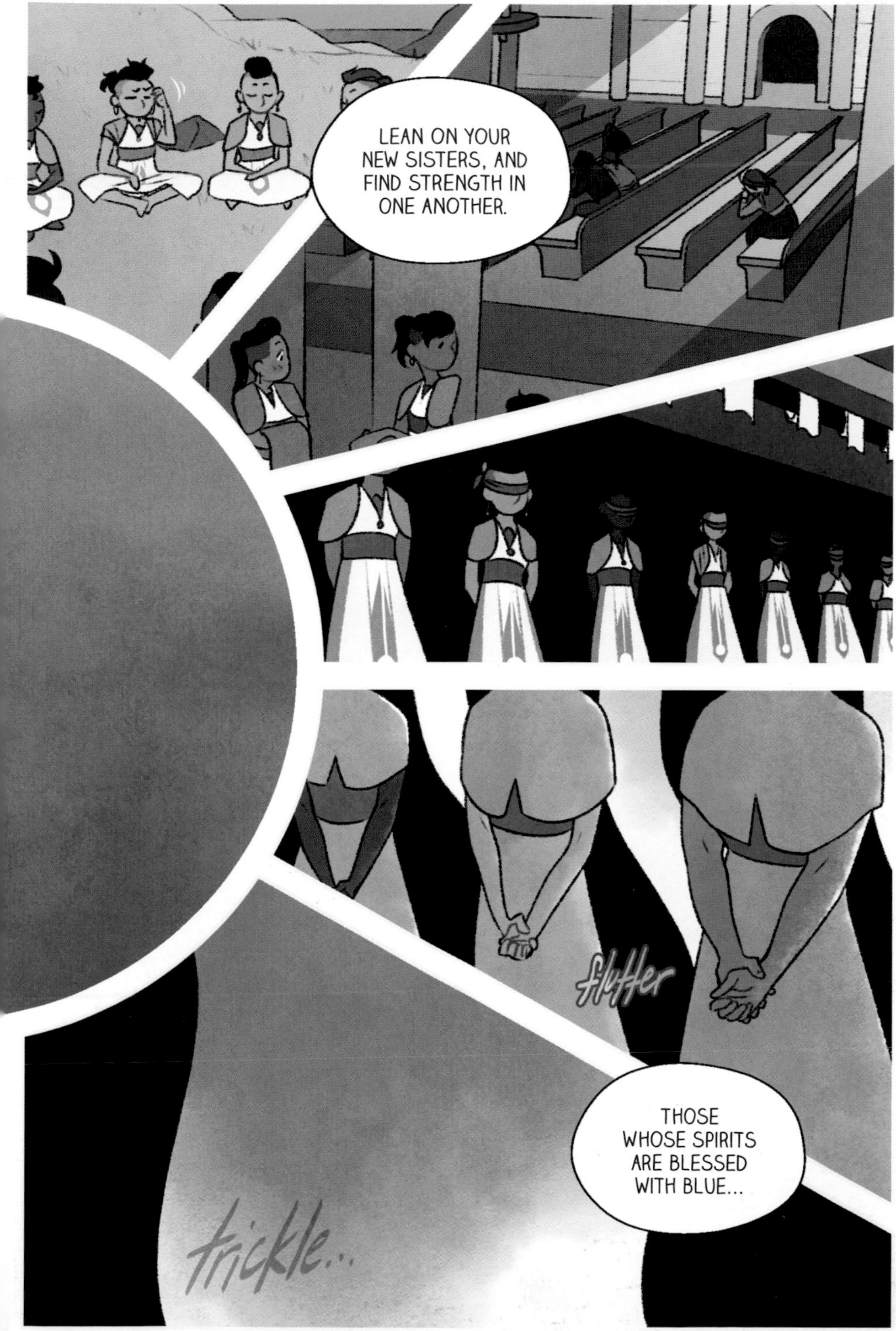
LEAN ON YOUR NEW SISTERS, AND FIND STRENGTH IN ONE ANOTHER.
flutter
THOSE WHOSE SPIRITS ARE BLESSED WITH BLUE...
trickle...

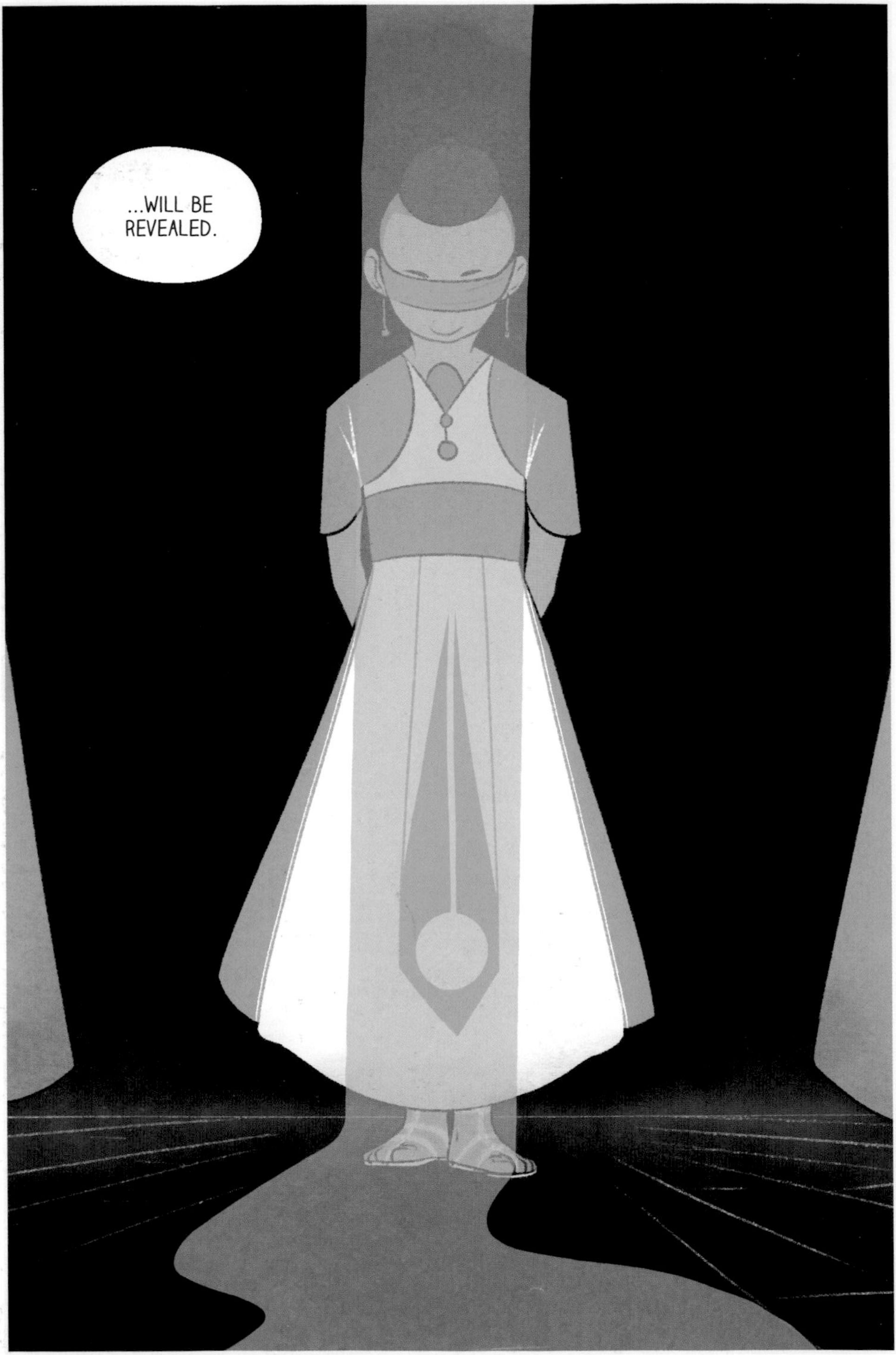
...WILL BE
REVEALED.

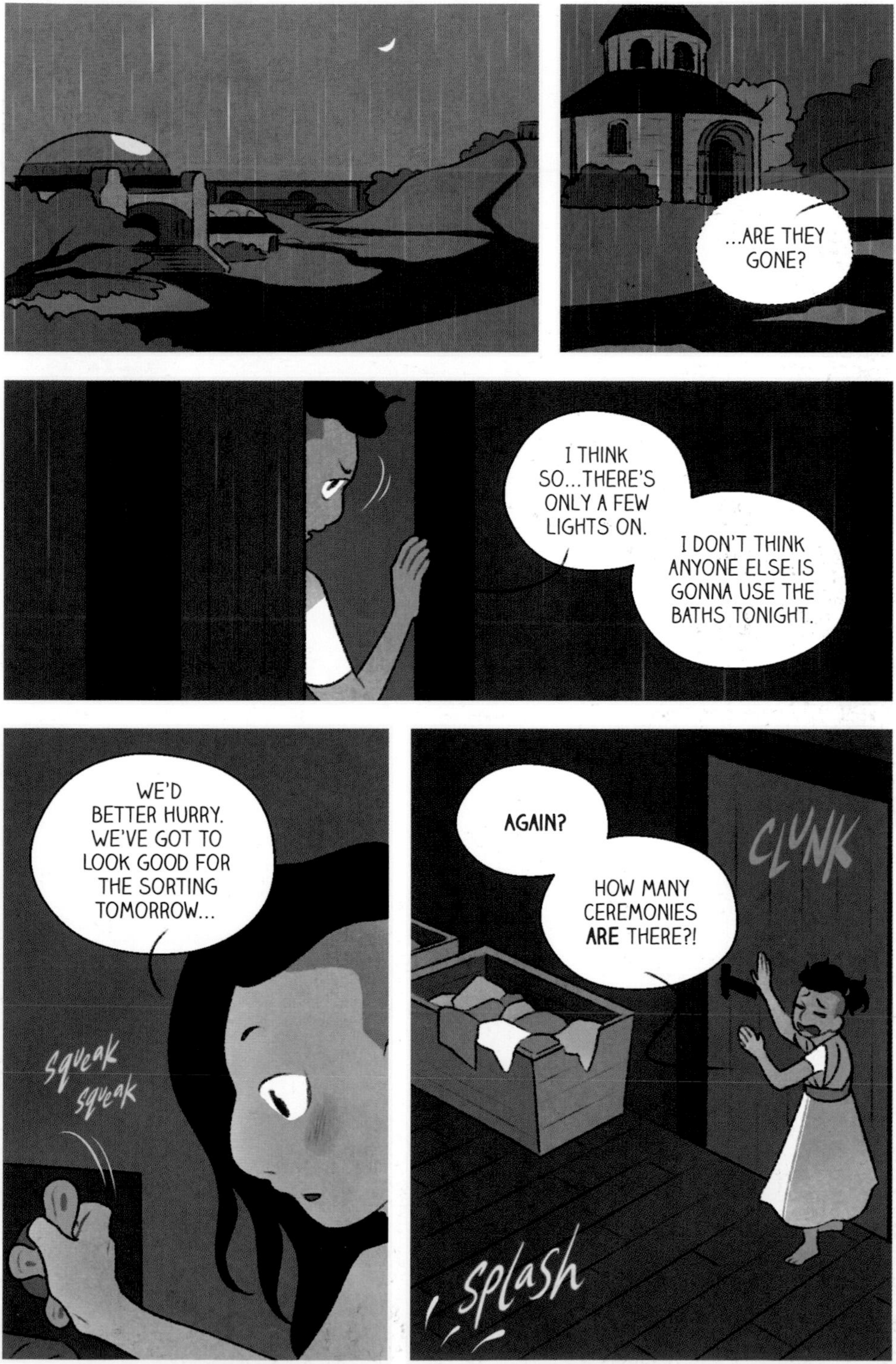
...ARE THEY GONE?
I THINK SO...THERE'S ONLY A FEW LIGHTS ON.
I DON'T THINK ANYONE ELSE IS GONNA USE THE BATHS TONIGHT.
WE'D BETTER HURRY. WE'VE GOT TO LOOK GOOD FOR THE SORTING TOMORROW...
squeak squeak
AGAIN?
HOW MANY CEREMONIES **ARE** THERE?!
CLUNK
SPLASH

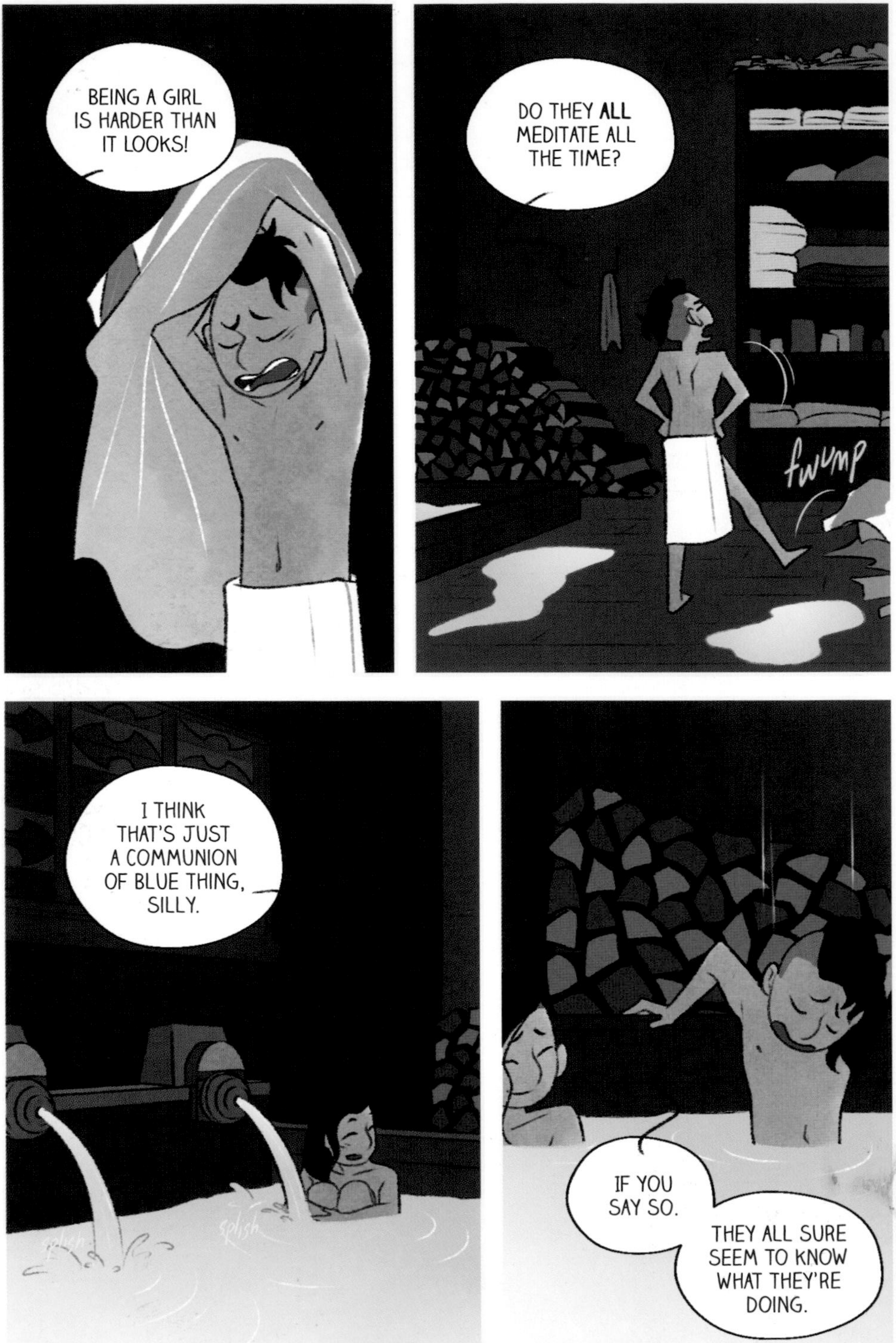
BEING A GIRL IS HARDER THAN IT LOOKS!
DO THEY **ALL** MEDITATE ALL THE TIME?
fwump
I THINK THAT'S JUST A COMMUNION OF BLUE THING, SILLY.
splish
splish
IF YOU SAY SO.
THEY ALL SURE SEEM TO KNOW WHAT THEY'RE DOING.

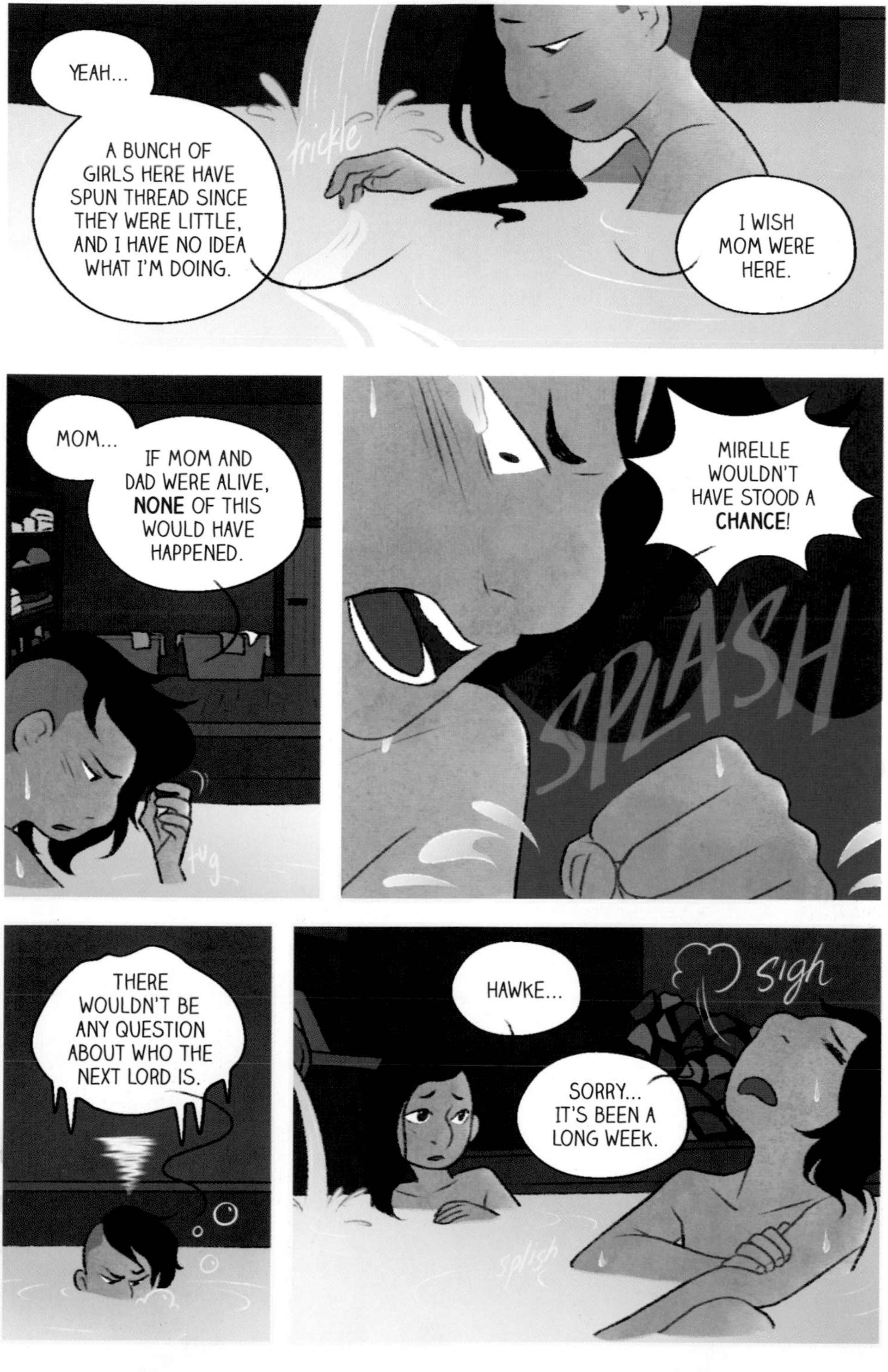
YEAH...
A BUNCH OF GIRLS HERE HAVE SPUN THREAD SINCE THEY WERE LITTLE, AND I HAVE NO IDEA WHAT I'M DOING.
trickle
I WISH MOM WERE HERE.
MOM...
IF MOM AND DAD WERE ALIVE, **NONE** OF THIS WOULD HAVE HAPPENED.
tug
MIRELLE WOULDN'T HAVE STOOD A **CHANCE**!
SPLASH
THERE WOULDN'T BE ANY QUESTION ABOUT WHO THE NEXT LORD IS.
HAWKE...
sigh
SORRY... IT'S BEEN A LONG WEEK.
splish

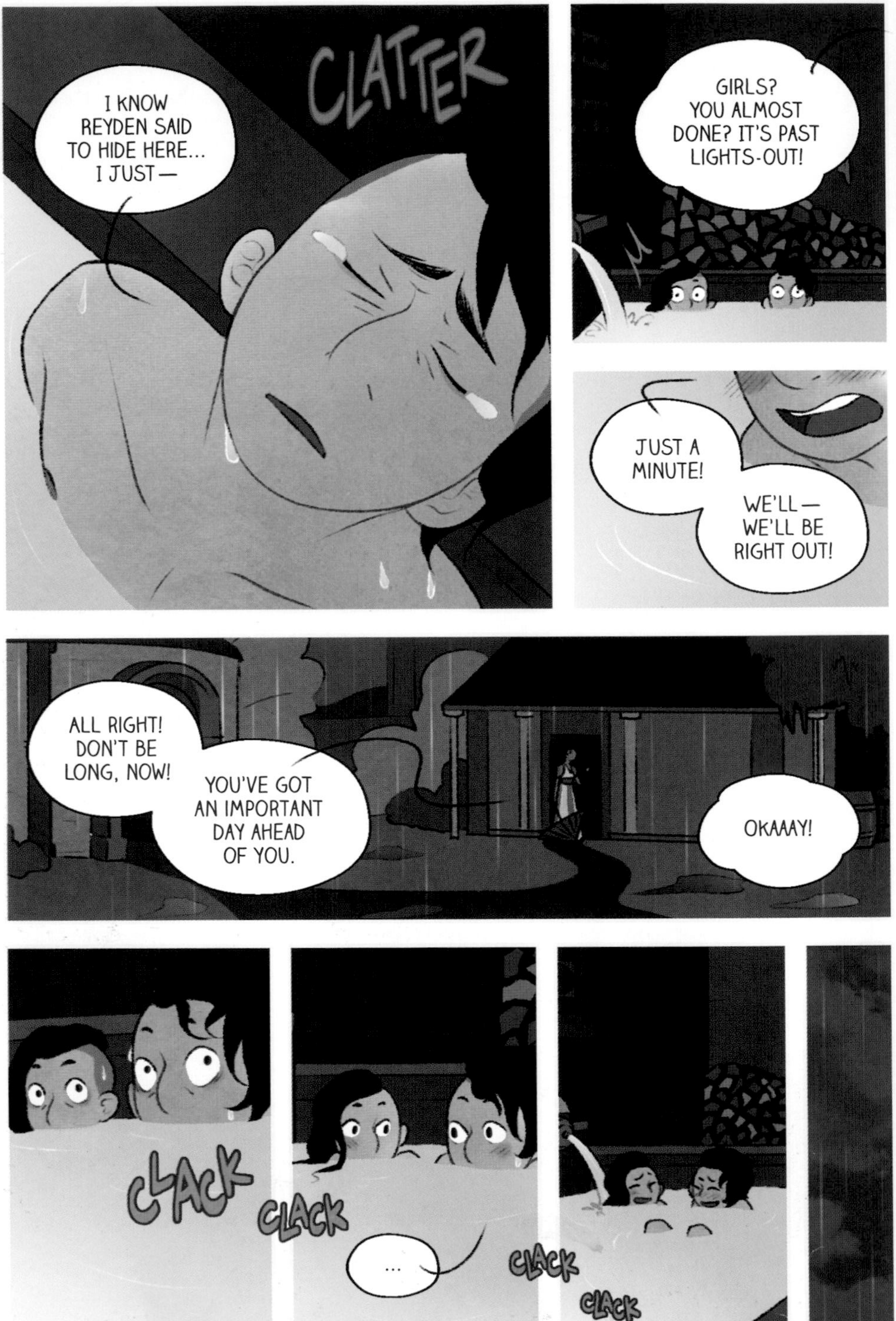
CLATTER
I KNOW REYDEN SAID TO HIDE HERE... I JUST—
GIRLS? YOU ALMOST DONE? IT'S PAST LIGHTS-OUT!
JUST A MINUTE!
WE'LL— WE'LL BE RIGHT OUT!
ALL RIGHT! DON'T BE LONG, NOW!
YOU'VE GOT AN IMPORTANT DAY AHEAD OF YOU.
OKAAAY!
CLACK
CLACK
...
CLACK
CLACK

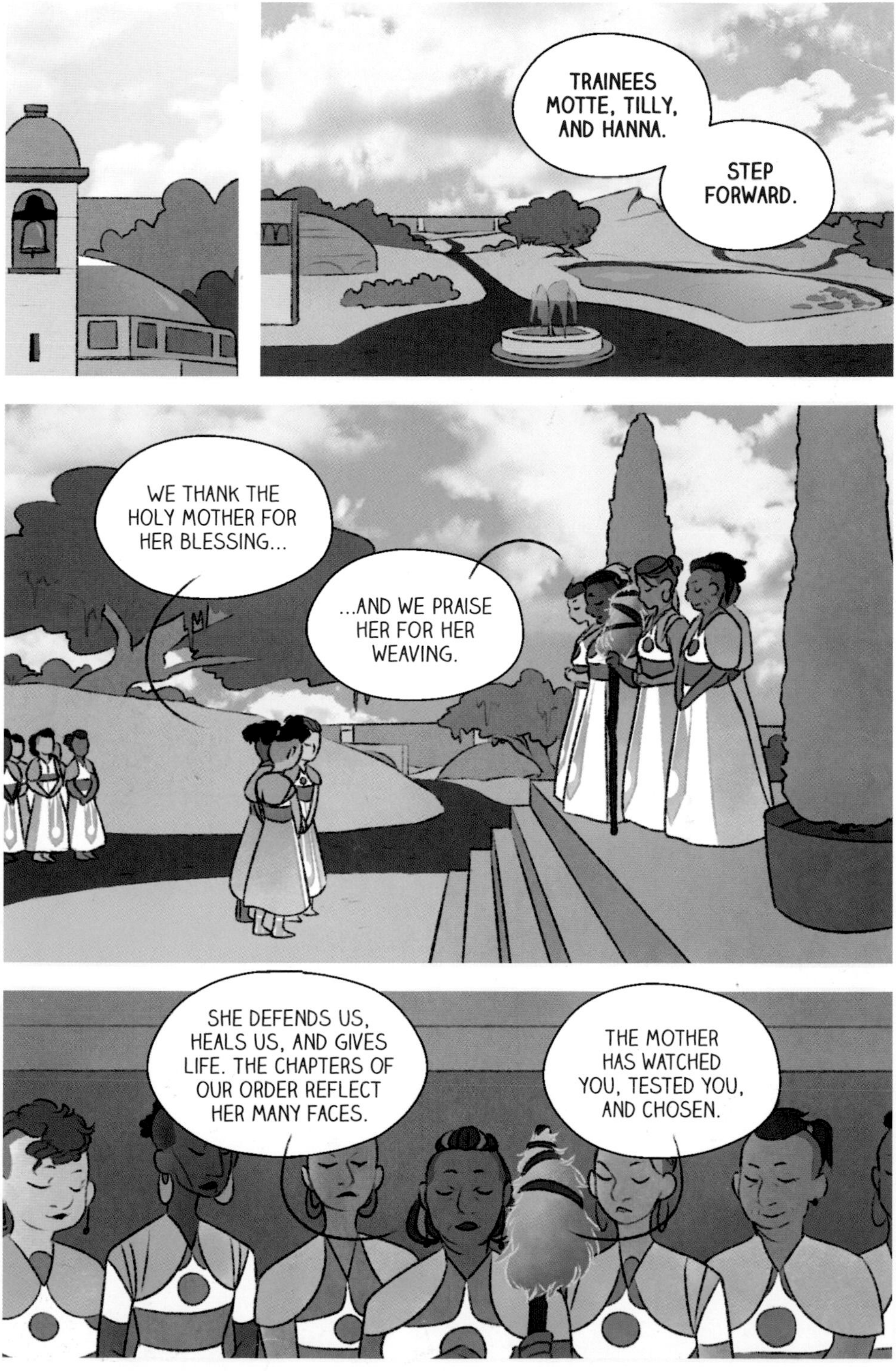
TRAINEES MOTTE, TILLY, AND HANNA.
STEP FORWARD.
WE THANK THE HOLY MOTHER FOR HER BLESSING...
...AND WE PRAISE HER FOR HER WEAVING.
SHE DEFENDS US, HEALS US, AND GIVES LIFE. THE CHAPTERS OF OUR ORDER REFLECT HER MANY FACES.
THE MOTHER HAS WATCHED YOU, TESTED YOU, AND CHOSEN.

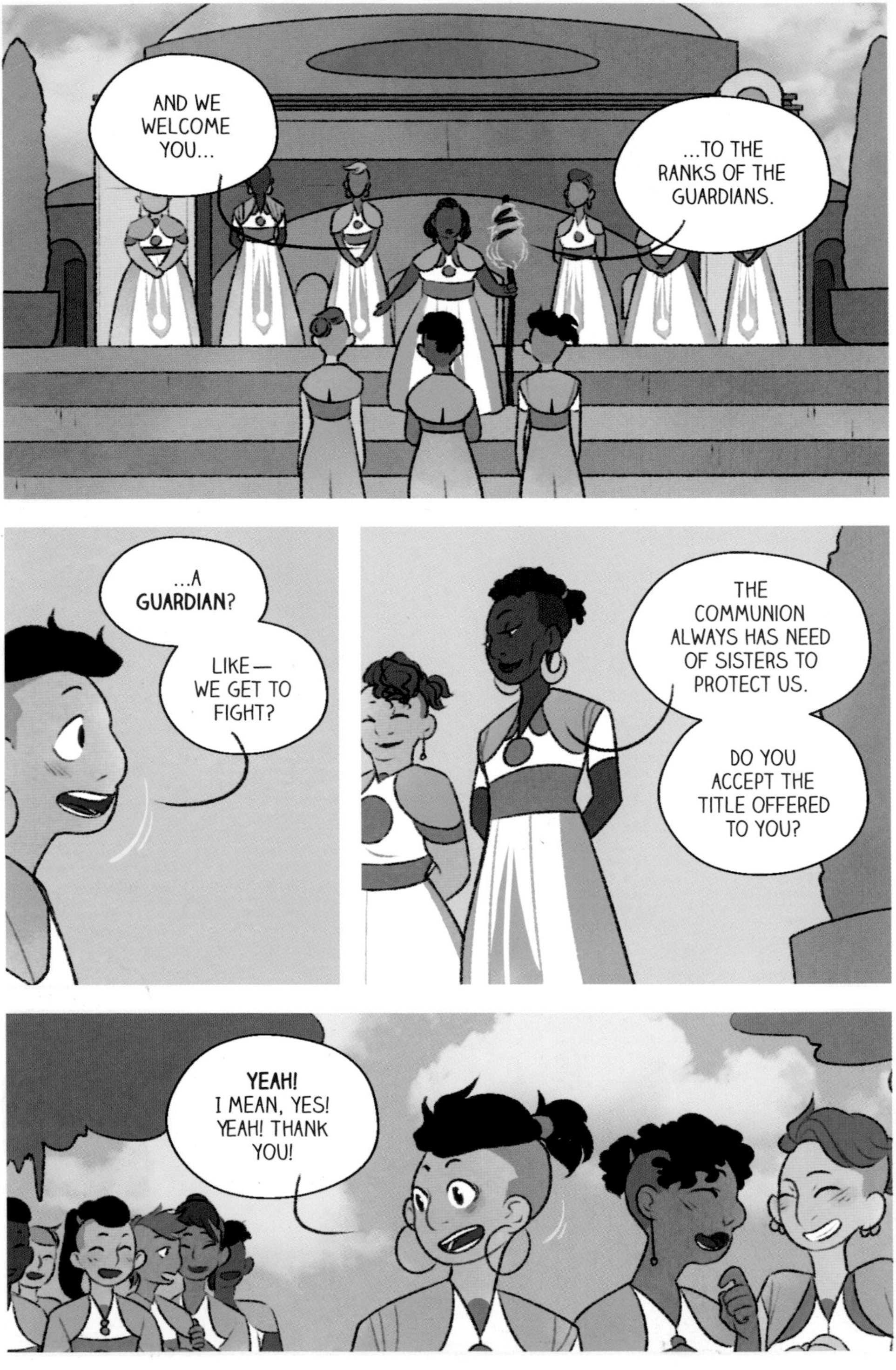
AND WE WELCOME YOU...
...TO THE RANKS OF THE GUARDIANS.
...A **GUARDIAN**?
LIKE— WE GET TO FIGHT?
THE COMMUNION ALWAYS HAS NEED OF SISTERS TO PROTECT US.
DO YOU ACCEPT THE TITLE OFFERED TO YOU?
YEAH! I MEAN, YES! YEAH! THANK YOU!

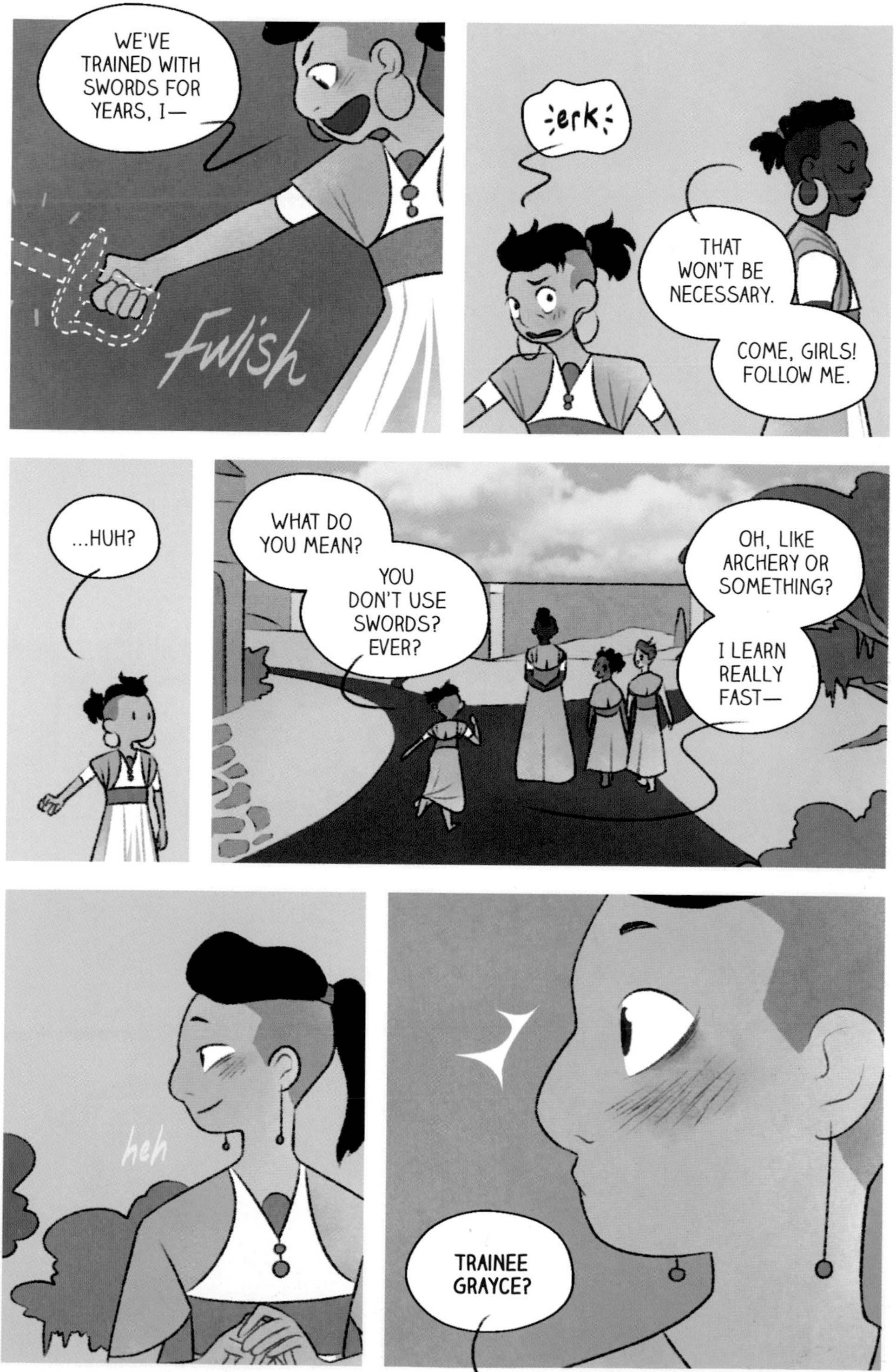

WE'VE TRAINED WITH SWORDS FOR YEARS, I—
fwish
erk
THAT WON'T BE NECESSARY.
COME, GIRLS! FOLLOW ME.
...HUH?
WHAT DO YOU MEAN?
YOU DON'T USE SWORDS? EVER?
OH, LIKE ARCHERY OR SOMETHING?
I LEARN REALLY FAST—
heh
TRAINEE GRAYCE?

STEP FORWARD.

THE MOTHER HAS WATCHED YOU, TESTED YOU, AND CHOSEN.

I...I THANK THE HOLY MOTHER FOR HER BLESSING.

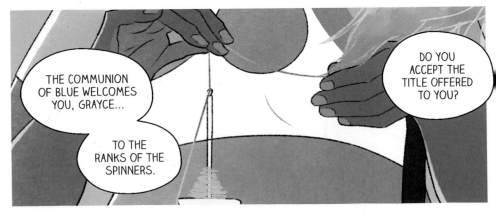

THE COMMUNION OF BLUE WELCOMES YOU, GRAYCE...

TO THE RANKS OF THE SPINNERS.

DO YOU ACCEPT THE TITLE OFFERED TO YOU?

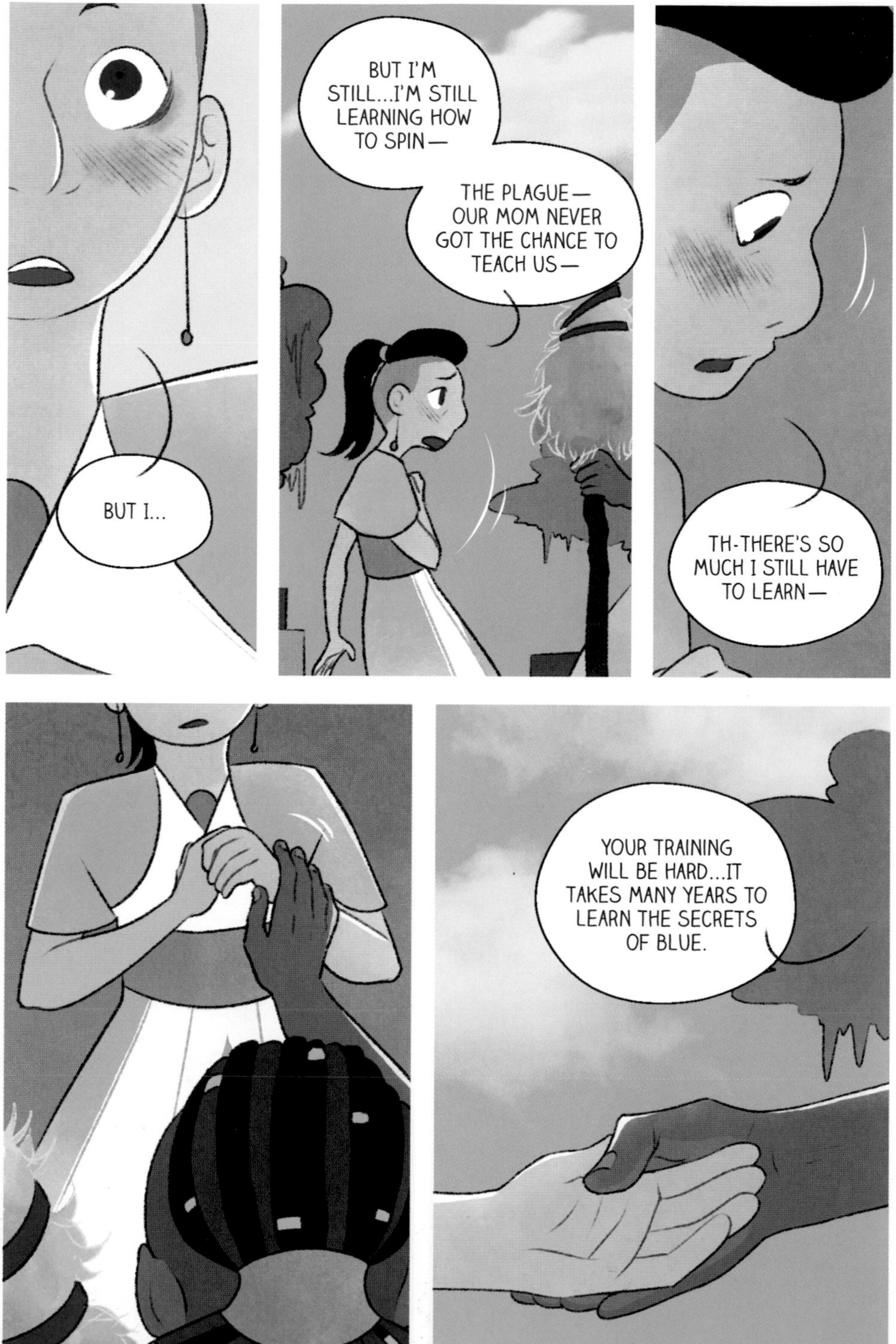
BUT I...
BUT I'M STILL...I'M STILL LEARNING HOW TO SPIN—
THE PLAGUE—OUR MOM NEVER GOT THE CHANCE TO TEACH US—
TH-THERE'S SO MUCH I STILL HAVE TO LEARN—
YOUR TRAINING WILL BE HARD...IT TAKES MANY YEARS TO LEARN THE SECRETS OF BLUE.

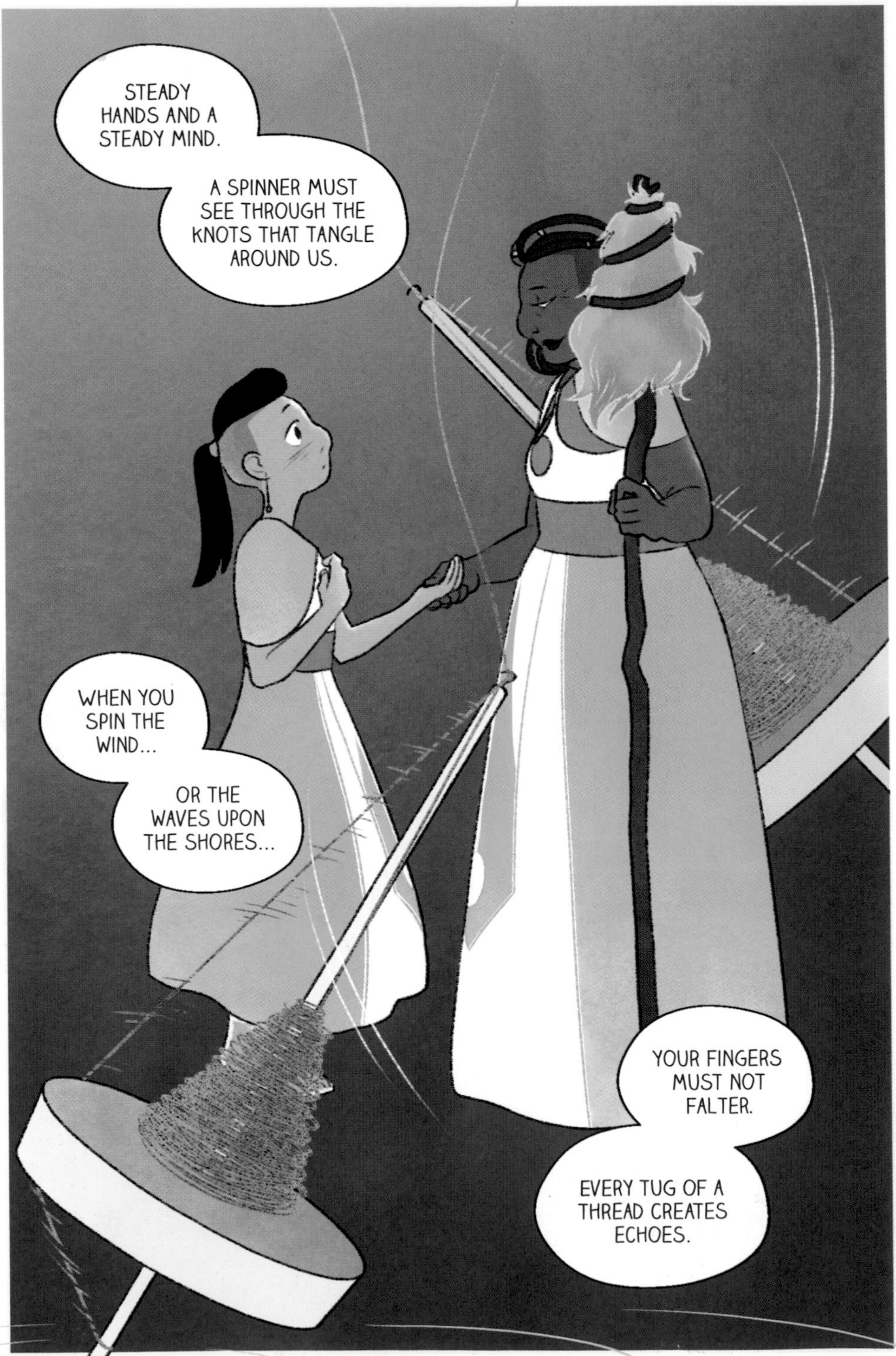
STEADY HANDS AND A STEADY MIND.
A SPINNER MUST SEE THROUGH THE KNOTS THAT TANGLE AROUND US.
WHEN YOU SPIN THE WIND...
OR THE WAVES UPON THE SHORES...
YOUR FINGERS MUST NOT FALTER.
EVERY TUG OF A THREAD CREATES ECHOES.

AND WHAT WAS WOVEN TIGHT...
...MAY FRAY WITH TIME.
YOUR PATH MAY DIVERGE FROM THAT OF YOUR TWIN.
ARE YOU PREPARED FOR THAT?
I—

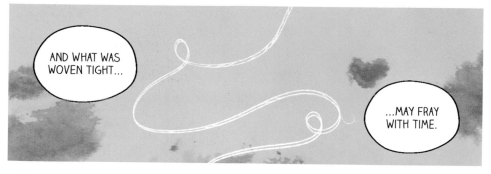

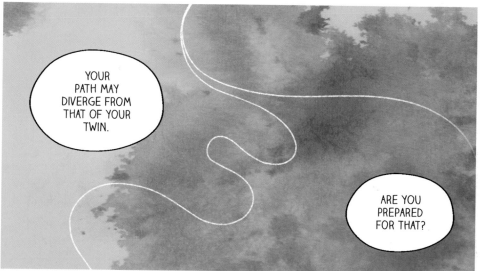

DO NOT BE AFRAID. YOU WILL NOT BE SEPARATED SO SOON.

ALL NEW INITIATES SHARE THEIR FIRST YEARS IN THE DORMS.

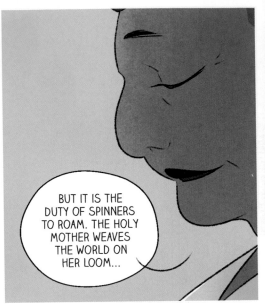

BUT IT IS THE DUTY OF SPINNERS TO ROAM. THE HOLY MOTHER WEAVES THE WORLD ON HER LOOM...

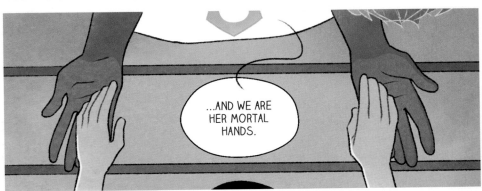

...AND WE ARE HER MORTAL HANDS.

THERE WILL COME A DAY WHEN YOU WILL LEAVE THE TEMPLE TO FIND THE THREADS THAT BIND ALL THINGS.

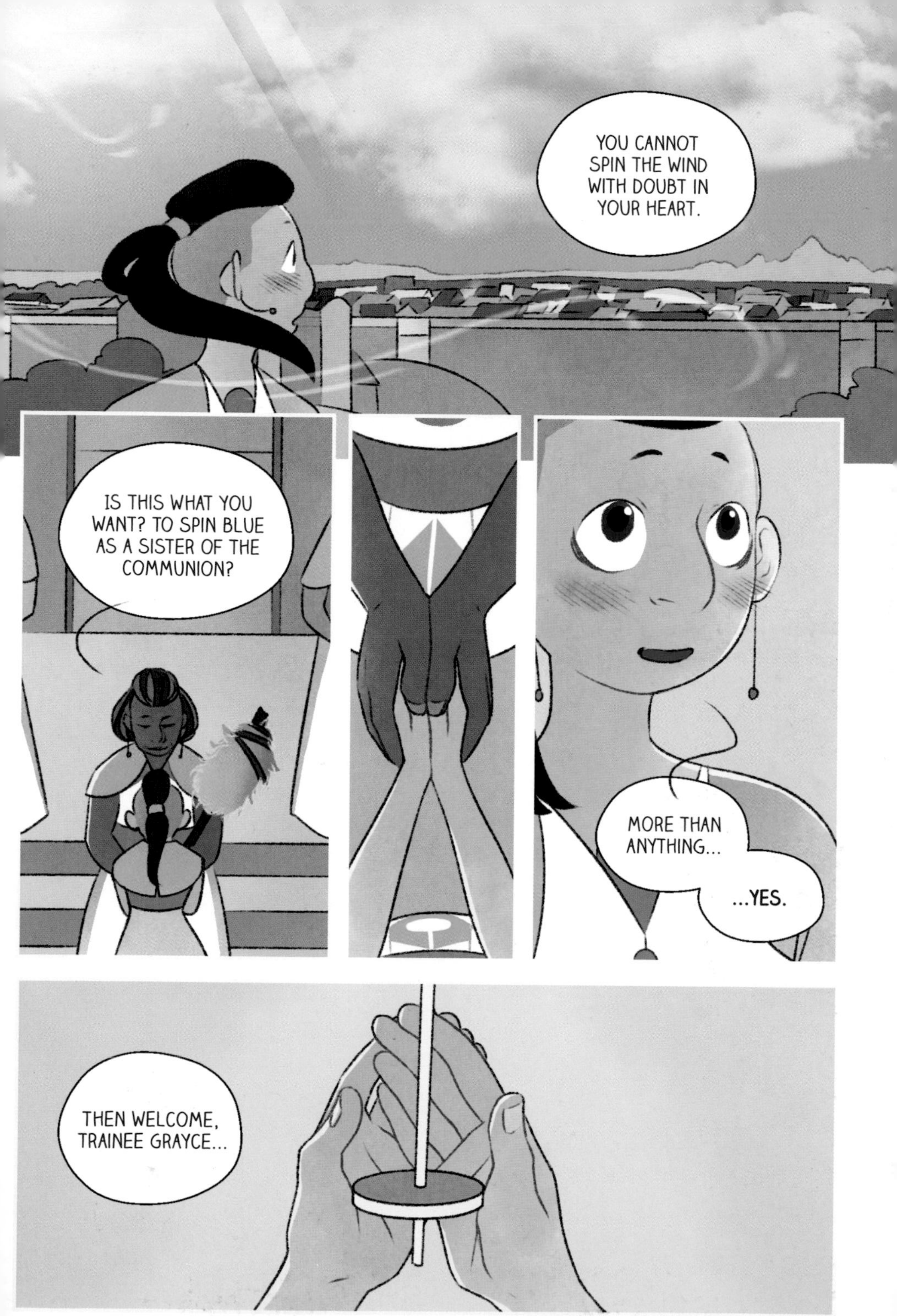
YOU CANNOT SPIN THE WIND WITH DOUBT IN YOUR HEART.
IS THIS WHAT YOU WANT? TO SPIN BLUE AS A SISTER OF THE COMMUNION?
MORE THAN ANYTHING...
...YES.
THEN WELCOME, TRAINEE GRAYCE...

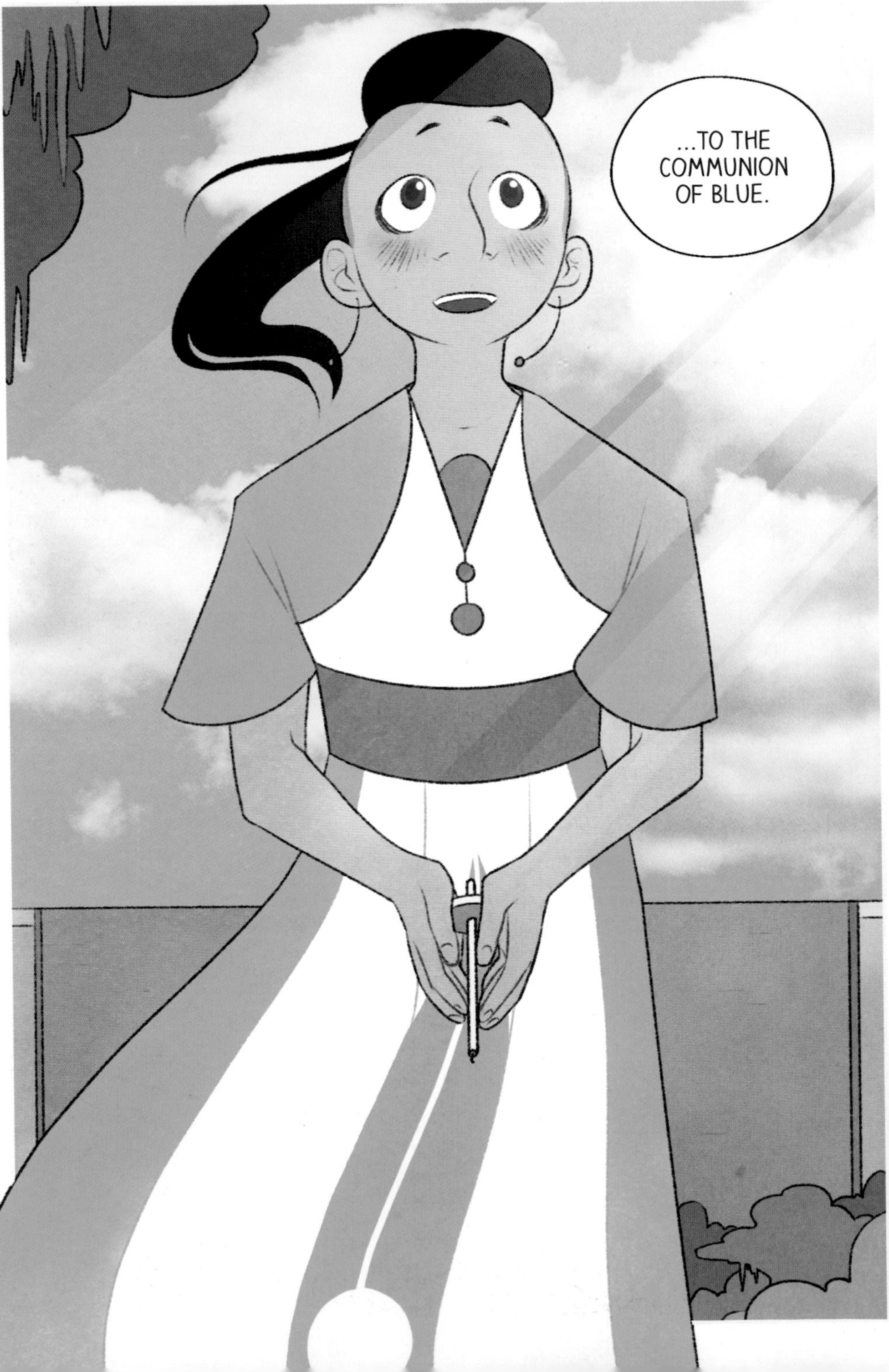
...TO THE COMMUNION OF BLUE.

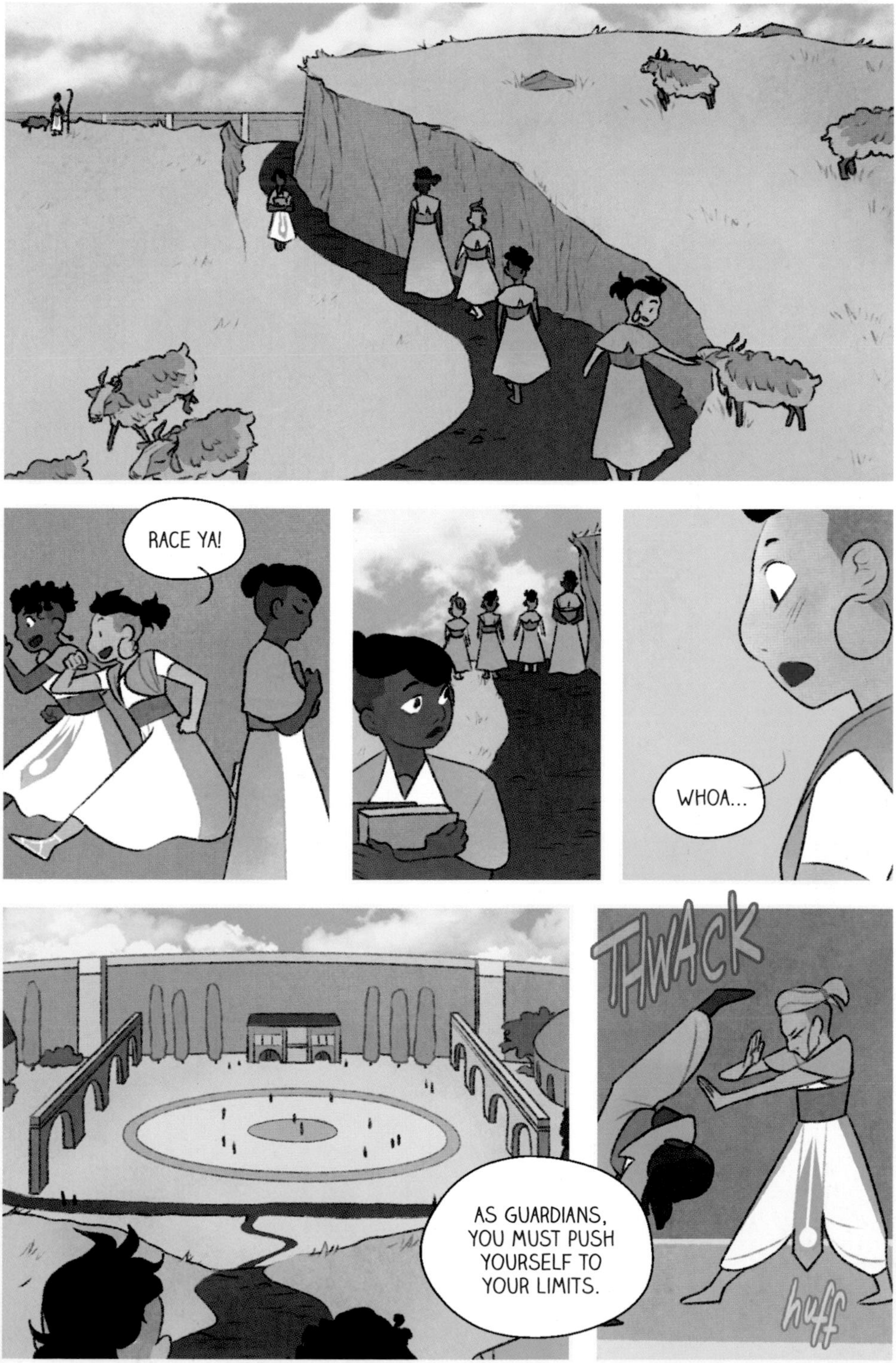
RACE YA!
WHOA...
THWACK
AS GUARDIANS, YOU MUST PUSH YOURSELF TO YOUR LIMITS.
huff

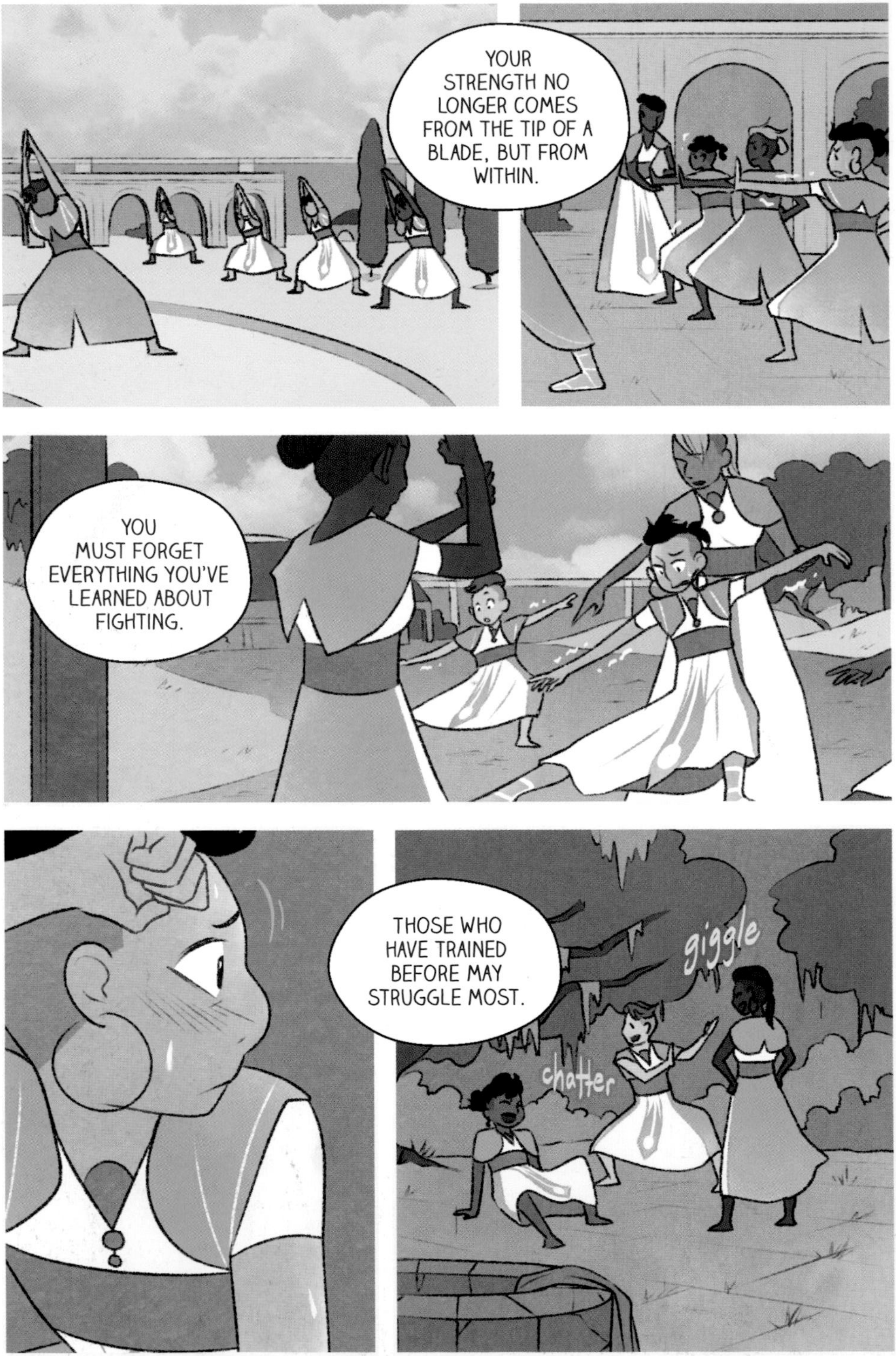
YOUR STRENGTH NO LONGER COMES FROM THE TIP OF A BLADE, BUT FROM WITHIN.
YOU MUST FORGET EVERYTHING YOU'VE LEARNED ABOUT FIGHTING.
THOSE WHO HAVE TRAINED BEFORE MAY STRUGGLE MOST.
giggle
chatter

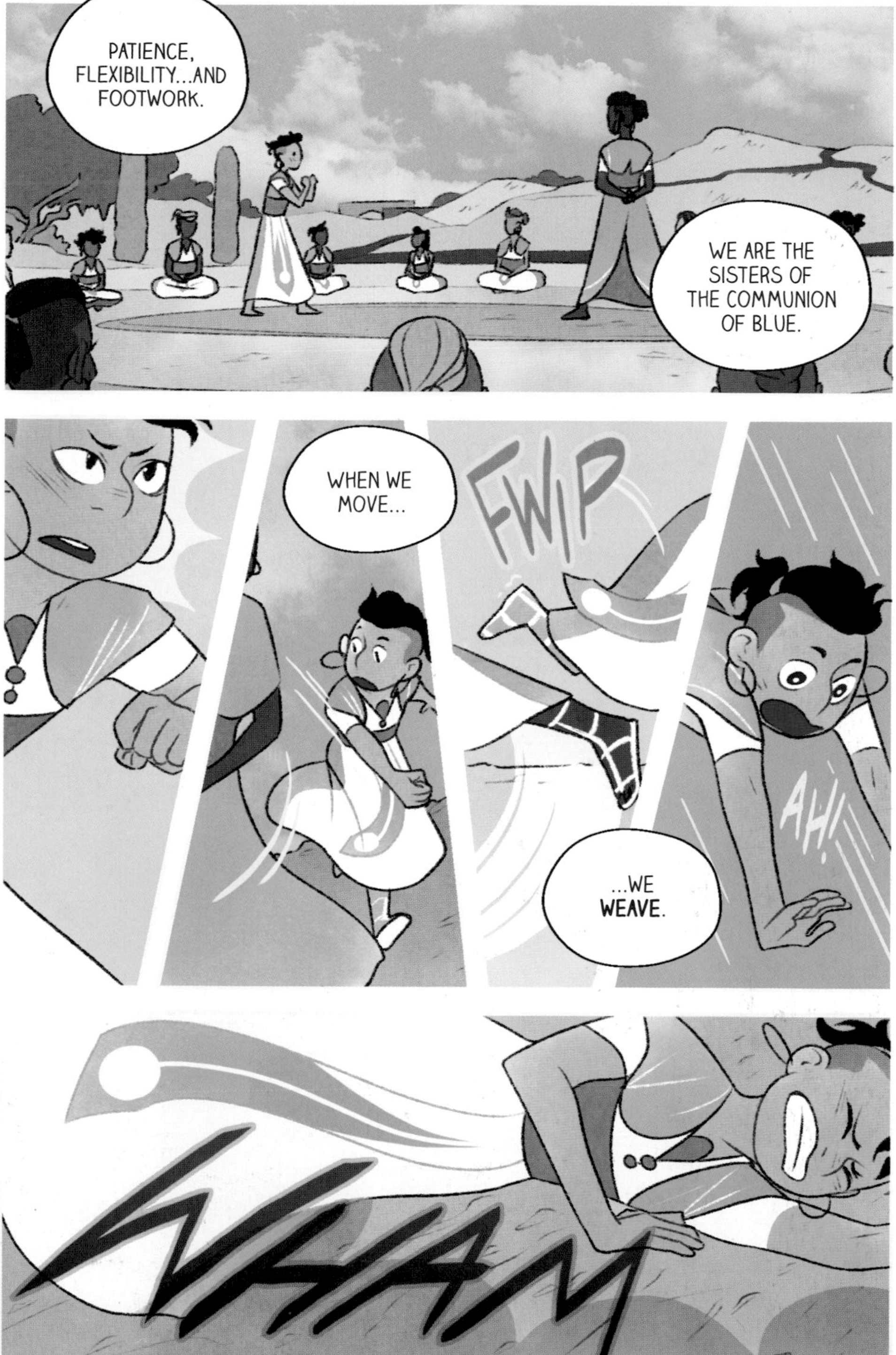
PATIENCE, FLEXIBILITY...AND FOOTWORK.
WE ARE THE SISTERS OF THE COMMUNION OF BLUE.
WHEN WE MOVE...
FWIP
...WE **WEAVE**.
AH!
WHAM

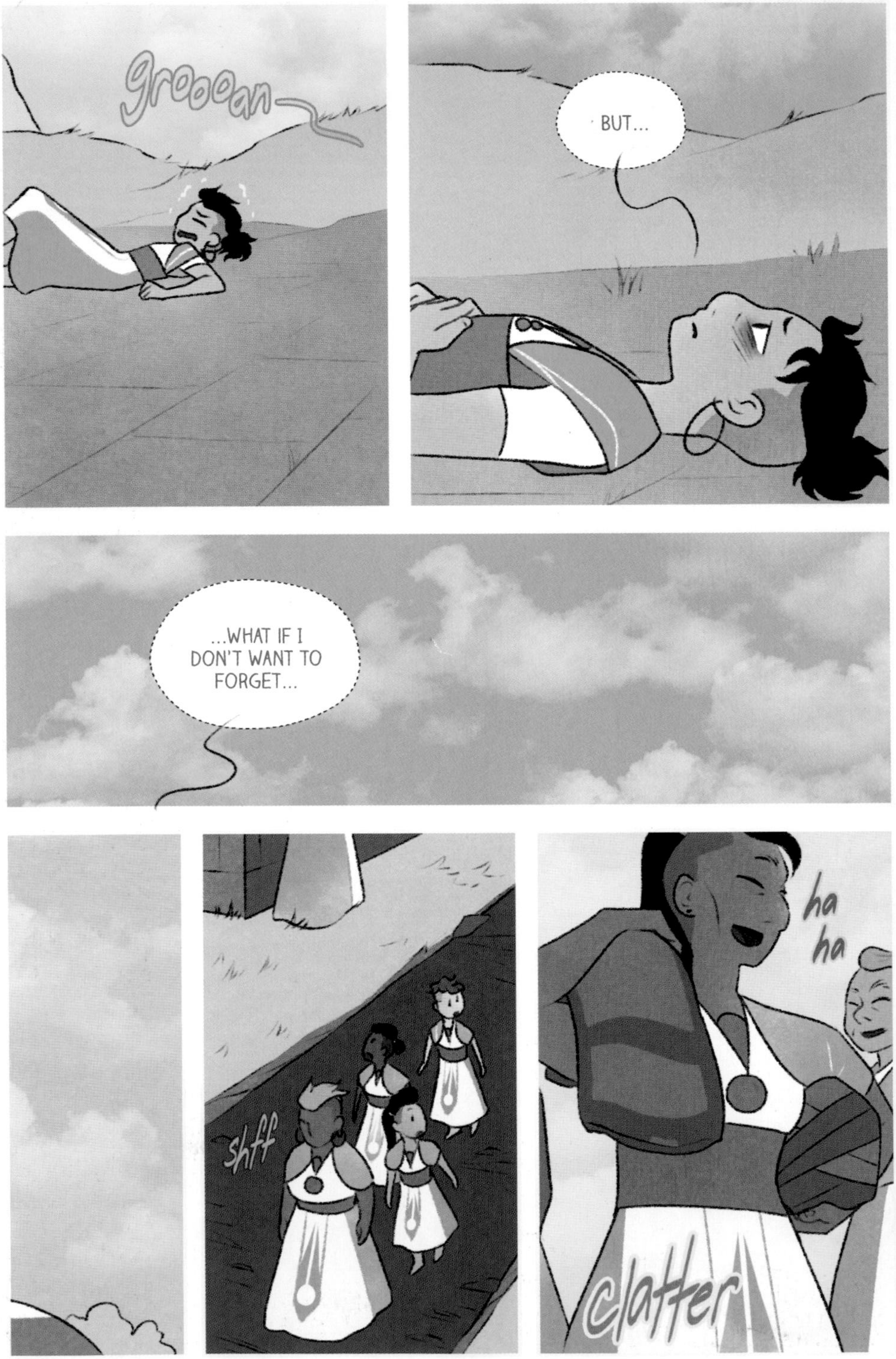
grooоan
BUT...
...WHAT IF I DON'T WANT TO FORGET...
shff
ha ha
clatter

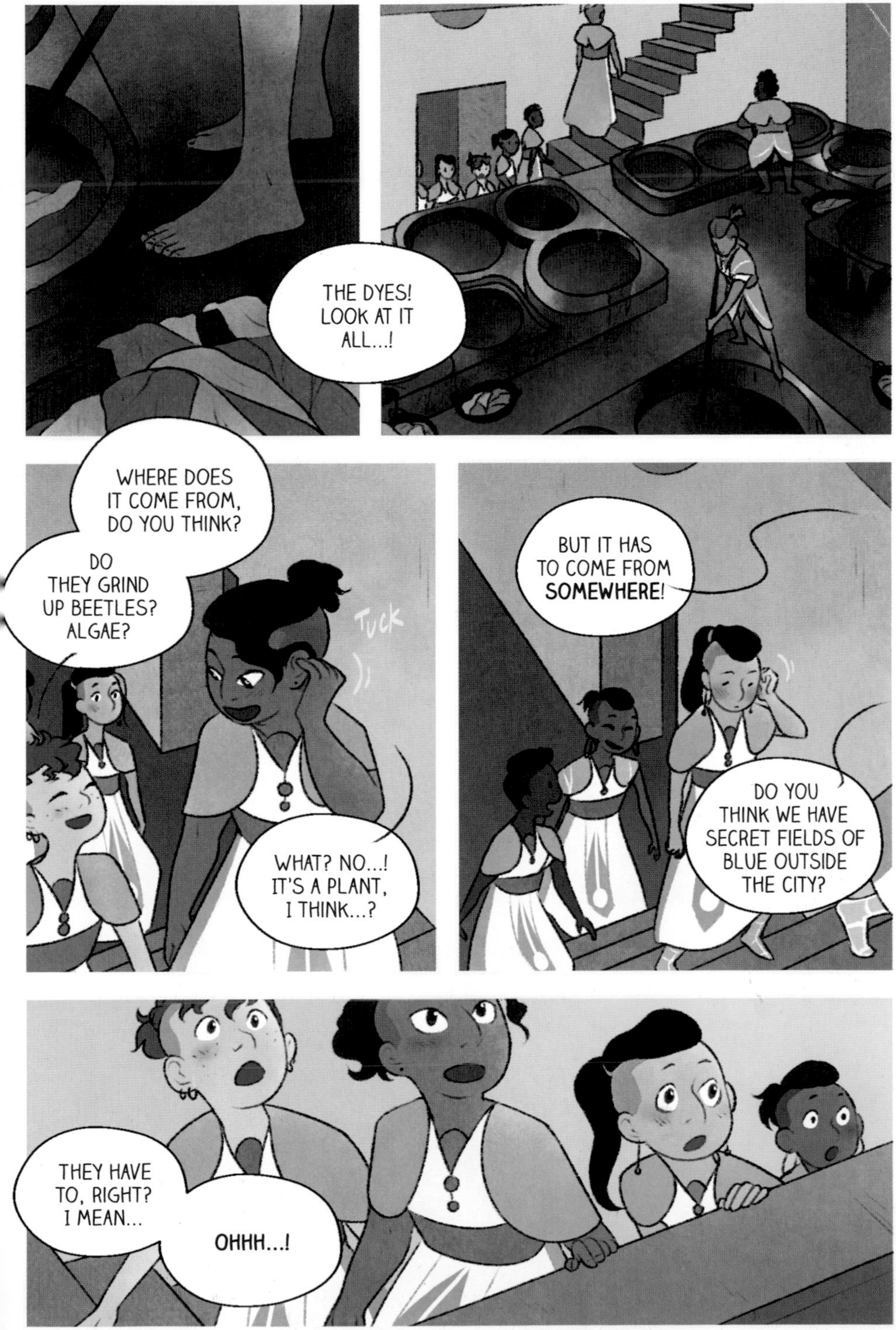
THE DYES! LOOK AT IT ALL...!
WHERE DOES IT COME FROM, DO YOU THINK?
DO THEY GRIND UP BEETLES? ALGAE?
TUCK
WHAT? NO...! IT'S A PLANT, I THINK...?
BUT IT HAS TO COME FROM **SOMEWHERE**!
DO YOU THINK WE HAVE SECRET FIELDS OF BLUE OUTSIDE THE CITY?
THEY HAVE TO, RIGHT? I MEAN...
OHHH...!

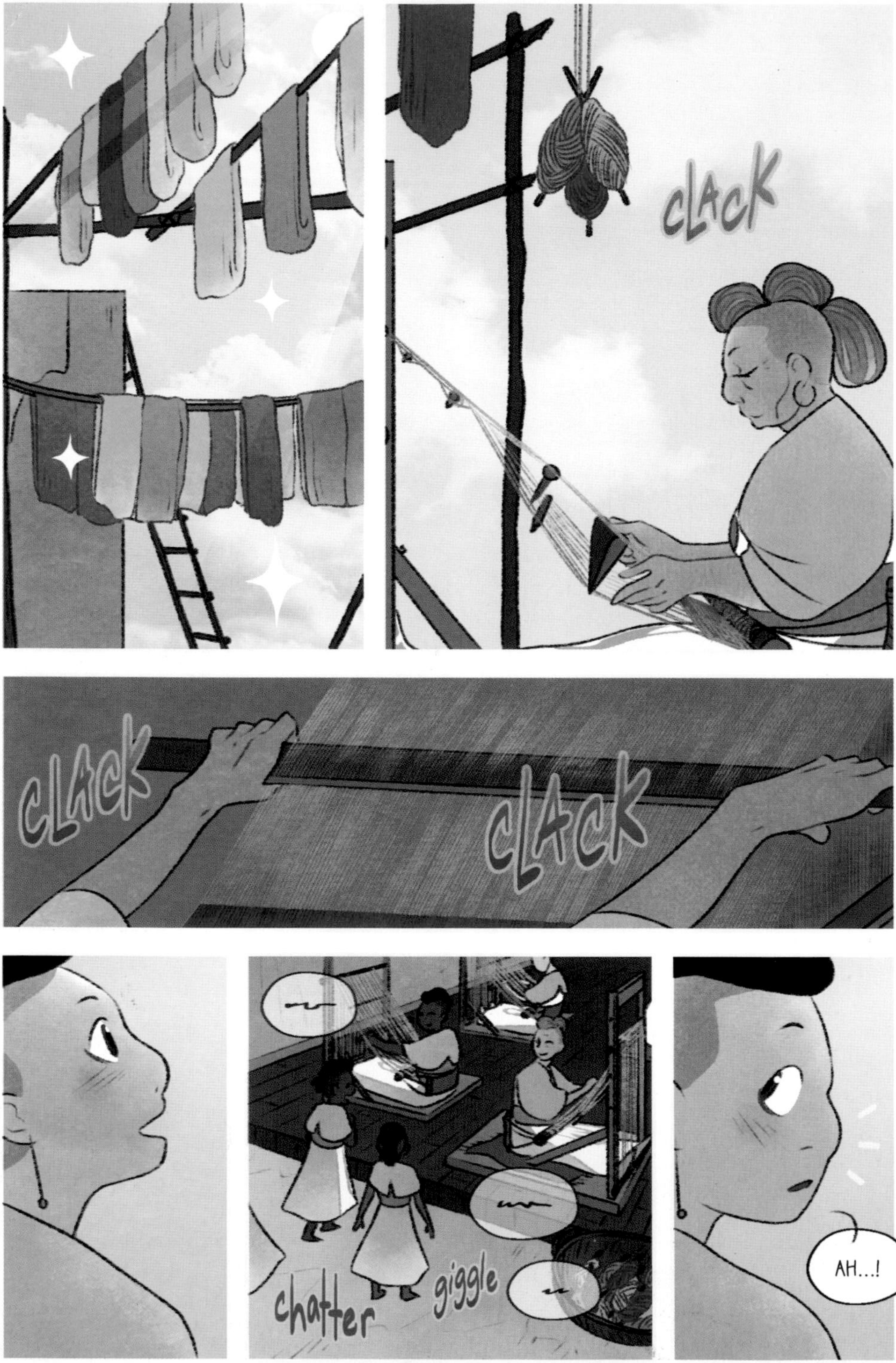
CLACK
CLACK
CLACK
chatter
giggle
AH...!

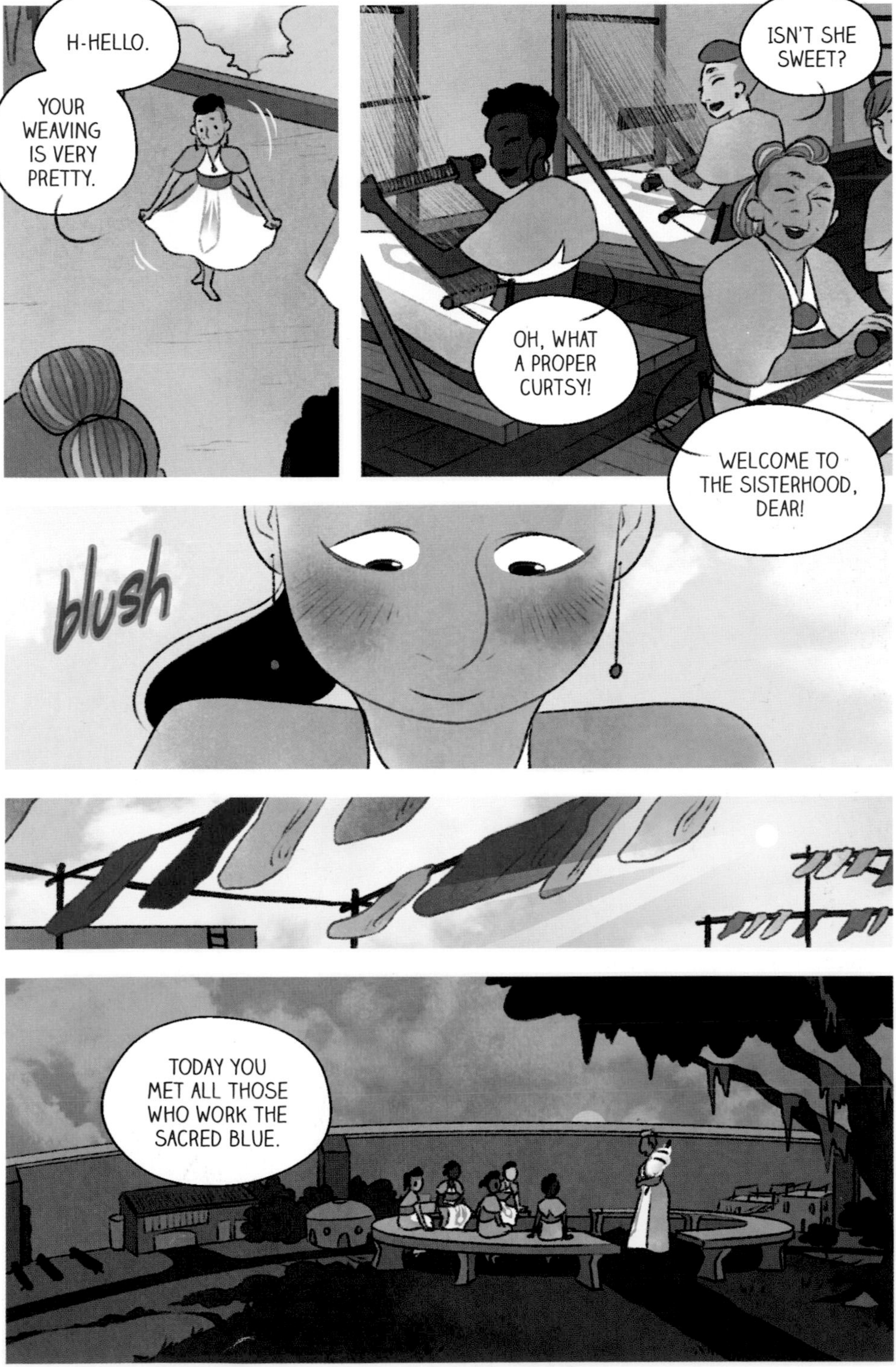
H-HELLO.
YOUR WEAVING IS VERY PRETTY.
ISN'T SHE SWEET?
OH, WHAT A PROPER CURTSY!
WELCOME TO THE SISTERHOOD, DEAR!
blush
TODAY YOU MET ALL THOSE WHO WORK THE SACRED BLUE.

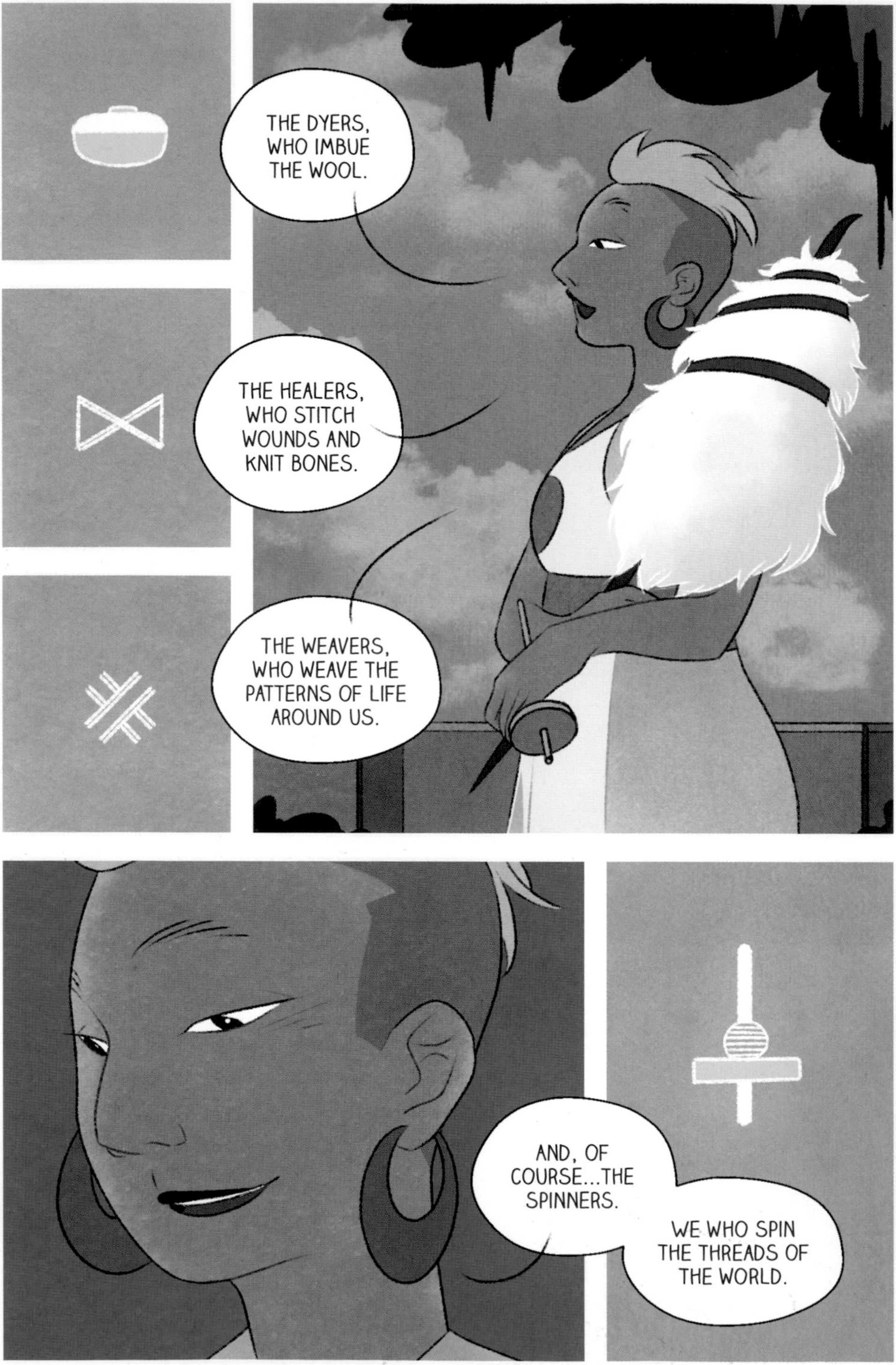
THE DYERS, WHO IMBUE THE WOOL.
THE HEALERS, WHO STITCH WOUNDS AND KNIT BONES.
THE WEAVERS, WHO WEAVE THE PATTERNS OF LIFE AROUND US.
AND, OF COURSE...THE SPINNERS.
WE WHO SPIN THE THREADS OF THE WORLD.

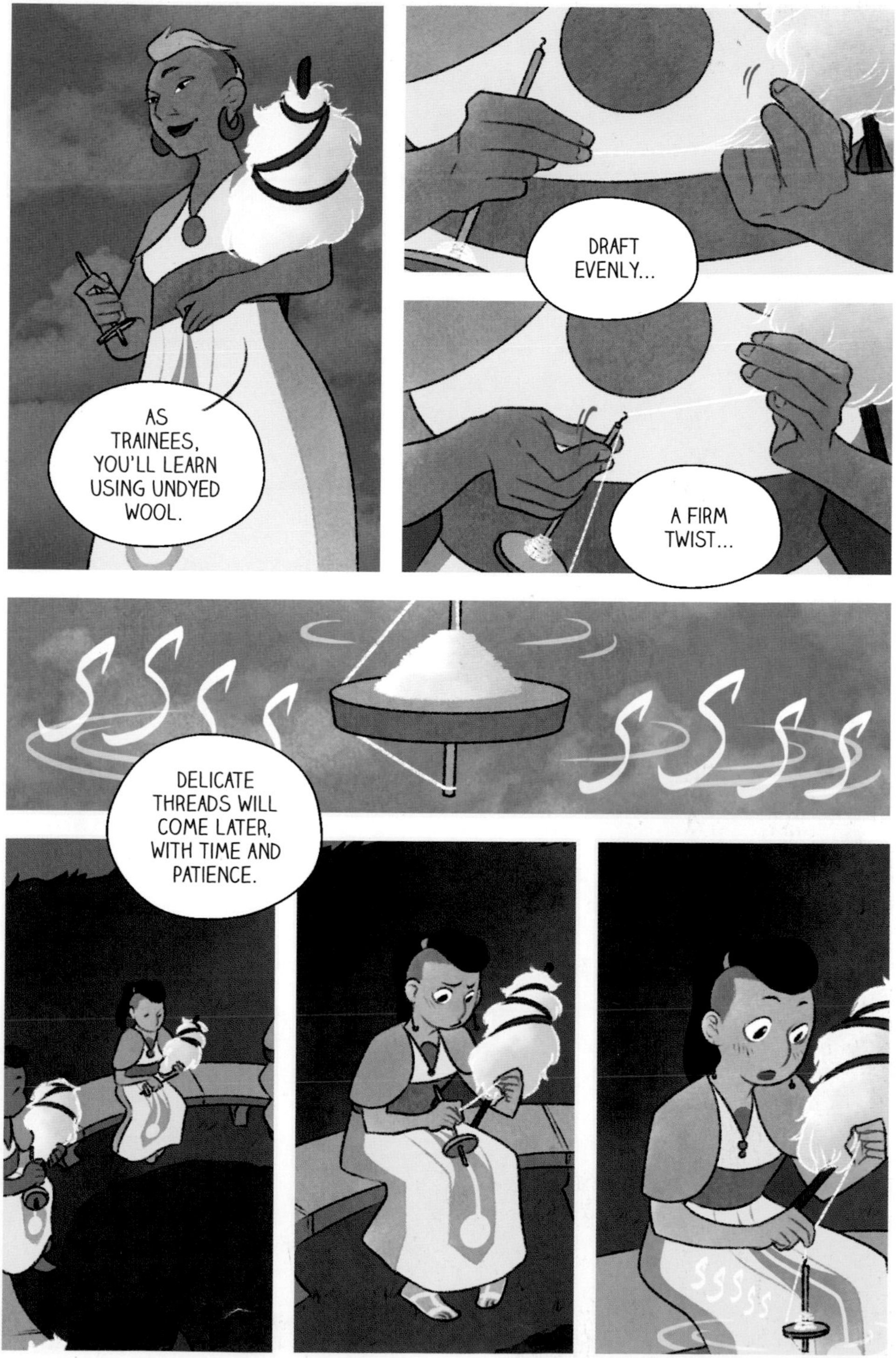
AS TRAINEES, YOU'LL LEARN USING UNDYED WOOL.
DRAFT EVENLY...
A FIRM TWIST...
DELICATE THREADS WILL COME LATER, WITH TIME AND PATIENCE.

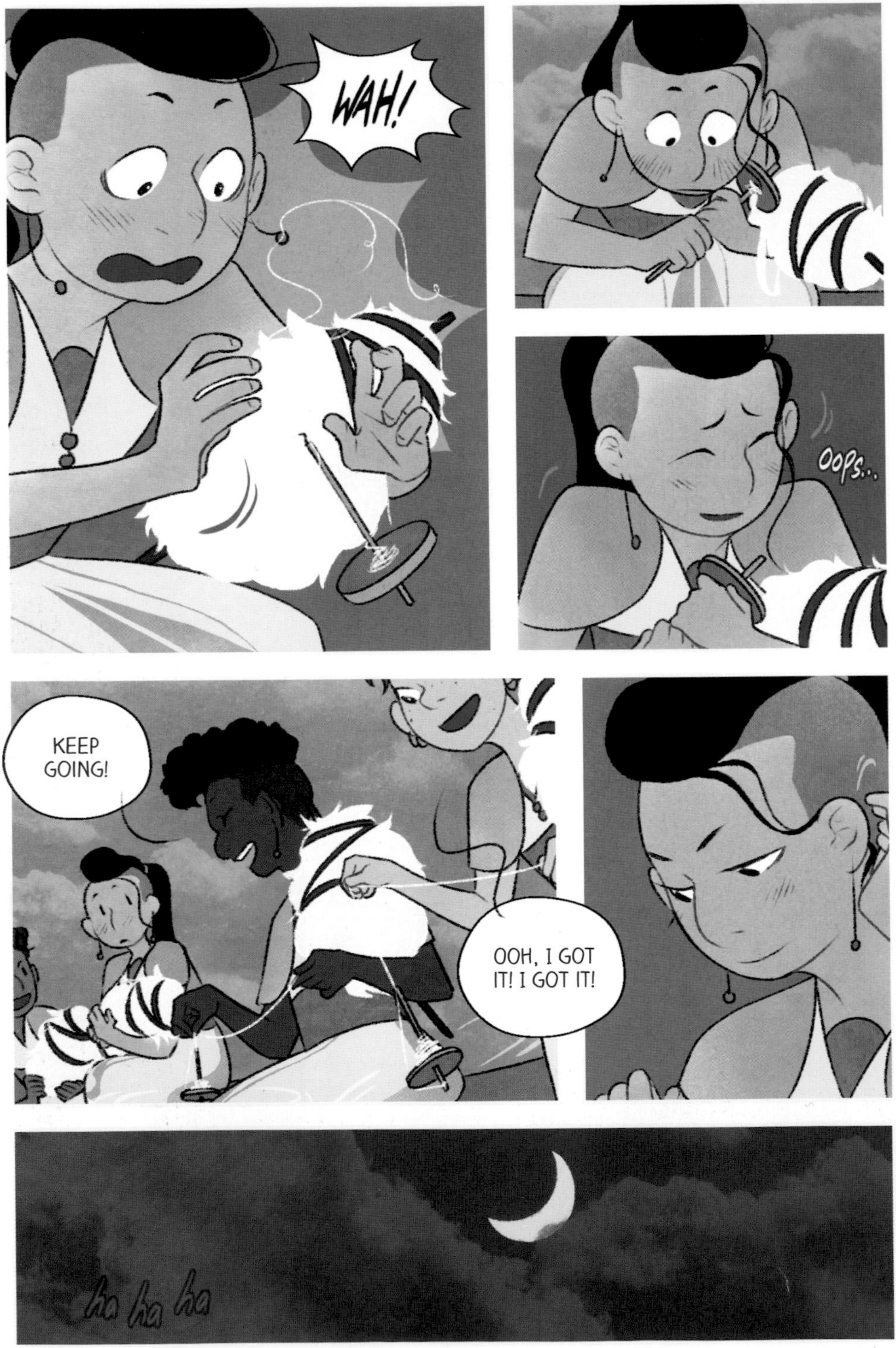
WAH!
OOPS...
KEEP GOING!
OOH, I GOT IT! I GOT IT!
ha ha ha

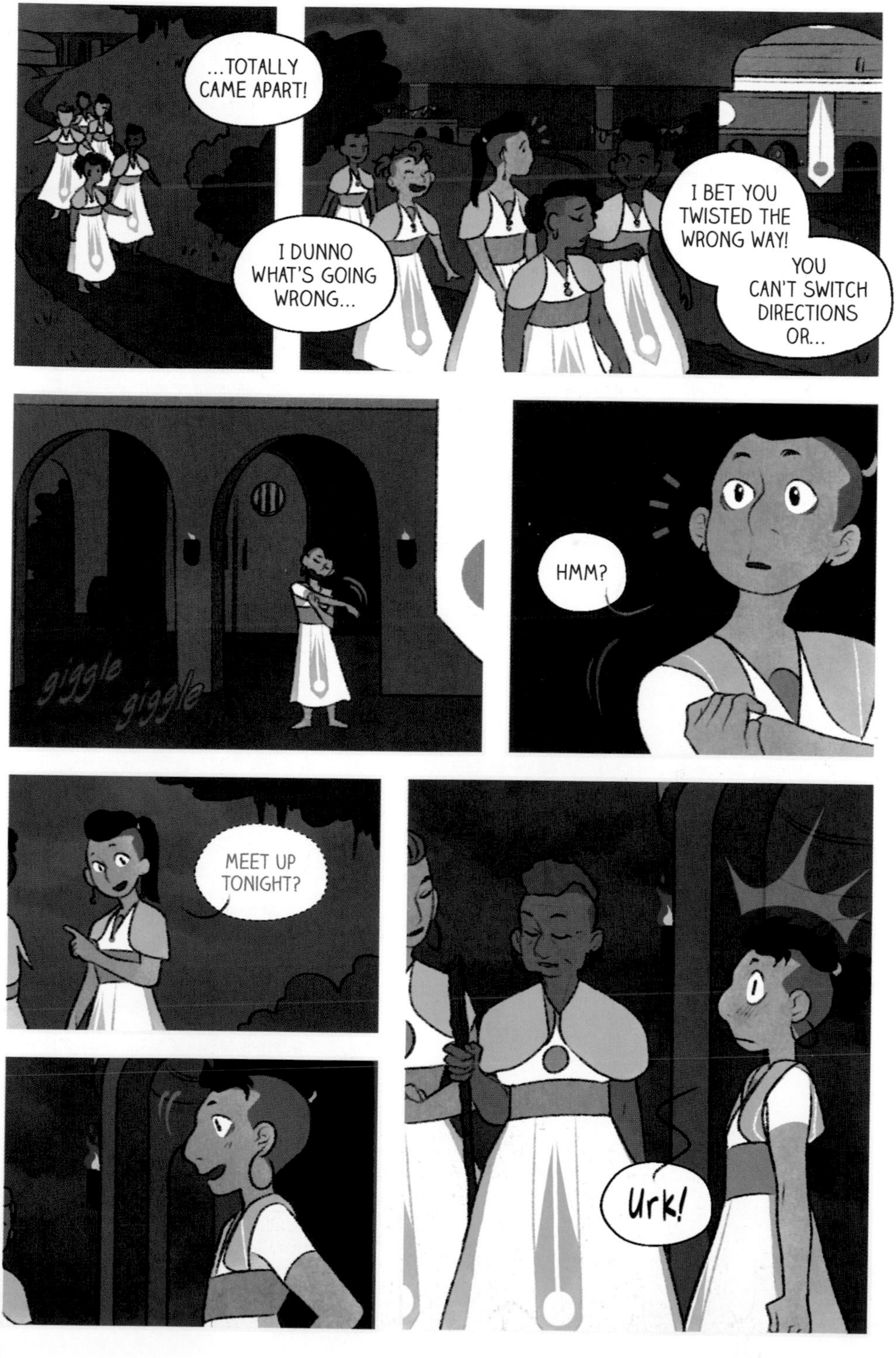

...TOTALLY CAME APART!
I DUNNO WHAT'S GOING WRONG...
I BET YOU TWISTED THE WRONG WAY!
YOU CAN'T SWITCH DIRECTIONS OR...
giggle giggle
HMM?
MEET UP TONIGHT?
Urk!

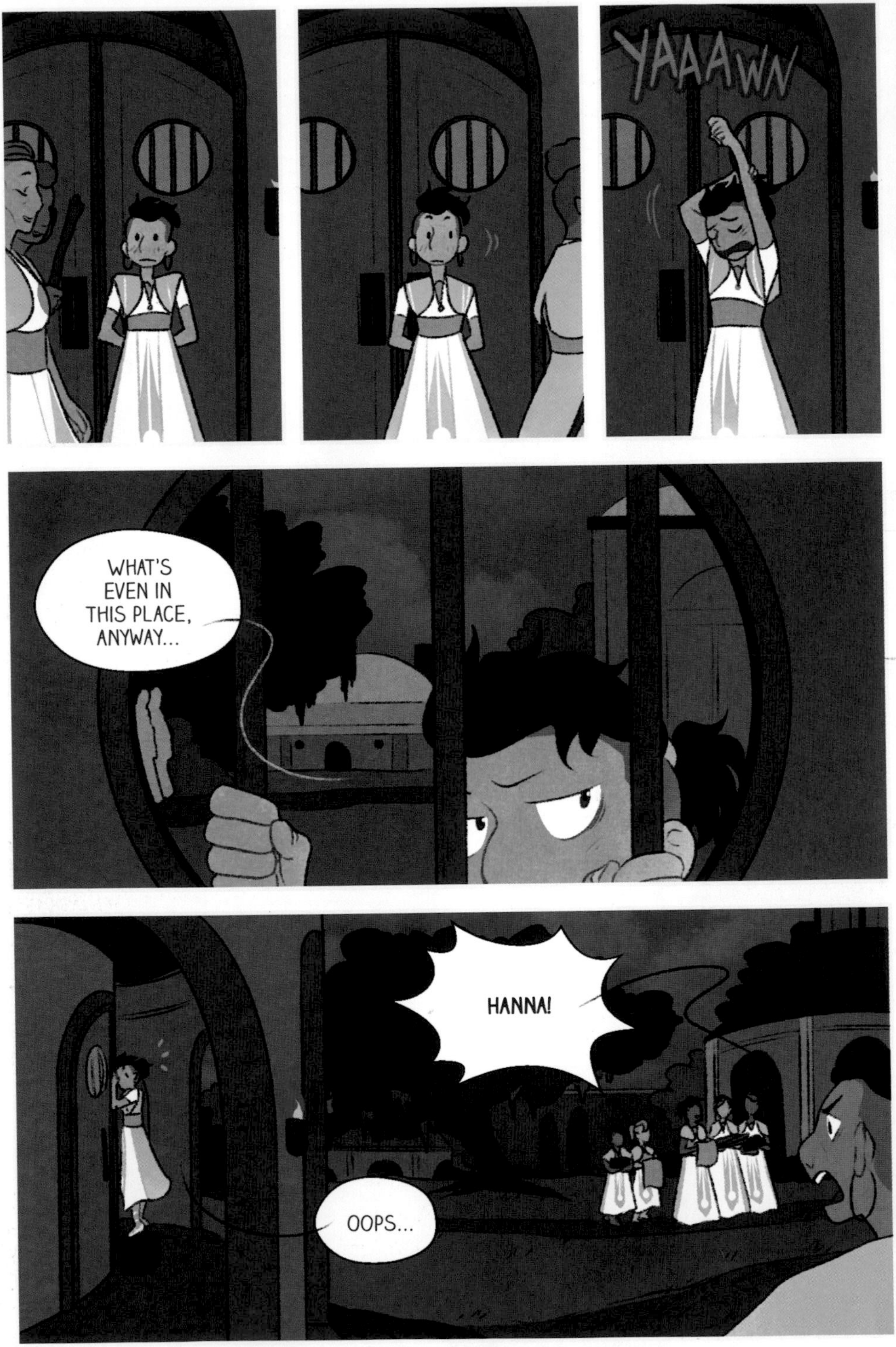
YAAAWN
WHAT'S EVEN IN THIS PLACE, ANYWAY...
HANNA!
OOPS...

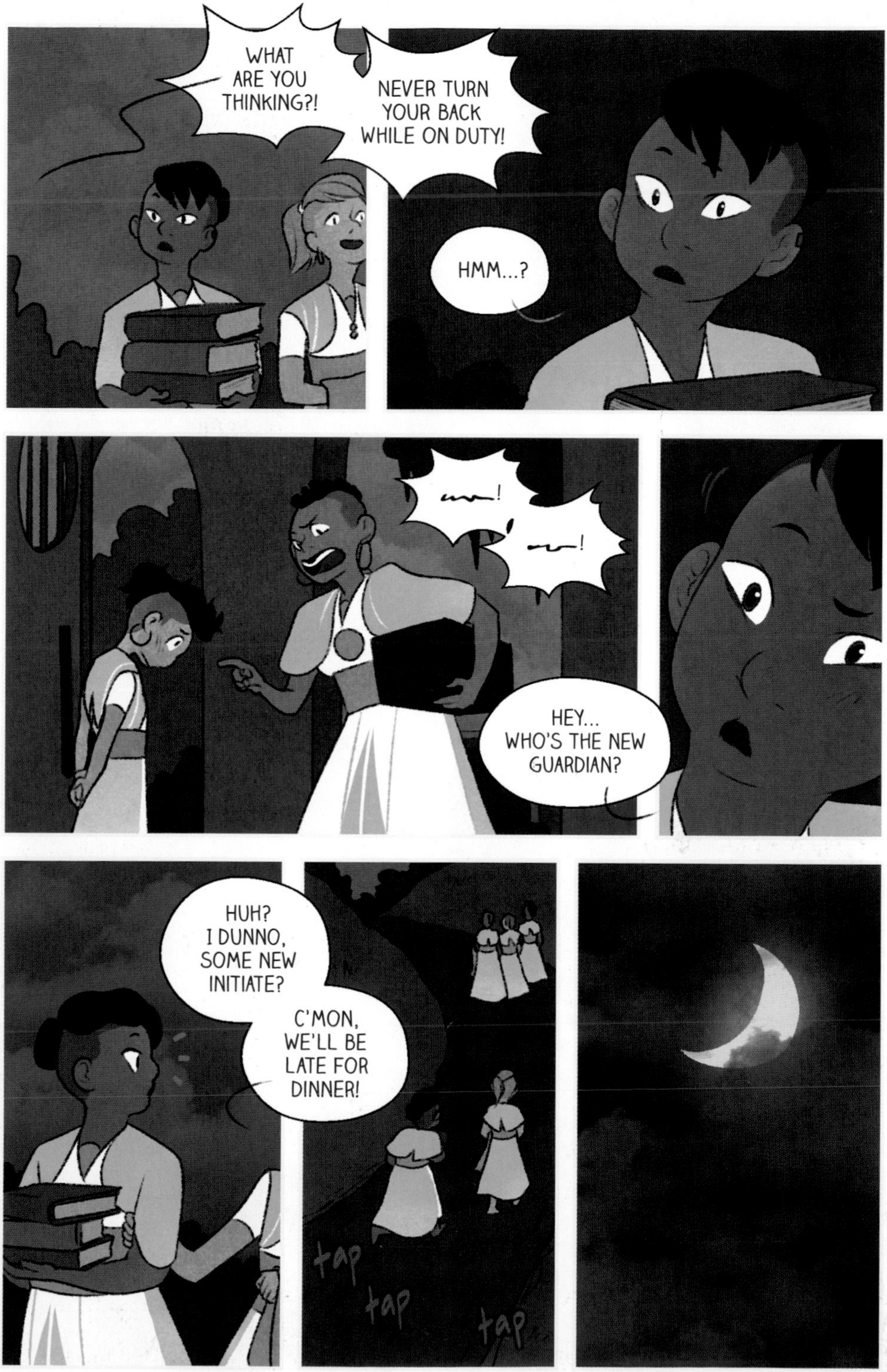
WHAT ARE YOU THINKING?!
NEVER TURN YOUR BACK WHILE ON DUTY!
HMM...?
HEY... WHO'S THE NEW GUARDIAN?
HUH? I DUNNO, SOME NEW INITIATE?
C'MON, WE'LL BE LATE FOR DINNER!
tap
tap
tap

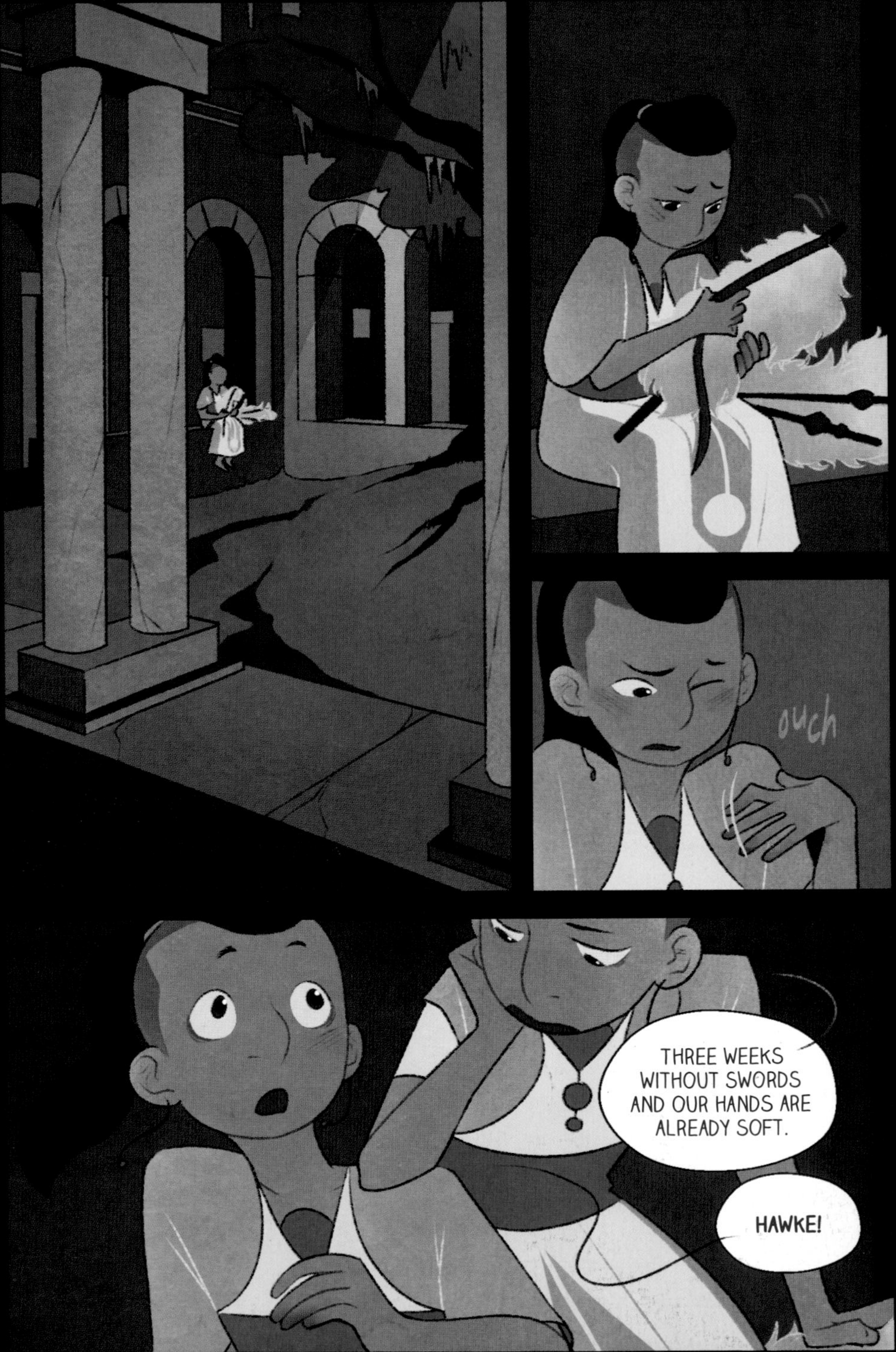
ouch
THREE WEEKS WITHOUT SWORDS AND OUR HANDS ARE ALREADY SOFT.
HAWKE!

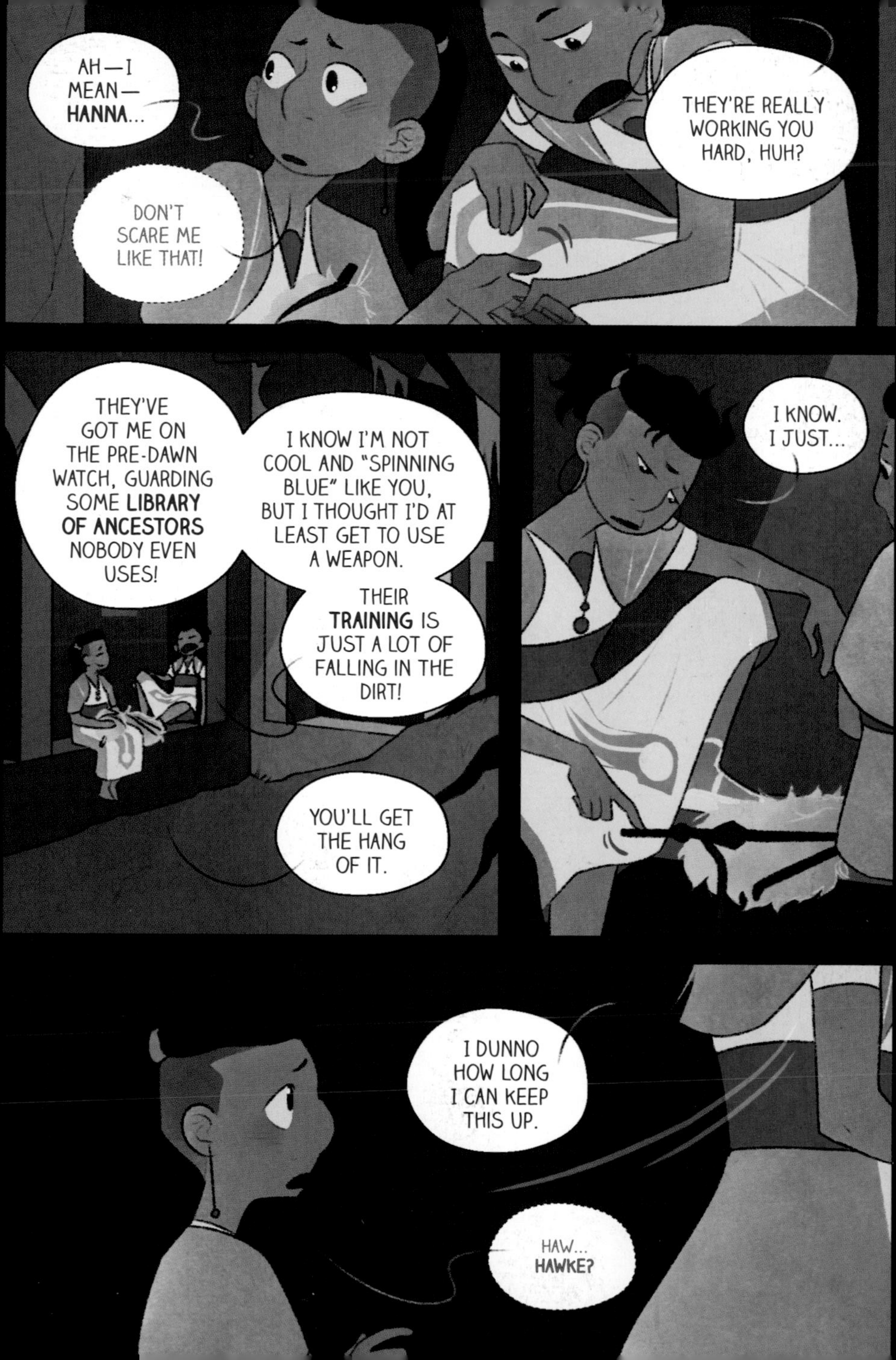
AH—I MEAN— **HANNA**...
DON'T SCARE ME LIKE THAT!
THEY'RE REALLY WORKING YOU HARD, HUH?
THEY'VE GOT ME ON THE PRE-DAWN WATCH, GUARDING SOME **LIBRARY OF ANCESTORS** NOBODY EVEN USES!
I KNOW I'M NOT COOL AND "SPINNING BLUE" LIKE YOU, BUT I THOUGHT I'D AT LEAST GET TO USE A WEAPON.
THEIR **TRAINING** IS JUST A LOT OF FALLING IN THE DIRT!
YOU'LL GET THE HANG OF IT.
I KNOW. I JUST...
I DUNNO HOW LONG I CAN KEEP THIS UP.
HAW... **HAWKE?**

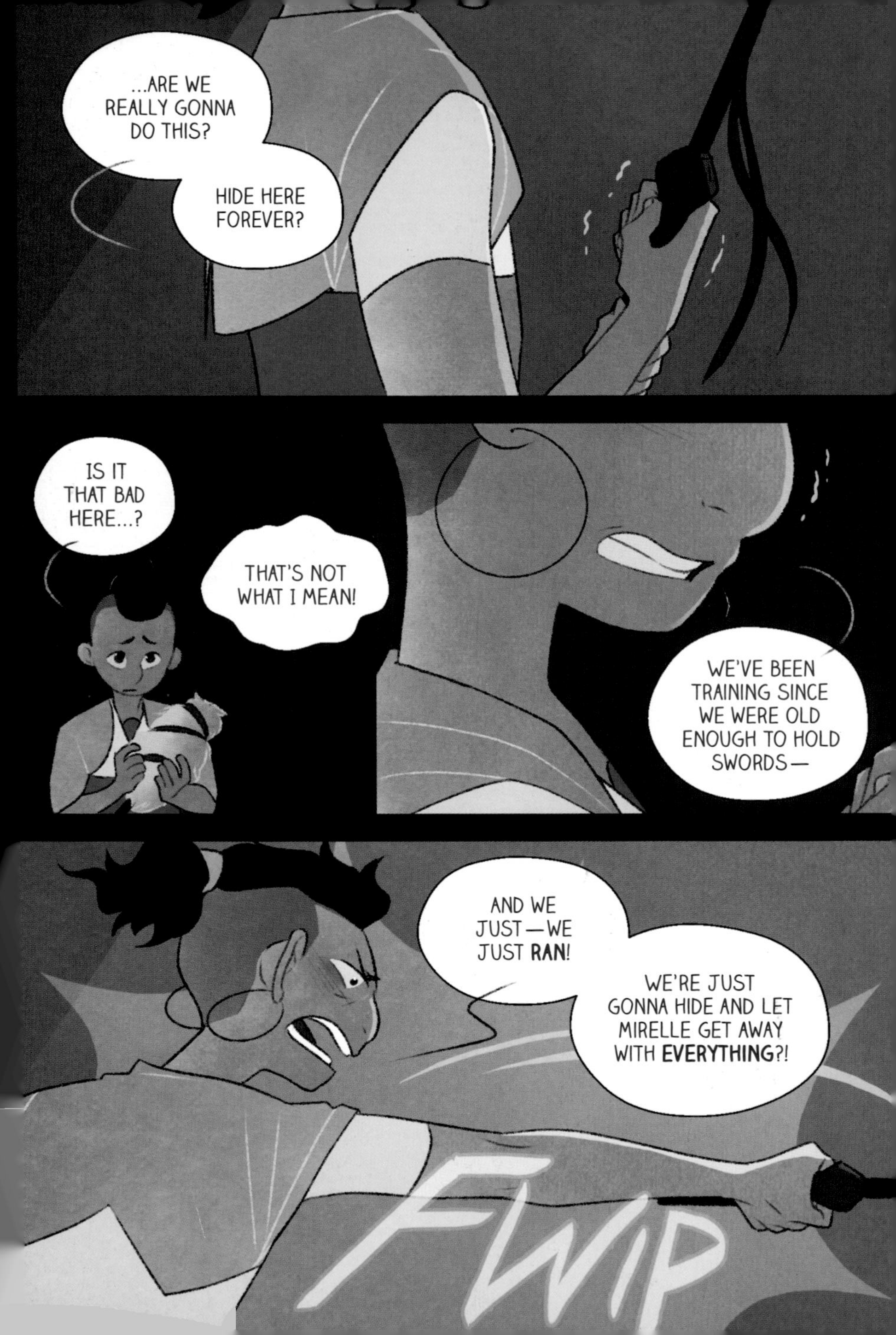
...ARE WE REALLY GONNA DO THIS?
HIDE HERE FOREVER?
IS IT THAT BAD HERE...?
THAT'S NOT WHAT I MEAN!
WE'VE BEEN TRAINING SINCE WE WERE OLD ENOUGH TO HOLD SWORDS—
AND WE JUST—WE JUST RAN!
WE'RE JUST GONNA HIDE AND LET MIRELLE GET AWAY WITH EVERYTHING?!
FWIP

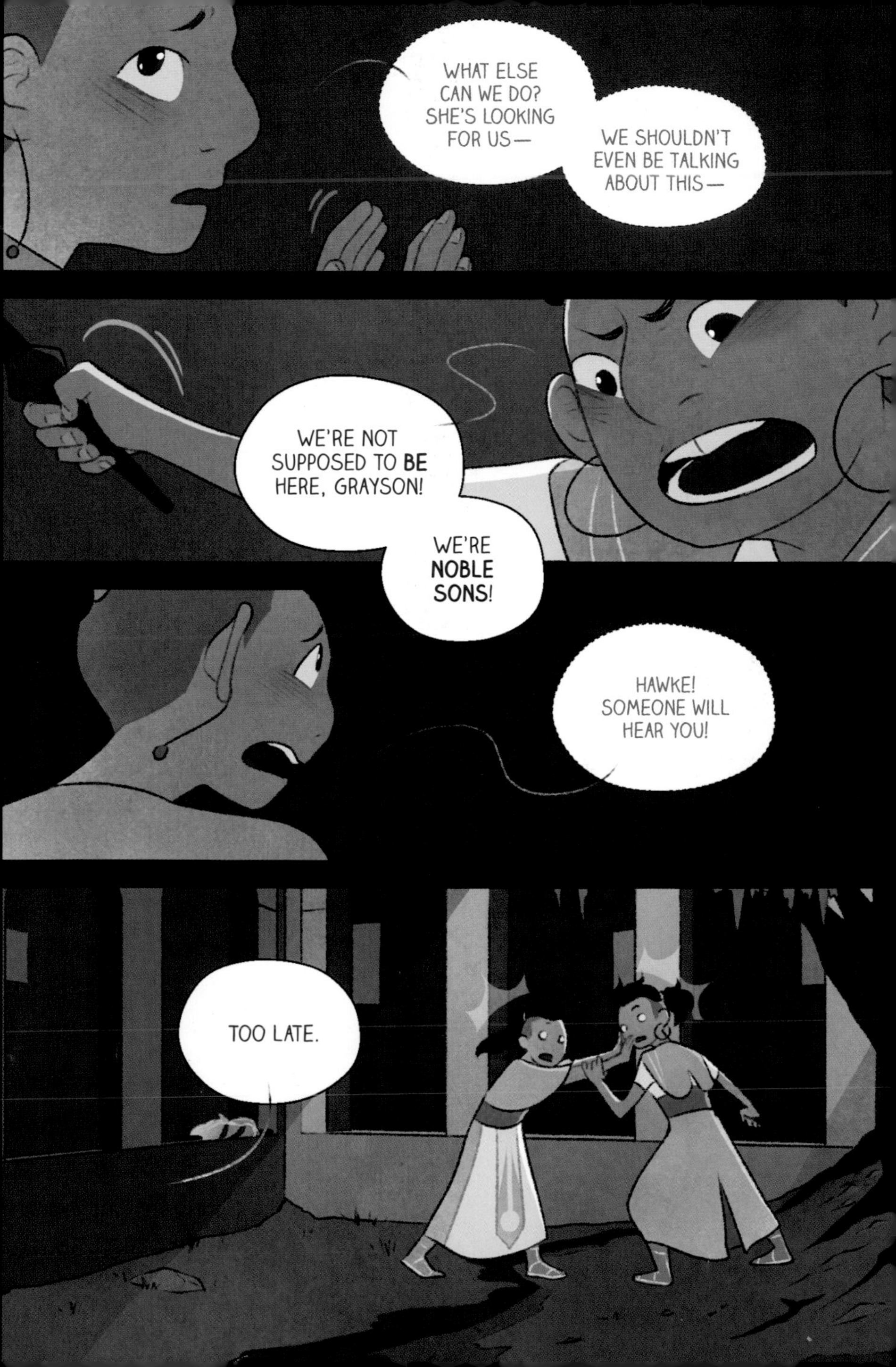
WHAT ELSE CAN WE DO? SHE'S LOOKING FOR US—
WE SHOULDN'T EVEN BE TALKING ABOUT THIS—
WE'RE NOT SUPPOSED TO **BE** HERE, GRAYSON!
WE'RE **NOBLE SONS**!
HAWKE! SOMEONE WILL HEAR YOU!
TOO LATE.

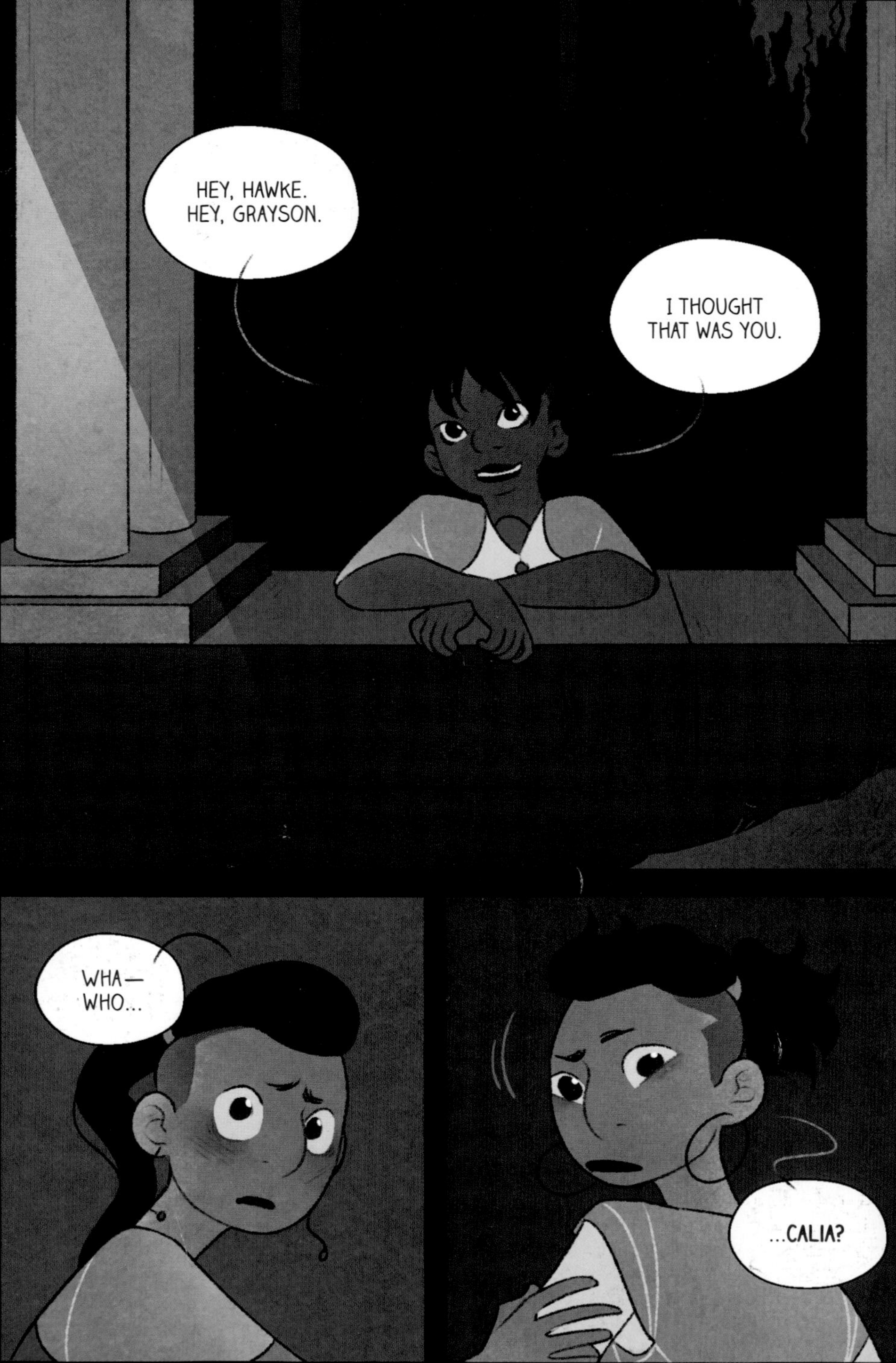
HEY, HAWKE.
HEY, GRAYSON.
I THOUGHT
THAT WAS YOU.
WHA—
WHO...
...CALIA?

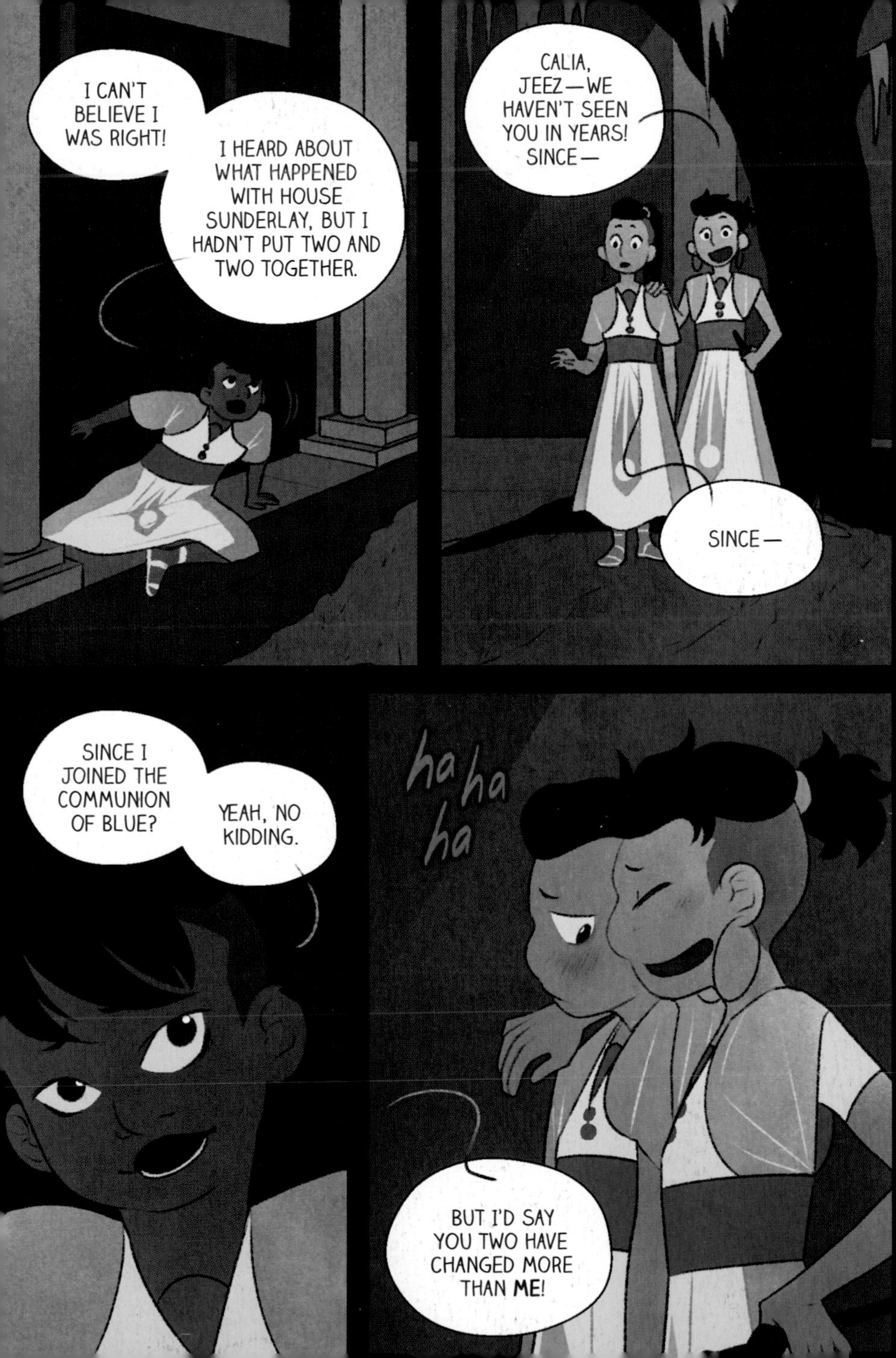
I CAN'T BELIEVE I WAS RIGHT!
I HEARD ABOUT WHAT HAPPENED WITH HOUSE SUNDERLAY, BUT I HADN'T PUT TWO AND TWO TOGETHER.
CALIA, JEEZ—WE HAVEN'T SEEN YOU IN YEARS! SINCE—
SINCE—
SINCE I JOINED THE COMMUNION OF BLUE?
YEAH, NO KIDDING.
ha ha ha
BUT I'D SAY YOU TWO HAVE CHANGED MORE THAN **ME**!

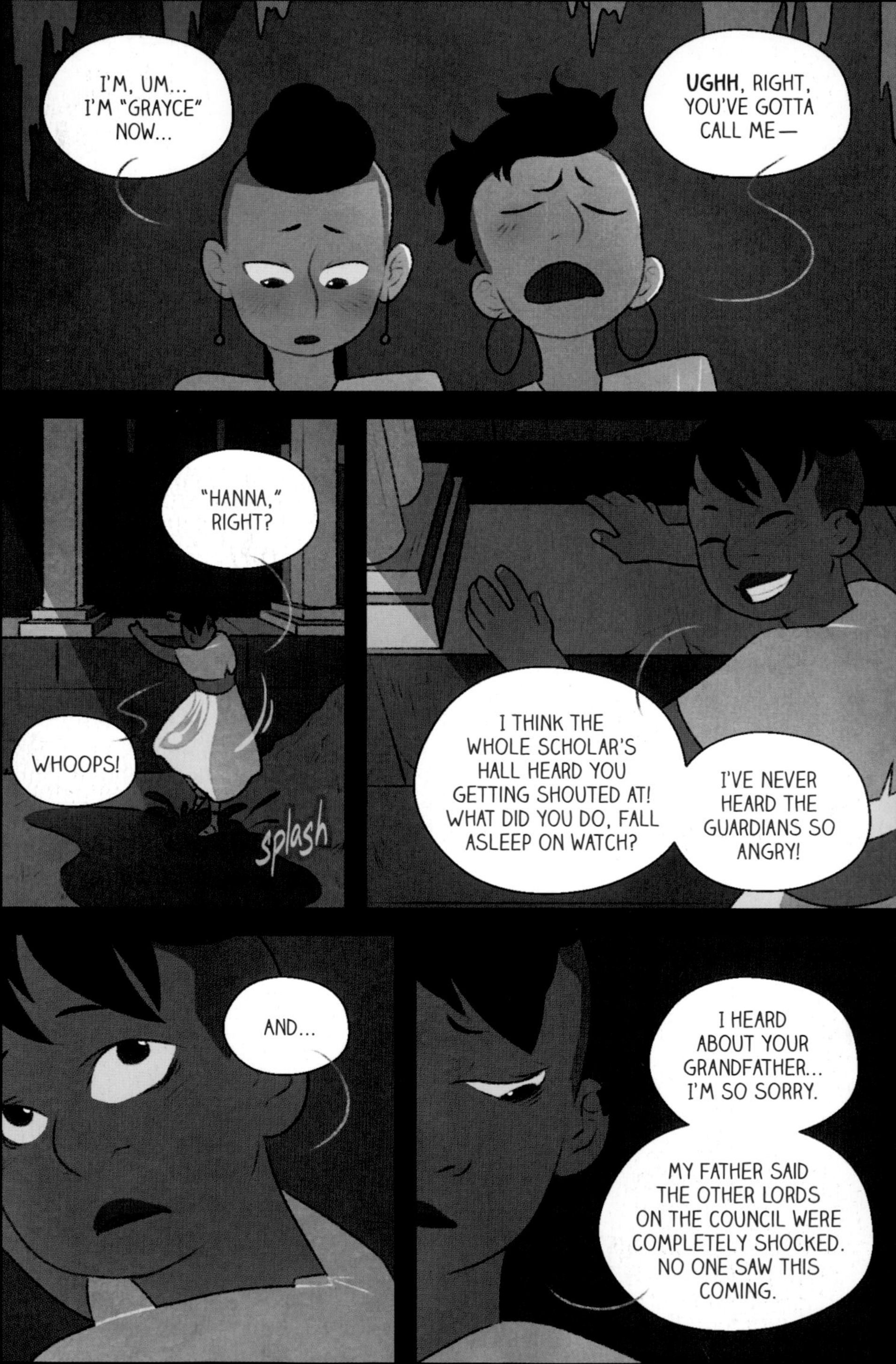

I'M, UM... I'M "GRAYCE" NOW...
UGHH, RIGHT, YOU'VE GOTTA CALL ME—
"HANNA," RIGHT?
WHOOPS!
splash
I THINK THE WHOLE SCHOLAR'S HALL HEARD YOU GETTING SHOUTED AT! WHAT DID YOU DO, FALL ASLEEP ON WATCH?
I'VE NEVER HEARD THE GUARDIANS SO ANGRY!
AND...
I HEARD ABOUT YOUR GRANDFATHER... I'M SO SORRY.
MY FATHER SAID THE OTHER LORDS ON THE COUNCIL WERE COMPLETELY SHOCKED. NO ONE SAW THIS COMING.

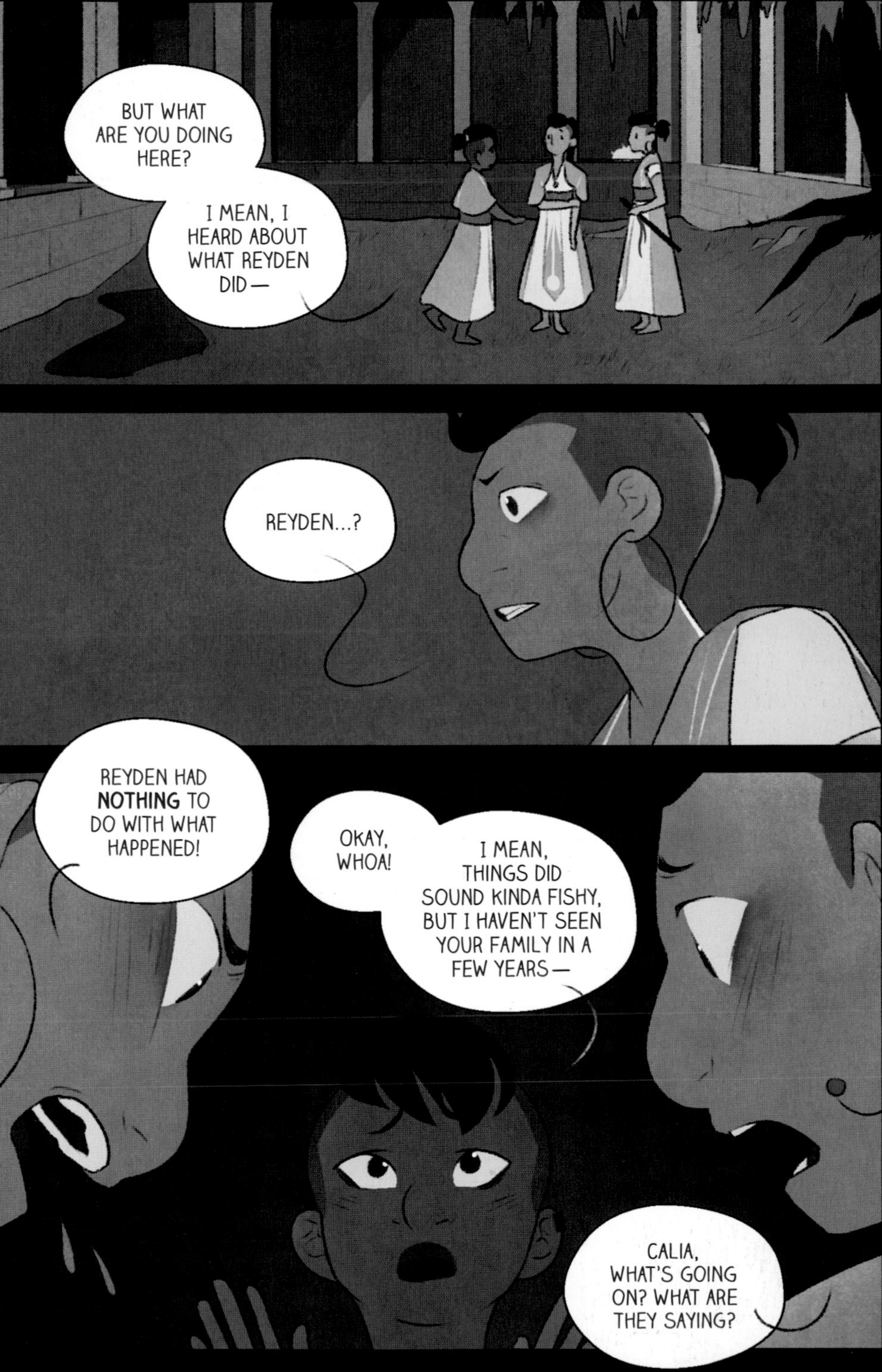
BUT WHAT ARE YOU DOING HERE?
I MEAN, I HEARD ABOUT WHAT REYDEN DID—
REYDEN...?
REYDEN HAD **NOTHING** TO DO WITH WHAT HAPPENED!
OKAY, WHOA!
I MEAN, THINGS DID SOUND KINDA FISHY, BUT I HAVEN'T SEEN YOUR FAMILY IN A FEW YEARS—
CALIA, WHAT'S GOING ON? WHAT ARE THEY SAYING?

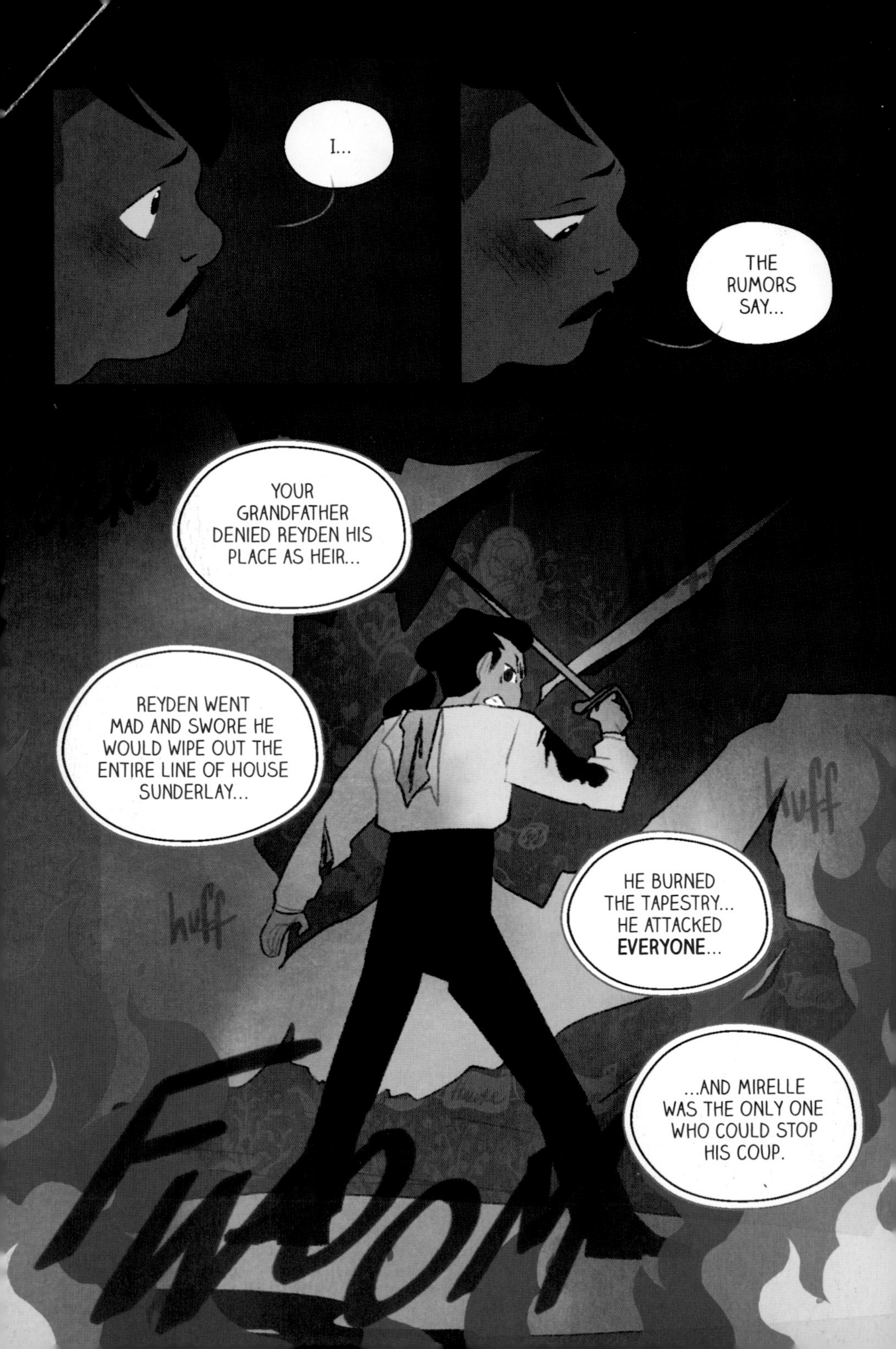
I...
THE RUMORS SAY...
YOUR GRANDFATHER DENIED REYDEN HIS PLACE AS HEIR...
REYDEN WENT MAD AND SWORE HE WOULD WIPE OUT THE ENTIRE LINE OF HOUSE SUNDERLAY...
huff
huff
HE BURNED THE TAPESTRY... HE ATTACKED **EVERYONE**...
...AND MIRELLE WAS THE ONLY ONE WHO COULD STOP HIS COUP.
FWOOM

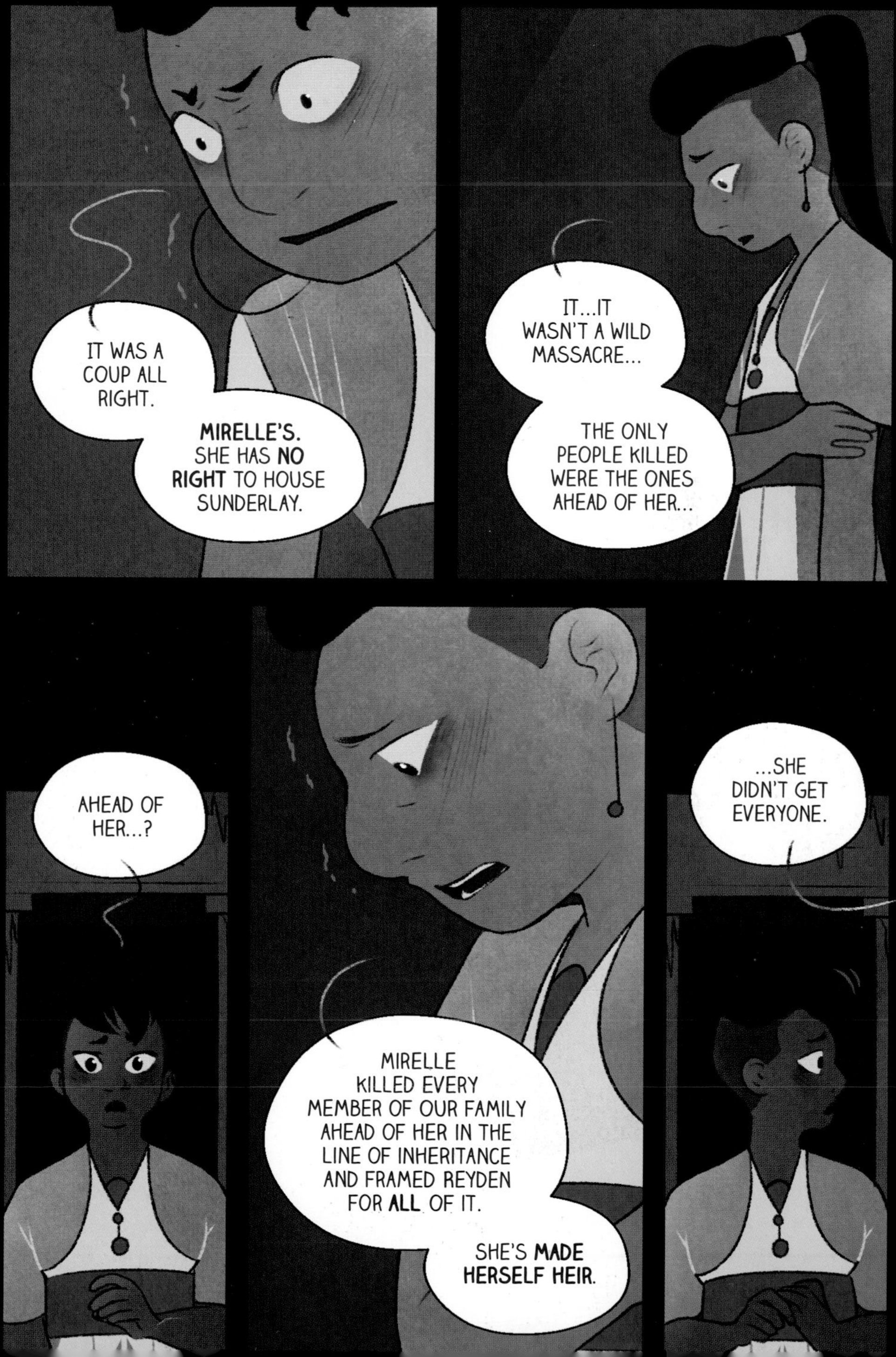
IT WAS A COUP ALL RIGHT.
MIRELLE'S. SHE HAS **NO RIGHT** TO HOUSE SUNDERLAY.
IT...IT WASN'T A WILD MASSACRE...
THE ONLY PEOPLE KILLED WERE THE ONES AHEAD OF HER...
AHEAD OF HER...?
MIRELLE KILLED EVERY MEMBER OF OUR FAMILY AHEAD OF HER IN THE LINE OF INHERITANCE AND FRAMED REYDEN FOR **ALL** OF IT.
SHE'S **MADE HERSELF HEIR**.
...SHE DIDN'T GET EVERYONE.

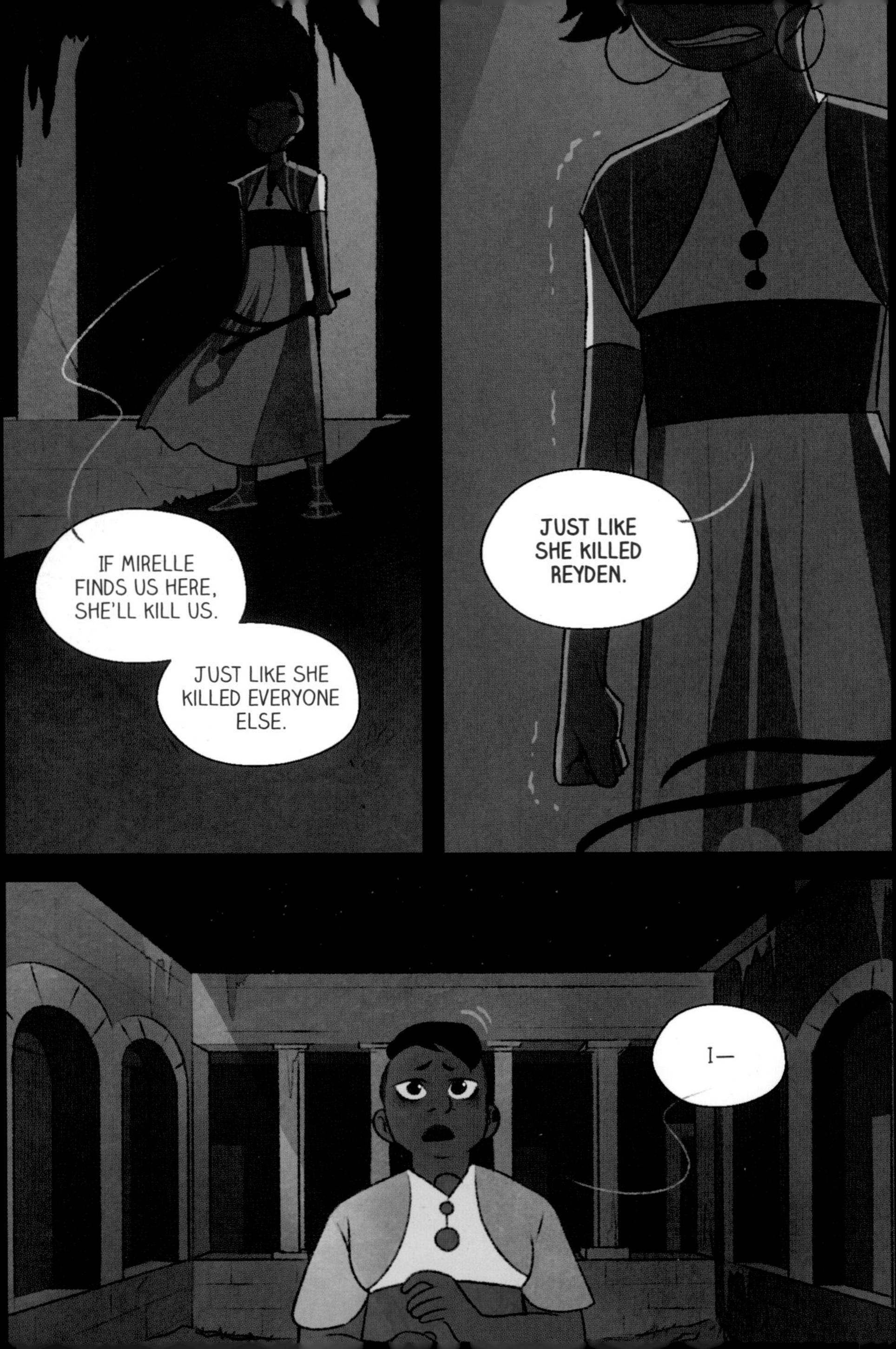
IF MIRELLE FINDS US HERE, SHE'LL KILL US.
JUST LIKE SHE KILLED EVERYONE ELSE.
JUST LIKE SHE KILLED REYDEN.
I—

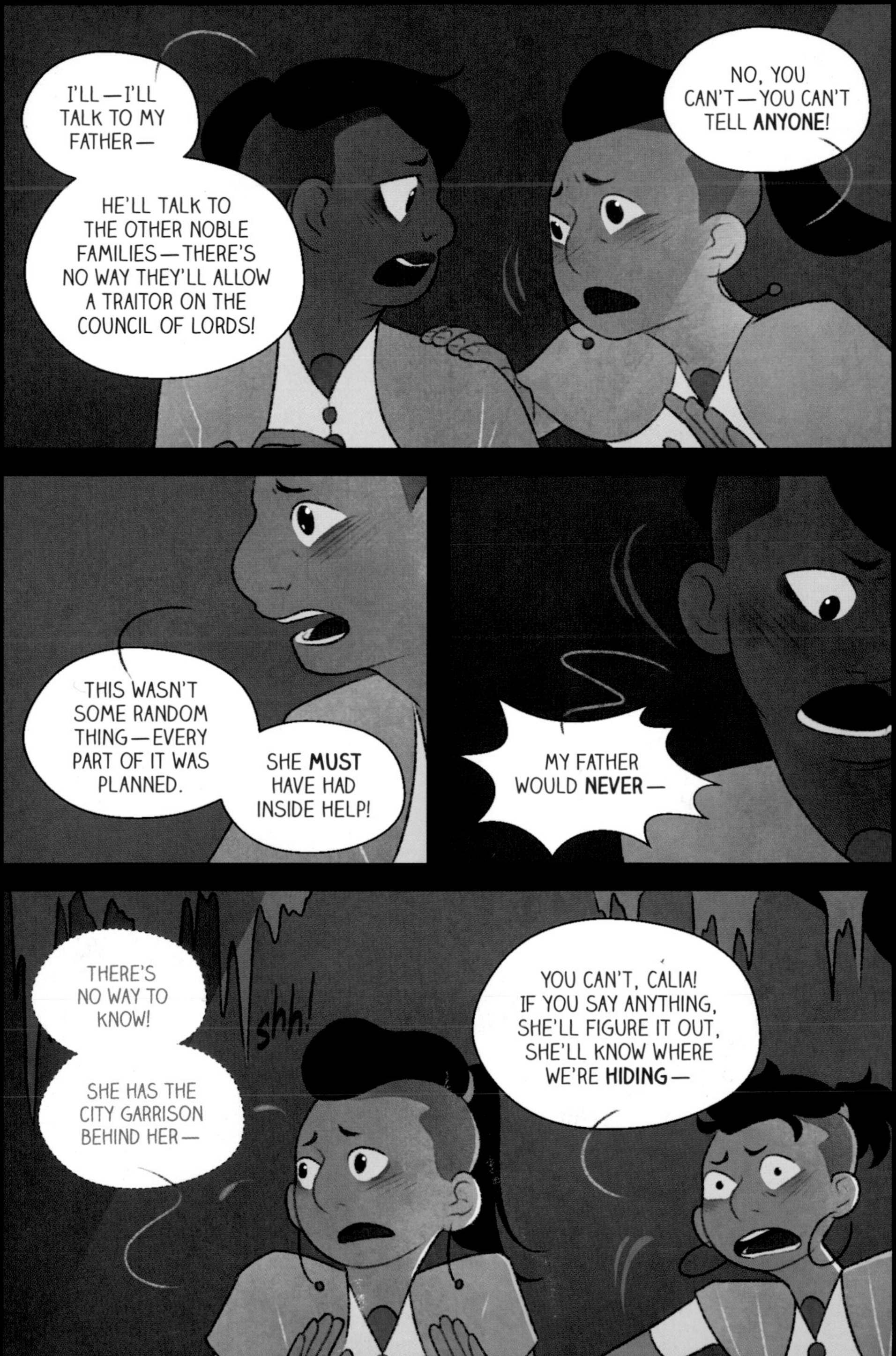

I'LL—I'LL TALK TO MY FATHER—
HE'LL TALK TO THE OTHER NOBLE FAMILIES—THERE'S NO WAY THEY'LL ALLOW A TRAITOR ON THE COUNCIL OF LORDS!
NO, YOU CAN'T—YOU CAN'T TELL **ANYONE**!
THIS WASN'T SOME RANDOM THING—EVERY PART OF IT WAS PLANNED.
SHE **MUST** HAVE HAD INSIDE HELP!
MY FATHER WOULD **NEVER**—
THERE'S NO WAY TO KNOW!
SHE HAS THE CITY GARRISON BEHIND HER—
shh!
YOU CAN'T, CALIA! IF YOU SAY ANYTHING, SHE'LL FIGURE IT OUT, SHE'LL KNOW WHERE WE'RE **HIDING**—

MIRELLE WILL FIND US.
IF IT'LL KEEP YOU SAFE...
OKAY. YOU WIN.
I WON'T TELL ANYBODY.

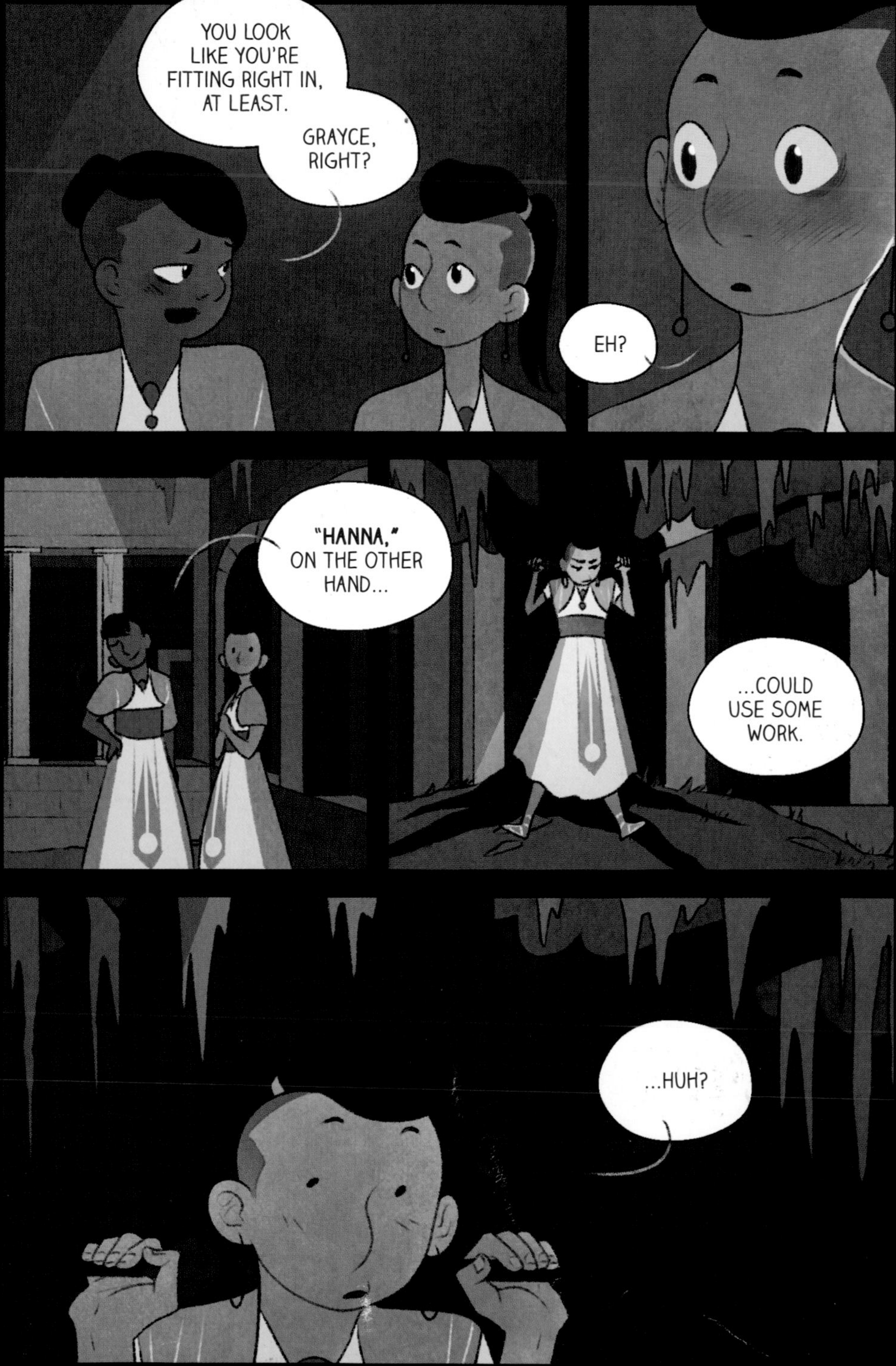
YOU LOOK LIKE YOU'RE FITTING RIGHT IN, AT LEAST.
GRAYCE, RIGHT?
EH?
"HANNA," ON THE OTHER HAND...
...COULD USE SOME WORK.
...HUH?

ha ha
ha ha ha
LOOK, YOUR SKIRTS ARE ALL TWISTED.
YOU KNOW THESE THINGS HAVE POCKETS, RIGHT?
THOSE BUTTONS ARE THERE FOR A REASON...
??
?!?
I TRIED TO TELL HIM!

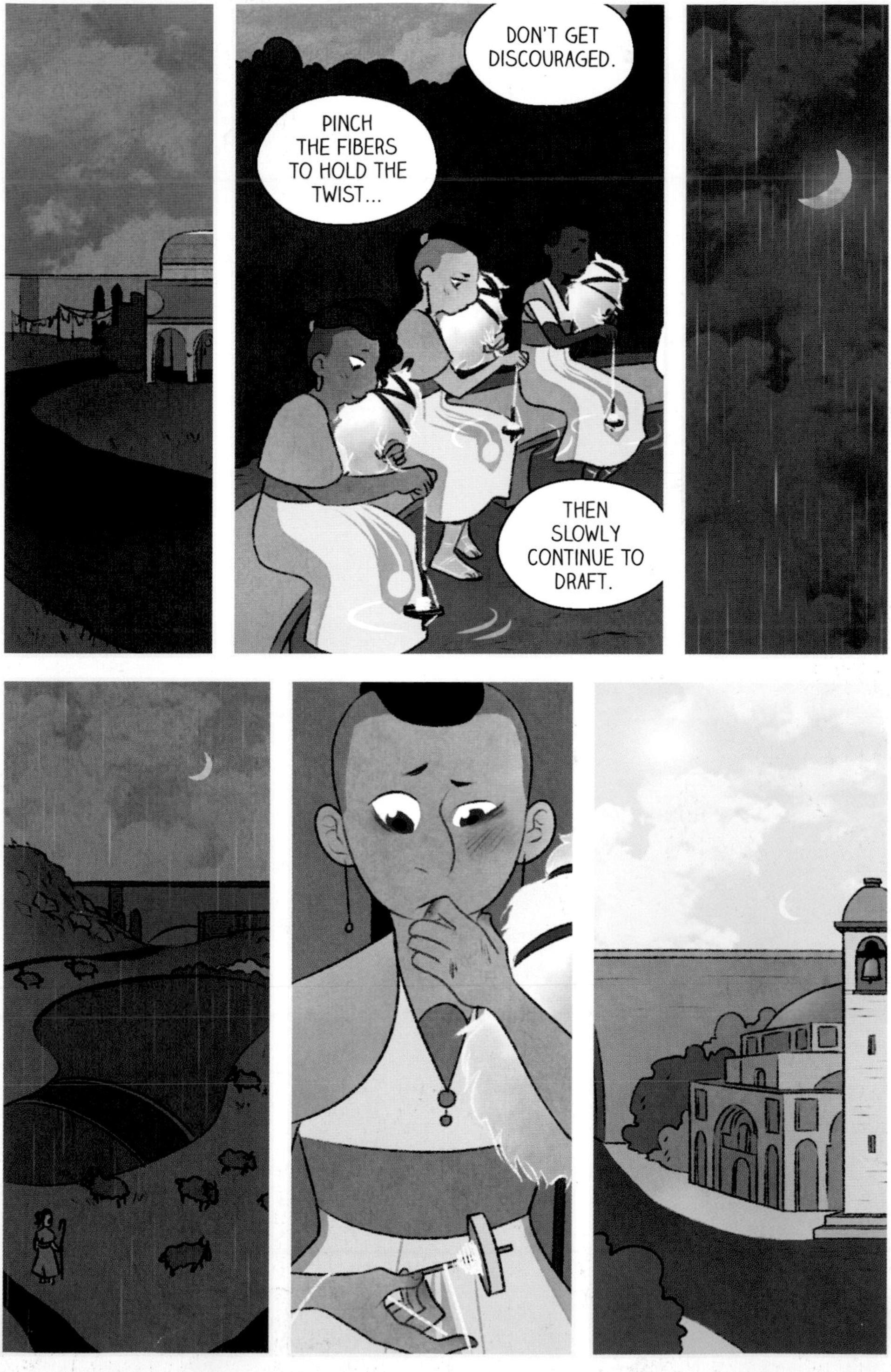
DON'T GET DISCOURAGED.
PINCH THE FIBERS TO HOLD THE TWIST...
THEN SLOWLY CONTINUE TO DRAFT.

WHEN YOUR SPINDLE IS FULL, IT WILL BECOME UNBALANCED.

WE SOAK THE FINISHED YARN AND HANG IT TO DRY...

SEE, IF IT COMES APART YOU CAN JUST OVERLAP IT WITH SOME NEW WOOL!

ooh...

WHEN YOU SPIN AGAIN IT'LL BE JUST AS STRONG!

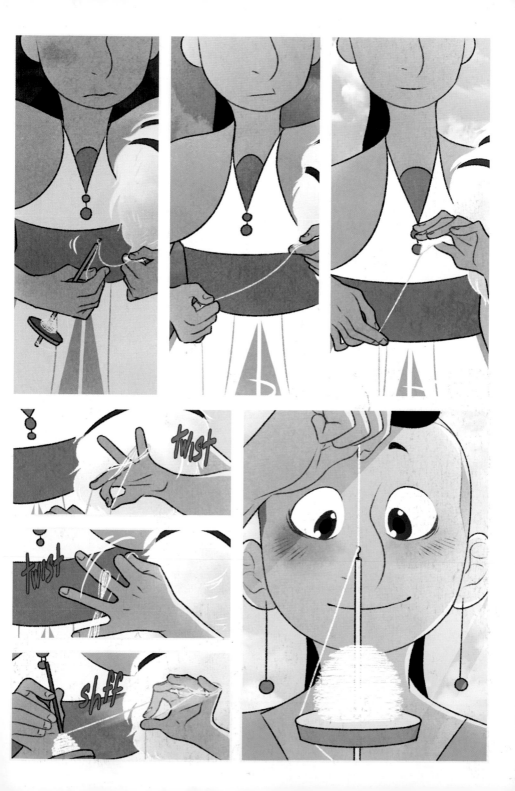

twist

twist

shff

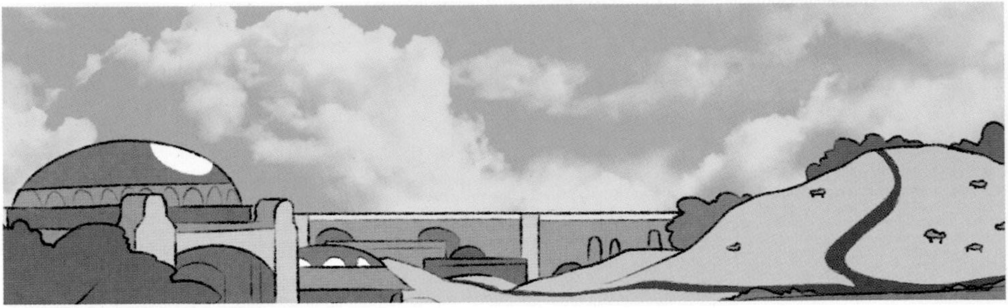

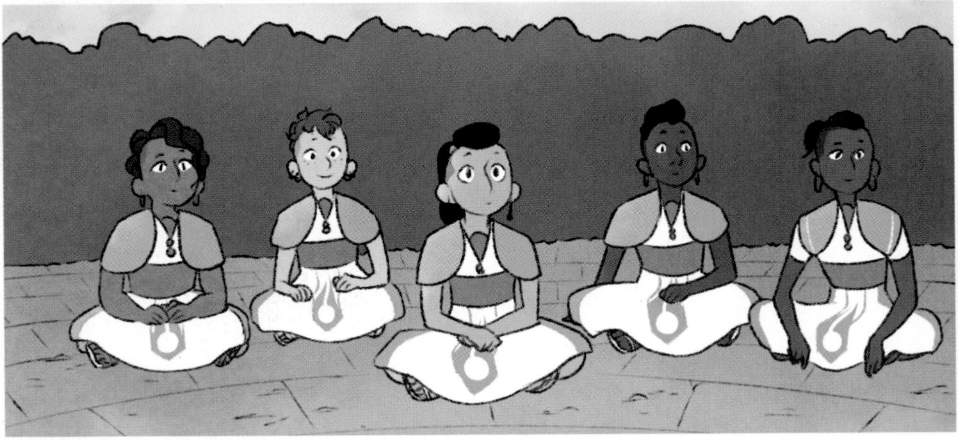

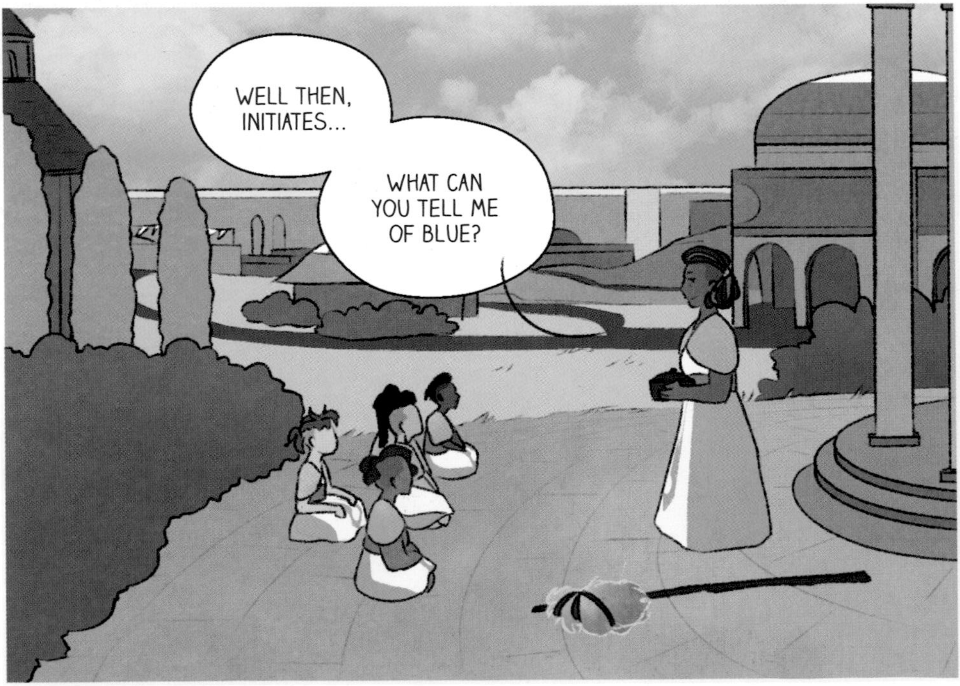
WELL THEN, INITIATES...
WHAT CAN YOU TELL ME OF BLUE?

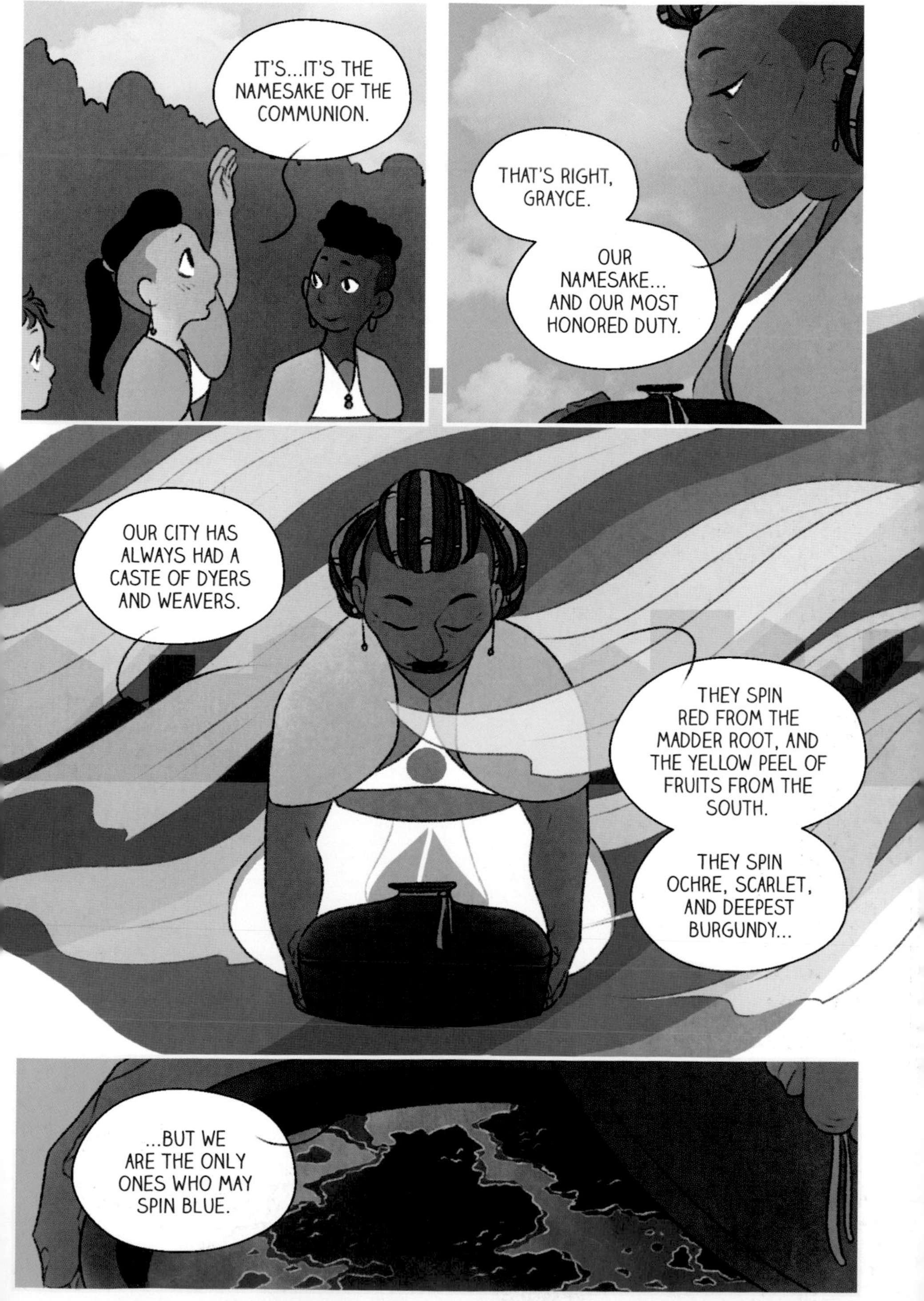
IT'S...IT'S THE NAMESAKE OF THE COMMUNION.
THAT'S RIGHT, GRAYCE.
OUR NAMESAKE... AND OUR MOST HONORED DUTY.
OUR CITY HAS ALWAYS HAD A CASTE OF DYERS AND WEAVERS.
THEY SPIN RED FROM THE MADDER ROOT, AND THE YELLOW PEEL OF FRUITS FROM THE SOUTH.
THEY SPIN OCHRE, SCARLET, AND DEEPEST BURGUNDY...
...BUT WE ARE THE ONLY ONES WHO MAY SPIN BLUE.

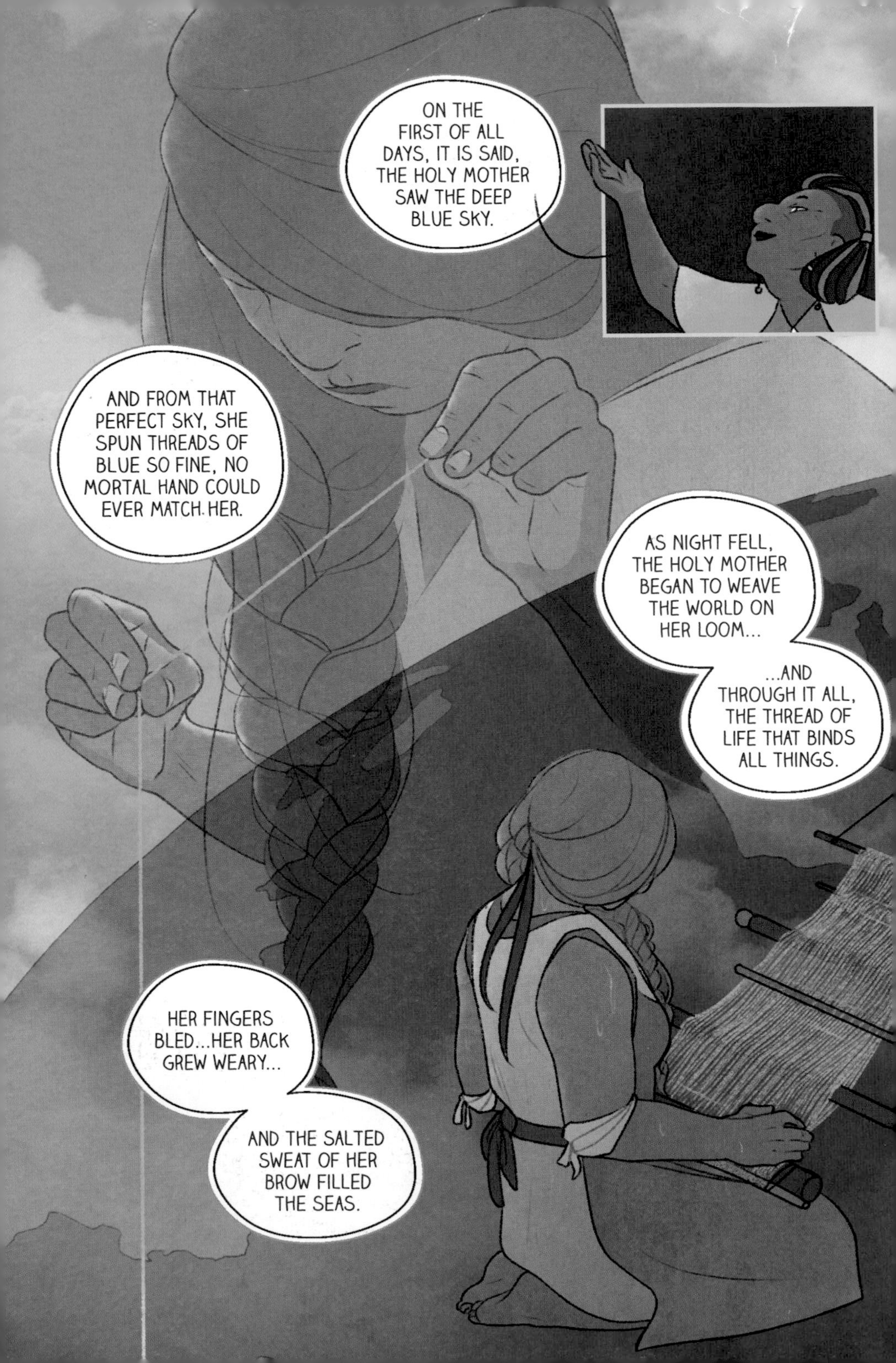
ON THE FIRST OF ALL DAYS, IT IS SAID, THE HOLY MOTHER SAW THE DEEP BLUE SKY.
AND FROM THAT PERFECT SKY, SHE SPUN THREADS OF BLUE SO FINE, NO MORTAL HAND COULD EVER MATCH HER.
AS NIGHT FELL, THE HOLY MOTHER BEGAN TO WEAVE THE WORLD ON HER LOOM...
...AND THROUGH IT ALL, THE THREAD OF LIFE THAT BINDS ALL THINGS.
HER FINGERS BLED...HER BACK GREW WEARY...
AND THE SALTED SWEAT OF HER BROW FILLED THE SEAS.

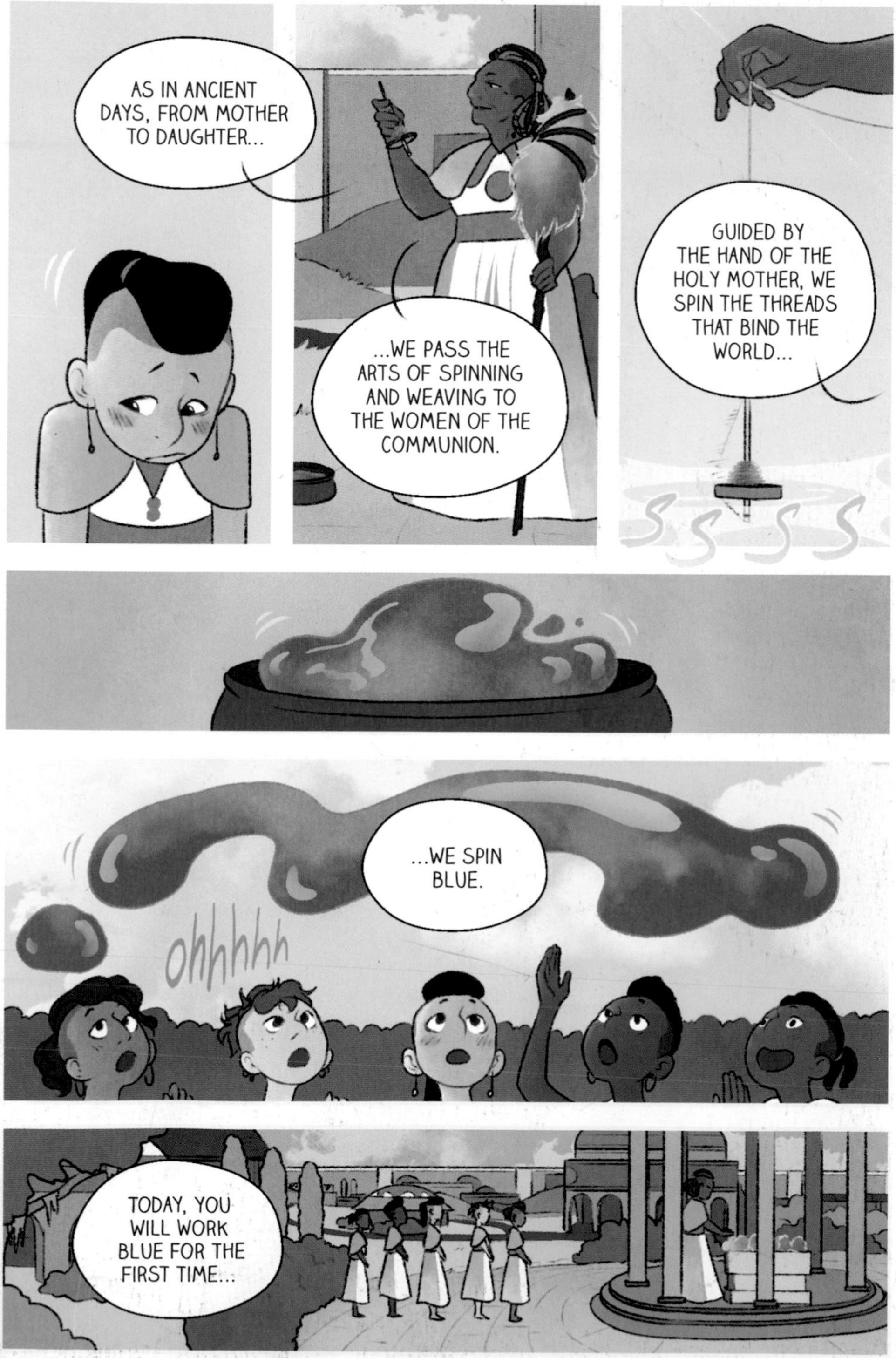
AS IN ANCIENT DAYS, FROM MOTHER TO DAUGHTER...
...WE PASS THE ARTS OF SPINNING AND WEAVING TO THE WOMEN OF THE COMMUNION.
GUIDED BY THE HAND OF THE HOLY MOTHER, WE SPIN THE THREADS THAT BIND THE WORLD...
...WE SPIN BLUE.
ohhhhh
TODAY, YOU WILL WORK BLUE FOR THE FIRST TIME...

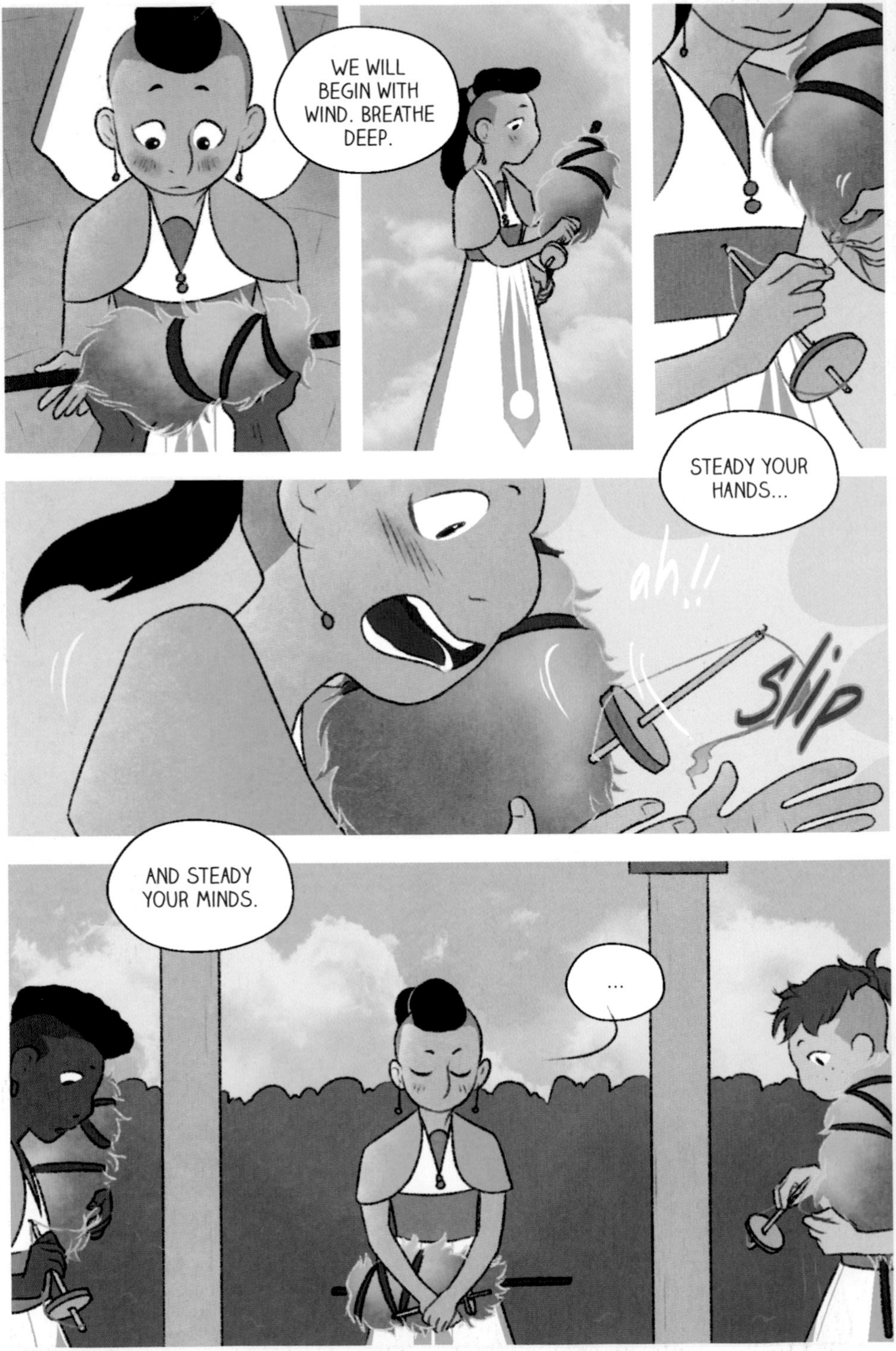
WE WILL BEGIN WITH WIND. BREATHE DEEP.
STEADY YOUR HANDS...
ah!!
slip
AND STEADY YOUR MINDS.
...

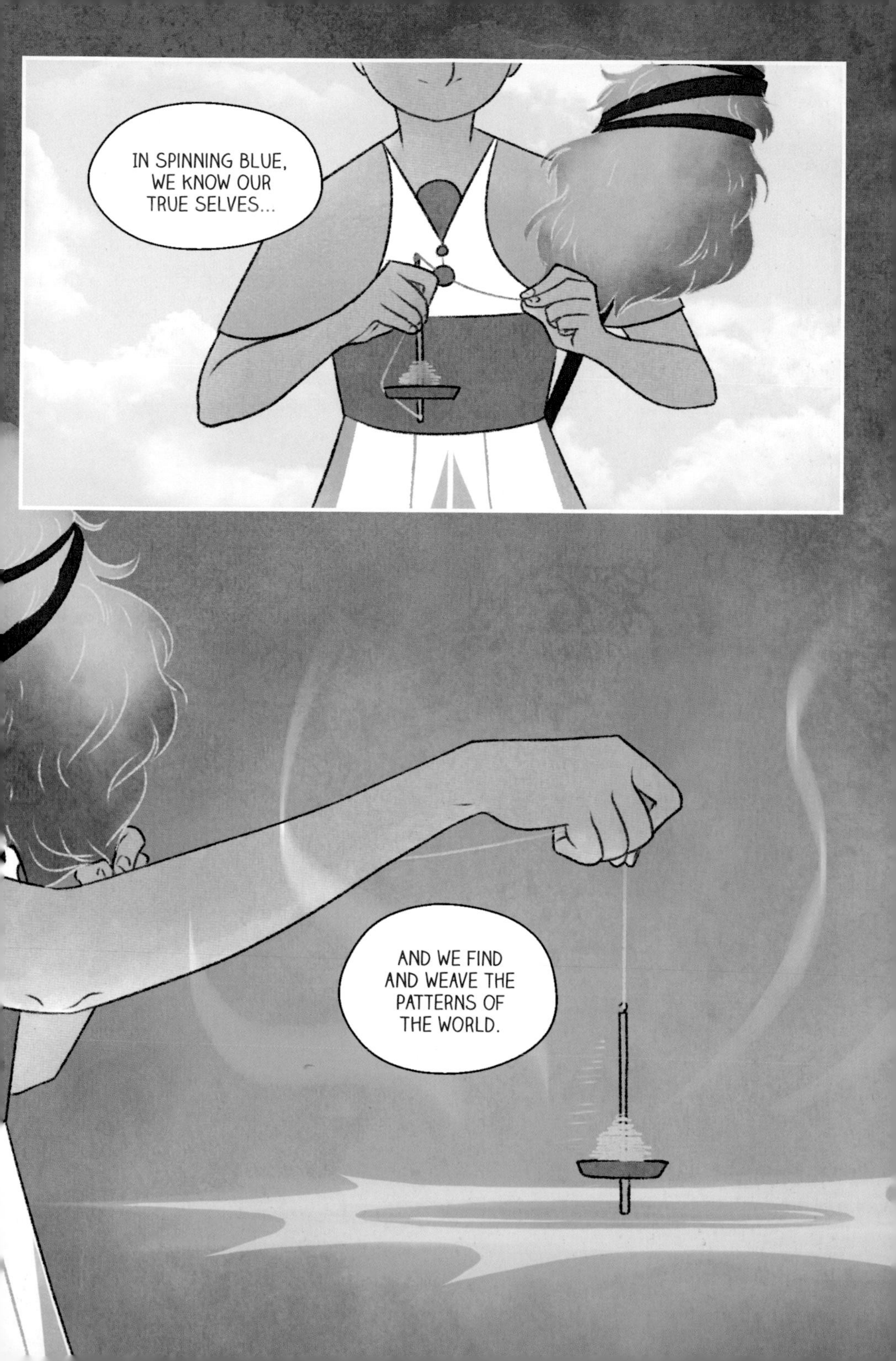
IN SPINNING BLUE, WE KNOW OUR TRUE SELVES...
AND WE FIND AND WEAVE THE PATTERNS OF THE WORLD.

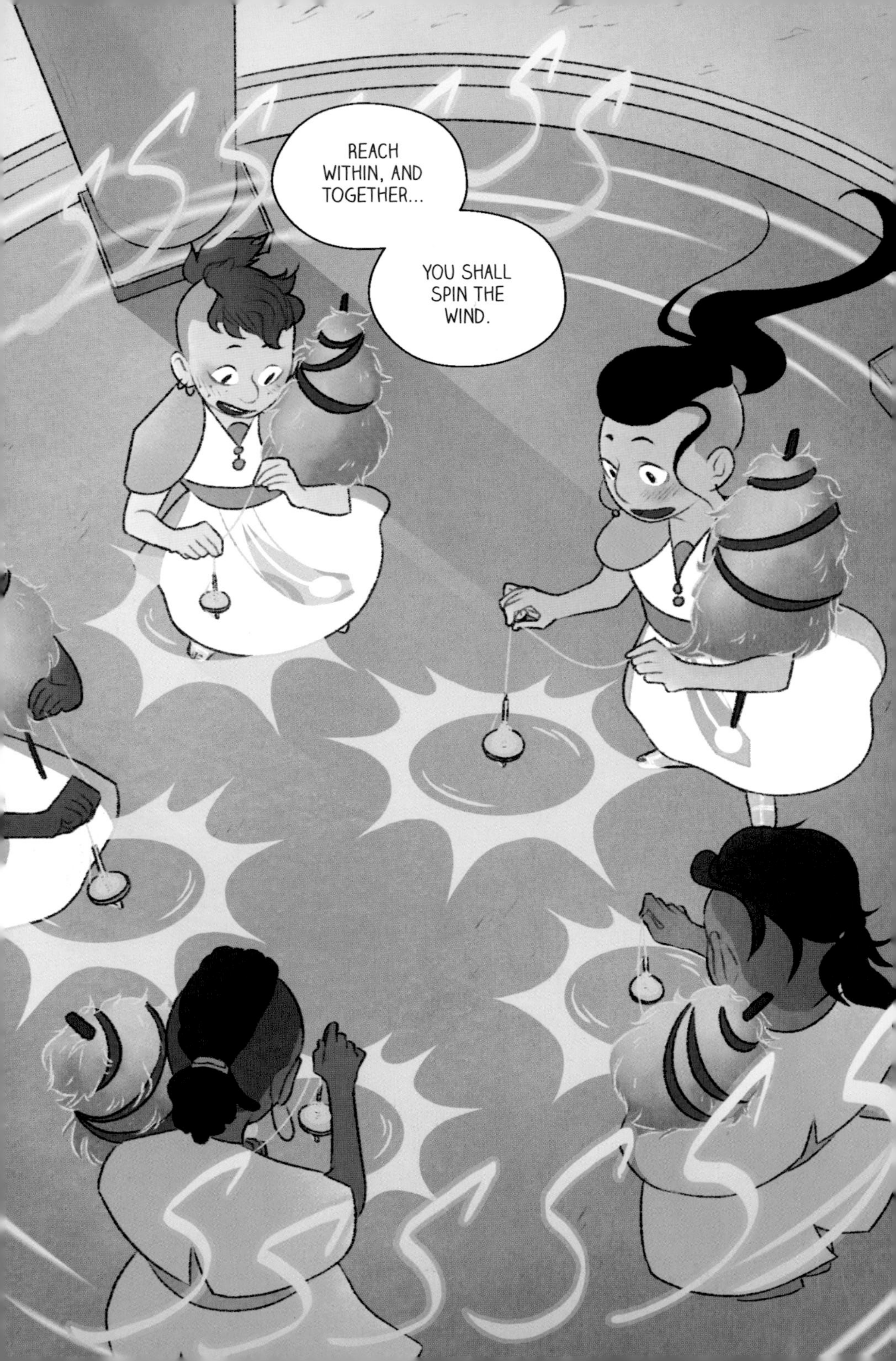
REACH WITHIN, AND TOGETHER...
YOU SHALL SPIN THE WIND.

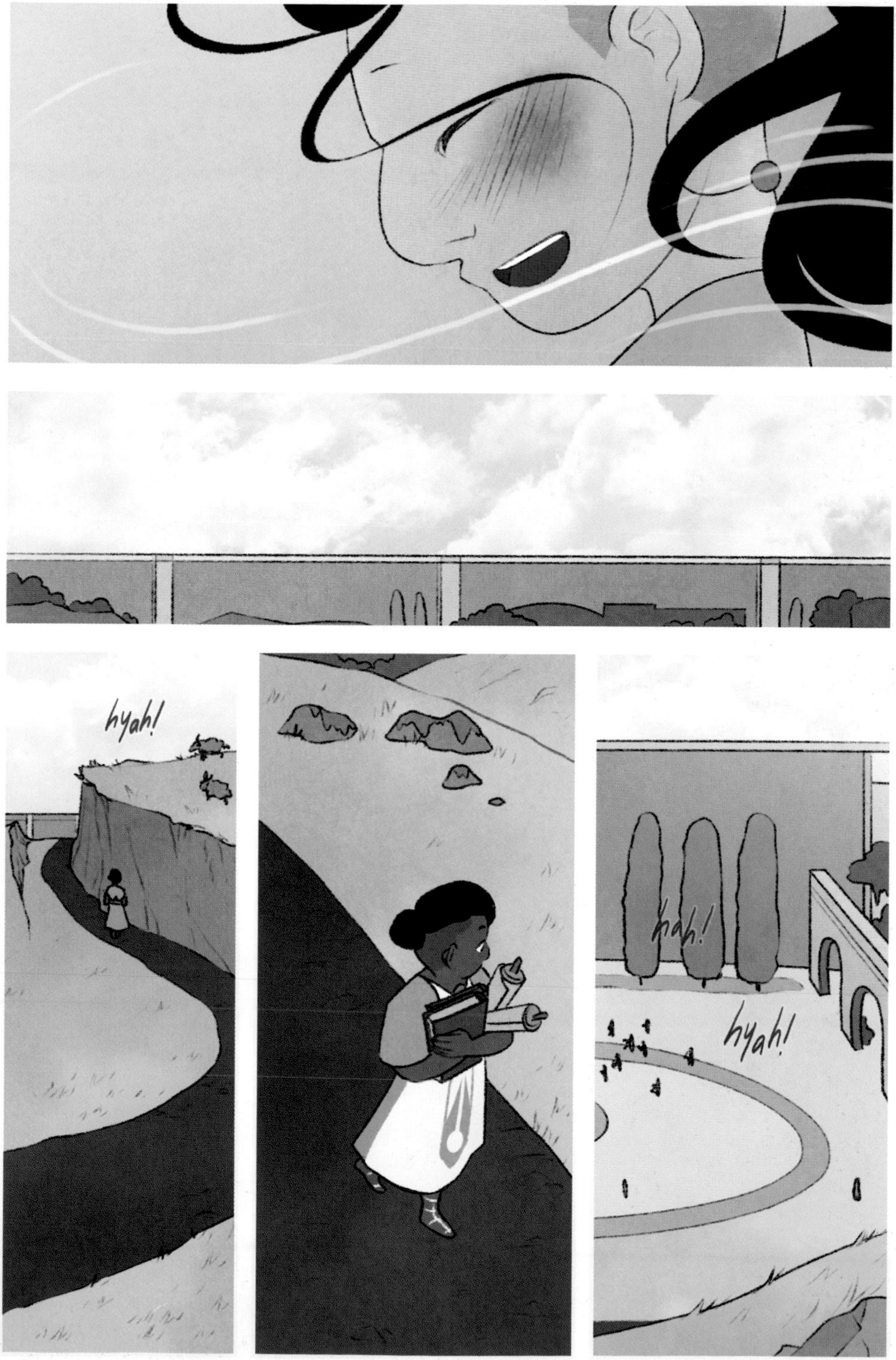
hyah!
hyah!
hyah!

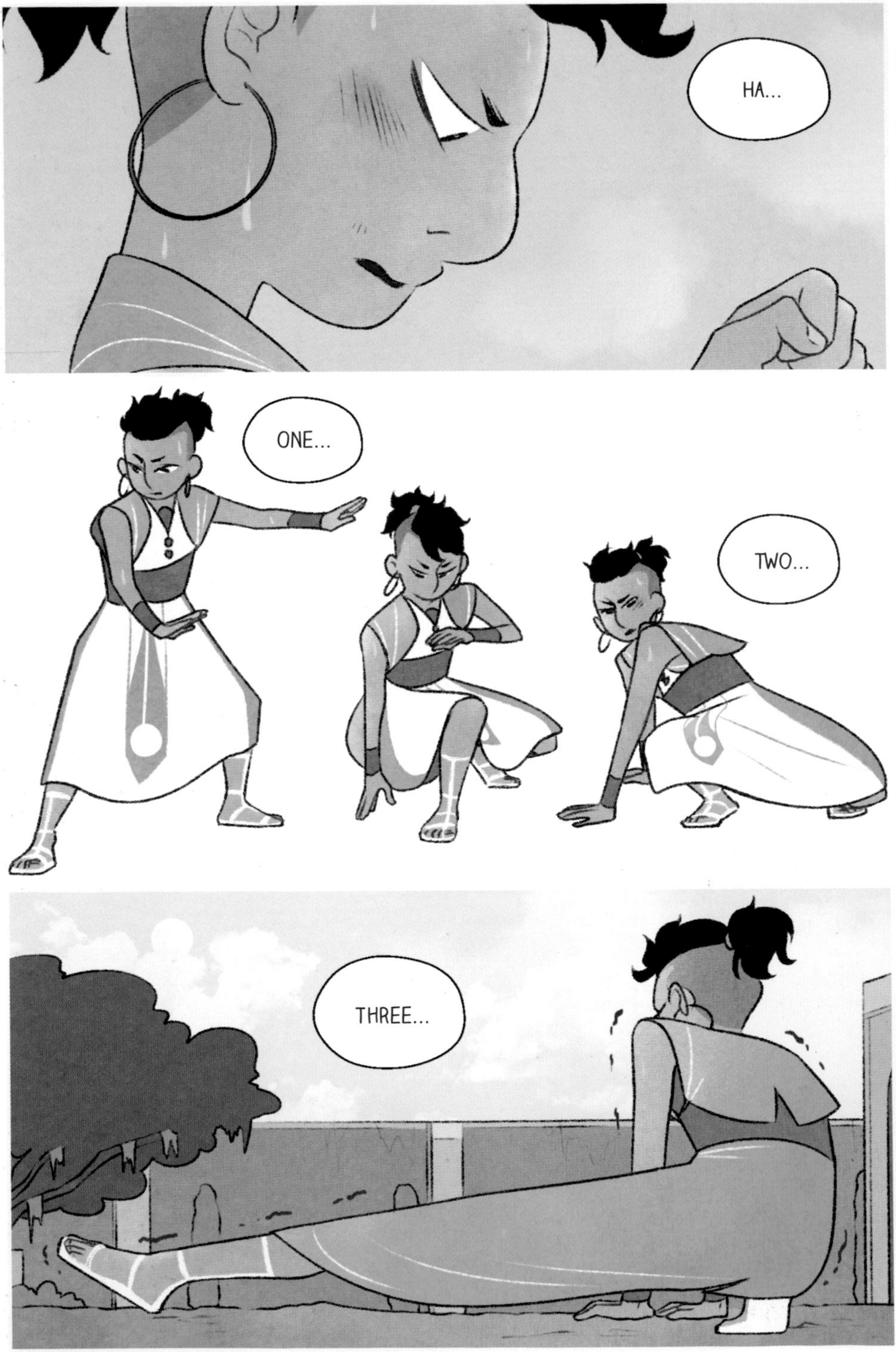
HA...
ONE...
TWO...
THREE...

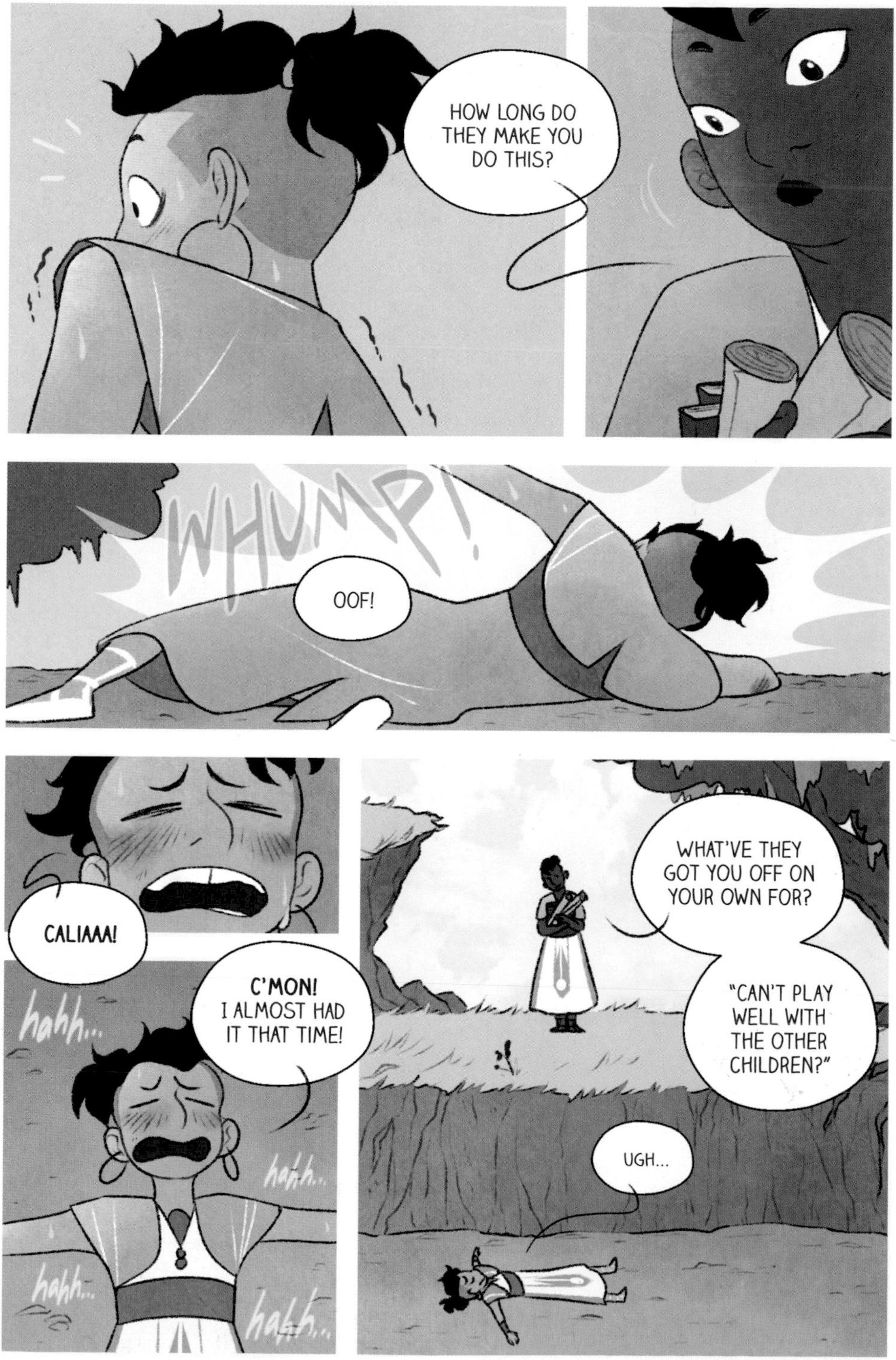
HOW LONG DO THEY MAKE YOU DO THIS?
WHUMP!
OOF!
CALIAAA!
C'MON! I ALMOST HAD IT THAT TIME!
hahh...
hahh...
hahh...
hahh...
WHAT'VE THEY GOT YOU OFF ON YOUR OWN FOR?
"CAN'T PLAY WELL WITH THE OTHER CHILDREN?"
UGH...

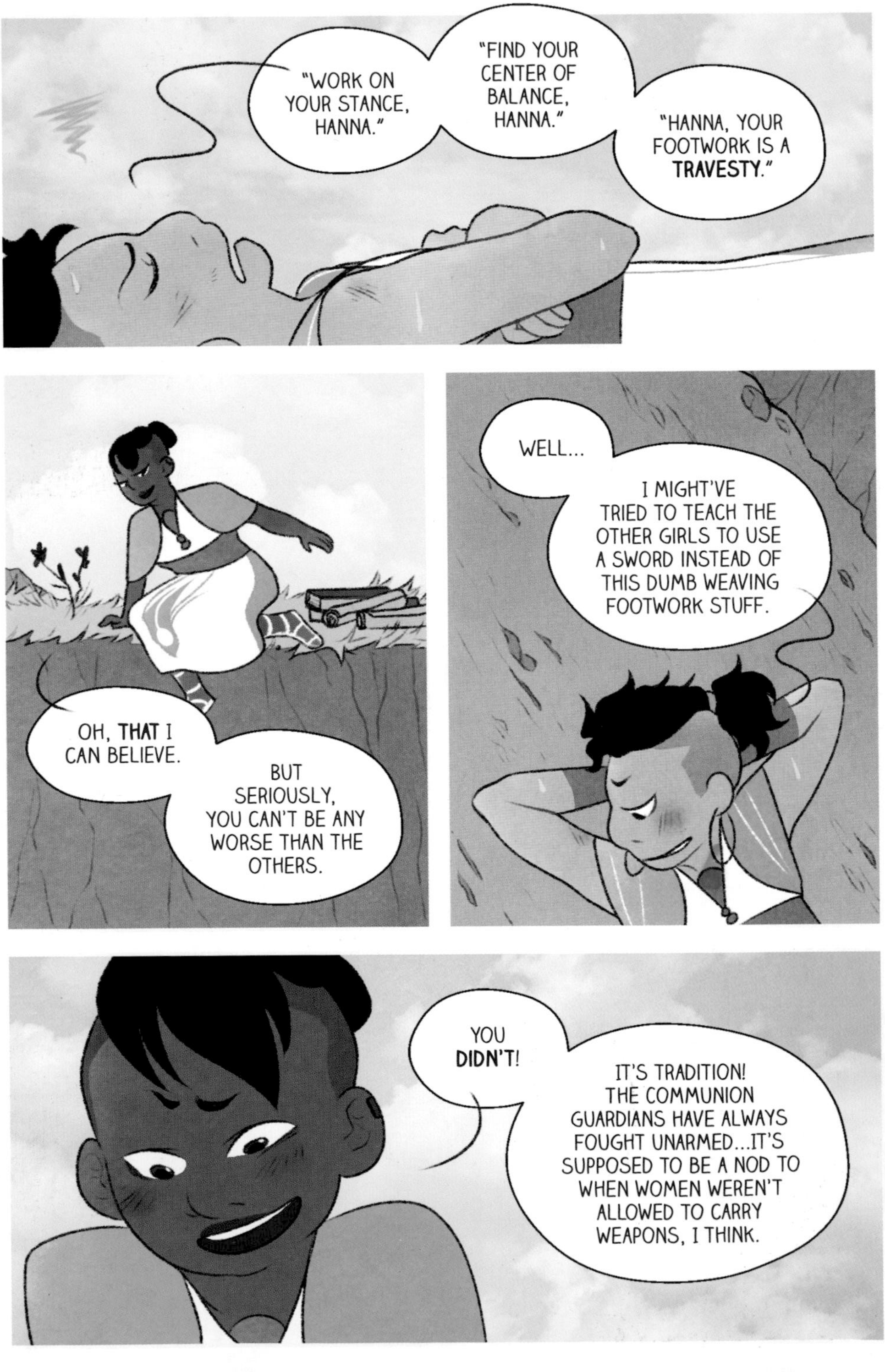
"WORK ON YOUR STANCE, HANNA."
"FIND YOUR CENTER OF BALANCE, HANNA."
"HANNA, YOUR FOOTWORK IS A **TRAVESTY**."
OH, **THAT** I CAN BELIEVE.
BUT SERIOUSLY, YOU CAN'T BE ANY WORSE THAN THE OTHERS.
WELL...
I MIGHT'VE TRIED TO TEACH THE OTHER GIRLS TO USE A SWORD INSTEAD OF THIS DUMB WEAVING FOOTWORK STUFF.
YOU **DIDN'T**!
IT'S TRADITION! THE COMMUNION GUARDIANS HAVE ALWAYS FOUGHT UNARMED...IT'S SUPPOSED TO BE A NOD TO WHEN WOMEN WEREN'T ALLOWED TO CARRY WEAPONS, I THINK.

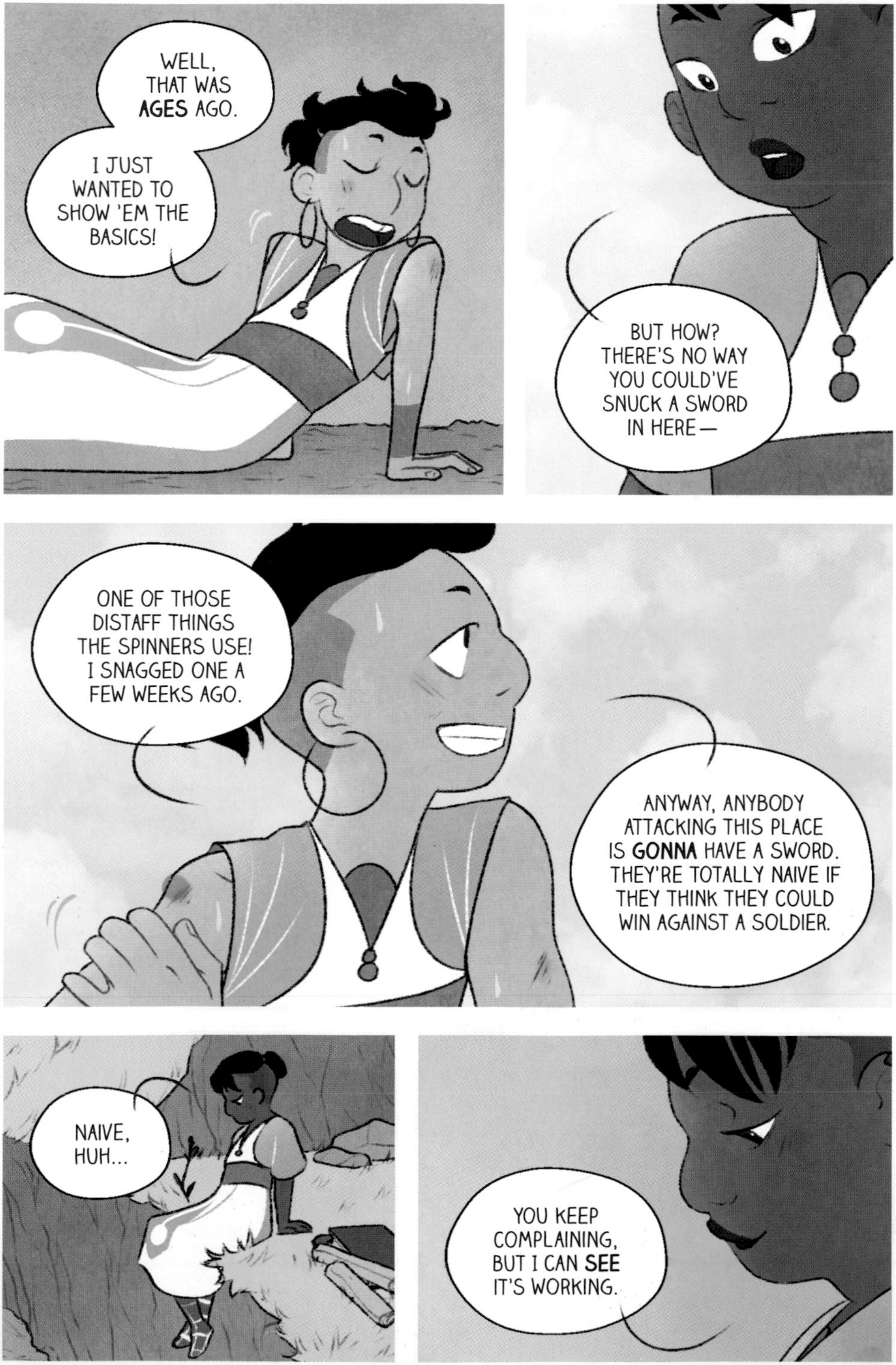

WELL, THAT WAS AGES AGO.
I JUST WANTED TO SHOW 'EM THE BASICS!
BUT HOW? THERE'S NO WAY YOU COULD'VE SNUCK A SWORD IN HERE—
ONE OF THOSE DISTAFF THINGS THE SPINNERS USE! I SNAGGED ONE A FEW WEEKS AGO.
ANYWAY, ANYBODY ATTACKING THIS PLACE IS GONNA HAVE A SWORD. THEY'RE TOTALLY NAIVE IF THEY THINK THEY COULD WIN AGAINST A SOLDIER.
NAIVE, HUH...
YOU KEEP COMPLAINING, BUT I CAN SEE IT'S WORKING.

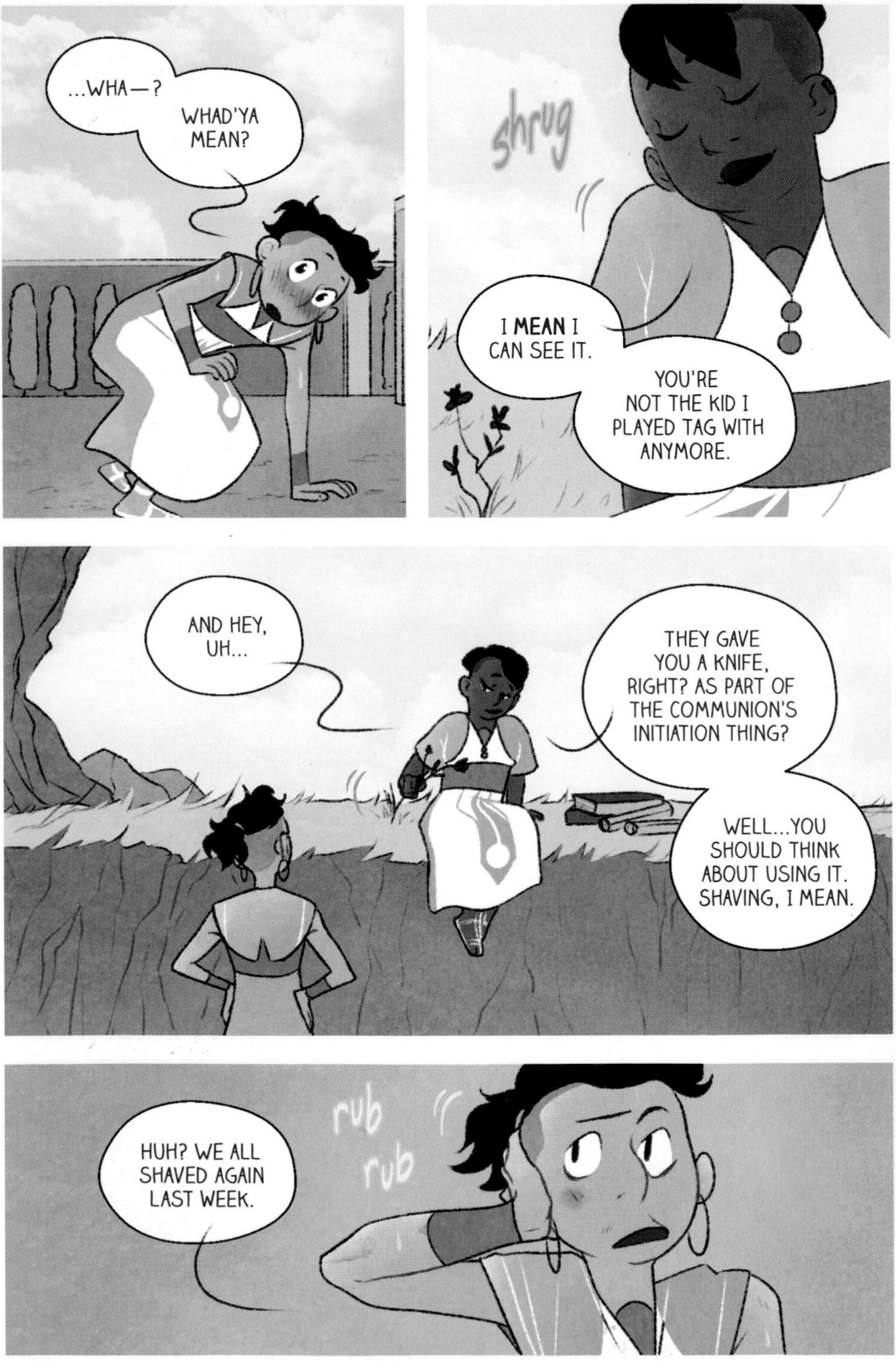
...WHA—?
WHAD'YA MEAN?
shrug
I **MEAN** I CAN SEE IT.
YOU'RE NOT THE KID I PLAYED TAG WITH ANYMORE.
AND HEY, UH...
THEY GAVE YOU A KNIFE, RIGHT? AS PART OF THE COMMUNION'S INITIATION THING?
WELL...YOU SHOULD THINK ABOUT USING IT. SHAVING, I MEAN.
HUH? WE ALL SHAVED AGAIN LAST WEEK.
rub rub

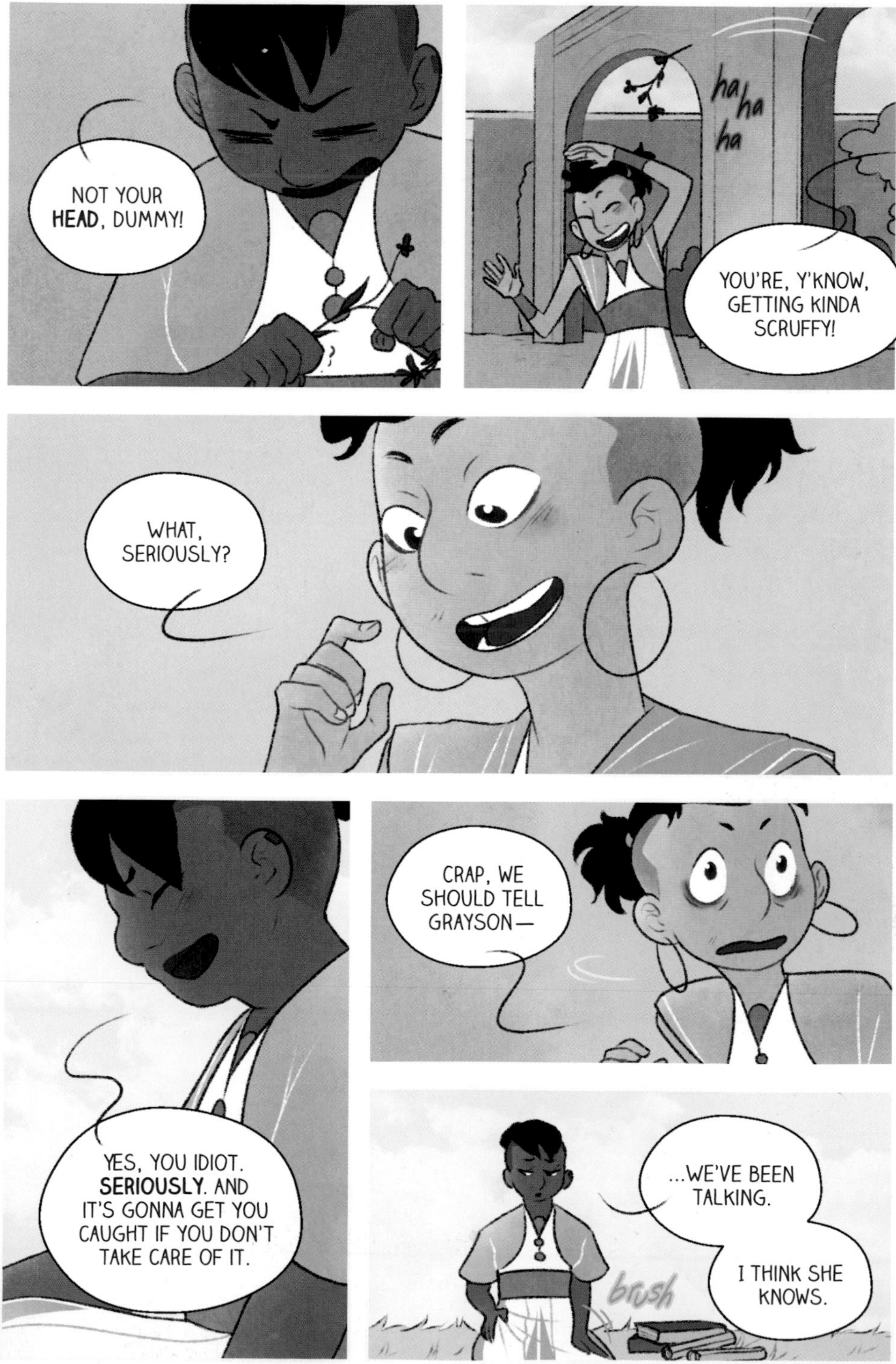
NOT YOUR **HEAD**, DUMMY!
ha ha ha
YOU'RE, Y'KNOW, GETTING KINDA SCRUFFY!
WHAT, SERIOUSLY?
YES, YOU IDIOT. **SERIOUSLY**. AND IT'S GONNA GET YOU CAUGHT IF YOU DON'T TAKE CARE OF IT.
CRAP, WE SHOULD TELL GRAYSON—
...WE'VE BEEN TALKING.
I THINK SHE KNOWS.
brush

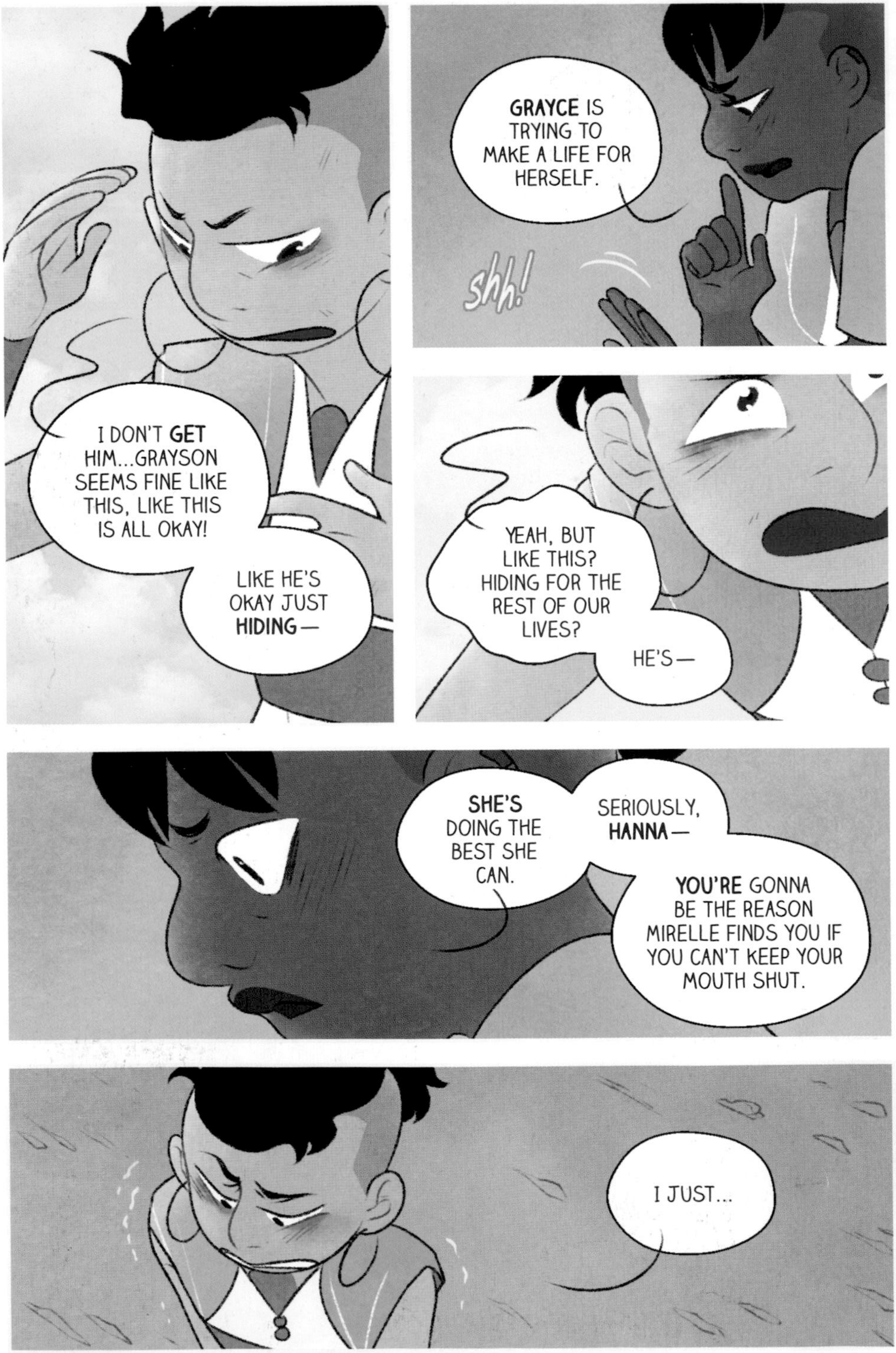
I DON'T **GET** HIM...GRAYSON SEEMS FINE LIKE THIS, LIKE THIS IS ALL OKAY!
LIKE HE'S OKAY JUST **HIDING**—
GRAYCE IS TRYING TO MAKE A LIFE FOR HERSELF.
shh!
YEAH, BUT LIKE THIS? HIDING FOR THE REST OF OUR LIVES?
HE'S—
SHE'S DOING THE BEST SHE CAN.
SERIOUSLY, **HANNA**—
YOU'RE GONNA BE THE REASON MIRELLE FINDS YOU IF YOU CAN'T KEEP YOUR MOUTH SHUT.
I JUST...

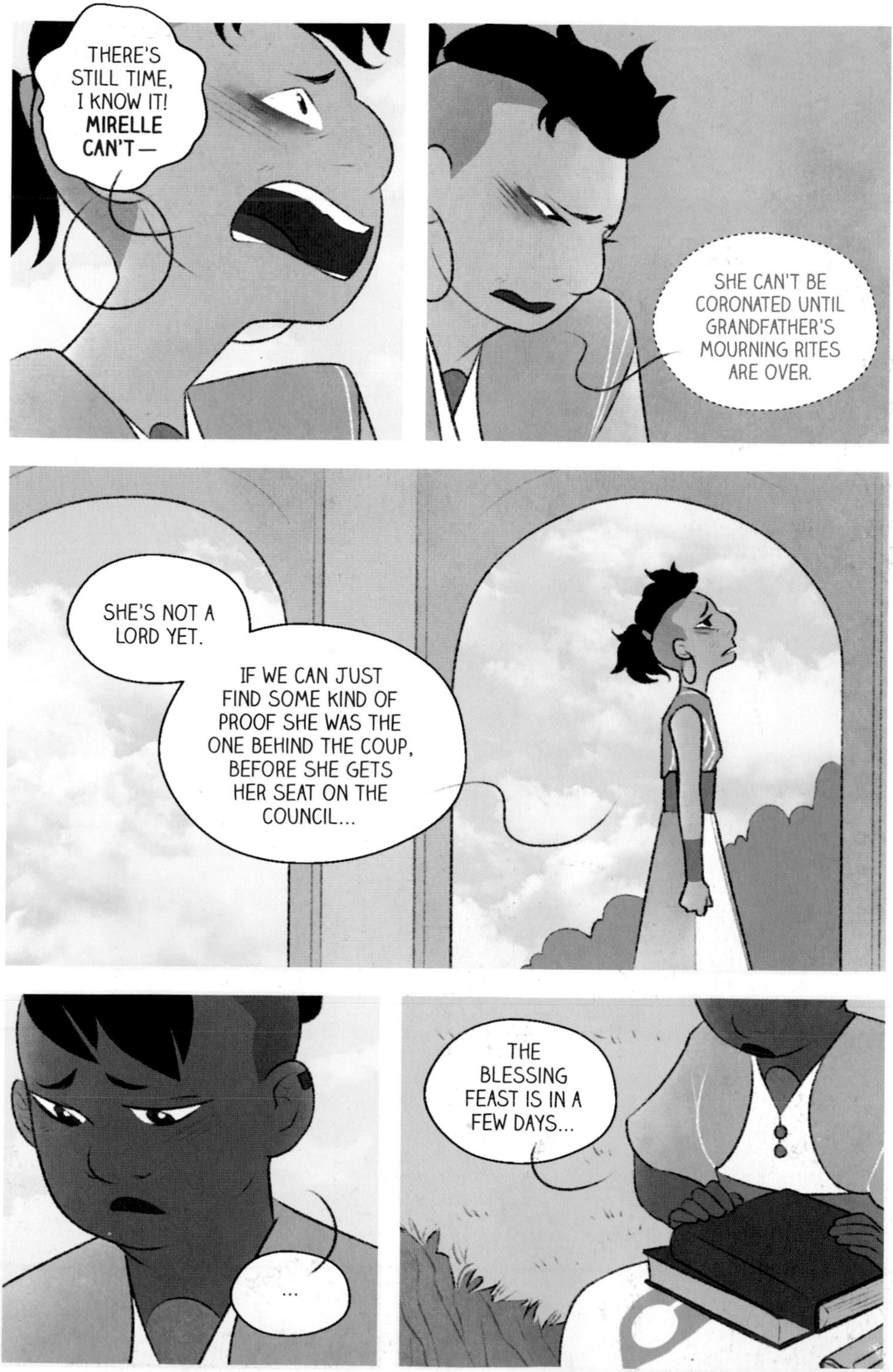
THERE'S STILL TIME, I KNOW IT! **MIRELLE CAN'T—**
SHE CAN'T BE CORONATED UNTIL GRANDFATHER'S MOURNING RITES ARE OVER.
SHE'S NOT A LORD YET.
IF WE CAN JUST FIND SOME KIND OF PROOF SHE WAS THE ONE BEHIND THE COUP, BEFORE SHE GETS HER SEAT ON THE COUNCIL...
...
THE BLESSING FEAST IS IN A FEW DAYS...

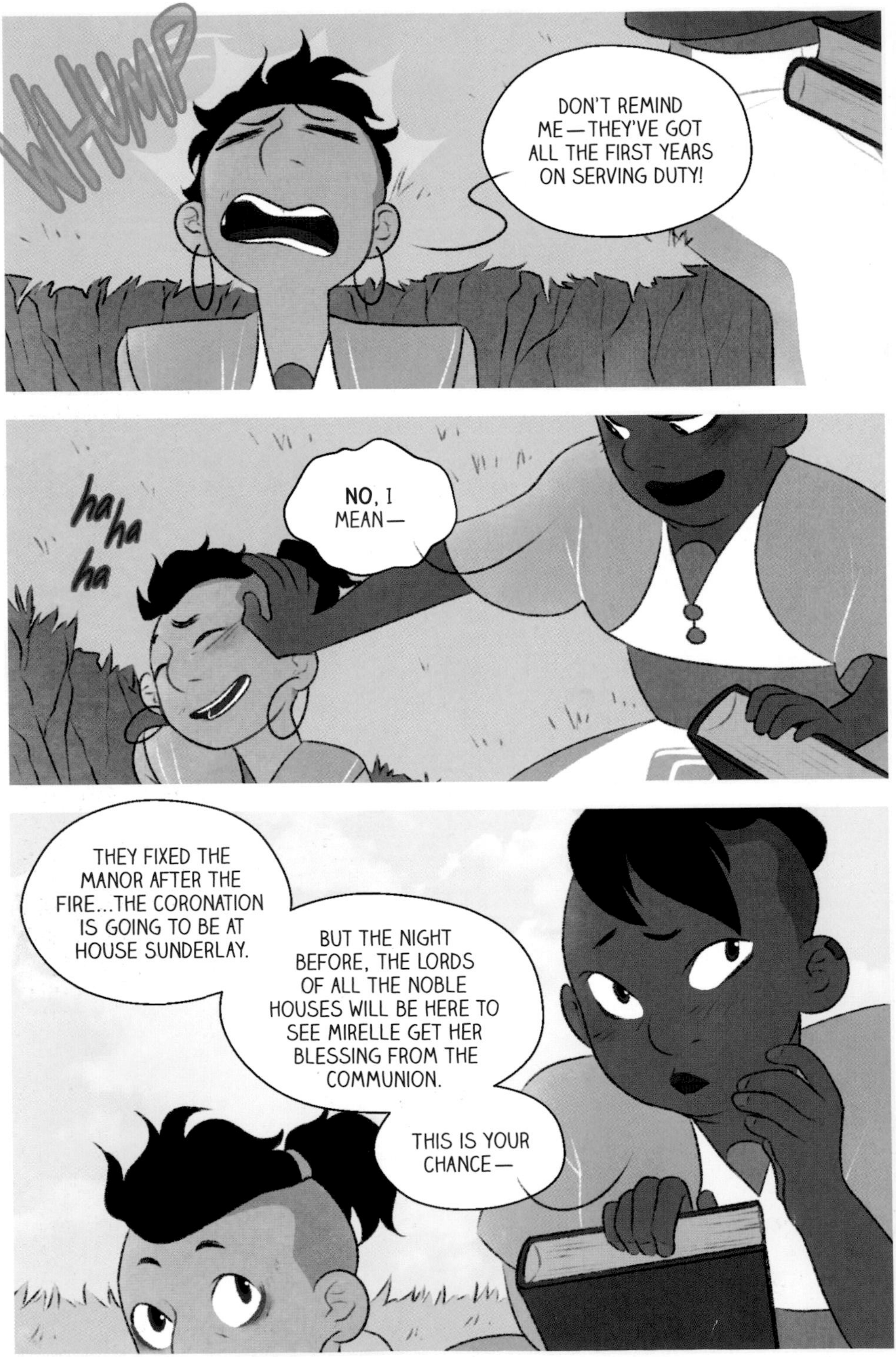
WHUMP
DON'T REMIND ME—THEY'VE GOT ALL THE FIRST YEARS ON SERVING DUTY!
ha ha ha
NO, I MEAN—
THEY FIXED THE MANOR AFTER THE FIRE...THE CORONATION IS GOING TO BE AT HOUSE SUNDERLAY.
BUT THE NIGHT BEFORE, THE LORDS OF ALL THE NOBLE HOUSES WILL BE HERE TO SEE MIRELLE GET HER BLESSING FROM THE COMMUNION.
THIS IS YOUR CHANCE—

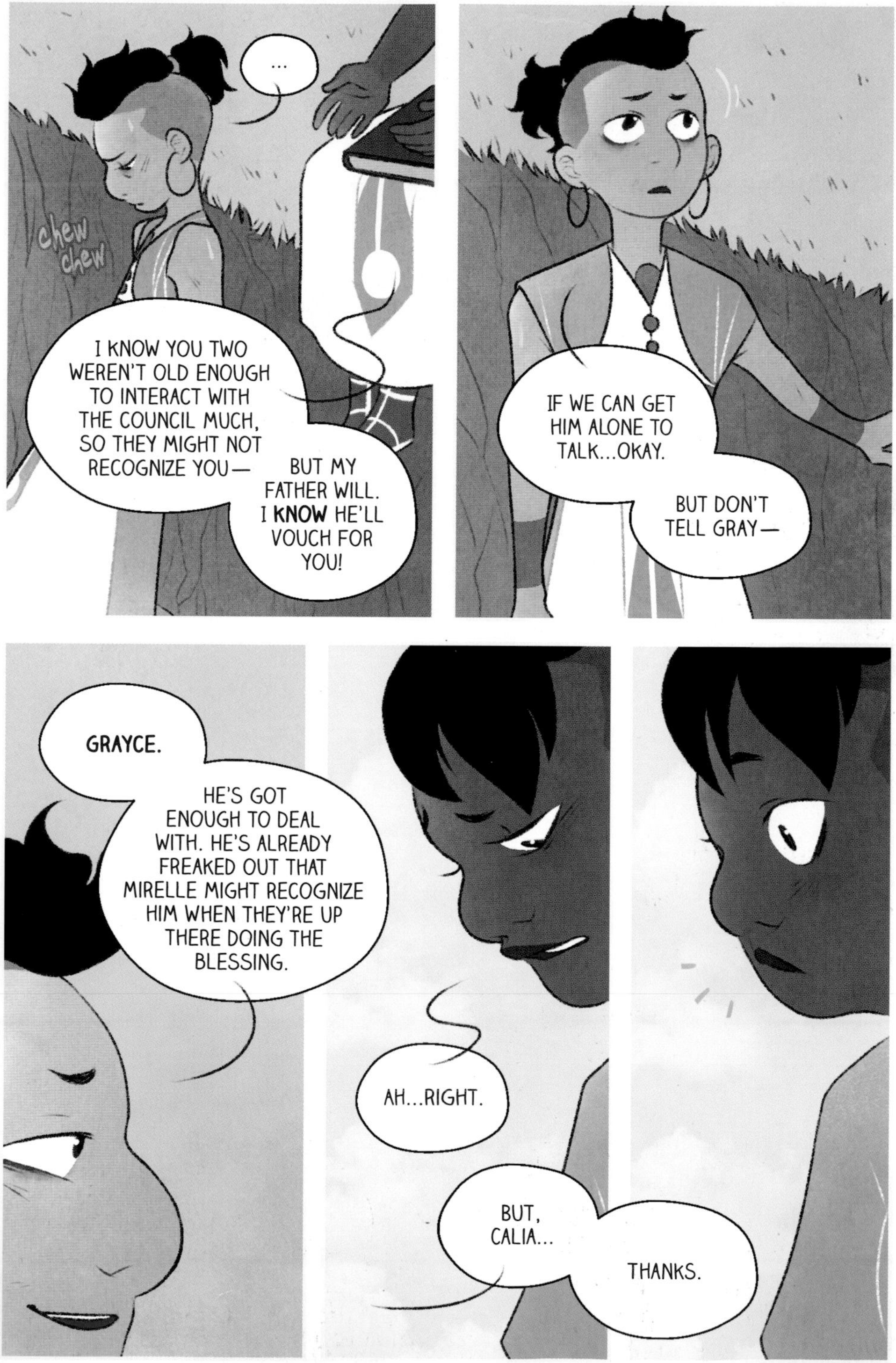
...
chew chew
I KNOW YOU TWO WEREN'T OLD ENOUGH TO INTERACT WITH THE COUNCIL MUCH, SO THEY MIGHT NOT RECOGNIZE YOU—
BUT MY FATHER WILL. I **KNOW** HE'LL VOUCH FOR YOU!
IF WE CAN GET HIM ALONE TO TALK...OKAY.
BUT DON'T TELL GRAY—
GRAYCE.
HE'S GOT ENOUGH TO DEAL WITH. HE'S ALREADY FREAKED OUT THAT MIRELLE MIGHT RECOGNIZE HIM WHEN THEY'RE UP THERE DOING THE BLESSING.
AH...RIGHT.
BUT, CALIA...
THANKS.

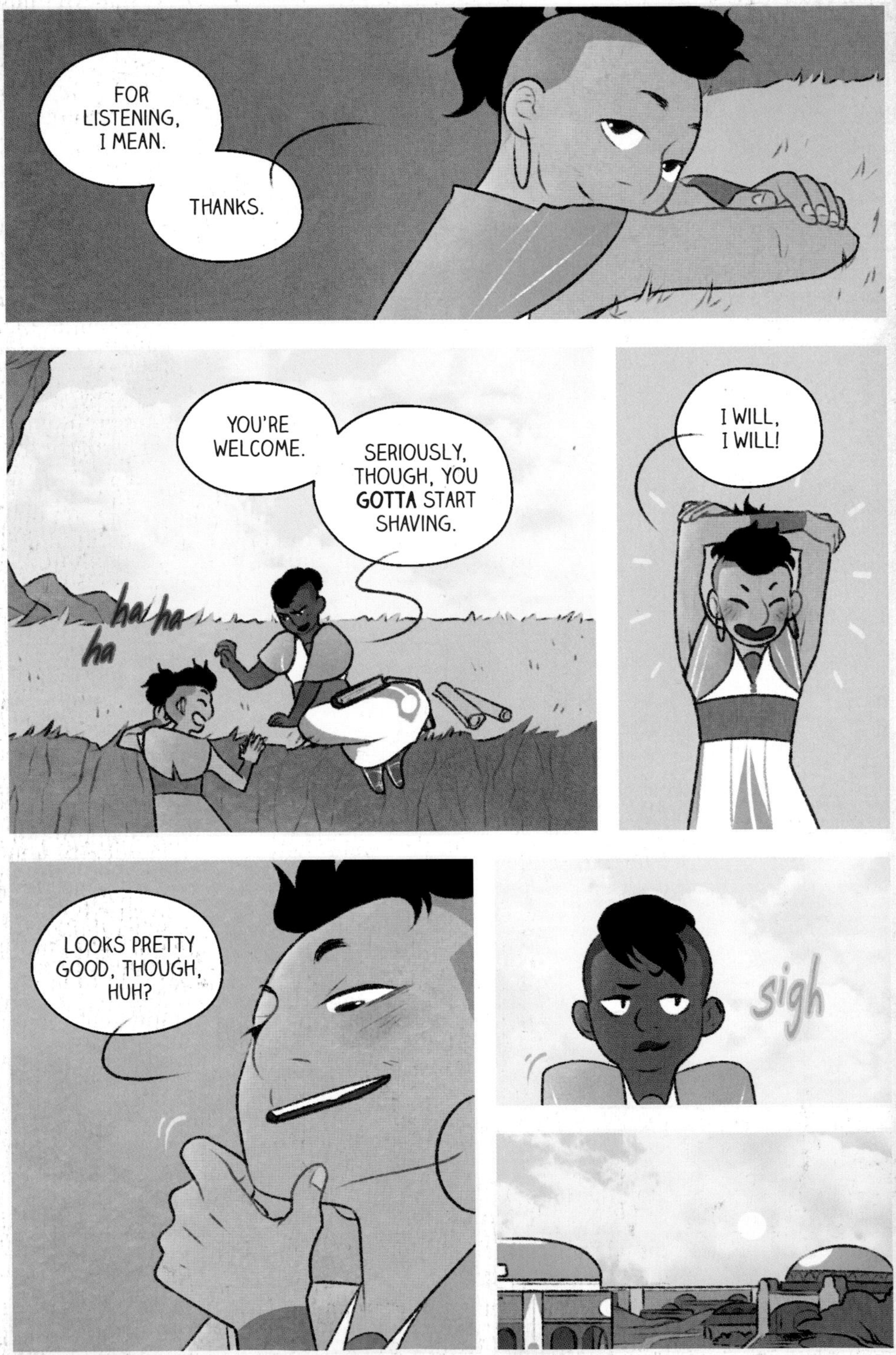
FOR LISTENING, I MEAN.
THANKS.
YOU'RE WELCOME.
SERIOUSLY, THOUGH, YOU **GOTTA** START SHAVING.
ha ha ha
I WILL, I WILL!
LOOKS PRETTY GOOD, THOUGH, HUH?
sigh

CHAPTER III
HOME

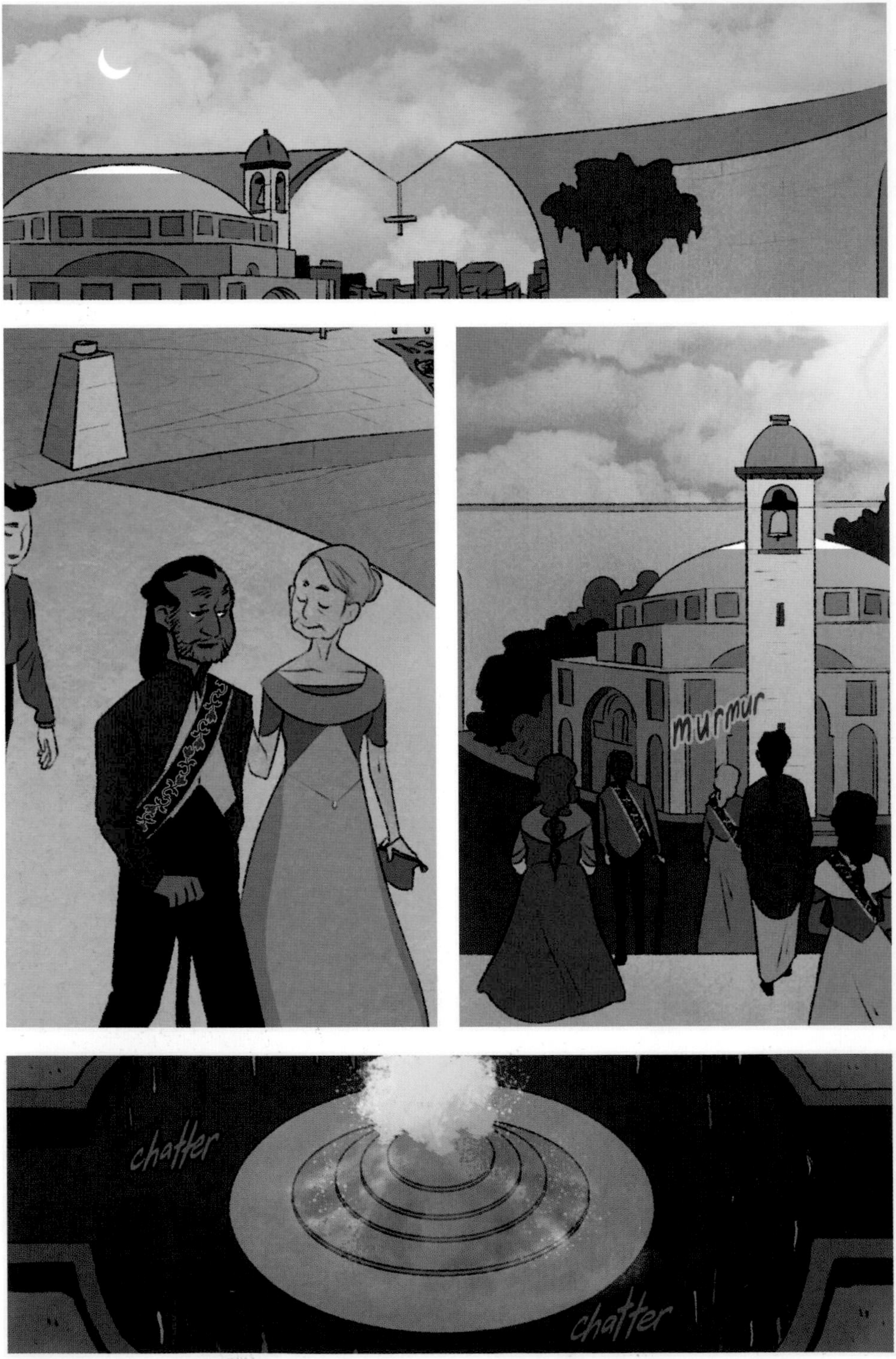
murmur
chatter
chatter

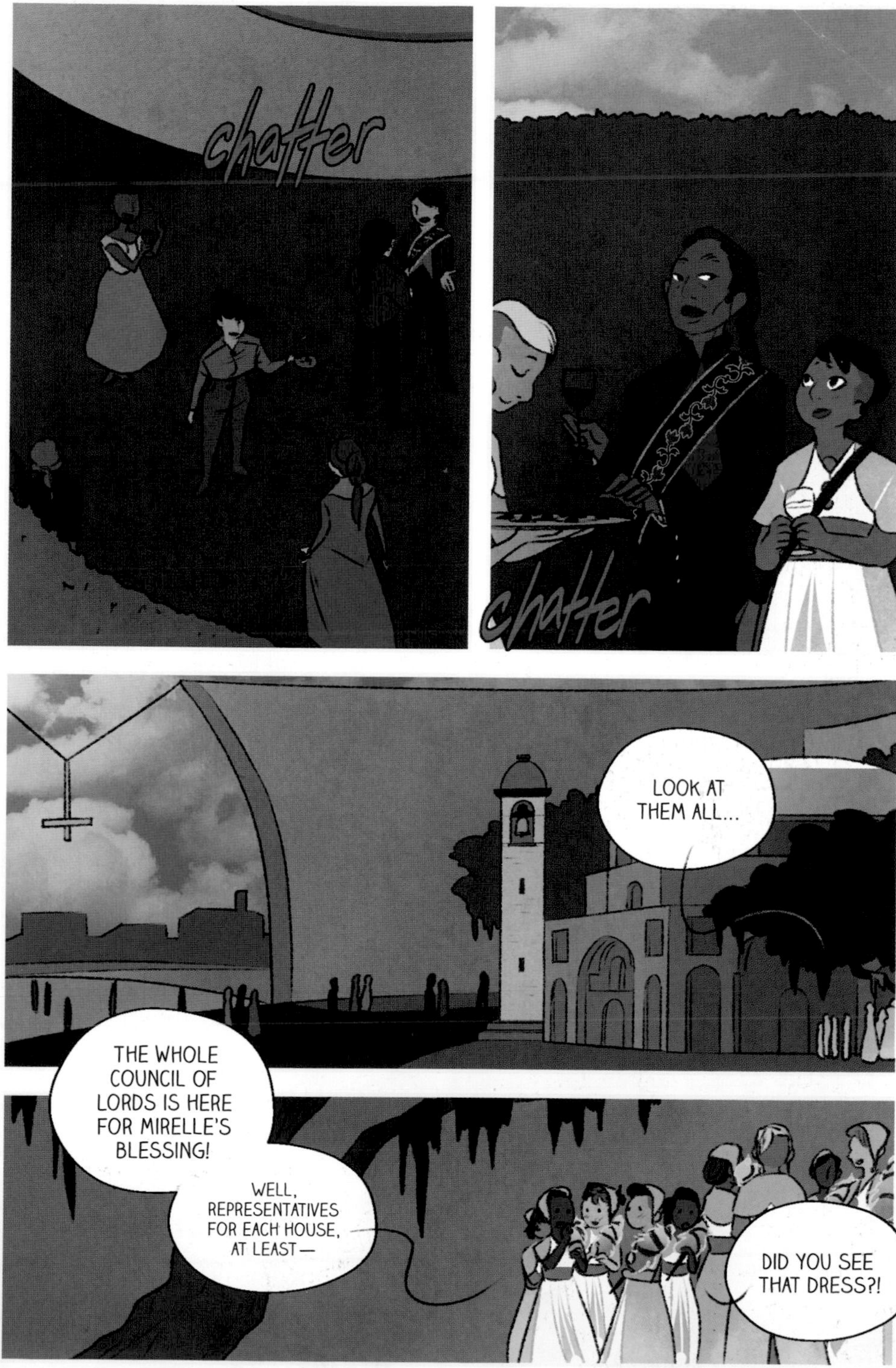
chatter
chatter
LOOK AT THEM ALL...
THE WHOLE COUNCIL OF LORDS IS HERE FOR MIRELLE'S BLESSING!
WELL, REPRESENTATIVES FOR EACH HOUSE, AT LEAST—
DID YOU SEE THAT DRESS?!

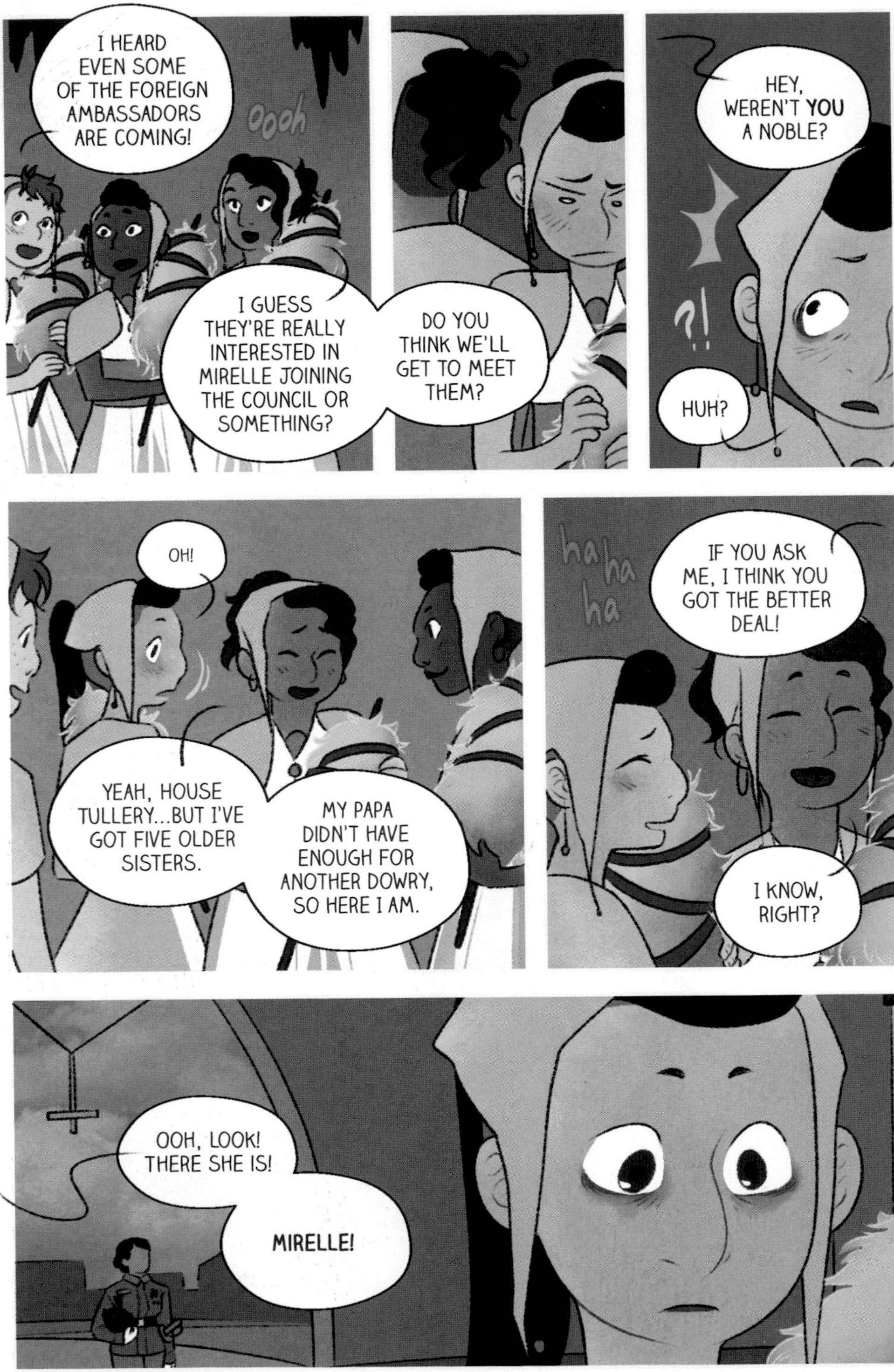
I HEARD EVEN SOME OF THE FOREIGN AMBASSADORS ARE COMING!
oooh
I GUESS THEY'RE REALLY INTERESTED IN MIRELLE JOINING THE COUNCIL OR SOMETHING?
DO YOU THINK WE'LL GET TO MEET THEM?
HEY, WEREN'T **YOU** A NOBLE?
?!
HUH?
OH!
YEAH, HOUSE TULLERY...BUT I'VE GOT FIVE OLDER SISTERS.
MY PAPA DIDN'T HAVE ENOUGH FOR ANOTHER DOWRY, SO HERE I AM.
ha ha ha
IF YOU ASK ME, I THINK YOU GOT THE BETTER DEAL!
I KNOW, RIGHT?
OOH, LOOK! THERE SHE IS!
MIRELLE!

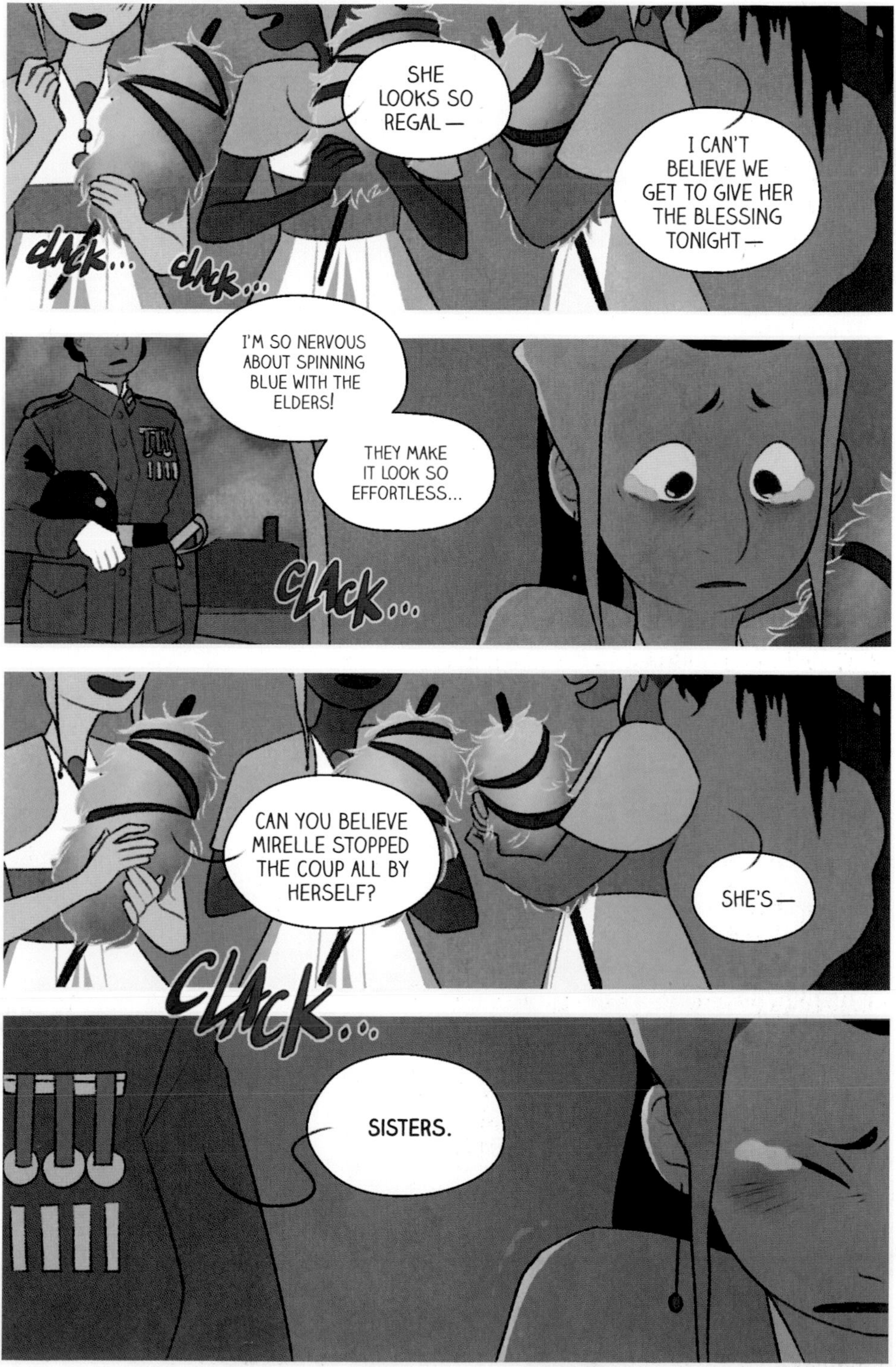

SHE LOOKS SO REGAL—
I CAN'T BELIEVE WE GET TO GIVE HER THE BLESSING TONIGHT—
CLACK...
CLACK...
I'M SO NERVOUS ABOUT SPINNING BLUE WITH THE ELDERS!
THEY MAKE IT LOOK SO EFFORTLESS...
CLACK...
CAN YOU BELIEVE MIRELLE STOPPED THE COUP ALL BY HERSELF?
SHE'S—
CLACK...
SISTERS.

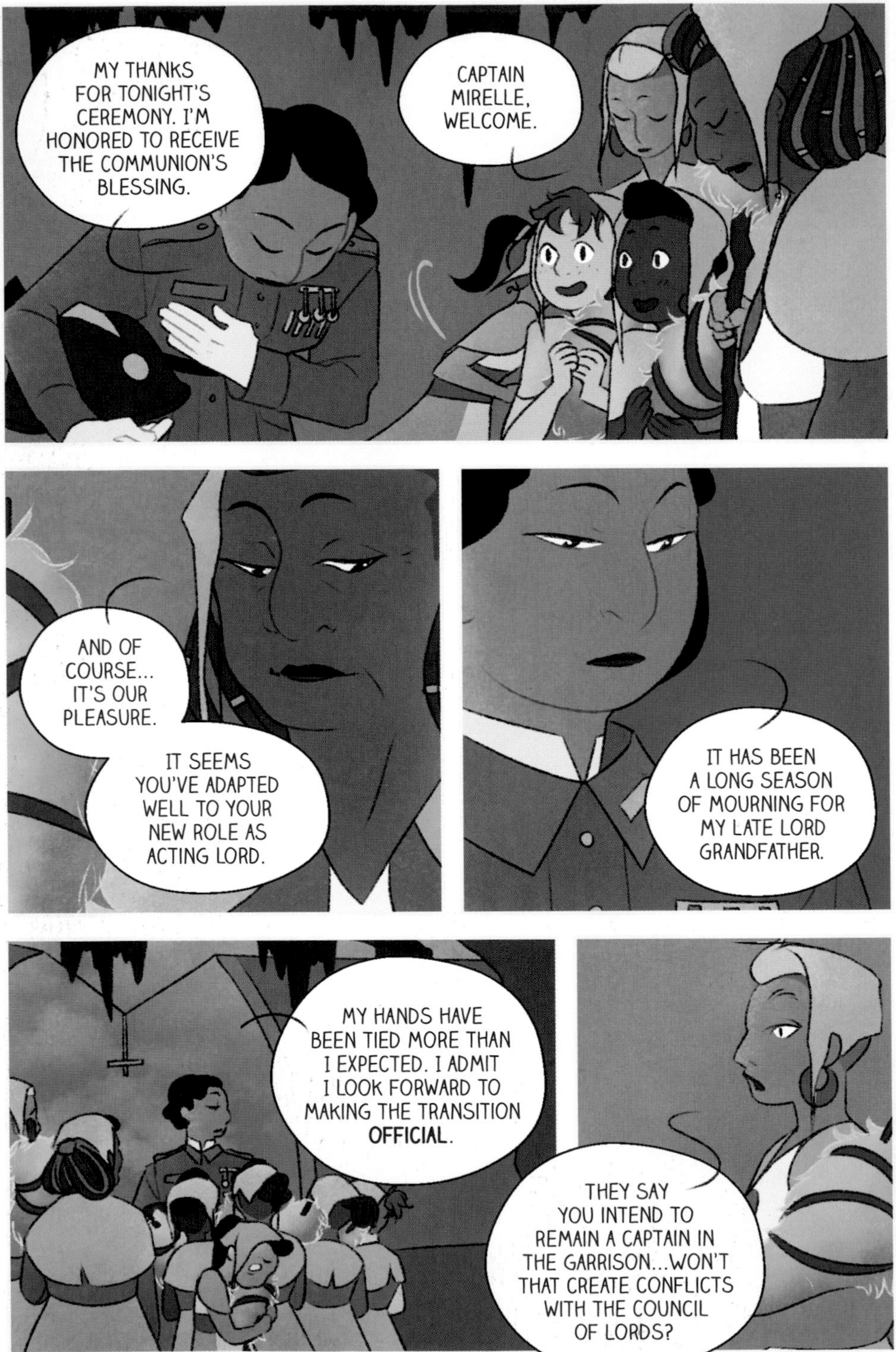
MY THANKS FOR TONIGHT'S CEREMONY. I'M HONORED TO RECEIVE THE COMMUNION'S BLESSING.
CAPTAIN MIRELLE, WELCOME.
AND OF COURSE... IT'S OUR PLEASURE.
IT SEEMS YOU'VE ADAPTED WELL TO YOUR NEW ROLE AS ACTING LORD.
IT HAS BEEN A LONG SEASON OF MOURNING FOR MY LATE LORD GRANDFATHER.
MY HANDS HAVE BEEN TIED MORE THAN I EXPECTED. I ADMIT I LOOK FORWARD TO MAKING THE TRANSITION **OFFICIAL**.
THEY SAY YOU INTEND TO REMAIN A CAPTAIN IN THE GARRISON...WON'T THAT CREATE CONFLICTS WITH THE COUNCIL OF LORDS?

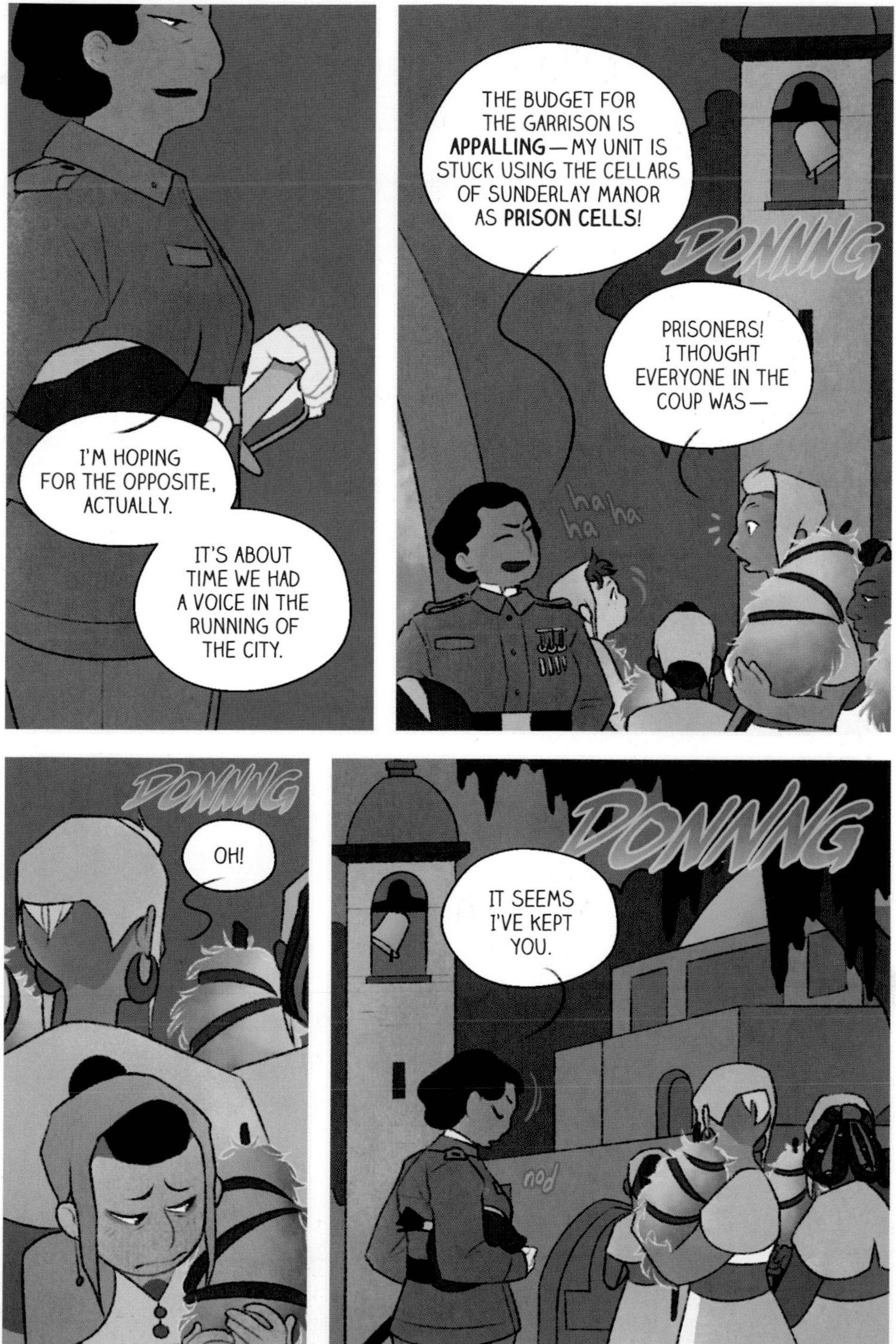
I'M HOPING FOR THE OPPOSITE, ACTUALLY.
IT'S ABOUT TIME WE HAD A VOICE IN THE RUNNING OF THE CITY.
THE BUDGET FOR THE GARRISON IS APPALLING—MY UNIT IS STUCK USING THE CELLARS OF SUNDERLAY MANOR AS PRISON CELLS!
DONNNG
ha ha ha ha
PRISONERS! I THOUGHT EVERYONE IN THE COUP WAS—
DONNNG
OH!
DONNNG
IT SEEMS I'VE KEPT YOU.
nod

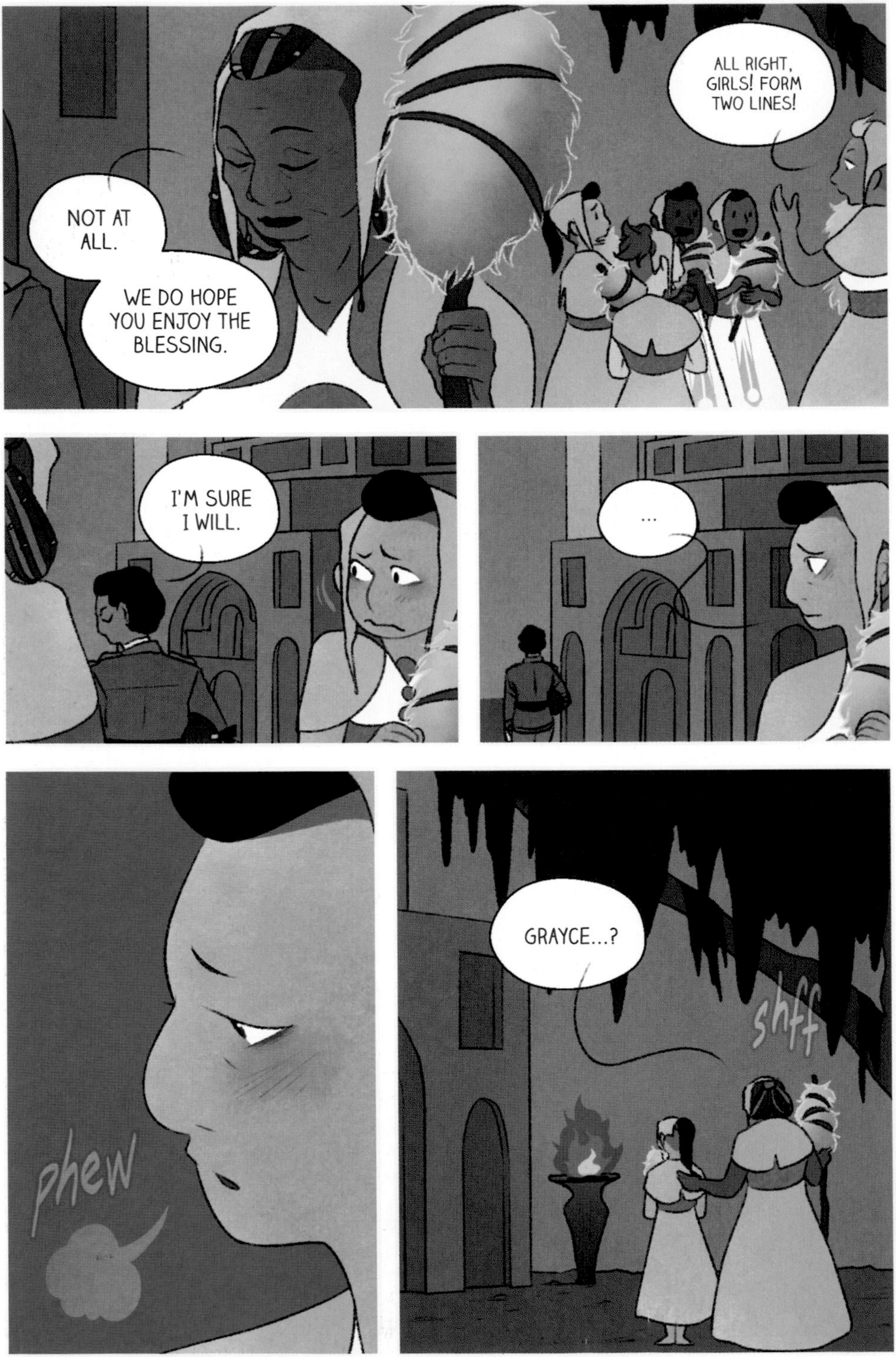
NOT AT ALL.
WE DO HOPE YOU ENJOY THE BLESSING.
ALL RIGHT, GIRLS! FORM TWO LINES!
I'M SURE I WILL.
...
phew
GRAYCE...?
shff

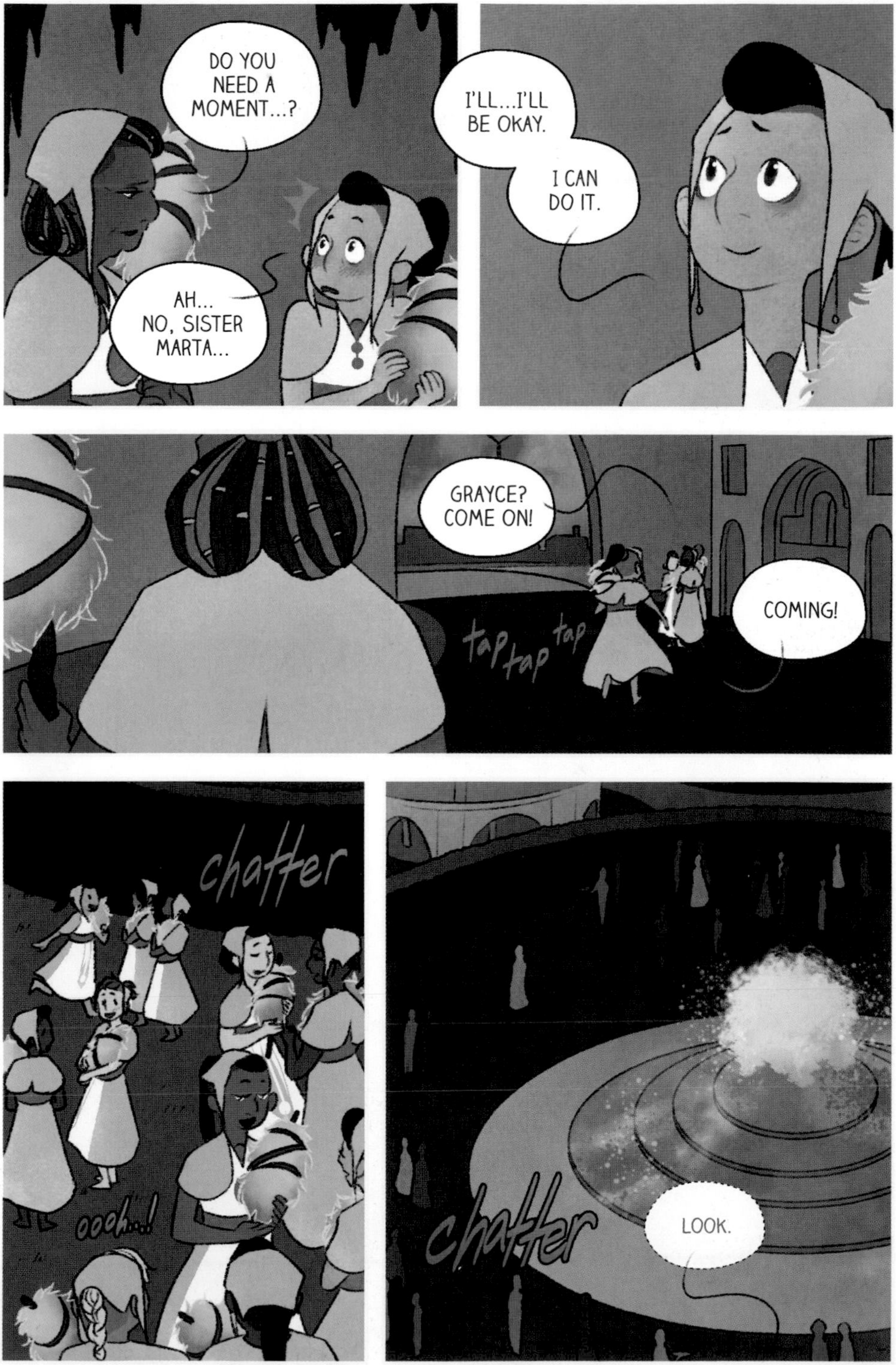
DO YOU NEED A MOMENT...?
AH... NO, SISTER MARTA...
I'LL...I'LL BE OKAY.
I CAN DO IT.
GRAYCE? COME ON!
tap tap tap
COMING!
chatter
oooh...!
chatter
LOOK.

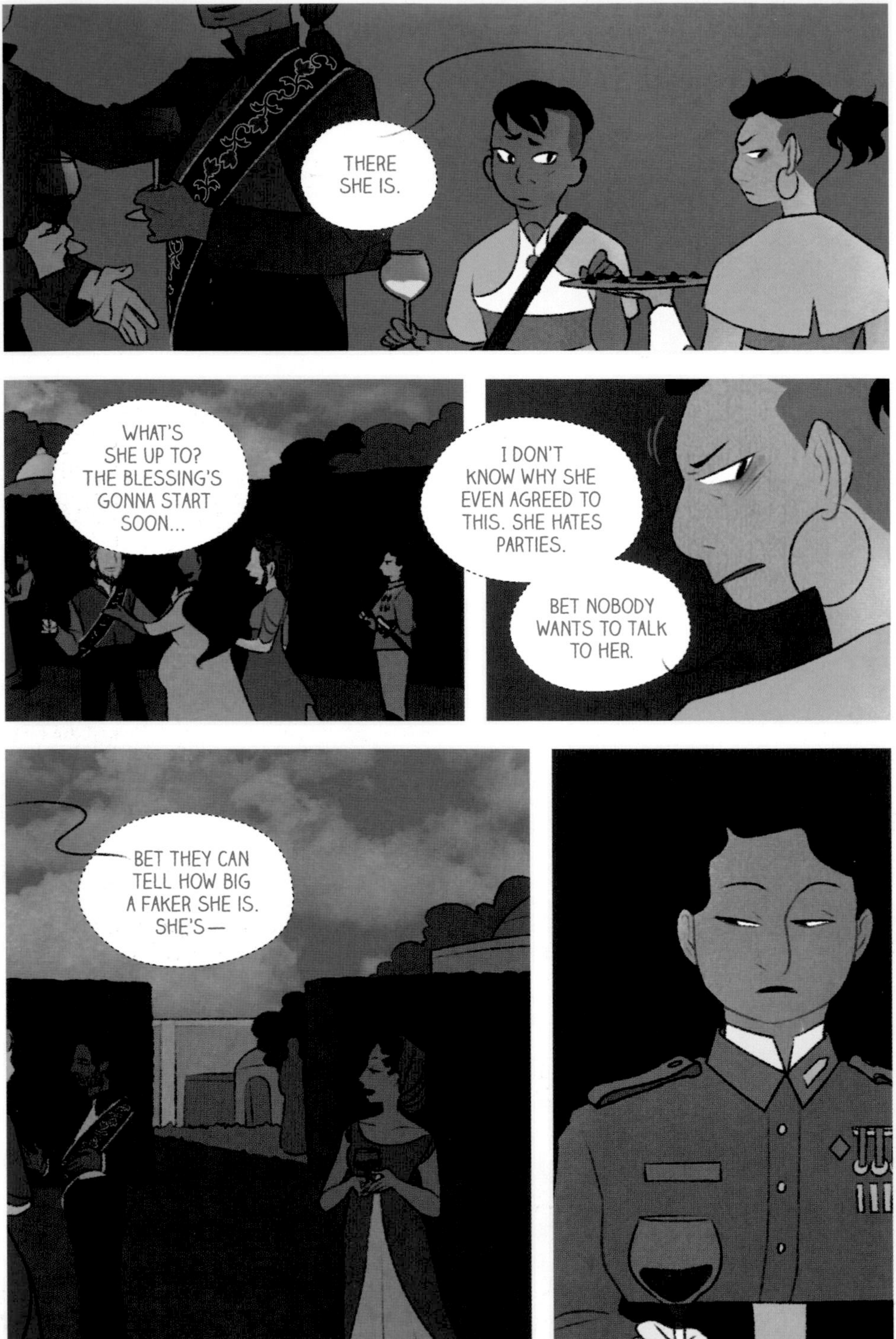
THERE SHE IS.
WHAT'S SHE UP TO? THE BLESSING'S GONNA START SOON...
I DON'T KNOW WHY SHE EVEN AGREED TO THIS. SHE HATES PARTIES.
BET NOBODY WANTS TO TALK TO HER.
BET THEY CAN TELL HOW BIG A FAKER SHE IS. SHE'S—

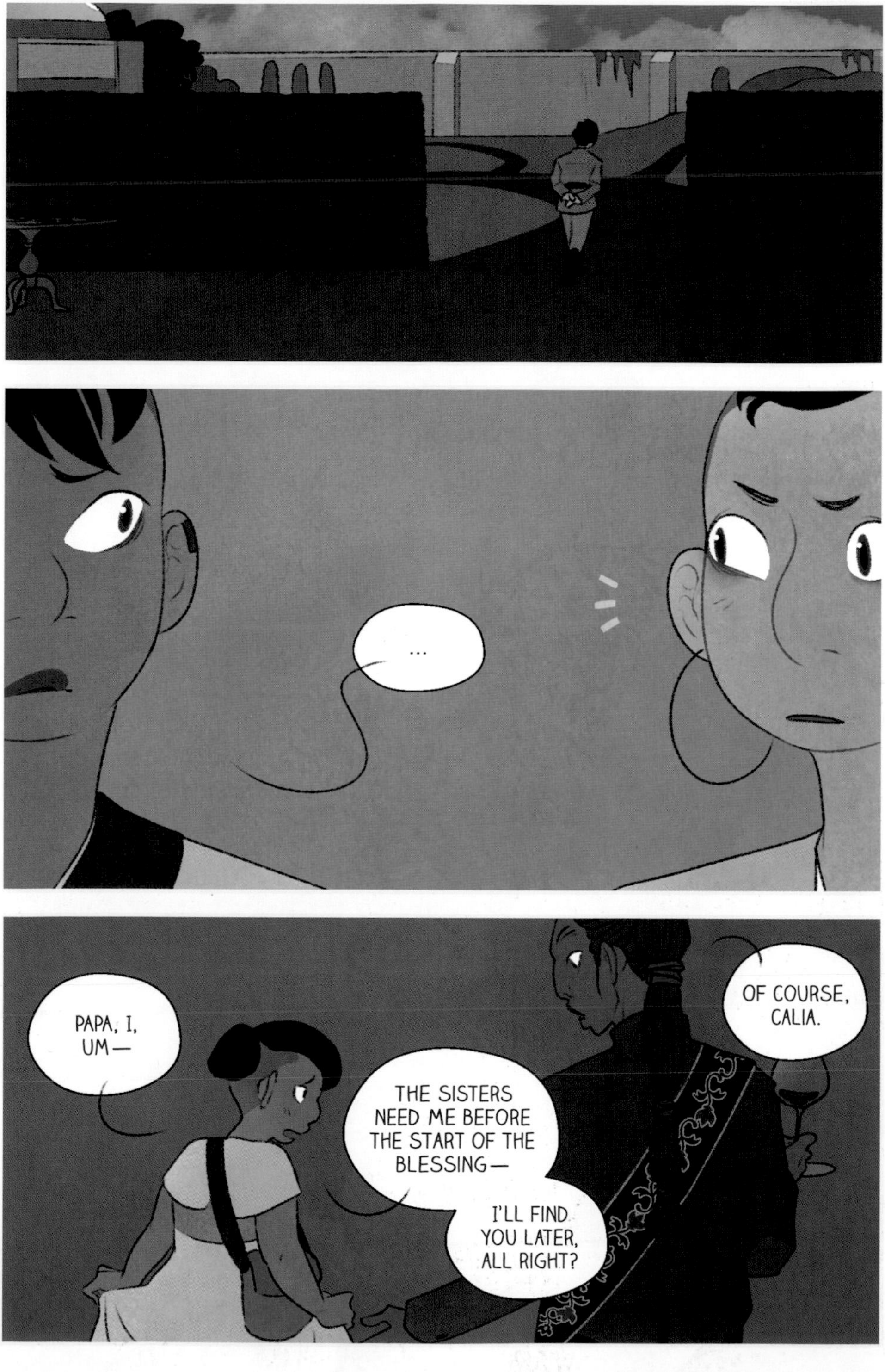
...
PAPA, I, UM—
THE SISTERS NEED ME BEFORE THE START OF THE BLESSING—
I'LL FIND YOU LATER, ALL RIGHT?
OF COURSE, CALIA.

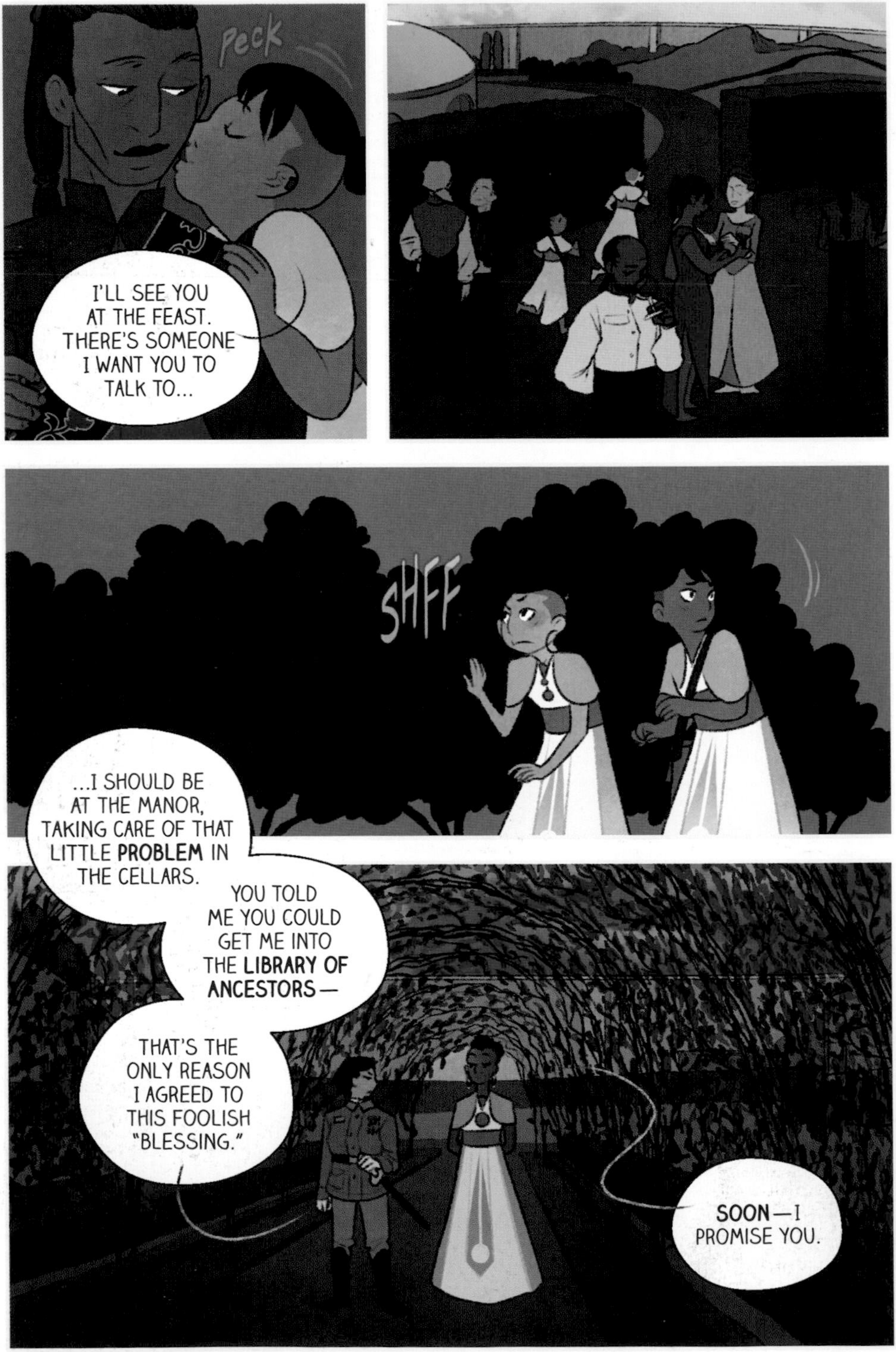
PECK
I'LL SEE YOU AT THE FEAST. THERE'S SOMEONE I WANT YOU TO TALK TO...
SHFF
...I SHOULD BE AT THE MANOR, TAKING CARE OF THAT LITTLE PROBLEM IN THE CELLARS.
YOU TOLD ME YOU COULD GET ME INTO THE LIBRARY OF ANCESTORS—
THAT'S THE ONLY REASON I AGREED TO THIS FOOLISH "BLESSING."
SOON—I PROMISE YOU.

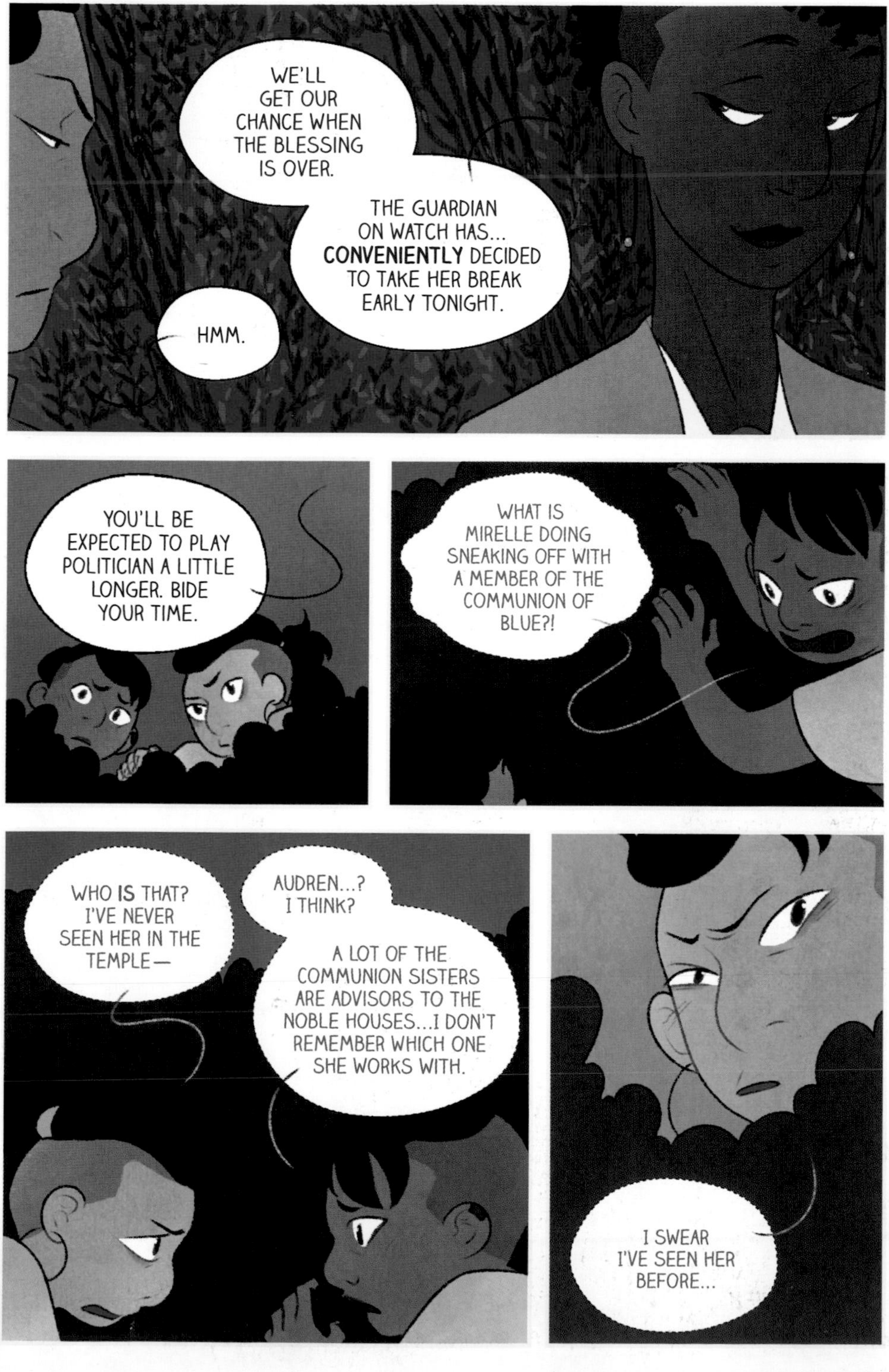
WE'LL GET OUR CHANCE WHEN THE BLESSING IS OVER.
THE GUARDIAN ON WATCH HAS... **CONVENIENTLY** DECIDED TO TAKE HER BREAK EARLY TONIGHT.
HMM.
YOU'LL BE EXPECTED TO PLAY POLITICIAN A LITTLE LONGER. BIDE YOUR TIME.
WHAT IS MIRELLE DOING SNEAKING OFF WITH A MEMBER OF THE COMMUNION OF BLUE?!
WHO **IS** THAT? I'VE NEVER SEEN HER IN THE TEMPLE—
AUDREN...? I THINK?
A LOT OF THE COMMUNION SISTERS ARE ADVISORS TO THE NOBLE HOUSES...I DON'T REMEMBER WHICH ONE SHE WORKS WITH.
I SWEAR I'VE SEEN HER BEFORE...

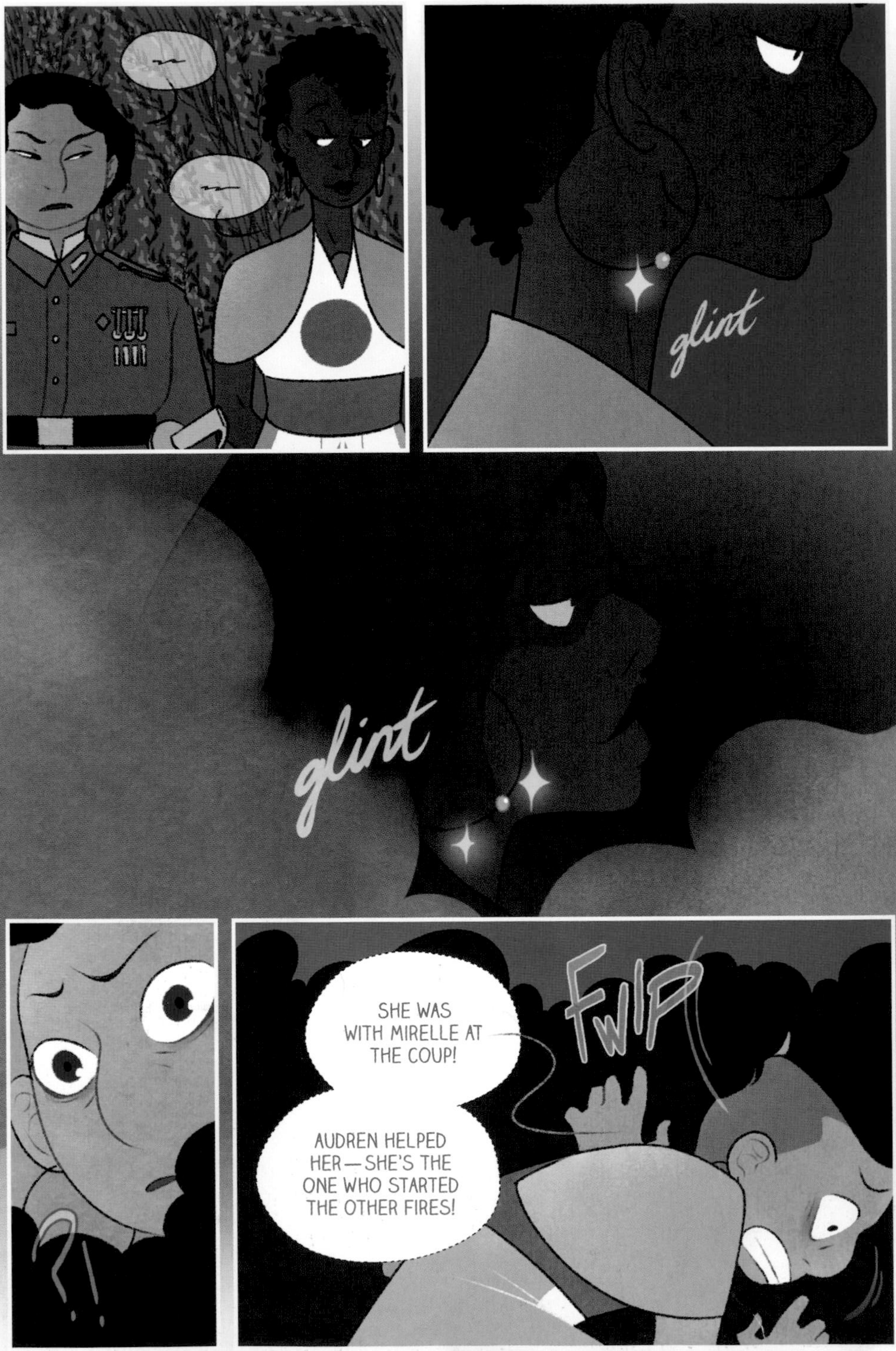
glint
glint
SHE WAS WITH MIRELLE AT THE COUP!
AUDREN HELPED HER—SHE'S THE ONE WHO STARTED THE OTHER FIRES!
FWIP
?!

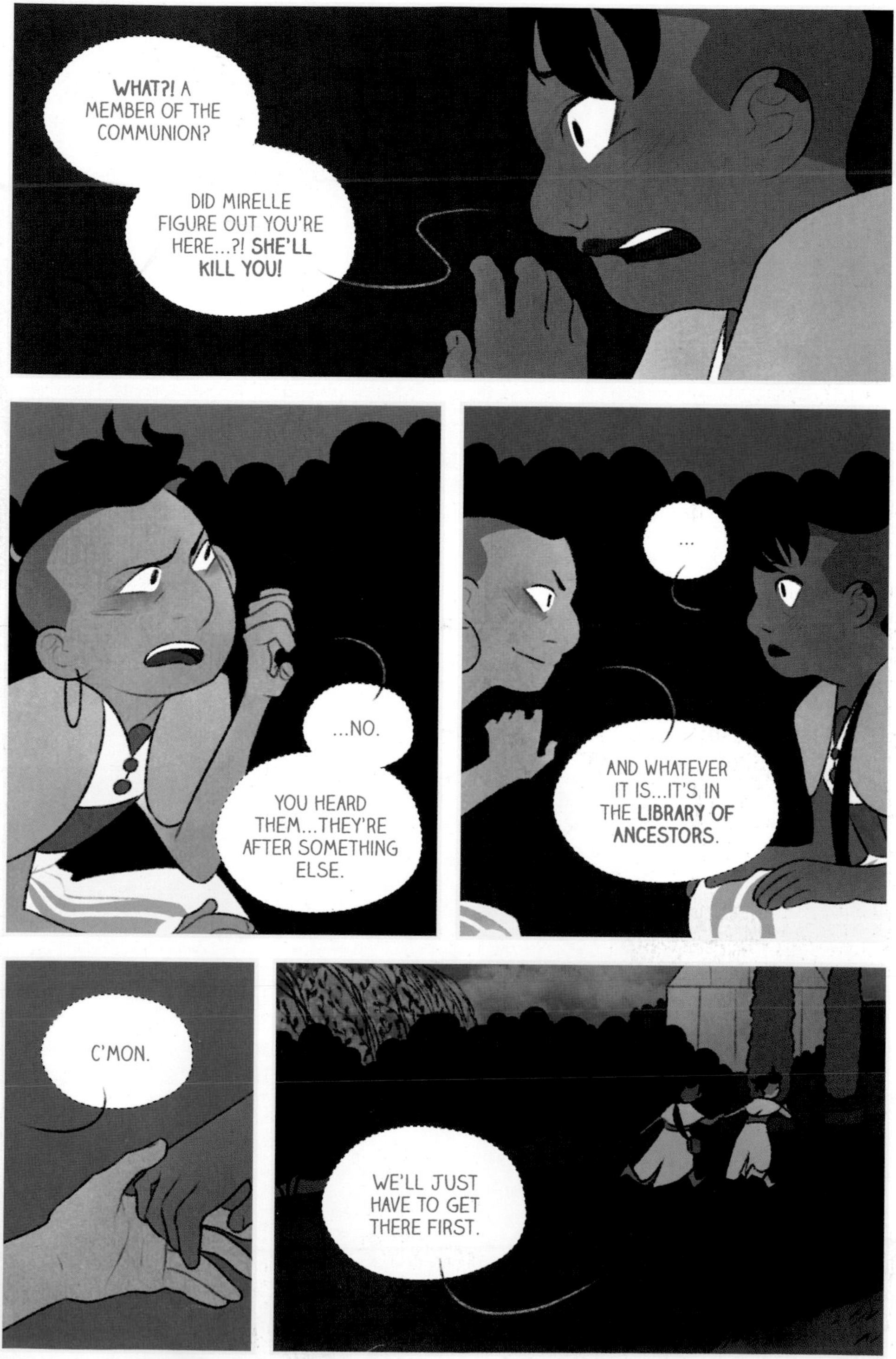
WHAT?! A MEMBER OF THE COMMUNION?
DID MIRELLE FIGURE OUT YOU'RE HERE...?! SHE'LL KILL YOU!
...NO.
YOU HEARD THEM...THEY'RE AFTER SOMETHING ELSE.
...
AND WHATEVER IT IS...IT'S IN THE LIBRARY OF ANCESTORS.
C'MON.
WE'LL JUST HAVE TO GET THERE FIRST.

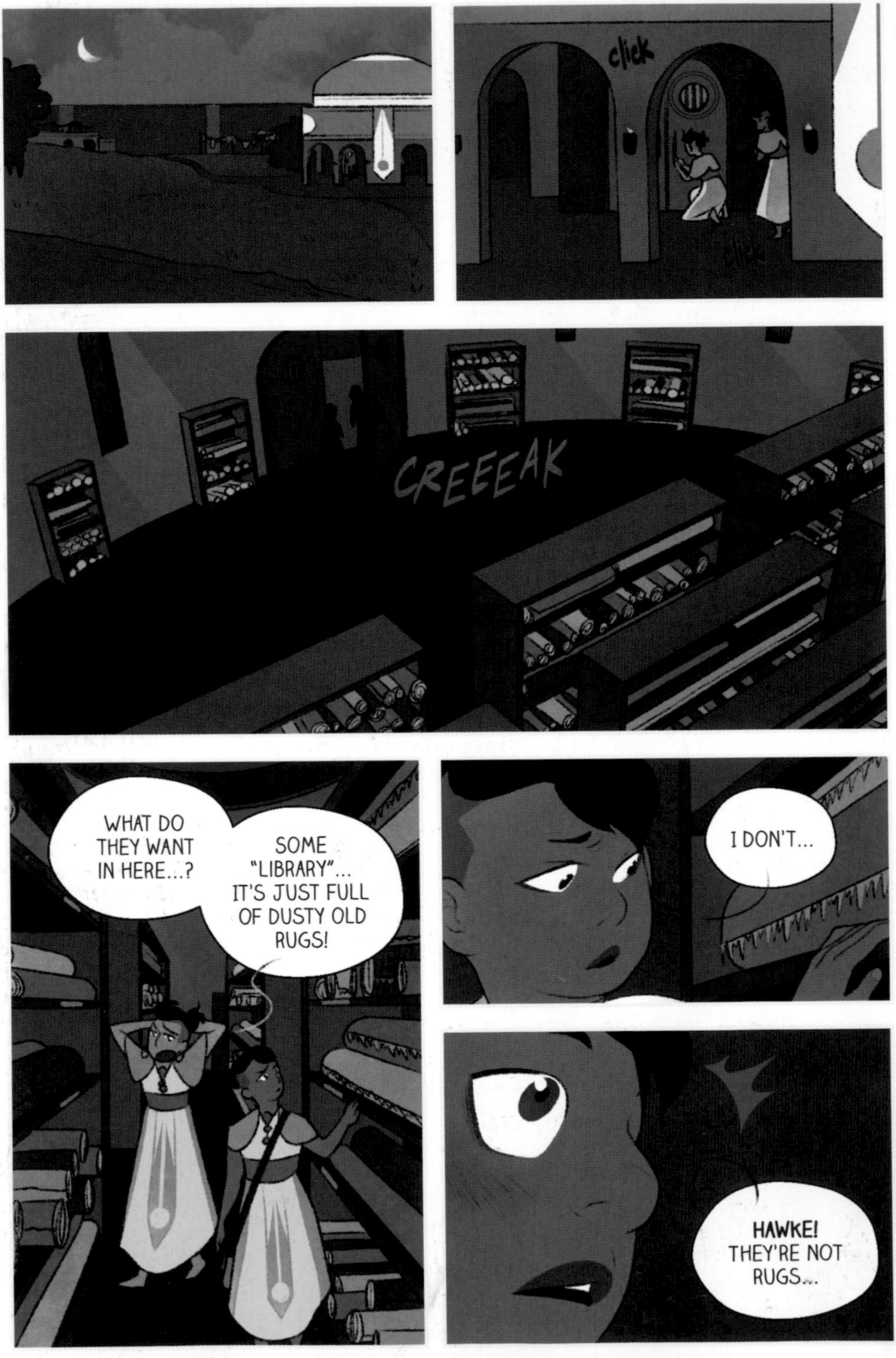
click
click
CREEEAK
WHAT DO THEY WANT IN HERE...?
SOME "LIBRARY"... IT'S JUST FULL OF DUSTY OLD RUGS!
I DON'T...
HAWKE! THEY'RE NOT RUGS...

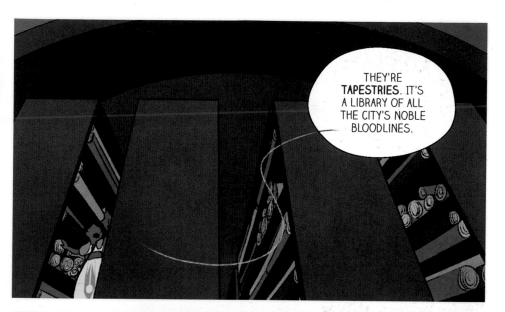

THEY'RE **TAPESTRIES**. IT'S A LIBRARY OF ALL THE CITY'S NOBLE BLOODLINES.

LOOK! THESE TAPESTRIES GO BACK FOR HUNDREDS OF YEARS!

SHFF

BACK BEFORE THE COUNCIL OF LORDS, BEFORE THE CIVIL WAR!

THERE ARE NOBLE FAMILIES HERE THAT DIED OUT **AGES** AGO— THEY'RE ALL HERE! THIS IS INCREDIBLE!

cough

OKAY...THEY'RE A BUNCH OF DUSTY **TAPESTRIES**. WHAT'S THE POINT OF KEEPING THEM LOCKED UP HERE IN THE DARK?

cough

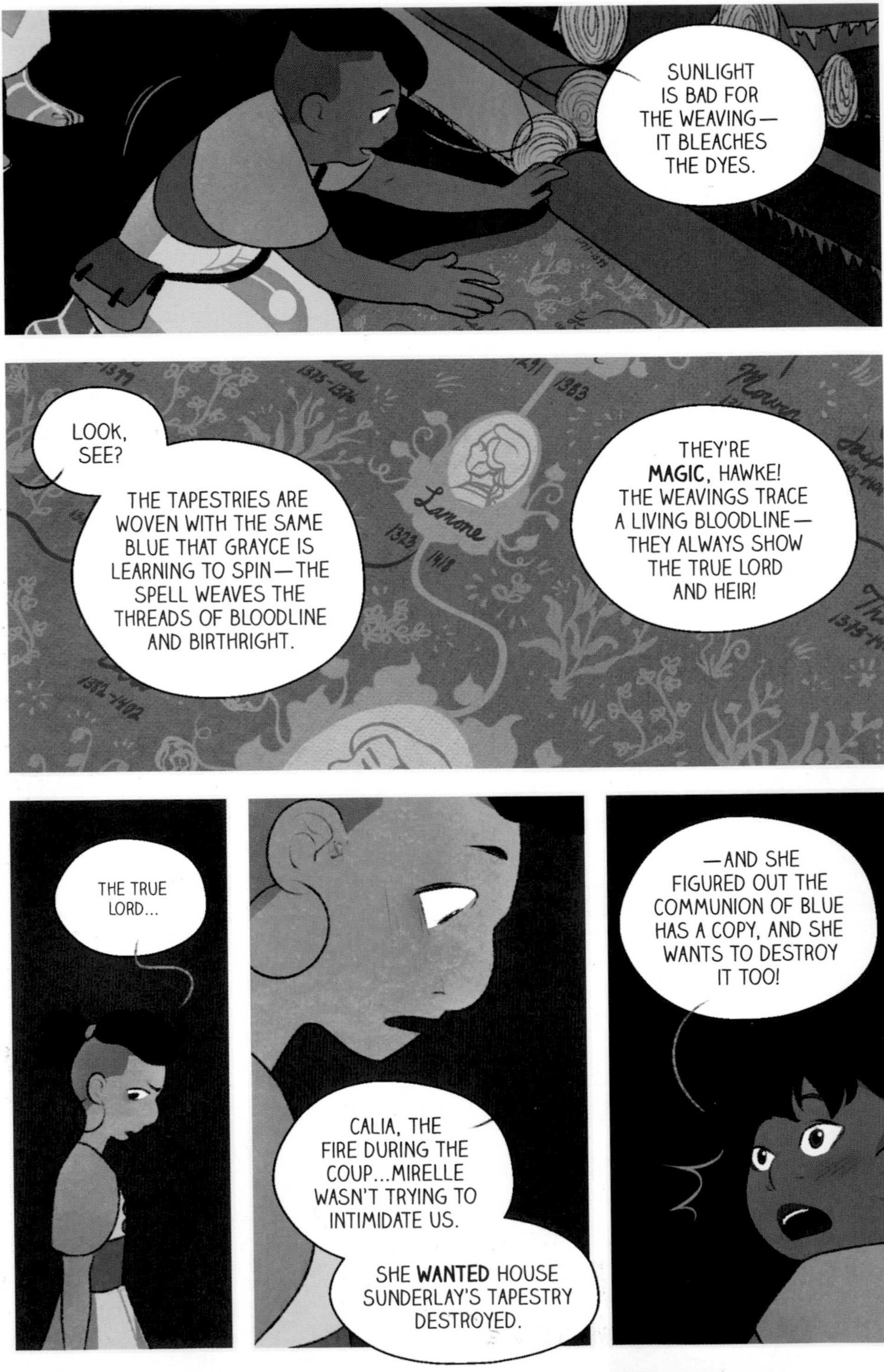
SUNLIGHT IS BAD FOR THE WEAVING—IT BLEACHES THE DYES.
LOOK, SEE?
THE TAPESTRIES ARE WOVEN WITH THE SAME BLUE THAT GRAYCE IS LEARNING TO SPIN—THE SPELL WEAVES THE THREADS OF BLOODLINE AND BIRTHRIGHT.
THEY'RE **MAGIC**, HAWKE! THE WEAVINGS TRACE A LIVING BLOODLINE—THEY ALWAYS SHOW THE TRUE LORD AND HEIR!
THE TRUE LORD...
CALIA, THE FIRE DURING THE COUP...MIRELLE WASN'T TRYING TO INTIMIDATE US.
SHE **WANTED** HOUSE SUNDERLAY'S TAPESTRY DESTROYED.
—AND SHE FIGURED OUT THE COMMUNION OF BLUE HAS A COPY, AND SHE WANTS TO DESTROY IT TOO!

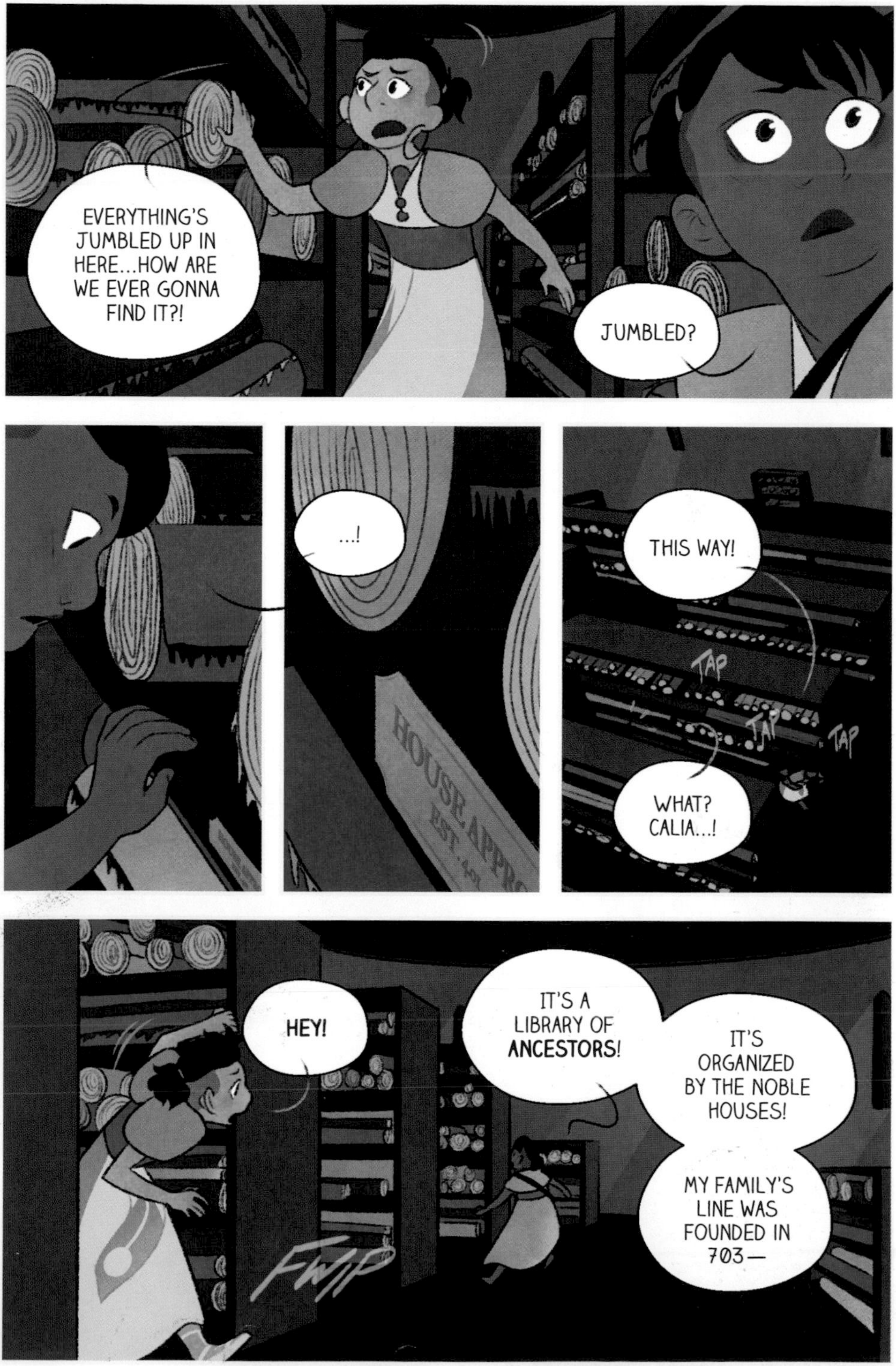
EVERYTHING'S JUMBLED UP IN HERE...HOW ARE WE EVER GONNA FIND IT?!
JUMBLED?
...!
THIS WAY!
TAP
TAP
TAP
WHAT? CALIA...!
HEY!
IT'S A LIBRARY OF **ANCESTORS**!
IT'S ORGANIZED BY THE NOBLE HOUSES!
MY FAMILY'S LINE WAS FOUNDED IN 703—
FWIP

YOURS WAS TWO HUNDRED YEARS LATER. THINGS WERE CHAOTIC FOR A WHILE, AFTER THE FIRST GREAT PLAGUE—
NOT THE PLAGUE WHEN WE WERE LITTLE, THIS ONE WAS **AGES** AGO—
AH, SORRY— YOUR PARENTS... RIGHT...
WELL...WELL, ANYWAY, THE FOUNDING WAS AFTER THE GREAT SPLIT ON THE COUNCIL, I THINK—
IT'S ACTUALLY REALLY FASCINATING.
CALIA...
HERE!
HOUSE SUNDERLAY
...THIS IS IT.
THE TWIN OF THE TAPESTRY BURNED IN THE COUP.

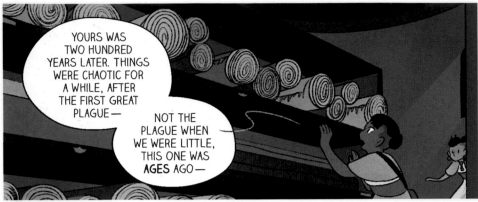

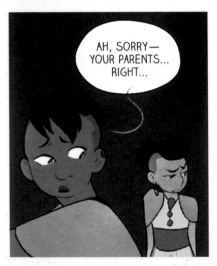

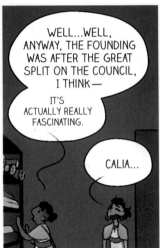

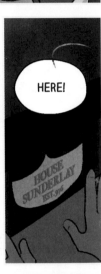

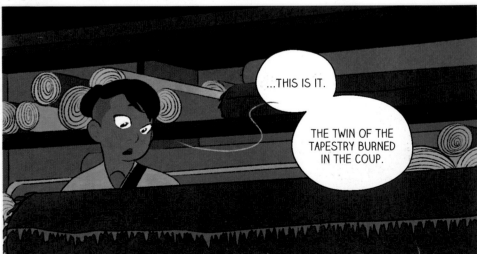

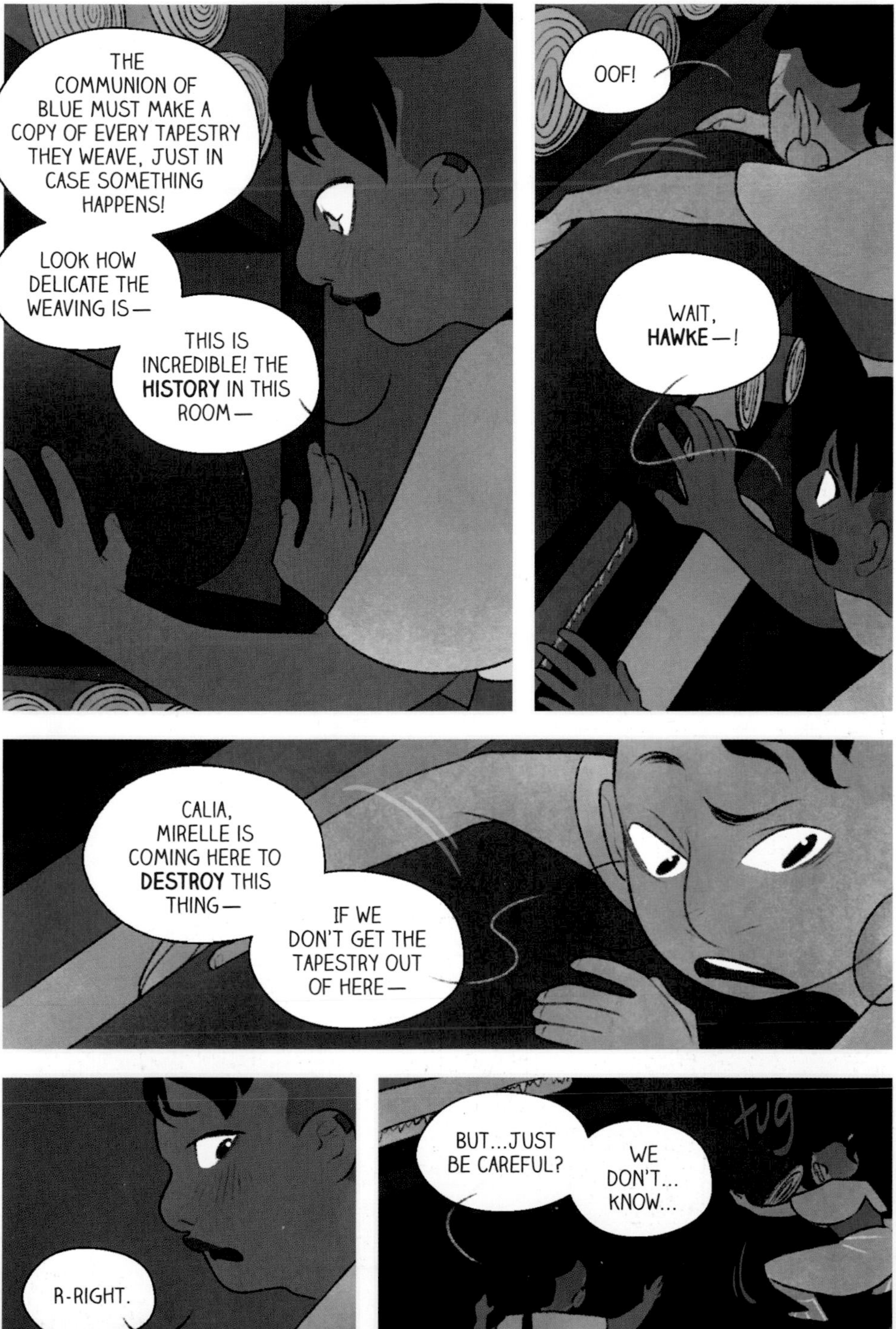
THE COMMUNION OF BLUE MUST MAKE A COPY OF EVERY TAPESTRY THEY WEAVE, JUST IN CASE SOMETHING HAPPENS!
LOOK HOW DELICATE THE WEAVING IS—
THIS IS INCREDIBLE! THE **HISTORY** IN THIS ROOM—
OOF!
WAIT, **HAWKE**—!
CALIA, MIRELLE IS COMING HERE TO **DESTROY** THIS THING—
IF WE DON'T GET THE TAPESTRY OUT OF HERE—
R-RIGHT.
BUT...JUST BE CAREFUL?
WE DON'T... KNOW...
tug

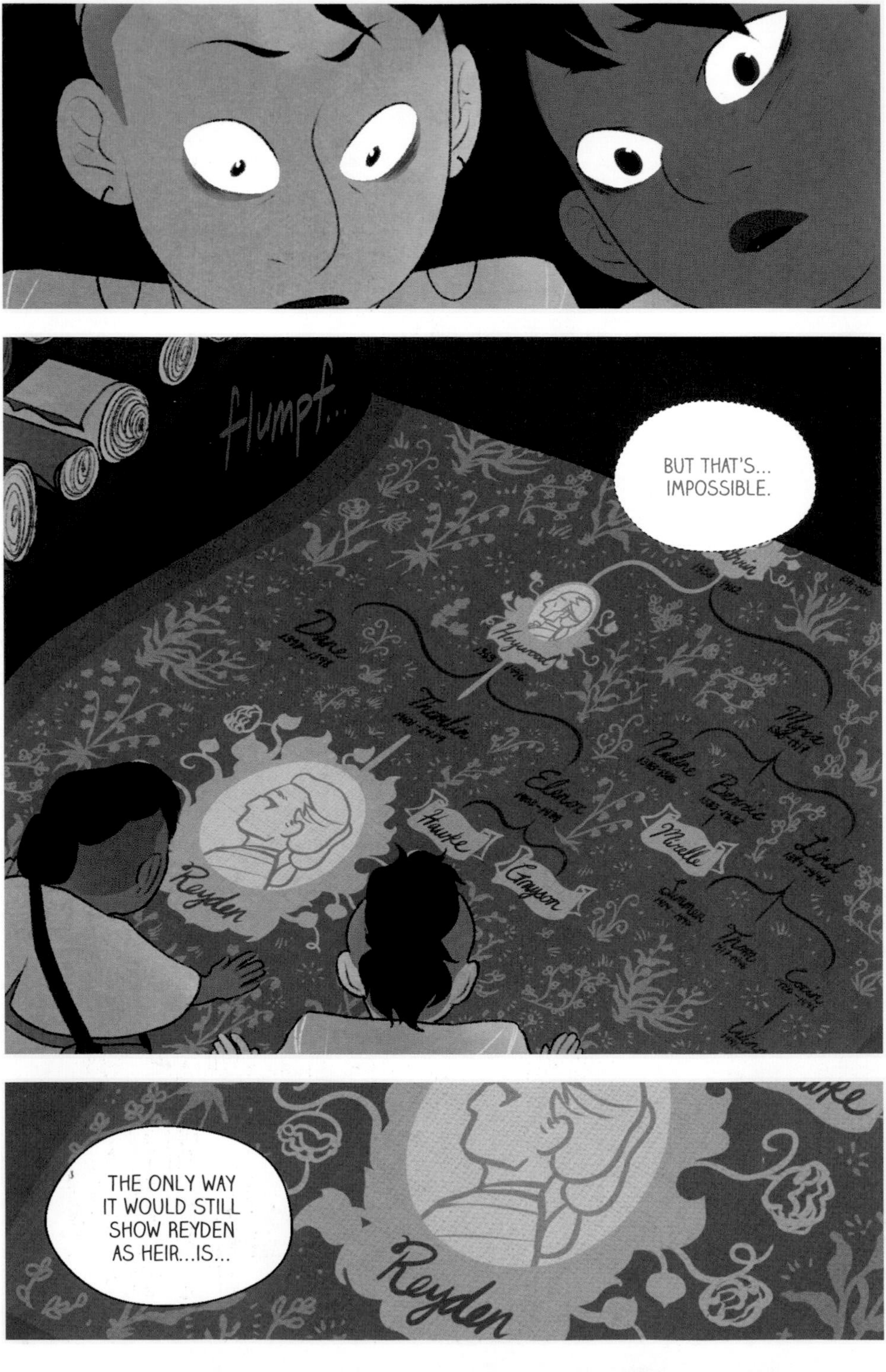
flumpf...
BUT THAT'S... IMPOSSIBLE.
Dane
Heywood
Reyden
Hawke
Grayson
Mirelle
THE ONLY WAY IT WOULD STILL SHOW REYDEN AS HEIR...IS...
Reyden

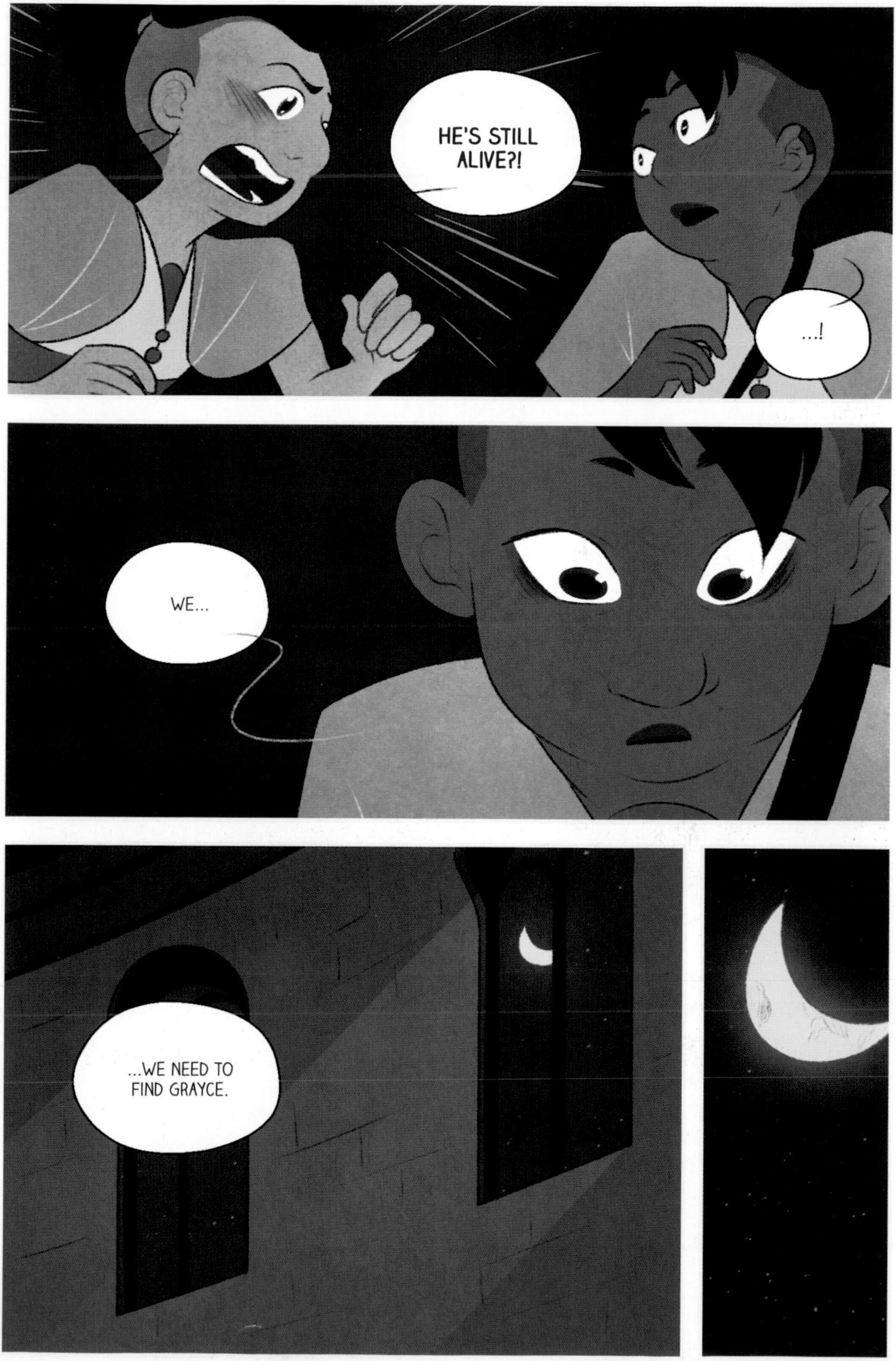

HE'S STILL ALIVE?!
...!
WE...
...WE NEED TO FIND GRAYCE.

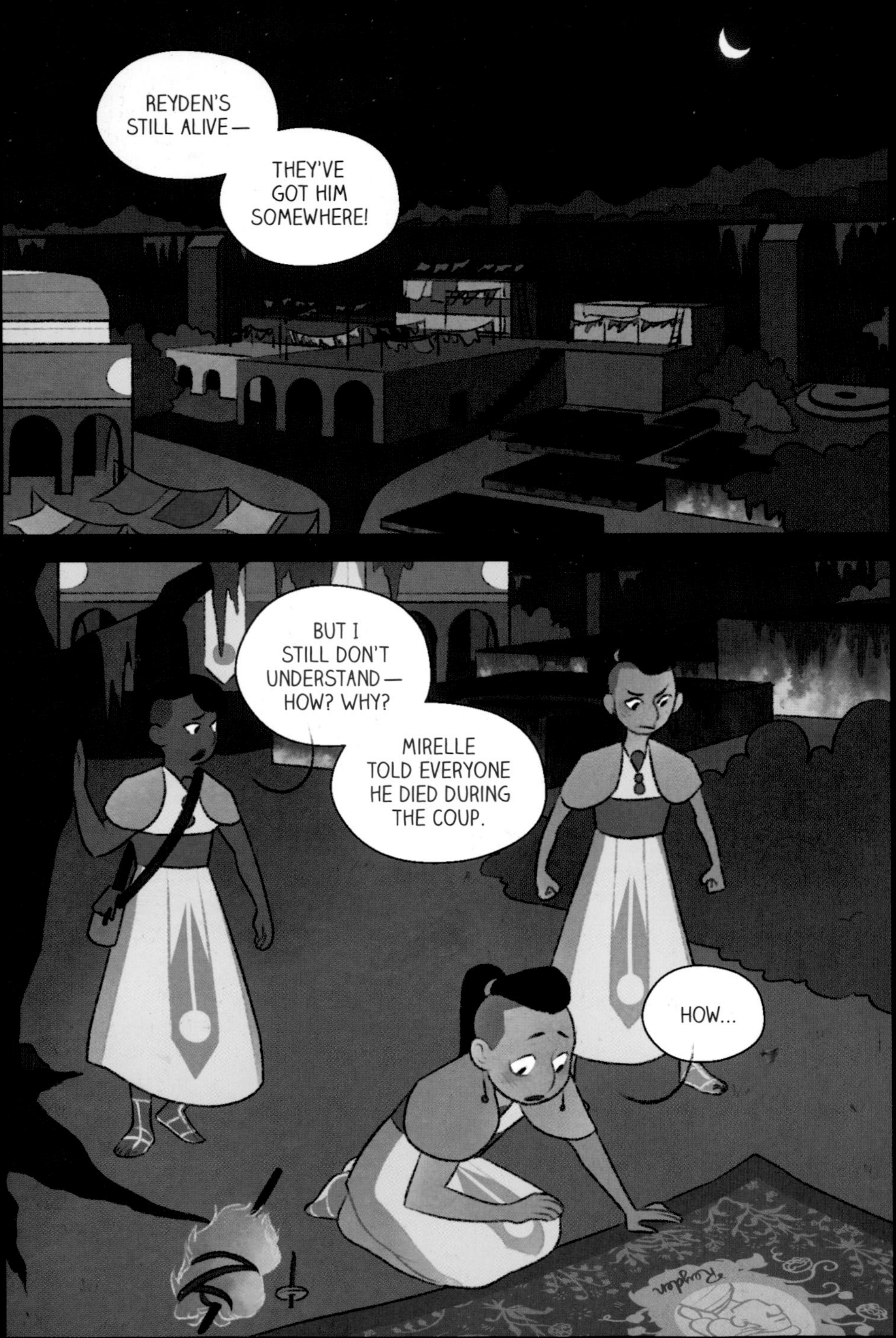
REYDEN'S STILL ALIVE—
THEY'VE GOT HIM SOMEWHERE!
BUT I STILL DON'T UNDERSTAND— HOW? WHY?
MIRELLE TOLD EVERYONE HE DIED DURING THE COUP.
HOW...

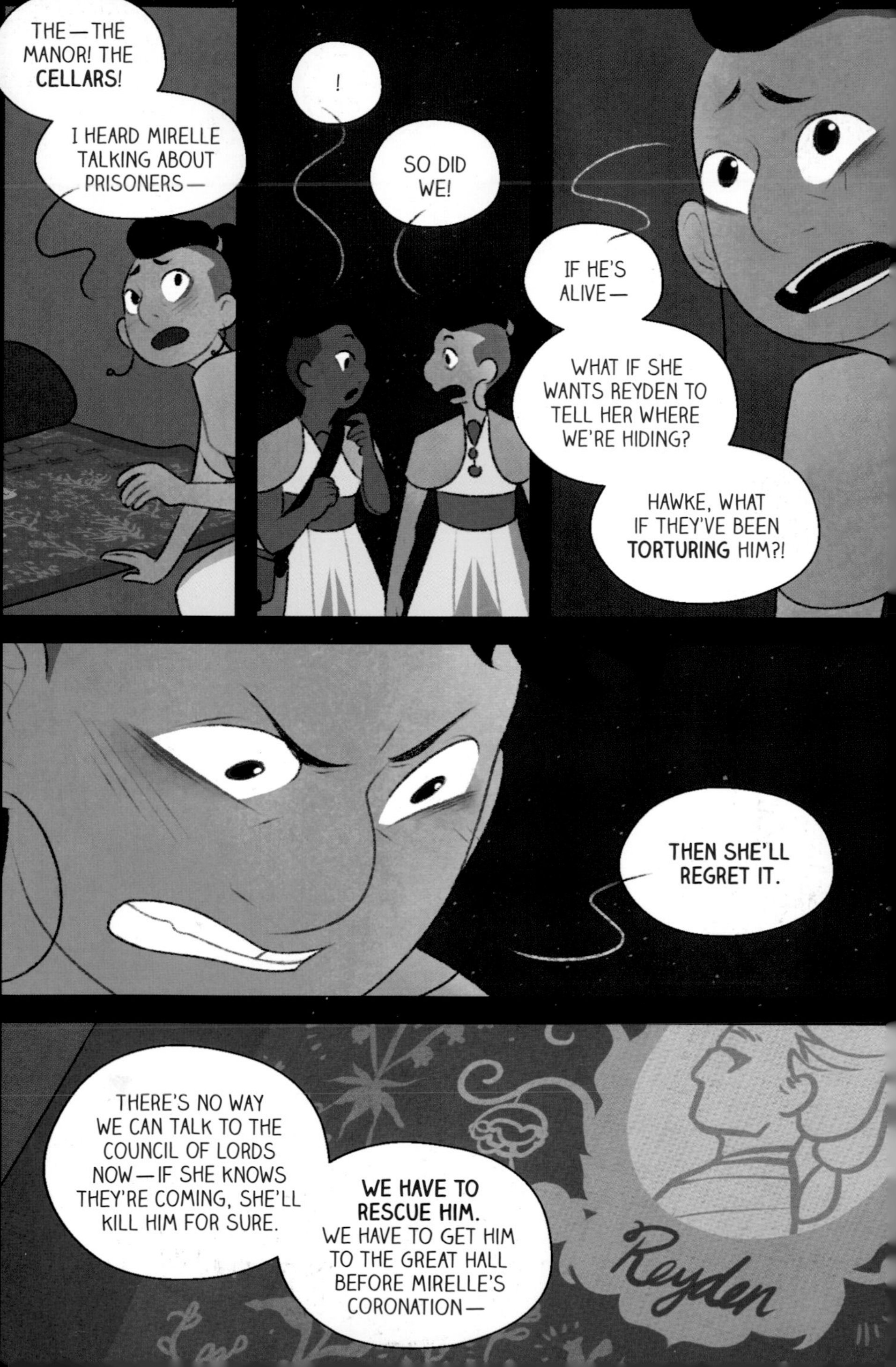
THE—THE MANOR! THE CELLARS!
I HEARD MIRELLE TALKING ABOUT PRISONERS—
!
SO DID WE!
IF HE'S ALIVE—
WHAT IF SHE WANTS REYDEN TO TELL HER WHERE WE'RE HIDING?
HAWKE, WHAT IF THEY'VE BEEN TORTURING HIM?!
THEN SHE'LL REGRET IT.
THERE'S NO WAY WE CAN TALK TO THE COUNCIL OF LORDS NOW—IF SHE KNOWS THEY'RE COMING, SHE'LL KILL HIM FOR SURE.
WE HAVE TO RESCUE HIM. WE HAVE TO GET HIM TO THE GREAT HALL BEFORE MIRELLE'S CORONATION—
Reyden

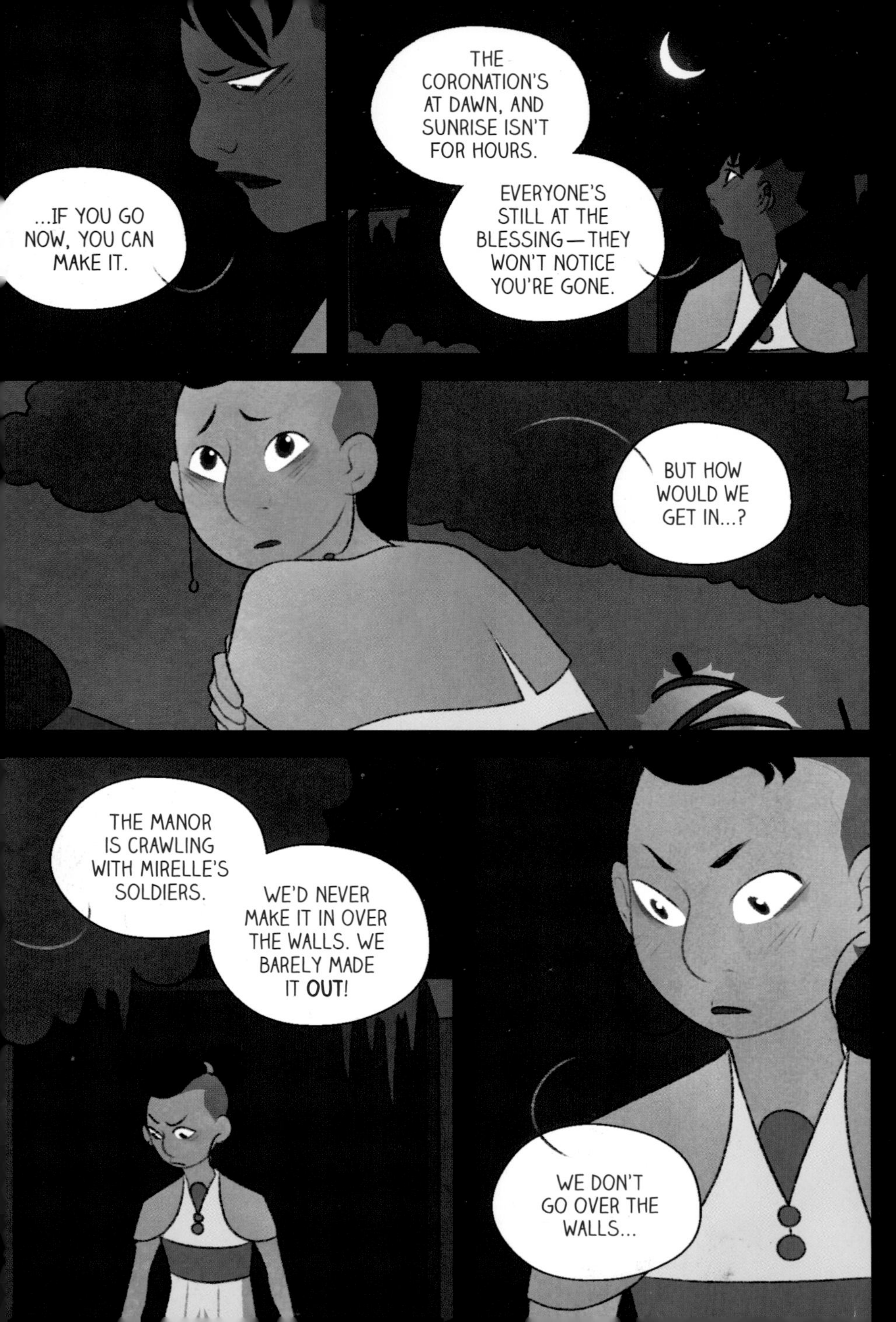
...IF YOU GO NOW, YOU CAN MAKE IT.
THE CORONATION'S AT DAWN, AND SUNRISE ISN'T FOR HOURS.
EVERYONE'S STILL AT THE BLESSING—THEY WON'T NOTICE YOU'RE GONE.
BUT HOW WOULD WE GET IN...?
THE MANOR IS CRAWLING WITH MIRELLE'S SOLDIERS.
WE'D NEVER MAKE IT IN OVER THE WALLS. WE BARELY MADE IT **OUT**!
WE DON'T GO OVER THE WALLS...

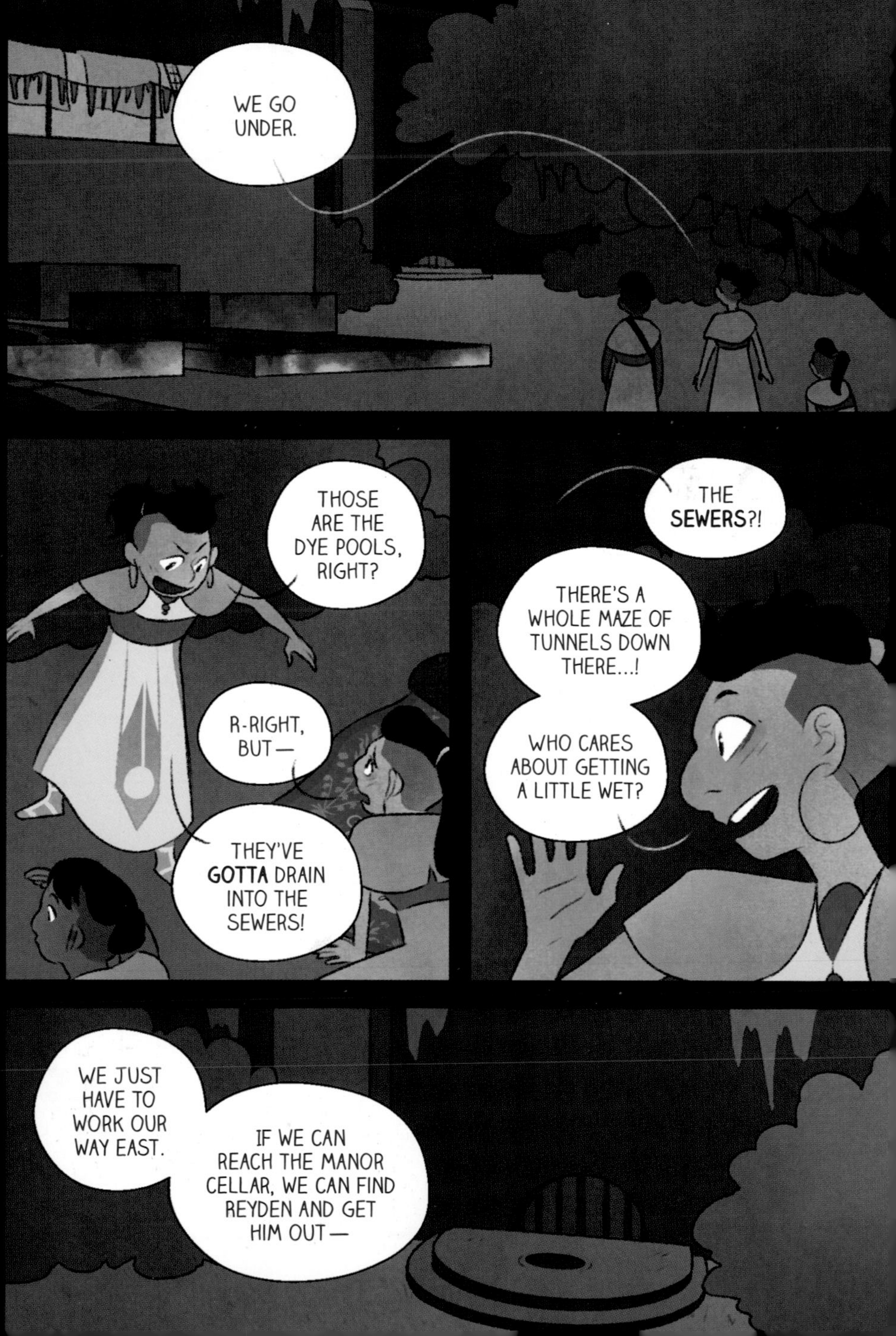
WE GO UNDER.
THOSE ARE THE DYE POOLS, RIGHT?
R-RIGHT, BUT—
THEY'VE **GOTTA** DRAIN INTO THE SEWERS!
THE **SEWERS**?!
THERE'S A WHOLE MAZE OF TUNNELS DOWN THERE...!
WHO CARES ABOUT GETTING A LITTLE WET?
WE JUST HAVE TO WORK OUR WAY EAST.
IF WE CAN REACH THE MANOR CELLAR, WE CAN FIND REYDEN AND GET HIM OUT—

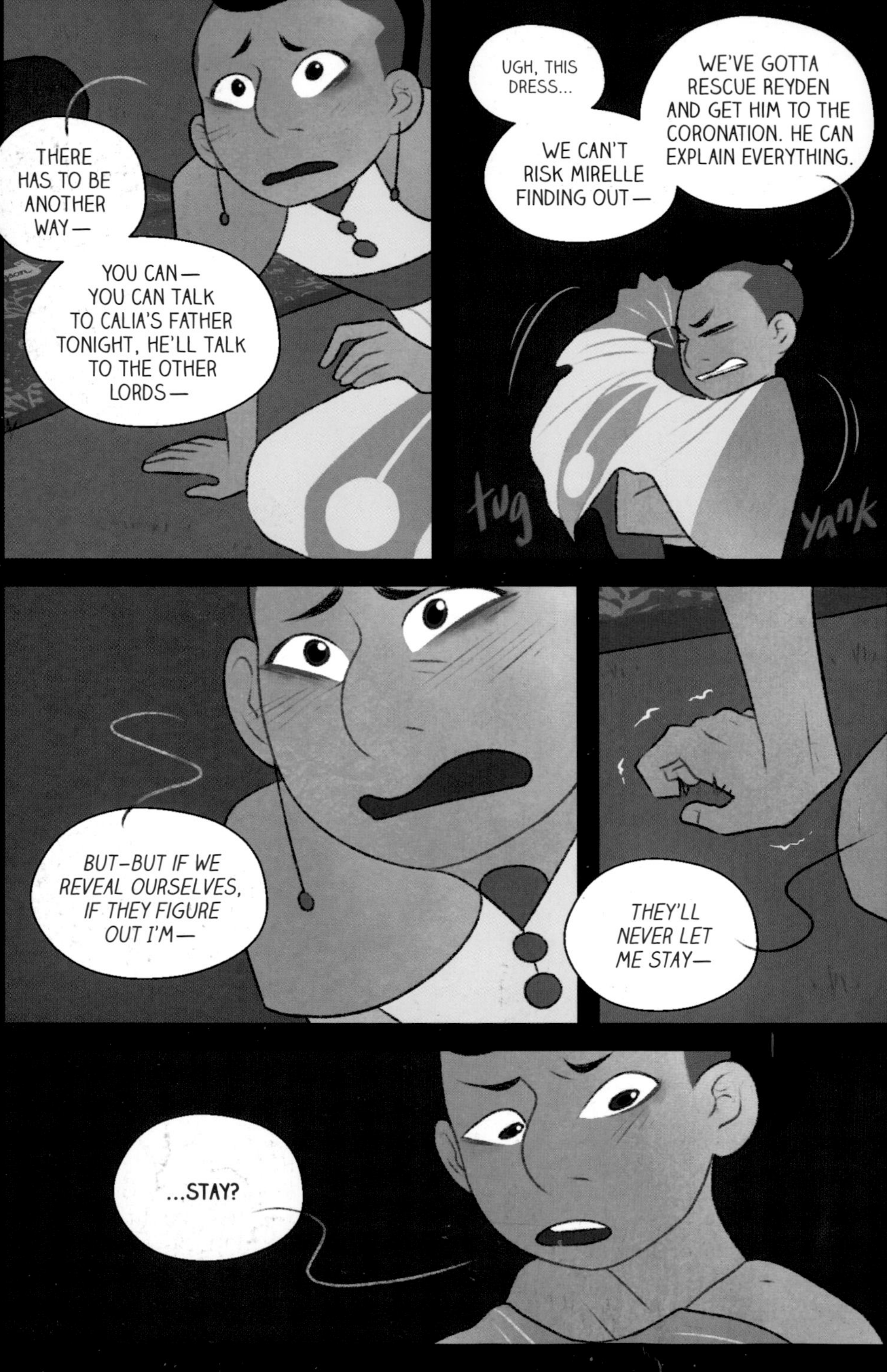
THERE HAS TO BE ANOTHER WAY—
YOU CAN— YOU CAN TALK TO CALIA'S FATHER TONIGHT, HE'LL TALK TO THE OTHER LORDS—
UGH, THIS DRESS...
WE CAN'T RISK MIRELLE FINDING OUT—
WE'VE GOTTA RESCUE REYDEN AND GET HIM TO THE CORONATION. HE CAN EXPLAIN EVERYTHING.
tug
yank
BUT—BUT IF WE REVEAL OURSELVES, IF THEY FIGURE OUT I'M—
THEY'LL NEVER LET ME STAY—
...STAY?

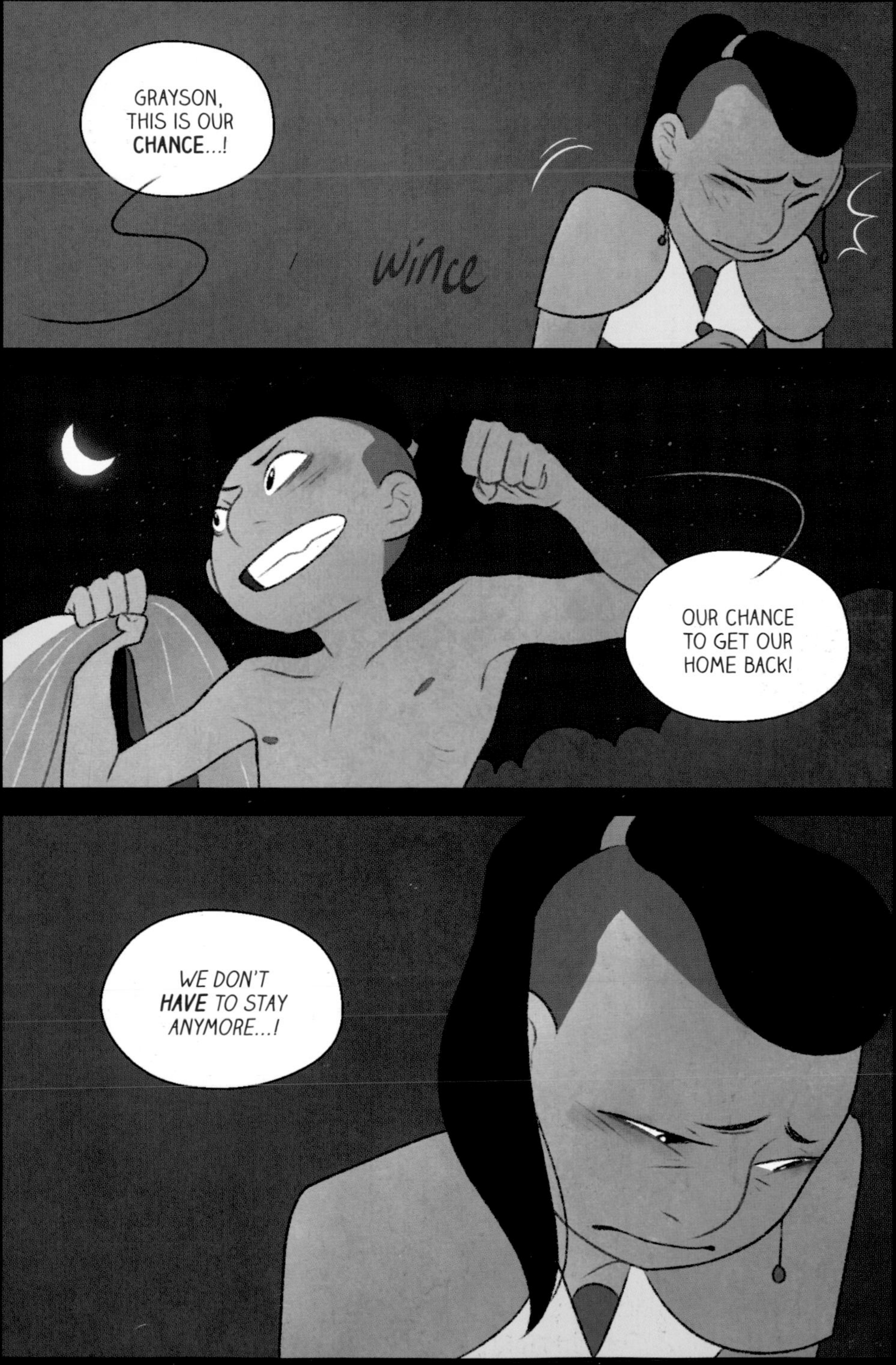
GRAYSON, THIS IS OUR **CHANCE**...!
wince
OUR CHANCE TO GET OUR HOME BACK!
*WE DON'T **HAVE** TO STAY ANYMORE...!*

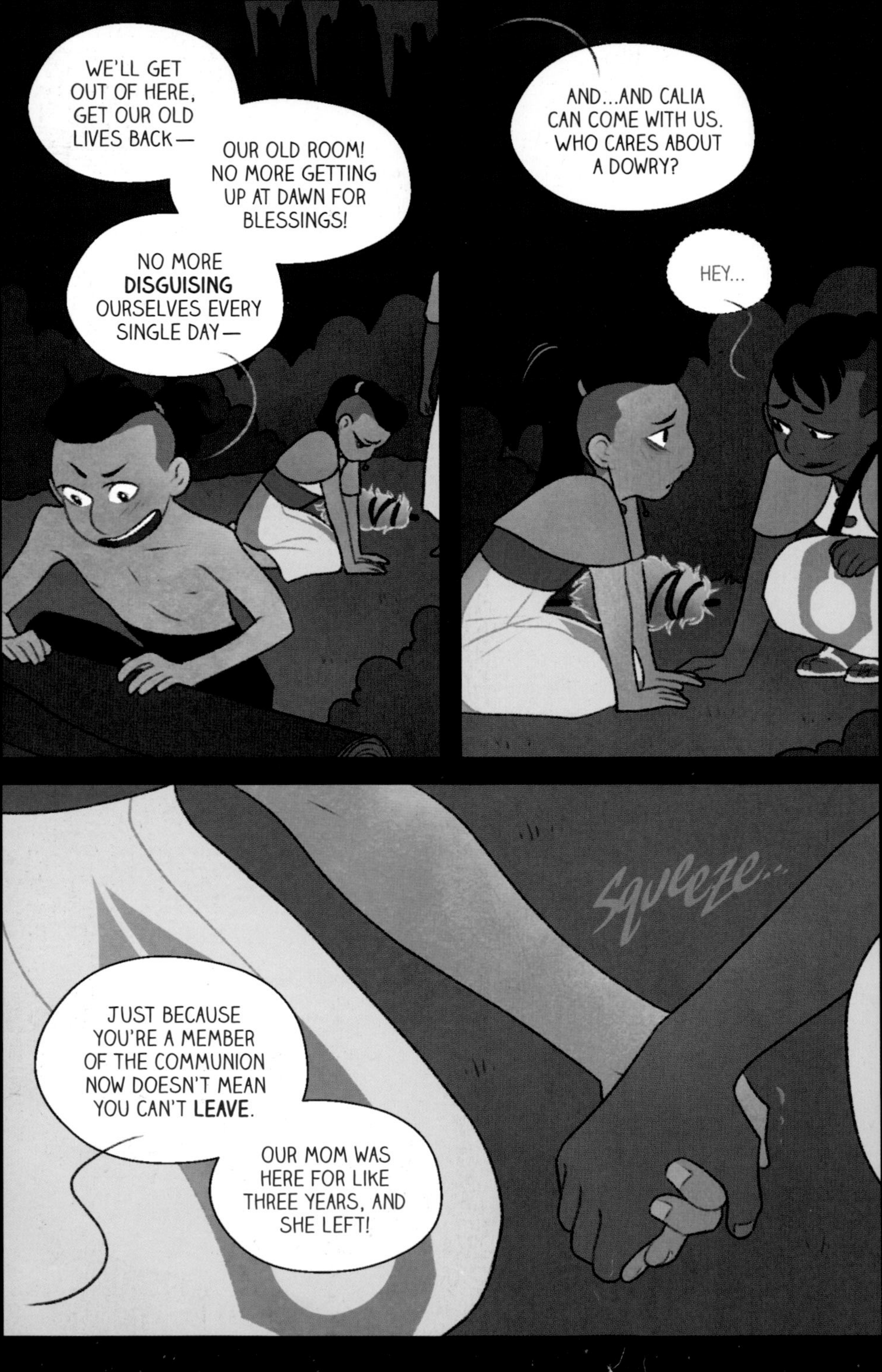

WE'LL GET OUT OF HERE, GET OUR OLD LIVES BACK—
OUR OLD ROOM! NO MORE GETTING UP AT DAWN FOR BLESSINGS!
NO MORE **DISGUISING** OURSELVES EVERY SINGLE DAY—
AND...AND CALIA CAN COME WITH US. WHO CARES ABOUT A DOWRY?
HEY...
SQUEEZE...
JUST BECAUSE YOU'RE A MEMBER OF THE COMMUNION NOW DOESN'T MEAN YOU CAN'T **LEAVE**.
OUR MOM WAS HERE FOR LIKE THREE YEARS, AND SHE LEFT!

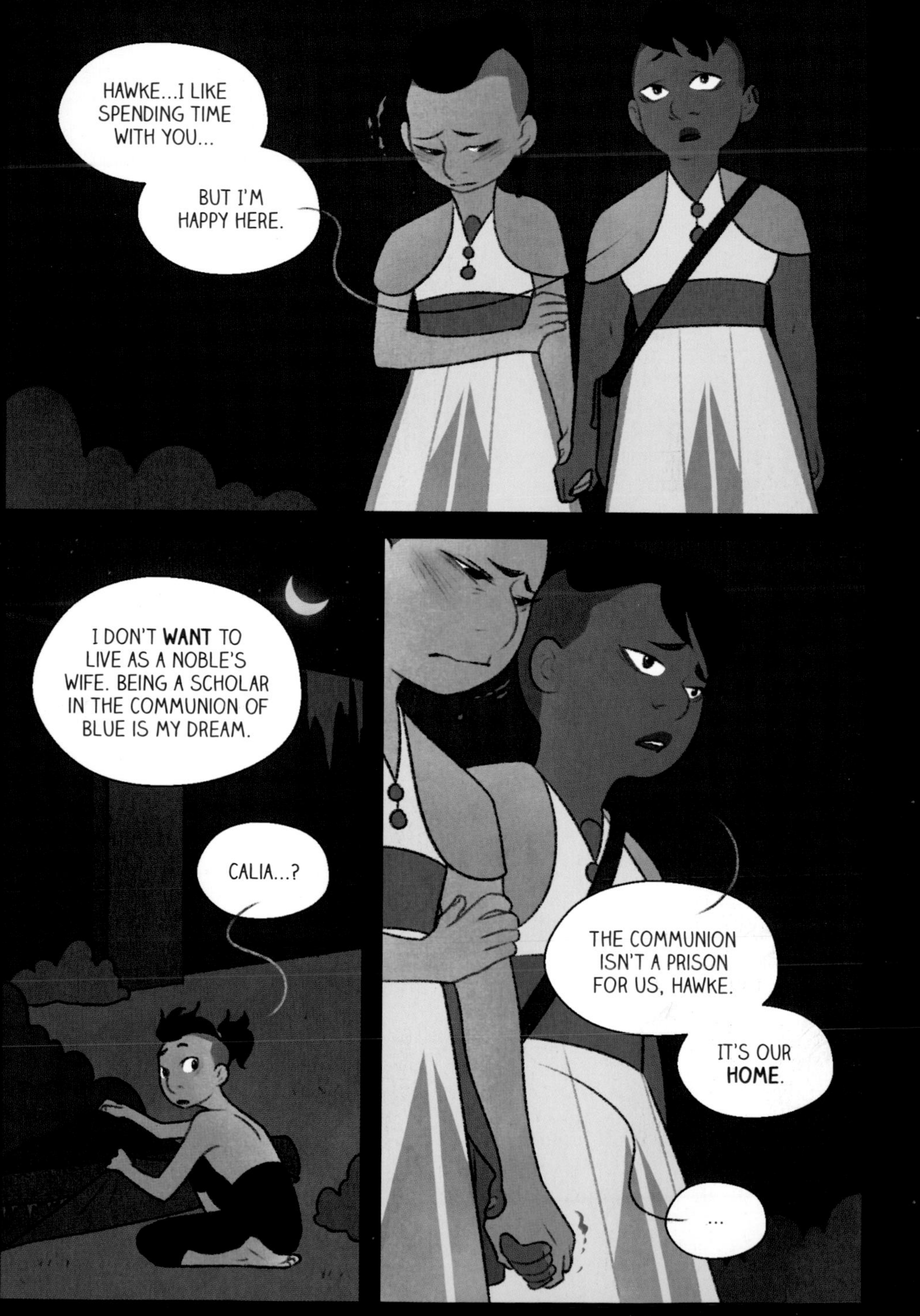
HAWKE...I LIKE SPENDING TIME WITH YOU...
BUT I'M HAPPY HERE.
I DON'T **WANT** TO LIVE AS A NOBLE'S WIFE. BEING A SCHOLAR IN THE COMMUNION OF BLUE IS MY DREAM.
CALIA...?
THE COMMUNION ISN'T A PRISON FOR US, HAWKE.
IT'S OUR **HOME**.
...

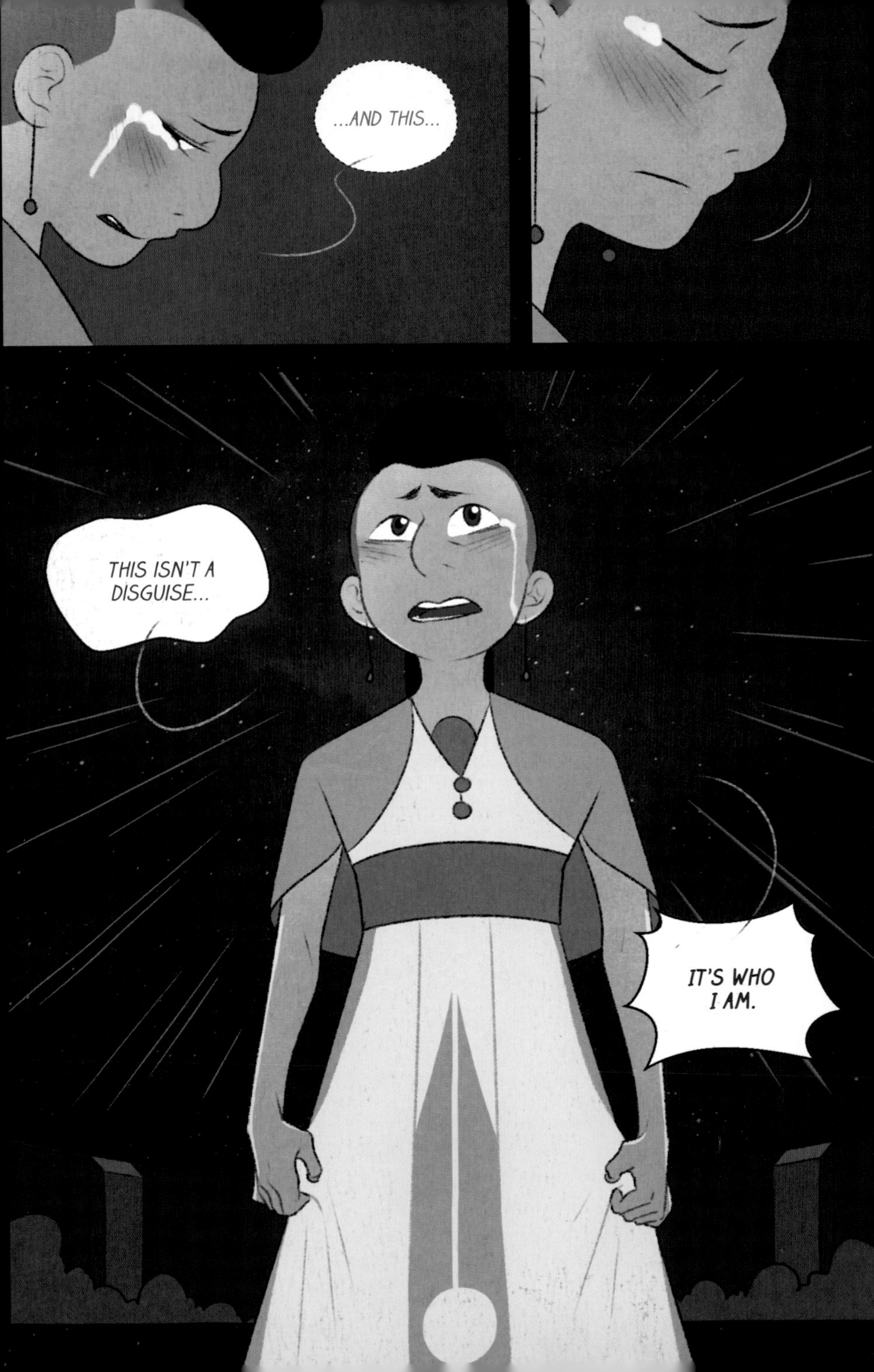
...AND THIS...
THIS ISN'T A DISGUISE...
IT'S WHO I AM.

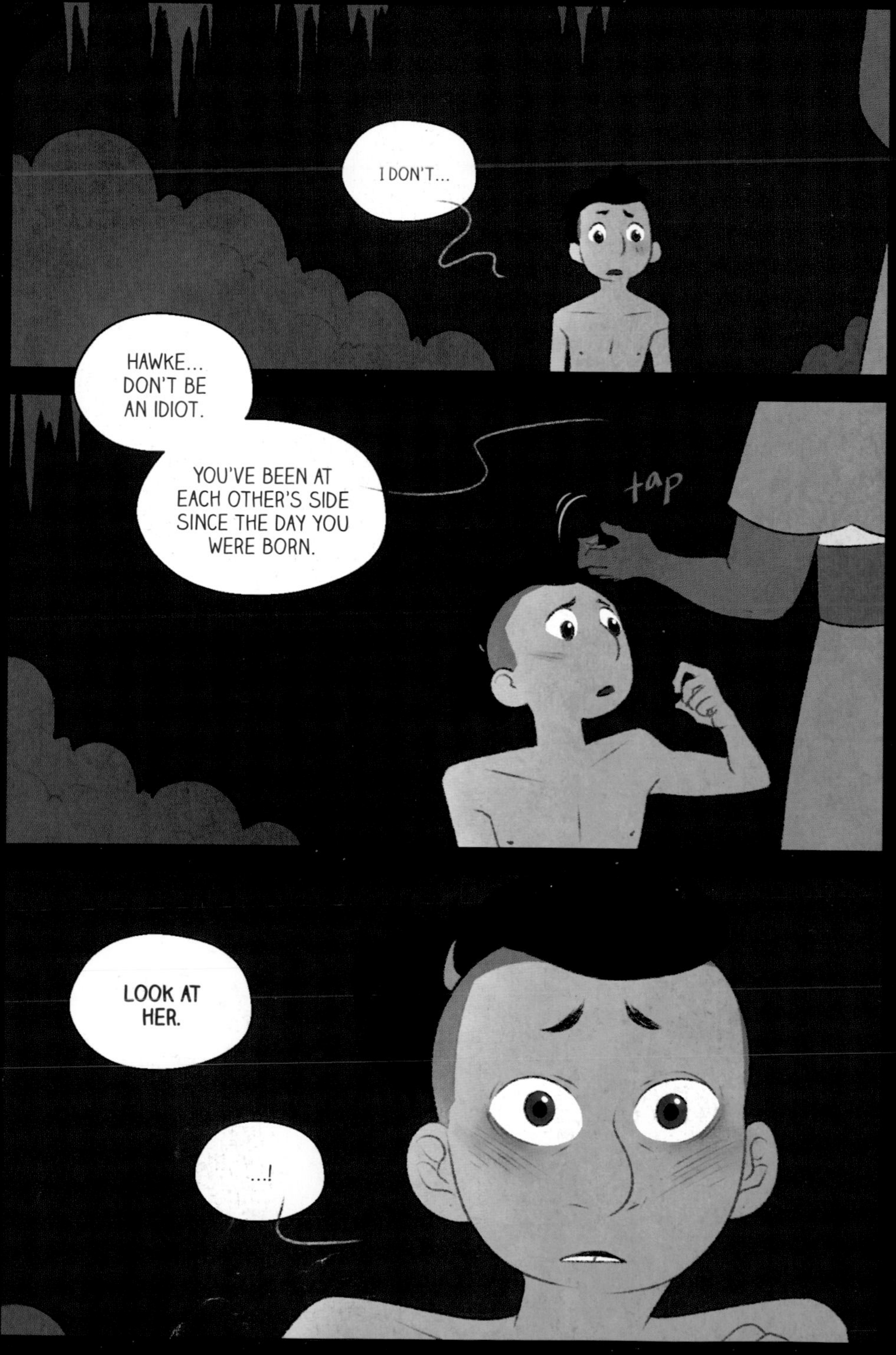
I DON'T...
HAWKE... DON'T BE AN IDIOT.
YOU'VE BEEN AT EACH OTHER'S SIDE SINCE THE DAY YOU WERE BORN.
tap
LOOK AT HER.
...!

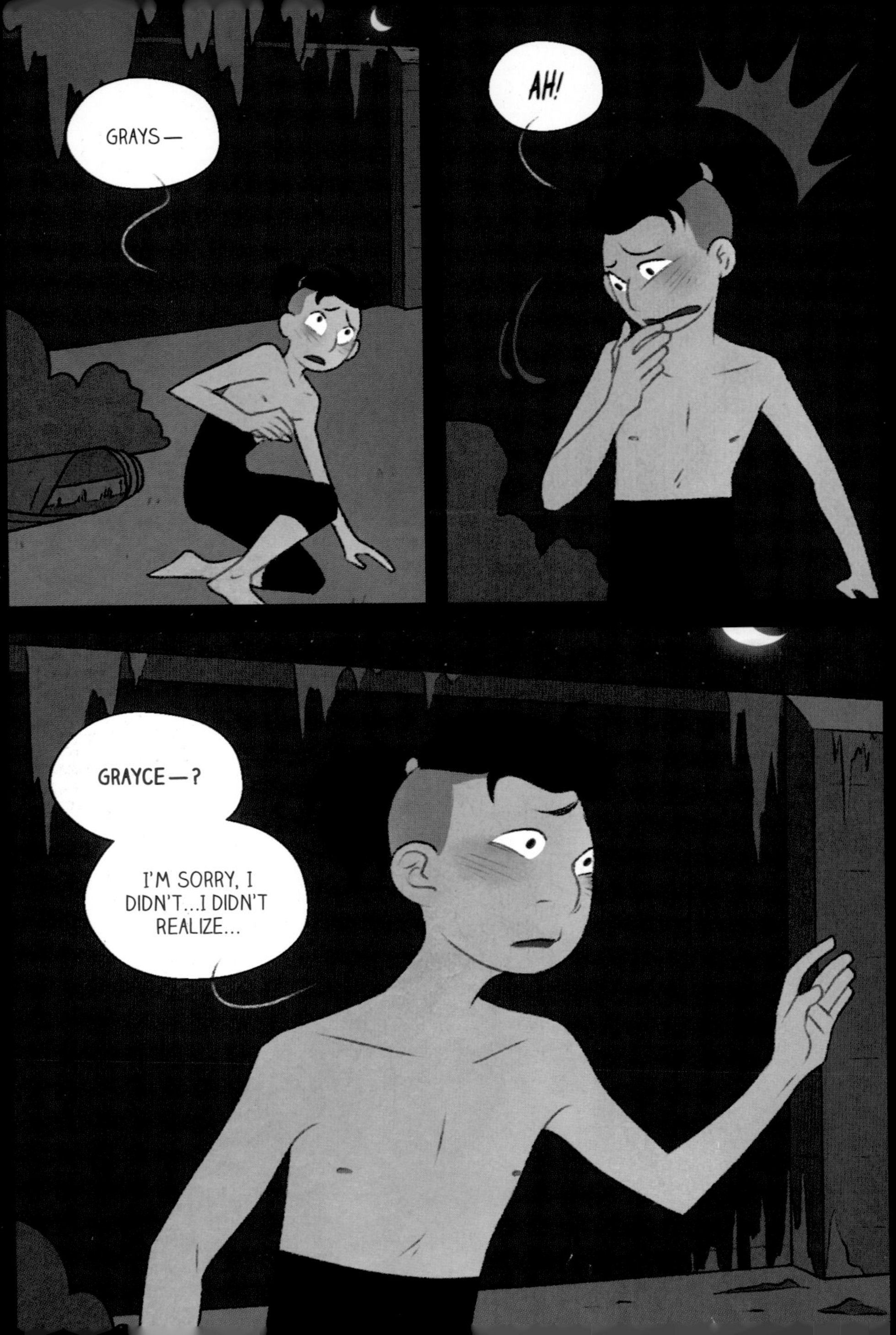
GRAYS—
AH!
GRAYCE—?
I'M SORRY, I DIDN'T...I DIDN'T REALIZE...

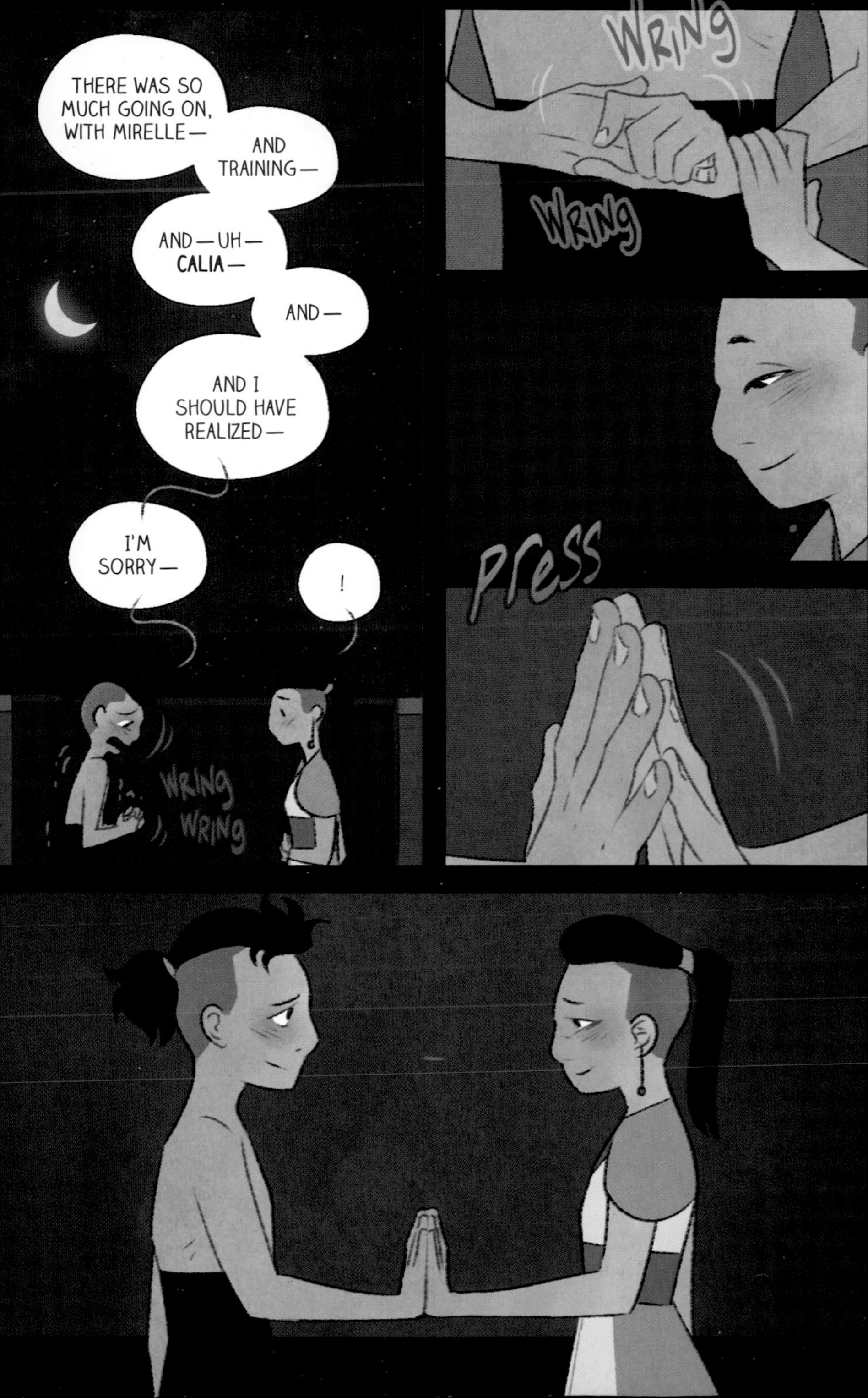

THERE WAS SO MUCH GOING ON, WITH MIRELLE—
AND TRAINING—
AND—UH— **CALIA**—
AND—
AND I SHOULD HAVE REALIZED—
I'M SORRY—
!
WRING WRING
WRING
WRING
PRESS

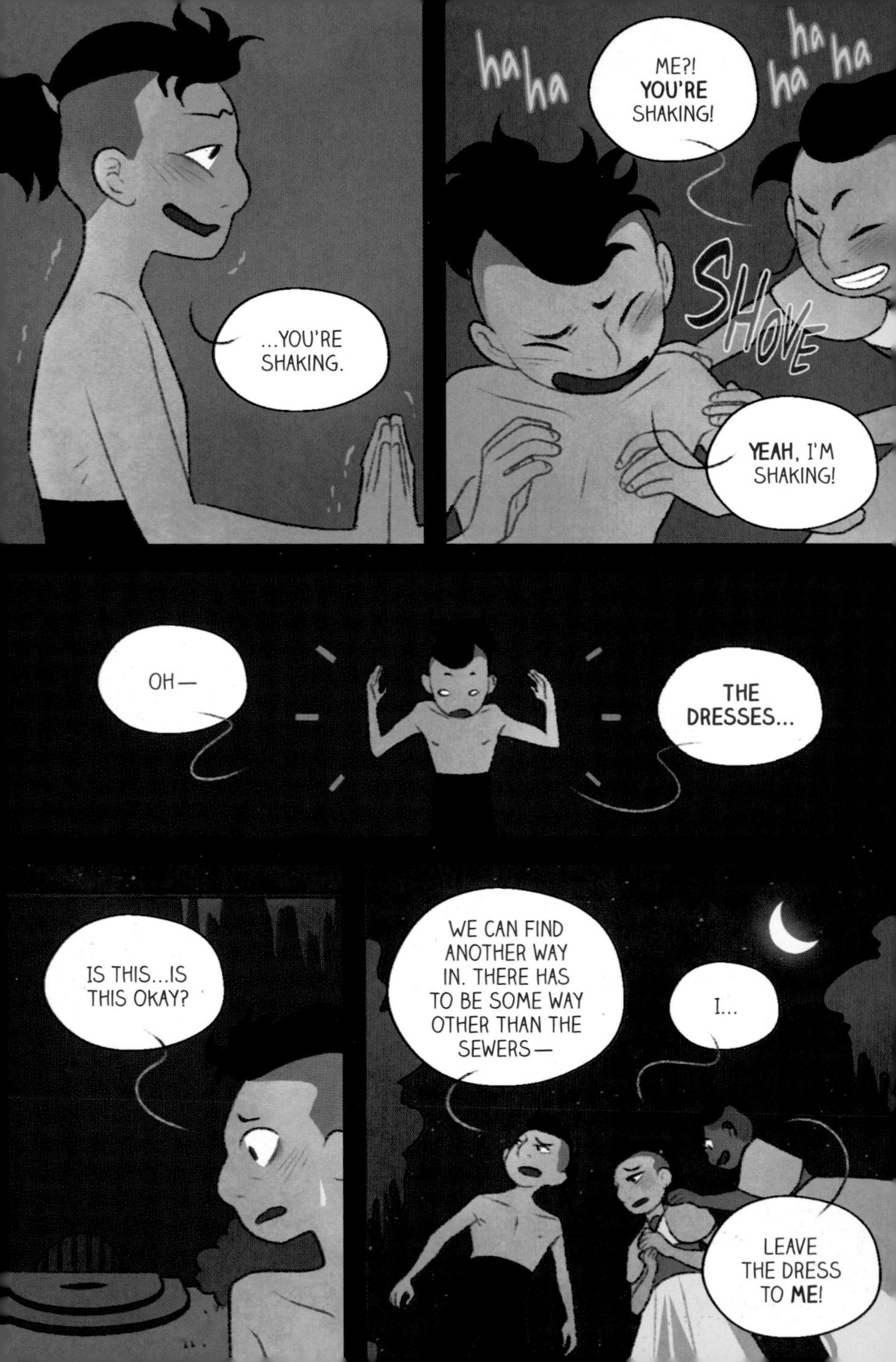
...YOU'RE SHAKING.
ha ha
ME?! YOU'RE SHAKING!
ha ha ha
SHOVE
YEAH, I'M SHAKING!
OH—
THE DRESSES...
IS THIS...IS THIS OKAY?
WE CAN FIND ANOTHER WAY IN. THERE HAS TO BE SOME WAY OTHER THAN THE SEWERS—
I...
LEAVE THE DRESS TO ME!

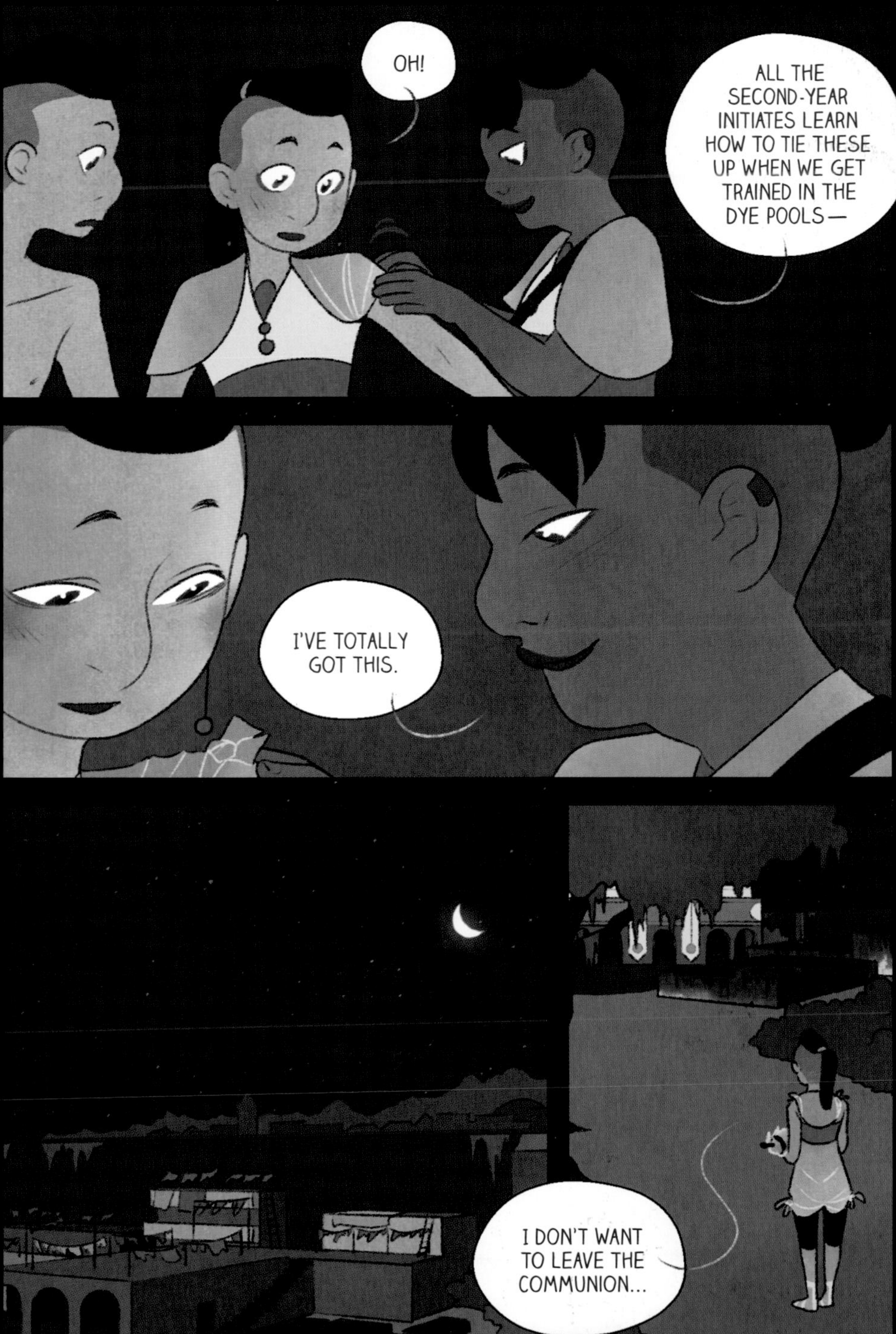
OH!
ALL THE SECOND-YEAR INITIATES LEARN HOW TO TIE THESE UP WHEN WE GET TRAINED IN THE DYE POOLS—
I'VE TOTALLY GOT THIS.
I DON'T WANT TO LEAVE THE COMMUNION...

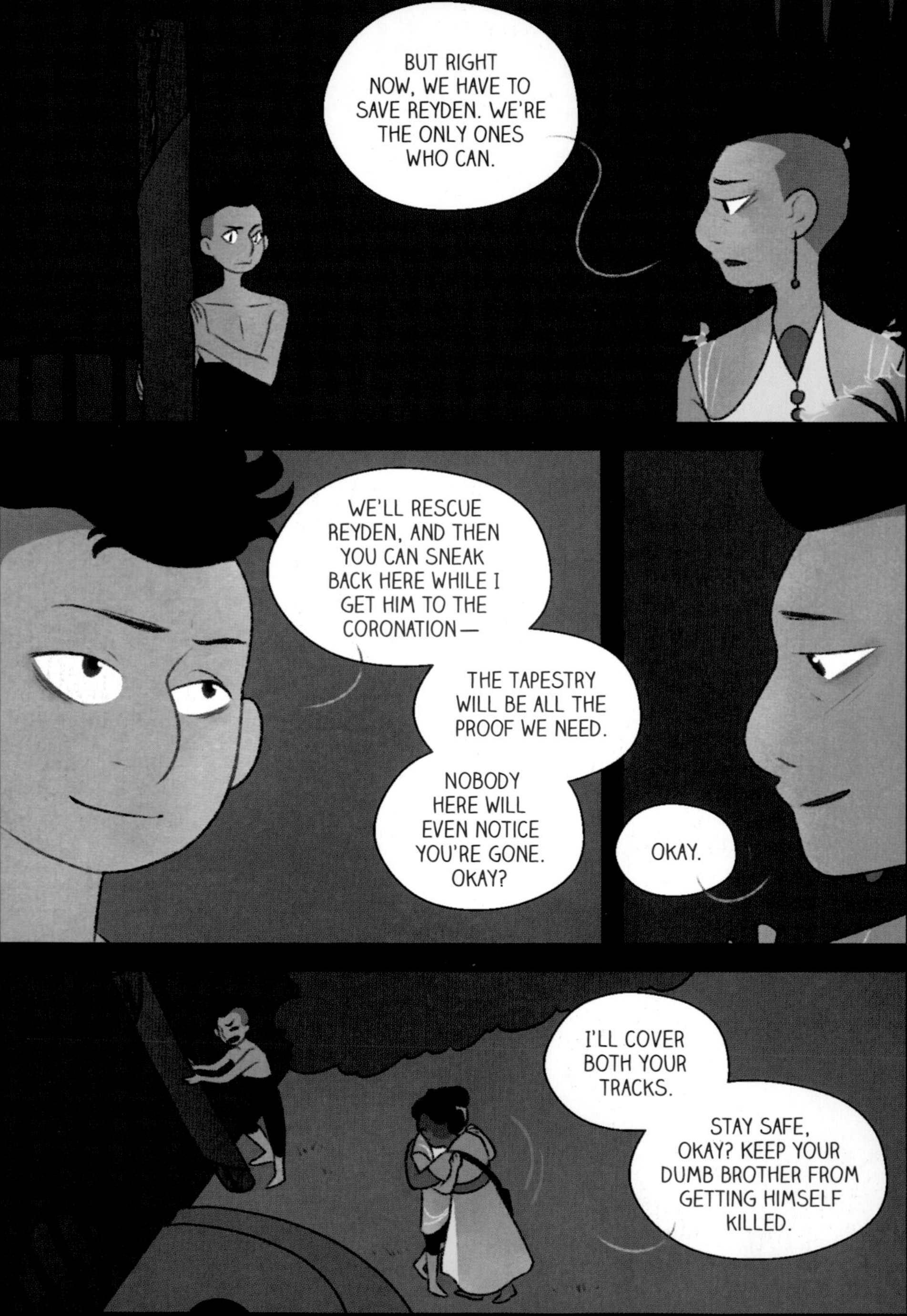
BUT RIGHT NOW, WE HAVE TO SAVE REYDEN. WE'RE THE ONLY ONES WHO CAN.
WE'LL RESCUE REYDEN, AND THEN YOU CAN SNEAK BACK HERE WHILE I GET HIM TO THE CORONATION—
THE TAPESTRY WILL BE ALL THE PROOF WE NEED.
NOBODY HERE WILL EVEN NOTICE YOU'RE GONE. OKAY?
OKAY.
I'LL COVER BOTH YOUR TRACKS.
STAY SAFE, OKAY? KEEP YOUR DUMB BROTHER FROM GETTING HIMSELF KILLED.

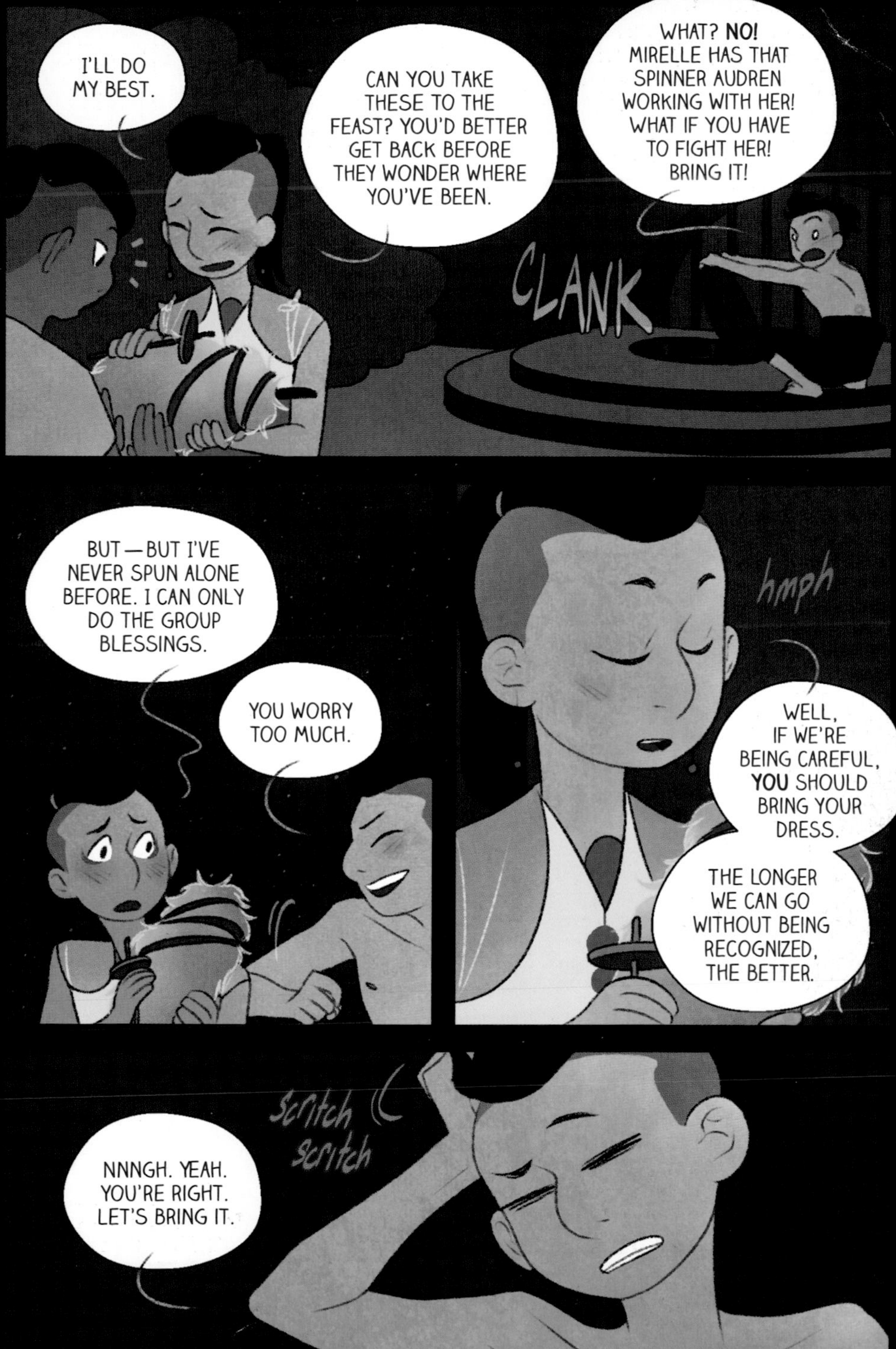
I'LL DO MY BEST.
CAN YOU TAKE THESE TO THE FEAST? YOU'D BETTER GET BACK BEFORE THEY WONDER WHERE YOU'VE BEEN.
WHAT? **NO!** MIRELLE HAS THAT SPINNER AUDREN WORKING WITH HER! WHAT IF YOU HAVE TO FIGHT HER! BRING IT!
CLANK
BUT—BUT I'VE NEVER SPUN ALONE BEFORE. I CAN ONLY DO THE GROUP BLESSINGS.
YOU WORRY TOO MUCH.
hmph
WELL, IF WE'RE BEING CAREFUL, **YOU** SHOULD BRING YOUR DRESS.
THE LONGER WE CAN GO WITHOUT BEING RECOGNIZED, THE BETTER.
scritch scritch
NNNGH. YEAH. YOU'RE RIGHT. LET'S BRING IT.

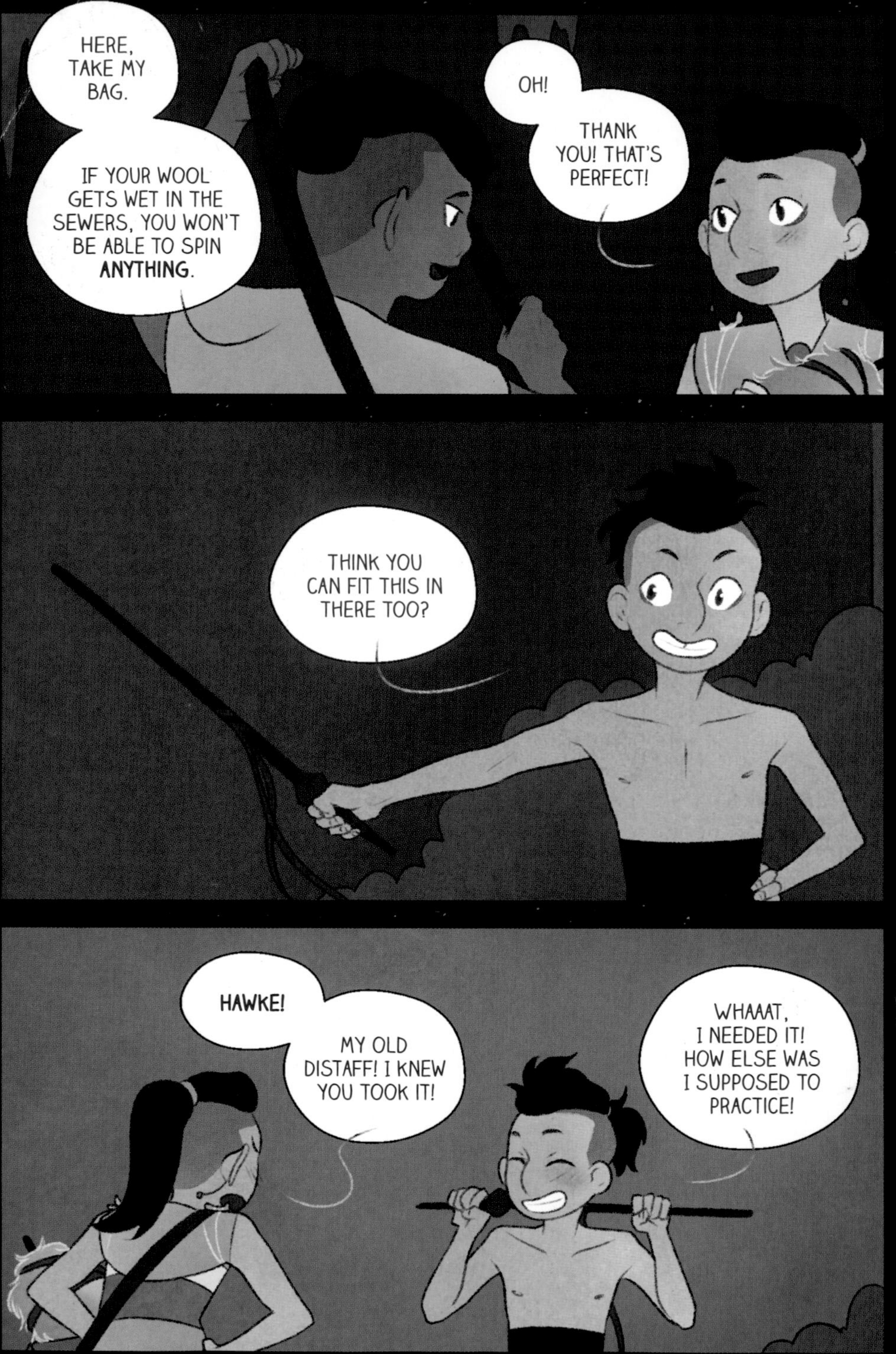
HERE, TAKE MY BAG.
IF YOUR WOOL GETS WET IN THE SEWERS, YOU WON'T BE ABLE TO SPIN **ANYTHING**.
OH!
THANK YOU! THAT'S PERFECT!
THINK YOU CAN FIT THIS IN THERE TOO?
HAWKE!
MY OLD DISTAFF! I KNEW YOU TOOK IT!
WHAAAT, I NEEDED IT! HOW ELSE WAS I SUPPOSED TO PRACTICE!

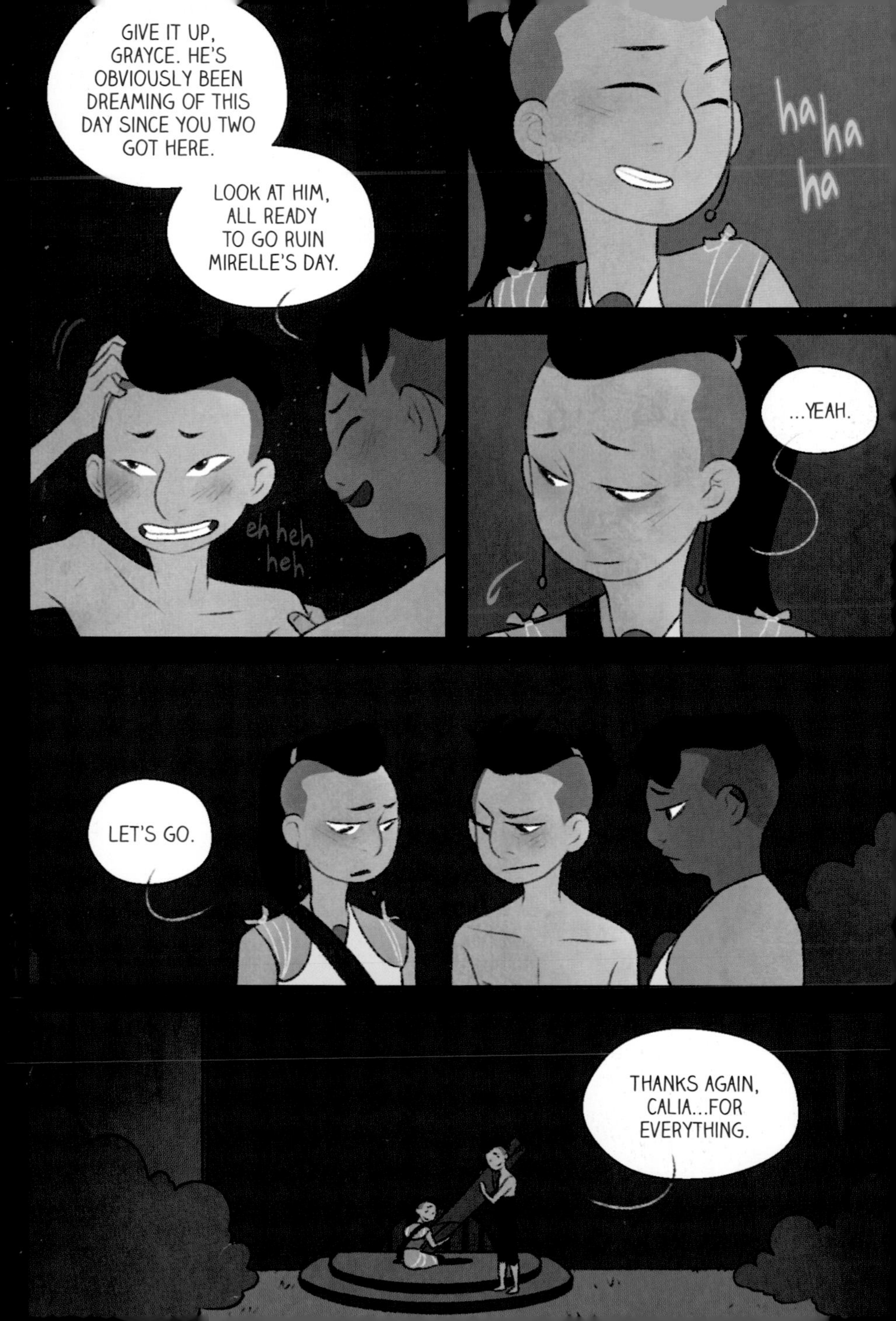
GIVE IT UP, GRAYCE. HE'S OBVIOUSLY BEEN DREAMING OF THIS DAY SINCE YOU TWO GOT HERE.
LOOK AT HIM, ALL READY TO GO RUIN MIRELLE'S DAY.
ha ha ha
eh heh heh
...YEAH.
LET'S GO.
THANKS AGAIN, CALIA...FOR EVERYTHING.

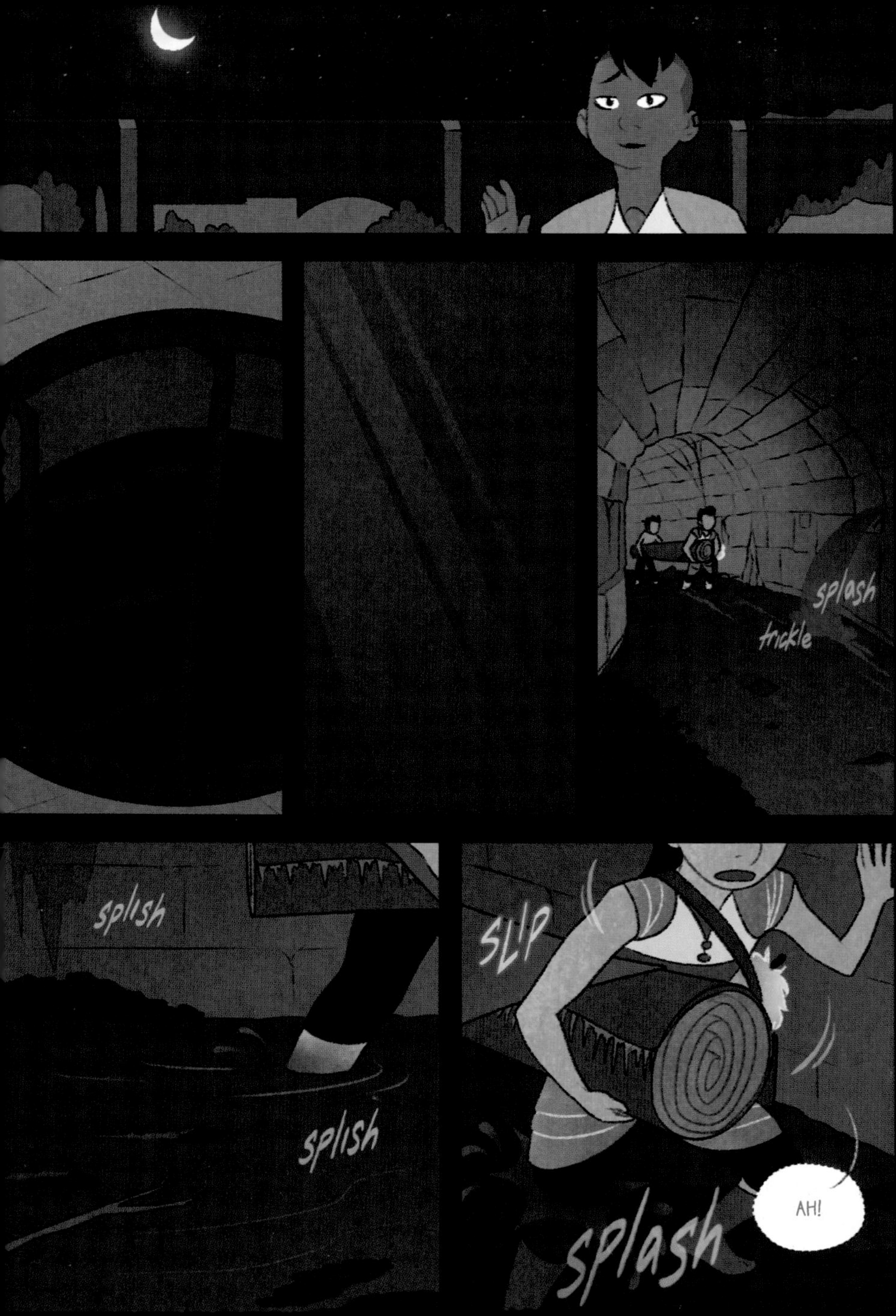
splash
trickle
splish
splish
SLIP
AH!
splash

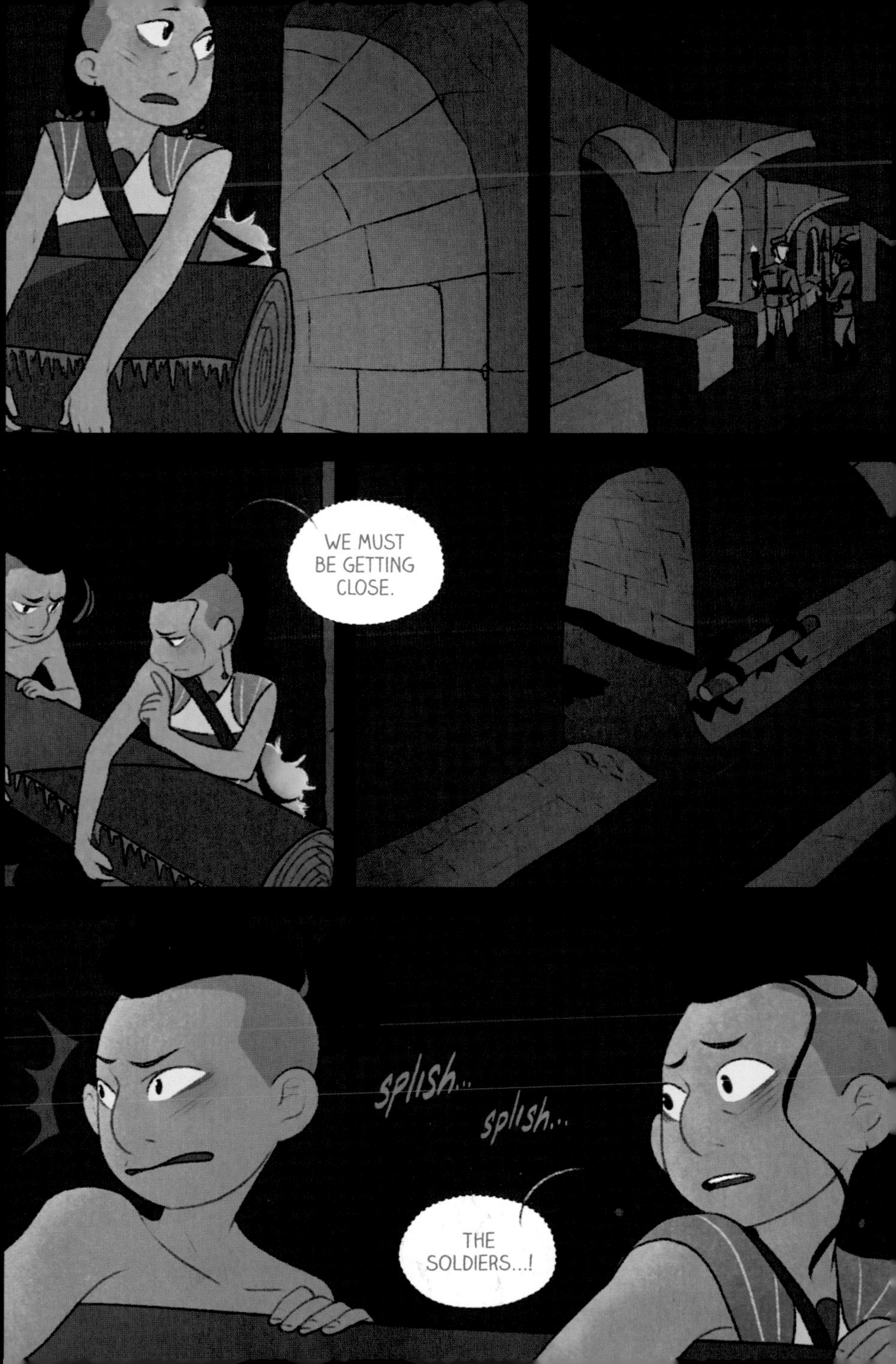
WE MUST BE GETTING CLOSE.
splish...
splish...
THE SOLDIERS...!

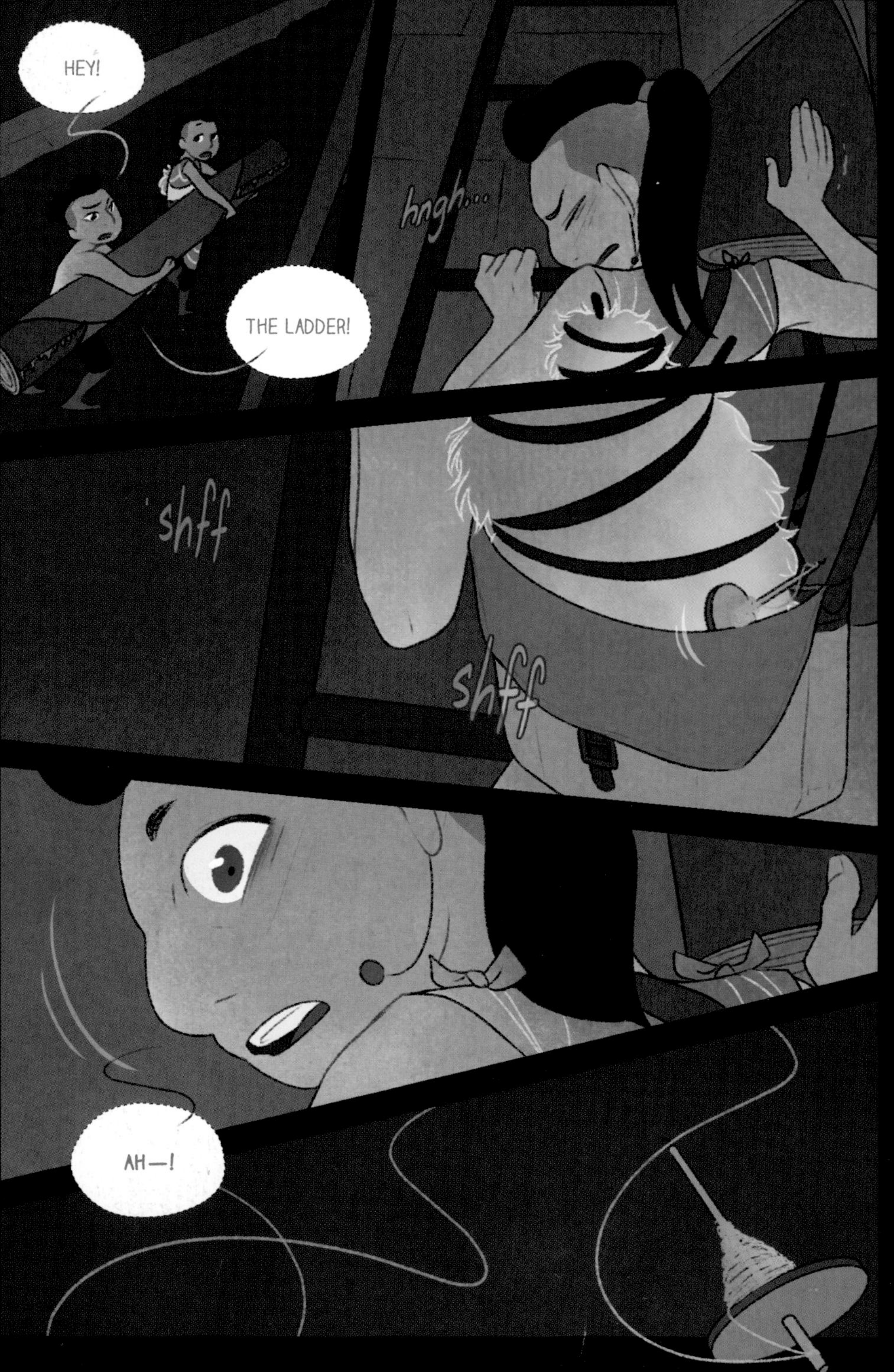
HEY!
hngh...
THE LADDER!
shff
shff
AH—!

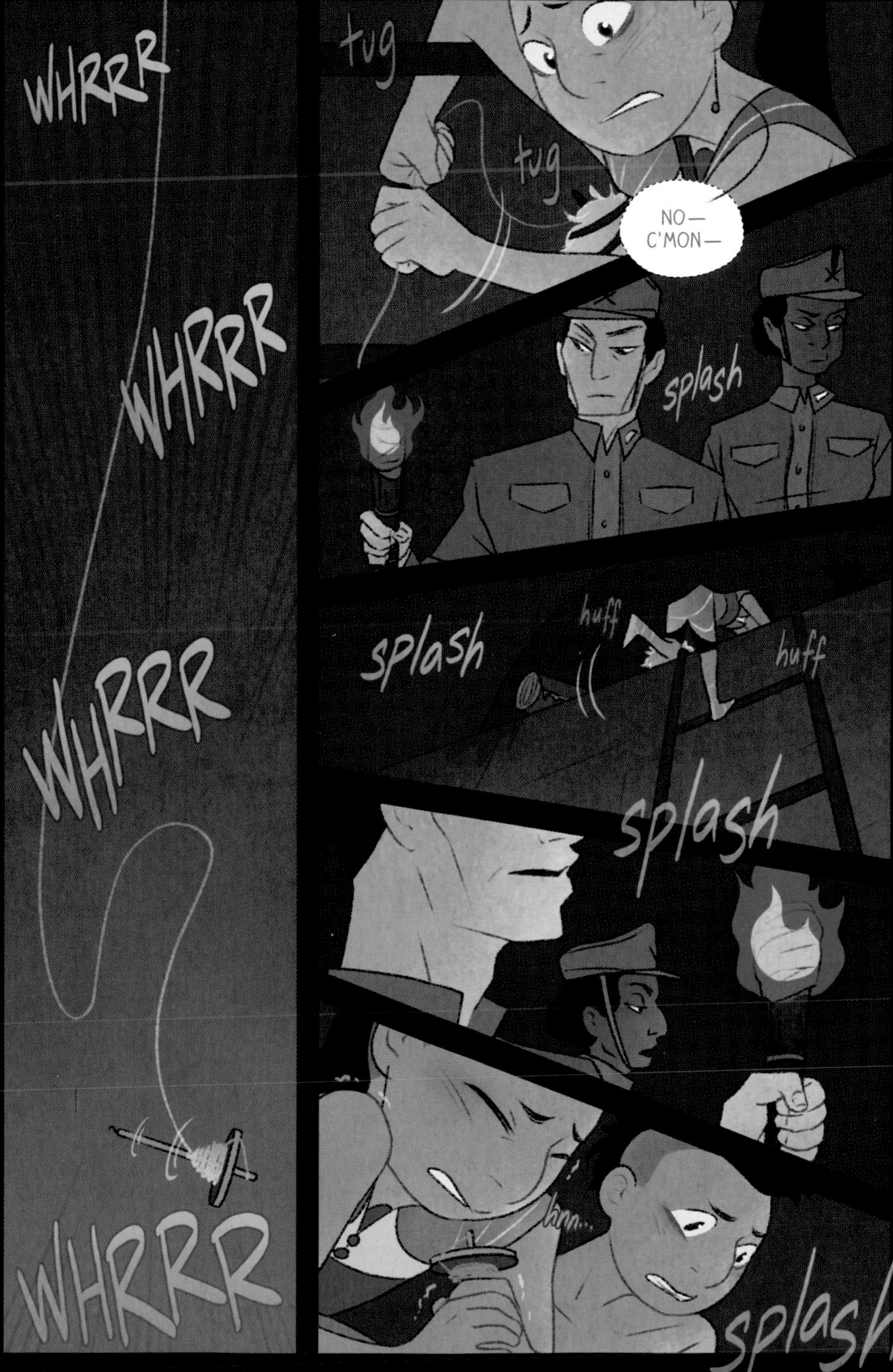
WHRRR
tug
tug
NO— C'MON—
WHRRR
splash
WHRRR
splash
huff
huff
splash
WHRRR
hnn...
splash

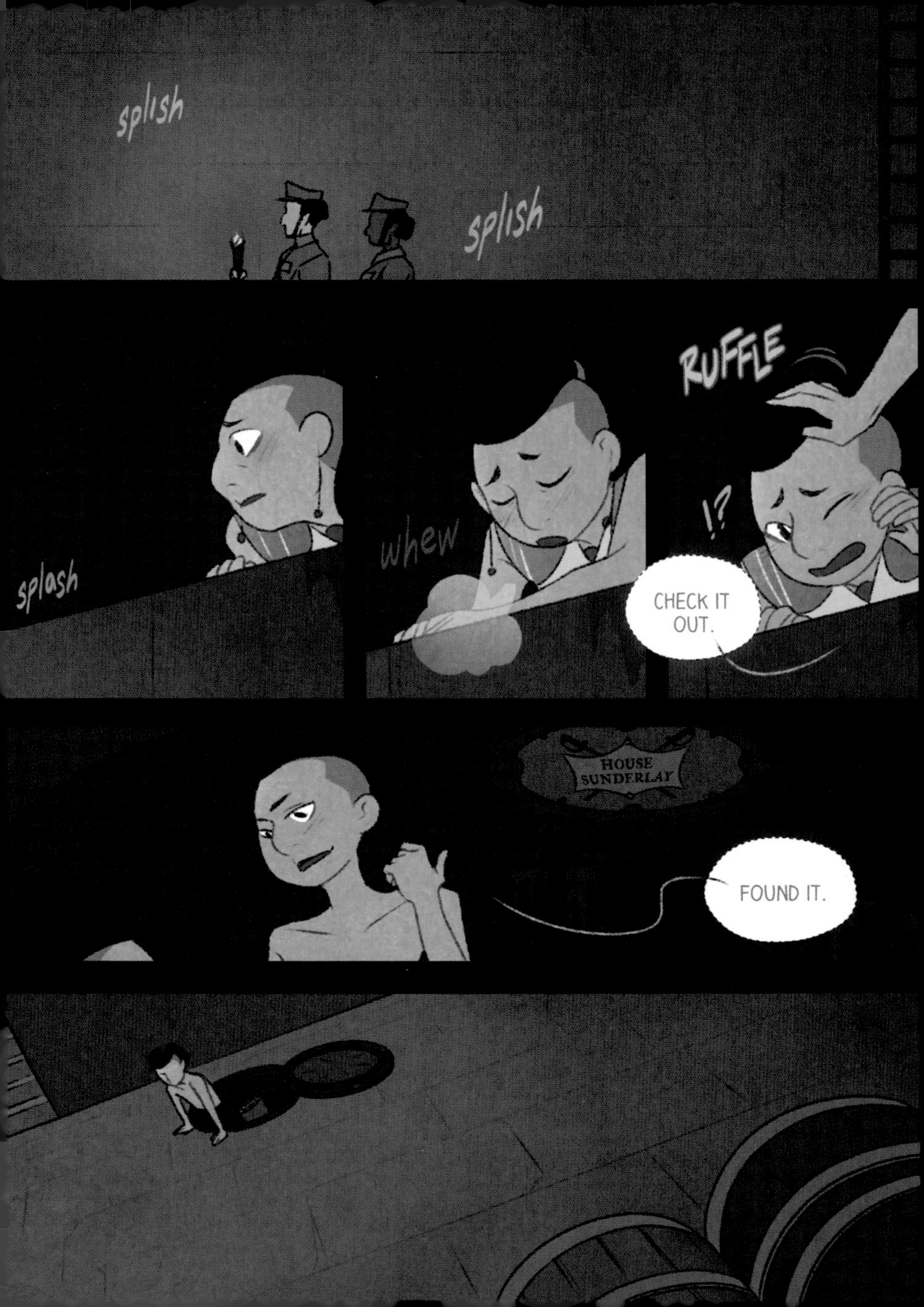
splish
splish
splash
whew
RUFFLE
!?
CHECK IT OUT.
HOUSE SUNDERLAY
FOUND IT.

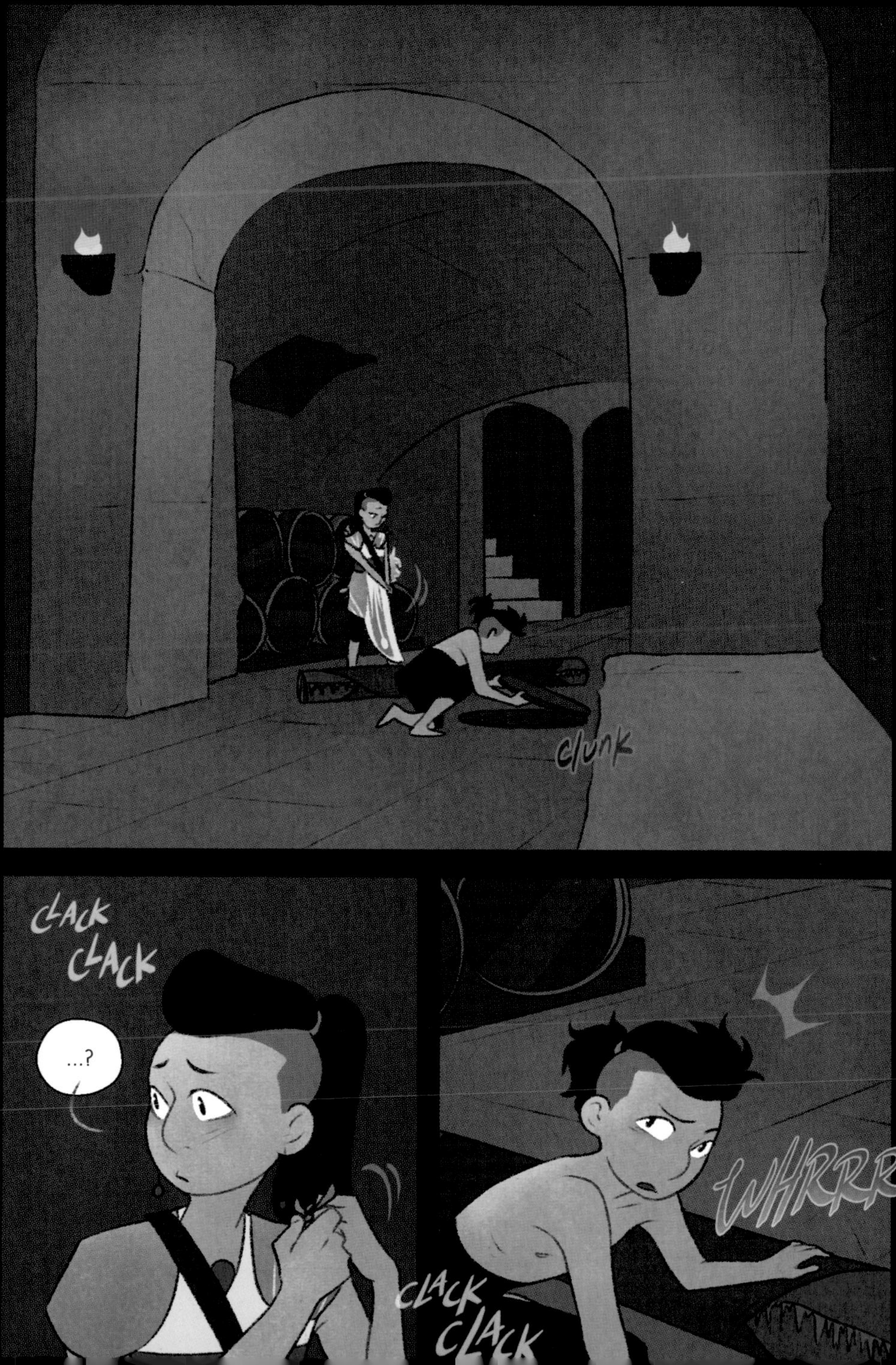
clunk
CLACK
CLACK
...?
CLACK
CLACK
WHRRR

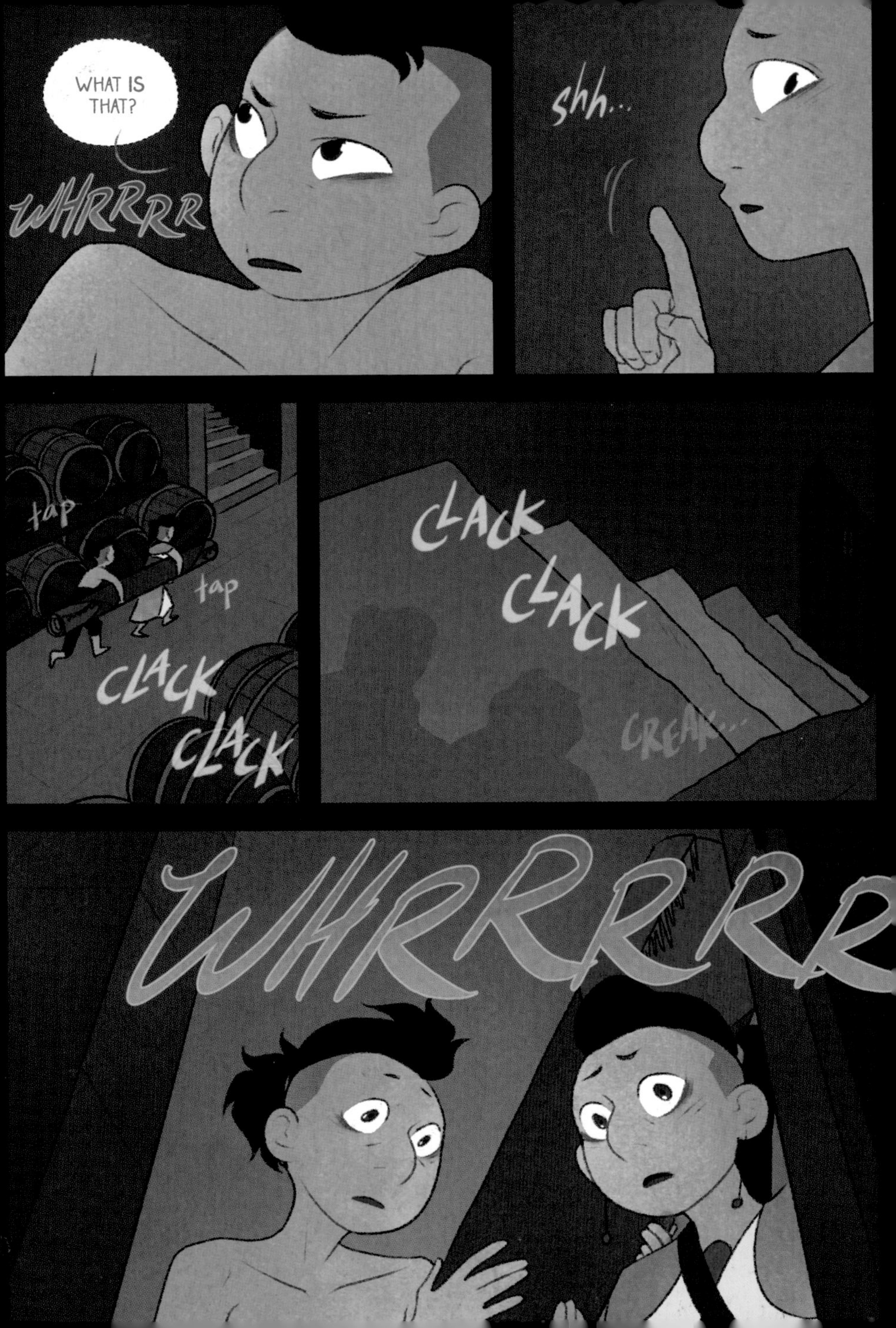
WHAT IS THAT?
WHRRRR
shh...
tap
tap
CLACK
CLACK
CLACK
CLACK
CREAK...
WHRRRRR

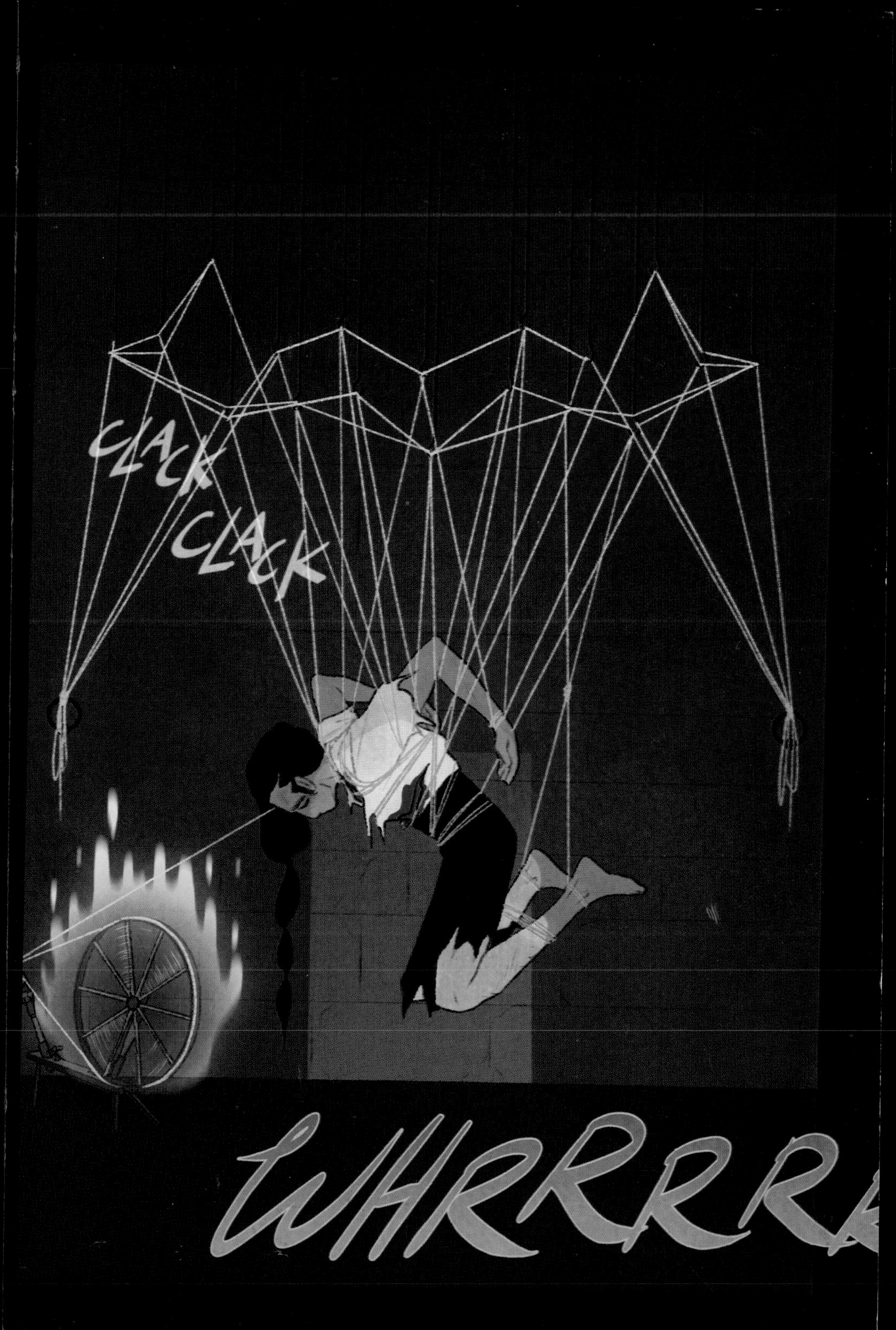
CLACK
CLACK
WHRRRR

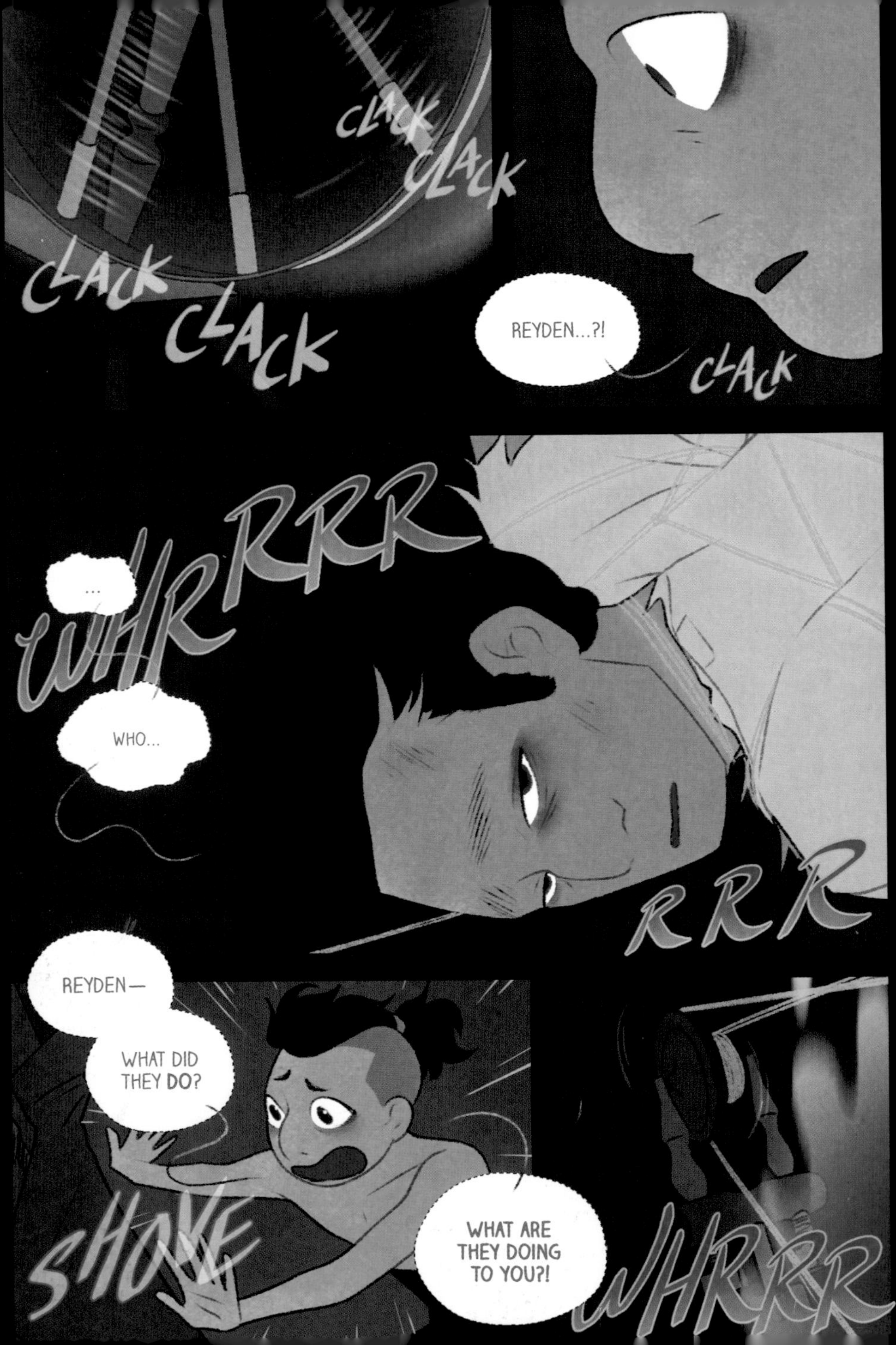
CLACK
CLACK
CLACK
CLACK
REYDEN...?!
CLACK
WHRRRR
...
WHO...
RRR
REYDEN—
WHAT DID THEY DO?
SHOVE
WHAT ARE THEY DOING TO YOU?!
WHRRR

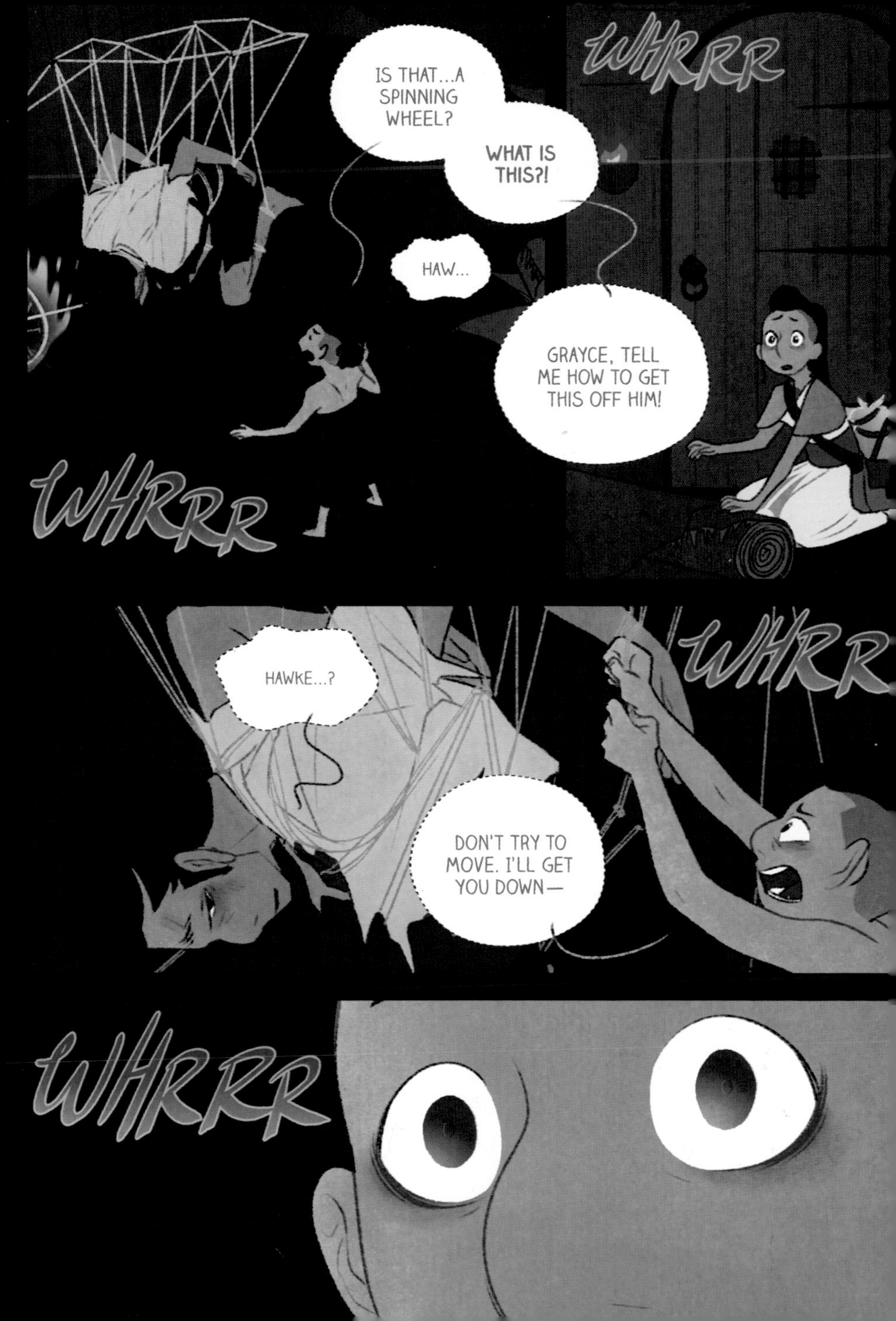
IS THAT...A SPINNING WHEEL?
WHAT IS THIS?!
HAW...
WHRRR
GRAYCE, TELL ME HOW TO GET THIS OFF HIM!
WHRRR
HAWKE...?
WHRR
DON'T TRY TO MOVE. I'LL GET YOU DOWN—
WHRRR

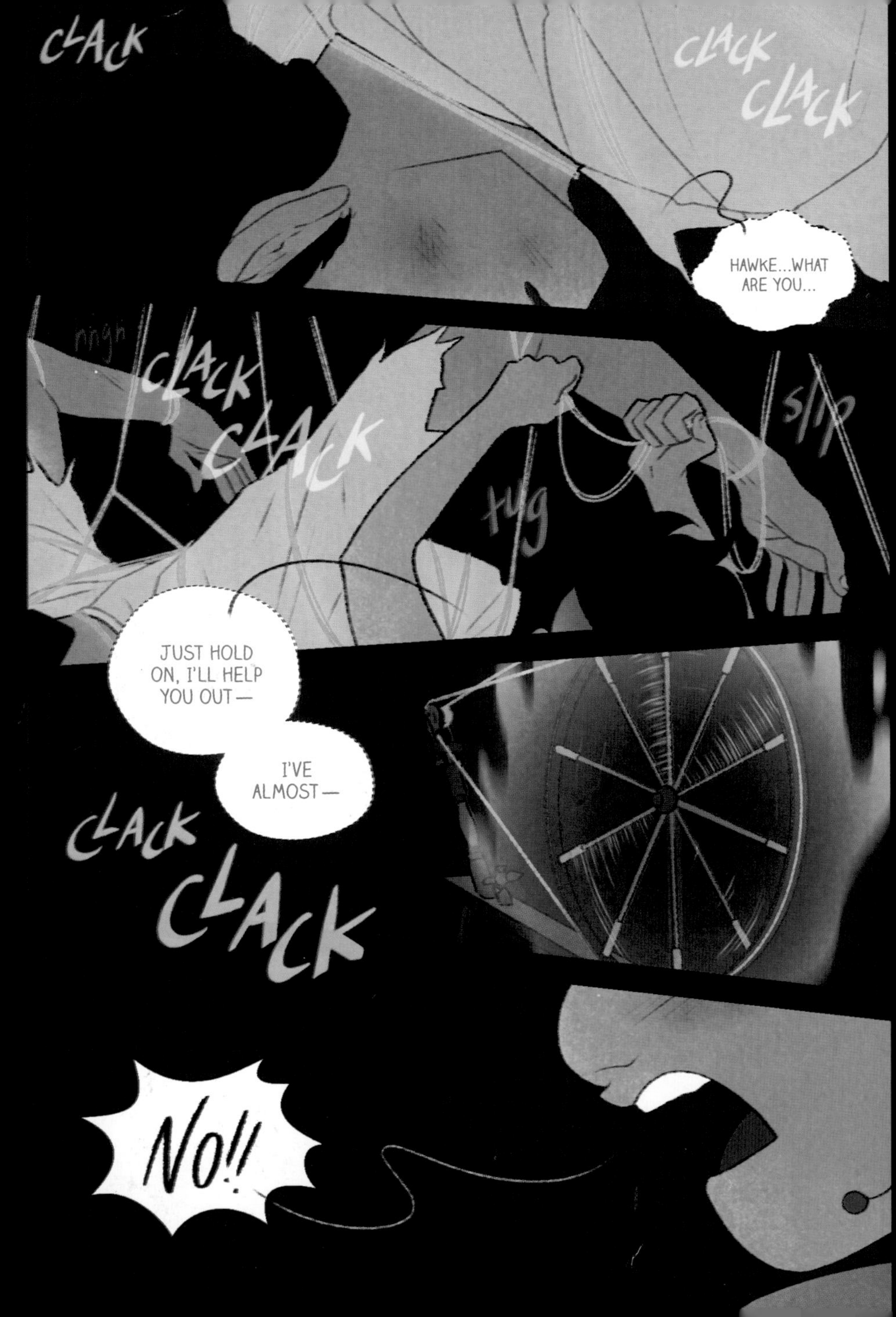
CLACK
CLACK CLACK
HAWKE...WHAT ARE YOU...
nngh
CLACK CLACK CLACK
tug
slip
JUST HOLD ON, I'LL HELP YOU OUT—
I'VE ALMOST—
CLACK CLACK
NO!!

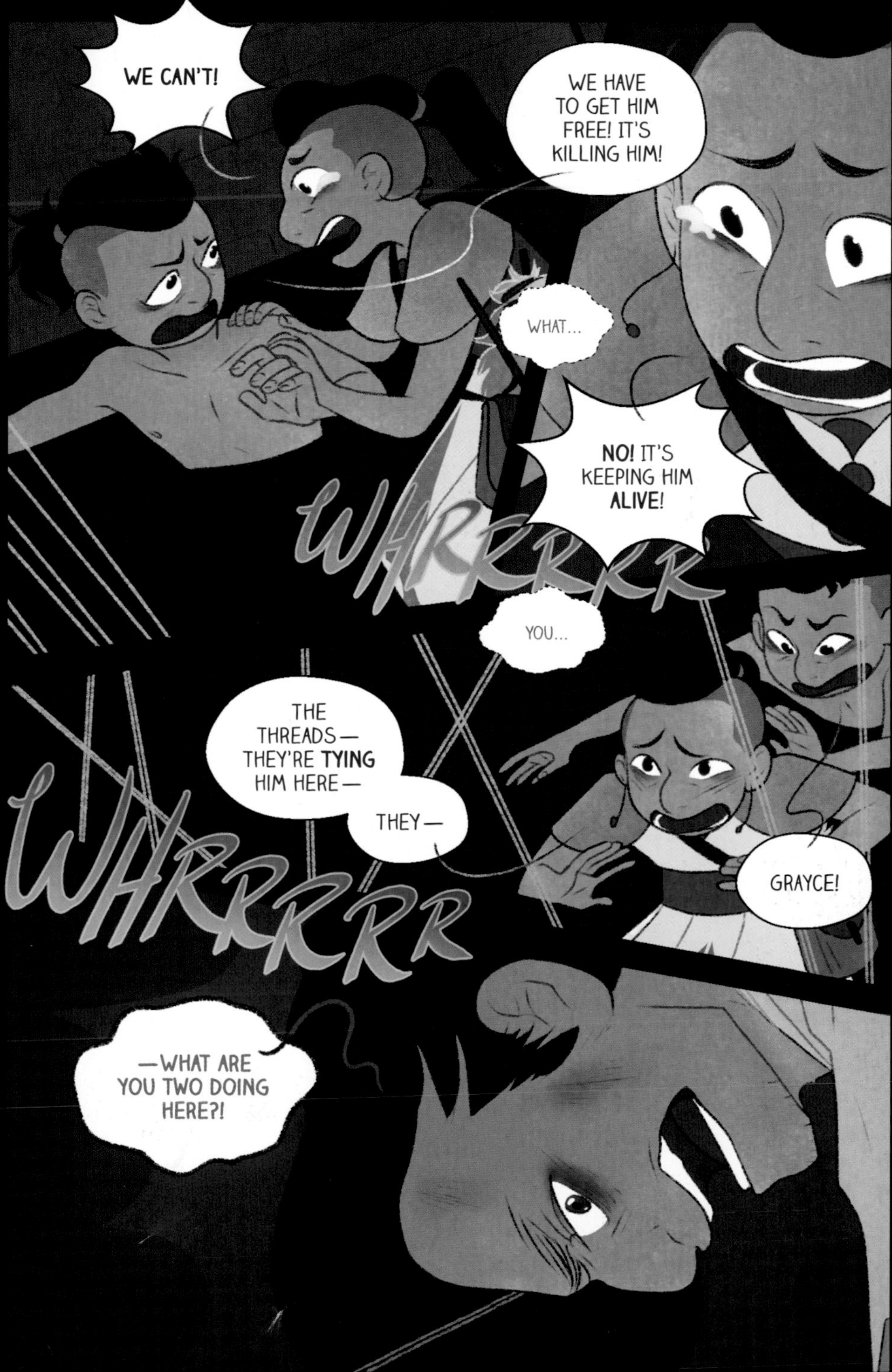
WE CAN'T!
WE HAVE TO GET HIM FREE! IT'S KILLING HIM!
WHAT...
NO! IT'S KEEPING HIM ALIVE!
WHRRRRRR
YOU...
THE THREADS— THEY'RE TYING HIM HERE—
THEY—
GRAYCE!
WHRRRRRR
—WHAT ARE YOU TWO DOING HERE?!

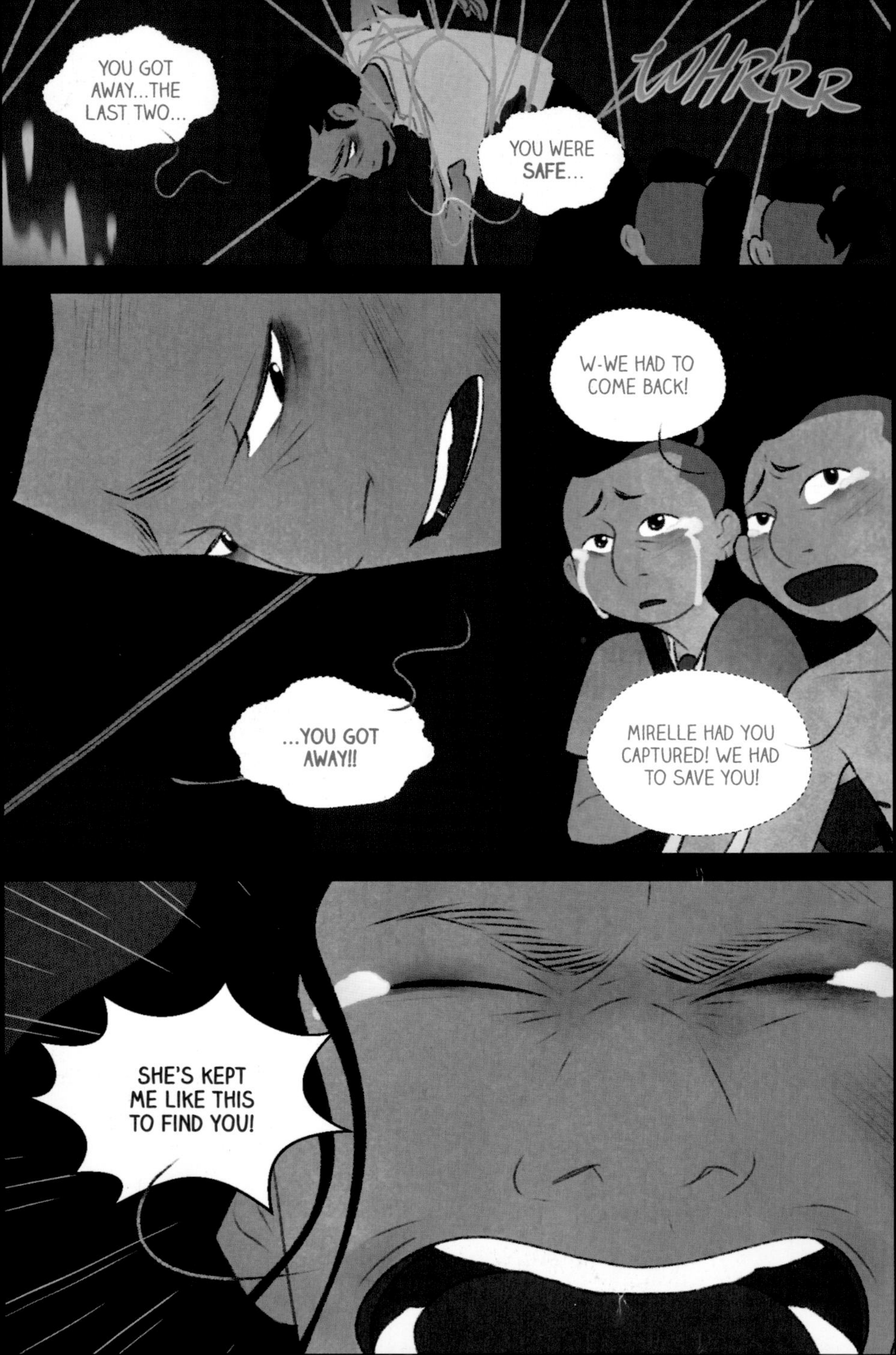
YOU GOT AWAY...THE LAST TWO...
WHRRR
YOU WERE SAFE...
W-WE HAD TO COME BACK!
...YOU GOT AWAY!!
MIRELLE HAD YOU CAPTURED! WE HAD TO SAVE YOU!
SHE'S KEPT ME LIKE THIS TO FIND YOU!

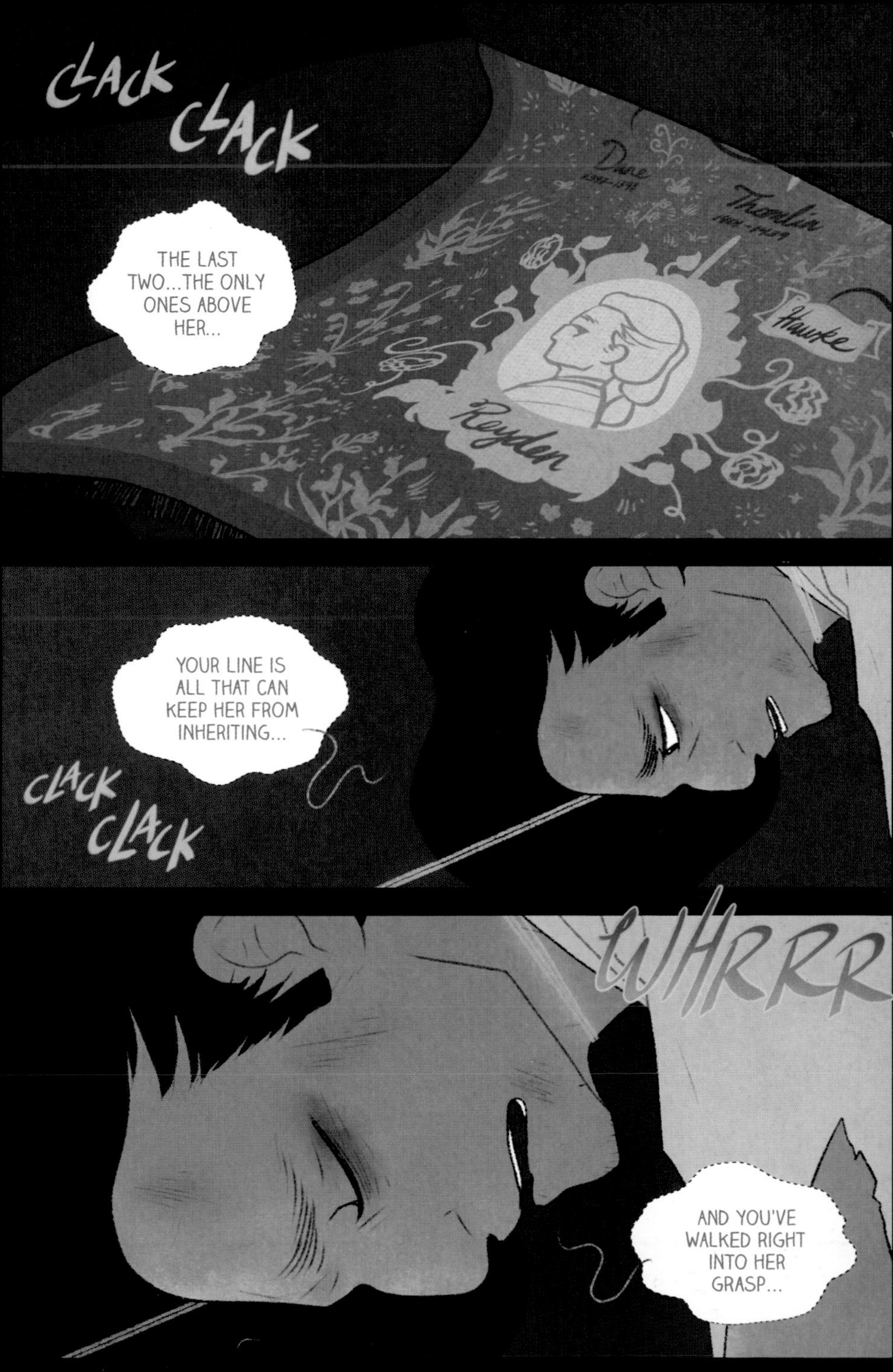
CLACK CLACK
Dane
Hawke
Reyden
THE LAST TWO...THE ONLY ONES ABOVE HER...
YOUR LINE IS ALL THAT CAN KEEP HER FROM INHERITING...
CLACK CLACK
WHRRR
AND YOU'VE WALKED RIGHT INTO HER GRASP...

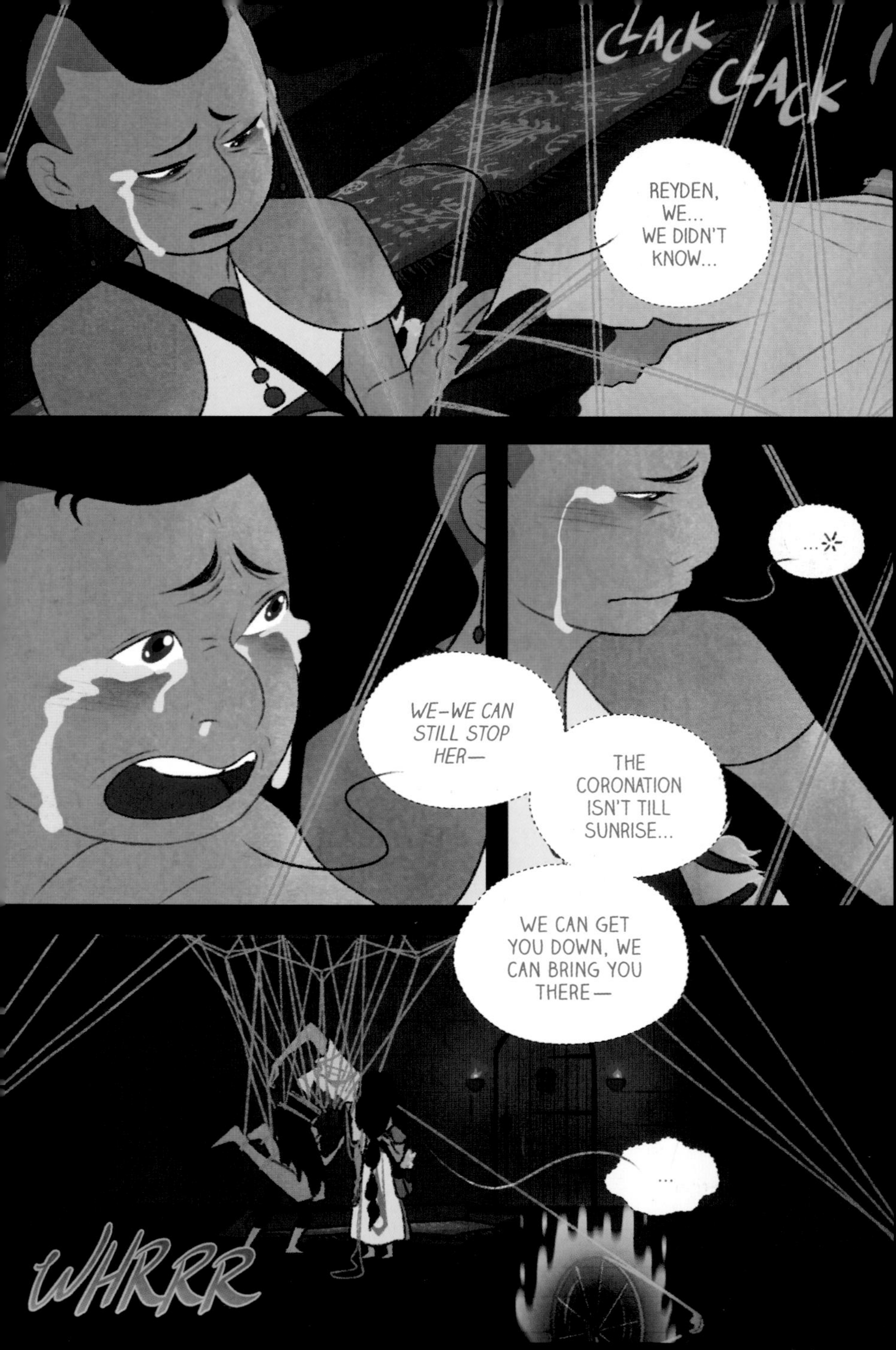
CLACK
CLACK
REYDEN, WE... WE DIDN'T KNOW...
...*
WE–WE CAN STILL STOP HER—
THE CORONATION ISN'T TILL SUNRISE...
WE CAN GET YOU DOWN, WE CAN BRING YOU THERE—
...
WHRRR

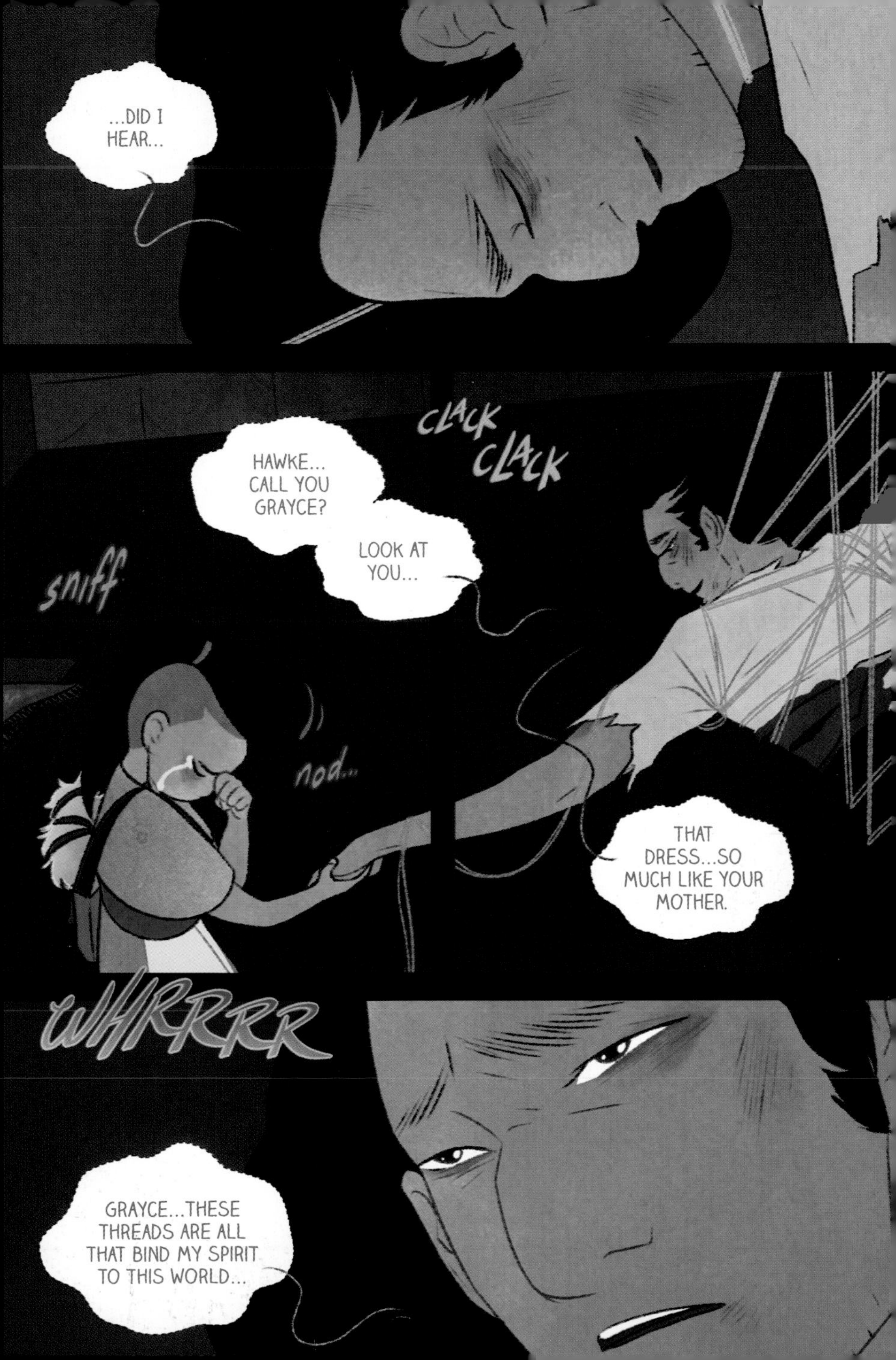

...DID I HEAR...
CLACK CLACK
HAWKE... CALL YOU GRAYCE?
LOOK AT YOU...
sniff
nod...
THAT DRESS...SO MUCH LIKE YOUR MOTHER.
WHRRRR
GRAYCE...THESE THREADS ARE ALL THAT BIND MY SPIRIT TO THIS WORLD...

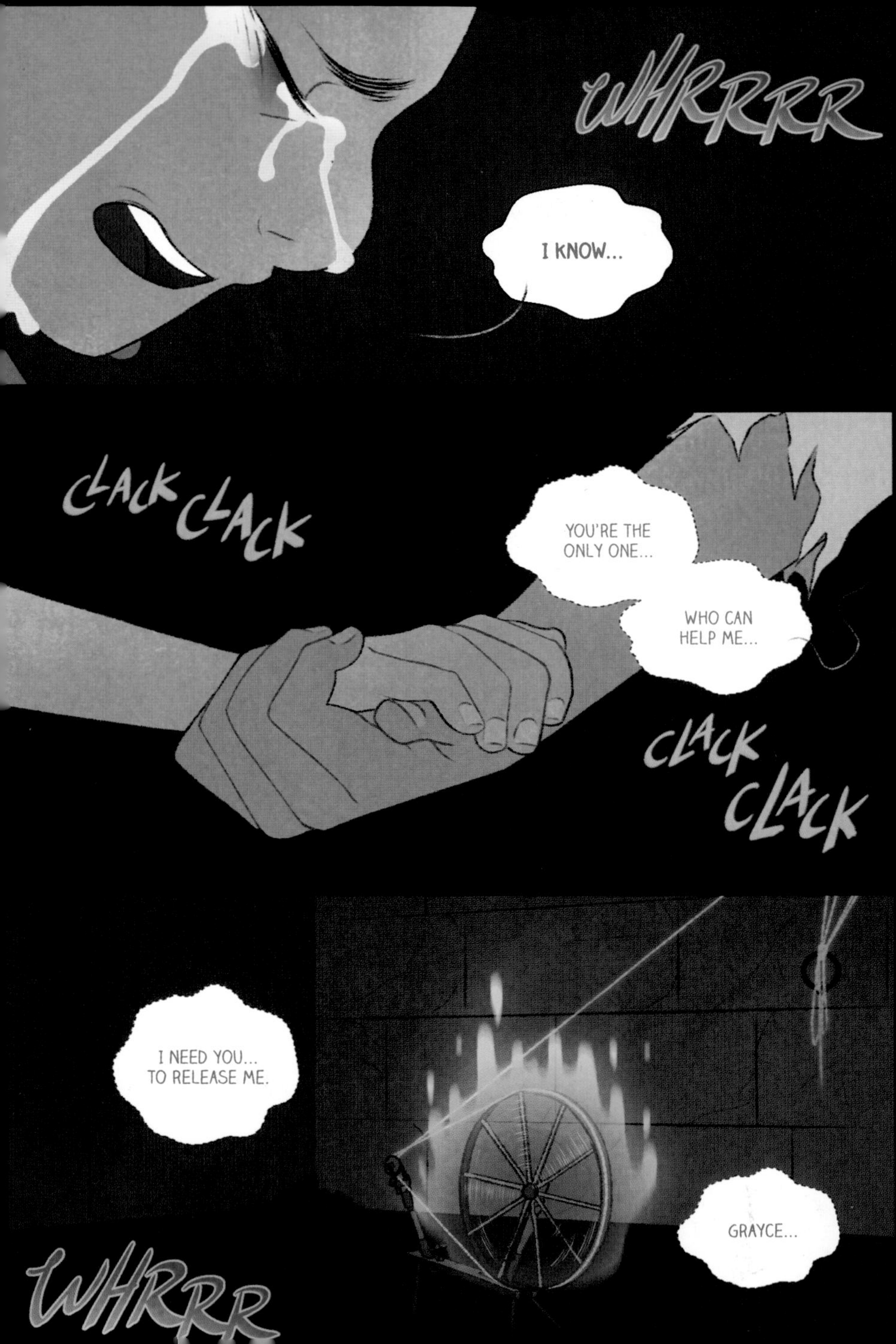
WHRRRR
I KNOW...
CLACK CLACK
YOU'RE THE ONLY ONE...
WHO CAN HELP ME...
CLACK CLACK
I NEED YOU... TO RELEASE ME.
GRAYCE...
WHRRR

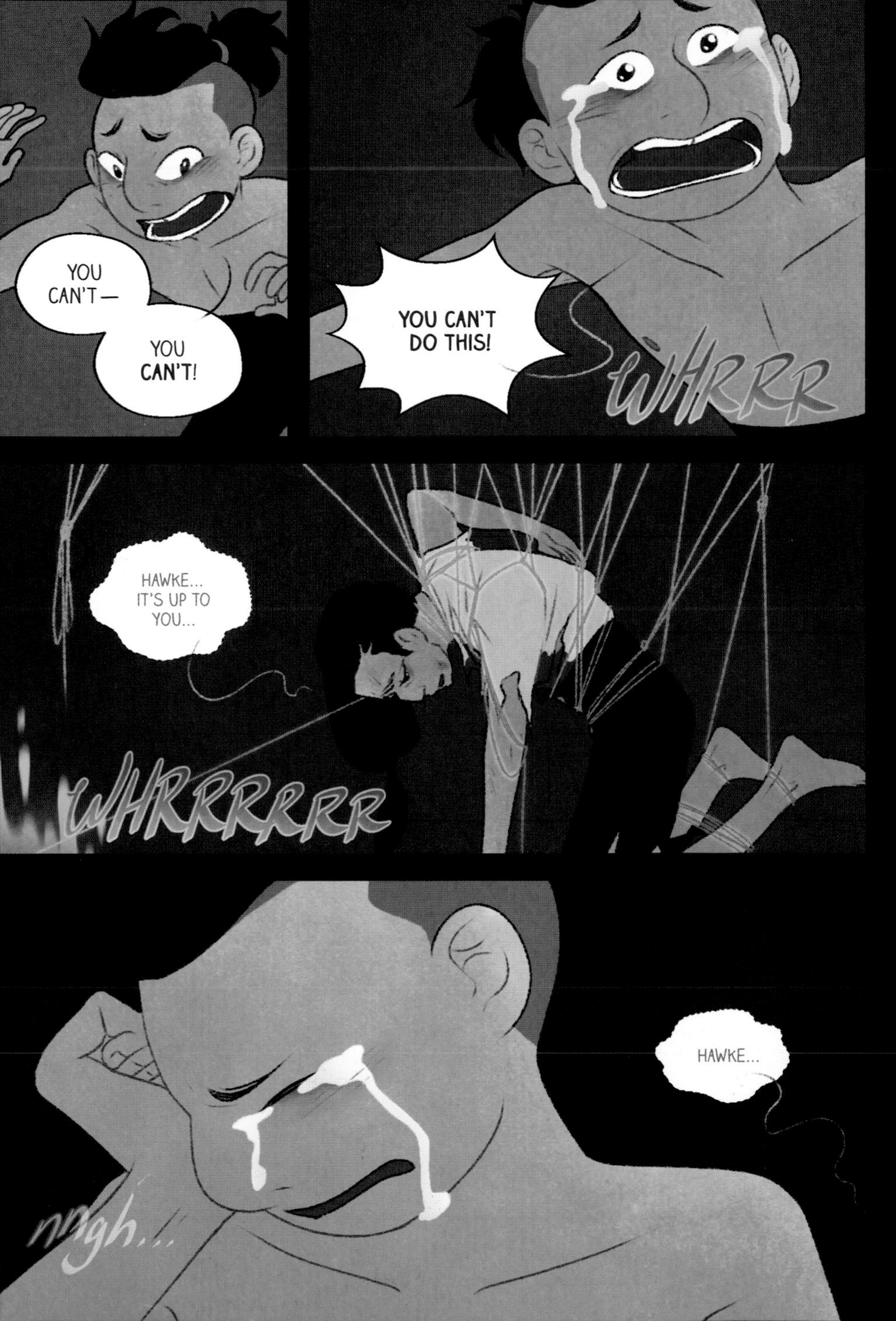
YOU CAN'T—
YOU CAN'T!
YOU CAN'T DO THIS!
WHRRR
HAWKE... IT'S UP TO YOU...
WHRRRRRR
HAWKE...
nngh...

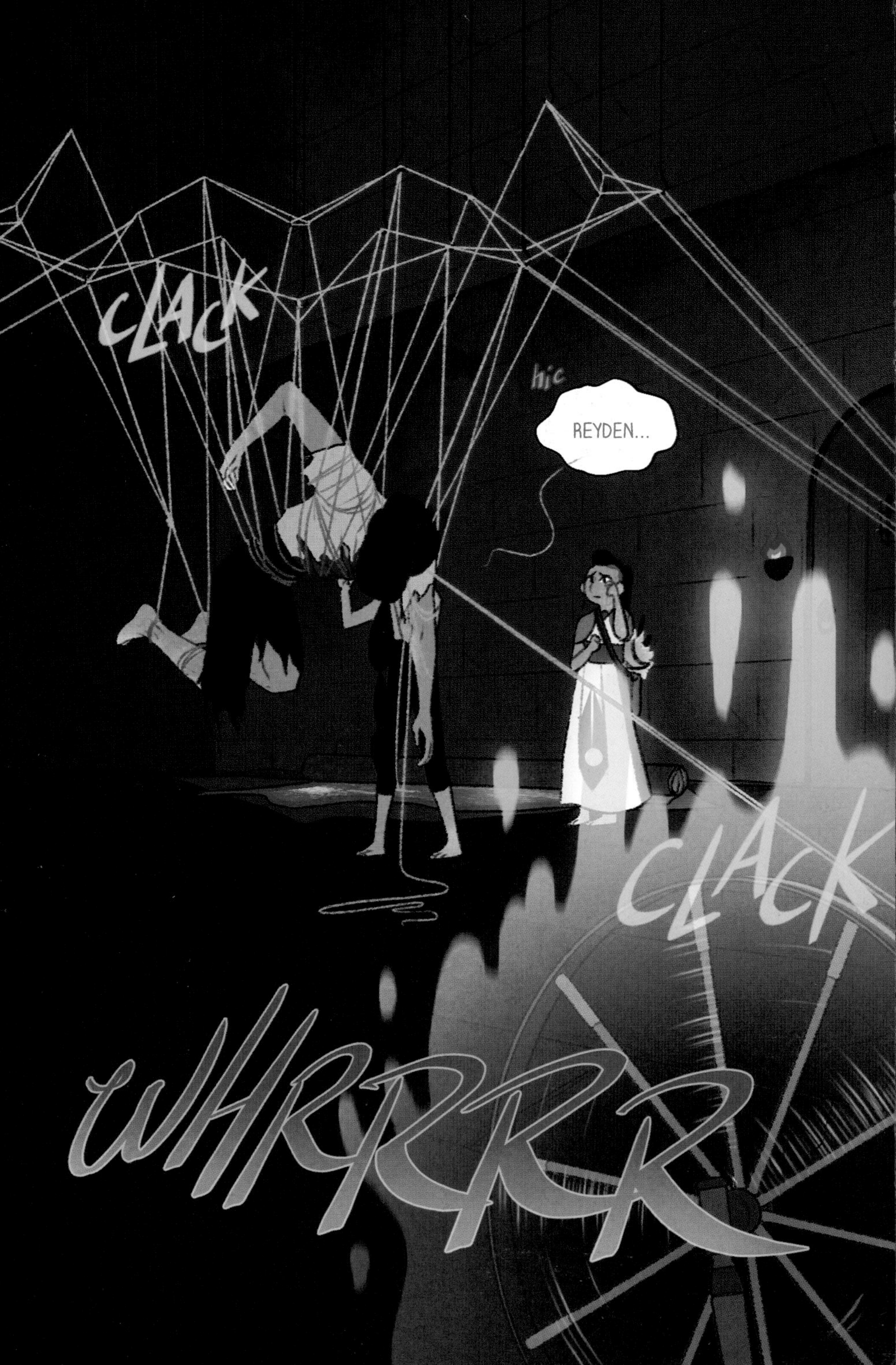
CLACK
hic
REYDEN...
CLACK
WHRRR

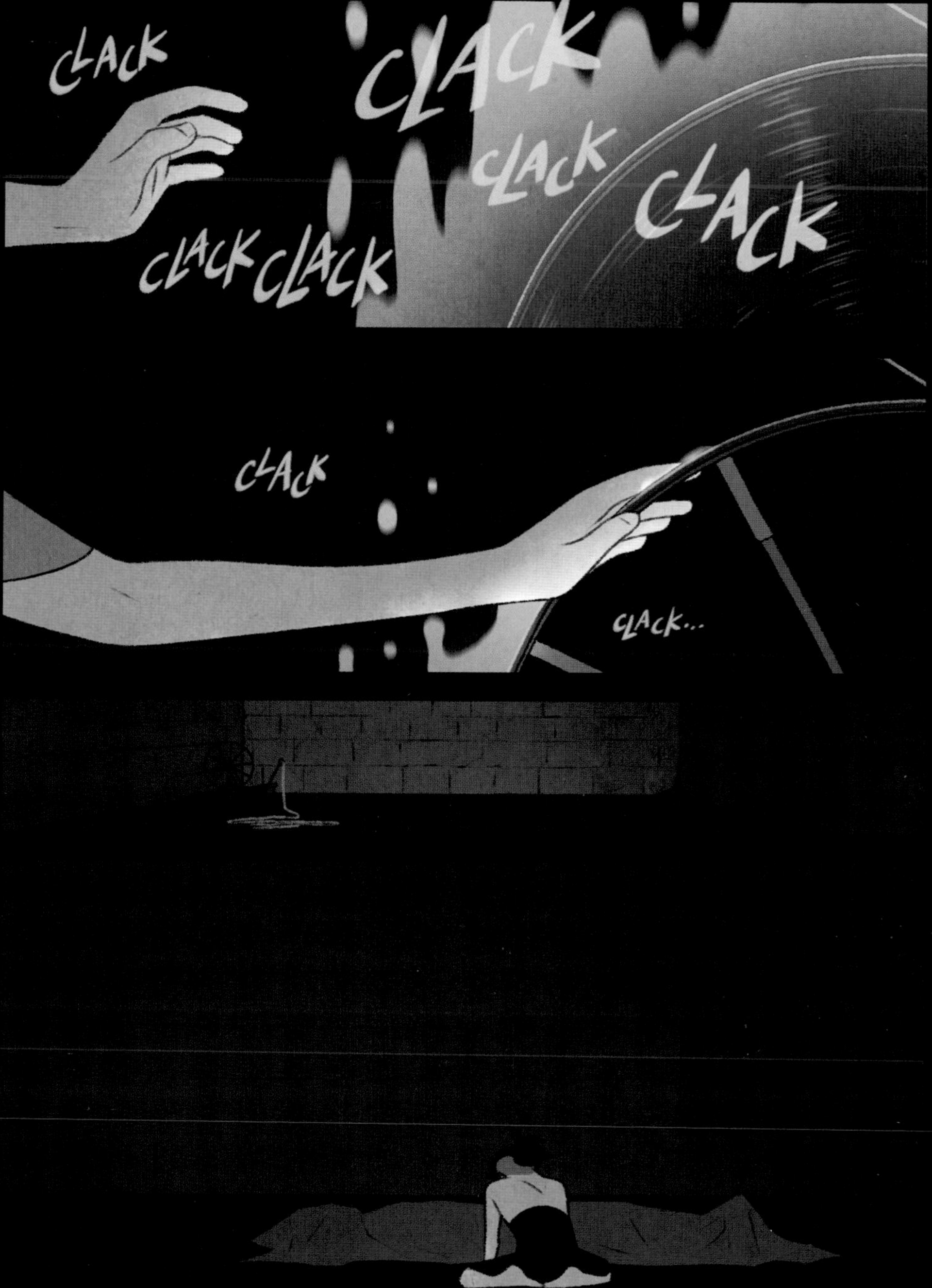
CLACK
CLACK
CLACK
CLACK
CLACK
CLACK
CLACK
CLACK...

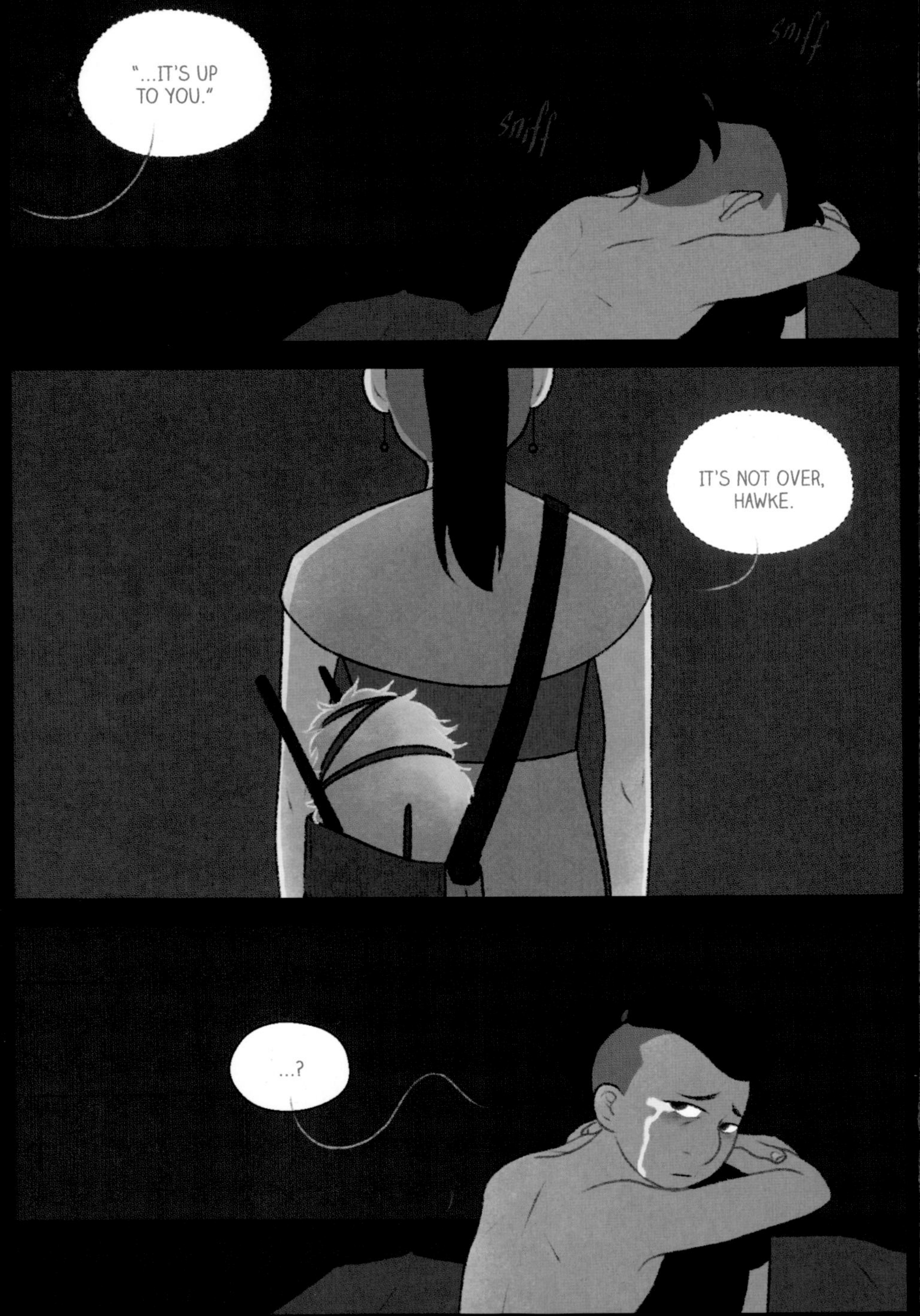
"...IT'S UP TO YOU."
sniff
sniff
IT'S NOT OVER, HAWKE.
...?

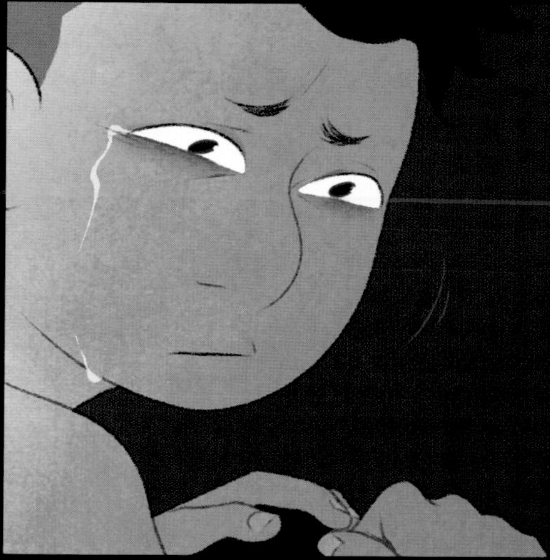

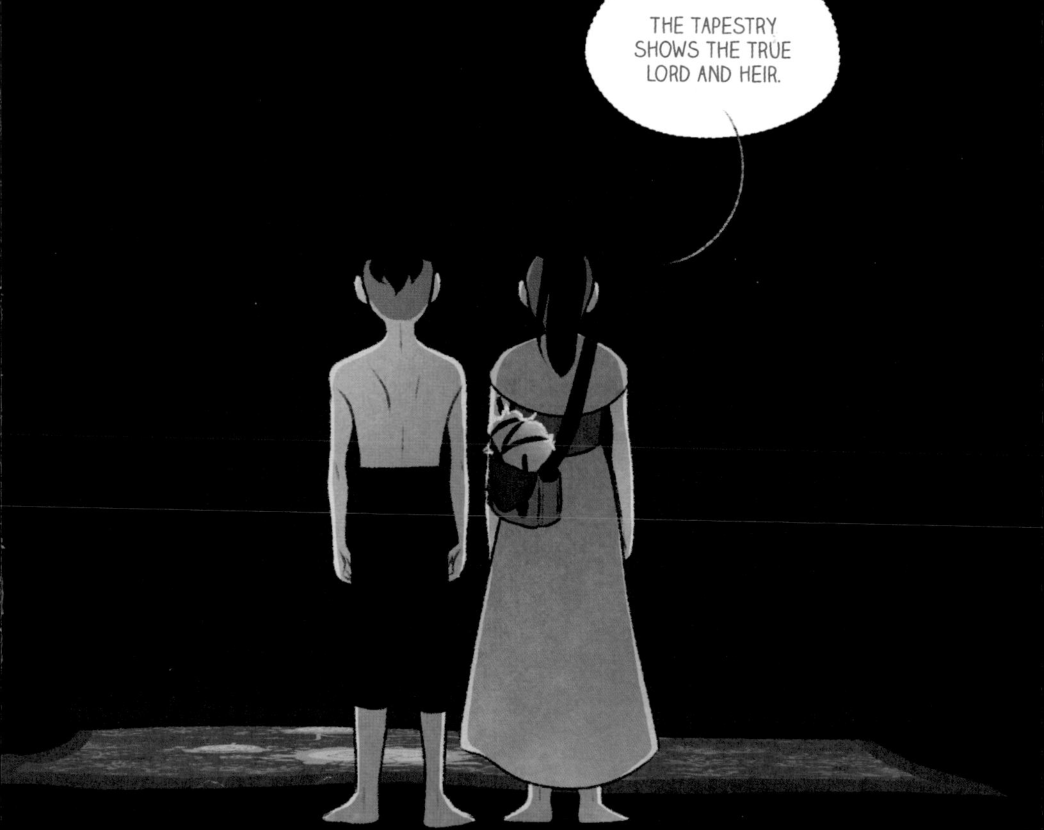
THE TAPESTRY SHOWS THE TRUE LORD AND HEIR.

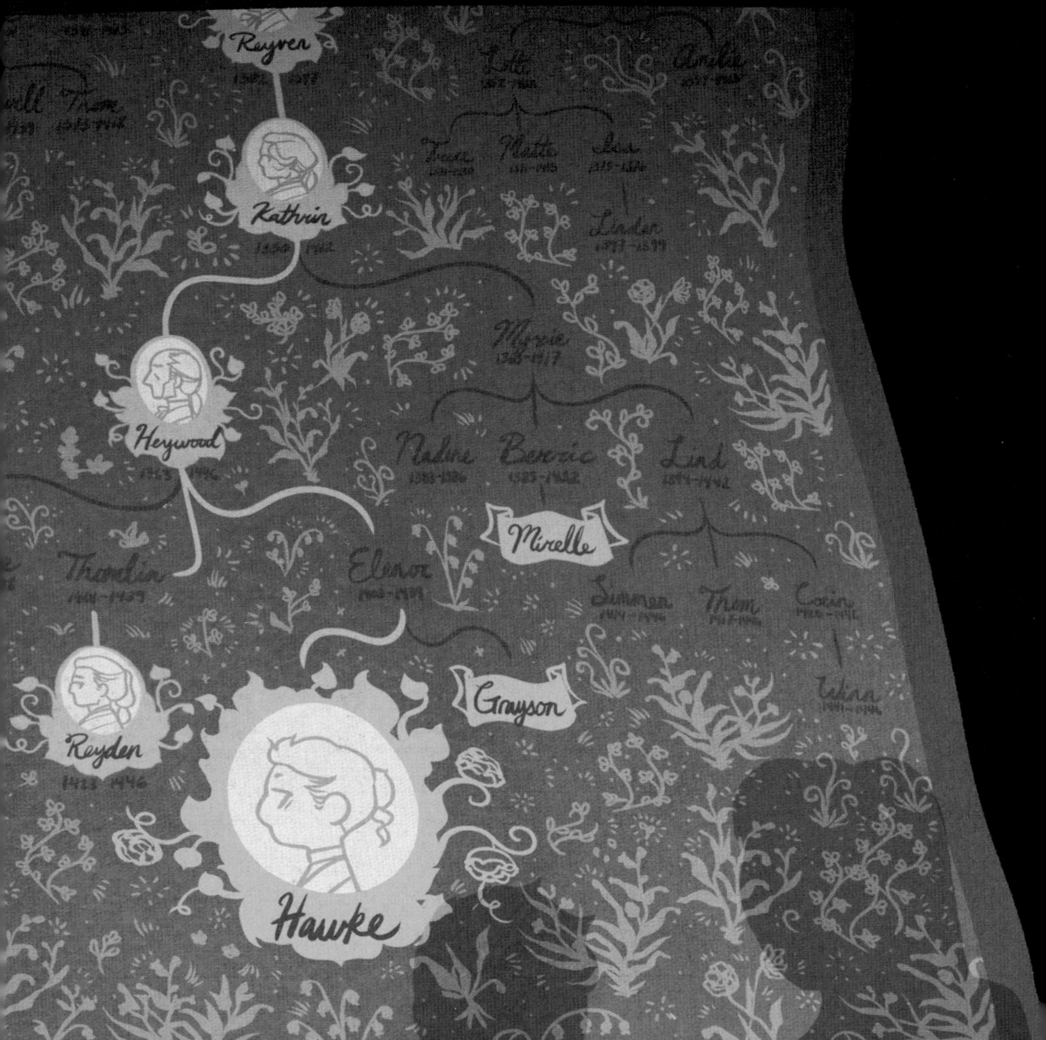

Reyren
Kathrin
Heywood
Nadine
Lind
Mirelle
Elenor
Reyden
Grayson
Hawke

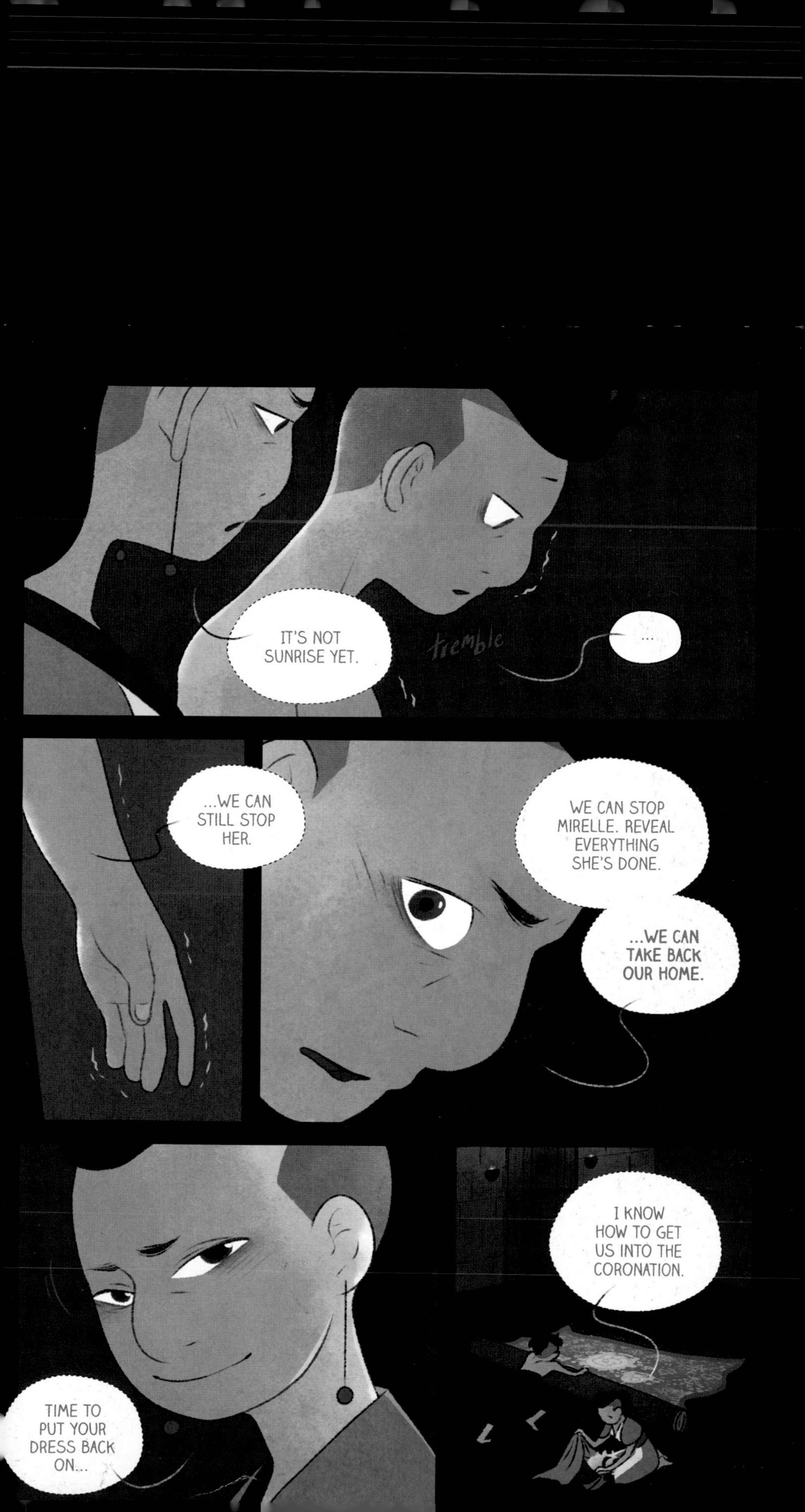
IT'S NOT SUNRISE YET.
tremble
...
...WE CAN STILL STOP HER.
WE CAN STOP MIRELLE. REVEAL EVERYTHING SHE'S DONE.
...WE CAN TAKE BACK OUR HOME.
I KNOW HOW TO GET US INTO THE CORONATION.
TIME TO PUT YOUR DRESS BACK ON...

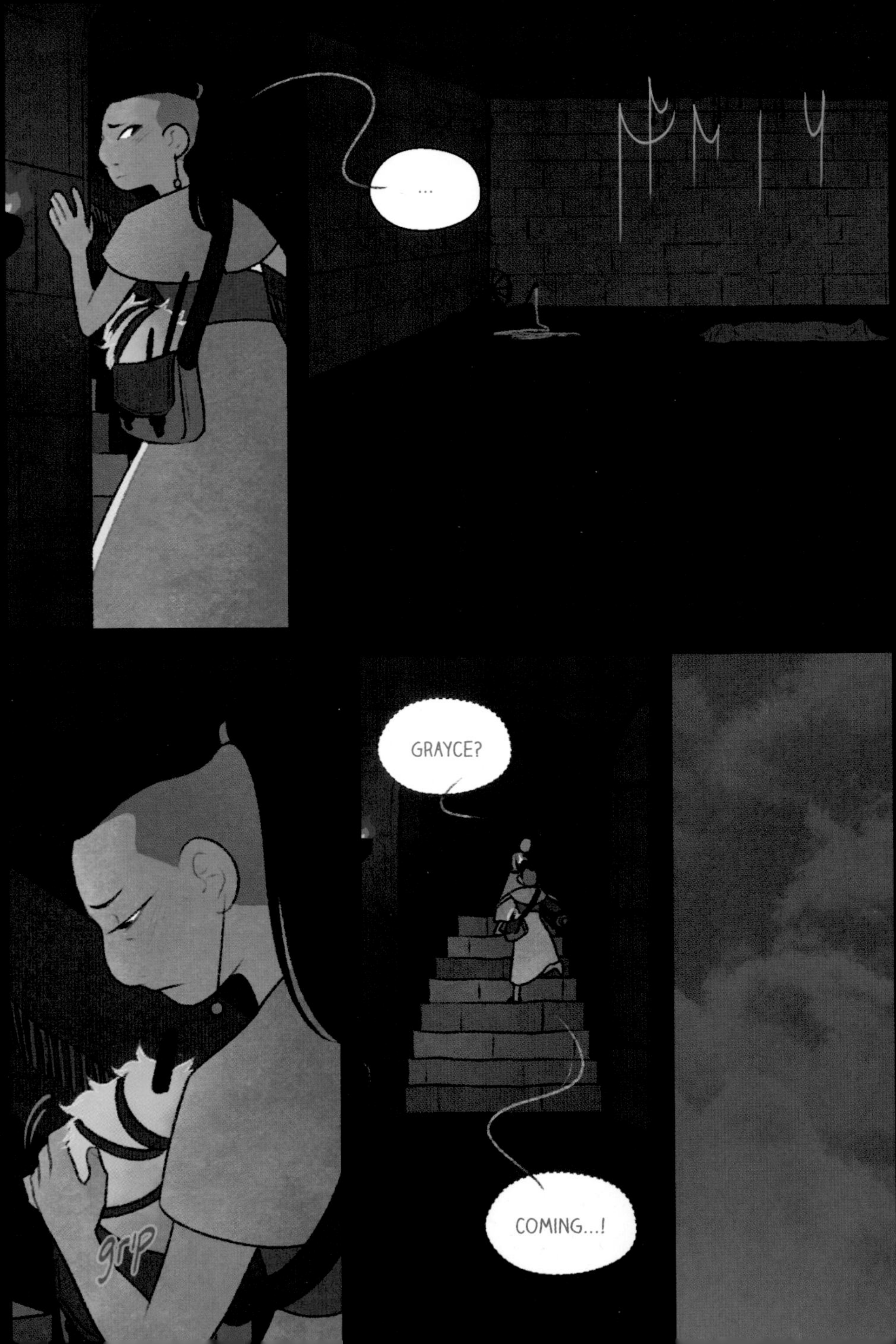
...
GRAYCE?
COMING...!
grip

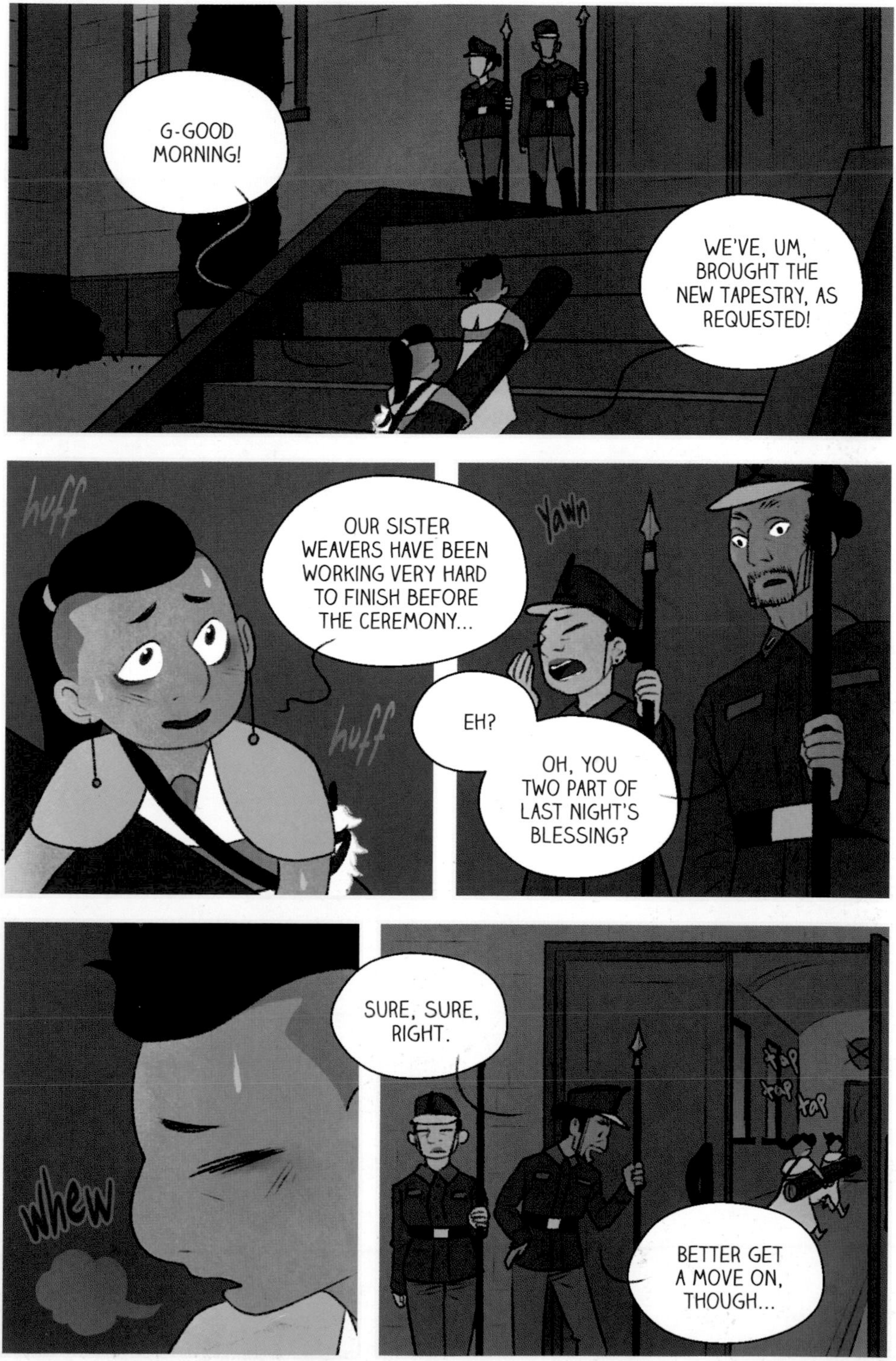
G-GOOD MORNING!
WE'VE, UM, BROUGHT THE NEW TAPESTRY, AS REQUESTED!
huff
OUR SISTER WEAVERS HAVE BEEN WORKING VERY HARD TO FINISH BEFORE THE CEREMONY...
huff
Yawn
EH?
OH, YOU TWO PART OF LAST NIGHT'S BLESSING?
SURE, SURE, RIGHT.
whew
tap
tap
tap
BETTER GET A MOVE ON, THOUGH...

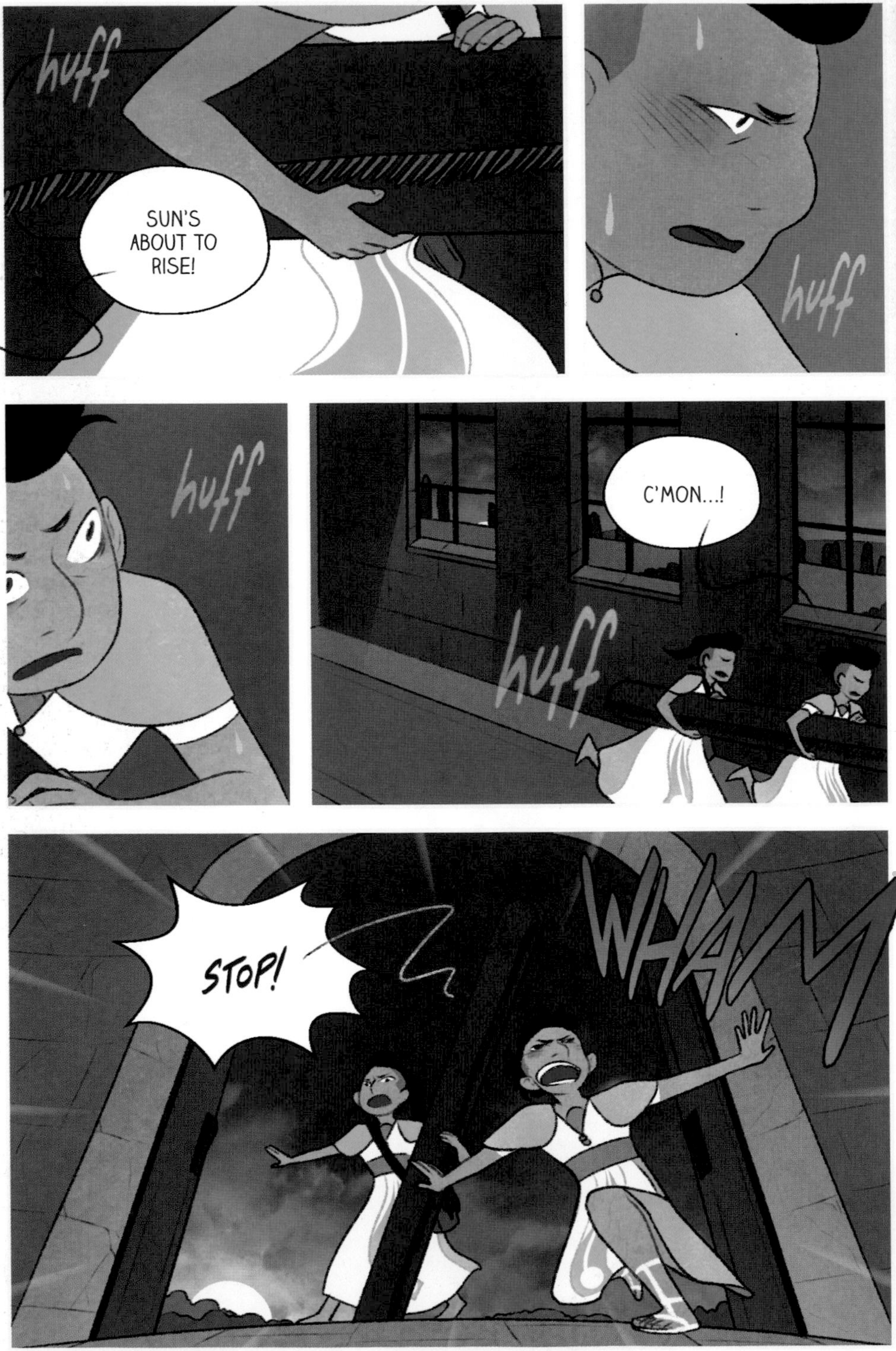
huff
SUN'S ABOUT TO RISE!
huff
huff
C'MON...!
huff
STOP!
WHAM

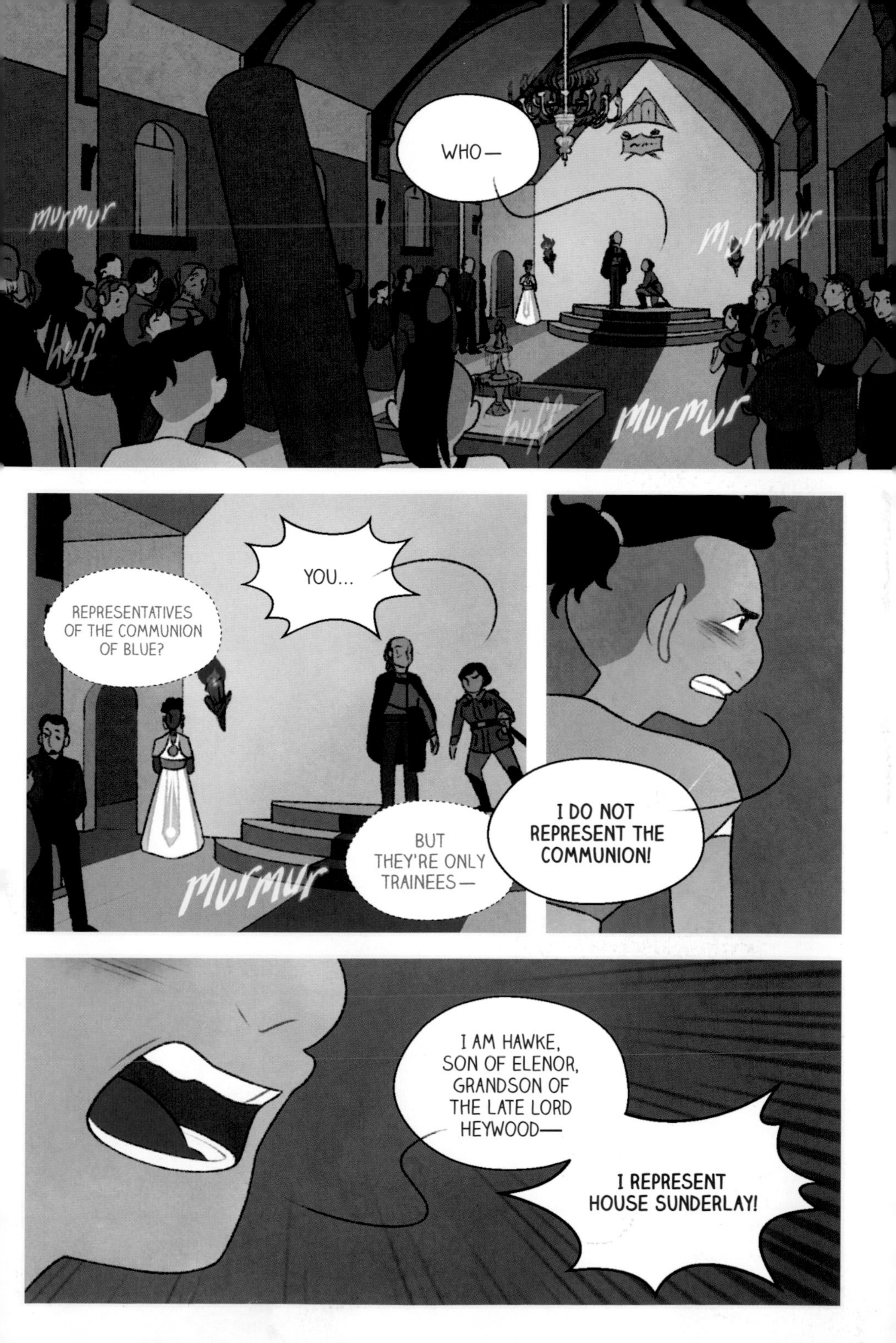
WHO—
murmur
murmur
huff
huff
murmur
YOU...
REPRESENTATIVES OF THE COMMUNION OF BLUE?
BUT THEY'RE ONLY TRAINEES—
murmur
I DO NOT REPRESENT THE COMMUNION!
I AM HAWKE, SON OF ELENOR, GRANDSON OF THE LATE LORD HEYWOOD—
I REPRESENT HOUSE SUNDERLAY!

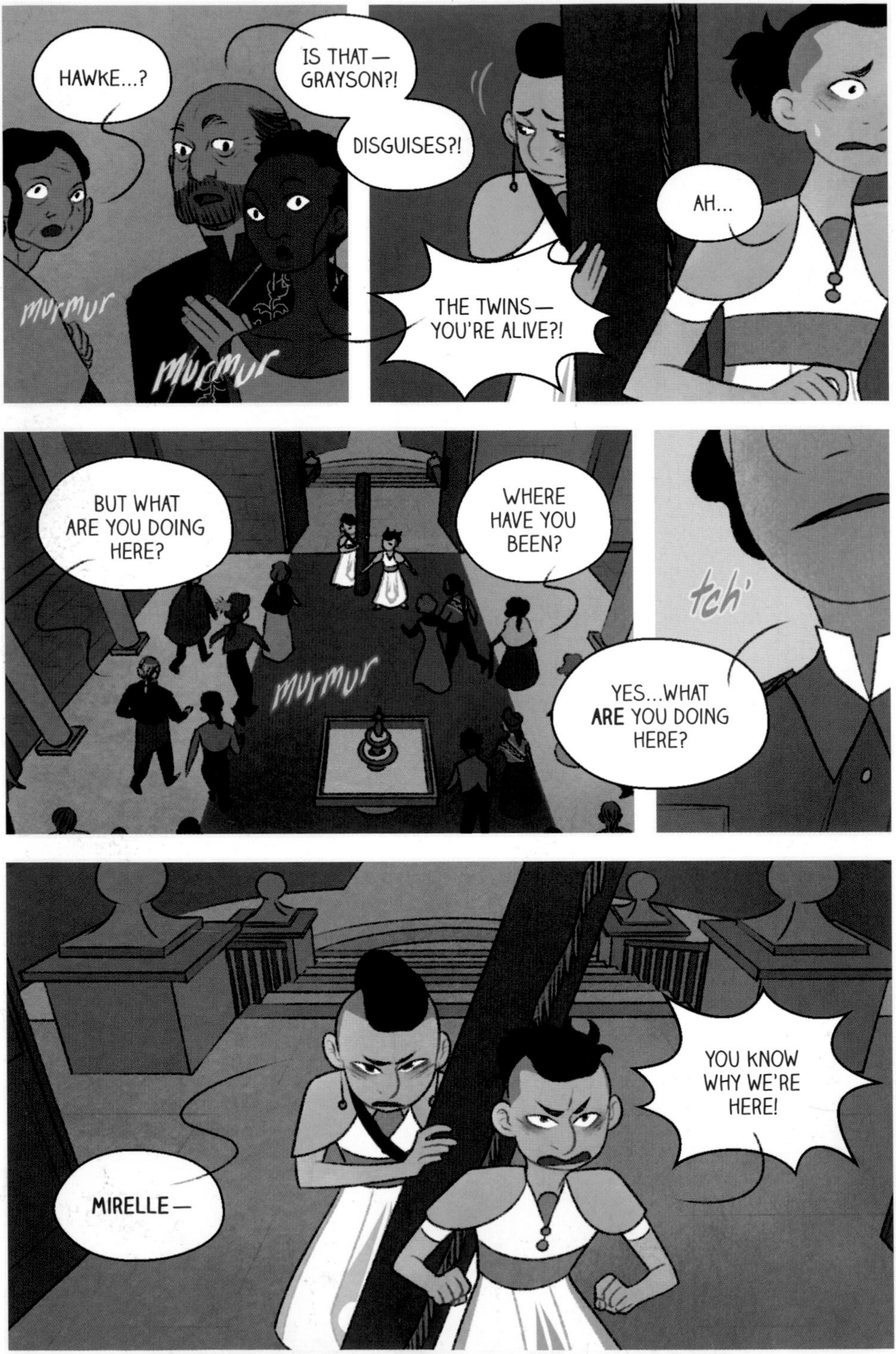
HAWKE...?
IS THAT—
GRAYSON?!
DISGUISES?!
murmur
murmur
AH...
THE TWINS—
YOU'RE ALIVE?!
BUT WHAT
ARE YOU DOING
HERE?
WHERE
HAVE YOU
BEEN?
murmur
tch'
YES...WHAT
ARE YOU DOING
HERE?
YOU KNOW
WHY WE'RE
HERE!
MIRELLE—

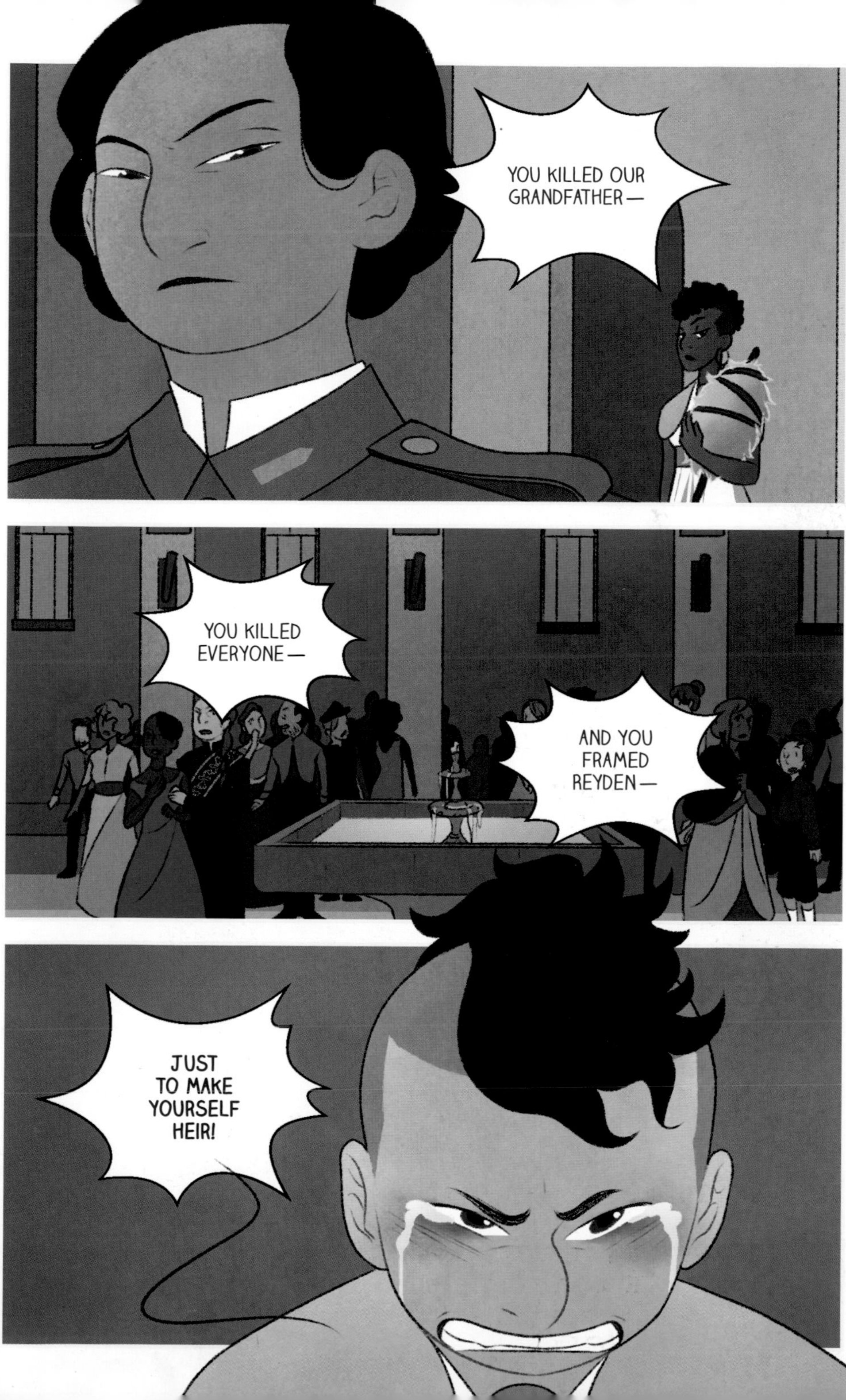
YOU KILLED OUR GRANDFATHER—
YOU KILLED EVERYONE—
AND YOU FRAMED REYDEN—
JUST TO MAKE YOURSELF HEIR!

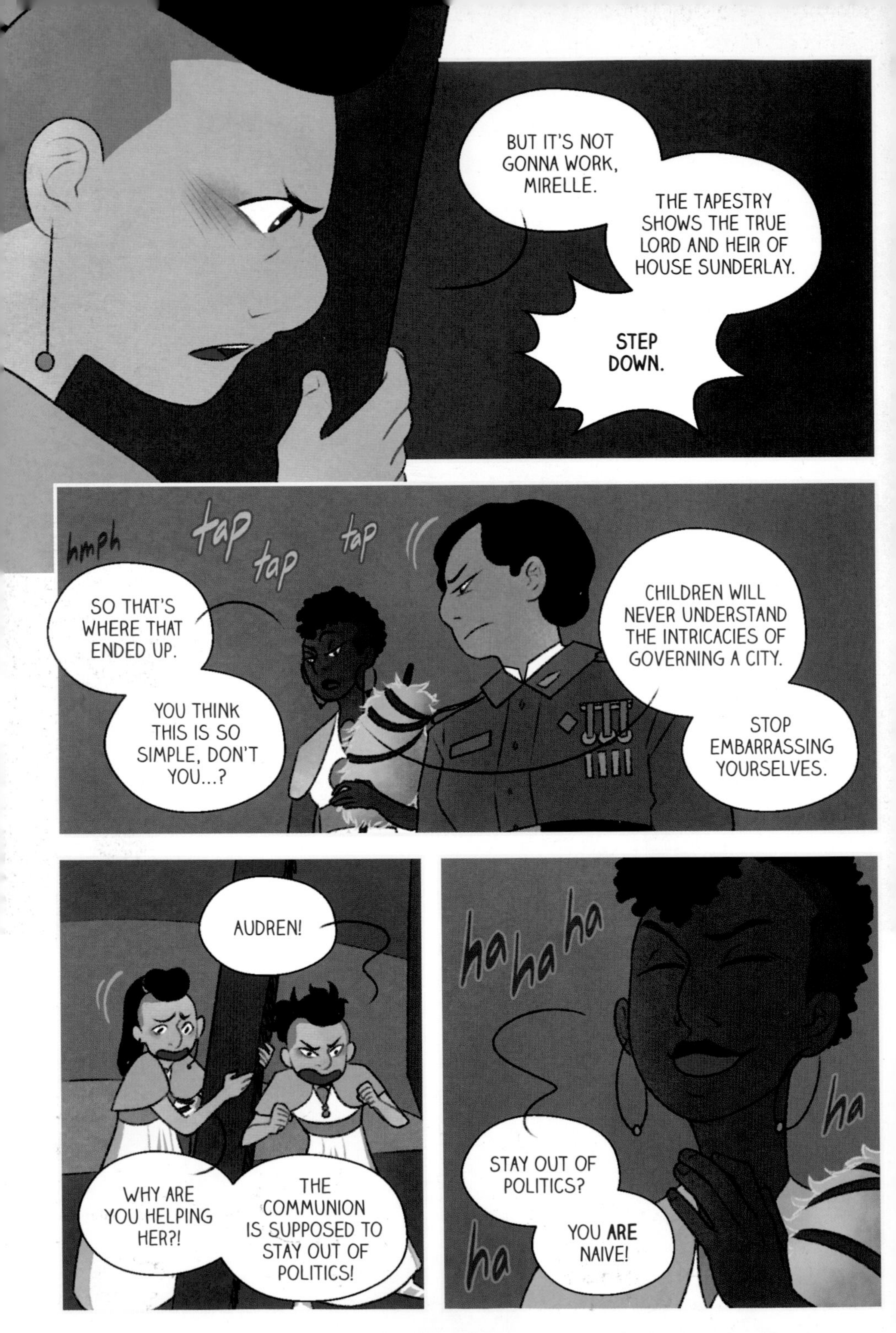
BUT IT'S NOT GONNA WORK, MIRELLE.
THE TAPESTRY SHOWS THE TRUE LORD AND HEIR OF HOUSE SUNDERLAY.
STEP DOWN.
hmph
tap tap tap
SO THAT'S WHERE THAT ENDED UP.
YOU THINK THIS IS SO SIMPLE, DON'T YOU...?
CHILDREN WILL NEVER UNDERSTAND THE INTRICACIES OF GOVERNING A CITY.
STOP EMBARRASSING YOURSELVES.
AUDREN!
WHY ARE YOU HELPING HER?!
THE COMMUNION IS SUPPOSED TO STAY OUT OF POLITICS!
ha ha ha
STAY OUT OF POLITICS?
YOU ARE NAIVE!
ha
ha

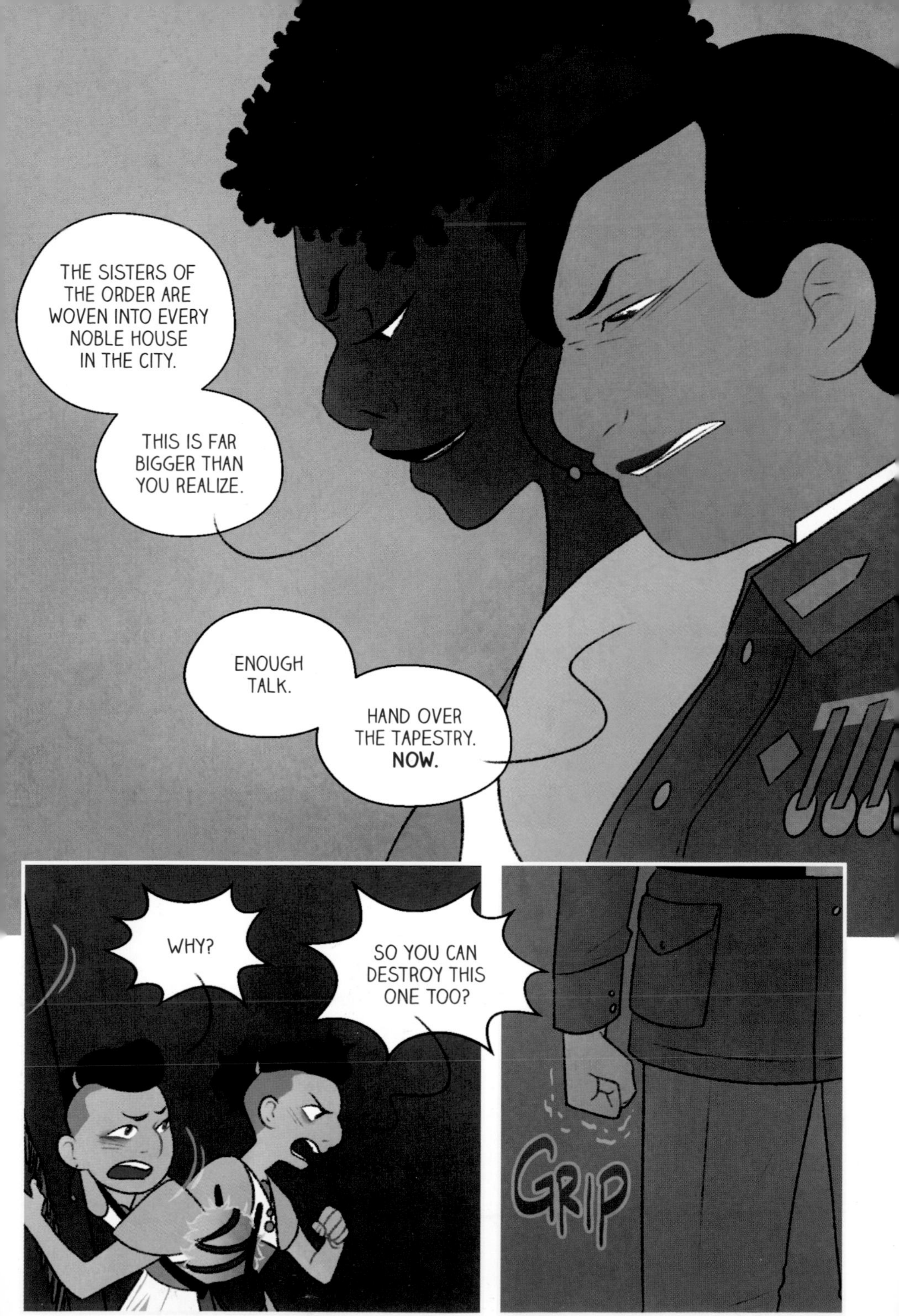
THE SISTERS OF THE ORDER ARE WOVEN INTO EVERY NOBLE HOUSE IN THE CITY.
THIS IS FAR BIGGER THAN YOU REALIZE.
ENOUGH TALK.
HAND OVER THE TAPESTRY. **NOW.**
WHY?
SO YOU CAN DESTROY THIS ONE TOO?
GRIP

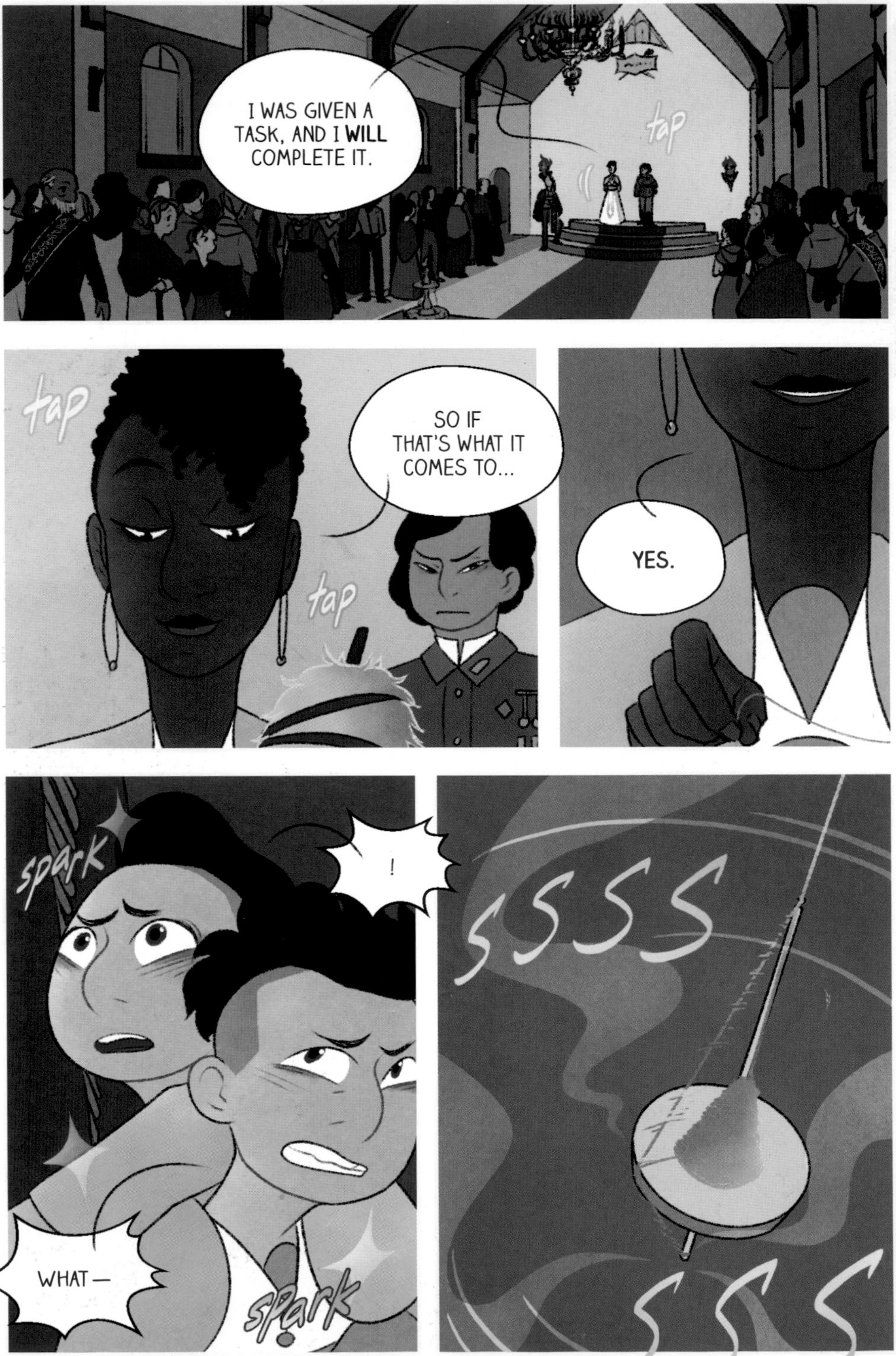
I WAS GIVEN A TASK, AND I **WILL** COMPLETE IT.
tap
tap
SO IF THAT'S WHAT IT COMES TO...
tap
YES.
spark
!
SSSS
WHAT—
spark
SSS

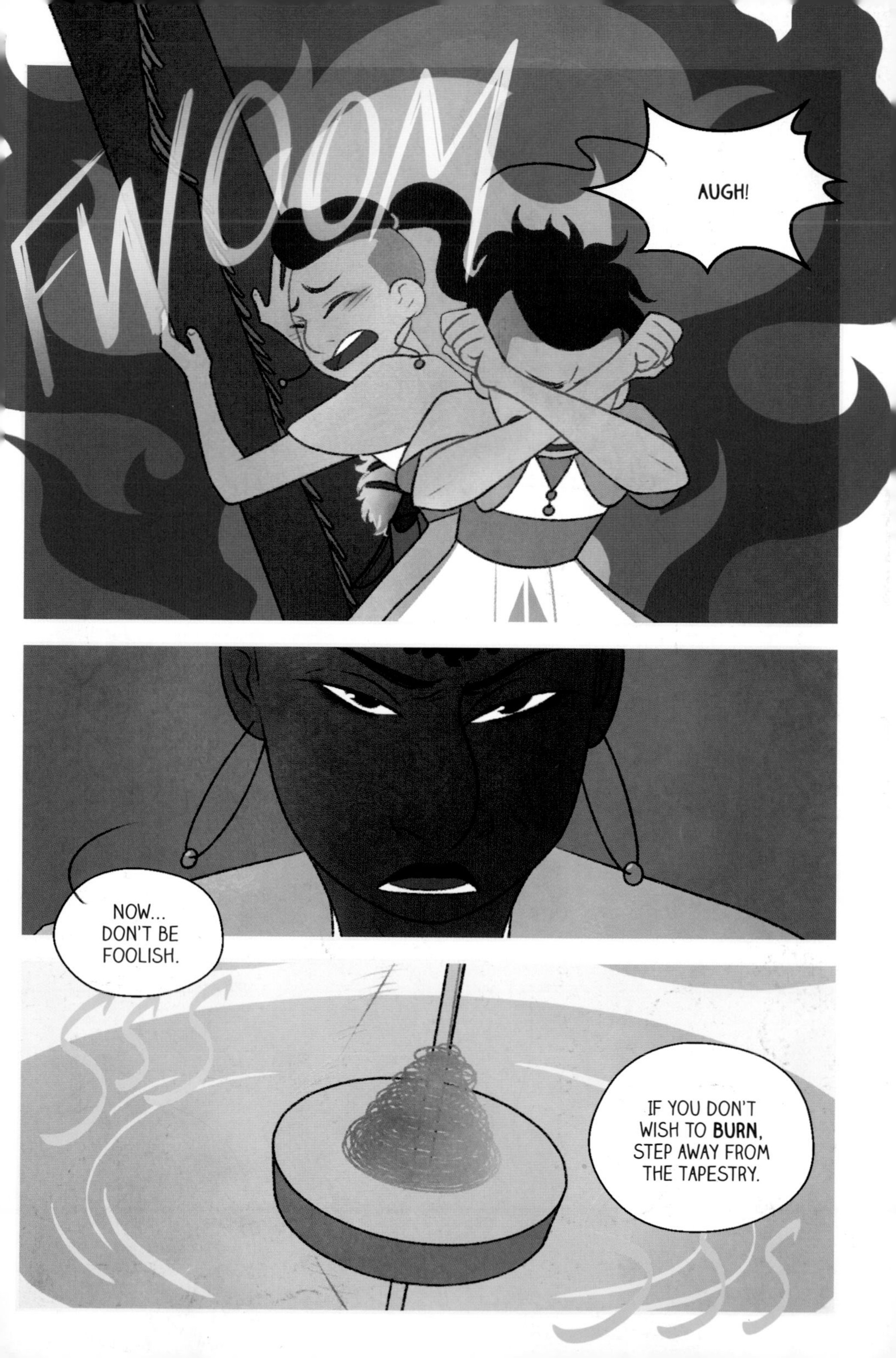
FWOOM
AUGH!
NOW... DON'T BE FOOLISH.
SSS
IF YOU DON'T WISH TO **BURN**, STEP AWAY FROM THE TAPESTRY.
SSS

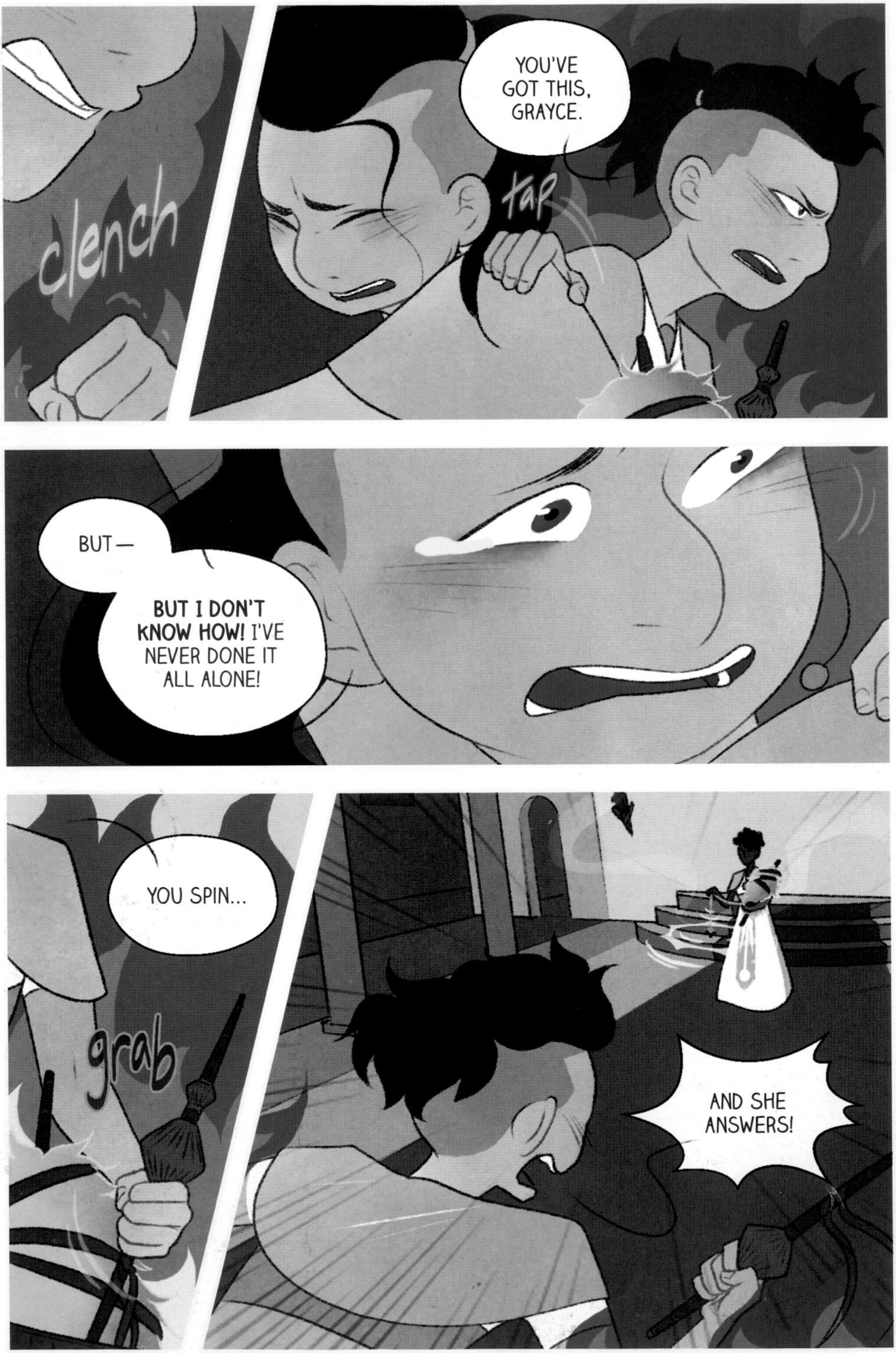
clench
YOU'VE GOT THIS, GRAYCE.
tap
BUT—
BUT I DON'T KNOW HOW! I'VE NEVER DONE IT ALL ALONE!
YOU SPIN...
grab
AND SHE ANSWERS!

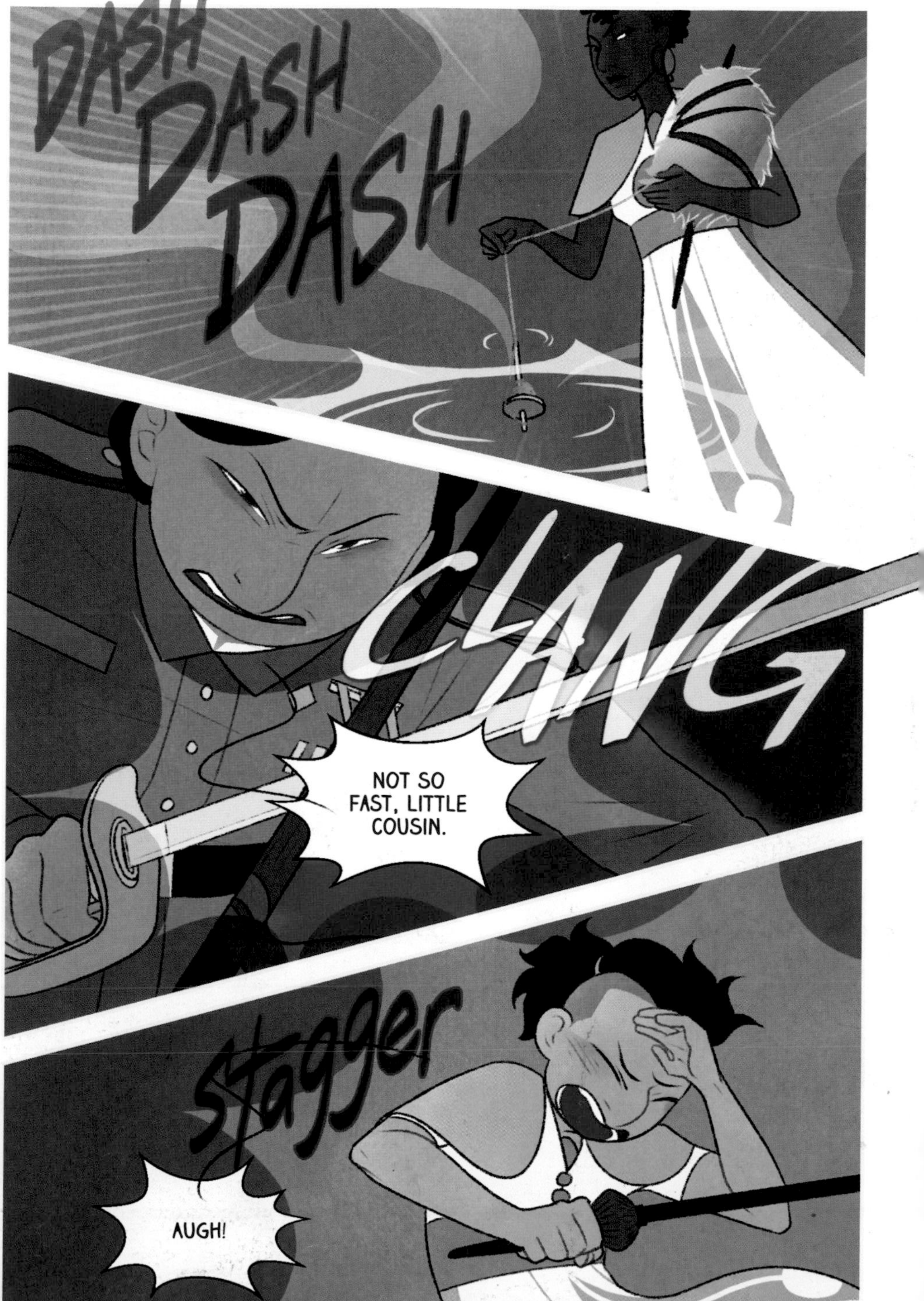
DASH DASH DASH
CLANG
NOT SO FAST, LITTLE COUSIN.
stagger
AUGH!

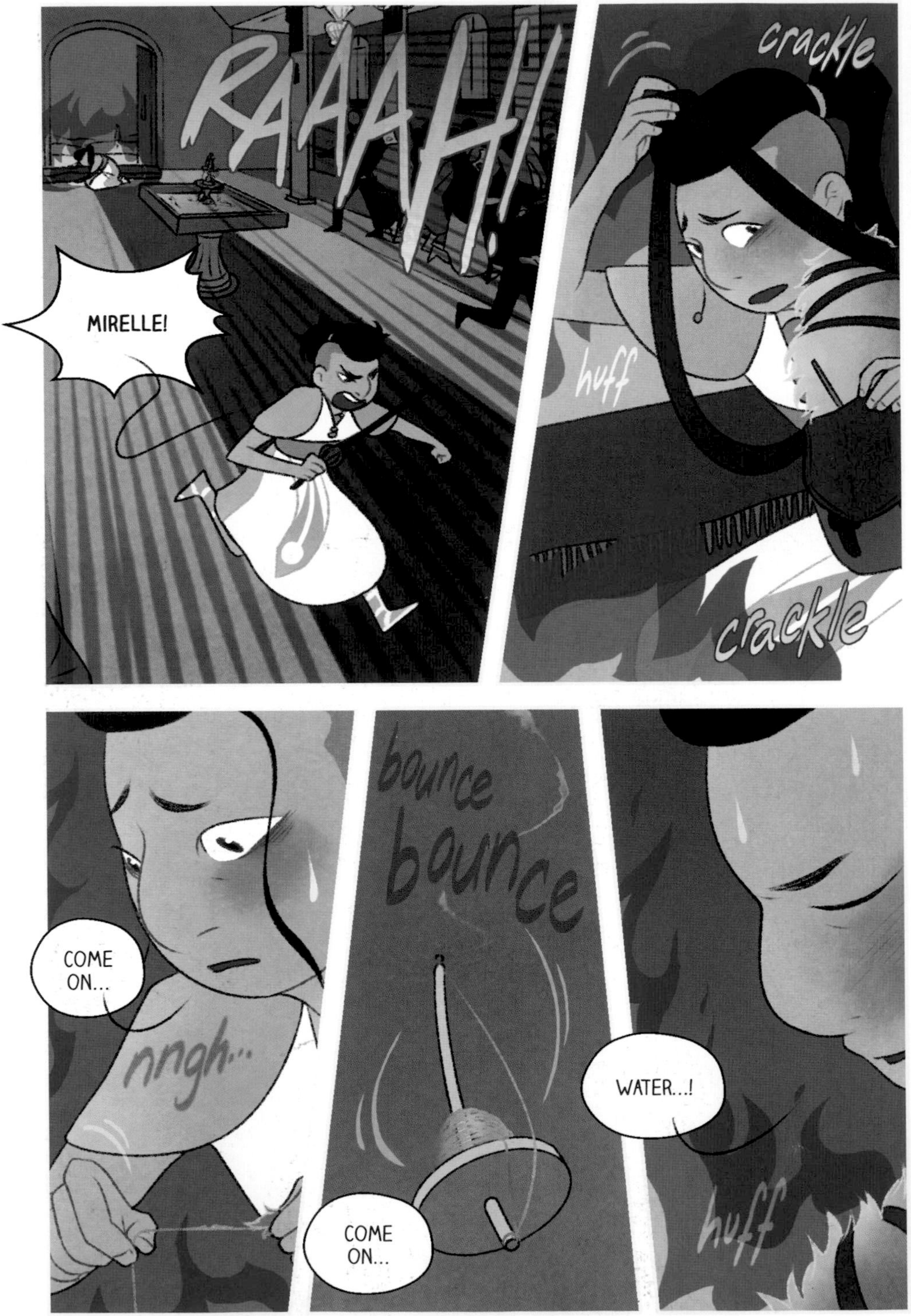
RAAAH!!
MIRELLE!
crackle
huff
crackle
COME ON...
nngh...
bounce
bounce
COME ON...
WATER...!
huff

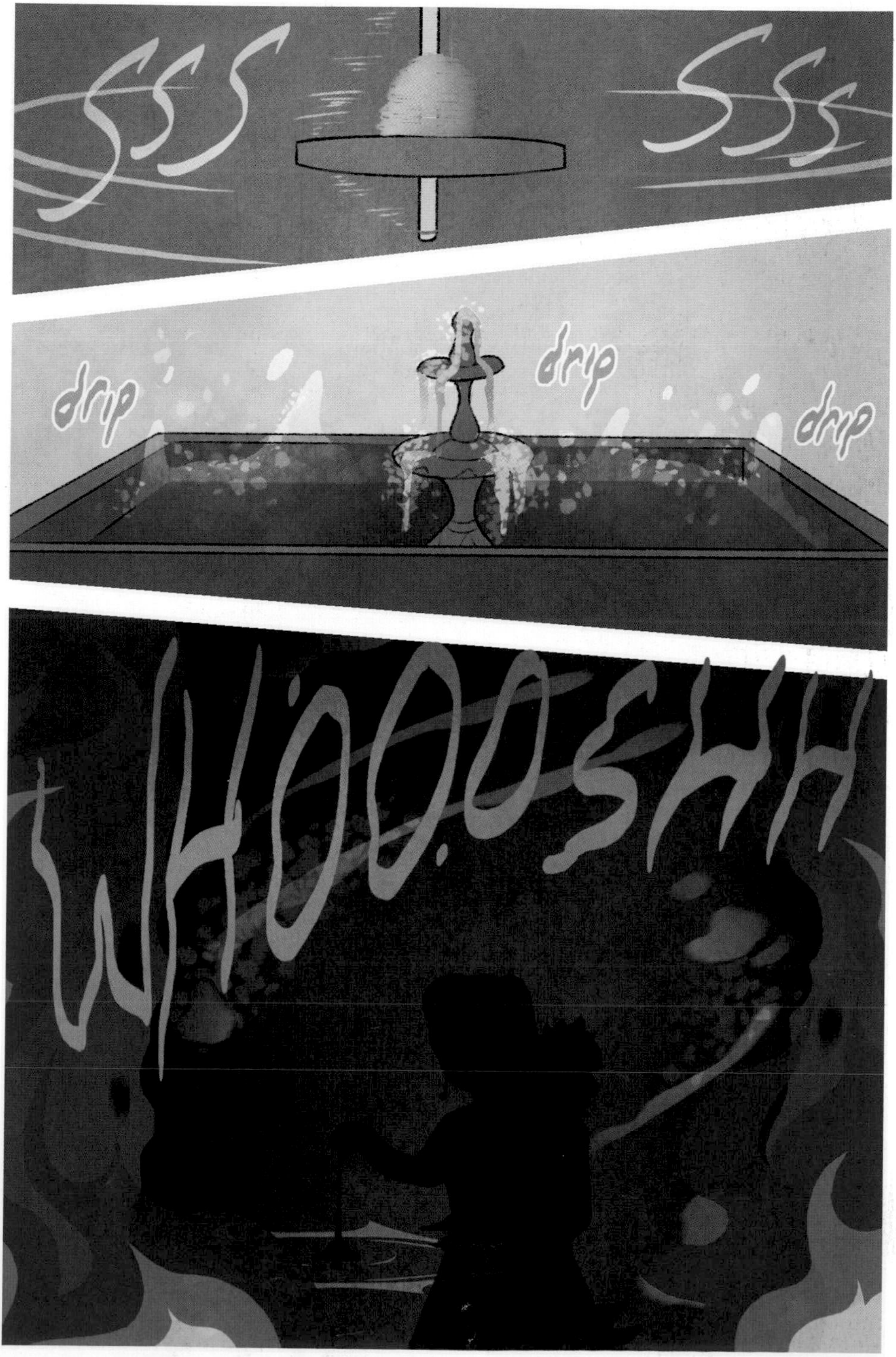
SSS
SSS
drip
drip
drip
WHOOOSHH

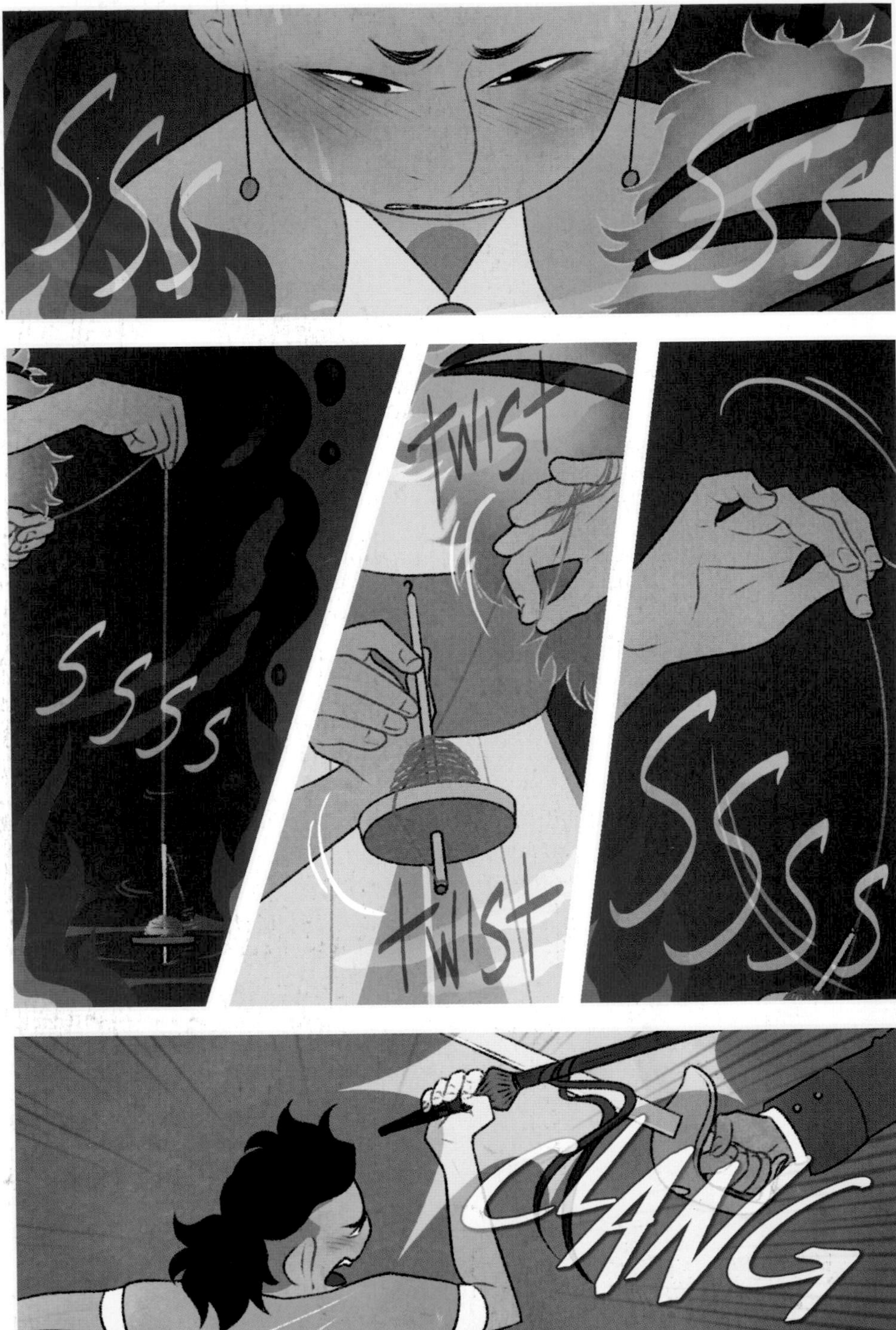
SSSS
SSSS
SSSS
TWIST
TWIST
SSSSS
CLANG

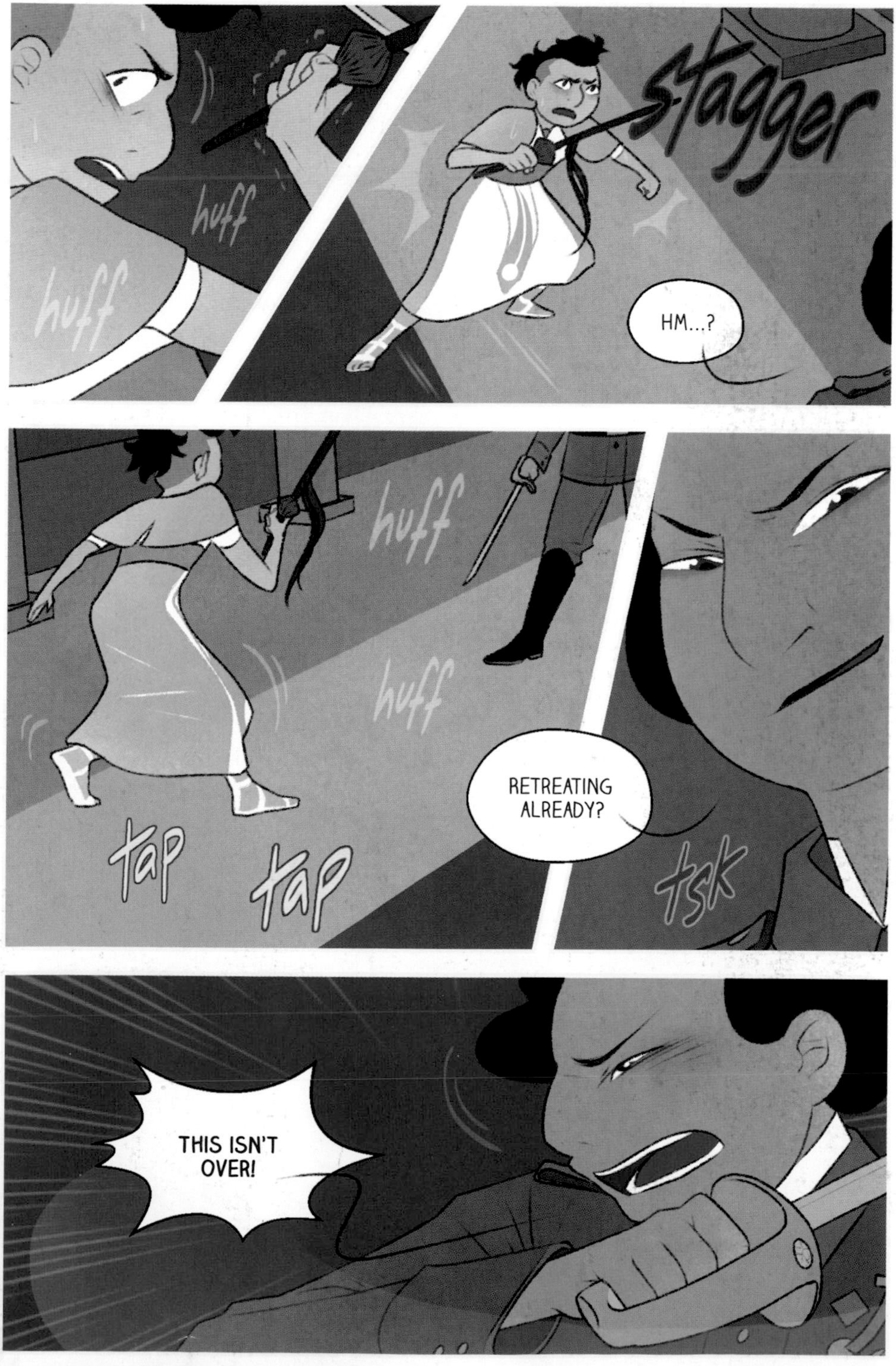
huff
huff
stagger
HM...?
huff
huff
tap
tap
RETREATING ALREADY?
tsk
THIS ISN'T OVER!

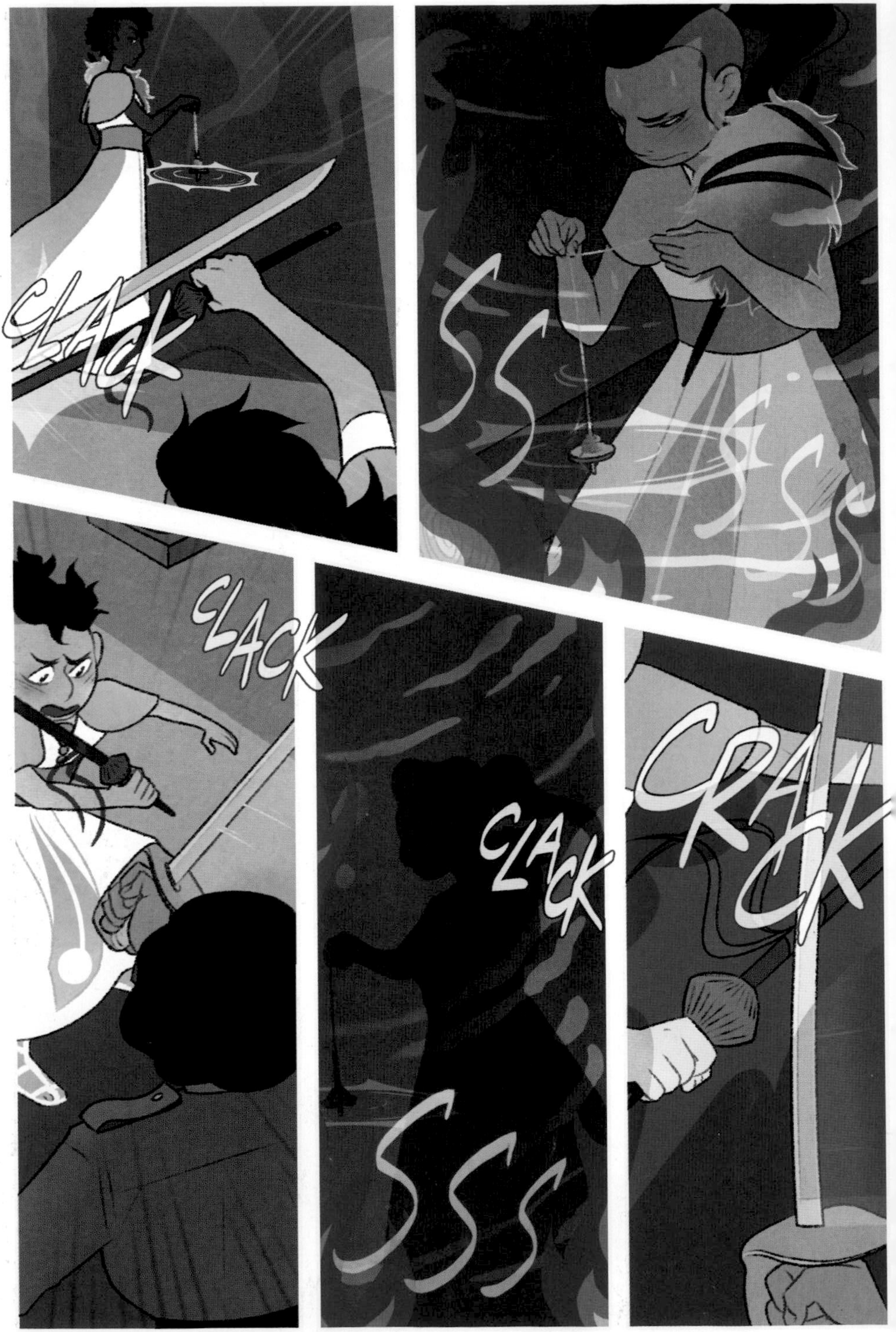
CLACK
SSS
SSS
CLACK
CLACK
SSS
CRACK

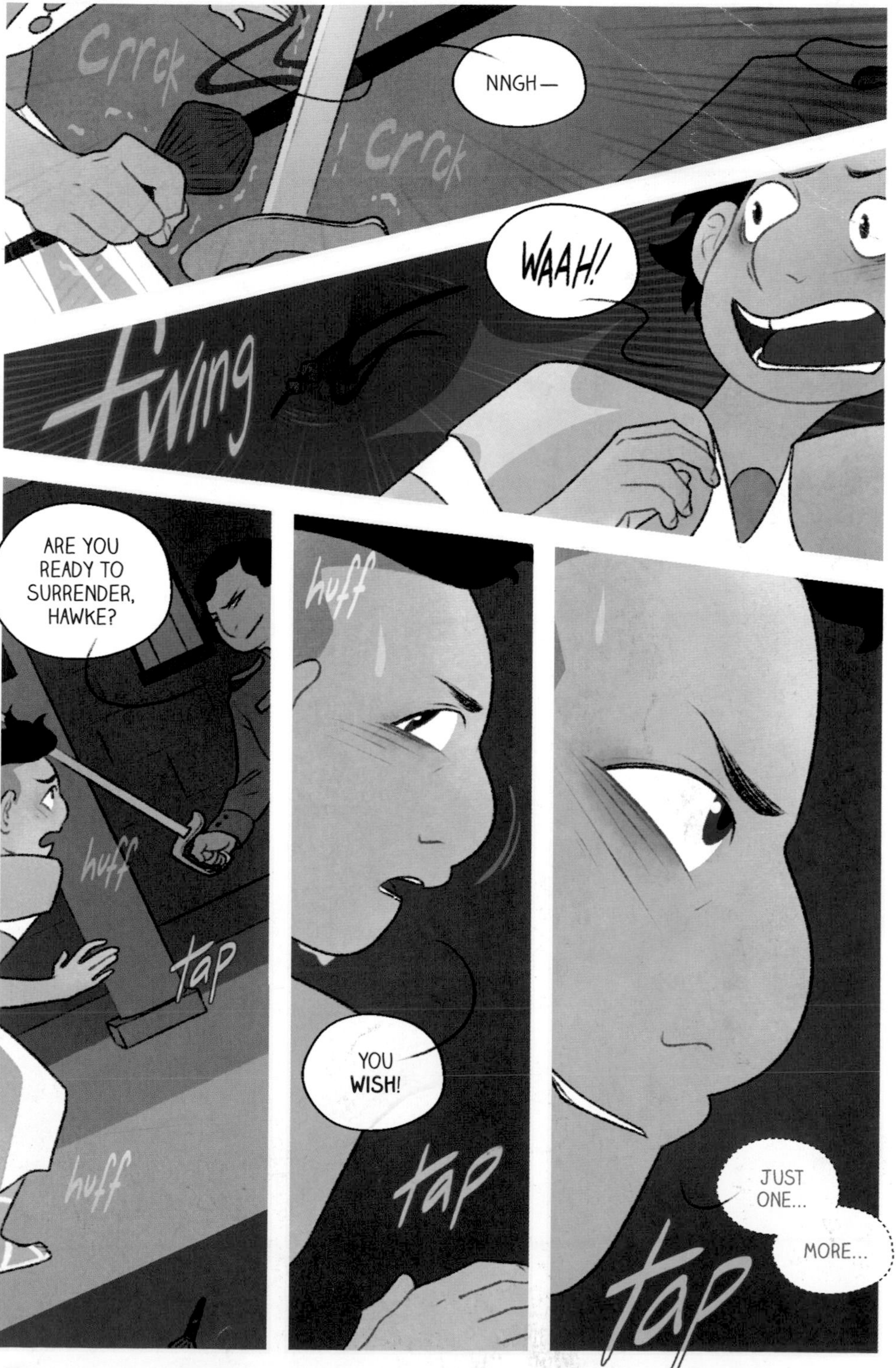
crrck
crrck
NNGH—
WAAH!
fwing
ARE YOU READY TO SURRENDER, HAWKE?
huff
huff
tap
huff
huff
YOU WISH!
tap
JUST ONE...
MORE...
tap

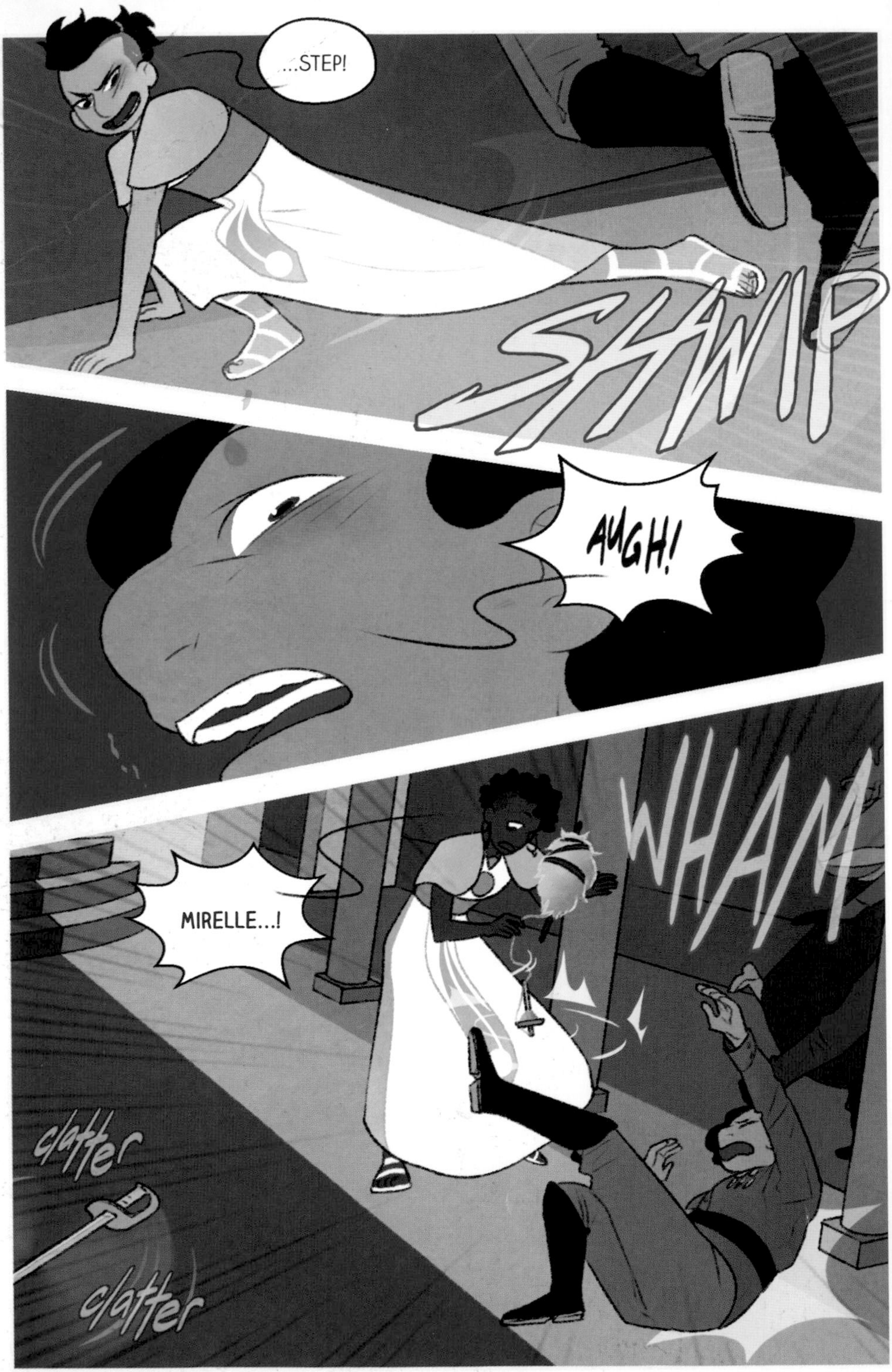

...STEP!
SHWIP
AUGH!
WHAM
MIRELLE...!
clatter
clatter

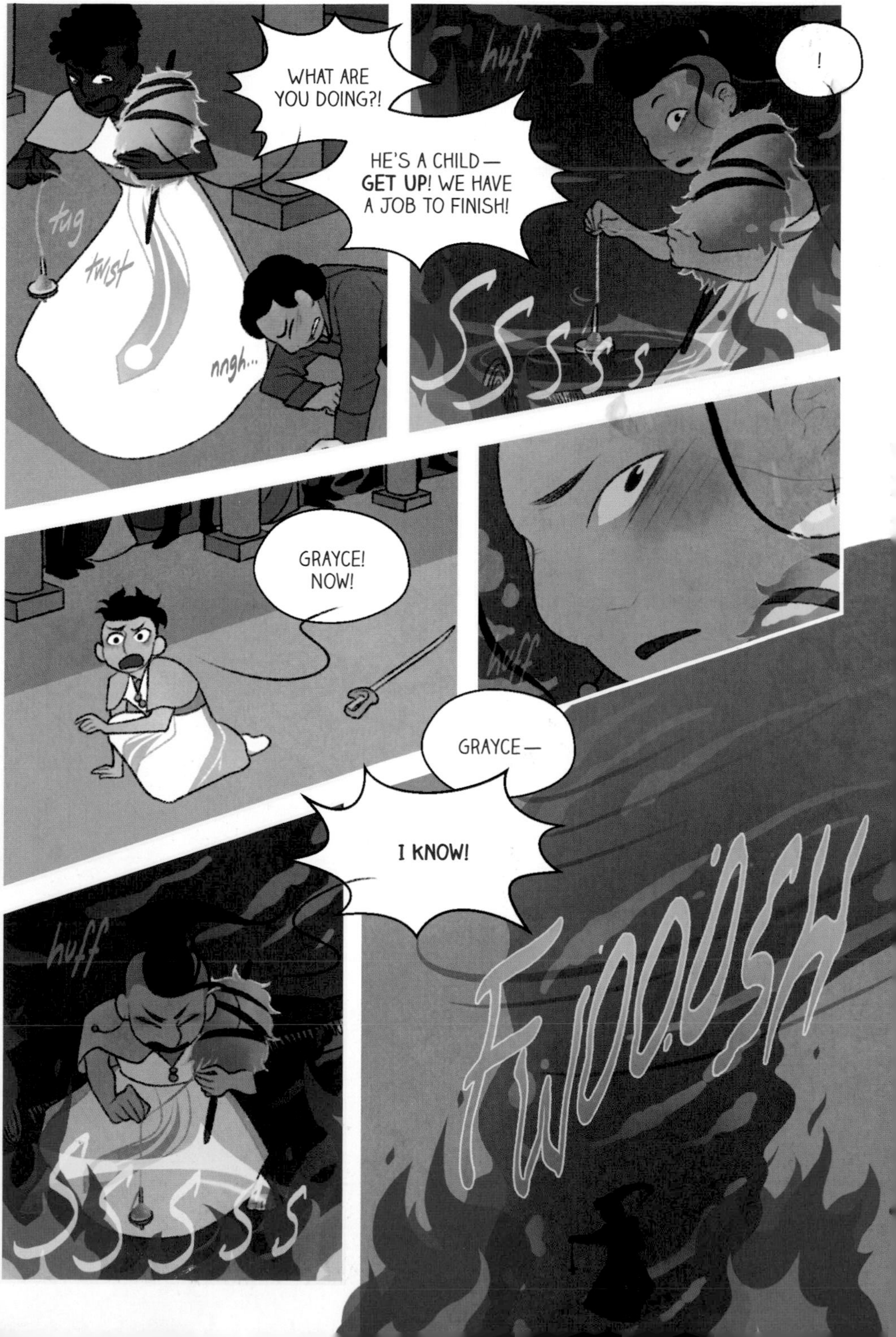

WHAT ARE YOU DOING?!
HE'S A CHILD— **GET UP**! WE HAVE A JOB TO FINISH!
tug
twist
nngh...
huff
!
SSSSS
GRAYCE! NOW!
huff
GRAYCE—
I KNOW!
huff
SSSSS
FWOOOSH

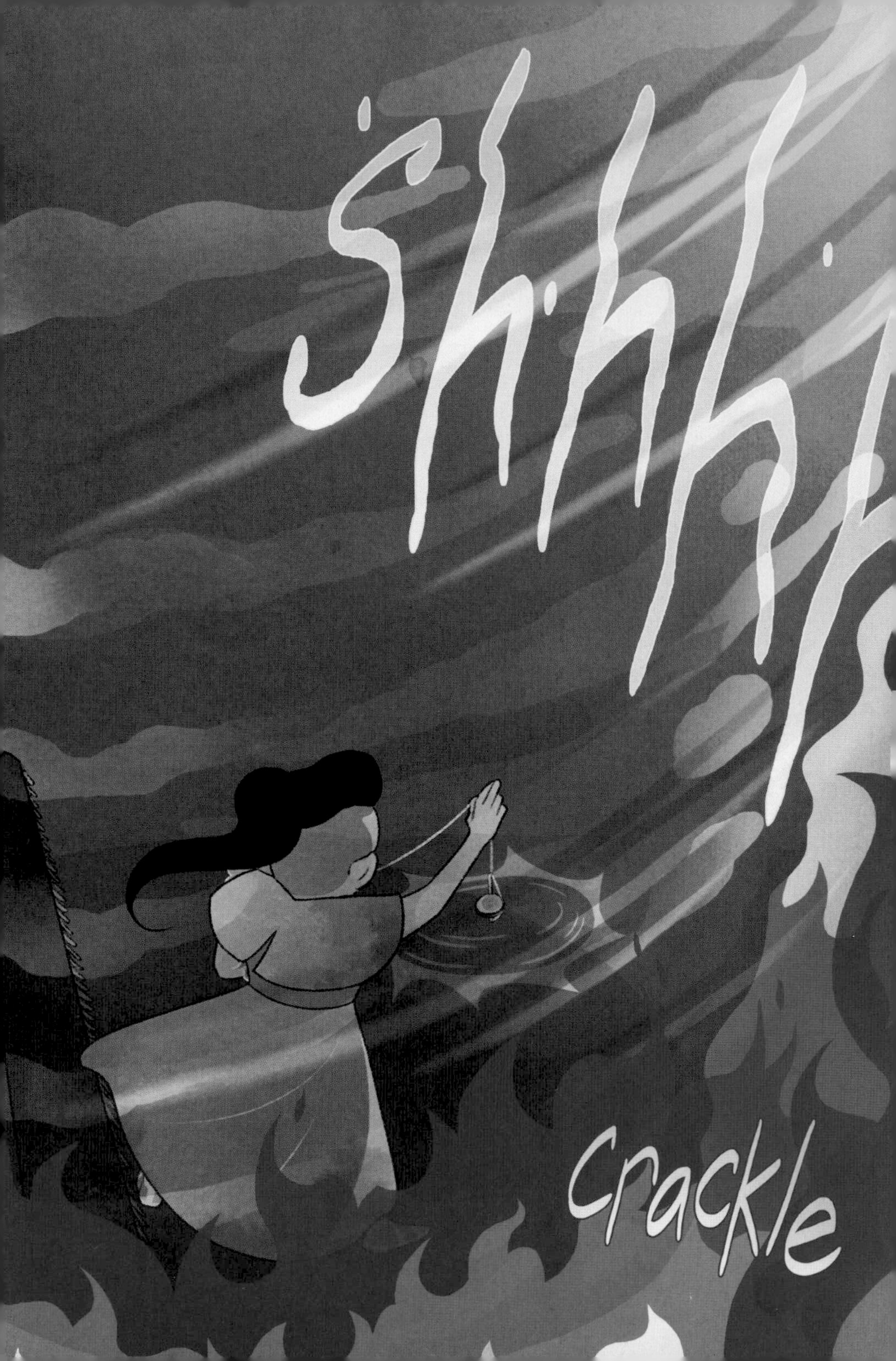
Shhhh
Crackle

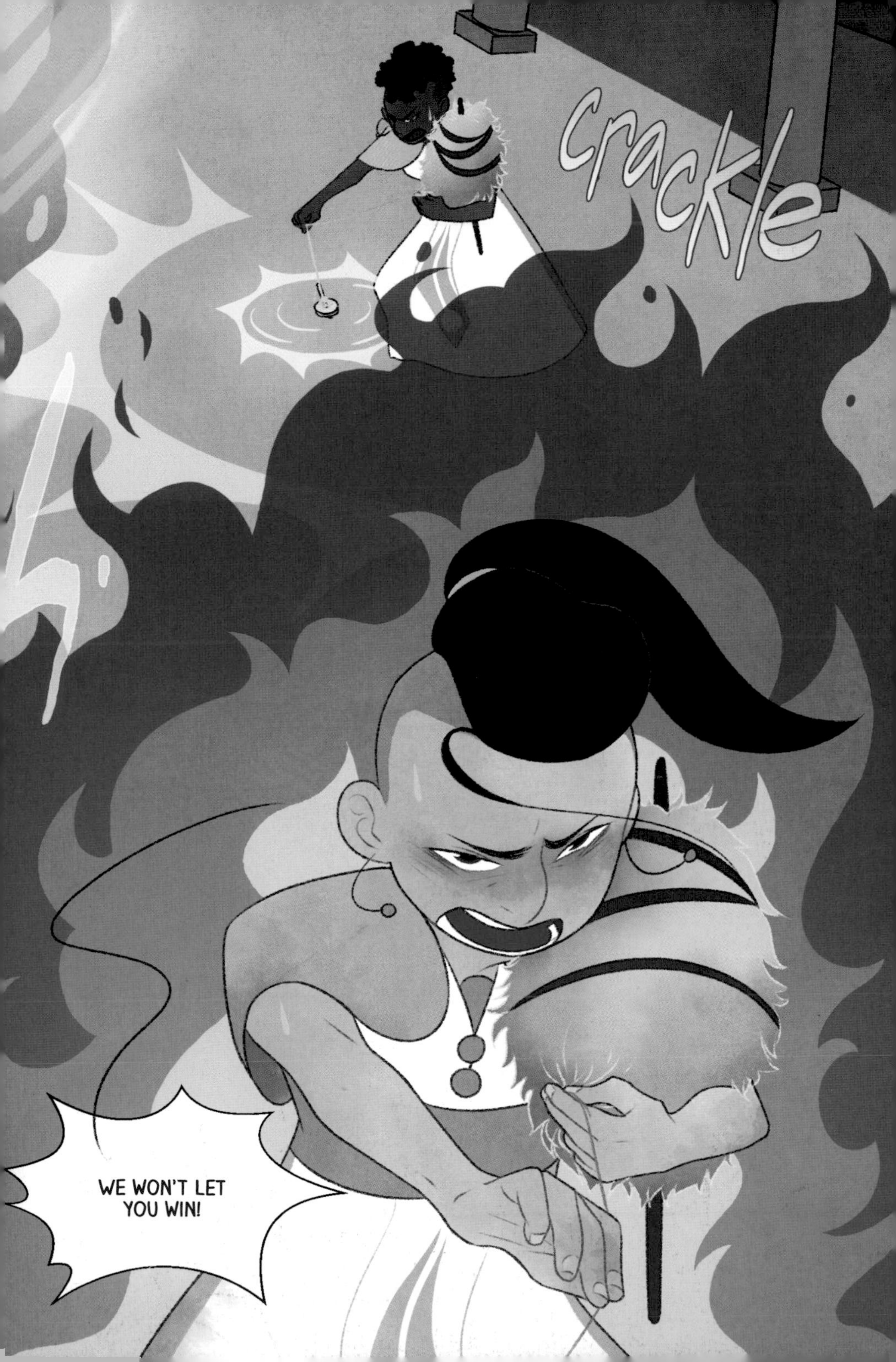
crackle
WE WON'T LET YOU WIN!

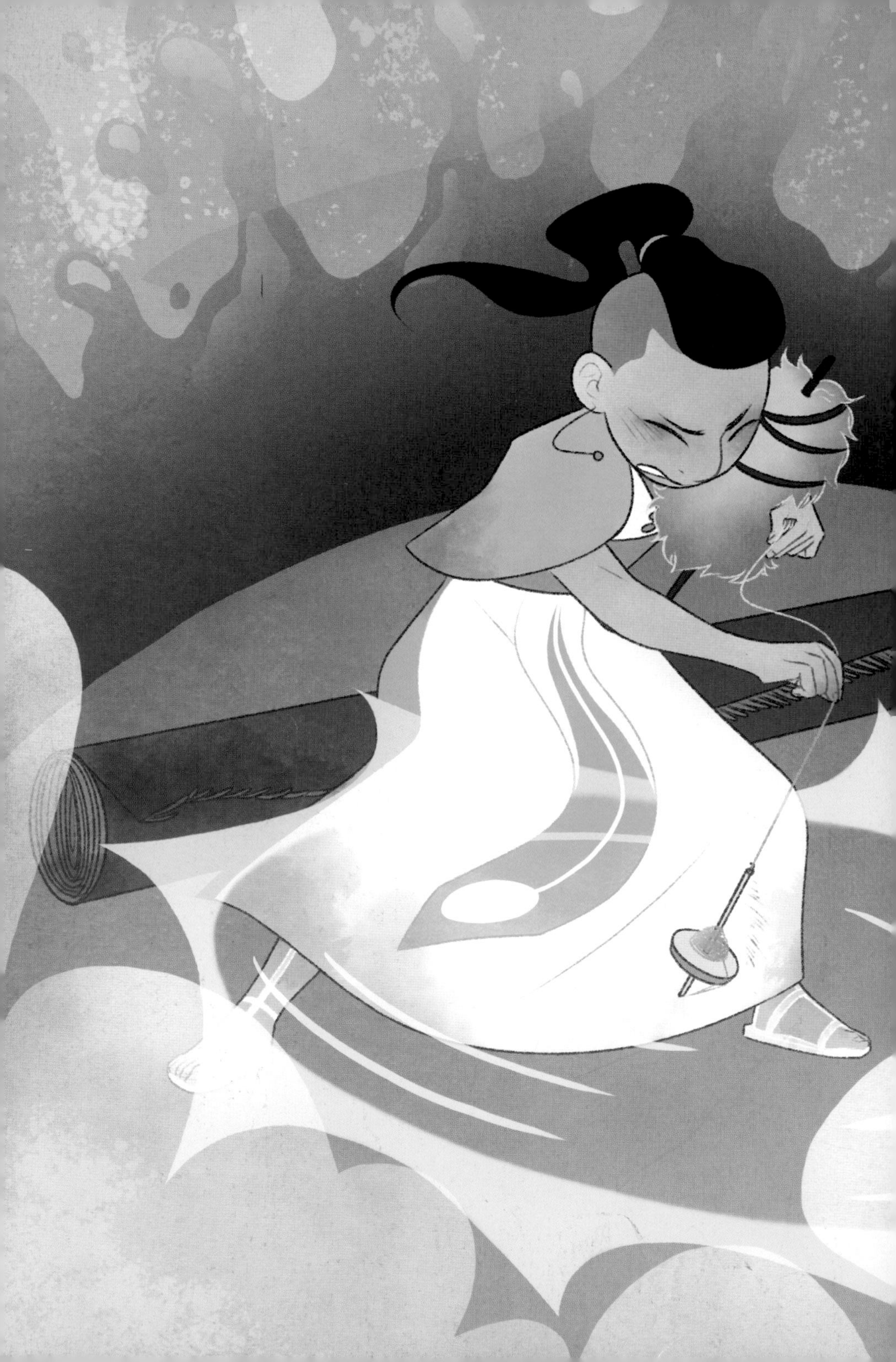

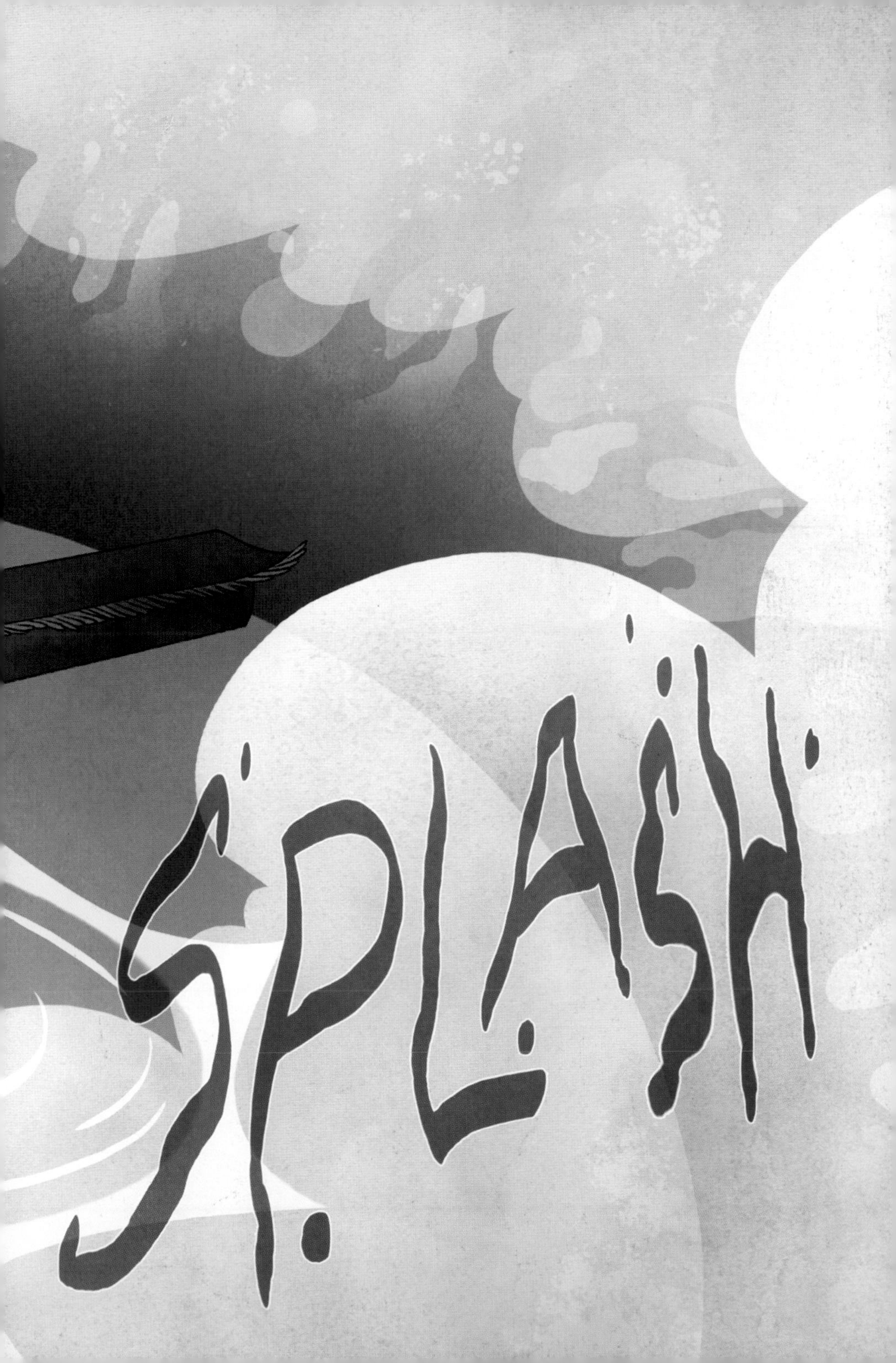
SPLASH

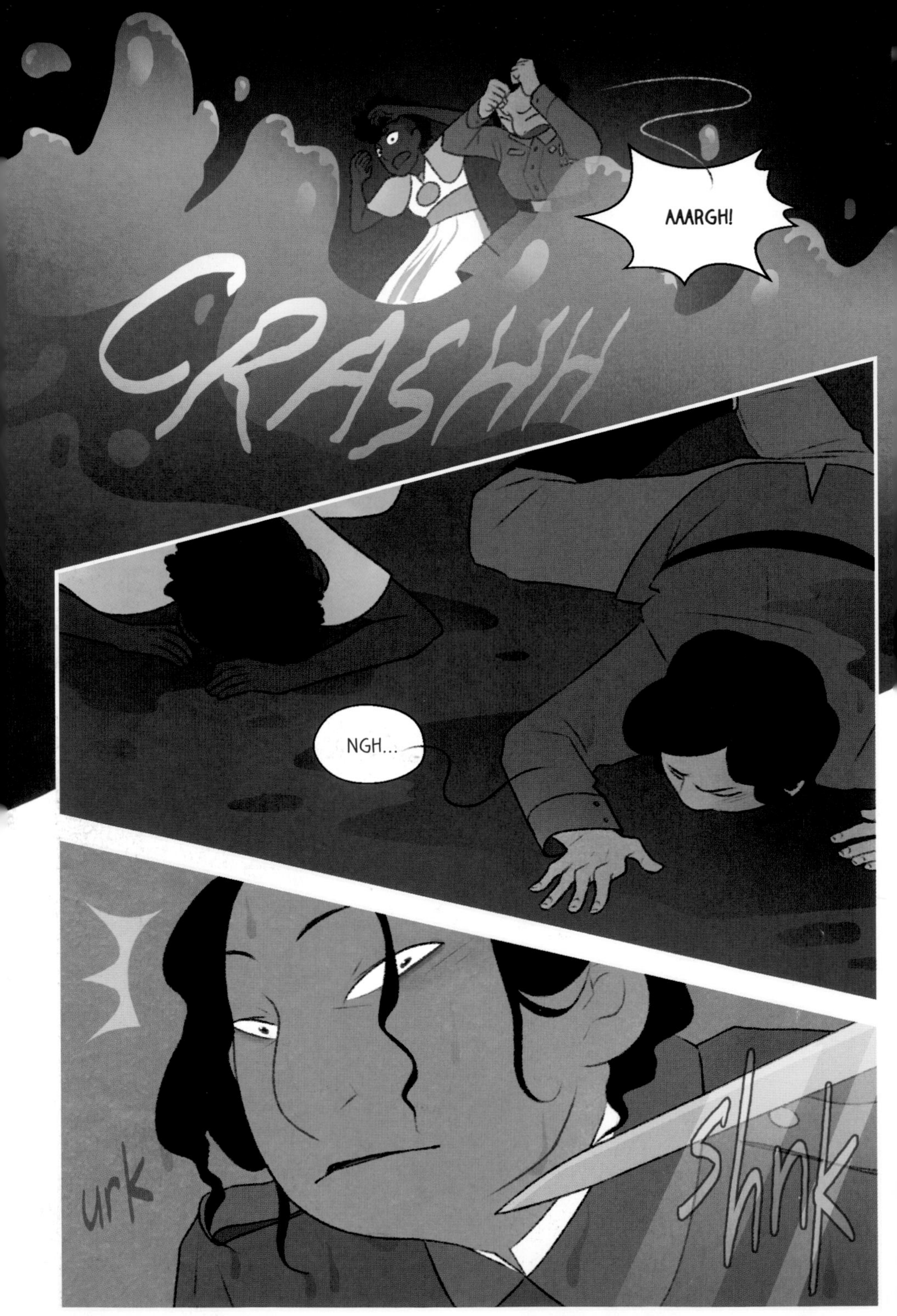
AAARGH!
CRASHH
NGH...
urk
shnk

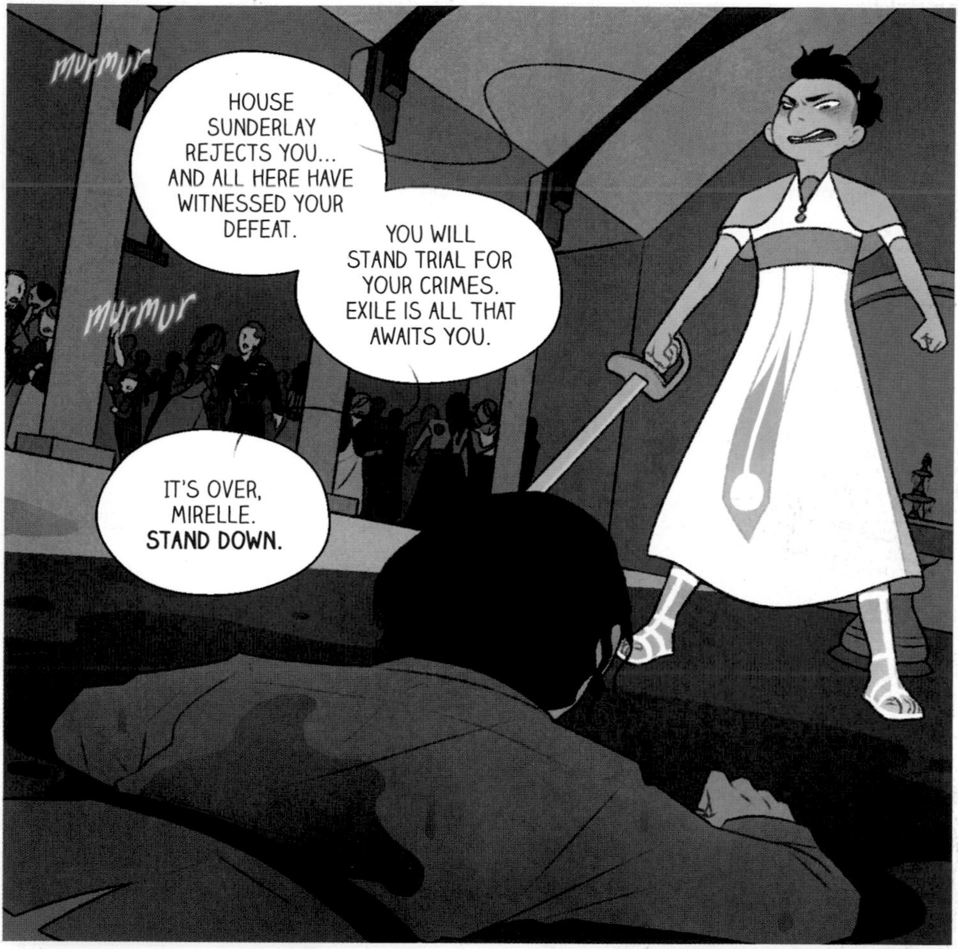
murmur
HOUSE SUNDERLAY REJECTS YOU... AND ALL HERE HAVE WITNESSED YOUR DEFEAT.
murmur
YOU WILL STAND TRIAL FOR YOUR CRIMES. EXILE IS ALL THAT AWAITS YOU.
IT'S OVER, MIRELLE. **STAND DOWN.**

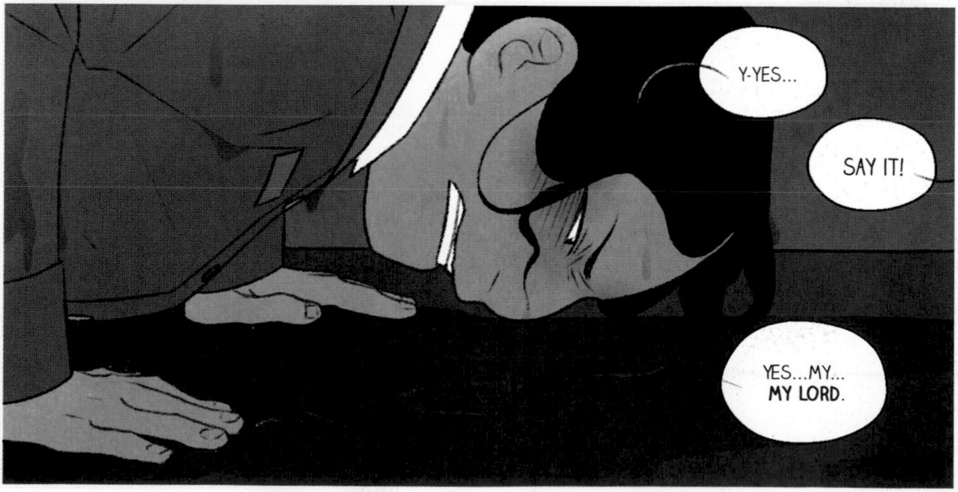
Y-YES...
SAY IT!
YES...MY... **MY LORD**.

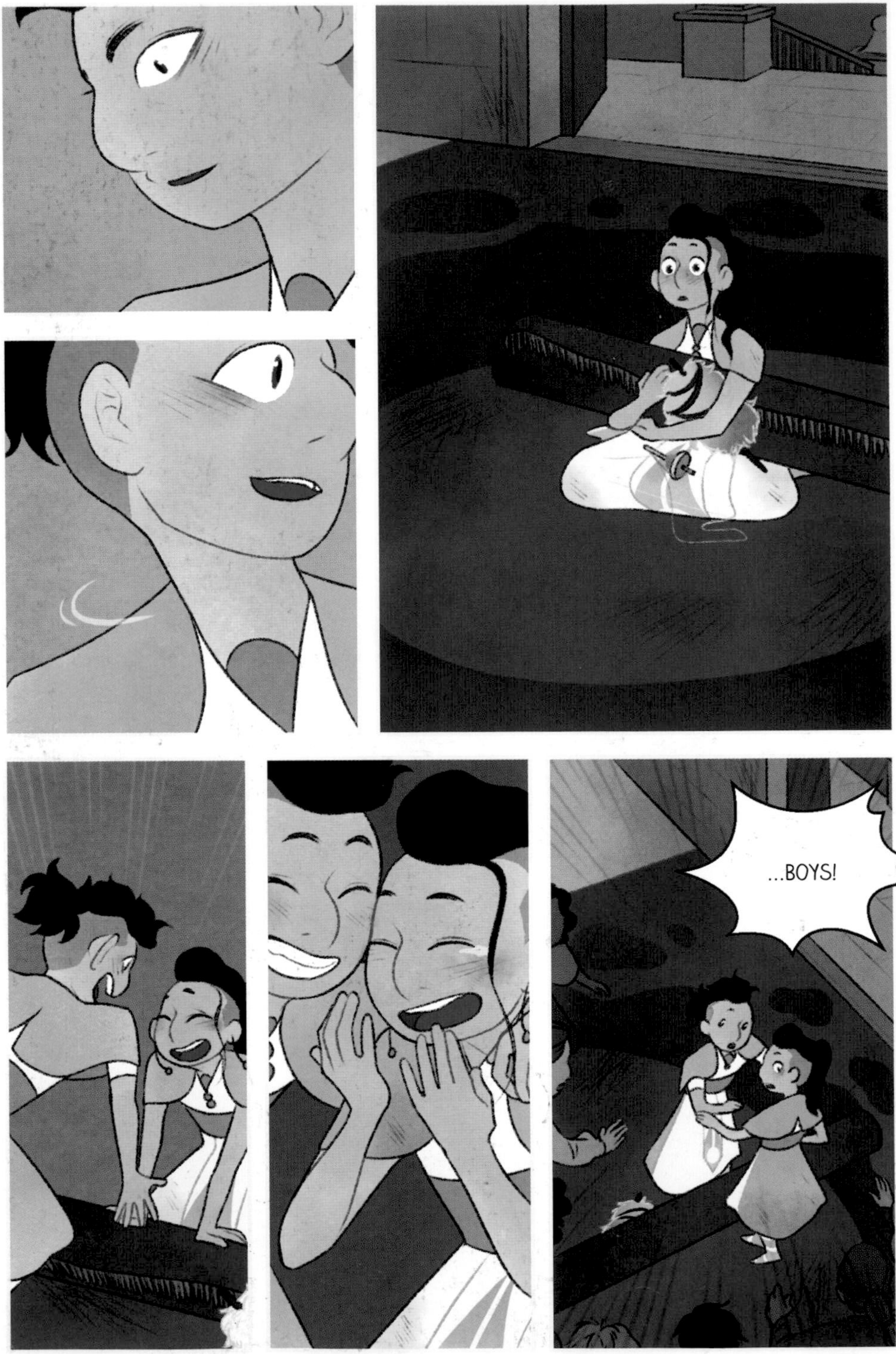
...BOYS!

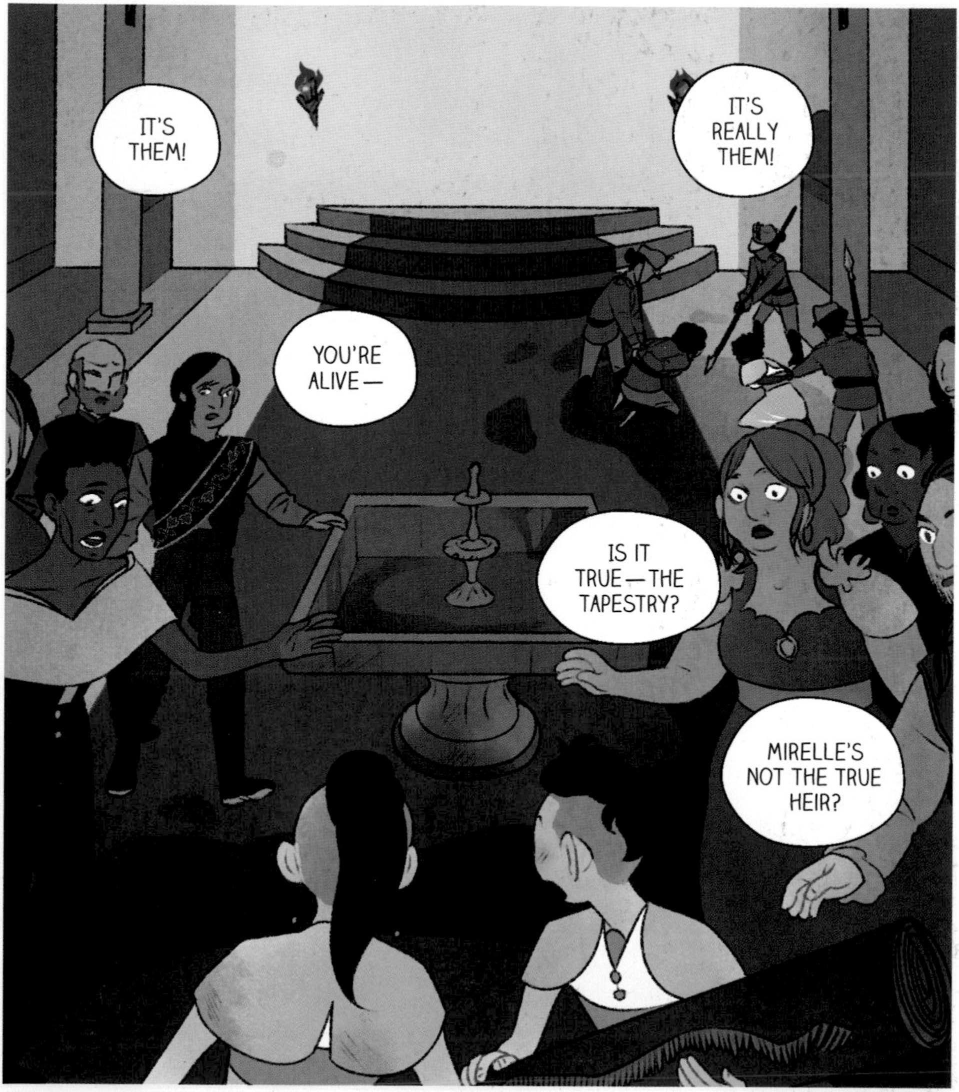
IT'S THEM!
IT'S REALLY THEM!
YOU'RE ALIVE—
IS IT TRUE—THE TAPESTRY?
MIRELLE'S NOT THE TRUE HEIR?
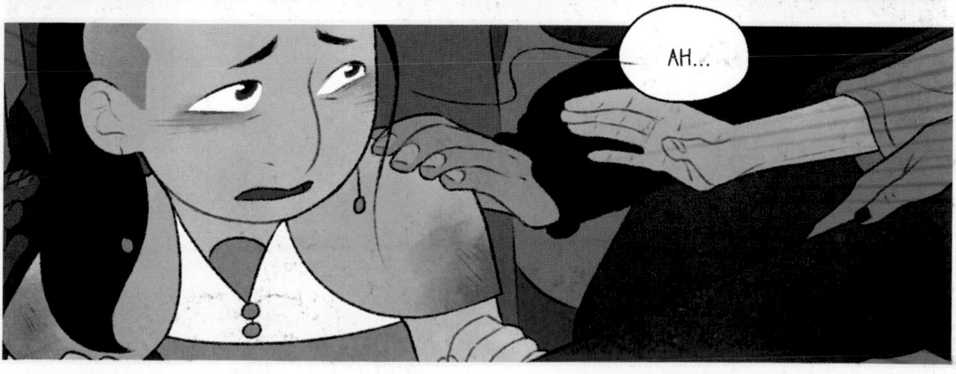
AH...

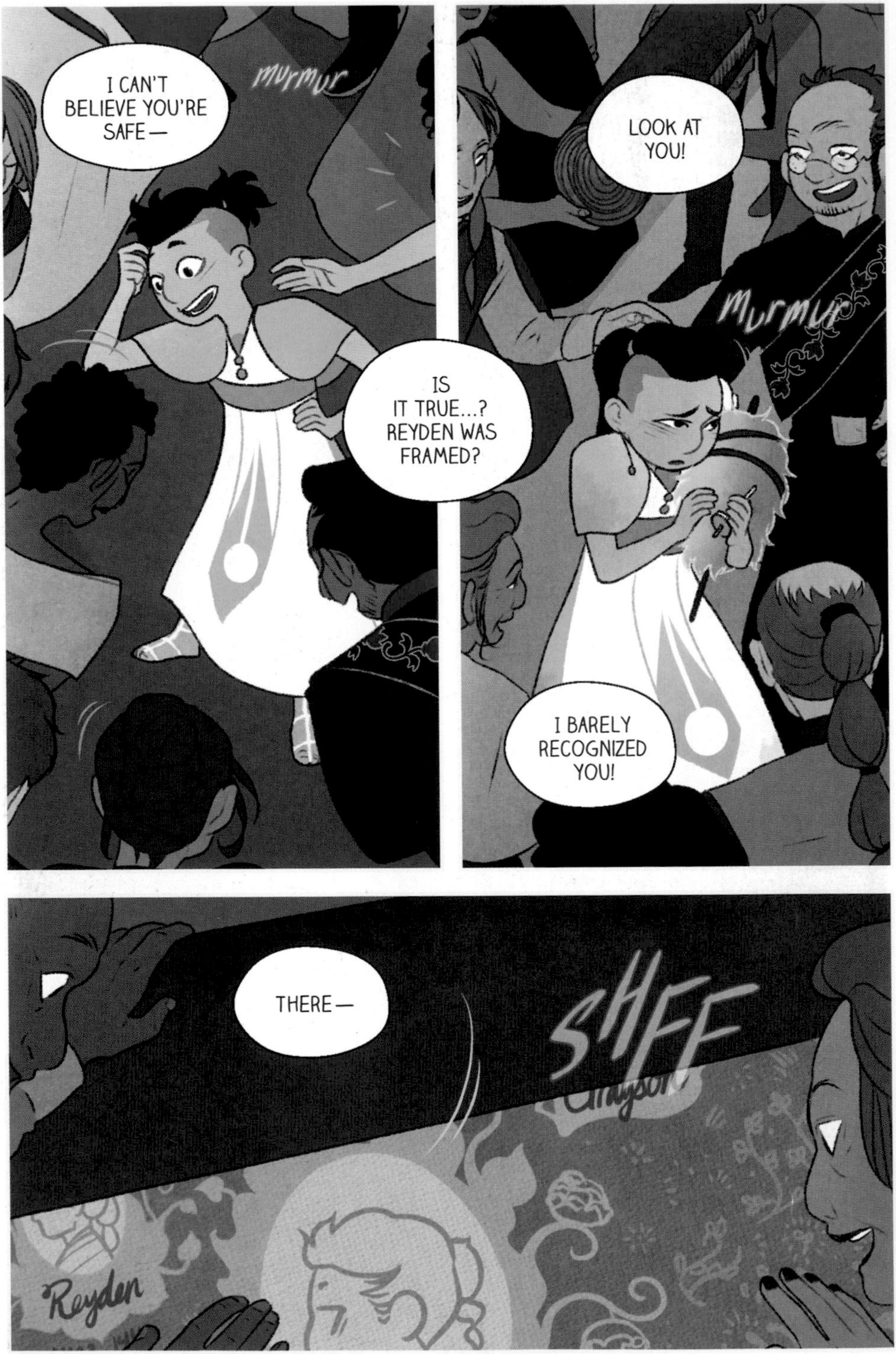
I CAN'T BELIEVE YOU'RE SAFE—
murmur
LOOK AT YOU!
IS IT TRUE...? REYDEN WAS FRAMED?
murmur
I BARELY RECOGNIZED YOU!
THERE—
SHFF
Reyden

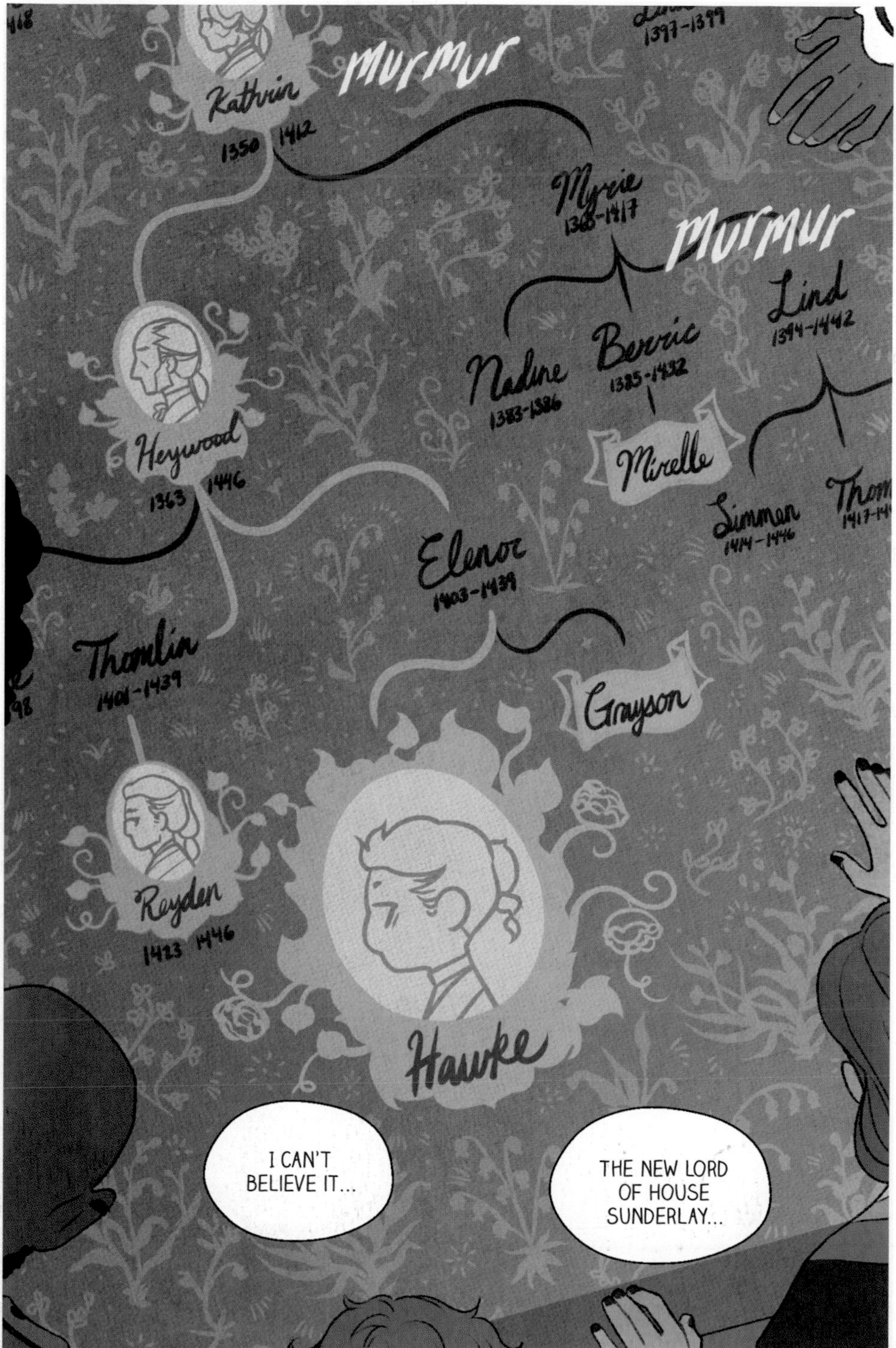

Kathrin
1350 1412
MURMUR
Myrie
MURMUR
Lind
1394-1442
Nadine
1383-1386
Berric
1385-1432
Mirelle
Heywood
1363 1446
Simmen
1414-1446
Elenor
1403-1439
Thomlin
1401-1439
Grayson
Reyden
1423 1446
Hawke
I CAN'T BELIEVE IT...
THE NEW LORD OF HOUSE SUNDERLAY...

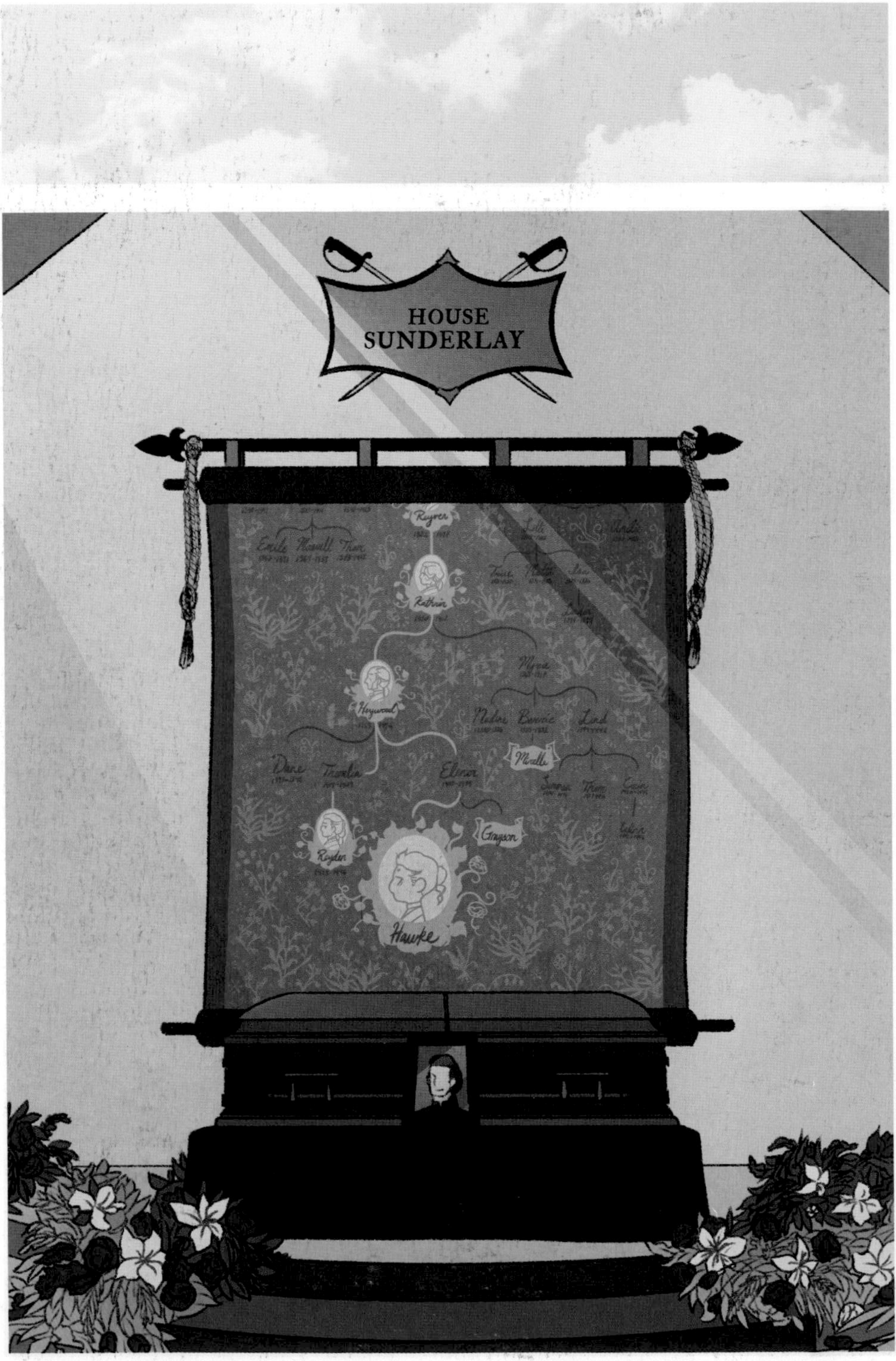

HOUSE SUNDERLAY
Rayner
Emile
Maxwell
Kathrin
Heywood
Dane
Elinor
Grayson
Royden
Hawke

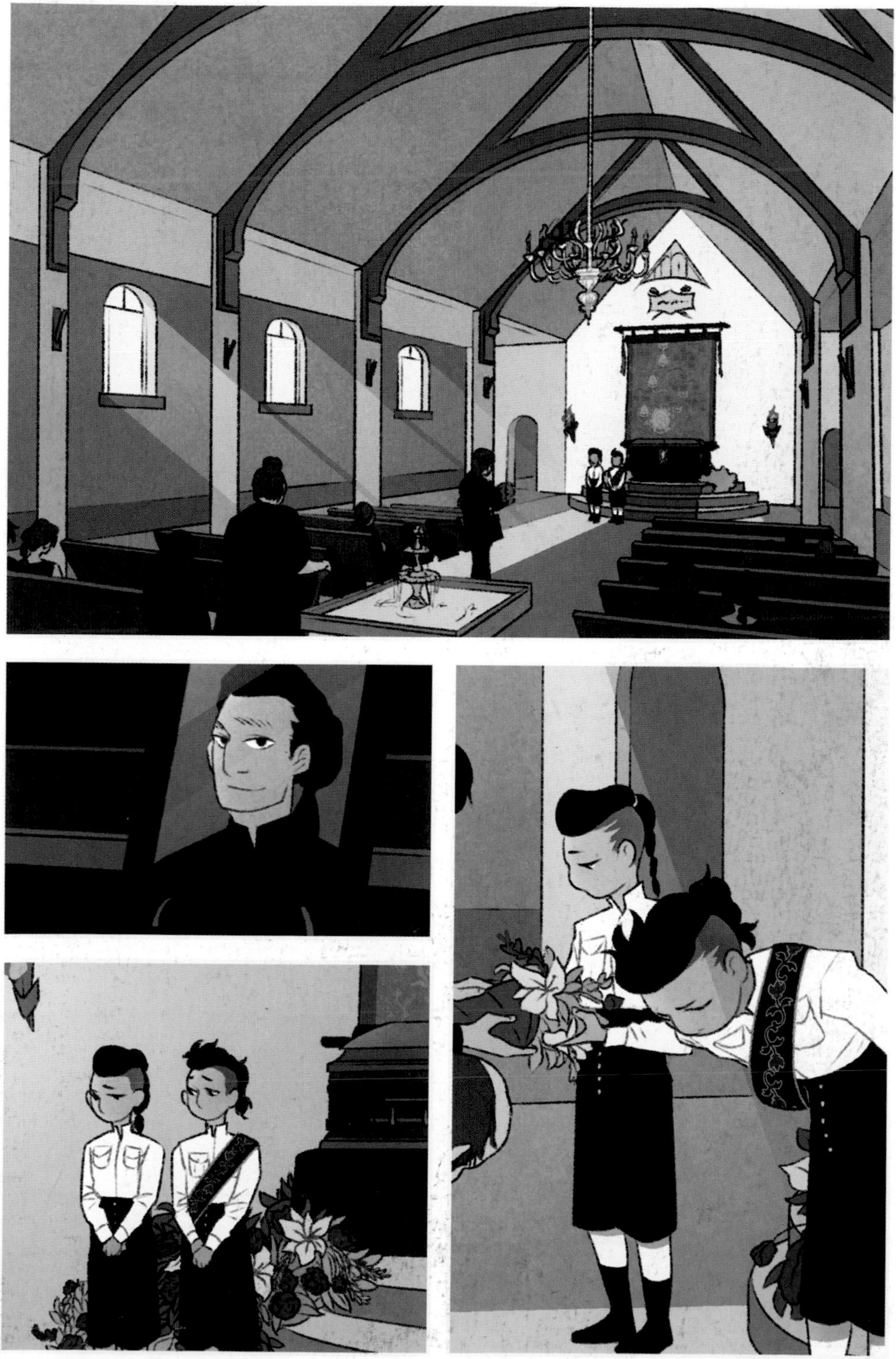

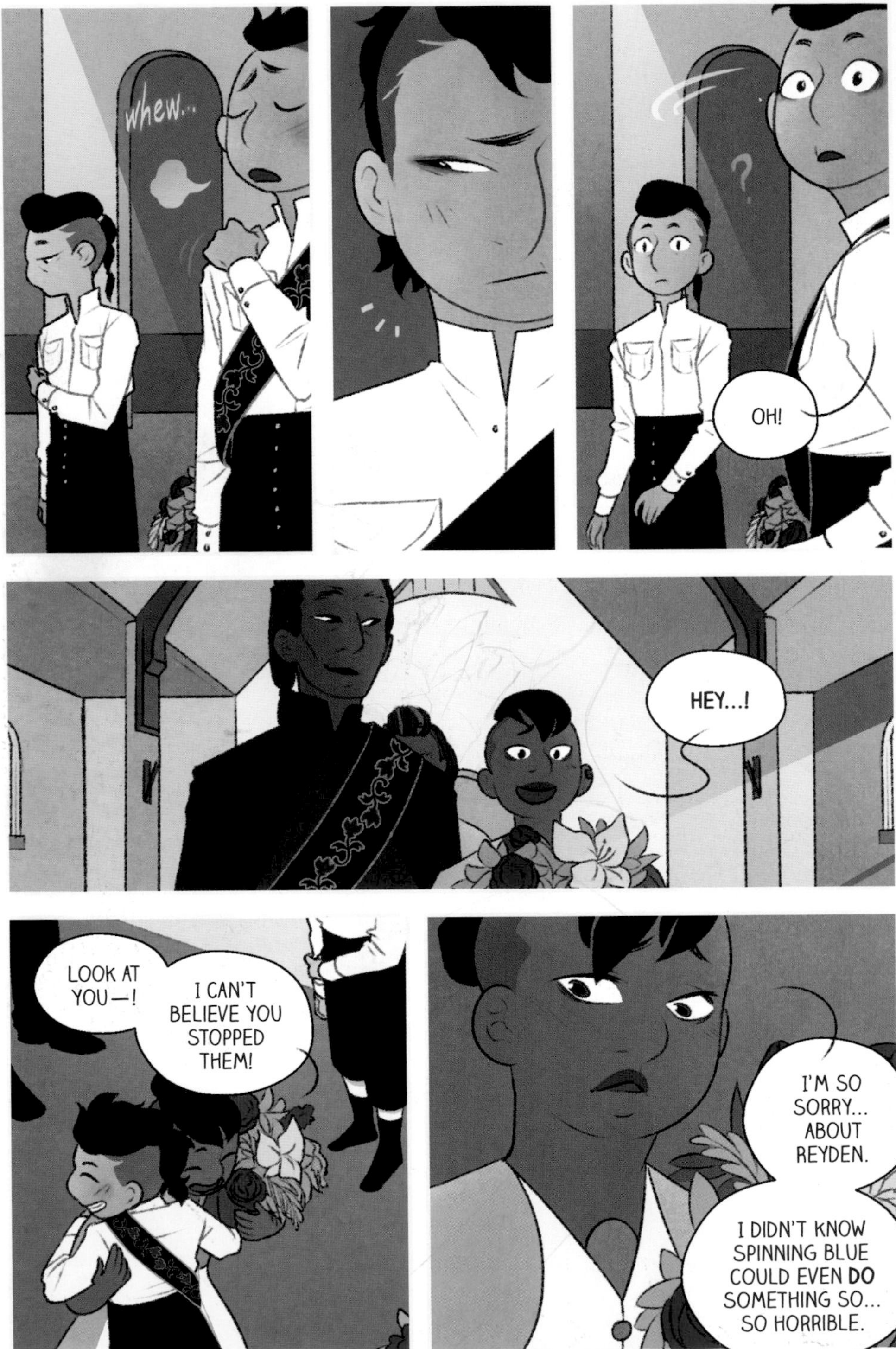
whew...
?
OH!
HEY...!
LOOK AT YOU—!
I CAN'T BELIEVE YOU STOPPED THEM!
I'M SO SORRY... ABOUT REYDEN.
I DIDN'T KNOW SPINNING BLUE COULD EVEN **DO** SOMETHING SO... SO HORRIBLE.

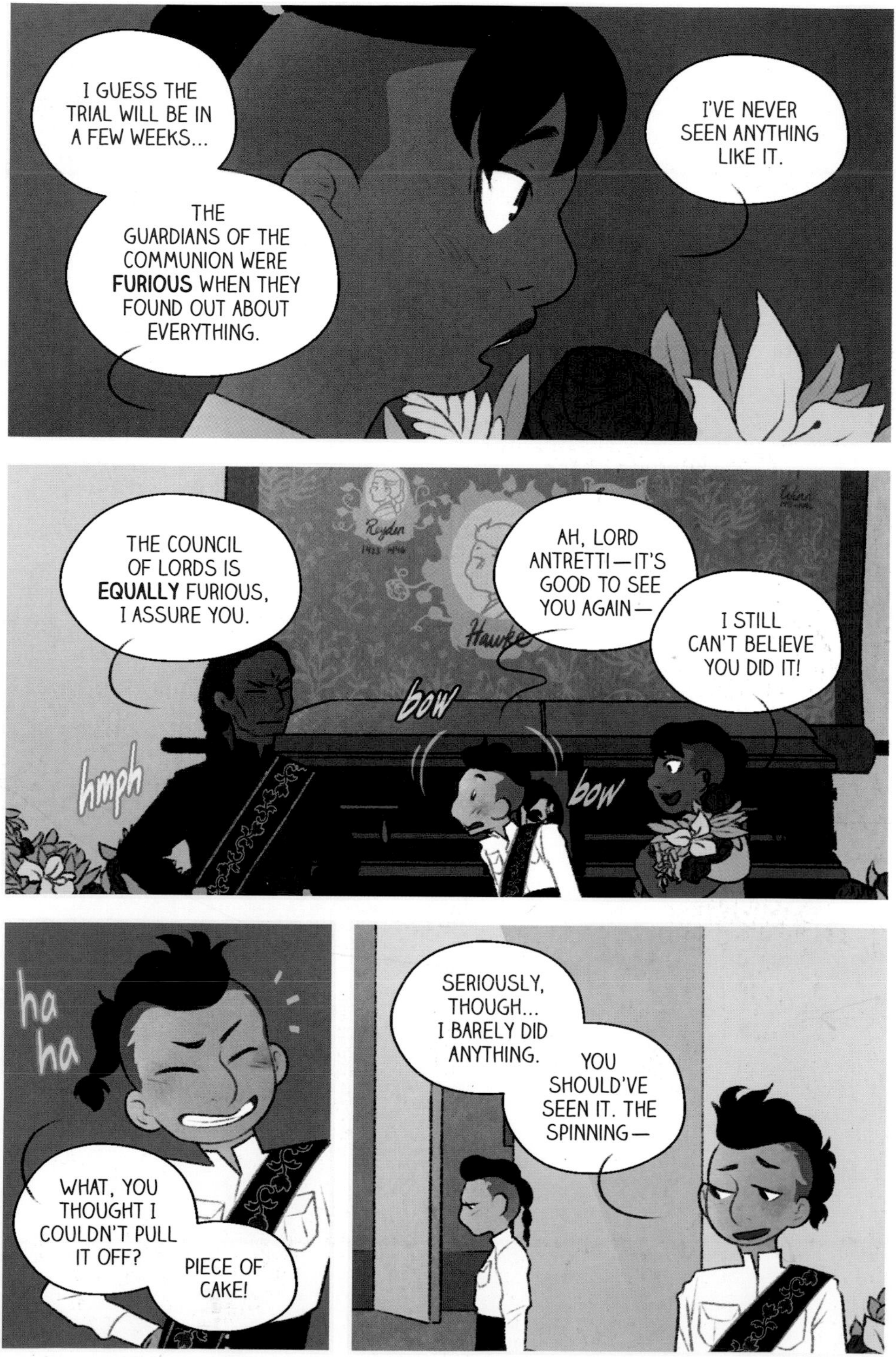

I GUESS THE TRIAL WILL BE IN A FEW WEEKS...
THE GUARDIANS OF THE COMMUNION WERE **FURIOUS** WHEN THEY FOUND OUT ABOUT EVERYTHING.
I'VE NEVER SEEN ANYTHING LIKE IT.
Reyden
Hawke
THE COUNCIL OF LORDS IS **EQUALLY** FURIOUS, I ASSURE YOU.
hmph
AH, LORD ANTRETTI—IT'S GOOD TO SEE YOU AGAIN—
bow
bow
I STILL CAN'T BELIEVE YOU DID IT!
ha ha
WHAT, YOU THOUGHT I COULDN'T PULL IT OFF?
PIECE OF CAKE!
SERIOUSLY, THOUGH... I BARELY DID ANYTHING.
YOU SHOULD'VE SEEN IT. THE SPINNING—

HEY...

IT SOUNDS LIKE YOU WERE AMAZING...

I'LL GO FIND SOMEPLACE TO PUT THIS.

...

WE'RE LOOKING FORWARD TO SEEING YOU ON THE COUNCIL SOON.

Y-YES! MY CORONATION'S NEXT WEEK!

Hawke

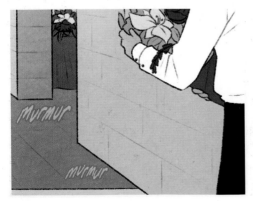

murmur

murmur

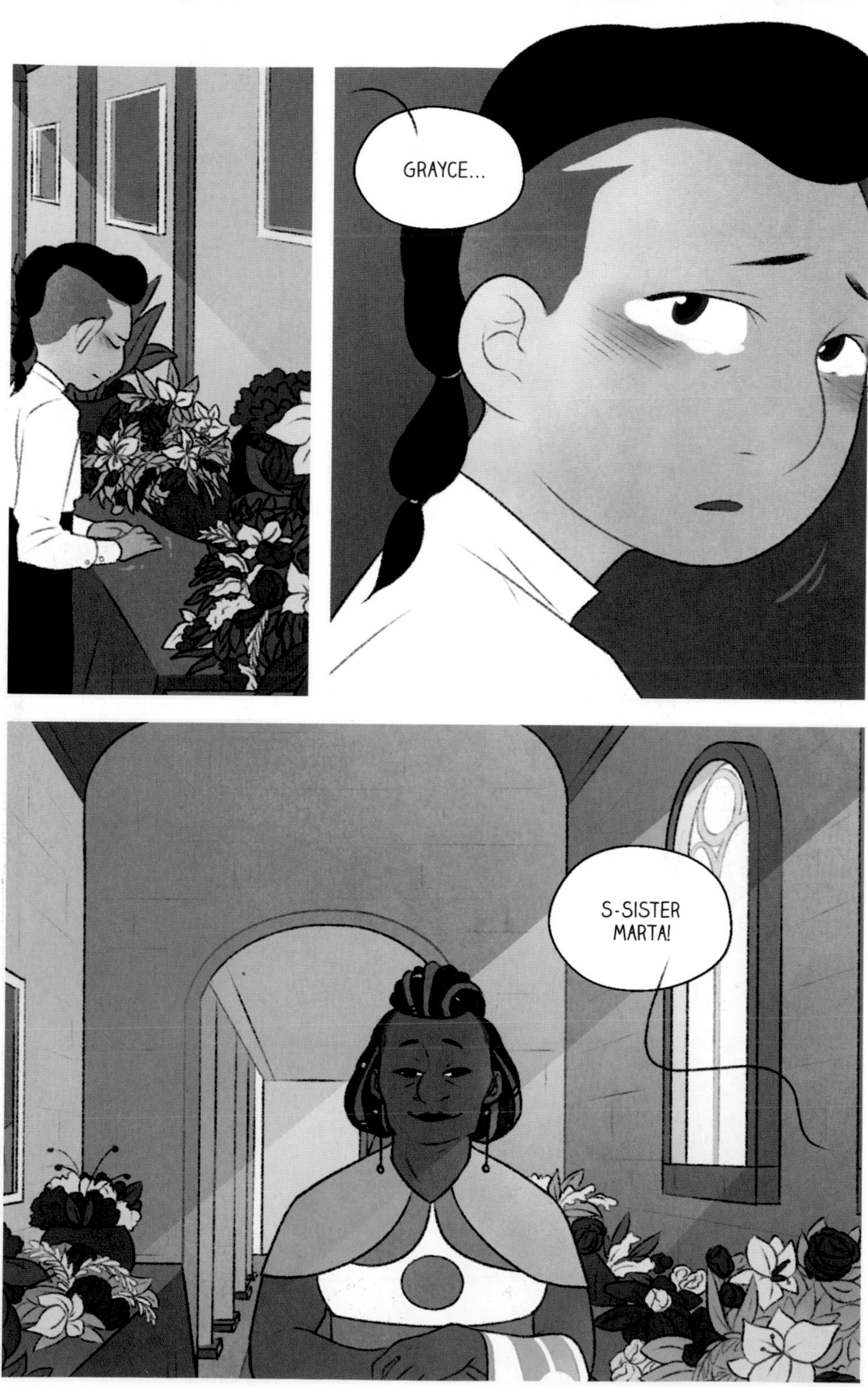
GRAYCE...
S-SISTER MARTA!

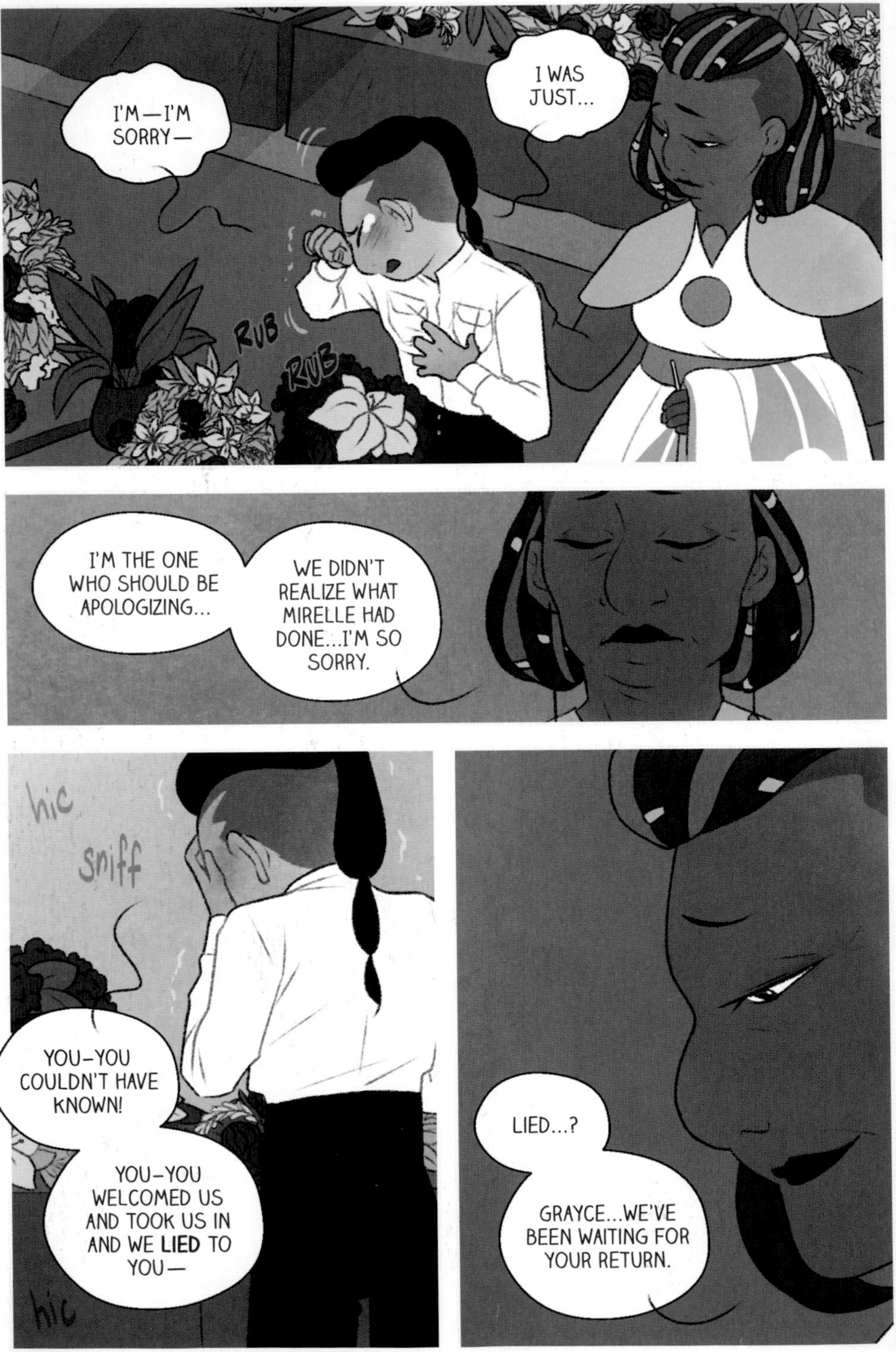
I'M—I'M SORRY—
I WAS JUST...
RUB
RUB
I'M THE ONE WHO SHOULD BE APOLOGIZING...
WE DIDN'T REALIZE WHAT MIRELLE HAD DONE...I'M SO SORRY.
hic
sniff
YOU-YOU COULDN'T HAVE KNOWN!
YOU-YOU WELCOMED US AND TOOK US IN AND WE **LIED** TO YOU—
hic
LIED...?
GRAYCE...WE'VE BEEN WAITING FOR YOUR RETURN.

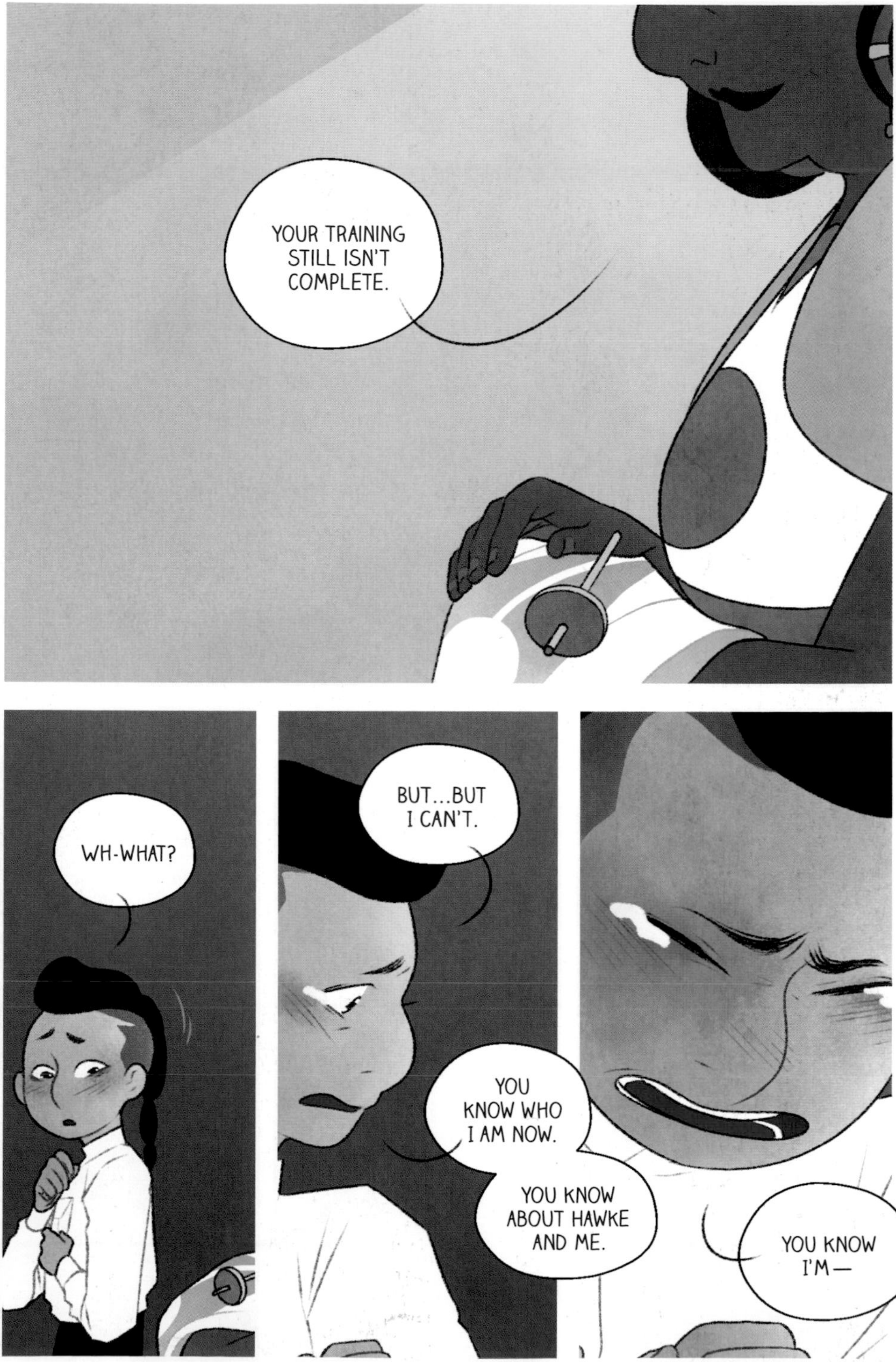
YOUR TRAINING STILL ISN'T COMPLETE.
WH-WHAT?
BUT...BUT I CAN'T.
YOU KNOW WHO I AM NOW.
YOU KNOW ABOUT HAWKE AND ME.
YOU KNOW I'M—

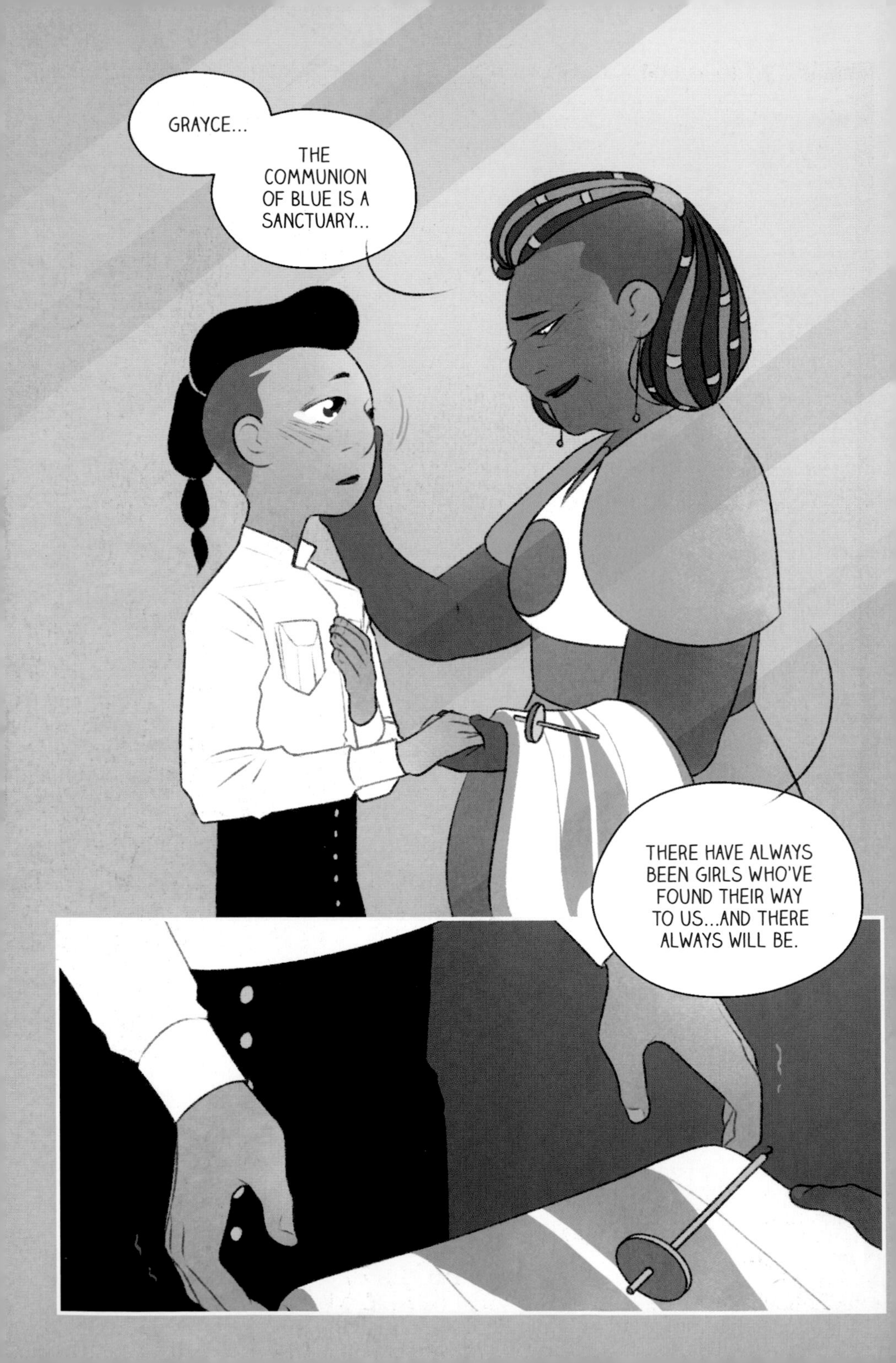
GRAYCE...
THE COMMUNION OF BLUE IS A SANCTUARY...
THERE HAVE ALWAYS BEEN GIRLS WHO'VE FOUND THEIR WAY TO US...AND THERE ALWAYS WILL BE.

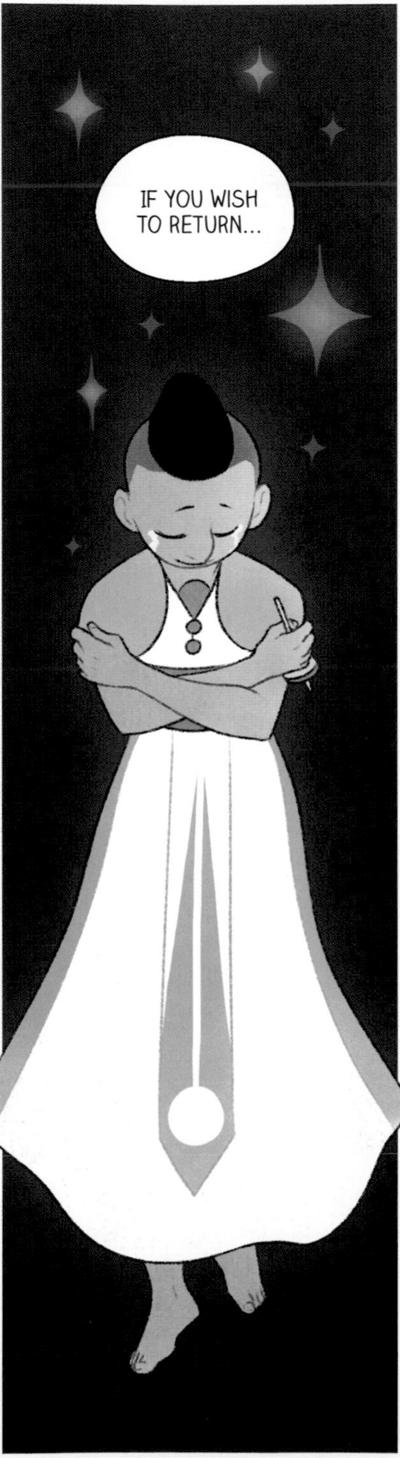
IF YOU WISH
TO RETURN...

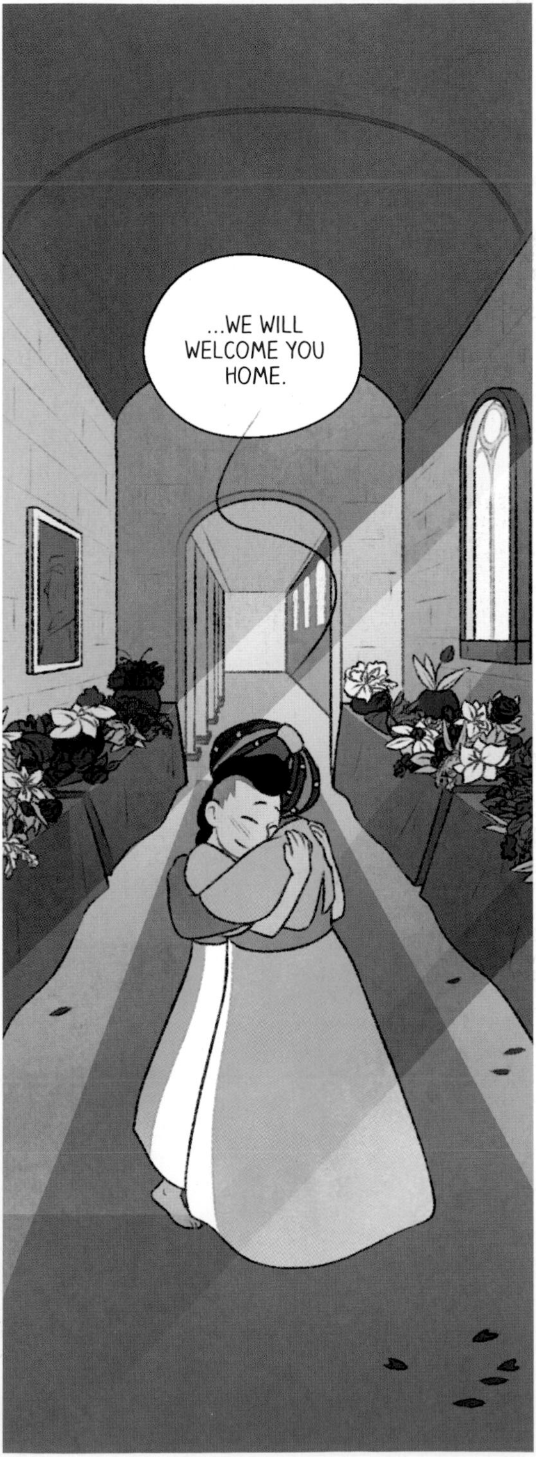
...WE WILL
WELCOME YOU
HOME.

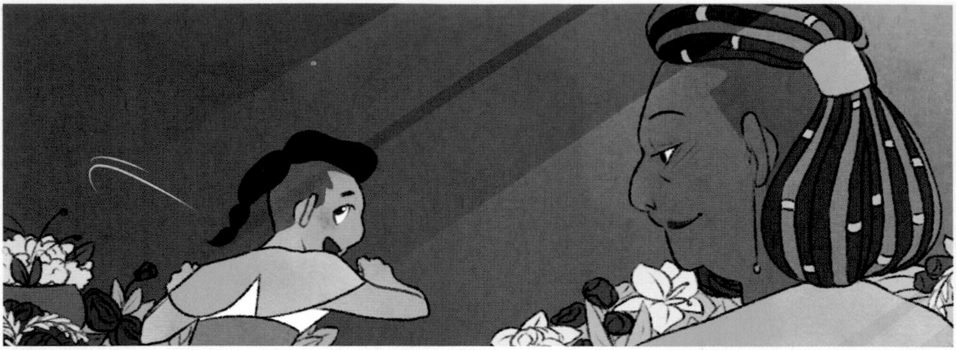

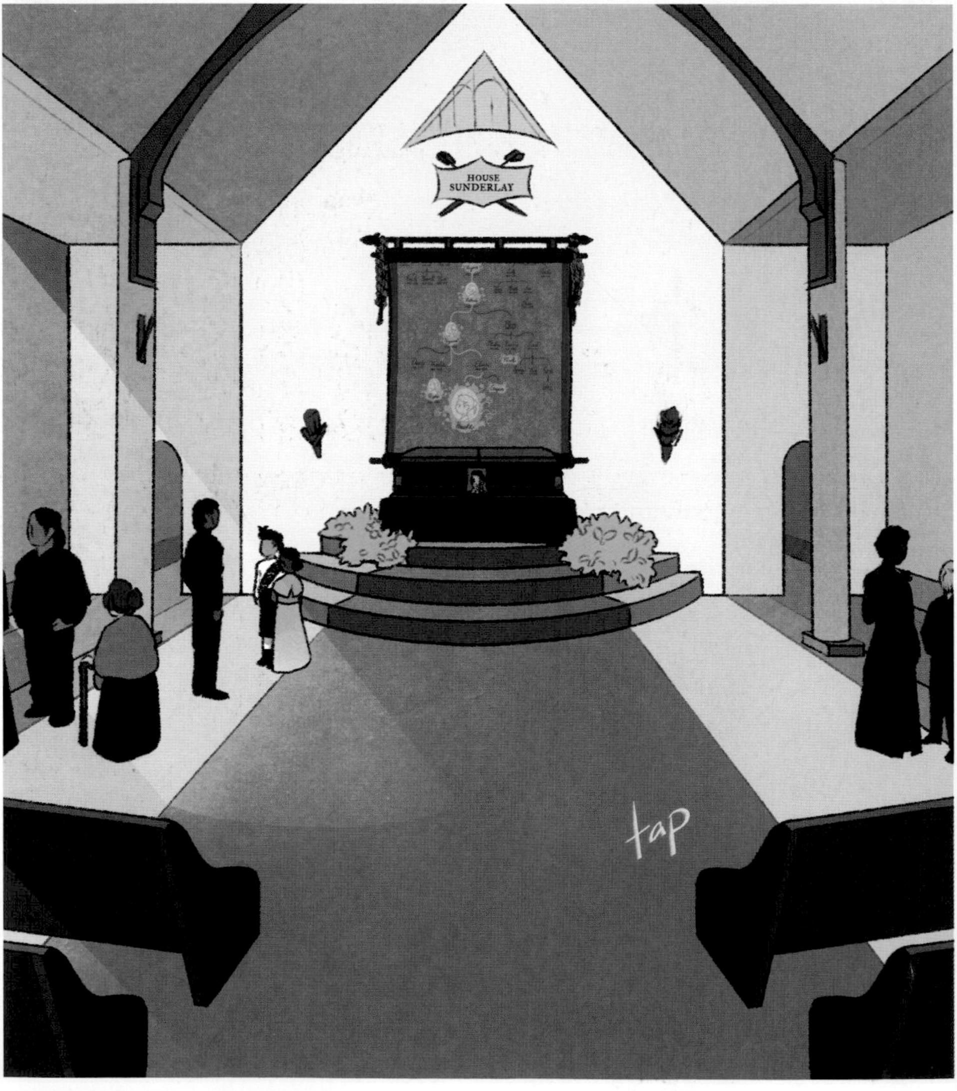
HOUSE
SUNDERLAY
tap

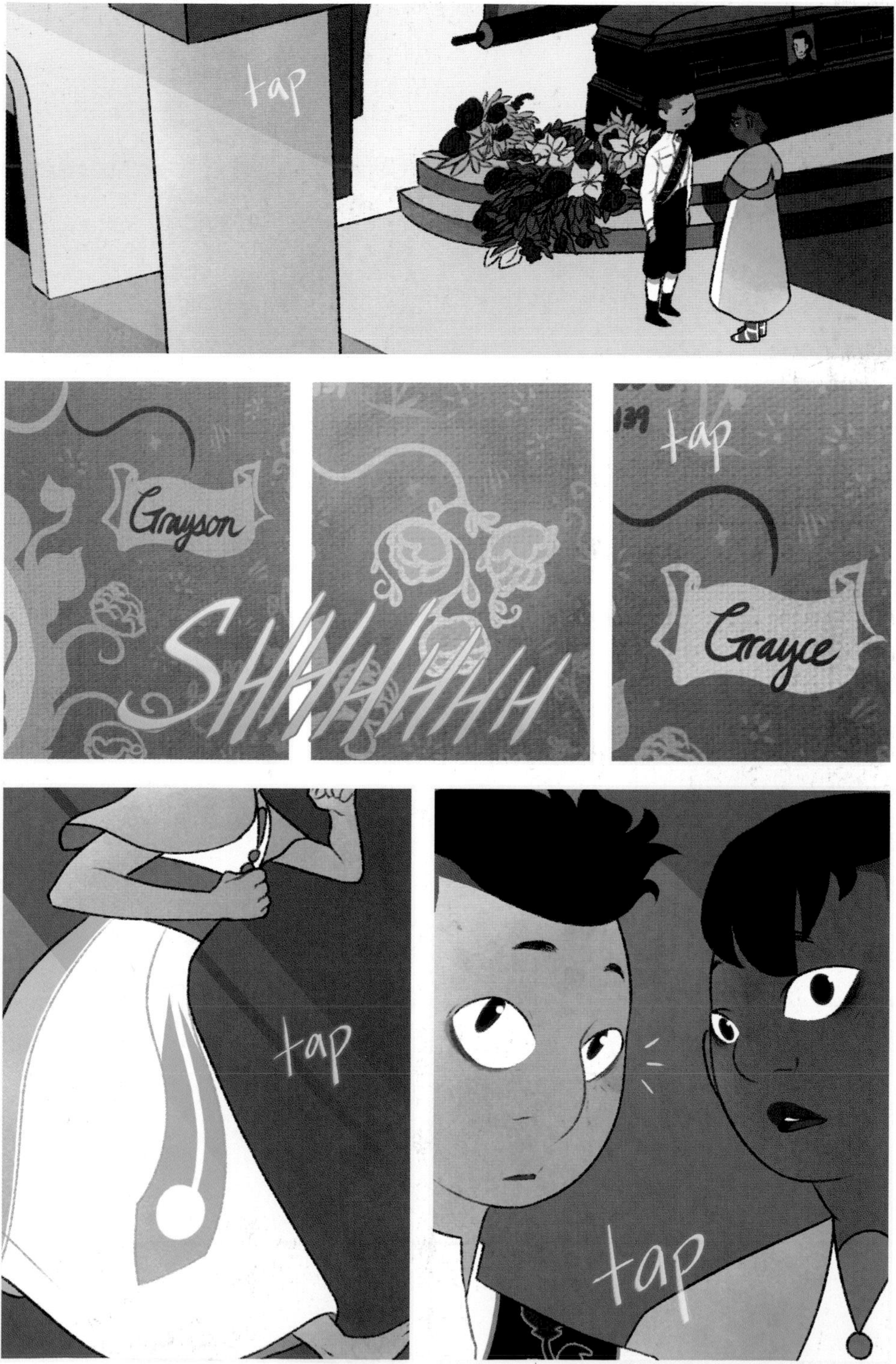
tap
Grayson
SHHHHHH
tap
Grayce
tap
tap

THE END

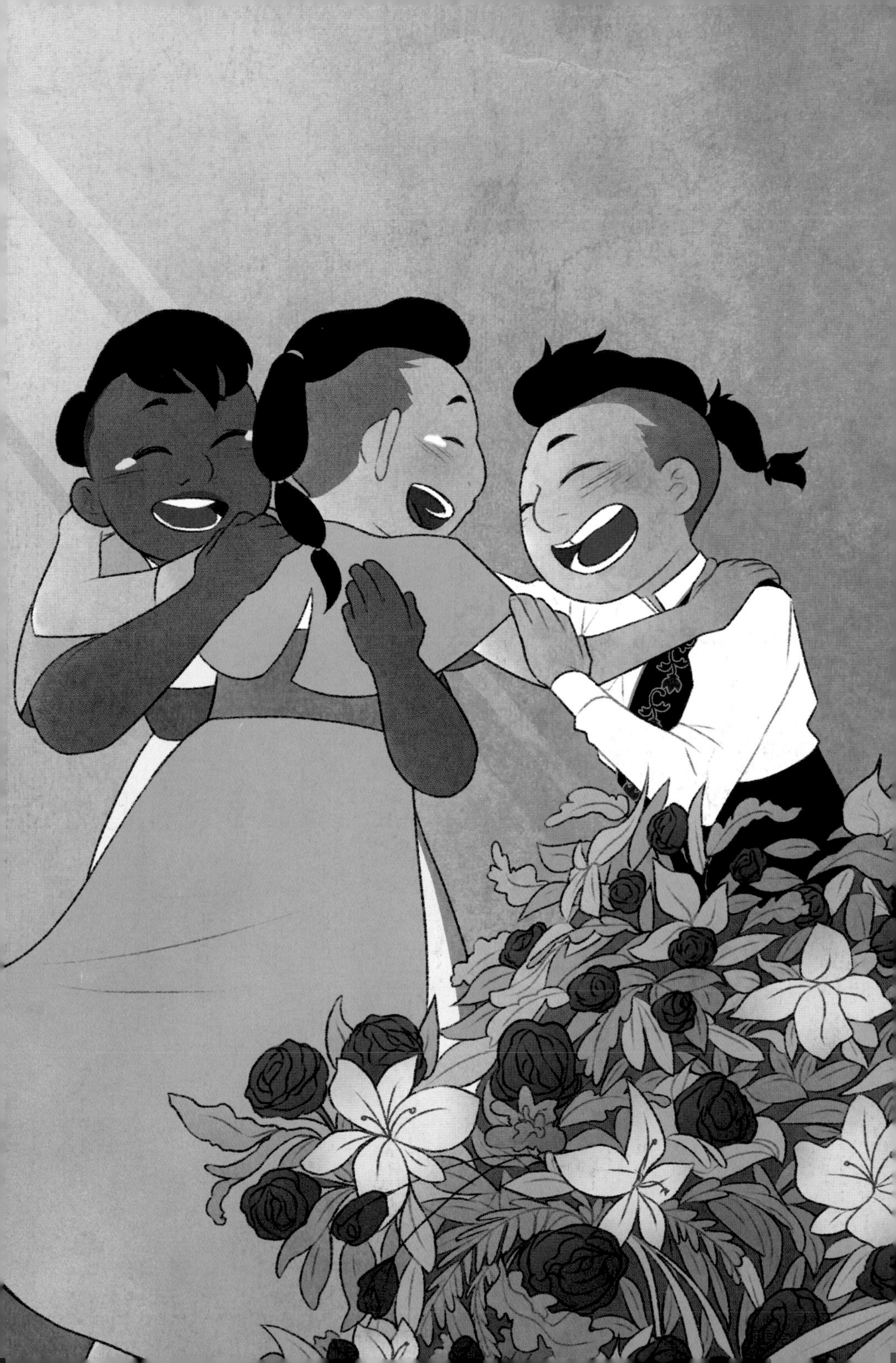

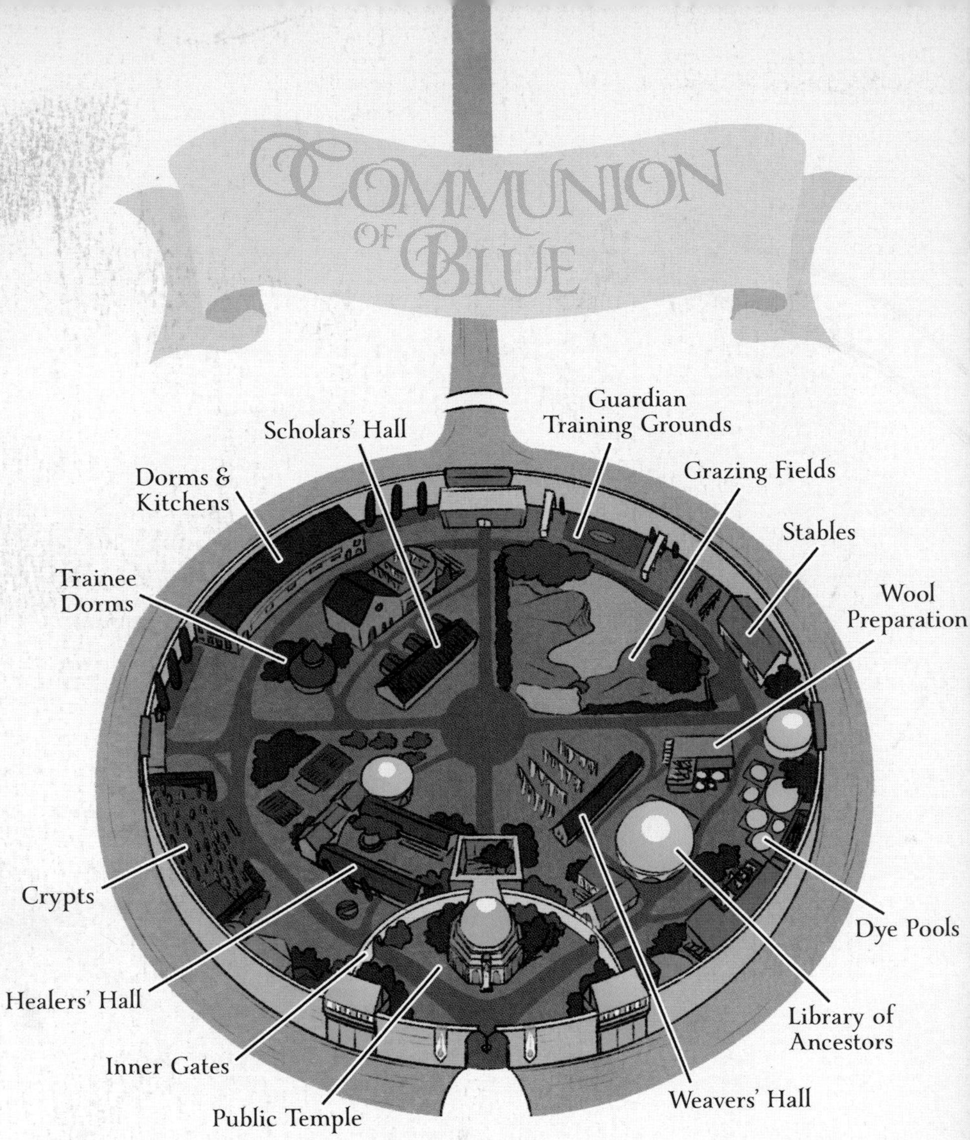
Communion of Blue
Guardian Training Grounds
Scholars' Hall
Dorms & Kitchens
Grazing Fields
Stables
Trainee Dorms
Wool Preparation
Crypts
Dye Pools
Healers' Hall
Library of Ancestors
Inner Gates
Weavers' Hall
Public Temple

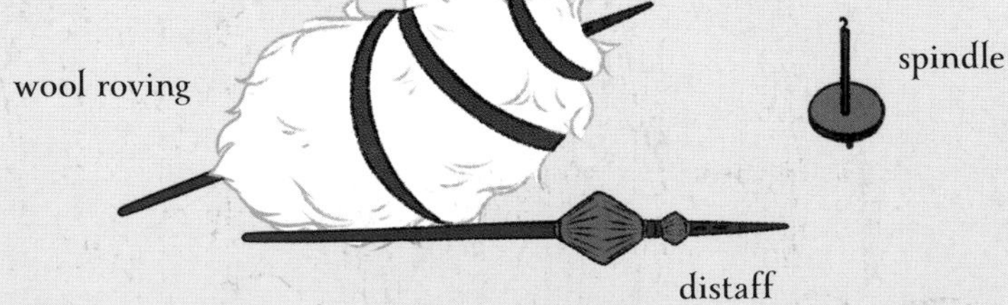
wool roving
spindle
distaff